MW01115816

A KINGDOM OF DEATH AND DESPAIR

BOOK THREE

WHITNEY'S VERSION

THE FOUR KINGDOMS
BOOK THREE

WHITNEY DEAN

UNDYING
RAVEN
PRESS

Copyright © 2023 Whitney Dean — All rights reserved.

Rights and Permissions: Undying Raven Press

No part of this book may be reproduced in any form or by an electronic or mechanical means, including storage and retrieval systems, without written permission from the author, except for the use of brief quotations in a book review or certain other noncommercial uses permitted by copyright law.

This book is a work of fiction. The entirety of any names, places, characters, businesses, locations, incidents, or events are strictly products from the author's imagination or created for fictitious manner. Any resemblance to actual persons, living or dead, or actual events are purely coincidental.

Author's Instagram: authorwhitneydean

Cover Design: Averil (bookishaveril)

Art: zoehollandartwork & jessamyart (No AI was used!)

Whitney's Version Stamp: Lindsay (itsonemorechapter)

Undying Raven Press Logo: Frankie (escape.to.fantasy)

For the ones who said no but couldn't fight back.
Raven said no. She fought back.
For you. For me.

AUTHOR'S NOTE

For the overall theme of the book, I suggest you download and listen to '<u>We Go Down Together</u>' by Dove Cameron and Khalid. The lyrics are eerily perfect to Zeke and Raven's story.

This is very, very dark.
      Please visit HERE for content warnings.

PREFACE

This is their growth.

PROLOGUE

R AVEN
I was not made to surrender.

PART ONE

I WAS NOT MADE TO SURRENDER.

01

ZEKE

Since the night Leonidas took Raven twenty-five years ago, my days had consisted of weights strapped to my ankles while I dragged them across the ocean floor. It was dark and endless, and breathing wasn't necessary because no matter how many breaths I took, everything still burned. I did not understand why everything around me seemed like such an endless void until my mother showed me the memory of our first meeting as children.

My soul had been split into two, and I did not dare to believe I would ever feel whole.

Until the night she breathed purpose into me.

Raven did not try to pull me up from the abyss. Instead, she stayed at the bottom with me. She would resurface long enough to draw in enough oxygen for both of us before returning to dance with me in the depths.

It was her alone that made me want to come back to life.

It was her that slowly brought me to the surface.

Being without her would be what dragged me back down. The freedom she had awarded me by removing the chains of my regret would return, and her absence would bring me to my knees. I would *crawl* across the ocean floor if it meant I had to breathe without her. I would live without the light of another day because the darkness would swallow me whole without her nearby.

And as everything around me blurred while rounding the corner of the castle into the courtyard, I realized that a home wasn't made of sticks or stones. It wasn't a roof or walls. It wasn't libraries, throne rooms, or dining rooms so grand that they seemed pointless. Home was not a place to gather.

At least, not for me.

Home was Raven's smile. It was the sound of her laughter and the taste of her lips after she drank wine. It was the gentle sway of her dress when I chased her down the hall. It was how she rolled her eyes, her frustrated sighs, and the way she always forgave me.

Home was not the shards of glass at my feet or the echoes of screams from the chaos ensuing around me. It wasn't the pitiful number of guards scouring the island looking for her, nor was it my mother on her knees, tending to Godfrey's wound as he slowly bled out.

Raven was my home.

Her warmth, her wild hair, her goddamn stubbornness.

She was the one that stars sang to every night.

Every ember ignited throughout eternity was because someone with a soul like hers existed.

Raven was my home.

And standing here without the strength to form a complete thought, I was a man without his home. I was an aimless wanderer moving in slow motion as I searched for any sign of where she could be, where Cade could have taken her, and how he managed to get back on the island.

I was a hunter searching for his greatest treasure.

≈

THE BLOOD WAS STILL FRESH.

Time had stood still since Cade had stolen her away in the darkness like the coward he was, but only moments had dragged by since discovering Godfrey.

Time had lost all meaning.

Guards ran past me in a blur, their words muffled and drowned by my panic, Jeanine's blonde hair flying behind her as she darted across the courtyard to gather as many details as possible about where Raven could be, and I just...ached with pulsing regret. My heart and mind couldn't sync together to fully grasp the moment of realizing that Raven would not be in my arms tonight.

Sprinkled droplets of her blood covered the ground. Pieces from a bottle of her favorite wine were clumped together in one spot. And Godfrey had collapsed in shock, mumbling nonsense about sun faeries and snow-covered roses. "Get her to the roses," he kept saying over and over, each time weaker than the last.

I had no time to entertain the stories of a dying man, which was what he would be if he didn't stop moving around to allow my mother to stop the mass amount of blood pouring from just beneath his ribcage.

We had trusted too much and too easily.

Our soldiers didn't even wear armor. Raven was the greatest treasure, the most wanted person in our realm, yet we hadn't even thought to protect her.

I watched Godfrey's memories while he slipped in and out of consciousness and made out enough from the obscureness to learn that Cade had poisoned Raven with aconite by disguising it in her wine. He had carried her limp body out of the courtyard and into the forest; I all but received confirmation from Grace as she blubbered and wailed about leaving the castle in time to see him cross the border through the trees.

Before Grace could finish speaking, I ran past the trees into the forest and felt Raven everywhere.

She was the wind spurring me forward. She was the warmth of spring. And she was the cold emptiness pulsing through me at the lack of her presence—at the gnawing uncertainty of where she could be and why she wasn't in my arms.

And the feeling in my chest, well beneath my heart and pumping black, belonged to her. It ached for the freedom to find her.

I had become so accustomed to having her beside me that I felt misplaced without her—like I was living in a nightmare I had somehow created for myself.

A nightmare that I could not wake up from.

I needed to feel her in my arms and hear her laugh. I wouldn't be upset if she popped out from behind a tree and told me this was an elaborate trick, because it would mean she was safe. I would carry her back to the castle and fight with her about it. I hated fighting with her more than I hated anyone looking at her, but I would fight with her all night if it meant I could hear her voice again.

I would fight with her until she rolled her eyes and then kiss her until the sun rose.

But as I approached the dock at our spring—the spring where I had made her mine—and saw the outline of a ship in the distance, I knew I was indeed living my worst nightmare. I wouldn't be able to recover her yet. And when I noticed her drying blood on the dock, my panic was replaced by unabashed, untethered rage.

GRIEF-STRICKEN AND PALE, John rose from the ground beside the bodies of two guards. Both men had been at the gate of the courtyard since Raven was a child.

I hadn't stopped running since finding her blood on the dock, but slowed long enough to hear his request that I grab weapons from the armory.

"I am the fucking weapon," I growled, searching the courtyard for Godfrey.

"Luca and another guard got him to the infirmary," John explained. "Your mother will stay by his side."

"Where would Cade take her? He's traveling by ship."

Jeanine appeared at my side with two bows and quivers full of arrows. She wanted to go with me to find her. After meeting Raven, Jeanine had been my partner when stalking her. She expected that I would ask her to accompany me, but as I looked at the bows in her hands, I had to decide quickly. "The heathens only listen to us because of their fear of Raven and me. Without us, you're all at risk."

The three of us exchanged looks before I shook my head slightly. "I don't have time to kill all of them. I can only shatter one mind at a time and don't have time to try. Send them back to Reales."

They chased after me as I ran toward the harbor, Jeanine shouting for clarification. "Send them back to Mira," I said. "I'm finished, Jeanine. I am so fucking finished with all of this."

Throwing a bow and quiver on one of our smallest and fastest ships, I squinted at the fading outline of Cade's ship in the distance. "My entire reason for existing is on a ship with her abuser and the man who tried to rape her. And it's because I was fucking tied down to an army, which I want nothing to do with."

I turned to John. "Send them back to Mira. Evacuate the island if you feel it's necessary. Send everyone to Thoya." I ran a hand through my hair. "Fuck, I don't care what you do. Tell me where Cade would take her."

"Thoya turned them away," John spoke hurriedly while searching for the ship I continued to stare at. "It would be Reales or Perosan. Perosan leads into the vast forest. Reales is a risk."

"The forest is a risk!" Jeanine exclaimed, watching as Cade's ship shrank in the distance. I was running out of time to close the gap between us. I wouldn't be able to catch him overnight, but I could stay on his tail long enough to see where he was headed.

"Why would Petra allow Cade into Perosan?" Jeanine asked. "She knows Raven...."

"Perosan is surrounded by rocky shores," I answered. "If Cade knows how to access them, he will. Petra won't be aware until it's too late."

Too late.

Too late.

Those two words were like rocks in my gut.

The shores posed a problem not only because Cade wasn't a sailor, but because they stretched for miles and were hidden behind jagged rocks that jutted out from the ocean floor like an underwater army. They made it nearly impossible to dock anywhere unless you anchored far enough away to attempt swimming to dry land.

"I have to tell the village." John doubled over, putting his hands on his knees.

I patted his back. "I am going to find her. I will not return until I have her."

"If she dies..." He stood, and for the first time in a long while, I watched my father cry. "If she dies, if he kills her, I won't see you again."

I ran my tongue across the roof of my mouth to keep myself from caving. "I will not let that happen."

"Son, I..."

Grabbing his shoulder, I stopped him by shaking my head and speaking before he could. "We are not saying goodbyes. I am coming home, and that little witch will have a very long reign."

I ran up the ship's ramp and turned quickly to put my hands on either side of the railings. Jeanine cursed and tried to shove past me, but I held firm. "You're second in command and an adviser. You must stay here and assist John in keeping our people safe."

"I am coming with you!" she shouted while shoving my chest. "You cannot order me to stay here. I am no longer your subject and do not answer to you!"

This was the one time I regretted my suggestion that Jeanine and Luca become residents of Seolia.

I grabbed her flailing arms and held them still. "You're right, Jeanine. I can't order you to stay here. But I implore you to think of what Raven wants you to do. She is your queen, and while she's gone, you represent her."

Her fear and anxiety were stifling and sharp, colliding with my panic, but she was needed here. She was Seolia's strongest chance of remaining safe.

A frustrated look of understanding passed over her face as she yanked her arms free from my grip and descended the ramp back to the dock. "Do not expect me to forgive you for this," she muttered.

I feared she wasn't being dramatic.

As I prepared to pull the ramp up, Luca came barreling down the dock and lunged past me before I had the chance to stop him. "You can't do this alone," he said on an exhale. "You think you can, but you can't. You're going to need me."

I couldn't waste any more time arguing. As he took over pulling the ramp up, I went to the ship's helm and pushed us off the dock. I didn't need to look at Jeanine to know she was glaring at me, and I could see John's immense worry for his sons leaving, but nothing mattered to me more than getting to Raven as quickly as possible.

I had already lived a lifetime without her.

Her absence wasn't something I could quite wrap my mind around yet, but when she was away from me, it felt as if half of me was missing—and it was always the better half. Without her nearby, I was angry and impatient. With her, I wanted to be the man she needed—the one who might earn a throne beside hers one day.

Luca came to stand next to me after securing the ramp and hoisting the sails. It was one of the rare times that I didn't mind reliving my past with him—I had taught him how to sail just a few years ago. I hadn't seen the need, but he insisted, and now I was glad for it.

Cocking my head, he followed my gaze to the map pinned against the wall. "Chart a course to Perosan."

"That's four fucking days away," he snapped, using his finger to trace an outline of the route between us. "That's too much time. He could change his mind, change course...."

"Luca," I interrupted. "It's the only plan I have. Nowhere else will allow him to enter the kingdom with Raven. We won't be far behind him. The breeze is on our side."

On cue, it brushed against the back of my neck and made the hairs stand on end. It pushed against our ship's sails and spurred us faster toward Raven.

Her. She surrounded me.

I could only hope that she was fighting against the poison and sending me the breeze herself—that perhaps I would see Cade's ship burst into flames and him burning along with it. Maybe he hadn't thought this through and the aconite would wear off quickly—perhaps I would see my little demon swimming toward me at any moment.

But the pessimist in me knew that Cade had spent years drowning her fire any way he could. He would find a way to keep her from weaponizing herself.

I craved her warmth.

I had come to rely on it.

"We should've done more," Luca said, standing at the ship's side and staring over the black water. He looked ready to dive in. "We should've stationed guards everywhere. At every entrance. Every fucking doorway." He looked at me then, his jaw tight, his brows drawn in, and his pain only adding to mine. "We should've been prepared for this."

Of course, we should've done more. I should've stayed by her side. I shouldn't have allowed her to walk alone. I was beginning to hate that island, even though it was where we had found each other. We were trapped on land where anyone could find her, grab her, and take her from me.

I wanted to go somewhere no one could ever find us.

Because I had a feeling that someone would always try.

I feared Cade was only the beginning.

DAY ONE, and I was in hell.

It wasn't the hell that spawned Raven and me—this was a hell that took pleasure in shredding souls into pieces and setting them aflame. There wasn't anything romantic or grand about the agony threatening to break my chest into two.

This was the madness Arthur had alluded to when speaking of what twin flames go through while apart. My mind was clouded, my skin felt tight, and the volume of bodies I wanted to tear apart would shock the damned.

I wanted to fill the ocean with nothing but blood.

The hatred Raven had worked to dispel was being rebuilt each second we were apart, and the ashy taste of my apparent shadows was pooling on my tongue.

Could this be what freed them?

And worst of all, I thirsted for her blood. The farther away she went, the more I wanted it. With her blood running through me, I knew she was safe. It was like having a part of her with me at all times. And standing here, full of sorrow and hysteria, I couldn't remember the last time I had bitten her.

Cade's ship was gone. It had somehow pulled ahead overnight. Or, perhaps, I had imagined all of it.

Since I hadn't slept, none of this felt real. It couldn't be. She had trusted me to protect her from monsters like him, but he had pounced the second she was away from me.

I released a heavy sigh when Luca disappeared into the cabin below deck. I was trying to stay strong for both of us, but holding the wheel to keep us on course was the only reason I remained standing. If I let go, I would crumble.

"My love," I whispered, tears wetting my eyes at the thought of never hearing her light and airy voice again. "I don't pray, Raven, but I am praying to find you."

Looking toward the sky, I choked back my fear, my apprehension, and my heart splitting into two. "Whoever or whatever can hear me, please don't take her from me yet."

Chest heaving with a stuttering cry, I wiped my eyes with the sleeve of my shirt. "I am not ready yet," I continued to beg and plead with whoever listened. "I am not ready to find out if we get another life together."

Because I didn't believe we would.

Our flashes of lives before this one didn't seem full of magic, except for the love between us. They looked rather plain, and we never looked older than we did now. Neither of our glimpses showed us living the happily ever after we so desperately craved. And with Raven's glimpse into our future, I couldn't help but wonder if this life was the one we had been trying to reach...

...which meant that if Cade did kill her, the last time I would ever see her would be meeting her amongst the flowers and blue sky of our meadow.

~

I NEEDED HER.

I couldn't think straight without her. I kept rewatching memories of her, particularly the one of us laughing on my ship as we sailed to Reales — teaching her how to sail, making love on deck, promising to love only each other. I felt such peace at that moment, imagining a future where that was all we would do.

It would have been enough.

"You need to eat," Luca said, appearing at my side. We hadn't spoken much since leaving Seolia. "Sleep. Let me take the wheel."

Shaking my head, I tightened my hold on the one thing keeping me upright. I couldn't stand around and do nothing. I needed to be here because every second meant I was one closer to holding her again.

"You haven't moved in two days, Zeke. Restore your energy."

As I shook my head again, he put his hand on the wheel. "It's what Raven would want."

That was a gut punch.

Of course, he was right. Raven always took care of me. Despite my pleas for her to stop, she put my needs before hers. She would agree with Luca and coerce me into rest.

For her, I would step back and eat something.

Releasing the wheel, I allowed Luca to take my place. He dipped his chin toward a wicker basket on the floor. "Eat. Mom threw in as much as she could."

I sighed and lowered to dig through the basket full of fruits and slices of bread. Bringing a pear up, I brushed my fingers over the soft skin.

Our bond. Our combined scent of pear and pine.

Something so simple drew us to one another. And now, I was hunting her to save our lives.

Finally allowing the weight of her absence to sit on my shoulders, I sat on the floor. I couldn't breathe as I attempted to pull in sharp breaths through my nose and stared at the pear in my hand.

My wife, my wife.

My mate.

My heart beating outside of my chest.

Luca kneeled in front of me and said something, but his words were mangled syllables, and Raven was the only thing that made sense. I only wanted to hear her laugh and the sounds she made when I kissed her.

He patted my arm and squeezed until I met his eyes. "All she wanted to do was show me things from our childhood home, Luca. She wanted to show me everything she had brought back. She wanted to hear my stories and memories, but I couldn't...."

Luca's eyes lined with silver.

"I didn't take the time to show her. I didn't take the time to look. John told me to try, but I couldn't. I still held a grudge and felt the pain of all of it, but now...."

"No, Zeke." He moved his hands to my shoulders. "We will find her and bring her home. We will put aside an entire day for her to show us anything she wants. We'll tell her stories of our childhood."

"I can't lose her, Luca. I can't. I'm not ready for it to be over."

"It won't be." His voice held nothing but determination. "We will not lose her."

I needed her. We all needed her. This couldn't be it. We'd been in bliss for only two weeks. We finally surrendered to one another. We were a gift; our strand was golden. The gods wouldn't have bestowed that upon us only to give us mere months together. It hadn't even been a year since I found her.

This couldn't be real.

I tried to shatter it, convinced it was a nightmare.

But it stayed. It was real.

She wasn't in my arms, and it was real.

I TRIED TO SHATTER IT, CONVINCED IT WAS A NIGHTMARE, BUT IT STAYED.

02

Zeke

The warming rays of the dawning sun slightly comforted me as Perosan came into view. Unable to stop pacing, my steps were surprisingly steady opposite the rocking of the ship while Luca guided us in. Choppy waves sloshed against the outstretched shores, unwelcoming against the dark sand. Every ounce of self-control I had left stopped me from diving into the water. I had barely slept because of the memories that haunted me. Each time I opened my eyes, the crushing weight of her absence sat upon my chest.

"Where do you want me to go? Do we search the shores?" Luca asked, then cursed as our ship dipped from the impact of a significant wave.

"No, that would take longer than docking in the harbor. Their shores expand across miles. I need to get my bearings first. It's been a while since my last visit."

Unlike Seolia and Reales, but similar to Thoya, Perosan was colorful. Perched on a large ledge with several artificial waterfalls underneath it, their castle appeared as if floating in the middle of the ocean. But once you pushed past the enchantment, underneath the castle, and through the waterfalls, jagged rocks and hidden caves awaited you. The sun couldn't illuminate the shores, dark and concealed beneath the kingdom, even when high and bright in the sky.

The outer banks of Perosan led into the vast forests beyond. Only a few had explored them and lived to tell about it.

Accessible by only one main gate, the castle's courtyard connected to the town by a peachy, wide walkway. Though there was only one castle, it was unnecessarily large and appeared like five miniature castles morphed into one. And without heirs, the space was wasted on Petra and Elric.

Perosan was the second largest kingdom in our realm and the one all the others seemed to want the most. The forest and the unknown that lurked beyond it drew travelers.

Running a hand through my hair as Petra's guards lined up along the dock, I sighed. After signaling us to pull in and tie up, I stood by Luca and searched the line of men until I recognized the captain. "Direk," I muttered, nodding subtly toward the man glaring at me. "He isn't fond of me and is the one to escort me from the kingdom whenever I visit."

"What do we do? I can't stall."

Rolling my neck, I tugged at the sleeves of my jacket and wished I had thought to bring my crown. Royalty intimidated Direk, which contributed to his abhorrence of me. "Let me do the talking."

"I don't know if that's the smartest idea," Luca mumbled.

"Fuck off," I returned, kicking the ramp down to connect to the dock and debarking the ship. Three guards stood before me, preventing me from going any farther.

"Move," I snarled.

With a grin twitching at the corner of his mouth, Direk made his way to the center of the line. I narrowed my eyes, the annoyance I felt toward him mirroring his feelings of me. "I don't have time for your fucking inspection, Direk. I'm here to retrieve Raven."

In a pathetic attempt to intimidate me, he balanced his palm on the pommel of his sword. "The Queen of Seolia is not in Perosan."

"Cade took her, and I have reason to believe he is hiding her somewhere amongst your shores." Ignoring Luca's warning behind me, I stepped closer. "Get the fuck out of my way, Direk. I am royalty in this realm and do not need to explain myself to you."

"We do not take kindly to the royalty of Reales making demands that they are in no position to make," Direk remarked.

"I can demand whatever I please and do not like repeating myself. Get out of my way." I shoved past him only to be faced with two more guards.

Impatience nestled into the back of my neck.

"You know what I am capable of!" I thundered. "I do not wish to remind you, Direk, but you will leave me with no choice if you do not advise your men to stand down."

"Are you confirming the rumors about you are true?" he asked, his boots clomping against the dock as he neared me. "If so, that would make you a threat to our land..."

"I have always been a threat to you, Direk." Turning, I caught his wrist just as he raised his sword. "You do not want to take this path with me."

Surrounding me, soldiers drew their swords and pointed them at me. Luca sighed. "I told you I should've done the talking."

Without breaking my stare with Direk, I crawled into one of his soldiers' minds and pulled from the deepest part of the buried memories. As I brought one forward, he shouted in agony and dropped his sword onto the dock.

Direk looked at him in alarm, but I remained still.

Releasing his mind, I moved to another, and a grin broadened across my lips as he shouted in dismay at the memory his subconscious had been shielding him from.

Direk's gaze slowly returned to me, his determination mixed with fear. Releasing his arm, I casually slid my hands into my jacket pockets. "If you do not let us go, I will be forced to shatter the minds of each and every one of your men."

Calling for Luca to follow me, we jogged down the remaining length of the dock and to the courtyard. "Fucking waste of time," I snapped, looking in each direction. Dark archways led to wooden bridges to cross underneath the castle and the shores.

"Zeke..."

Looking over my shoulder, I sighed in annoyance as we were surrounded by soldiers again. Before I could take another step, Luca's hands were secured behind his back in cuffs.

Cold sweat pooled at the base of my spine at the idea of Luca returning to a cell. He would not be locked away again because of me. "I do not have time for this!" I shouted, head-butting Direk when he came for me and swinging at the guard holding Luca. Bone cracking and blood pouring from his nose, he released Luca as two more came for me.

Dodging their punches, I returned them with my own and kicked another who charged at me. I had to get to her before it was too late. I was not proud of my abilities, but I would destroy worlds for her, even if it meant shattering minds.

Closing my eyes, I grabbed the first mind I could find and shattered it into pieces before grasping for another, repeating the process until his mind was nothing but broken fragments in my hands. The men who had grabbed me stumbled backward, looking around in confusion.

Direk growled, but before he could move, I crawled into his mind and squeezed. He froze, his eyes widening while I tunneled through his subconscious.

"Every memory," I snarled, "Every good moment, every woman you've ever fucked, and every piece of your life belongs to me, Direk. I swear to the gods that you will never create another memory if you do not release my brother and me. You will beg for your life to end because of the mental torment I will cause."

His pupils dilated as I swiftly flickered through his memories and released him. He stumbled to the side, but I shoved into his mind again to prove my point. "You will not follow us. You will allow me to retrieve my mate."

The shadows that Morana had introduced me to pushed at my chest and wound tightly around my ribs, causing breathing to become difficult. They craved the freedom to find Raven on their own.

And to kill. They wanted to kill him. Badly.

Releasing the hold on Direk's mind, I looked at the soldier holding Luca. "Release him, or you'll be next."

Luca's handcuffs fell to the ground and he rubbed his wrists. I glowered at Direk. "Touch another member of my family and your heart will be dragged across the very ground you stand on."

Not waiting for an answer, I turned and chose the closest archway to run toward, but slowed when I recognized the cocky grin staring back at me, his shoulder leaning against a mossy wall. "You always knew how to make an entrance, Ezekiel."

"Edmund," I said, shocked. "How?"

"John sent us a letter. I came as soon as I heard." Unlike the distance Seolia maintained from each kingdom, Perosan and Thoya were only separated by a day's worth of land. "We will find that exquisite creature, Ezekiel."

"Yes," I confirmed, because there wasn't another choice.

He glanced behind me. "Brother?"

Luca extended a hand. "Luca."

"We need to go, Edmund. Direk has delayed me."

Edmund frowned. "I came by carriage. There were many ship-wrecks along the shores, Ezekiel. I am fearful..."

"I cannot entertain that idea, Edmund. I have to believe that she isn't one of those. She's alive."

Edmund nodded, but then sighed as he studied us. "No weapons, Ezekiel. Really?"

Realizing I had left our bows on the ship, I shrugged and jogged past him toward the pitch-black bridge. "Did it look like I needed any fucking weapons?"

~

A DECAYING and rickety bridge stood between the kingdom and its shores. Each step we took across it was met with bated breaths. The split wooden planks held us above tragic ends. Nothing but darkness and water lurked beneath.

While waiting for Edmund and Luca to cross, I looked around the misty shores and trees that touched the sky. While Perosan was bright and cheerful on the outside, it harbored darkness down below. Rumors of the forest were similar to those of the Black Forest in Seolia. Many had attempted to make it to the other side to find what lies beyond, only to disappear and never be heard from again.

While the rocky shores were dangerous and not a place I would want Raven to be, I feared the forest even more. It was endless. If Cade dragged her into it, my chances of finding her unharmed substantially diminished.

I tore my gaze away from the intimidating trees to look along the shoreline. It could take days to explore entirely, which was time I did not have.

Scattered amongst protruding rocks and rough waves were broken pieces of splintered wood from ships that had failed to settle along the bank. Barnacles on cracked wood planks proved the length of time they had spent in the water, and bone fragments from lives lost were strewn about the sand like rocks.

"This place is spine-chilling," Luca said, looking around the bone-littered shore. "Have you been here before?"

I shrugged a shoulder. "I haven't explored it. I've walked down here but left shortly after because something about it didn't feel right."

Though it was spring, the air remained crisp and cool. I was already cold without her, and this didn't help.

"Petra typically has this area guarded," Edmund said. "I am partially surprised that no one stopped us from entering."

"They're hoping I don't come back alive," I muttered, beginning our trek down the shore. "His ship had one sail, but that's all I saw. Cade isn't a sailor, so the chances of us finding his ship intact..."

31

Trailing off, I blinked back tears at the thought of her being harmed somewhere along the coast. "We need to move quickly."

Foam from the shallow waves covered our boots as we trudged through the moist sand, looking for any sign of Raven or life of any kind, for that matter. We were the only ones around, and besides the howling of wind and waves, there was only silence.

Nothing about Raven was silent. She made her presence known, which added to my hopelessness of locating her quickly.

"Talk about her." Edmund's tone was gentle. "It will help you."

Frowning, I looked across the deep water and spun the ring around my finger with my thumb. "Her wedding dress was green and ivory," I murmured. "My mother's partner in Reales made it. I delivered the tulle of her skirt to her shoppe before Mira locked my mother away."

I closed my eyes briefly, pulling the memory of Raven walking across the deck during the happiest night of my life. "I remember looking at the tulle when I delivered it, and I wondered if someday..." I swallowed. Vulnerability was foreign to me. "If someday, I would find someone who would allow my mother to make her a wedding dress made of ivory.

And then I saw her eyes — quickly and without reason since we hadn't met as adults, but I saw them." I put my inked knuckles against my lips. "I held onto that. I often saw her eyes in my dreams but never knew why. I could never understand it."

"Until you saw her at the festival," Luca said quietly.

"Until that night. It all made sense, Luca. Everything in my life led to her. Not a day goes by that I do not regret my decisions that led to you and mom being locked away, but Raven healed us. She's brought joy back into our lives."

Luca squeezed my shoulder. "She has."

"Her light is addicting," Edmund said with a soft laugh. "Not a day passes that we don't talk about her."

I glanced at Edmund. "Has Gisela said anything interesting about her?"

He lifted an eyebrow. "Should she have?"

After noticing a shipwrecked vessel with flags from the older days of Reales, I wondered which men we lost that day. "She has musings about where Raven could have come from. She doesn't believe...."

"Zeke!" Luca shouted.

A small ship with one sail sat between two rocks. One of them had sliced through the ship's side.

"Raven!" I yelled in hopes she would pop out from behind one of the rocks and run into my arms. "Raven!" I called over and over as we neared the vessel, nearly stumbling once I saw the flag from Reales.

Why did Cade have a ship from Reales?

I didn't have time to dissect that right now.

Running to the side that wasn't impaled, I jumped and hoisted myself over. Luca and Edmund stayed on the shore to search for any sign of her.

Skidding down the steps beneath the deck, my nostrils flared as her scent hit me. I smelled her everywhere. Pieces of broken bottles were scattered along the floor, the lingering drops of aconite wafting into my nose and blending with the sweetness of her.

"Ezekiel!" Edmund shouted. I reappeared on deck to see him pointing to the sand. "A trail!"

From my vantage point, I spotted two separate trails of footprints — one with steps much closer together than the other, meaning one had run while the other had slowly chased. Why was my wife constantly seeking refuge in dark forests of death?

But a few feet away from her trail of footprints was another — one that didn't lead into the forest or anywhere else. No, it was a set that ended where it began, as if whomever it belonged to had appeared and disappeared in the same spot.

"This would have been a good time to have weapons!" Edmund shouted to me, motioning toward the forest. "There is a good chance Thoya will be left in my sister's hands."

I jumped from the ship's deck to the ground and rolled my sleeves up. "I can assure you, Edmund, that I am the only weapon you'll need."

As I walked toward the tree line, I heard him sigh behind me and mutter to Luca, "Being mated to Raven has gone to his head."

THE SUN COULDN'T ILLUMINATE THE SHORES, EVEN WHEN HIGH AND BRIGHT IN THE SKY.

03

Zeke

Knee-high woven tree roots latched onto my pants every time I stepped over one. It was the only reason I wished I had a sword. The tree cover barely allowed enough light to create a pathway for us, but even if I had more sunlight, it wouldn't have helped. Overrun by mud and leaves, the trail wasn't a trail at all.

We were walking blindly into the darkness.

Calling her name would be risky. Alerting Cade that we were nearby would make him feel threatened, which might cause him to drag her farther into the forest.

Though the mud prevented me from seeing anything, it didn't block my other senses. The faint aroma of our scent spurred me on.

No sign of her blood gave me hope she was unharmed, though the uptick in my heartbeat made me wonder if it was a result of adrenaline or if she was afraid.

Edmund and Luca lagged behind by only a step. It was eerily quiet in a forest so vast. "Are we not going to discuss these?" Edmund whispered as he caught up to my side. I had hoped they would overlook the skeletons scattered across the ground and perched against trees.

The forest floor was a bed of bones.

"Go ask their name if you're so goddamn curious," I muttered, cursing as another root grabbed my leg and nicked the exposed skin.

"Ezekiel, we need to get our bearings. We could be walking away from her and not closer to her."

"I can't stop, Edmund." I paused momentarily to face him. "I smell her. She's in here. Cade abused her and tried to rape her before we banished him from Seolia."

"I know," he responded painfully. It was evident that the thought bothered him. He had grown to love her dearly. "We prevented him from entering Thoya after receiving John's initial letter." He put his hand on my shoulder. "I am anxious to find her, but we need direction. We need light."

A loud and unrecognizable caw above had us searching the treetops, but we saw nothing. Luca spun around in a slow circle. "Zeke, I don't have a great feeling. There's a reason no one is allowed in here. Petra and Elric wouldn't have declared it unsafe otherwise."

"What do you expect me to do then? Leave her in here?" I shook my head. "You two can leave. I am not giving up on finding her."

"Ezekiel, we are not leaving. We simply want a plan."

"I don't have time to make a plan, Edmund!" I shouted. "The longer we're here, the more we remain at risk — the more Raven is at risk. It's been days since I saw her, Edmund. I have to keep going."

He and Luca exchanged a quick glance before he nodded. "Of course. I apologize, Ezekiel."

Sighing and exhausted, I ran a hand down my face. I was grateful he was here with me. He didn't need to leave his kingdom to help find my wife. He was already doing more than I could've ever asked for. We both stood to inherit kingdoms in this realm. If we lost our lives, it would change the trajectory of our people forever. "Don't apologize. Just help me find her."

"I am not a hunter, and she is your prey," he said with a slight grin. "Please lead the way."

Leaves bristled and crunched under our steps. The simple noise sounded louder in the silent forest. All three of us were on high alert for anything irregular or threatening, which was... everything.

I felt Luca's unease. "What's the history of this place?" he asked. "We didn't learn much about it as children."

"There's a reason for that," Edmund muttered.

I couldn't answer that. It had garnered the nickname of *The Forest Beyond* — the center of all horror stories children would tell to one another, stories about creatures and deaths without any hard proof behind them. The skeletons at my feet made me wonder if there was some truth to the stories.

Edmund knocked down tree roots with a large stick. "Unfortunately, I do not know much. Petra and Elric have remained secretive about it, much like Leonidas did about the Black Forest in Seolia. Each forest seems to have its own dark story attached to its history."

"The rumors about the Black Forest are untrue," I said. "I lived in that forest for three months. The only strange thing about it was the caves. Other than those, it's just a forest."

Edmund's chuckle was deep. "Petra and Elric claimed the same thing about this one. However, no forest of Thoya ever caused deaths. No man has ever feared lands like they do the forests of Perosan and Seolia."

"Something about forests," I grumbled. "The forest of Reales supposedly houses a cabin that Celestina enchanted. Only Raven has access to it."

"Does it not seem strange to anyone else?" Luca asked. "All of the kingdoms in our realm have had witches as leaders, except for Petra, unless she's one, too. Three out of four have magical forests. That can't be a coincidence."

I hadn't thought about it before. "It's not a coincidence. The leaders of this realm have secrets that remain unshared. Have you ever asked your mother about it, Edmund?"

"Many times," he answered. "She evades my questions."

I couldn't help but grin. "The only witch who doesn't ever seem to know what's going on is Raven, yet she is the most wanted," I said. "My father believes she is the key to something."

"I believe it," Edmund quipped. "My mother talked about Raven for many years, even before her identity was confirmed. She would never allow me to visit Seolia, though."

"Not for lack of trying." I looked at him with a raised brow. "You sent letters to Raven."

He threw his head back in laughter. "I wondered if you'd ever learn of those. She never wrote back to me. Rumors of her beauty had every man's curiosity piqued. I had to try my hand."

I debated whether I should tell him the truth or construct a lie about how she was just waiting for me. But the fact was, Raven would've liked Edmund. She would have entertained his offer to court her. Hell, maybe even Gisela would've won her over. Both siblings were too charming.

Luca snorted. "Cade burned all of your letters before she could read them."

Edmund guffawed. His jaw dropped open in shock. But then, a broad smile stretched across his mouth. "It was for the best. Once they met, I wouldn't have wanted to battle Ezekiel for Raven's hand."

"It is for the best," I added with the tiniest smile I could manage. "She would've loved you easily."

Ever the dramatic one, he put a hand over his heart and groaned. "Do not tell me that, Ezekiel."

"It would've been over for both of us if she met Gisela first," I admitted. It held more truth than I was willing to reconcile with.

"Gisela has taken many lovers," Edmund said. "But I believe Raven would have settled her had that happened. Gisela enjoys having her fun, but despite what she says, I know she is looking for someone to expect more of her."

"I think we all wish for a pairing." Luca reached up and squeezed the back of my neck as my thoughts drifted back to my mate. "You two have given all of us something to hope for."

This had become a much deeper conversation than anticipated, and not one I would have believed I'd be having in a forest full of human remains while looking for my wife, but the gesture and words were kind. Our brokenness and personal tragedies may seem unfair, but our love was the only thing that mattered at the end of each day.

It was ironic that others found what we deemed strange and confusing to be endearing and something to wish for. So when I looked at Luca and said, "Thank you," it was genuine.

I NEEDED to know how Raven had made it this far into the forest. We had walked miles and still found no sign of her. We couldn't have been that far behind them. A silence had drawn out between the three of us — they all circled back to Raven despite our best intentions of distracting ourselves with conversation. She was entwined into so many of our stories and memories.

But when a familiar warmth crept across my spine, I stopped and looked around. Slowly, the sound of leaves turned into something else. A whisper. A soft howl. The hairs on the back of my neck stood as I turned in a slow circle, holding my hand up to keep Luca and Edmund quiet while I listened.

Similar to what I had heard in the forest of Seolia all those months ago, my lips parted when her name echoed off the trunks. It was slow at first and so low that I thought I imagined it. But the whispers started coming from multiple voices and increasing in volume the longer I stood still.

Frantic. The voices were hysterical.

Worried, frazzled, and overbearing. My fingers curled because I didn't know which way to look.

Bones rattled.

"Do you hear that?"

Their lack of answers told me I was the only one listening to her name being repeated through the trees. "Raven," I said, taking small, hesitant steps forward. "Raven."

The whispers ceased.

But from behind me, a gust of wind rushed up, blowing my hair over my eyes.

I took off sprinting, following the breeze and watching as the branches swayed in the direction I needed to go.

I didn't have answers. I didn't have time to question it. Edmund and Luca called my name, but the whispers drowned out their voices with only her name.

Raven. Raven. *Raven.*

It didn't matter how it was happening. It didn't matter why the trees seemed to talk when it had anything to do with her. All that mattered was that I did not need anything other than her in my arms. The trees opened into a clearing next to a large pond.

My little demon stood swaying next to a body.

Wearing a tattered white dress, covered in blood, and with flames lit on her palms. Raven looked as if she might have been dreaming when her eyes slowly lifted to meet mine, and relief flooded her body.

Bruises and cuts covered her face and arms, her eyes were black and hollow, and her wrist was bruised in too much purple. Her red hair was matted and stuck to her skin. Blood from her bottom lip dripped down her chin and throat.

Before she could fall to her knees, I was running toward her. Her eyes rolled back as she hit the ground, her fire seeping back into her skin, her pulse slowing as I felt mine grow weaker — almost as if she was waiting to see me again before giving in to the swift hand of death.

"Baby, please stay with me."

Dying. She was dying in my arms.

I caught her before her head hit the ground, and I brushed her bloodied hair from her face, crying her name, begging her to stay with me just a little longer.

Cold. She was so cold, even as Blaze.

Sudden rain fell down upon us, wetting the blood on her skin and dribbling down my hands as I held her in my arms.

Her eyes were a mixture of pine green and flames as she tried to focus on me. It took a considerable effort from her to put her hand against my cheek. She tried to say my name, her voice barely a whisper and broken. I cried her name when she coughed up blood, adjusting her in my arms and pressing my lips to her forehead.

And the last words I heard before she drifted were ones I had been waiting to hear since I met her.

"Kill him."

THE FOREST FLOOR WAS A BED OF BONES.

04

Raven

YESTERDAY

Thump. Thump. Thump.

My pulse pounded in my throat, tingling the back of my skull and discharging uncomfortable sensations down the length of my spine. With stiff muscles, I brushed my fingertips across the raw skin in the crook of my arm and winced from the swelling. Moving even an inch shot pain through my shoulder. I groaned and then coughed from the dryness of my throat.

I felt like I had been asleep for days.

The sluggish movements of my limbs felt too familiar, the burning of aconite like an old friend, and I desperately needed water.

Sweat stuck hair to my face and neck, either from a fever or Blaze working overtime to burn through the poison.

Zeke.

I had grown used to his arms wrapped around me each time I slept and felt out of sorts by myself. After an entire life spent sleeping alone, the weeks with him had replaced all feelings of loneliness. And wherever he was, I knew he hadn't slept while trying to figure out where I could be.

Rubbing my eyes, I slowly peeled them open and blinked colors away. Two slender rays of sun peeked through the cracks of a latched door, providing me very little light. Stagnant air surrounded me, making me wonder just how long I had been stowed away.

Sitting up slowly, I extended my fingers and muttered obscenities at the pain that flooded down my ribcage and across my chest. When I tried to shift into Blaze, fire pinched my veins and I hissed, wanting to physically slap my most stubborn shift.

"Fine," I muttered as if she were a separate person. "Take your time, I guess. You could at least allow Frost to soothe the burning, you stubborn demon."

Clutching the worn blanket between my fingers, I held it toward the fragment of light streaming through the door, confirming that the crusty residue on the white fabric was my blood. Immediately dropping the sheet, I searched my body, tugging at my clothes, relieved to find I was still dressed in the top and pants I had put on before leaving the castle.

And I didn't feel...violated. At least, not in the truly irreparable way, though I doubted I would ever be whole again after this.

I needed to get back to Zeke. I would swim if I had to.

Throwing my feet over the bed, I took a step too fast and stumbled sideways, knocking into a table in the middle of the small cabin. I didn't recognize this ship. I hadn't sailed much, but I knew which ships were in my harbor and this wasn't one of them.

My eyes lifted as feet stomped across the deck. Crumbled on the floor in a ball, I braced myself as the latched door opened, and a face I had grown to loathe looked down into the cabin. "You're awake," he said with a sigh.

"Observant," I replied with an eye roll, my voice raspy and

41

strained. "I would like to extend my heartfelt appreciation for drugging me and stealing me away from my husband, Cade. Always the gallant one. And you wonder why I didn't choose you."

I never imagined wishing I still had a spirit of death lurking inside me more than I did at this moment, though when the words tumbled from my lips, I froze and gauged the look on his face. I was at his mercy in this cabin and remarks like that might not play to my advantage anymore–our typical jesting back and forth was no longer playful and wouldn't lead to him being the kind, protective friend I once knew. He was much more willing to harm me now.

Chuckling, he descended the ladder into the cabin and walked to a shelf mounted on the wall. "You'll learn to love me again, Raven." He took a small vial between his fingers. "You'll forget about him after some time."

"No," I said defiantly, rising to my knees, "I won't, Cade. He is not a chapter you can rewrite. I will escape you, or he will find me. This will not end in your favor."

Turning toward me with a malicious grin, he shrugged a shoulder and spun a needle between his fingers. "Raven, I plan on fucking you so often that you won't remember your own name, let alone his."

Panic and disgust coated me like a heavy cloak. "You will not fucking touch me, Cade. I would rather die."

"Always so dramatic," he said, walking swiftly across the cabin. "Now, be still."

Standing quickly, I walked backward around the small cabin. Dizziness wafted over me from my lack of movement lately. The rocking of the ship didn't help, either. "Do you not find it pathetic that you must drug a woman to be with her?" I held the table between us like a shield.

He lunged for me, but I shoved the table against him and ran to the opposite side. Growling, he kicked the table to the side. "I fucked plenty of women while you were in Reales, Raven, and each time I came inside them, I yelled your name."

I cringed, looking around the cabin for anything I could use as a weapon. "I didn't even want to say your name each time you fucked me, so I can't relate."

He pounced so quickly that I could only think to jam my elbow into his nose as I had once watched Zeke do to him. The pop of bone made me squeal with delight and triumph.

Zeke would be so proud of me.

My name was mangled with a string of curse words. I took advantage of the temporary distraction to run toward the ladder.

His arms wrapped around my waist, the blood pouring from his nose spreading across my neck as he tried to keep me still. I tried to knock the needle free from between his lips, but he dodged me.

"Cade!" I screamed, kicking the wall hard enough to propel us backward.

Falling into a heap on the bed, he pinned me between his legs and jammed the needle into the swelling on my arm. I cried out in agony as the liquid entered my bloodstream and sent a fresh wave of burning through my veins.

Blood covered his lips and cheeks as he watched me fade, nothing discernible in how he looked at me. I could no longer recognize the man I had spent so many years with.

"I hate what you've made me become," was the last thing I heard. His fist was the last thing I felt.

$\sim$

SUNLIGHT WAS NO LONGER POURING through the door's cracks when I opened my eyes. The wind howled and the boat dipped and rocked against its side. Maybe it would throw Cade overboard.

Not only was my arm swollen, but now my eye felt fractured. I could barely open it, and attempting to heal it with my fingertips did nothing other than cause me to cry in pain. And no matter how hard I tried, I could not stop shivering.

Since my healing wasn't magic, it seemed to work quicker than Blaze at dispelling the poison and keeping the bruises on my body bearable to touch. Since trauma was spread across my body, it couldn't decide where to heal first.

All I wanted was my elements back, silently cursing at how nearly undetectable the smell of aconite was, even the taste of it easily masked—hence the ingenuity he displayed at pouring it into my wine bottle. If I could just push through it, everything else could come later. Bruises were a daily occurrence with Zeke's desire to consume me like a meal, so those I could handle. It was the thought of Cade finding a way to fuck me that made me ache in the worst way.

I needed to find a way off of this ship, but destroying the supply of aconite was my first priority. Blinking rapidly to adjust to the darkness of the cabin, I slowly scooted to the edge of the bed and drew a deep breath. Without the ability to ignite the tips of my fingers, I needed to rely solely on smell and touch alone—a rarity for someone like me who always had an arsenal of personal weapons at their disposal.

Cade. All I smelled was Cade—the stench of an unwashed man, though if Zeke were here, he'd smell the lies and deceit wafting off Cade.

Standing on shaky legs, I hobbled around the room, biting back curses as the boat rocking sent me knocking into a table and tripping over the leg of a chair. I held my arms out as if I were tightly wrapped in wads of fabric, blindly dancing across the room until I reached the shelf hanging on the wall from where he had retrieved the bottle.

Empty.

Inaudible frustrations tumbled from my lips as I kept dragging my fingers across the wooden plank, hoping I was wrong. Lifting my head to look at the closed latch door, I considered my options. I could stay down here, wait until he sought me out again, and bide my time, or I could bravely try to find the poison myself by going on deck.

Every inch of my body was sore, but Zeke would want me to fight. Jeanine would *expect* me to fight. I refused to cower and accept this as my fate. I would find my way back to them somehow, even if it meant facing the man who had made his intentions clear on repossessing my body again.

Despite my anger and frustration, the part of me that had grown up around Cade couldn't believe that he was the same man who was upstairs—that he was the man trapping me purely to own me.

Had I truly caused him to do this? Had my actions somehow led to the desecration of the man he used to be?

Was this because of me?

A clear mental picture formed of Jeanine rolling her eyes at me.

No, Raven, she would say.

Cade was a mirage. The man I had built up so high in my head wasn't real. He was the one I should've been protecting myself against. He no longer deserved my forgiveness or devotion, and I had to stop lying to myself while trying to explain away his actions.

Staring at my hands, which were nearly invisible in the dimly lit cabin, I blinked while considering my options. I wasn't able to shift yet. There wasn't any magic for me to use against him. I would have to use the pathetic amount of training I had to bring him down.

I could inject him with the aconite if I managed to find it, but I wasn't sure he would have the same reaction to it as me. And I remained unsure of where we were. I couldn't waste time trying to find land only for him to wake up.

Inhaling a deep breath, I slowly climbed the ladder and pushed on the latched door. The room around me shrunk as I realized I was stowed away with no escape. My palms clammed up with sweat, goosebumps pimpled across my skin, and I screamed as I banged on the door with my fists.

I refused to be held hostage. I couldn't be locked down here. I needed to burn through the wood; if only I could light my palms...

The door flew open, and I gasped as if I hadn't been breathing, the crisp ocean air filling my nostrils and welcoming me. "Please let me out," I pleaded, climbing one step higher. "I need air, I need water, I need...."

He held his hand up to silence me and stared while contemplating. Finally, he took a small step back. I took the steps as fast as possible and pulled myself up to the deck, rolling to my back and smiling at the night sky full of stars.

Freedom. Zeke.

Sitting up on my knees, I looked around in hopes of recognizing something, but all I saw were harsh waves and a flag of Reales whipping through the air.

That was why I couldn't recognize it.

I glanced over at him as he stared at me with arms crossed. "Why do you have a ship from Reales?" With a swollen eye, visibility was a chore. I stood and limped to the ship's side. The absence of the outline of anything numbed my fight to survive, just a little.

And the sight of a picnic basket in the corner gave me an ounce of hope that maybe the poison was hidden in there, though I doubted he'd keep it near his food.

He stood behind me and put his arms on either side, nuzzling his nose against my hair. I jerked at the contact and tried to shove away from him, but he stayed locked around me. "We went to Mira," he said quietly, resting his chin on my shoulder.

I was still as death, except for when he dangled a half-empty canteen in front of me, which I grabbed like a thief. Water had never been my favorite, I only drank it when I was forced or reminded, but now I would never take it for granted again.

"I begged her, Raven. I told her I would be on her side if she'd let me take you and kill him." He moved the hair away from my neck and brushed his lips across my skin. The contact made me sputter the water from my lips as a wave of fear rinsed over me. "But then she informed me that if he dies, so do you."

Sighing, he moved to rest his hands on my waist. I trembled in his hold, my heartbeat hammering in my ears, trying to open a crack in my chest to spill to the floor, just so it wouldn't be near him. As he fidgeted behind me, I braced for the worst, but then parted my lips when I felt the warmth of his jacket enveloping my shoulders. Tears pooled in my eyes at the gesture that mirrored the man I once knew— and for a second, I doubted my resolve to get away from him. I wanted him to stop touching me, but I needed more information. I needed to know what he saw and who he might have met.

He took the empty canteen from my hands and tossed it to the ground. "Unfortunately, I had to create my own plan to have you. One night, I stole one of their ships and left my parents there."

My eyebrows drew in slightly. "Did she allow them to stay in Reales?"

He nodded against my head. "She said they would be welcomed in Reales and introduced me to an adviser on her court, who assured me that we would be well taken care of."

I cleared my throat to keep my voice steady. "Had we met him before?" Did he seem *unbreakable*?

"Raven," he whispered against my ear, pressing me into the ship's side. "I can't wait to be inside of you again."

I pushed my elbow back with surprising force, shoving his arm off as he grunted from the blow to his stomach. "No, Cade, you will not have me ever again."

He took slow steps toward me as I continued to back away. "I will, Raven. I will fuck you as often as I want because you are mine. You always have been."

"No," I said again through clenched teeth. "I belong to *him*. That will not change just because you are holding me hostage like a fucking coward."

"You are mine!" he shouted, lunging and growling as I moved out of his grasp. "And you will be again."

Swim. I would have to swim.

I would rather drown than allow him to touch me. I would rather risk the rumored bloodthirsty sirens living at the bottom of the ocean than feel his body again.

Running to the ship's side, I managed to get my knee on the railing before he pulled me off and threw me down.

I screamed and rolled to my stomach, crawling toward the opposite side, but he grabbed my ankle and yanked me backward. I balled my hands into fists and hit any part of him that I could reach, tears welling in both eyes and stinging as they pooled against the swelling. "No!" I screamed repeatedly. "Zeke!" I shouted.

Cade crawled over me and tugged at my shirt, the fabric tearing and stretching underneath his fingers.

Clasping my hands together, I put every ounce of energy I had left into knocking them against his temple. He cursed as he fell to the side, clutching his nose and giving me a chance to make it to my feet.

But as I ran toward the side of the ship, I stumbled down into the opening of the cabin and cried out in pain as I landed on the floor, the bones in my left wrist splitting. I wailed and clutched it against my chest, crawling away from the ladder into a dark corner and hoping he wouldn't find me.

I needed to heal extremely quickly.

My panting and whimpers gave me away as he slid down the ladder, coming right to me and pulling me up by my elbow. His hands shoved into the waistband of my pants, but I brought my knee up and managed to buy myself another few seconds as he doubled over in pain.

"Broken," I rasped, tears sliding down my cheeks. "I broke my wrist, Cade. Please don't touch me, please don't touch me right now, please let it heal," I begged.

"Goddamnit, Raven!" he yelled, rising up and wrapping his fingers around my throat. "You can't fight me forever, wench."

I clawed at his wrist with my good hand, trying to draw in breaths as he restricted my air flow. "Cade," I said with a wasted breath.

"Sleep, Raven."

HE TOOK THE EMPTY CANTEEN FROM MY HANDS AND TOSSED IT TO THE GROUND.

05

RAVEN

I sat up with a gasp. Time had lost all meaning. I never knew how many days had passed each time I opened my eyes, and without food, I was weakening. I couldn't remember the last time he had left a half-full canteen of water down here, but the dryness of my tongue told me that if he wasn't the one to kill me, dehydration would handle it.

Wrapped in a shirt and aching, I placed my wrist on my chest only to find I had been changed into a white dress that I had twisted around my body while thrashing in my sleep.

Nightmares. I had nightmares without Zeke with me to shatter them. I constantly ran toward him, only to be caught and dragged away by Cade. He would shout my name while Cade covered my mouth to muffle my screams.

My nightmares didn't differ much from my reality.

Grimacing, I pushed up on my palm and leaned against the wall. "Zeke," I whispered through the burning in my throat. "If you find me and search my memories, I need you to know that I fought. If I'm dying, I need you to know that I gave it everything I had, and I need you to know that I loved you with a fierceness that will never be matched by anyone else."

"Especially anyone else," I continued grumbling to myself, "Because if you don't die with me and move on to someone else, I will find a way to kill you."

Delirious, I started laughing to myself, because even while I was trapped and possibly dying soon, my envy was as strong as ever.

My laughter ceased as the latched door swung open. I shut my eyes at the sudden burst of light, mentally and physically bracing myself for whatever he wanted to try next.

The bed creaked and sank from his weight beside me, and I jerked from the feel of metal against my thigh. Squinting, I peeked at the canteen and grabbed it, quickly bringing it to my lips. Warm water shot down my throat, and I could have sworn I had never tasted anything better.

Taking the empty canteen from me, he tossed it toward the ladder and placed his hand on my bare thigh. The dress he'd chosen for me was short and gave him easy access if he decided to take it. "Raven, it doesn't have to be this way."

There wasn't any other way it could be. I would never love him the way he wanted me to, and while fighting him daily seemed like the more tiring option, I wouldn't give in.

I wouldn't betray Zeke.

Rolling my head against the wall, I stared at the man I once loved. All the memories we had created together would now be tainted. And while I still recognized him physically, even that had differed. Cade had always been fit; even after leaving our guard to be an adviser, he continued caring for himself. There had been mornings when I sat at the border of the Black Forest and waited for him to jog around the island before returning to me so we could start our day together.

But under the direction and guidance of my husband and Jeanine, while training the armies in Seolia, Cade had changed. His muscles became more defined, the lines around his eyes and mouth had hardened from the days under the sun, and I knew he could easily overpower me.

He might not be the smoothest fighter, but his determination to keep me outweighed that—not that I was any better. I hadn't taken part in training nearly enough to be an actual threat to him, especially without my elements, but I was enough of a threat to fight my way to freedom, even if it meant my life in the end.

"Why are you doing this?" I asked in a small whisper. "How long have you been planning this?"

Sighing, he adjusted on the bed until we faced one another. "You're so naive, Raven. I suppose I am partially to blame for that."

Something about how he spoke to me always made me feel...less. Less than enough, less than him, less. When Zeke communicated with me, it was as with his equal. Cade talked to me as if I was beneath him.

"Whether I keep you here or take you somewhere, it would be no different than how we've always lived."

I must've been more incoherent than I thought, because that didn't make sense. "I don't recall you ever locking me away on a ship, Cade."

His fingertips brushed across my arm. I drew in a breath through clenched teeth as he applied pressure to the swelling. "Not a ship, perhaps."

Still, I couldn't detangle his riddles and wished he'd get to the point.

"For the entirety of your reign, I kept others away and prevented you from leaving the island, especially after..." He paused, his fingers wrapping around my arm until I winced. "Well, especially after I overheard John speaking to Leonidas about his son."

I blinked. "You knew about Zeke?"

"I did not know who John's son was, only that he had one that he wanted you to marry." He laughed then, but the laugh wasn't one I recognized. "John was the one who encouraged my father to bring me to the castle, yet changed his mind and told Leonidas that I was an *unhealthy* friend for you."

"But Leonidas trusted you...."

He dipped his chin in a slight nod. "Leonidas did not know me well and died before he could heed John's advice. Leonidas groomed me to become obsessed with you, Raven. He forced me to watch you and implored me to stay by your side while you grew. And while I'll admit you were quite a strange child, I came to care for you."

My eyes lined with water. "You're blaming someone else for your obsession with me? Even now, you can't take accountability?"

"I did not want this life," he snapped. "And well"—a perverse grin spread—"once you reached adulthood, not only were you beautiful, you possessed magic. I would've been foolish to set you free and give you to someone else. If anyone else found you and discovered our secret, I would be forced to share you."

I cried out as he pinched my broken wrist between his fingers and released me. "I would not allow John's eldest son to steal what was mine."

Nausea swept through me like a storm. I had been nothing more than a pet to him—something to keep bound and desperate for his attention when he had always known I belonged to someone else. I could've had a family.

I turned my head away when he ran his thumb across my bottom lip. "You were so desperate for love, Raven, and so needy for attention that you didn't care that I fucked other women as long as you had me every morning."

Embarrassment heated my cheeks as my eyes lowered to the ground. "You were my best friend."

Laughing almost manically, he grabbed my chin and turned my head toward him. "I was your only friend, Raven. You made it so easy for me." His jaw ticked. "Until him."

He sighed through his nose. *He* looked stressed. *I* was fighting for my life, but he looked downright burdened to be talking about this. Selfish fucking—

He interrupted my thoughts with, "I knew my freedom was slipping away, and I would have to seduce you to keep your mind on me. Though, leaving you in Reales was a nice break." His grin turned spiteful. "Old habits, I suppose. I never could turn down the blondes."

I rolled my eyes. "If you expect me to be jealous, you'll be disappointed. I was highly satisfied in your absence. Zeke..."

He backhanded me and I fell sideways, wailing at the sting on my cheek. "You will stop saying his name in my presence, Raven! Your time with him is over."

"Zeke," I said again, louder than before. "Zeke, Zeke, Zeke!" I shouted, rising up again. "I will never stop saying his name. You will have to cut out my tongue before I *ever* stop saying his name, you fucking bastard."

He plied his fingers into my mouth and gripped my tongue, tugging it. "That can be arranged, Raven...."

I bit down on his fingers and pinched until I tasted his blood. He shouted obscenities at me as he jimmied his fingers from my grasp. He stared at the break in his skin before narrowing his eyes on me, then backhanded me again and yanked my hair to keep me upright. "You will annul your marriage and marry me."

I shoved at his chest with my hands, ignoring the pain. "I won't! I will never be free of him, Cade. You will never have me the way you want me. No amount of time will change that. I am his mate. I belong to him."

His lips thinned into a straight line as he pressed his fingers into my thighs and sent chills across me. "You are my bride, Raven. Look how beautiful you are in your dress. I chose it for you."

"You are fucking insane, Cade. You have completely lost it." I tried to peel his fingers from my thighs. "Stop touching me. I do not want you."

He leaned forward so fast that I knocked the back of my head against the wall. I groaned as I tried to rub the sting out. Pressing his lips against my ears, his voice was hoarse as he asked, "Don't you remember how I felt inside of you, Raven? How you used to moan for me?"

"Because I thought of him," I bit out, yanking my head away. "He shattered every memory of when you touched me, Cade, because I couldn't stand to think about it."

"Oh, Raven." He pushed my legs apart with his hands, attempting to crawl between them. "I'll remind you."

I wasn't sure what he thought it would prove if he reclaimed me, but he was deranged if he believed he would ever come close to the pleasure Zeke brought me.

My broken wrist did nothing to assist me in shoving him off, but when my fingers caught the waistband of his pants, hope blossomed. My thrashing instability hid my secret and continued to make him believe I was shoving him off, when I actually needed him closer. Trying to keep the smile from my lips, I wrapped my fingers around the needle and slid it from his waist to behind my back. Pure adrenaline kept me from crying out at the sharp and sudden movements of my wrist, shoving logic through my mind that I would heal—and even if I didn't, the risk was well worth it.

When he leaned forward and pressed his lips to mine, I fumbled with the needle. My grip was shaky at best, but my newfound relief of possibly finding a weapon quickly dissipated as the crack in my wrist shot nearly unbearable pain through the length of my arm. But when his tongue pushed against my lips and I jumped at the contact, he grinned as if taking my reaction as a positive one. It wasn't until he noticed my hand go still beneath me that his eyes slowly shifted downward.

"What do you have, Raven?"

"Nothing," I barely got out, wrapping my fingers tightly around the needle. "I don't have anything."

Glowering, he took my broken wrist and squeezed it until I cried out. "Show me what you have!"

Instead of revealing it to him, I attempted something I had only seen Zeke do once before. I brought my head against Cade's with all the strength I could muster, immediately regretting it as colors shot through my eyes and a pounding headache formed.

"Fuck!" he shouted, palming his forehead and falling backward on the bed.

I sat up and switched the needle to my good hand, though even that one shook from nerves, and screamed as he grasped for me. I thrashed against him, biting his tongue as he tried to shove it in my mouth again.

Spitting out his blood, he brought his hand up to slap me again, but I sat up quickly and jammed the needle into the side of his neck. His eyes widened as I squeezed the poison out, feeling for the needle and pulling it out, staring at it as he swayed enough to give me hope that it worked.

Not that I had time to think about it.

But fuck, my head hurt.

Holding my forehead in my hand and wrist against my chest, I shakily ran toward the ladder and climbed it. Cade fell to his side on the bed with his eyes shut.

I had only attempted sailing once on my own and had failed the test, according to Zeke. All I remembered was something about foam and wind, which wouldn't prove helpful at this particular moment.

Temporarily blinded by the sun, I blinked while running toward the ship's helm. The air was chilly, and I remained cold without my elements, but time was limited, and swimming somewhere was out of the question.

Squinting, I looked in every direction. The sun directly blocked what looked like a castle, but not one I recognized. Surely we hadn't traveled outside of our realm, but I hadn't visited Perosan in fifteen years.

No matter where we were, anything was safer than this.

Grabbing the wheel with one hand, I groaned and twisted it in the castle's direction. I released an exerted cry of frustration as the ship barely moved, and attempted again to turn the wheel.

"Please," I whispered. "Just a little bit of Terra to guide me closer."

I didn't shift, nor did I feel her, but a heavy breeze collided with the water and gave the ship enough boost to turn in the direction of the sun-covered kingdom. "You could've spent a little more time teaching me and a little time less flirting with me," I said aloud to Zeke.

It was almost as if I could hear him say, *that will never happen,* and it made me smile for the first time in days.

Delirium was evident, but I would take it happily if it gave me visions of him.

I needed food. I needed more water.

Glancing around, I located the picnic basket opposite the helm. Biting my lip as I looked again toward the unfamiliar kingdom, I decided it wouldn't make a difference if I took a few minutes to grab something small to eat. I needed to replenish some of my energy to be able to dock.

I paused on my way to the basket to kick the latch door shut, fumbling with the lock until I was convinced he couldn't escape. When I flipped open the lid on the basket, excitement had me falling into a heap on the floor. I grabbed an apple and took a bite bigger than I could adequately chew.

A few more moments, and I would be safe again.

I leaned my head against the ship's side while practically inhaling the apple, reaching into the basket to grab another one when I heard him. He was climbing the stairs and grunting, his fist banging against the locked door. I whipped my head back and forth, looking for something, anything, that could keep the door closed, but the deck was empty. Using one hand, I crawled toward the door, nearly throwing my body across it to keep it shut, but when he broke the weak hinges and the door flew open, I froze and cowered behind it.

It wasn't enough. I hadn't injected him with enough.

He didn't notice me as he looked toward the helm, cursing and limping toward it. When he moved to turn it in the opposite direction, I screamed for him to stop and stood to run toward him.

He glanced over his shoulder at me and dipped to knock me with his shoulder as he turned the wheel. I stumbled backward a few steps, but I had gotten this far.

I would not give up.

I would not surrender.

Channeling Jeanine, I curled my hand into a fist and went for his temple, taking the wheel from him as he faltered a step. "Goddamnit, Raven!" he bellowed, grabbing a chunk of my hair and yanking it until I had to release the wheel. "You cannot change the outcome of this!"

Growling, I kicked his ankle repeatedly. "You have tried to control me for too long!"

His weakened state from the poison worked in my favor as he

shuffled to the side, giving me a chance to stand back up and retake the wheel.

He held on and fought me, trying to turn in the opposite direction and hitting my ribs with his fist.

I was nothing more than a walking bruise by now, but the only thing that would stop me from trying to get away from him was death.

So, I screamed. I screamed and fought and put every last bit of valor into keeping the ship turned toward the kingdom. But as the sound of wood scraping against rocks sounded off underneath us, we both jerked our heads toward a shoreline that was coming up way too quickly.

"Fuck!" we shouted in unison, and I released the wheel for him to attempt to avoid the rocks.

Darkness; so much darkness lay ahead of us with black rocks and gray sand surrounded by trees that seemed to welcome death with open arms.

But I didn't feel threatened.

At least, not until I heard rocks colliding with the ship.

The last thing I remembered was flying.

NAUSEA SWEPT THROUGH ME LIKE A STORM.

06

RAVEN

"Why are you always getting yourself into these situations, Raven?"

My eyes fluttered open at the sound of a voice I didn't recognize. The wet sand was coarse against my cheek and coils of bitterly cold air wrapped around me. Groaning, I rolled my wrist. It no longer felt broken, only sprained. My healing was working faster now that it had been over a day since my last injection.

Whispers of my elements crawled through my legs, though I remained cold against the sand. "Zeke," I whispered, hoping the voice would be clearer if I heard it again.

In my line of, albeit fuzzy, vision, black shoes stood before me—shiny and pristine and not at all like something that belonged on a coast.

Blinking and squinting an eye, I attempted to look up to see whom the shoes belonged to, but my vision was impaired, though the person staring back at me looked familiar.

"Go to the forest, Raven. You'll be safe there."

"So tired," I muttered, closing my eyes again. "Hurts."

"You always were the stubborn one," the voice said with a sigh. "I can't do this for you, Raven."

"I don't recall asking you to do anything." A shoe nudged my sore ribs. *Everything* was sore. I hissed and lazily swatted at it with my hand. "Go away. I need to heal."

"We're going to run out of time, Raven. I can't use my magic here. You need to go to the forest."

Magic. His magic.

Opening my eyes again, I blinked rapidly to focus on the face staring back at me, but I had to be hallucinating. He loathed me; why would he be here trying to help me?

"River," I breathed.

I could've sworn the corner of his mouth twitched. "Ever the observant one. Go into the forest, Raven. That is thrice I've told you. I cannot help you here."

"Why can't you use your magic here?"

He looked behind me before nudging me again with his shoe. "He's waking up. Go, Raven. Go, now."

"Help me," I whispered, whimpering as I raised up on my elbows. "My elements aren't back yet, and I'm so tired."

"I am not supposed to be here, Raven. You will be safe if you'll listen for once in your life and go to the forest."

"Why are you here?"

He didn't move, but cold water rushed underneath me. I yelped, moving quickly to my hands and knees. My head snapped toward the forest as the trees seemed to sway in response to the magic used, but when I looked for him again, he was gone.

Only the imprint of his shoes remained.

I WAS CONVINCED I had dreamt him up in my dehydrated state, but I crawled toward the forest. I didn't particularly trust him, but it seemed safer than staying only feet away from Cade, who had unfortunately not died.

I needed to regain strength before running down the shoreline toward the kingdom. But as I crawled, Cade groaned behind me. Without looking back, I rose to my feet ungracefully, drawing in sharp breaths through my nose at the pain shooting through my legs.

I must've landed harder than I thought.

My run was more like a hobble, but it was all I could manage as I headed toward the trees, hoping Zeke would find me. Being in a forest shouldn't shock him, though being chased through them was growing tiresome.

I didn't recognize where I was, so I would most likely not see Zeke for a while—not until I managed to kill Cade and escape. I was confident whatever kingdom I was in would look upon me in terror in my ragged dress and bloodied body, but my chances of surviving this were dwindling, and there was no other option.

Zeke would eventually find me.

It wasn't until I crossed into the trees that I glanced behind me to see Cade wobbling as he stood, zeroing in on me with a hardened glare. He wouldn't go down without a fight.

Neither would I. This would end with one of us dead.

I jumped, then cursed, as I noticed the skeletons...everywhere. It was odd enough to be in a forest with bones, let alone fully preserved ones still intact and staring at me through the black holes in their skulls.

As if watching me.

I might have been foolish to trust River.

Mud from the ground stuck to the bottoms of my feet, numbing me from the cold. I wouldn't make it to day's end if I didn't find a shelter of some sort.

"It would be nice if you'd ignite soon," I snapped at Blaze.

"Raven!" Cade called out, his voice too close for comfort.

At the mention of my name, the trees seemed to react the same way they had when River used his magic. Branches rustled above me, and roots seemed to move out of my way, clearing a pathway as I continued limping.

Stopping, I doubled over and placed my hands on my knees. My chest burned, and drawing in deep breaths was impossible. "I can't," I choked, coughing. "I can't keep going." I stumbled a step forward to lean against the trunk of a tree. "Zeke," I squeaked in a rasp. "I can't keep going, Zeke. I can't."

Bracing myself against a trunk to remain upright, I planted my feet and prepared to fight Cade with what I had left. My legs could give out at any moment, and everything was hazy through my exhaustion, but I refused to surrender.

But ahead of me and just out of reach, a small burst of flame hovered in the air and disappeared before I could touch it. Blinking, I turned my head as another appeared on my left. I grasped for it, but it vanished and reappeared a few feet away.

Pure curiosity had me moving my feet, slowly chasing the small bursts as they created a pathway through the trees for me to follow. Maybe if I caught one, it would bring Blaze back. Or, I could wield it somehow.

This had to be a forest of illusions.

In no natural universe could I see flames and glowing snowflakes creating trails for me to run toward, bouncing and spinning like they often danced together, blending into their embraces.

It was beautiful and mesmerizing and I chased them, driving deeper into the forest and slowly regaining some of the evaporated strength I had lost.

He knew. Somehow, River knew what lurked in this forest.

You always were the stubborn one, he had said to me, making it seem like he…knew me.

"River," I said aloud, pausing when the flames and snowflakes did. They stopped dancing and moving, hovering above me, almost as if they stared at me the same way I watched them. "Why can't River come in here?"

I took small steps closer toward them. They remained still in the air, but their glow brightened. "Where am I?"

A gust of wind behind me rattled the bones around me. I snapped out of my trance and remembered that now was not the time to search for answers. The elements seemed to remember, too, as they took off faster than I could keep up with. My legs quickly grew tired again, and bark from the trees as I knocked into them cut my skin and caused fresh blood to pool and drip.

The trees opened into a large clearing, similar to the one in the Black Forest. Almost too similar, if you had asked me on a sane day. And seeing a small pond brought tears to my eyes as I thought of Zeke. "My love," I cried, palming my eyes.

I was ready, I decided. I was prepared to meet him in the meadow if it allowed me to see and touch him again. I could apologize for giving up, for not fighting hard enough.

We could find a way to stay there together. We could live amongst the flowers and springtime air until it was time for us to rebirth in another lifetime.

We could find our happy ending somewhere else.

I was so tired. My body hurt in places I didn't realize could hurt. Blood, both dried and fresh, covered me. I was hallucinating my elements, which had to mean my time was up. The universe was letting me say goodbye to them.

My body could become part of the forest, living peacefully amongst the trees with the other lost souls.

Warmth surrounded me, and when I dropped my hands from my eyes, they widened. I spun in a slow circle.

I was enclosed by multiple bursts of flames. Glowing. Expanding as if creating a wall of fire around me—vibrant and popping like bonfires from the festivals at home.

So many that I couldn't look at all of them.

"Blaze," I whispered, reaching out to touch one. I was so close— just mere inches away from feeling my fire again.

Crying out in surprise and pain, I was tackled to the ground. The flames around me scattered but beamed so brightly that I had to close my eyes.

Cade put every bit of strength into keeping me on the ground, pinning my wrists above my head and sneering. "I am going to *kill* him, Raven. I will force him to watch me fuck you before I end him."

I couldn't help but laugh at the threat. "You have never been man enough to take him on."

"It is his fault this has happened!" he lied. "If he had never come to Seolia, we would be *fine*!"

We wouldn't. I would've still been living my life as a lie. I never would've known what true love felt like, what having a friend like Jeanine could do for my self-confidence, or feel the fierce protectiveness of a brother like Luca.

I never would've known *myself*.

And I was worth saving.

"I told her, you know." He leaned in closer. "I told Mira of your marriage to him, of the army you're raising to fight against her." His sneer turned into a spiteful grin. "She said she'll take care of it."

I didn't miss the bright orange flames morphing into purple, nor when they slowly began enclosing Cade. "Say it again, Cade," I said with a grin. "Tell me again what you want to do to him."

"I will bring him back to Reales...."

My fingers slowly curled.

"I will throw him at the feet of Mira, Raven."

Sparking, simmering, surrounding.

"And then I will watch as she hangs him."

Jerking my head to the side, the flames followed my direction and attacked him, setting his clothing aflame. He howled in surprise, in pain, but I didn't fucking care about anything other than crawling out from underneath him.

"You will not threaten my husband, Cade." At the flick of my wrist, the flames left his body to wait above me.

He crawled toward the pond, screeching from the burns and crying out in frustration. And I waited. I gave him a moment to believe I would show him mercy.

Because that was what he was used to.

He was used to my forgiveness. My second chances.

Casually trailing behind him, I brought the flames with me. "I loved you," I said honestly, tears filling my eyes from watching my best friend crawl across the ground in pain and wanting nothing more than to see him suffer.

He said my name like a curse, grabbing my ankle as I kicked him to his back and he attempted to pull me down. But with another flick from my wrist, the flames morphed together.

Hovering above him in a mixture of orange and purple, furious and heartbroken, grew an outline of a blossoming, fiery fox.

She was a sight of gleaming brilliance.

Her body was made of purple, orange, and red. Her flaming hair sparked and glimmered, growing brighter as I said Zeke's name aloud. She was ready to protect and defend, and for the first time in my life, I stared at my element come to life and felt immense pride.

Her eyes were the same bright red that mine changed to every time I shifted into her, glowing and glaring. Her tail curved upward into a sharp point like a scorpion's, the mixture of purple and orange rich and the epitome of my fury.

She was my anger—my bloodthirsty addiction. She was what he demanded I bury for the entirety of my life, and now she was here to seek revenge.

Such poetic justice.

He stared at her in shock, his lips parting as she bared her flaming fangs at him.

"Cade, I would like to formally introduce you to Blaze."

I cocked my head, and the fox lowered to the ground, graceful in her prowl toward him. He quickly rose to his palms and backed away hastily.

I would have been lying if I had said there wasn't slight hesitation in what I had to do next. This was Cade—the man I had spent years protecting and making excuses for. The man I spent nearly every birthday with, collapsing in a drunken heap on our balconies. A man I had temporarily given my body to, falling asleep in the comfort of his arms every night.

While he was never the one to own my heart, he had been an integral part of my life. He had provided me with memories and a feeling of family. And now, I was ready to let him go.

No one could threaten Zeke and get away with it.

"I will never forgive you for this," I whispered, making a fist at my side to keep Blaze still. "I hate you, Cade, for making me love you and breaking my heart."

His eyes were not kind as he slowly shifted them from Blaze to me. "You were never enough for me, Raven."

Coughing out a cry at his final words to me, I said my last one to him, "Likewise."

Nodding once, I turned as Blaze lunged for him. I hated how good it felt as he wailed in pain. I felt the power of the flames as they seared away his life, scream by scream.

More than anything, I worried about how good this amount of power in my hands felt—how easy it was to release it on someone I once loved and admired.

Swaying, and positive I would pass out soon from exhaustion, I looked toward the trees.

"Blaze," I whispered, commanding her to stop. She disintegrated and returned home, seeping into my palms. I shivered as all three of my shifts flooded my body, stealing what was left of my energy as I shifted into my fiery friend.

Zeke.

We locked eyes, relief and fear swirling in his, not at all like the vengeance and exhaustion in mine.

I would give my husband this gift.

As he ran toward me, I collapsed to the ground from relief and joy at the feel of his skin against my palm. If this was it, if his face was the last thing I ever saw, all of the pain would be worth it.

For him, I fought.

For myself, I resisted.

Zeke found me like he promised he always would.

SHE WAS A SIGHT OF GLEAMING BRILLIANCE.

07

ZEKE

"Stay with me, Raven. This isn't the end. Breathe, baby. Breathe." I pulled her limp body into my lap and stood with her in my arms. "Edmund!" I bellowed. All I wanted to do was hold her, see her eyes, hear her voice, but I made a promise to her long ago that I would always give her what she wanted—and his life would satisfy us both.

I shifted her body into Edmund's arms, leaning down to kiss her forehead. "Start back toward the castle. She needs a physician. I'll be right there."

"Ezekiel, she'll want you there when she wakes...."

"She asked me to kill him, Edmund." I peered down at her body, my fists clenching at the sight of bruises on her face. "Look at her! She deserves to know he's gone. I will be right behind you. I swear it."

He didn't have time to argue with me, nor did I feel any trace of disagreement in him as he glanced at where Cade lay on the ground. "Do not be long."

I watched him leave with her in his arms, shoving down my need to follow him, until I could no longer see him through the trees, but Luca stayed. My little brother; always shadowing behind me even when he shouldn't.

I shook my head at him, motioning for him to go. "You don't need to see this, Luca. Go with Edmund. Make sure they make it out of the forest alive. Protect her at all costs."

Luca looked toward where Edmund had disappeared. I could sense his internal struggle, so I took a small step forward and forced a grin. "I promise you, Luca, I will be right behind you. This will be quick."

He backed away slowly with a slight nod before turning to jog after Edmund and Raven.

I turned to Cade on the ground. He crawled toward the small pond that seemed to darken the closer he got to it.

Raven had done quite a bit of damage to him on her own. His face was covered in blood and burns, and his hand was nothing but bone. She had burned the skin right off.

Out of pure curiosity, I stood for a moment and waited. My head cocked to the side as he threw his charred body into the pond, immediately squalling in pain as black water changed into a thick, inky, and steamy substance around him.

Burning him, I realized. Finishing the job.

All around me, trees whispered her name.

And as sweet as it would be to savor this moment—this moment I had waited so long and somewhat patiently for, Raven needed me more.

I wasn't sure what possessed me to do it, but I asked aloud for the forest to allow me to finish him off instead. Slowly, the whispers ceased, and the blackened water lightened enough to give me the confidence to step into it without burning.

The Forest Beyond seemed to favor my mate.

My steps into the pond were sloppy and quick, and he knew better than to fight me when I pushed him underwater and held him there until he believed he would die by drowning. It was only then that I gifted him another breath, bringing him to the surface, and then repeating. I shoved his head low enough to feel it smashing into the pond floor.

Grabbing the shredded fabric on his shirt, I dragged him out of the pond and threw him on the ground. "I wish she would've burned you alive," I said, lowering to my knees on either side of him. "But she loves me, Cade, and she wanted your death to be a gift for me."

Do you often leave one another human beings? Melik had asked me in Reales, and I couldn't help but smile at the irony.

Cade's face, barely recognizable from the burns, scowled at me. He raised his hands to shove me off, but all I did was broaden my grin at the pathetic attempt. "You've lost, Cade. You lost the moment I locked eyes with her."

"She would've chosen me if you hadn't returned," he said in a garbled slur of words.

"No, Cade, she wouldn't have. And you don't get to live with that victimized belief anymore."

I wanted to free whatever was inside my chest, building pressure and pulsing uncomfortably, but I didn't know how. The smoky ash was building in my throat and spurred my hatred.

I placed my hands on either side of his face. "I will never be able to harm you enough for you to feel the irreparable damage you've done to my mate, but I will be able to live knowing you no longer breathe."

With such force that surprised even myself, the memory of holding her limp and bloodied body in my arms had me applying enough pressure to his skull that the bone split between my hands.

He couldn't make a noise, he couldn't take a breath; all he could do was stare blankly with widened eyes as blood poured from the cracks in his head, as the veins in my hands turned black, as the leaves around us lifted from the ground, breezeless but reacting to whatever I possessed.

And I loved every fucking second of it.

I loved that I held two sides of his head in my hands. I clamored for the power I felt from destroying someone who had harmed her — who had touched her and known her body as I had. The intense feeling of pure force in the palm of my hands had me itching for more.

But when I released him and stared at the blood on my hands, I climbed off him and crawled away backward.

I thought of when I met him and the possessiveness he showed over her then. I remembered seeing her naked body stroll onto the balcony, the regret in her eyes for finally giving him power over her.

How he yanked her up in Duck's and forced her to kiss him.

The bruises on her shoulders.

The way she defended him over and over.

Watching her memory of how he tried to force himself upon her in Reales. Hearing her screams for me as he attacked her in Seolia. Godfrey bleeding out from his side, the two dead guards at her gate who had stood by her side from the beginning.

And while I hated him for doing this to her, I hated myself more for allowing it to reach this point. I had let her down. I hadn't keep her safe.

His life was gone, but his actions would live with us for the rest of time. The ramifications of his abuse and manipulation would linger. And my wife, the most joyful and endearing creature to ever exist, would never be the same.

As I stumbled to my feet, my hands covered in blood and fragments of bone, I clenched my fists and screamed.

I fell to my knees and cried her name. I thought of her tattered body and shouted obscenities at the sky, the gods, and myself. I fell forward and dug my fingers into the earth, tears streaking down my cheeks, my stomach twisted in knots and bound by hatred.

Cade was only one threat.

We still had so much more to go.

I couldn't think about that now. I needed to be with her. I needed to promise never to let anything like this happen to her again.

Taking one last look at what remained of Cade as I stood, I felt no remorse for the soul that no longer had a home.

A soul that no longer *belonged*.

EDMUND AND LUCA had made it more than halfway down the shore by the time I caught up to them, panting and trying to catch my breath. Our heartbeat was alarmingly slow, but I needed her in my arms, even if it meant we would die on this coast together.

Jogging in front of Edmund, I turned and held out my arms. "Give her to me."

"Ezekiel, you look like you might keel over at any moment," he said. "I will carry her until we reach the kingdom, and then I will—"

"Give her to me," I growled, interrupting him before he could finish. "She is my mate, and I am demanding that you return her to me."

"Ezekiel, this is not a war between us," he spoke softly, sidestepping around me. "I am doing this for your protection and hers."

He was right. I knew he was right and that he had most likely slept and eaten more than I had these last four days, but that didn't stop me from remaining at his side and stroking the top of her head. I just needed to touch her.

"You will give her back to me when we set foot in the kingdom," I said, scrunching her dry, tangled hair between my fingers.

"Yes, Ezekiel," he replied with an exasperated sigh. "I have no intention of keeping your mate. Control your urge to kill me and focus on getting there quickly."

"I don't want to kill you," I lied, rolling my neck. Because I did, and I didn't understand why. Edmund was my best friend, and I knew he wasn't purposely keeping her from me. But right now, the gnawing feeling inside my chest told me that everyone who looked upon her was an enemy.

Luca cleared his throat. "Is he dead? Did you…"

"Yes," I answered, clenching my fists. "He will never touch her again."

Before we could utter another word, the clattering of boots against the wooden bridge ahead had us on high alert. I prepared to shatter as many minds as possible, but when Petra stepped out from the middle of the gathered soldiers, I raised an eyebrow.

I hadn't spent much time with Petra. She never wanted to see me when I visited Perosan, and I didn't particularly care to exchange pleasantries with the royals of a kingdom who saw me as their enemy.

Realistically, I didn't give a fuck about past wars or the intentions of previous rulers of Reales. Technically, I had no actual relation to any of them. Their battles were not mine.

Like Raven, Petra was gentle in demeanor. I would've assumed her black hair was long if she ever let it down, but it was always pulled back and strung together by relics I never cared to look too closely at. I remained unaware of the history of her lineage, but she appeared younger than I would've imagined her to be and never seemed to age—no matter how long it had been since I'd last seen her.

Petra and Elric had been king and queen of Perosan for as long as I could remember.

And they both loathed me.

There was nothing but resolve in Petra's eyes as she met my gaze. I stepped in front of Edmund and gave him no other choice but to move Raven into my arms. He stepped in front of me, either to prevent me from barreling through the crowd of soldiers or to use the people skills I did not possess to persuade Petra to let us into the kingdom.

But before he could do either of those things, Petra looked at Raven in my arms and immediately called for us to follow her.

I kept my lips pressed against Raven's forehead as we jogged after Petra, crossing the wooden bridge into the kingdom and toward a carriage waiting at the end.

I hesitated briefly and gauged Petra as she motioned for us to climb inside. I stepped back, tightening the hold on my wife and shaking my head. "I can't...feel you."

It was as if she had a shield around her, preventing me from sensing anything she felt, which was not something I had ever encountered before.

As she stared at me, whatever blocked her emotions was slowly lowered to reveal concern. "I have no ill intention toward Raven, Ezekiel. Quite the opposite. Please get in the carriage so we can examine her."

Looking down at my broken mate, I had to think quickly. She needed a physician. I didn't know where to find one on my own, and she wasn't healing quickly enough to entertain other ideas.

"Direk informed me of what you can do, Ezekiel. If I break my word to you and harm comes to Raven, you will be free to take my mind."

That worked for me.

Shifting Raven in my arms, I climbed into the carriage and sat beside Luca, allowing him to rest her head on his lap while I kept one of her hands pressed against my lips.

Her other hand was severely bruised and showed signs of traumatic injury around her wrist. The bones didn't feel broken, but that didn't mean they hadn't been at some point.

Petra sat beside Edmund and stared at Raven with a deep frown. "How long has she been like this?"

"About half an hour," Edmund replied quietly. "We came as fast as we could."

"And why is she not healing?"

At her question, all three of us looked to Petra. I had been told that Petra and Damiana were aware of Raven's magic, but I was given no further details about why or how.

Her ability to raise and lower some kind of shield around herself made me hyper-aware that she held secrets of her own. Maybe Luca was right—maybe Petra was also a witch and had kept it secret all these years.

It was Luca who finally answered. "Poison. He poisoned her to keep her elements paralyzed."

"Her healing isn't magic," I responded, brushing my thumb across the bruise on Raven's cheekbone. Damiana had said once that her healing was a gift from the gods. While her elements might have been paralyzed, it wouldn't have stopped her from healing. "It was trying to heal too much too quickly. Physically, she looks better than when we found her, but mentally...."

I couldn't finish. I scooped her up again to rest against my chest. "I love you," I repeatedly whispered against her forehead. "Gods, I love you, Raven. I'm so sorry, my love."

Petra's constant examination of Raven made me uneasy until she finally asked, "How did she end up in the forest?"

"I don't know," I answered quietly, looking at her tattered face and the cuts along her arms. "Her mind is quiet. I can't see anything yet."

"You do not need to look, Ezekiel," Edmund said with a heady warning in his tone. "Do not subject yourself to that. It will not change the outcome."

"I need to know what he did to her, if he touched her—"

"She will tell you," he interrupted. "Give her time to heal, and let her decide how much she wants to tell you."

"She won't want to tell him anything," Luca said, speaking precisely what I was thinking aloud. "She'll want to protect him from all of it."

She wouldn't have to know I looked...

As if hearing my thoughts, Petra said, "Trust is freely given until it's not, Ezekiel."

I looked at Petra with a frown.

"Do not break hers."

THE REST of the carriage ride to the castle was silent, as was carrying her in and lying her on a bed so soft that it felt like a cloud. I cleaned her with a warm cloth as best I could while we waited for the physician. The blood from her skin had soaked entirely through the rag.

So much blood from a tiny, delicate soul.

Blood that belonged to me and not on the bed sheets.

And it was everywhere. It covered her.

When the physician arrived and asked me to leave the room, I protested heavily and demanded I be allowed to stay. But it was Petra's gentle promise of no harm befalling Raven that made me relent and stand right outside the door.

I knew what everyone believed, even without having to feel them. If I saw Raven's body and all that was done to her, I wouldn't be able to control the urge to seek revenge—no matter who might be on the receiving end.

The door creaked open and I stepped back enough to allow Petra and the physician to come out into the hallway. I tried to peek in on Raven, but Petra shook her head slightly and left the door open only a sliver.

The physician, an elderly woman, kept touching my arm as she spoke about Raven's injuries. None of them surprised me. A cracked wrist, a broken rib, a concussion, nothing that we couldn't work through quickly.

The bruises would fade, and she would be good as new...

"And she lost the baby."

My heart stopped. I blinked.

"She wasn't far along from what I could tell. Maybe a few weeks. It was most likely a result of the stress and physical trauma she endured."

I couldn't hear her correctly. My ears rang, and a cold sweat doused my skin. Breathing was difficult, and nothing about anything made sense anymore.

Because we had a baby.

Part of her, part of me.

Our own kind of magic. We created...

I couldn't form a complete thought.

Luca's hand was on my shoulder, squeezing. I looked at him. Staring. Unmoving. Disbelieving.

All I could think about was when I saw Raven as a baby. A beautiful, green-eyed baby. And we wanted that.

We wanted a family.

"You did not know," Petra said through my heartbreak and rage.

Cade took that from me. He nearly killed my mate and took my child; all I did was take his life.

It wasn't nearly enough.

I stepped toward Raven's door, but Petra risked herself and moved to block me. I growled as I tried to step around her, but she stopped me with a hand on my chest. Whatever I felt inside, she felt it, too. She stared at her hand before raising her tearful eyes to mine. "Go. She will not wake for a while. Whatever you feel right now does not need to come into this room."

I clenched my jaw, my nostrils flaring.

"Go," she repeated, shoving me back a step. "No one will stop you. Do what you must before you return."

I didn't need assurance before I turned and walked away, my fists constricting, everything burning. I knew Edmund and Luca would kill anyone who dared come near her with ill intentions, and there was something I needed to do.

"TRUST IS FREELY GIVEN UNTIL IT'S NOT, EZEKIEL."

08

ZEKE

All I saw was red.

Was this the correct way to grieve?

Was there a correct way?

No one stopped me. Direk saw me and looked the other way. Soldiers stared in fear and confusion at the Prince of Reales and his hidden abilities.

Good. They needed to know I could render them useless.

I hadn't stopped jogging since I left the castle. I knew exactly where I was headed and what needed to be done.

I ran across the wooden bridge and down the shoreline until I stood in front of the shipwreck that once flew the flag of Reales. I recognized it from our history books. It hadn't been used since before Rudolf became king. Our colors had always been black and green, but he redesigned our crest when he was sworn in.

The colors on the flag were faded, and the fabric was hard to fold from the years of water-log, but it was easy enough to wrap around my wrist and hand.

Cracking Cade's skull wasn't enough.

I needed to rip out his heart.

Turning from the ship, I studied the dark forest of whispers and illusions. I had very little time. I needed to return to Raven before she woke, but my bloodlust was tremendous, and it wouldn't be satisfied until this was done.

I tightened the laces of my boots and trudged past the tree line. Branches swayed and leaves rustled, but I feared nothing here. Somehow, in ways that remained unknown, forests welcomed my wife with open arms, and as long as I remained loyal and faithful to her, they allowed me to move through them freely.

The skeletal remains in The Forest Beyond reminded me of the men Raven often left in The Black Forest. That had to be a coincidence, though it was an odd connection between the dark forests.

I placed my hand against a tree trunk with the bones of two bodies at its roots and whispered her name. Branches swayed in response.

I had to be delirious. I hadn't slept in days, surviving off pure adrenaline. I couldn't be talking to trees. Cats, caves, trees...the occurrences of my non-human conversations had increased since meeting Raven.

Forging ahead, I moved down the same pathway we took to find her. I didn't have time to figure out why caves and trees whispered her name. I didn't want to know what connections she had here.

I wanted penance for the man who took our child away from us. I wanted his heart fed to the beasts that lurked within these trees.

Because I could feel them. I was being watched.

The hairs on my arms stood as I traveled alone toward the clearing, convinced that eyes stared at me through the darkness. They weren't eyes of reds and blacks from nightmares; these were eyes of white and bright blues. Some were golden, similar to Raven's when she shifted as Terra. A breeze pushed against my back when I spotted a pair.

Either spurring me on or encouraging me to leave.

I wouldn't leave. Not yet.

Passing through the clearing, I stomped through the murky pond where I had left his body to rot on the other side. I would rip him apart limb by limb. He wouldn't feel the pain, but mine would be enough for the both of us.

He had crushed our dream.

We weren't ready for a child. We wanted to wait, but that didn't mean it should've been stolen from us. We weren't allowed to accept it, celebrate, or witness what the love between us could create.

I would never meet the child we lost. I would never have the chance to know who they wanted to be, the color of their eyes, the sound of their voice, or the dreams they might have.

I would've created dreams of magic for them.

And I would never forget this feeling.

Is it still a loss if we didn't know we had something to lose?

The crack in my heart told me *yes*.

Stepping out of the pond, my lips parted as I whipped my head back and forth, scanning the ground. Lying where a fleshed body should be was nothing but bones—a skeleton with a cracked skull and a blanket of dried blood beneath it.

I crouched down to study it. It was Cade. His skull was split in all the right places, but his organs were gone. There was nothing that remained of him.

Clenching my jaw as I stood, I shouted to the watchers, "You took this from me! He took my child away!" I barged through the trees, driving farther into the forest and closer to the sets of eyes on me. "I wanted his heart! I wanted to rip apart his limbs!"

I punched the trunks as I went, kicking roots and weeds and shouting obscenities at whoever they could be. "Raven miscarried! She lost our child!"

Leaves rustled. The sky darkened.

"She is mine! Whatever claim you feel you have on her needs to end. She is *my* mate, *my* twin flame, *my* wife!"

Tears ran down my cheeks, but I kept going. I continued chasing what stared at me, eyes that seemed to glow brighter at the mention of her name. "Who are you?" I bellowed, growling at the silence. "How do you know her well enough to protect her?"

The wind rushed up behind me and I turned, ready to fight. I would fight for her. She belonged to me, not a cluster of trees and eyes. But what I expected to be a physical being in front of me was something completely different.

It was a bright and glowing smoky haze, violet in color. I reached out to touch it, but it scattered. Replacing it and forming right before my eyes was a mixture of orange and red mist. It moved from in front of my face to my hand, circling around the flag wrapped around my wrist.

Untying it, I held it out toward the mist.

It *bounded*.

The mist encircled the old and ragged flag, simmering.

"I would venture a guess you are not fond of Reales."

The mist set the flag aflame in my hand.

I hissed at the burning and dropped the flag, shaking my hand in front of me. This wasn't Raven's fire. "She won't be happy you did that," I snapped at the flickering mist.

I fell backward as it charged at me, holding my arm over my face and preparing for it to burn me. Instead of heat, I felt the chill of ice against my skin. Peeking out from underneath my arm, I stared in shock at the white snowflakes hovering in the air and holding back the orange mist.

"So...it's feisty no matter who wields it," I grumbled.

It attempted to lunge at me again, but the violet haze returned to assist the snowflakes in holding it back.

"I have to be imagining things." I ran a hand through my hair and blinked rapidly, expecting the illusion to disappear, but each color remained in place.

These were the colors of her elements. The chaos of the mixed colors was what I saw in her eyes in Reales.

They...existed, but these didn't belong to her.

Clearly. Since one of them wanted to kill me.

"I am her flame. You cannot hurt me if you care for her."

But you are not her mate.

79

Whipping my head around at the whisper, I searched for the source. I was hesitant and a little frightened but slowly stood. "Say that again," I challenged, attempting to touch the mist or snowflakes.

All three colors scattered and dissipated.

"She is my mate," I argued, "how can I not be hers?"

Silence. No colors, no eyes, nothing but the rustling of branches as if trying to convince me that I had imagined all of this. "Hey!" I shouted. "Don't be a fucking coward! Come out here and talk to me!"

An unnerving sound had me taking slow steps backward. I regretted everything I said as the clanging and soft pops of bones rattled around me.

These skeletons—they weren't sacrifices.

Maybe they had been at one point, but now...

As three unevenly built skeletons emerged from the depths of the darkness, bones reattaching and twisting together, my eyes widened as I gaped at death moving toward me.

I could hear Edmund saying, *I told you so*. Because I couldn't shatter these minds—there were no minds *to* shatter. I had no weapon of my own to use against them.

I wouldn't go like this—not by someone else's hand...or bones. No one was allowed to take me from Raven.

Unfortunately, my confidence meant nothing as towering skeletons surrounded me, standing shoulder-to-shoulder, bones popping and clicking from rubbing together and sending chills straight down my spine in terror.

I backed away slowly. For the first time...ever, I did not feel like a threat. It was evident that this forest had been off-limits for a reason, and the reason stood before me, growing taller as the final bones snapped into place.

Their bony fists curled when I whispered Raven's name, hoping they might take pity on me. It only seemed to anger them further.

These skeletons were guards of the forest.

And I was their target.

～

As I ran through the forest like my life depended on it, I suddenly missed when magic didn't exist, because I understood why it scared the fuck out of everyone.

I had managed to get so far back into the forest that I wasn't confident I was running in the right direction, and death moved surprisingly fast. Either that or because I was severely outnumbered by the remains in this goddamn forest.

Cursing as one appeared before me, I kicked it as its bony fingers reached for me, and shattered it to the ground. It began rebuilding as I ran, looking for any way out of here, but all I saw were dark trees.

I had to get back to Raven.

She was my driving force and had me running faster than I ever had. "She would want me alive!" I shouted through mangled breaths, as if it mattered. "You're only going to piss her off!"

I had to stop and catch my breath, doubling over as I tried to find my bearings, but there were none. There was nothing but trees and no sign of the clearing. Above me, a darkening sky signaled dusk with no stars to guide me out.

And all around me, the sound of vibrating bones.

They would find me in a matter of seconds.

I needed to run to get ahead of them again, but I froze before I could lift a foot.

Between two trees, the first skeleton to find me tilted its cracked skull and stretched its fingers. It wobbled and didn't look ready for a fight, but there was an eerie determination as I held its hollowed gaze.

I bared my teeth, my nails digging into my palms.

"You're using *him* to protect you?" I rolled my neck, suddenly uncaring that this forest might eat me alive if I stayed any longer, but I would not leave him here to defend the place where he died. "Is this his soul that lingers?"

"Can you hear me, Cade?" I took steps closer, matching his. "Are you still trying to keep me from her?"

I was well aware that I was surrounded by dead souls and their remains, talking to trees and mists, and would most likely have nightmares of this place if I made it out alive, but no part of him deserved to live.

His head crooked to the side as I swung for it. He had an unfair advantage. I couldn't move my limbs like that.

I reached up to finish tearing his skull into two pieces, but his bony fingers wrapped around my throat and pressed into my windpipe, quickly cutting off my air supply.

With his skull still cocked, it was almost as if I could see him smiling at me—the slight upturn of his cheekbones.

But what he had consistently underestimated, even as a mortal, was my devout determination to keep him from her and to return to her with the promise he would never touch her again.

Choking on my growl, I reached up toward a low-hanging branch, struggling to get a good enough grip to pull it down.

Breathe for me, my love.

You said you would always breathe for me.

The thought of her allowed me to wrap my fingers around enough of the branch to tear it from the trunk. I swung hard enough to knock his head to the ground, gasping for air as his fingers released my throat.

His skull rolled far enough away to give me time to dismantle his ribs next, watching as they fell to the ground one by one.

And for moments I worked, taking him apart piece by piece. I cried her name while stepping on his bones each time they tried to rebuild, shattering his skull underneath my foot until it was nothing but fragments.

I thought of our child.

I broke his ribs in half across my knee, throwing them into the darkness to hopefully be gnawed on by rabid beasts. As the last of him tried to rebuild, I fell to my knees, tearing apart any piece I could find, snapping bones, and stabbing them into the mud.

I was made of flesh and a beating heart, yet I felt as empty as the guards of this forest. I was held together by the memory of her, by the thought of returning to her and having her in my arms.

Without her, I was nothing more than bones and regret.

I would roam forests to find her. I would protect the magic that inhabited her. I would guard her with whatever was left of me and keep her from what waited outside of these trees.

I collapsed to my back, staring up at the starless sky.

Because without her near me, they didn't exist.

"Raven," I whispered.

I had become a man who was solely existing to love her. All I wanted to do was love her—why was that never enough?

Why was the universe always trying to take her from me?

Being with her in the meadow seemed more enticing than constantly chasing her through a life that didn't seem to want us together. We could be together there. We would be at peace. I wouldn't let our souls separate. I would find a way for us to be together.

I picked up a rock with jagged edges and held up my arm, putting the sharpest point against my wrist. "I can fix this for us," I whispered. "I can prevent more pain for you, my love."

I would meet her amongst the bright flowers and endless sunshine. We would have many lifetimes together and never again know the pain that living brought us.

Before I could drag it across my skin, the orange mist reappeared and burned my hand. I dropped the rock back to the ground. Growling, I rolled over and reached for the rock again, but the violet haze pushed against me forcefully with a gust of wind.

"You don't understand!" I shouted. "You do not know of the suffering we have been through!"

The white snowflakes rested upon my skin and soothed the burn. It was the same feeling Raven always brought as Frost whenever I was hurt.

The snowflakes rose to mingle with the orange mist and violet haze, combining into colored chaos. Rising to my feet, I watched as the colors of her elements created a silhouette of her.

Her laugh bounced off the trees, her smile spreading in bright red and orange, her hair flowing effortlessly in a mixture of violet and white.

Tears filled my eyes as I took in the beauty of her elements, reaching for her hand and gasping as it latched onto mine. It pulsed through me the same way it always did in our dreams, causing me to laugh and cough on a choked cry. "Raven," I whispered, my palm lying flat against hers.

The orange mist didn't touch any part of my skin. While it

appeared like my mate's, these elements weren't hers. But it did help me realize that I wasn't ready to leave yet.

We still had more to do here—things I could understand, paths we needed to take, but all that mattered was that we would be together. That was the point of all of this.

The misery couldn't last forever.

"Help me," I pleaded gently. "Please help me get to her."

Tearfully, I watched the outline of her fade, and when the brightness of the colors dimmed, I was staring directly at another skeletal guard. I braced for what was about to happen, but instead of attacking, he walked straight past me.

I watched him in awe and bewilderment and was convinced I was in delirium. I felt utterly mad and deranged, blinded by passion and grief.

Turning, I looked once more toward the trees, meeting the golden eyes of...something. I touched my heart while dipping my chin. I was leaving with my life intact. "Thank you," I murmured, waiting until they faded away before I slowly followed behind the guard toward whatever might lie ahead.

LYING WHERE A FLESHED BODY SHOULD BE WAS NOTHING BUT BONES.

09

ZEKE

The eagerness to cross the tree line back to the sandy shore was a mixture of hysterics and terror. The skeletal guard stared at me as I passed him, his hollowed gaze guaranteeing that my trepidation of this place would stay with me.

Vomiting on the ground as I fell to my knees reminded me that I was not as invincible as I believed I was.

I had the worst fucking luck with forests.

As I wiped my mouth with the back of my sleeve and looked up from where I kneeled, I stared directly at King Elric. I immediately stood, panic rising as I looked toward the kingdom. "Raven..."

"Is still asleep," he finished for me. "You have time. Catch your breath. You look...pale."

Fisting my hair in my hands, I was convinced I had imagined all of it. My nightmares and sorrow had created those illusions of her and fighting Cade's remains. "What is this place?"

Elric took a step forward and stared into the forest, the corner of his mouth tilted upward in a grin. "Whatever you might need it to be, I suppose. Or what it needs to be."

"I don't understand," I said on borrowed breath, since I couldn't find mine. "The things I saw in there couldn't be real, Elric. Magic has been gone in our realm for over a century."

"I believe your abilities alone prove otherwise."

Direk didn't waste any time sharing what I possessed. I expected a lecture on etiquette from Elric, but his expressions spoke for him. He didn't seem surprised or question how I possessed such deathly and dangerous qualities. If I had time, I could render an entire army useless. If leaders were smarter, I'd be locked away.

Unlike Petra, Elric was beginning to show his age...whatever it might be. His lineage remained as mysterious as hers, with shockingly little information about Perosan's history of rulers. His gray hair would have led me to believe he was the same age as John if it weren't for the hints of black at the ends. It was his eyes, though, that gave me pause.

They were such a bright blue that they seemed painted. His skin was golden like mine, most likely from living on the coast, but unlike mine that came to be that way from years of training as a soldier, his was not calloused or scarred.

Standing here with him, I recalled just how little time I had spent conversing with the man who never greeted me whenever I visited. He had always kept his distance.

He caught me staring. "Why did you come back here, Ezekiel?"

I was reminded of my grief and anger and lowered my hands from my hair to clench my fists at my sides. I had destroyed Cade as a mortal and a soul, but it still didn't feel like enough.

"Raven miscarried our child. The physician said it was from the stress and physical trauma she endured under his hands." I swallowed harshly. "I wanted to return and rip him apart. I wanted his heart, Elric. I wanted to shred it. But when I found him, he was nothing but bones. His flesh and organs were gone. It doesn't make sense. I've killed a lot of men, Elric. It takes far more than an hour to disintegrate."

"Is that all you saw?"

My gaze slowly moved back to the trees, scouring the darkness between the trunks for the eyes that had watched me. "No," I whispered. "I saw more than that — things I could never explain, but when I did find him, I made sure no part of him would ever exist again."

"The forest gifted you with his soul."

He said it like it was a regular occurrence.

"Yes," I replied. "His soul is gone."

And what an extraordinary gift that was.

The silence drew out between us as he turned to face the water. I needed to return to Raven, but like Petra, I couldn't gauge his feelings. It piqued my curiosity enough to give him a few more moments.

Finally, after watching waves crash against jagged rocks along the coast, he said, "Direk said you referred to Raven as your mate."

Direk had a big mouth.

"She is my twin flame and mate; he is lucky to still be breathing after delaying me."

His chuckle was low and deep in his throat. "You cannot fault those who don't understand pairings and laws of magic, Ezekiel."

"I can fault anyone who prevents me from recovering my mate, Elric." I rolled my shoulders back as I faced him. "And you need to inform him of that. I am not fond of your captain and will not hesitate to take his mind next time. I will take pleasure in shattering his memories."

Elric motioned toward the castle. "We should return. Perhaps you can sleep before she wakes."

Sleep. It seemed like a foreign concept now. I didn't mind losing sleep when it came to making love to my wife, but this served as a reminder of how weak I truly was when I went without blood or any form of her for days at a time.

My addiction to her served a purpose. It fed more than just my desire for her.

As we trekked back toward the castle, Elric cleared his throat. "I lost a child once while sacrificing for the greater good. I am deeply sorry for your loss, Ezekiel."

"The greater good," I repeated. Silver lined my eyes as I looked at the castle ahead, wherein lay my broken and beaten wife, who didn't yet know of our loss. "I will never see any good come from this loss, Elric. The death of our child serves no purpose, and I am now tasked with sharing the news with my mate, who wants a family of our own. Raven is—" I had to stop for a moment to collect myself. "Raven is the gentlest soul. She did not deserve this."

"No," he replied gently. "She did not. You are free to seek refuge in our kingdom, Ezekiel. No one will bother you while she heals." He paused with a sigh, clasping his hands behind his back. "Our ties with you have been unwelcoming in the past, but we understand that you have no ill intention toward our kingdom."

"I never did, Elric. Wars fought by men in the past have nothing to do with me. My title as Prince of Reales isn't legitimate and does not belong to me. The only titles that matter to me are that of her husband and flame."

"You are already wed."

"Yes," I confirmed. "I will not hide that any longer. Mira is planning a war between our kingdoms and has tried to use us to entice you to visit Reales for our wedding, but I am tired of these games. After these last few days, I have learned that I care about nothing other than the well-being of Raven."

"And what of Seolia?"

"I will prevent as much heartbreak for her as possible if Seolia is invaded, but I need to be standing with her at the end of all of this, Elric. No matter how we get there, that is my sole purpose and intention. I can fight wars, but it will always be for her safety and life. Nothing else matters to me."

I was growing impatient, but when he stopped to face me, I paused and waited. "This has always been bigger than our realm, Ezekiel. It was not only the realm we were trying to protect. It became more important as more people became residents of our kingdoms, but it was never the sole purpose."

Lifting an eyebrow, I followed his gaze to the forest. I already knew the answer, and I dreaded it. No matter how many people I killed or how far away I dragged her from this realm, she would always be wanted. "Raven," I said with a knowing sigh. "This has everything to do with Raven, doesn't it?"

"Raven," he confirmed, "and you and River."

"River." I crossed my arms over my chest. "You know of River? How? He tried to drown Raven. I can't imagine anything I could have in common with him."

"You have more of a history than you may realize, Ezekiel."

My conversation with Elric was interrupted by a frantic Derik as he came barreling across the bridge to inform the king that a carriage flying flags of Reales was nearing the mainland.

Elric, concern behind his eyes, turned to me. "Go, Ezekiel. Go to her now!"

∾

I DIDN'T UNDERSTAND the panic, but it didn't prevent me from running back to the castle. It was most likely Mira coming to check on her investment.

Luca and Edmund were still in Raven's room. Petra had left, and according to Luca, a servant had burst into the room to share that someone from Reales was close.

I paced the length of the room and debated with them about how long it would take to move Raven away from the castle. "I told Elric," I informed them. "I told him of Mira's plan and didn't mention that she would drown Seolia if she found out we weren't planning to hold up our end of the bargain."

Edmund sighed and braced his palms against the table. He stared at Raven for a moment before hanging his head. "You must stop getting us into these predicaments, Ezekiel."

"I don't fucking care about any of this, Edmund!" I shouted, tangling my hands in my hair. "I don't want to do this anymore!"

"But she does!" he bellowed back, pointing a finger at my sleeping wife. "Raven does! She cannot wake up to discover that you have sentenced her entire island to death, Ezekiel! Those are her people that she has spent her entire life protecting. You had no right—"

"Do not speak down to me, Edmund. I am your equal and have the right to make these decisions...."

"For *your* kingdom," he argued, "last I checked, Seolia is not."

I was taken aback by his remark, my eyes widening at the insult. In return, he sighed and rose to his feet. "Ezekiel, you are in a difficult position. You are married to a kingdom queen in this realm, but because your allegiance is tied to Reales, you do not hold the right to make decisions for her, despite your marriage."

"I am her husband, Edmund."

He crossed his arms over his chest. "That does not matter, Ezekiel. Not with our laws."

"Fuck the laws." I sank down to the edge of the bed, burying my face in my hands. Edmund was correct, and I hated it. Because of my allegiance to Reales, my hands were tied. Without Raven's permission, any decisions regarding Seolia were out of my control. Jeanine held more power as an adviser than I did as Raven's husband.

"So, what you're saying"—I lifted my head to look at him, resting my elbows upon my knees—"is that I might have drowned her island and risked every inhabitant by telling Elric."

He walked around the table to sit on the edge closest to me, crossed his feet at the ankles, and sighed deeply through his nose. "We will not know until someone walks through that door and tells us, but yes, Ezekiel. You might have."

"Before I left," I said quietly, "I told Jeanine to evacuate the island because of Mira's army. I didn't think they would be safe without us. I told her to send them back to Reales...."

"You did *what*?"

I was startled at the sleepy, broken voice behind me and winced. Blinking her eyes open slowly and staring at me as if she were in a dream, Raven repeated her question.

My heart pounded wildly at the sight of her open eyes, and she clutched her chest at the sudden uptick of our heartbeat. "Raven," I whispered, my eyes filling with tears.

The glow of her green eyes was muted ever so slightly as she continued to stare at me, disbelief and confusion pouring out of her.

For a moment, I worried she had hit her head somewhere along the way and all of her memories had fallen away, but then her face twisted, and she reached for me.

"Zeke," she cracked, twisting my shirt between her fingers and pulling me down. "Zeke..." She wrapped her arms tightly around my neck.

"Raven," I said, wanting to be gentle with her and squeeze her until she lived solely inside me so nothing like this could ever happen again. "My love, I have never been more relieved to see your eyes...."

"Zeke," she cried, burying her face into my neck and soaking my skin with her tears.

Pain. There was nothing but heartbreak and fear in her. And my name from her lips sounded more like a cry for help rather than genuine happiness.

"Baby, you're safe," I promised between her cries, "please, Raven, calm down and look at me." I tried to peel her arms from around my neck, but she only held on tighter. "Raven, please..."

"Don't leave me, Zeke, please."

I could barely understand her through her sobs, but I shook my head and kept my hands on her neck, trying to push her chin up to look at me. "Raven, I'm not going to leave you. You're safe, baby. Please look at me."

"His blood!" she shouted, her body trembling in my hold. "His blood is all over me. Get it off, get it off...."

"Raven, you're broken and bruised in so many places...."

"Get it off!" she screamed. Her hair was matted and plastered to her face with tears. "Get it off, get it off...." Her hands shook, and her body temperature dropped the more panicked she became.

"Ezekiel," Edmund called in a gentle warning. "She doesn't know where she's at. She doesn't know she's safe...."

"She's delirious," Luca said, standing beside the bed and crouching to rub Raven's back.

She cowered from his touch and pressed against me, covering her ears with her hands. "No, no, no."

I felt helpless. All I could do was hold her against me, stroking the back of her head while promising her that nothing like this would ever happen to her again.

But all she did was scream and thrash, begging for his blood to be off her skin, quivering in my arms. Her mind was an endless void of colors as her elements fought to readjust.

Luca hung his head. "You have to do it, Zeke."

I shook my head slightly. "I can't, Luca. I can't do that to her."

"She's scared. She needs rest."

Edmund took a step forward. "What is he talking about?"

Raven clawed at the dried blood on her arms, creating scratches and drawing her own. I put her wrists in one of my hands and brought her to my chest by the back of her head. "I can scare people awake, but I can also"—I hesitated—"put them to sleep temporarily."

I had only tried it a handful of times and always on Luca when he annoyed me as a child. I didn't like intruding on someone's subconscious to force them into slumber, but Raven was frantic in my arms. Her body wasn't ready to face our new reality, nor was her mind.

"She won't even remember," Edmund assured me.

I pushed into her mind and focused on her subconscious. It was full of fear and bleakness—the complete opposite of the delight that typically accompanied her.

Balancing a subconscious in such a state of panic needed to be done with delicacy and gentleness. Though Raven trusted me, I could never anticipate how a mind would react to outside touch.

Raven, I murmured into her mind, *Rest*.

No sound emitted from me physically, but my voice in the depths of her mind soothed her. She stopped thrashing in my arms, her screams dying into whimpers.

And then, within a secret I would never share with anyone, I hummed a melody between our minds. It was one that I had known my entire life but never pinpointed the source of where I learned it.

It just *was*.

I hummed until her muscles loosened, until Luca told me she was falling asleep. I opened my eyes to see hers fluttering closed. Blaze warmed her skin, the roots of her hair turning red. I was startled at the sight of her shifting while asleep and pushed into her mind again to see her fire at the forefront, staring right back at me.

Let her sleep, I whispered to the demon, the flame barely

morphing into an outline of a creature with fearsome, glowing eyes, sending chills across me.

Blaze only burned brighter.

≈

EDMUND AND LUCA STAYED.

None of us could sleep. We needed to, but we still hadn't heard about the visitor from Reales. We were none the wiser if a war was happening outside these doors.

A servant had brought us food trays, but I couldn't eat. I couldn't do anything but stare at Raven as she slept peacefully. I would check on her dreams every few moments to ensure they stayed calm, but didn't push past that.

Edmund and Petra were right. I couldn't infringe on her memories without her permission. I would have and used to, but we were partners now. I wanted her permission.

Edmund stood by the window overlooking a large courtyard beneath the mezzanine. This castle wasn't as golden and bright as Edmund's, but it was nicer than ours. The choice of coral-colored embellishments everywhere was a head-scratcher.

Luca sat in the corner of the room, tossing an apple in the air while leaning against the wall. He wasn't only staying for Raven's sake. He was worried about my mental state.

They asked where I disappeared after learning of Raven's miscarriage, but I didn't divulge details of the forest I had roamed, speaking with the dead and misty elements that prevented me from meeting Raven in the meadow. I wasn't sure I would ever share those stories, even with my mate.

Edmund broke the silence with, "Gisela wanted to be here. I ordered she stay in Thoya in case something happened to me."

"I am sure she loved being ordered to do something," I responded with a chuckle. "She's like Raven in that way."

"Masochists," Luca said, "we're all masochists for the company we keep with these women."

"I assume you are referring to Jeanine." I grinned slightly. "I will not be returning to a warm welcome from her, either."

Luca mirrored my grin, but it changed into a frown as his gaze shifted to Raven. "Will you tell her?"

Sitting on the floor beside the bed, and at his question, I rolled my head against it to look at Raven. "Of course," I answered. "But I want to give her time to recover. Our loss will destroy her."

Edmund's tone was gentle as he turned his head to give me a small smile and said, "When your child returns to you someday, I will make an excellent uncle."

"Not as good as me," Luca jested.

Edmund's gaze shot to Raven and he nodded toward her. Luca flattened the chair back to the ground, the apple falling from his hands and rolling across the floor. My brows knitted together before I turned to see that Raven had shifted from herself to Blaze and opened her eyes.

Her eyes glistened as they searched the room before settling on me and blinking her tears away. Her voice was scratchy as she whispered my name.

Rising to my knees, I grabbed her hand and put it against my lips. "My love."

She wasn't screaming or thrashing. She wasn't panicking or fearful. She was simply heartbroken and relieved.

Edmund and Luca crowded around me. Her eyes widened from the attention thrust upon her, but she relaxed once she recognized their faces. "Hello," she squeaked in the way of greeting.

We all laughed through tears and emotions. Edmund ran a hand down her red hair while Luca took her other hand with his. "You had us worried," Edmund said.

Raven sniffled and tried to smile. "I apologize for the inconvenience."

Edmund lowered beside me and shook his head. "Nothing about your existence will ever inconvenience me, love. Don't you know that by now?"

I rolled my eyes. "Shameless."

Edmund winked at her before slapping Luca on the shoulder. "Come, Luca. Let us leave these two."

Luca squeezed her hand and then my shoulder as he nodded. I waited until the door closed before I moved to sit on the bed. She immediately sat up, crawled into my lap, and bundled herself against me.

I would've been content to stay like that forever.

Rubbing her arms, I pressed my lips against her head. "Raven," I whispered. "Allow me to see your eyes."

Her tears soaked through my shirt. I shifted her in my arms until I could lie on the bed. She cried my name again and curled into a ball.

I feared she would never feel safe again.

Hastily removing my shirt, I threw it to the ground before I lay beside her and pulled her against my chest. "Feel me, Raven." I grabbed her wrist and placed her palm against my chest. "I am right here. You're not in a nightmare or on that ship anymore. You are in my arms, my love. Breathe, Raven."

Warmth flooded her body, and I couldn't help but smile.

Breathe, Raven.

I whispered it in her mind until her breathing steadied, and she responded to my cues to trust me. And when her muscles relaxed in my hold, I gently took her chin between my fingers and lifted it until her red eyes focused on me.

"There's my little demon."

They refilled, water lining the rims as she closed them again and dipped her forehead until it rested against my lips. "Zeke," she murmured, "you found me."

Three simple words had me coughing out a cry as I wrapped her so tightly in my arms that it was a wonder she didn't crack in two. "Raven, I will always find you."

"I didn't know," she tried to say but had to stop to regain her composure. "I didn't know if I would ever see you again."

"Oh, Raven." I threaded both hands in her hair, scrunching the strands between my fingers. "Nothing will ever keep me away from you. You are my mate."

But you are not hers, I heard the words from the forest repeated in my head. I couldn't focus on that right now, nor did I believe I'd heard it correctly. She belonged only to me.

"I need you to tell me that you didn't watch my memories." She gnawed on her bottom lip as she peered up at me. "Promise me, Zeke. I need you to promise that you never will."

Swallowing, I searched her eyes. I wanted to. I wanted to see what she went through to experience it with her. I didn't want her to go through this alone, and I wouldn't understand how she felt until I felt...her.

"Raven," I whispered, but she quickly shook her head.

"Promise me, Zeke. I will tell you some of it, but not if you don't promise me that you will not watch them."

I closed my eyes briefly before I shook my head once. "Raven, I can't promise you that. I'm sorry."

She tensed in my arms, and I felt her heat flare. "They are my memories, Zeke. Not yours."

I clenched my jaw, grinding my teeth together. "You are mine, Raven. Every inch of you belongs to me."

"Not this," she whispered meekly. "What happened to me cannot be ours. It needs to remain mine alone."

Cade beat my wife, bruising and breaking her. He stole our child from us, and she honestly asked me not to live those moments with her, not to share her pain the way I so desperately wanted to.

And this was not the conversation I wanted to be having with her as soon as she woke up. I wanted time to *be* with her, give her a complete examination, and promise that it would never happen again.

"Did he"—I paused to breathe deeply through my nose, bracing myself for the answer—"rape you?"

There was nothing left of him for me to destroy, but I would find my way into hell depending on her answer.

"No," she replied. "I will not lie to you and say that he did not try, but I stopped him each time."

"And he hit you?"

"Zeke, please." She put my face between her hands, causing my eyes to widen and fill with tears at her touch. She took notice and mirrored my emotion, pressing our foreheads together and breathing in each breath I released as if I were breathing for her. "No one has had me but you. Please let that be enough for now."

"Gods, Raven." My voice was weak and shaky, and I couldn't help but laugh at her words. "You are breathing. That will always be enough for me."

"Then promise me, Zeke."

Sighing, I asked myself silently if this was a request I could honor —if I could give her the space and privacy she was demanding of me. But I never wanted to be the man who went against her wishes, no matter how much I might want to. It wouldn't stop me from asking her again someday, but for now, I could abide by her wishes.

I brushed the pad of my thumb across her cheekbone before I nodded once. "I promise."

I HAD THE WORST FUCKING LUCK WITH FORESTS.

10

ZEKE

The bathroom was connected to the bedchambers. She asked again to be allowed to wash off his blood, and I couldn't delay her any further. After explaining that her body still showed signs of injury and bruising, she agreed to move as if she were made of glass.

And with an eye roll, no less.

Whoever had come to Perosan from Reales had yet to make it inside the castle, and no one had sought us out to tell us what was going on. Luca checked in moments before and informed me nothing was out of sorts.

I wanted to leave with Raven.

I would take her away from all of it if she asked.

Night had fallen, leaving us with little to no light inside our suite. I had found matches, and she watched me with an amused expression from the bed as I walked around the room, lighting candles. "I don't want you to over-exert yourself too soon," I explained.

Even though she had shifted into Blaze, my decision seemed purely logical, but that didn't stop her from lighting the tips of her fingers in defiance. She hadn't shifted back to herself yet and I hadn't asked why. If I had to guess, I'd say it was a defensive measure and I would see my little demon more frequently than usual.

I carried her to the bathroom, which she didn't argue about. Despite what she said, her exhaustion was evident. Her eyes were glazed and sunken in, and she couldn't remain upright for long before she was forced to lean against a wall. Her fingers twisted tightly together in front of her.

I wasn't used to seeing her like this. Typically, I couldn't get her to stop smiling and laughing, even in her worst moods. She would always huff and roll her eyes, but a smile soon broke across her face as if she couldn't stand any other emotion. But now, I felt none of her joy.

There was only emptiness.

And soon, I would be adding to it.

Cursing aloud as water spilled onto my shoes, I shut off the water and ran a hand through my hair. "You put my world on pause every time, my love."

There was an effort to smile, but it was quickly replaced by sorrow. "I feel so..."—her palm rested against her stomach, causing my chest to hurt—"gone."

I braced my hands on either side of her and rested my lips against her forehead. Gripping my shirt tightly, her breathing became unsteady.

"Raven, you're not gone. If you would let me watch your memories, I could—"

"No," she interrupted. "No, Zeke, you can't have my memories. Nothing good would come from that."

Putting my hands on her neck, I gently tilted her head up. "Baby, I want to feel everything you are. I want to go through this with you. If you let me in, I could take away some of the pain."

Her flames burned so brightly behind her irises that I could barely see any white surrounding them. And her heat was so prominent that it warmed the entire bathroom, causing the mirrors to fog and sweat to bead on my skin.

"I wanted to meet you in the meadow," she said after moments of silence.

Nodding, I softly brushed across her cheekbones with my fingertips. "Me too." I wouldn't tell her yet about how I almost made it happen or how elements similar to hers came to life and burned my hand to prevent me from it.

When she tried to burrow into me, I held her still and kissed the tip of her nose. "Talk to me, my love. Don't hide."

"I fought." Her bottom lip puckered out. "I fought him as much as possible, but it still wasn't enough."

"Raven, it was. It was enough. You nearly killed him."

"The things he said... the threats." Her fire burned through the fabric of my shirt and nipped at my skin.

It felt like a heated torture chamber in here.

Grabbing her wrists, I wrapped her hands around my throat. "I am right here, Raven. No one will touch me."

"He said he would kill you for causing this." The orange morphed into purple as the flames behind her irises grew. I had seen her purple flames before, but never in her eyes. They were mesmerizing; dark violet in color like galaxies swirling with flames. "That was all it took, Zeke, for Blaze to come alive."

I opened and closed my mouth after she said that, raising an eyebrow. "What... what do you mean?"

Her eyes glowed so brightly that the white disappeared altogether. I worried she would burst into flames any moment. "Blaze was alive—she was *real*."

I had more to ask, but turned when I felt a burst of heat behind me. Fire spread across the floor behind us. I turned to her with widened eyes and took her face between my hands. "Little demon, I killed him. You do not need to seek revenge; you do not need to be fearful." I held her gaze, even as I was worried the entire roof would cave in on us at any moment. "Raven, I need you to breathe."

The flames in her eyes lessened. "Show me."

My head jerked back. "What?"

If she meant physically, there was nothing left.

Even as Blaze, I didn't recognize the look she gave me. "Show me how you killed him. Give me your memory."

"That hardly seems fair..."

"I deserve to see it!" she snapped. "I deserve to see his death. I have *earned* it."

"Raven, this doesn't sound like you..."

"You said you would always give me what I want," she interrupted. "Give me your memory."

I regretted making that promise to her.

She closed her eyes in anticipation. Sighing, I pulled the memory from my mind and melded ours together until it was one memory shared between us.

She watched it unfold with bated breath. Her breaths were hot on my lips as her inhales quickened, as the beat of her heart caused mine to jump. And when his skull cracked between my hands, she gasped and dug her fingers into my arms.

I wasn't sure which reaction or emotion I expected from her, but it certainly wasn't contentment or giddiness.

I tried to pull the memory, but she hissed at me.

This was not my Raven. Even with her bloodthirsty darkness, I had never seen this side of her.

As soon as Cade dropped to the ground, I took the memory from her mind and opened my eyes. Her eyes fluttered open, but the flames still beamed brightly. It wasn't enough to calm her.

The splintered wood behind us cracked. I needed to devise a solution quickly, or we would have to purchase Petra and Elric another castle.

So, I kissed her.

I kissed her for the first time since she was taken.

It was a kiss full of passion and fear; relief and anger. It was how we continuously poured our feelings out to one another—our own language. Because as the world imploded around us, this was always something we could understand.

It was wet from the tears of our desperation to reconnect. It was a kiss that lasted moments—a kiss that would never be long enough.

It was a kiss that twisted my stomach into knots from grief and longing.

The fire that was raging behind me soon wholly enveloped me. Her palms lit against my chest, and her tongue slipped past my lips and warmly collided with mine.

She created a circle of protection as if trying to keep the rest of the world away from me.

It would be easy to lose myself in her.

It was tempting to lock her away somewhere and have nothing but her body for days on end. I thirsted for her blood. But I still held a secret from her—something she might hate me for hiding, but I couldn't tell her. Not yet.

And I didn't feel right having her until she knew—until her body was healed fully and her mind was somewhat back to normal. So when I broke our kiss and pinned her wrists to the wall to keep her from reaching for me again, I kissed her softly once more. "I love you, Raven. I love how much you love me and want to protect me."

Her flames grew again behind her eyes, but I kissed her tenderly to keep them at bay. "I am yours, Raven. I am not going anywhere. He is gone and will not touch either of us ever again." I paused, contemplating if I should divulge more. "Not even his soul remains."

Her eyebrow lifted. I shook my head slightly and gave her a small yet hesitant smile. "Stories for another time. Let me wash you, please?"

"I don't…" she trailed off, looking down at her body, "I don't want you to see me."

Frowning, I released her wrists. "Do you not trust me?"

"It's not that, Zeke. I am… covered in bruises." A tear fell down her cheek. "I don't want to subject you to that. I don't want you to remember me like this."

"Raven," I said with a sigh, covering my heart with my palm. "Baby, you are beautiful in every single way. I want to take care of you. I promise to look at you just as I always have."

Millions of thoughts ran through her mind as she stared down at her body, again twisting her fingers nervously.

"I won't force you," I said softly. "But I would like to stay if you'd allow me."

Her eyes fell to the floor. "But will you still want me?"

I couldn't help but laugh. "Raven, I would want you even if you were a one-legged pirate." A grin broadened across my face when I saw a small smile on hers. "Even if you grew ten feet tall or shrank to be as small as a mouse, I would love you no differently than I do now."

She giggled through her tears. I pulled her from the wall and wrapped her in my arms. That was the only sound I had wanted to hear since she was taken—that addicting noise.

I kissed all over her face, nipped at her nose, and squeezed her until she laughed again. She threw her arms around my neck and returned my mini attacks of her face with some of her own until our lips locked in a sweet kiss.

"The water is cold by now," I said upon releasing her. "I can warm it up again."

"I can take care of it." She raised her arms above her head and winced at the tug of her ribs. "Bathe with me."

"I don't think you've looked at the size...."

"Of you? Many times."

I chuckled. "Of the tub. It doesn't look built for two."

"It wasn't a question." She slid out of the silky pajamas Petra had changed her into while I was away, the flames around us fading at the flick of her wrist.

I stared at the charred floor in amusement, dragging the tips of my fingers across my forehead as I thought of how to explain this to John.

When she dropped two balls of fire into the water, it lit her body enough for me to see the bruises she referenced. They were every-where. Purple and yellow battle wounds decorated her skin from her shoulders all the way down to her shins.

When she caught me looking, she frowned.

I slid out of my still-soaked shoes. "Raven, don't think for one-second that my opinion about you has changed."

She didn't acknowledge me but held out her hand to allow me to assist her into the tub, hissing from the hot water on her broken skin. I moved to hoist her out, but she held up a hand and shook her head.

There wasn't much of a shirt left, but I discarded what was left and dropped it to the floor. But for once, she wasn't watching me. She stared at the water, slowly turning red from the excess blood on her skin.

Her blood. His blood. The blood signaling our loss.

A demon in a pool of blood should be what nightmares were made of, but I craved hers. I had buried it down since finding her. I didn't want to steal from her while she recovered, but I wanted to taste it on my tongue.

Dipping her hands under the water, she cupped them together to bring up a small pool of bloodied water in her hands. "I hate that any part of him is touching me," she whispered.

"It's a reminder, Raven." I crouched and tucked her hair behind her ear. "This is all that remains of him. He touched what belonged to me, and now he no longer breathes."

"I should've let you kill him the first time he touched me." There was regret and anger in the way she spoke, in how her teeth clenched together after she said it, revealing her perfect jawline.

I skimmed my fingers across it, brushing my thumb across her cheekbone. Raven was beautiful; there was no denying that. I knew that every person who looked at her thought the same because even if beauty wasn't skin-deep, hers was evident... everywhere.

But as Blaze, Raven was unholy.

While blinding to look directly at, the sun lived within my wife. She embodied the very lifeblood of this world, and as each element, it was a gift to others to see it as more than dirt, snow, or light.

She was angry and had every right to be. But staring at her, being with her... I couldn't feel anything but grateful.

Grateful that she lived—she was here; our time here wasn't over yet, no matter what that meant for our future. Because that was what we would have: a wildly unhinged future of sun, snow, and soil.

The only sound that remained was the slight movement of water and flickering of candles as their flames began dying out. Soon, we would be masked in complete darkness.

"Let me take you back," I said softly, pulling down her bottom lip with my thumb. I wanted her so bad I could taste it, but not yet.

Only after I told her.

She turned her head toward me and searched my face, my eyes, knowing exactly how much I wished to have her. Confusion was apparent in how she held herself, but finally, she nodded. "You'll be there?"

My brows knitted together. "Where you are, I am."

She looked fearful, but not because of what happened. I waited patiently for whatever was working through her mind, tilting my head slightly in curiosity.

"This won't change anything between us, right?"

I didn't know where all of her doubt was stemming from, but I wanted to squash it. She never before had any reason to doubt my complete infatuation with her.

Leaning forward and using every last drop of self-control, I kissed across her jaw and up to her ear before whispering, "I have never loved you more than I do in this moment."

Whimpering, she covered her face with her hands. Her shoulders began to shake from heavy and silent sobs, her body slumping as she tried to lean against me. "I missed you," she whispered hoarsely. "Gods, Zeke, I talked to the wind." She sniffled and removed her hands, her eyelashes wet and darkened from tears. "I talked to you even though you weren't there."

Tears fell down my cheeks, but I didn't wipe them away. I needed her to know how much I ached for her, how I no longer wanted to breathe if she wasn't near me. "I was there, Raven. I was always with you." I put a hand over her heart. "I am always *here*. I feel everything you do. Any time *we're* apart, *I* fall apart. The matching beat of our hearts is the only reminder that even if we're not together, we are."

She rested her head against the rim of the tub, her eyes heavy from tears and exhaustion. "You're always saving me."

"And I always will," I promised.

Because I needed her.

I'd always known that—since the night I first saw her. But now, having almost lost her, I had never been more certain about anything. I needed her to survive. Not only because our hearts were so in tune with one another's, but because I needed her to keep me human. I needed her to remind me to smile, to laugh. Before her, I felt nothing but desolation. I was hopeless about everything in my life.

Raven came into my life like a shooting star, lighting everything in her path. Carrying darkness of her own, she took mine and promised to bring it alongside hers so I wouldn't ever feel dragged under again. She gave me a reason to believe again—that we could make it through this life as long as we had each other.

And though she was my wife, and I still couldn't understand the depths of our bond and how it worked, I understood this much—she was my mate. My mate, my mate. My other half, my tether to this world. The blood she spilled belonged to me and ran through me.

We were one and the same, and I needed her.

Magic or not, bond or not, flame or not—I would have found her. If I could leave this life sure of one thing, and only one thing, it was that she was meant to be mine.

And I was meant to be hers.

IT WAS A KISS FULL OF PASSION AND FEAR; RELIEF AND ANGER.

11

ZEKE

We slept for hours.

After finding new pajamas for her—nothing more than a nightshirt that fell right past her knees—Raven sat against the wall while I bathed.

Upon seeing the bruises on me, she inquired how I received them. I'd given her the bare minimum of information, blaming it mainly on the tree roots.

When she offered to waltz into the forest and burn them for me, I laughed so hard that my chest hurt. She was desperate to set something on fire for me. I promised to find something for her when we returned home, but I was not sending her back into that forest.

She fell asleep tucked against my chest.

It wasn't until someone shook my leg that I jerked awake, looking down at Raven as she remained asleep beside me.

My heart beat like a stampede of wild horses.

Blinking as I looked around, Luca's silhouette made me roll my eyes and lie back down on the pillow. This was the most I had slept since she was taken, and I needed more than this without the intake of her blood.

But when he said, "It's Mira," I jolted up.

Raven stirred slightly but didn't open her eyes.

"She's insisting she sees Raven," he whispered. The door to our room was cracked open. "She wants proof she lives."

"No," I growled. "She cannot see Raven. I am fucking finished with Mira, Luca. We owe her nothing."

Luca sighed. "She's causing problems for Elric and Petra, Zeke. She won't leave the castle grounds. She's acting a bit mad. More than usual."

Now I was just curious. Mira rarely showed emotion.

Looking at Raven, I cursed silently. I was growing tired of leaving her because of Mira. She would need me next to her when she woke up, but when Mira's voice raised from the hallway, I growled and uncurled myself from Raven. "I'll be her proof, but I can't be away long. If she keeps me from my mate, I will shatter her mind."

Rolling my neck to release the tension already building, I glanced again at Raven to ensure she was still asleep before stepping into the hallway and closing the door behind Luca and me.

Mira was utterly disheveled. Her hair was unkempt, her dress and long coat in disarray and wrinkled. She looked as if she hadn't slept in weeks.

Fear, panic, and anger poured from her, though her lack of concern for her sister wasn't the least shocking.

I positioned myself in front of Luca. He was safe between me, Petra, and Elric, but I still wouldn't take a chance on her taking him from me again. "What do you want, Mira?"

She hissed at me and I rolled my eyes. I was no longer afraid of her. She was weak and possessed no weapon other than River. If it wasn't for the threat of Raven losing her elements if I killed him, all of my problems could have been quickly eliminated.

She paced manically. I took the opportunity to explore her mind and gather what I could about the new legion she partnered with. After nearly losing Raven, I no longer took my gift for granted. I would use it to our advantage.

Before I could see anything more than her standing in front of River and two men I didn't recognize, she felt me in her mind and lunged for me from across the hall.

To my surprise, and very much unnecessarily since I could snap her into pieces with my bare hands, two of Petra's guards appeared behind columns and kept her away from me. "You bastard!" Mira shouted. "You have been the bane of my existence ever since Rudolf took pity on you!"

I remained unfazed, simply shrugging a shoulder.

I didn't quite understand it, but it didn't change anything. I was an heir of Reales, no matter what she tried to do to keep me from the throne. It would be mine long after we killed her.

"I am done playing your games, Mira. Raven is mine. I hold exactly what you need. I regret not realizing it sooner, but Raven has the support of our entire realm behind her. If it wasn't for fear, even our people would revolt against you."

"This is a battle you will not win, Mira," Petra said.

I looked at Elric. He silently conveyed that what I had shared with him was no longer a secret.

Mira's chest heaved. I understood her panic, but I didn't know what could possibly make her so frightened. "What did you get yourself into, Mira? Who are these men you've agreed to work with? And what did you promise them in return?" I asked.

The surprise on her face was satisfying.

Raven stepping out of our room just as River breezed in through the front door was not as satisfying.

They didn't look like twins, especially not with Raven still shifted as Blaze, but they paused when they locked eyes. Instead of the usual fear I felt in Raven when River was near, there was a genuine likeness. Gratefulness.

A bit of bewilderment.

And I realized there was something Raven hadn't told me about her brother.

Like Petra and Elric, I couldn't gauge River's emotions as he stared at my mate. He was stoic as per usual, but there was a difference in how he looked at her now compared to when they first met.

Edmund came up behind us and looked between them, bellowing a loud chuckle that echoed through the room. "It would make sense that the universe would want to brag about the beauty it created and boast it in twin form."

Petra and Elric looked between Raven and River, though Raven looked nowhere but at River while her hand wrapped around my wrist as she stepped closer to me. "River," she whispered.

He dipped his chin in a subtle nod. "Raven."

Edmund stretched his arms out dramatically and sighed. "Now, can you tell me why I was woken up?" He glanced over at Raven with a wink. "Not that I'd ever complain about seeing you, exquisite creature."

I rolled my eyes.

"Mira was about to concede," I said. "She has chosen a war she cannot win. She underestimated how beloved her sister is."

"Pity," Edmund said. "I was looking forward to seeing Ezekiel on the throne and arguing over trivial things such as taxes and imports. I know he loves nothing more than taking time away from our darling Raven."

Mira, looking utterly ravaged and glaring at me as if I had somehow ruined her life, opened her mouth to pour venom, but River spoke up first. "Yes, it seems our plan was not well-constructed. We were unaware that the threat of drowning Seolia would not be enough when you have such allied forces."

I tilted my head. He was *too* comfortable speaking to us as if we would listen to anything he had to say as a stranger in our realm.

"You did not honestly believe that threatening my people would get you anywhere," Raven said. "I might not be the most experienced royal, but I care for my kingdom and do not take your threats lightly. You were foolish to believe otherwise."

Raven fought to remain standing as she leaned against me. She hadn't recovered her energy yet, and seeing Mira was not something she needed. But she was stubborn and refused to show weakness.

I snaked an arm around her and brought her to stand in front of me, keeping my arm locked around her chest and pressing her tightly against me. My other arm wrapped around her waist while I narrowed my eyes at Mira. To them, it would seem as if I were protecting her, not just keeping her stable.

Raven kissed my hand in gratitude.

Mira eyed her from head to toe. "You look... well." She gained some of her lost composure and straightened. The envy in her eyes as she stared at Raven bewildered me, though I could understand it on a certain level. It was similar to how I felt about Luca being the true heir to the throne, but not the one who would one day sit upon it. "Well enough to travel?"

I barked out a laugh. "She is not going to Reales, Mira."

River stepped forward. Luca took position on Raven's other side. She was now sandwiched between Edmund and Luca, with me locked around her.

River paused with a slight grin and held his hands up defensively. "It is apparent that we have lost. We would like to extend our gracious apologies and show goodwill toward the realm."

"This isn't your realm," Edmund said. "You hold no position in any kingdom here. You are a threat to one of our queens. We will not stand for that."

"I can't feel you," I interjected. "I have no way of knowing that you mean what you say, and Mira is frightened by something. There is nothing but fear and panic coming from her. I will not allow my mate into your kingdom."

River's gaze shifted only to Raven. "We would like to hold a Four Kingdoms ball in Reales. No hidden agendas, no armies. It will be grand and our way of apologizing."

Edmund crossed his arms over his chest. "You expect the leaders of every kingdom in our realm to show up to Reales without protection and leave our kingdoms open to intrusions?"

"It can be one leader from each kingdom if you'd prefer." River looked directly at me then. "Reales is suffering without imports from the other kingdoms. More shoppes have closed down. People are starving."

He knew where to hit me.

Raven's hands squeezed my arm. We knew Reales was falling apart under Mira's control, but we had hoped it wouldn't reach a low point.

"There are three other kingdoms you could send your people to," Edmund said. "We will take your people in."

Mira gasped at Edmund's suggestion, placing her hand over her heart as if she actually had one. "And make everyone leave their homes? Some of our families have been in Reales since its birth. You cannot ask that of them."

Mira didn't care about our people, but she was correct. The families that remained in Reales were loyalists and wouldn't be keen on leaving the kingdom where they had raised generations of families.

I asked, "And what of your army, Mira?"

"The men in Reales are visitors from the kingdom where I've been," River answered. "They care nothing about the realm or the war. We've been entertaining them."

"Entertaining them," Raven repeated. "One of your captains came to Seolia petrified of these men."

Raven did not mention the letter he brought with him, unwilling to endanger the sender, even though we remained unsure who wrote it. And it only made me love her more, if that were possible.

"I did not say they weren't intimidating," River argued. "They have lived differently than you."

Petra and Elric, who had been surprisingly quiet throughout this entire exchange, looked at Mira. "And no harm would come to any of our kingdoms during our visit?"

I scoffed and accidentally squeezed Raven so tightly that she groaned. I kissed the top of her head before looking at Elric. "You're honestly considering this offer?"

"It is either this, Ezekiel," Petra said, shifting her gaze to me, "Or men die in battle. Being a ruler requires risk."

"And I will not risk Raven," I snarled. "She has already been through too much at their hands. Her brother tried to drown her, yet he stands here to offer a ball as a sign of peace."

Petra's gaze shifted to River. "You tried to drown Raven?"

A hint of amusement flickered across his eyes. I narrowed mine in a perpetual glare.

"It's not up to you what we decide," Raven said quietly, tipping her head backward to look at me with an apologetic grin. "It's up to us."

"Raven," I whispered. "Do not do this. I beg of you."

"I have to think of our people, Zeke. If it means we do not have to fight a war, then it's something I need to consider." She looked at Edmund. "As the Prince of Thoya, you act as a proxy for decisions regarding your kingdom."

I did not miss the look exchanged between my wife and friend, my head tilting slightly as I tried to gauge what it could mean. The smallest hint of mischief gleamed in Edmund's eyes, his emotions mirroring it. Raven, however, remained stoic.

Edmund looked at me, obviously torn between what his friend wanted and what his father would do in this situation. "Ezekiel, I apologize greatly, but our realm has maintained peace for a century. I cannot be at fault for not allowing them to apologize and come to a resolution."

"Mira wanted a war!" I roared. "She wanted to burn all the men! You cannot stand there and tell me that Damiana would ever trust her again!"

"This isn't about trust," Edmund argued. "It is about the well-being of our people, of *your* people."

I closed my eyes. Releasing Raven with a sigh, I ran a hand through my hair and took a few steps backward. After everything we went through, I now had to prepare for this.

"Take heart, Ezekiel," Mira said condescendingly. "At least you will not have to partake in a faux wedding."

Growling, I stepped in her direction but was held back by Luca and Edmund. "Do not think for one moment that I believe anything either of you is saying, Mira! You care nothing about this realm other than possessing it as your own. You locked away my family, you made me commit horrific acts—"

"I wish you had died that night," Mira interrupted with a sigh. "Next time."

One moment I was held back by Edmund and Luca; the next, I was covering my head as flames erupted in front of me, heading straight toward Mira.

She tried to back away, she screamed, but Raven didn't move. She lifted a hand and brought a gust of air toward the flames, spurring them on faster.

There wasn't anything any of us could do but watch as the fire first grabbed the bottom of Mira's dress, as she shouted for Raven to stop while stomping her feet and fanning her skirt only for it to spread higher.

"River," Petra said calmly.

As smoke reached the ceiling, Petra's guards looked at her for orders, but we were all too shocked to utter a word. And River looked authentically torn on whether he should help or allow her to burn. I remained still, observing him instead of the writhing, horrific woman dying before us.

Finally, with a swift jerk of River's arm, a burst of water appeared out of thin air and splashed across Raven's flames, suffocating them and leaving only the charred remains of Mira's skirt.

Raven sighed at the prevention of Mira's death. Everyone stared at her in shock; even Mira was speechless at the fact that Raven, the one known as the gentlest queen in our realm, had just tried to murder her sister in cold blood.

RAVEN HAD JUST TRIED TO MURDER HER SISTER IN COLD BLOOD.

12

RAVEN

T hat was disappointing.

Sighing as I watched River soak my flames with his water, I held Mira's stare with an annoyed one of my own. "You will not threaten Zeke again," I warned, moving my arm out of his reach when he tried to stop me from moving closer to her. But I was no longer fearful of Mira or her threats. River saved me. He wasn't cruel, maybe a bit condescending, but he showed genuine concern for my safety. There had to be a reason other than keeping me alive for Mira's needs.

"We will attend your ball, I suppose." A ball in the middle of an impending war seemed out of place and frivolous, which I had learned was the opposite of something River would do. This so-called peaceful movement clearly held plans of its own, but I had garnered a reputation of being too trusting, so it was a mask I would use to my advantage.

I wished my stride held more confidence, but I could pass out at any moment due to exhaustion. "But you will stop threatening my family. You will stay away from my island because I am not afraid of you, Mira."

When she lifted a foot to close the gap between us, River grabbed her arm and shook his head slightly. I looked between them curiously before an arm wrapped around my waist and pulled me back. "Stay away from him," I warned, teeth bared and flames lit. The thought of anyone causing Zeke pain caused an inhumanly feral instinct to over-take me. "River will not always be there to save you, and I look forward to that day."

My nostrils flared as an unrecognizable scent of honey and sea salt wafted across me. I blinked as a distant familiarity of the smell brought forth a foreign feeling of endearment. Similar to the memo-ries that were always caused by Zeke's bites, I couldn't see anything, however I was soothed by the scent. And when I shifted my gaze to River, he conveyed a replicated expression.

But I did not speak, nor did I ask why I could suddenly smell him and how I could recognize it even though we hadn't spent any time together. Instead, I said, "Stop," and watched as his eyes flickered with delight before the scent faded.

"We need a month of preparation," Mira said, refusing to look at me anymore. "It will be held on the day their wedding was supposed to take place, but it seems that is no longer needed."

"We married weeks ago," Zeke confirmed, his voice smug at finally revealing the secret we'd held from her, the control we took for ourselves. Without our faux-engagement, Mira was left with nothing she could use to gain the trust of the other leaders. "Every leader was made aware of the union. You have lost, Mira."

"So it seems," she remarked, hesitant in the way she looked at Zeke. "Send the army back to Reales."

I scoffed. "No. I am not returning men to you, Mira. You cannot be trusted with an army."

"I will handle the army," Zeke said, and I didn't need to ask what he meant by that. "And you will give us six weeks, not four."

"That is two weeks longer than we agreed!" Mira exclaimed.

"It is more than you deserve!" Zeke shouted, his voice bouncing off the walls in the atrium. "You will allow this, Mira, or you do not have a deal."

She couldn't decide where to look as her eyes darted back and forth between us. She was severely outnumbered with the realm siding with me instead of her. "You have one chance to undo what you've done, Mira," I said. "You can expect us to be prepared when we visit Reales. It might be best that you ask River's friends to leave."

There was nothing else she could say. No argument could be made for the choices she made. It was time to face the consequences of her decisions and threats. But what I didn't say aloud was that, though I didn't manage to kill her here, I would still find a way. She had nearly killed Zeke once before, threatened him, thrown Luca and Alice into a dungeon, and used me, and all of it was for nothing.

She had underestimated my devotion to Zeke and our people. The next thing I needed to do was learn why River had saved me but continued to stay by her side.

I did not move until Mira turned to leave; I did not look anywhere but at River as he dipped his chin in the way of goodbye but held my gaze the longest before following her outside. Petra motioned for her guards to follow them, assuring they returned to their carriage to leave this kingdom in peace.

And the second they were gone, I slumped against Zeke's chest. He breathed a sigh of relief, kissing the top of my head. "Quite the dramatics, little demon."

"I told you I would burn this world for you."

"I did not realize you meant it so literally."

Petra, Elric, and Edmund surrounded us in a miniature meeting of leaders. I wanted nothing more than to sleep—perhaps for days—but we had decisions to make. "I believe we all acted splendidly," I said in amusement.

Zeke sighed in relief. "I was hoping you weren't seriously considering attending a ball."

Elric held Zeke's gaze. "What did you feel from her?"

"I don't trust her," Zeke said first. "She's still hiding something. I tried to sift through as many memories as possible but focused more on protecting Raven. I did not recognize two of the men that frequented her memories."

Edmund stroked his chin. "How do we proceed?"

I shrugged a shoulder. "Cautiously. No bone in Mira's body means well. She has her sights on avenging Celestina."

"She said it's her sole purpose in life," Zeke added. "That will not be something she gives up easily."

Petra and Elric exchanged a look before focusing on me. "Then there is only one thing to do," Petra said. "We take Reales."

Edmund looked at Zeke.

Zeke squeezed my shoulders.

And then, I nodded. "We take Reales."

ZEKE WANTED ME TO REST. I tried to relax, but I couldn't sleep, and since he wouldn't touch me the way he wanted to, I asked him if we could go for a walk. I had suggested we return to the forest, but his experience there had evidently been very different from mine, and he immediately refused that request.

A bright glow from the moon lit the courtyard as we stood in front of the castle. I looked to him for guidance. It had been a long time since my previous visit, and at that time I had stayed within the castle walls. A midnight stroll might not have been the best way to see the kingdom, but the walk underneath the stars suited us.

Taking my hand in his, he gently tugged me toward town. We seemed to be the only two people out, but unlike Reales, Perosan didn't hold an eerie silence. It was serene and calming, the breeze light and warm as it encircled us, very different from the bone-chilling one on the shores. And we walked in complete silence until too many questions filled my mind with an urge to escape. "What will you do with the army?"

He stared straight ahead at the pale cottages and shoppes, even bright in the moonlight. I decided that Perosan, though seemingly joyful and unique, would not be a place I would ever want to live in. I enjoyed the golden brightness of Thoya but preferred my village to hold an edge of darkness, as it reminded me of where I belonged. It was why Seolia was the perfect blend of dark and light.

And Zeke, my living, breathing shadow, would look out of place anywhere with buildings the colors of peaches. "I don't know," he responded woefully. "If we fight Mira, we will need an army, but I do not know if I can convince them to switch their allegiance to me without the offer of freedom in return."

"And you do not want to do that?"

He shook his head. "No, Raven. I do not want to subject anyone else to their vileness. They committed horrific things, baby, things that I will never discuss with you. I am ashamed of bringing them to our island and wouldn't have done it if I didn't believe your life was at risk."

"But that is the monster you would be for me."

"Believe me, Raven. I would be much worse."

"But you are hesitating now when you would not have done so before. That shows you have changed, Zeke."

He chuckled in the deep and raspy way that always made me ache for him, and his eyes reflected the very monster he was always so ashamed to be. "I am not hesitating for their lives, Raven. I have not changed my need to kill. It is still very much an addiction, but it has been sated since finding you."

I gave him a small smile. "Is that what it is then? You are afraid of wanting something other than me?"

He brought my hand to his lips with a slight shake of his head. "No, Raven, I will never want anything more than you. I am hesitant because I want to be a better man for you. I do not want to be the one others fear..." he trailed off with a grin. "That is a lie. I want them to fear me when they are threatening you, but I do not want to be dreaded for simply existing."

"Zeke," I whispered, my heart aching from his words. "No one could ever dread you."

"I shattered men's minds upon my arrival here," he admitted, his voice showing a hint of remorse. "They kept me from you, so I broke their minds into tiny pieces. That is not something I can ever reverse, and now they look at me like I am every inch the horror Mira made me out to be."

"You were protecting what belonged to you, Zeke. There is no shame in that. Your powers are a gift, no matter how you decide to wield them."

He side-eyed me. "Is that what you told yourself when you nearly burned Mira alive tonight?"

I smiled at the memory of her screaming in terror as the skirt of her dress shredded from my flames. "I was protecting what's mine, too. It is what we have always planned to do; I just decided to escalate it."

"Mira and that army are no worse than me, Raven. I have murdered, bargained for their lives, and threatened them. I have performed dark things, Raven. Depraved things. And enjoyed them."

The insinuation that Zeke could ever be like those men made me shift uncomfortably, my hand leaving him to run through my hair. "You are not those men, Zeke. You do things to protect your family."

"And that excuses my actions?"

"Why are you doing this? Are you asking that I treat you the same way as I did Mira? My flames can't touch you, so if you need a physical punishment for your crimes, you will need to be a little more creative."

"I ask that we not act impulsively when faced with empty threats."

Pausing, I turned to face him with my hands on my hips. "Impulsively? You are guilting me about the decision to eliminate our problem, a problem that we have always planned to kill. Do not act differently because you have decided to grow a conscience."

"That is unfair, Raven. I can live with blood on my hands." His voice raised an octave, ricocheting off the walls of the empty village and making me shiver. Because no matter how powerful I believed myself to be, he would always be the one person who could intimidate me. "I would do it again and sleep fine knowing you are safe in my arms, but you are everything good in this world."

I turned away from him.

"You are hurting, Raven. You are angry about what happened to you. For some reason, you are fearful for my life when you shouldn't be. No one is going to touch me. You cannot burn every person who spits venom at us. I need you to understand what turning into this person will do to your soul."

Above us, a star shot across the sky and crossed the moon. And to me, we were no more than that. Zeke and I, we always burned. We always struggled to find a balance between what felt good and what was right. After everything we had gone through, separately and together, a little sip of vengeance wouldn't damage our souls any more than anything else already had. "I do not regret it," I murmured, watching as the star faded. "I felt her death at my fingertips. I tasted the ash on my tongue."

Slowly, I turned to face him, the flames in my eyes simmering. "Do not forget the first time you saw me. I have always wanted to set fire to those who deserve it, especially when they threaten my flame. It is what drew you to me, remember? My unyielding need for blood. We have always been the same."

Moving so swiftly that I didn't even have time to brace, he grabbed a chunk of my red hair and gently dragged my head backward. His other hand snaked around my neck and squeezed, sending a minor wave of pain down my spine.

Because even when I was broken and bruised, the darkness inside of him ached to control me, to never let me push *past* the point of simmering. He desperately wanted to keep my soul intact, sparing me from the cracks and crevices that his soul showed, no matter how often I patched it up. He would always be the man who stalked me like prey, the one who took lives with his bare hands for the sake of mine, who would gladly hand his soul over to the devil if it meant mine was safe and sound.

And it was apparent that we had both reached a point of not returning to the goodness we kept trying to claim. But I thirsted for blood, and he wanted mine. There was no balance regarding the shameless way we harbored our addictions. "You want to burn the world, little demon? Then do it."

Backing me into a wall, he leaned in and skimmed his lips along my jawline before finding my ear. "I will stand by you while it goes up in flames, but don't you dare, Raven"—he tugged my earlobe between his teeth—"don't you ever fucking say I didn't warn you."

The secrets he held from me were hidden behind his eyes, something inky with gloom that had very clearly shrouded his soul with wrath. Whatever it was, it was tearing him into pieces, and when he realized I was pulling it out of him with simply a look, he answered with a searing kiss before he released me, backing away and nearly blending into the night sky behind him.

"I am a mirror of you," I said. "You cannot change that. And whatever you are not telling me better be worth the mistrust between us right now."

His eyes watered. Running a hand through his hair and resting the other at his waist, he looked utterly devastated and exhausted. I wasn't sure what could be causing him so much grief since I stood here before him, alive and breathing. That was always his greatest fear, so whatever else this might be had to be extremely disheartening.

My face softened. "Baby, what is it?"

He pressed his forearm against the wall above his head and dug his face into the crook of his elbow. Running a hand down his back, I bit my bottom lip in anticipation as a million different thoughts ran through my mind. "Whatever it is, we'll get through it," I assured him, "but you must tell me."

I noticed a familiar silhouette approaching us from the corner of my eye, and once he reached us, his expression reflected the same sullenness that Zeke's did. "Ezekiel," Edmund said, grabbing Zeke's shoulder and shaking it gently. "You need to sleep. Rest. Dawn will break soon."

The night sky left illumination from the stars, but the beginning light of the sun crawled over the horizon. It was breathtaking, but all beauty now left a bittersweet taste as I feared our moments would never truly be joyous again. We would forever carry the weight of these last few days, and I would always reflect on the sunrise I witnessed in Perosan the day after Zeke found me. Cade would always linger.

"Must I flirt with your mate for you to listen to me?" Edmund patted Zeke's back twice. "Come now. I have a carriage waiting to carry me back to Thoya, but I will walk you back to the castle."

But still, Zeke did not move.

"My love," I whispered, squeezing between him and the wall where he had taken up temporary residence. Placing my hands against his chest, I searched for his eyes, but they remained lowered. "I feel your heart, Zeke. It still beats with mine. Fight this feeling, Zeke. Don't let it take you from me."

"It doesn't want to take me away from you, Raven. It wants me to destroy everything for you." Lifting his hand, he brushed his thumb across my cheekbone. "You were dying in my arms, Raven, barely breathing. I couldn't feel you."

"But I am here," I promised, removing his hand from my face to place it against my heart. "I am here and healing. We must survive this, Zeke, or it will all have been for nothing."

"Time will be your best friend right now," Edmund remarked, "for both of you. It has only been a day, Ezekiel, and you've barely slept since you left Seolia. Rest, my friend. Allow Raven to sleep for as long as she needs."

But Zeke didn't need sleep. He didn't *want* sleep. As his eyes lowered to the scar on my neck, I knew exactly what he wanted. And if staying awake until the end of times could prevent anything like this from ever happening to me again, he would do it. But blood was not what he needed right now.

He needed me. He needed assurance that I would make it to the other side of my fury and confusion. He needed to trust that he could share whatever secret he held with me and that I would not set fire to our world. So, I buried my need for blood and revenge and shifted into myself.

Relief flooded his eyes. I had no promises I could make to assure him that Blaze would not return, but for now, I would give him the trust he needed from me that I knew he would protect me from any harm. "I am safe," I said. "I am not a dream or a mirage. I am here."

Leaning in, he pressed his forehead against mine and drew in a deep inhale of my scent while twisting a strand of my hair around his finger. "You are here," he repeated, "but you are my dream."

"And mine," Edmund said.

Zeke sighed through his nose, tugging at my hair before straightening and grabbing my hand. "Didn't you say you were leaving?"

Edmund waved for us to follow him. "Tell me how we shall kill your sister, Raven."

I shrugged a shoulder. "I don't know. I no longer possess a spirit of death. We will need a new plan."

"I shall speak with my parents. We have been training our army since your visit. We will need to meet again before we visit Reales."

"Six weeks is not long," Zeke said. "Our army is small. We may need to train with yours."

"And you believe Seolia is safe?"

I nodded. "I don't know if I trust River completely, but he had a chance to harm me and didn't take it." I hadn't shared this with Zeke yet. "He's the one who told me to go into the forest. He was there after our ship was wrecked. He spoke to me like... like we were friends."

"Elric knows River," Zeke said. "I did not get a chance to learn how before we were interrupted, but I do not believe this is as simple as a plan for realm domination."

Edmund ran a hand down his face. "I miss the simple days of no magic aside from my mother."

I pouted. "But then you wouldn't have met me."

Edmund touched my back. "I am happy to see you alive, Raven, even if you frightened me."

"I apologize," I said. "I can safely say that Zeke will not let it happen again."

He squeezed my neck with a smile. "I'll see you soon, love. Tire of Ezekiel before then, yes? I will continue to wait for you to come to your senses."

"Fuck off," Zeke said through a chuckle. He put a hand on Edmund's shoulder. "Thank you for coming, Edmund. I am grateful."

"Ah," Edmund said with a wink. "I will think of ways for you to repay me." He glanced back at the castle. "I imagine this was not how you wanted to revisit Perosan?"

I frowned at the castle. Unlike Edmund's palace, this one wasn't nearly as charming. There were so many coral embellishments that I wondered if they took inspiration from a mermaid's undersea lair. Even the art on the walls was of fish and ships.

Zeke laughed when I wrinkled my nose. "Not your style, my love?"

"I miss our manor," I answered. "Please do not paint it coral as a gift for me, Edmund."

"Only if I ever have the itch to annoy you, love."

His way of goodbye was in proper Edmund fashion: a dramatic bow and quick peck on my cheek before Zeke could shove him away. He left us laughing as he climbed into a waiting carriage.

Zeke took my chin between his fingers and returned my focus to him. "You need sleep, little witch."

I rolled my eyes with a smile. "You think you know everything about me, don't you? How can you *possibly* know what I need?"

"Your eyes are the map to my world, little demon. They'll tell me when it's okay to breathe again."

I threw my arms around his neck. "I want everything you say tattooed on me."

He brushed his hands up and down my ribs with a grin. "I do not want this perfection ruined by my words."

"Oh, my love." I swayed with him amongst the silence and feeling of safety I enjoy every time I am in his arms. "Nothing you say could ever ruin me."

"BUT THAT IS THE MONSTER YOU WOULD BE FOR ME." "BELIEVE ME, RAVEN. I WOULD BE MUCH WORSE."

13

RAVEN

The news of Mira nearly dying by my hand spread across the kingdom like wildfire. It would make it to Seolia soon, which meant we would have questions to answer upon our return. While murmurs of why it had happened were the loudest, no one seemed to be making me out to be the villain. Mira wasn't exactly beloved in this realm, so I didn't believe anyone would lose sleep over it when we succeeded in killing her.

Direk, who I learned despised my husband, informed us while we sat with Petra and Elric for breakfast that the most common question amongst everyone was, what would happen to Reales if Mira died? Would it remain a kingdom in our realm?

I hadn't given it too much thought before. Could we alienate an entire kingdom from our realm? Since it was dying, residents might be better off seeking refuge in one of the remaining three.

But Zeke quickly answered the question with, "Reales was the first kingdom in our realm. It will remain as such."

The fierce devotion to his kingdom that he tried to deny so often was endearing. Though I was born in Reales, I did not feel an allegiance to it, but I couldn't discount that Zeke did. Rudolf trusted Zeke would care for it should the crown ever fall to him. I couldn't take that away from him.

While Direk droned on, I looked around the dining room in shock that anyone would want this much coral in their castle. The only piece of furniture not painted teal and inky pink was the black dining table we sat at, but even that was adorned with floral arrangements made of admittedly beautiful flowers. "What are these?" I interrupted, touching one of the delicate petals.

"Gladiolus," Petra answered. "Rare."

"Mm," I hummed, dropping my hand to dust across one of the seashells imprinted into the tabletop. "Was one of you a fish in a past life?"

No one answered, but Elric did grin.

Zeke leaned back in his chair with his elbow propped on the table, lazily holding an orange in his hand while glowering at Direk. I wasn't sure why they despised one another, but the glare that Direk returned to Zeke made it apparent that he did not appreciate Zeke dining with his king and queen.

I found Zeke's arrogance delicious. He glanced at me with a wink, peeling his orange back and popping a carpel into his mouth. It was the first time I had ever witnessed him actually get to consume an orange without squashing it between his fingers.

We had slept for nearly two days, barely spoke since we were rarely awake at the same time, and did not address the secret he still had not shared. This was the first time we had set foot outside our chambers since Edmund left, being fed from trays left outside our door and dressing in fresh clothing that was placed inside our wardrobe every morning.

But I didn't tell him about the nightmares, and he didn't ask why

I'd wake in cold sweats because he didn't need to. The nightmares would shatter into tiny pieces, and I would wake up to his gray eyes staring into mine before we'd drift away again.

It led to him not touching me, but that didn't prevent me from flirting with him. With a grin, I maintained eye contact with Zeke while asking Petra, "Petra, do you have any fudge lying around?"

Zeke narrowed his eyes on me.

Sighing, Petra held up a hand for Direk to stop speaking. We had all stopped listening to him a while ago. "Unfortunately not, Raven. We have shipments delivered weekly from Thoya, but it never lasts more than a day. Have you tried theirs?"

I attempted to hold back a smile. "Once. It was quite orgasmic."

Zeke choked on his juice and coughed. Petra's eyes widened, but a smile broke across her face as Elric chuckled. "I have not heard it described like that before, but I suppose you are correct," she said.

"Perhaps that is why it sells so quickly," Elric tacked on.

Highly perturbed that I had interrupted his debriefing, Direk placed his hands on his hips and stared at me with a raised brow. Zeke grinned at my annoyance, allowing me to handle this myself. "You don't care for me much, do you?"

Direk seemed surprised at my direct question, clearing his throat. "I apologize if I've given you that impression, Queen Raven."

Sitting up, I rested my elbows on the table and gifted him a sweet smile. "Think nothing of it, Direk. My husband is out of juice. Would you run along and fetch him some more?"

The muscles in his jaw flexed as he blinked, and a noise resembling a grunt came from him as he dipped his chin and backed out of the room.

Elric chuckled. Zeke grabbed one of my hands and tugged. Standing from my chair, I allowed him to pull me into his lap and rested against his chest while he softly grazed my arm. "This bewitching creature loves me," he said.

"Entirely too much," I teased.

He kissed my temple and intertwined our fingers, lifting my knuckles to his lips. And without dropping our gaze, he said, "I need the two of you to tell me why I cannot feel your emotions."

My head jerked to the side as I looked at Petra and Elric, unaware that anyone could prevent Zeke from sensing their emotions. Zeke leaned up and skimmed his teeth across my jawline, causing heat to rise along my spine, my blood warming at his touch.

Gods, Raven, I can smell it.

I closed my eyes at his whisper in my mind, tipping my head to rest my temple against his forehead. He hadn't asked for my blood once, and I couldn't say I hadn't wondered why.

Returning to rest against the chair and denying his temptations, he looked between Petra and Elric. "Don't everyone answer at once."

Petra sighed. "Ezekiel, we were having such a leisurely breakfast."

"I believe it's become evident that magic lingers in our realm," Elric answered nonchalantly, peeling the skin from an orange. "If we possess it, we do not have to disclose it."

"But you know River," I said.

Petra's eyes flared as she looked at Elric, who avoided her and flicked his eyes to the ceiling instead. I leaned forward, trying to catch one of their gazes. "How would you know of a twin I knew nothing about?"

"We were friends with Celestina," Petra replied as if that answer would suffice, but it was the same one Damiana had given me.

"That doesn't explain how you know him," I countered. "He's lived outside this realm."

"I did not say we knew him," Elric interjected. "Perhaps we knew *of* him."

"*Perhaps* there are things you are not telling us," Zeke said, his voice tight and defensive. "Like why you guard a forest with skeletal remains that... move."

Again, I turned to stare at him in bewilderment. "Move?"

"You were delirious from lack of sleep, Ezekiel," Petra said. "You were angry and hurt from your loss. I imagine someone who had gone through so much so quickly would see impossible things, too."

They were evading our questions, but something Petra said stuck with me, and I tilted my head. "His loss? I hardly believe he would consider Cade a loss."

Zeke stiffened. Our heartbeat quickened, making me realize that Petra was not referencing Cade's death. And suddenly, my mouth felt dry. "What loss is she talking about?"

Petra paled. "You have not told her."

Shoving Zeke's arms from around me, I twisted to look at him. With my heart caught in my throat and eyes watering, I wanted to be wrong. I didn't want to ask or imagine that he could ever hide something of this caliber from me, but when he looked at me with tearful eyes, I knew.

~

PETRA AND ELRIC had hastily excused themselves from our *leisurely* breakfast and closed off every entry into this nauseating room. The floral arrangements I once found beautiful would now be tied to this moment—the moment I prayed I was wrong.

Pacing the length of the table, I couldn't stop trembling. "Tell me it's not true, Zeke. Please tell me you did not hide this from me."

"Raven." He leaned against the table as he watched me. "Please stop and look at me."

I shifted into Blaze unwillingly as panic encased my heart in a locked box. Pausing to face him, I dug my nails into my palms to keep from lighting the room on fire and burning through all the watery embellishments. "Say the words."

"Raven, you were healing. Your mind was bleak. I didn't want to tell you until I knew you could handle it." He stepped toward me. "Baby, please."

I held up a palm. "Say the words, Zeke."

He put a fist against his lips as if physically stopping himself from uttering the words aloud. Tears slipped down his cheeks as he sank back down to the table, and the devastation I had witnessed from him the other night returned in full force.

He didn't want to tell me then, and now I understood why. I understood this was killing him, but he hid it from me. And part of me hoped I was wrong—that it was something else entirely, that this was all a nightmare I would soon wake up from.

But when he lowered his hand from his lips, inhaled a shaky breath, and said, "You miscarried," all I saw was black, red, and blood.

Terra came out. Falling to my knees as my world crumbled

around me, as the walls around us shook and pieces of ceiling fell to the floor, I screamed. I screamed so loudly and so heartbreakingly that windows shattered behind me. Pieces of glass flew across the room, Zeke covered my body with his own to protect me from the debris, but all I could do was scream.

Unreachable. Gone.

The floor shook, and cracks spread across the tile. He grabbed me to find my eyes, but I couldn't stop *feeling*.

Fury, despair, hopelessness. Everything bleak and weary wrapped itself around me. So much power; I held so much magic in my veins, yet I couldn't save my own child. Too weak and feeble; I could never do enough to stop losing everything.

I yearned for something that no longer existed.

The child I would never know—the one I would never be able to accept. The life we had created together from the unfathomable love between us.

It was gone. Taken away. The blood from the bath, oh gods, the blood in the tub was a mixture of Cade and the child I lost. "You knew," I rasped.

"Raven, I'm sorry...."

Shoving him off, I stood on shaky legs with tears streaming down my cheeks. "I can't be near you."

"Raven!" he called as he followed me out of the room, nearly tripping over the cracks in the floor.

I slammed doors shut as I ran through rooms, unaware of where to go or how to get there, but it had to be away from him.

He shouted for me. He *cried* my name.

Pieces that had mended together since meeting him deepened as they broke apart again.

How could I ever forgive him for this?

How could I ever forgive myself?

∽

PETRA FOUND ME FIRST.

Burrowed in a small pantry between the dining hall and a scullery, I lay in a puddle of tears and heartache. Time had no meaning anymore. Nothing might ever again carry purpose and reason, because one could not exist for this.

I couldn't get myself to move. Not a limb. Not a finger. All I could do was stare at the ceiling above me, convinced I had died that day in the forest. *My* Zeke wouldn't have hidden this from me. My best friend wouldn't have drugged me and dragged me to another kingdom simply to possess me.

All of this had been a chasmic dream.

I hadn't bathed in a pool of blood from the loss of our child. I hadn't been told about miscarrying by a queen I hardly knew. No, surely I was stuck in a nightmare. Maybe I was in Seolia, tucked away in Isla's cottage, and when I wake, she'll make tea, and we'll laugh about all of this. I pinched myself hard enough to bruise myself and wake up, but it didn't hurt because everything was numb.

We had dreamed of a family together. I often imagined what our children would look like. I hoped to have a son identical to his father, with hair black as night and skin so golden it appeared as if he had bathed in the sun. I wanted to hide in the hallways with him while Zeke sought us, giggling when he'd find us and wrap us up in his arms.

It was a daydream I held onto when thoughts of war or death overwhelmed me. It was be thoughts I shared with him before falling asleep so he could create dreams for us of a future that seemed possible.

He wanted a daughter that looked just like me—a small, feisty witch who would challenge him. He would speak of spoiling her since I rarely allowed him to spoil me.

We wanted miniature versions of one another because of our love. We couldn't get enough of each other and wanted to spread this ungodly love to our offspring.

And I lost that dream.

We weren't ready. We hadn't planned on having children this soon. It wasn't the best timing, but I still deserved a chance to choose, and that was taken away. Not only had I nearly lost my life, but I had also lost our child.

Petra did not ask questions as she closed the door behind her and lowered herself to sit on the floor next to me, moving my head into her lap. She remained silent even as I sobbed until the cries burned my throat. She said nothing when the skirt of her dress became soaked in tears of agony.

She brushed her fingers through my hair. "Grief is the hardest when it was an 'almost.'"

Whimpering, I covered my face with my hands.

An *almost*. Our dream was an *almost*.

My life consisted of almosts—almost had a mother, almost had a sister, a twin, a family, almost successfully killed Mira, almost broke down the wall between my husband and me, almost died, almost kept control over my magic, almost, almost, almost.

The idea became redundant.

Everything was nearly in my grasp before it fell away, leaving me with nothing but want.

"I was there when the physician discovered you were with child." Her voice quivered, her hand stilling in my hair. "You were not far along. And I was there when Ezekiel was informed."

As upsetting as him not telling me was, knowing how his heart must have broken hurt me the most.

"I have lived entirely too long, Raven. I have been part of many moments full of joy or sorrow, and I have never seen a man as devastated as Ezekiel."

I was positive my heart was in pieces on the floor because it could no longer beat inside my body.

"You will be whole again, Raven. You might not be the same, but there is beauty in loss, dear one."

Blinking away as many tears as I could, I met her eyes and waited for how I could ever possibly see anything other than suffering from this loss.

Her eyes shimmered as she brushed tears from my cheeks. "Hope rises with the sun, Raven. And for as long as I've lived, the sun has always risen again."

～

HOLDING MY HAND, Petra guided me into a large sitting room. Zeke sat on a chaise lounge in front of the lit fireplace, and I knew it was because he wanted to feel me in one of our darkest hours. Bent over with his elbows on his knees and face buried in his hands, it looked as if he hadn't stopped moving since I'd left him in the dining room. His clothes were rumpled, his hair disheveled, and he was the portrait of a broken man.

"Ezekiel," Petra called softly.

Relief washed over his face as he looked up and stood, but he did not rush to me as I expected him to. His throat bobbed as he held in a cry, his face stained with tears and his eyes resembling the dark thunderstorms that rolled in each time he was upset.

And with a darkened stare pinned to me, not from lust or desire but from pure guilt and grief, he remained as still as death as Petra left us and closed the door behind her.

"Raven." He rocked on his heels to keep his distance between us. "There are no words to express how sorry I am for keeping this from you."

My eyes closed as I lowered my head.

"I was scared, Raven." He took a moment to recompose. "You hadn't shifted into yourself yet, and then you tried to kill Mira. I wasn't sure what telling you would do to you, and I couldn't break your heart yet."

"That was not your decision to make," I managed to say. "You had no right to do that."

"I know," he said, his voice cracking as emotion overcame him. "I know it wasn't. I should have told you, but please try to understand, baby. You must understand that I did not withhold this from you to hurt you."

Of course, I knew that, but it didn't make it hurt any less.

I stepped back on instinct when he took a step toward me. His eyes widened at the rejection, and he clutched his shirt to his heart as if I had just stabbed it. But I couldn't move. My feet remained planted firmly on the ground.

He fell to his knees, his hands resting against his thighs as he slumped forward. "Baby, please. I can't live without you, Raven. You don't have to forgive me, but please tell me that you will not leave me because of this."

"I hate you at this moment," I whispered. "I hate you for coming into my life." My teeth chattered. "I hate you for making me feel like I could have this dream only for you to hide the loss of it from me when it happened."

His cries were nearly unbearable and the ache in my chest grew. "And I hate myself for ruining it for us."

He blinked rapidly as if he had misheard me. "Raven," he whispered, standing and coming to me. I flinched, but allowed him to close the space between us. "You did not ruin anything. How could you blame yourself for any part of this?"

"I lost our child." I could barely verbalize it. My bottom lip quivered and my entire body felt like it could collapse into itself at any moment. "That was our future."

"It *is* our future, Raven." Cradling my neck between his hands, he brushed tears from my cheeks with his thumbs. "Raven, we didn't have only one chance. We will mourn, but then we dream again. We never stop dreaming."

My bottom lip puckered out. "But you will resent me."

"Fuck, Raven." He lifted me by my waist and carried me to a high table against a window, setting me down so we were at eye level. "Nothing could ever make me love you any less. I would never resent you for anything that happens." He took my hand and placed it against my heart. "Hate me, Raven. Hate me all you want because my love for you, for us, will always outweigh your hatred."

Scrunching his shirt between my fingers, my forehead dipped against my fist. "I am so upset with you," I rasped.

He wouldn't stop touching me, as if this were the last time he would be able to. I wanted to reassure him that I would never leave him and that we would get through this and come out stronger for it. But my heart was broken, and our trust was severed.

Instead of making promises I wasn't sure I could keep, the only words I could manage were, "Take me home."

INTERMISSION

RAVEN

Days had passed since Zeke found me.

Saying goodbye to Petra and Elric was more challenging than I thought it would be. I didn't know them well, and it was evident that there were things they weren't telling us, but they opened their home to us and nursed me back to health until I was well enough to travel back to Seolia.

We left three days after the news of my miscarriage. Instead of dealing with it, I slept. I pushed aside my need to explore The Forest Beyond again and just... survived. It was all I could do right now.

I hadn't spoken to Zeke much since that day. He rarely slept and did not touch me. I wanted to forgive him. He was hurting as much as I was, but I couldn't view his secrecy as anything but a betrayal against us.

Before we left Perosan, Petra gifted me with a trunk full of new clothing. Similar to the dresses in Reales, the outfits were cut in ways I had never seen, and I realized that, while we always received shipments of textiles from Perosan, I had never inquired how they had such unique fabrics.

I was wearing one of those dresses now—an airy, short dress that skimmed across my knees. Zeke had grumbled something about it being too short, but that was the most we had spoken on the sail home.

It had been four days of awkward silence and making small talk with Luca, who knew better than to ask how I was feeling.

I tried sleeping in the cabin below deck, but as darkness enclosed me, my lungs constricted and I couldn't breathe. After a night of unsuccessfully falling asleep, I moved to the deck to sleep under the stars every night. And just as Zeke did on our trip to Reales together, he stayed awake at the helm while Luca slept below.

He visited my dreams every night. We danced under the stars or just held one another. Our escape from reality was the only way we communicated right now, but at least dreams kept us connected.

I will always find you in our dreams; he had promised me once and kept his promise.

But even in our dreams, I faded fast.

Even in a place where everything was fabricated, I still felt the heaviness between us. The silent discourse each look between us conveyed.

And I feared we would never recover.

I WILL ALWAYS FIND YOU IN OUR DREAMS; HE HAD PROMISED ME ONCE AND KEPT HIS PROMISE.

14

RAVEN

I
t was nightfall when we docked in Seolia.

Our sails swayed in the warm breeze, rustling the leaves of the trees in the Black Forest. Luca departed the ship after promising that everything would work itself out. He left to find Jeanine and explain everything that had transpired, insisting that Zeke and I spend time alone to prepare for the onslaught of questions we would receive—questions I would never be prepared to answer.

Zeke leaned against the ship's side, watching me. I gnawed on the inside of my cheek, making the flesh raw from the newfound anxiety I experienced every moment.

This was my home, yet I feared leaving this ship. Cade was gone, but he lingered around me like a ghost. He haunted each memory, reminding me that the trust I continuously gave to others had burned me worse than my own fire ever could.

Clearing my throat, I tore away at chipped wood planks decaying from years of use. "I would like to readjust to being here before we discuss what is to be done about Mira's army."

I breathed a curse word when the sharpened end of a plank pinched the tip of my finger and drew blood. Zeke was beside me instantly, watching as droplets of blood dribbled down my finger.

I held it out to him.

His tongue swiped across his bottom lip before he shook his head. "I do not deserve it."

"No," I whispered, "you don't. But I am offering."

He moved slowly to keep me at ease. I wasn't ready to give him everything, but I would give him this. Taking my wrist gently, he raised my finger to his lips, but instead of sucking from the break, he brushed my fingertip across his lips to smear the blood. He wiped it clean with his tongue in one stroke.

His entire body shuddered.

I didn't understand it. I wasn't sure I ever would.

His stare became dark. "The forest was alive." His voice carried a hint of fear. "It... *knew* you. It was guarded by magic that seemed implausible." He squeezed the tip of my finger to draw more droplets and grazed his lips again. "Raven, I need this. I can't explain it. I..."

A sigh of relief and footsteps on the deck had him cleaning the blood from his lips with his tongue. As John neared us, I pressed my fingertip into my palm to heal the cut.

Forcing myself to smile, I timidly stepped into John's open arms. I used to love being touched; communicating with others by hugging. Now, anyone's hands on me made me squeamish.

It was another comfort Cade had stolen from me.

"I am overjoyed to see you," John said softly. "Luca told me... everything."

"Miscarriage," I said since no one else would. We couldn't dance around it, and I wouldn't pretend it didn't happen. We had a child. It was a piece of myself I would never get back, and it didn't deserve to be buried down.

John's gaze swept to Zeke. "I am sorry about your loss. I can't imagine..."

Shifting uncomfortably as I tore myself away from him, I interrupted with a soft but firm voice. "I can't talk about it right now. I need sleep and normalcy for a few days. We will discuss Mira and what to do about the army then. For now, I need peace."

"Of course," John said, squeezing my arm. "Take all of the time you need, Raven."

Time would never be a solution. I would never heal from what we had endured and lost—from the permanent change it had made in my marriage.

Hesitating for a moment longer, I disembarked. Months ago, feeling unsafe in Seolia was unfathomable. And while I believed Mira to be my most significant threat, I was wrong. The most dangerous one had lurked in my bed, leaving marks on me that I would never recover from.

In the end, Cade won.

~

TWO DAYS HAD PASSED.

Every moment that passed by felt like sleepwalking. I couldn't remember the last time I felt like myself. I stayed shifted as Blaze day and night, burying Raven down until only a whisper of who I used to be remained.

Even though we didn't speak, Zeke never left my side. If anyone came to our door, he would talk to them, but for the most part, everyone left us alone.

Cade's chambers were being torn apart above us. His furniture would be replaced, and any trace of him existing in this castle would be wiped clean.

As my new adviser, Jeanine would move into his chambers once finished. The small suite she had lived in since returning from Reales wasn't fitting for someone of her title. And while I wasn't sure I could ever step foot into those chambers again, I couldn't think of a better way to move on from the memories I had created in there with Cade.

Zeke hadn't bitten me yet, but I would break skin for him every so often. His reaction was always the same. His eyes would darken, his energy would replenish, and he'd entertain himself by moving furniture around our chambers to keep from touching me.

At one point, he moved the desk into our bedchambers. After realizing it made no sense, he pushed it back. I would try to sit down, only to find that a chair had been moved to a separate room.

Boredom combined with missing me was a terrible combination for him.

After the first sleepless night in our bed, he moved a chaise to our balcony. It wasn't large enough for both of us, but the sounds of my village below calmed me enough to sleep.

He would lie down, feet hanging off and undoubtedly uncomfortable, before I would lie on his chest. His heart beating in my ear was always the last thing I heard before drifting off.

That was one thing between us that hadn't changed.

I wasn't dense enough to believe I could sleep without him. I still felt there wouldn't ever be a safer place for me than in his arms. He remained the most vital component in my universe.

And he kept the nightmares away.

When I would wake up crying from our loss or sweating from fear, he'd kiss away the tears until I calmed, whispering promises of nothing like this ever happening again.

I had woken moments ago, but he was in such a deep sleep that he didn't stir when I lifted my head from his chest. Since sleep was a rarity for us, I didn't want to wake him.

Barefoot and dressed in nothing more than the nightshirt I had lived in since returning, I crawled off of him to glance over the balcony. With dawn on the horizon, the village was quiet and empty.

Stealing another glance at my dozing husband, I tiptoed off the terrace and through our chambers until I stood at the downstairs staircase. My heart pounded in my chest to tell me I wasn't ready, but I rarely listened.

I passed by Jeanine and Luca's doors, contemplating if I should wake Jeanine. She had honored our request for time to heal, but I missed her and owed it to our friendship to show her I was alive.

Broken and bleeding, but alive.

I inched down the dark hallways and passageways Cade had

chased me through over the years. I passed the dining hall, where he had embarrassed me in front of my entire family, marking the beginning of the end to our friendship.

And the farther I walked, the angrier I became.

With one of my hands, I tried to free Blaze. I wanted to manifest her like before. I wanted to know if I had dreamed of the fiery fox from the forest or if she really could exist outside my body.

But when nothing came, I sighed heavily and shoved open the doors to the throne room. I stared at the throne in the center—the throne I never wanted, never asked for, the one that introduced me to Cade and this life of games and politics. The burden Leonidas had placed on me centered on this very chair. A chair made of gold and red plush, somehow signaling that I was better than everyone who kneeled before it.

Like I could fix their problems.

Like I had somehow earned respect for doing nothing more than existing; for being the bastard child of a witch and a weak king who never had the decency to introduce himself to me.

If he hadn't forced me onto this chair, I never would've left Reales. I would've met Zeke sooner. I wouldn't have lost my child because of the man he trusted to protect me.

Everything wrong in my life—every bad thing that had ever happened to me—was because of this throne.

I didn't want this fucking thing.

Without a second thought, I curled my hands into fists and lit the throne ablaze. It melted too slowly for my liking, so I added more and more flames until all I saw was orange.

Over a century of royalty had sat on this throne, declaring themselves to be the greatest protectors of this kingdom, but none of them had ever prevented this from happening.

I didn't prevent it.

I was not qualified to handle this on my own.

Upon hearing my name shouted, I turned to face Zeke and John as they ran into the room together. Their jaws fell slack at the chaos ensuing behind me.

I stood still, unfazed, watching the reflection of flames in their eyes. Zeke stared at me with concern and fear, saying something to me, but I heard none of it.

Walking past them and ignoring their calls for me to stop, I flicked my wrist to kill the flames, leaving the throne as nothing more than a pool of melted gold and a century of lies.

~

ZEKE FOLLOWED me into our chambers, grabbing my wrist to spin me around. The expression on my face remained unchanged except for the eyebrow I lifted, daring him to challenge me. I would have been lying if I said I wasn't looking for a fight. Anything would have been better than our constant silence.

"Raven," he said, but he seemed lost for more.

I wrangled my wrist free and walked into our bedchambers. I had no plan or purpose, but I was tired of being still.

"Raven, you can't just...."

I whirled. "Can't just what, Zeke? I can do as I please. This is my castle. I don't want the throne anymore."

He pinched the bridge of his nose. "You're acting impulsively, Raven, and I understand. You're upset with me and with... everything, but..."

I scowled. "I am not acting impulsively."

He dramatically motioned toward the door. "You set the fucking throne on fire, Raven! You're telling me that was planned? You woke up and thought that you would just meander downstairs to light the throne of Seolia on fire?"

I shrugged a shoulder and blatantly lied, "Yes."

"If you want to be angry, be angry with me. I am the one who deserves it. This kingdom doesn't."

"I protected this kingdom!" I shouted. "I stopped Mira's plan! We can win this war now with the full support of Thoya and Perosan."

"You cannot truly believe it is that easy."

Crossing my arms over my chest, I waited for him to continue. I wasn't particularly in the mood for a political conversation, or to be told I was wrong.

He rolled his shoulders back, switching into his role of the prince.

And though I was the queen of an entire kingdom, I wasn't naive enough to believe I was more well-versed in this subject. Zeke had been taught royal protocols, something I remained envious of.

Sensing my discomfort, he motioned toward the door again. "Would you prefer we have this conversation elsewhere?"

I rolled my eyes. "Why?"

"Because these are our bedchambers, Raven. This is where we exist as a couple, not as royals of two kingdoms who will most likely disagree about the next phases of our leadership."

"A couple," I huffed out with a laugh. "That's exactly the opposite of what we've been since you found me."

His eyes narrowed. "There has not been one moment that you have not belonged to me, Raven. There will be a day you get that through that thick skull of yours."

"I belong to no one," I muttered, knowing that was precisely the wrong thing to say right now, but it came out all the same.

I immediately regretted it as he bared his teeth, seeming taller than usual. His canines seemed sharper and primed, and the way his chest heaved told me he was one step away from draining me completely to prove his point.

"What?" I challenged, moving my hair to one side of my neck to reveal his scarred bite. "Continuing to hold back, Zeke? Because you know you fucked up. How long, hm? How long are we going to live like strangers?"

I continued, "How long will we pretend we haven't spent the last few months with you practically living inside me? How long will you act like you do not ache for my blood like the monster you are?"

"The monster *I* am?" He laughed, running the tip of his tongue over the point of his tooth. "I am not the one who tried to murder my sibling in cold blood. I am not the one who has changed the course of this realm for the rest of eternity."

"You cursed this realm the second you agreed to work with Mira," I spat out with venom behind my words. "Do not act as if you are any better than me. You were prepared to fight a war long before you ever met me."

"And I still would," he growled. "I would fight thousands of wars for you, Raven, and only for you. But there is a correct way to rule a kingdom, Raven, and what you did was not it."

"I tried to kill her for *you*!" I yelled. I ran my tongue over the roof of my mouth to prevent myself from crying. I would not show weakness for this. I would not feel guilty. "And I would do it again and again." I took a step forward. "Why are you allowed to kill for me, but I cannot do the same for you? It was always the plan, Zeke. I just tried to accelerate it."

"That is the point of having a plan, you infuriating witch!" He turned from me, resting his hands loosely on his hips and breathing slowly. "We had Edmund on our side. We were training your men to fight. You take a kingdom with dignity, Raven. The people of our kingdoms need to be able to trust you. Now, you are nothing more than the rumors."

My lips parted at the insult, but those words hit me heavily. Because he was right. I had become the dark witch that Mira wanted everyone to see me as. All of the trust I had worked to build, the lengths we had gone to convince everyone that it was Mira who was meant to be feared, had been diminished by my inability to think clearly whenever I was in pain.

"I didn't think... I..."

He turned to face me then, his features softening slightly. "That is always the problem, Raven. You react before we have a chance to talk about it. I didn't need you to kill her for me, Raven. Not yet." He took slow, tentative steps toward me. "You want to protect me. I understand that more than anyone. But now, my love... I will need to protect you. She will not let this go."

The tears I had been holding back pooled in my eyes. "River won't harm me," I whispered.

He stopped in front of me and shrugged his shoulders. "We don't know that, Raven. We know nothing about the men in Reales or about him. Maybe he did save you, Raven, but at what cost? He is still with her. He is still on her side."

I wasn't sure what to say. Every choice I had made was the wrong one, and now we were stuck in an endless cycle of the ramifications of my decisions.

"As for us being strangers," he said softly, tucking a strand of hair behind my ear, "if you'd allow me, there is something I would like to show you."

I hadn't meant it. If I knew anyone, it was him. But when he extended his hand to me, I just stared at it. I wanted to let him back in and knew I would eventually, but I had to ask myself if I was ready for that moment.

"Zeke," I said, intending to convey all of it.

When he whispered, "Please," with heavy emotion, I relented and took his hand.

"AS FOR US BEING STRANGERS, IF YOU'D ALLOW ME, THERE IS SOMETHING I WOULD LIKE TO SHOW YOU."

15

Despite never giving him a castle tour, Zeke knew it well. That didn't surprise me. With his stealthiness, I didn't doubt he had become familiar with the castle between flirting with me and training.

We descended staircases beyond the kitchen and sculleries that hadn't been utilized in decades, passing places that I had never ventured into. Vaulted cellars beneath the castle remained untouched. I had no idea what was in any of these rooms, let alone what could lurk in these dimly lit and forgotten corridors.

He stopped in front of a large wooden door with a partially

missing latch and kissed my hand. "I promised myself that when I found you, I would do this."

"Leave me for dead in our abandoned basement?"

He chuckled as he guided me inside. Ancient candelabras covered in dust hung on the walls. He crouched in front of me, waiting until I jumped on his back to take me around the room, waiting patiently while I lit each candle with my fingertip before setting me down in the center.

The candles slowly flickered to life and brought enough light into the room to reveal what he wanted to show me. The trunks, portraits, and trinkets I had brought back from his childhood home idly sat beside aged furniture covered in cloth sheets and cobwebs.

I didn't feel like these pieces of his life belonged next to the forgotten, but he had made it clear that he wanted no part of his previous life.

Standing awkwardly and rocking on my heels, I was unsure what to say. He had turned me down multiple times when I pried about his life before Mira, which left me uncertain of what to expect now.

He seemed just as uncomfortable as me. "While leaving you for dead is appealing," he said with a smile, "I promised myself I would bring you down here and tell you everything you want to know."

With only the candlelight, he looked haunted as he stood in front of his past, staring at his present. And I knew the effort this took on his part—having to open every old wound and revisit memories to regain my trust.

I sat on an old and covered chaise, ignoring the cloud of dust that followed. "I would love that."

$$\sim$$

HE DIDN'T HOLD anything back. He paused to breathe every so often, staring silently at his relics. We all had demons, things we didn't want to remember. Trauma. And this was his.

He was pushing past his heartbreak and shadowed reminders to let me in. He didn't owe me any of this. These things belonged to his life before me, and while I wanted to know everything about him, I had come to terms with the fact that there were pieces of his past that were too painful to revisit.

Clearing his throat, he grabbed the sleeve of a tunic nicer than any I had ever seen him wear. It looked far too small to fit the man he was now.

"When I was seventeen, Reales held a ball for the common folk." A small ghost of a grin appeared as he fingered the material. "I dreaded these kinds of events because I would be chased around the room by girls who wanted to dance with me."

"How awful that must've been," I teased.

"One of my tutors took pity on me." He tipped his head back and chuckled, staring at the low ceiling above us. "She kept me by her side all night and pulled me into a dance each time she saw a girl coming for me. She was a short, plump woman that smelled of parchment and ink, but I had never been more grateful for her than during those moments."

I gasped as he slid the memory into my mind. My smile was broad as I watched him attempt to hide behind columns in one of their grand ballrooms, only to be dragged out by the woman with a kind face and contagious laugh. He was beautiful, even then. "I would've tried to dance with you, too."

"I wouldn't have hidden from you."

Blush crept across my cheeks and I bit my upper lip as the memory faded. "You liked dancing with me."

"No," he said, shooting me a flirtatious grin. "I *loved* dancing with you, little demon. I was only good at it because of her."

"No formal classes for you?"

He dropped the sleeve with a smirk. "Gods-given talent."

I leaned back on the chaise with his beloved plush monkey on my lap. He had tossed it to me earlier, explaining that he'd slept with it every night as a child, only giving it up when he moved into the castle.

"Tell me something about your childhood. Please."

Nodding, he lowered to sift through one of the many trunks until he pulled out a yellowed and nearly shredded piece of parchment, bringing it to me. I could barely make out anything as I tilted my head to the side, tracing multiple lines centered on a giant X in the middle.

"Treasure map," he explained, sitting beside me. "Luca and I used to explore the forest. Once, when I was around ten, we took axes with us." He smiled, but not at me. It was my first time seeing his true joy since we started.

"We thought we could build a treehouse on our own." He chuckled and took the monkey from my arms. "Luca was only seven and could barely carry the axe into the forest. I don't know what made us believe we could swing the damn things."

Laughing aloud, I curled my legs underneath me.

"But did that stop us?" He shook his head. "We found the biggest tree and started swinging. Well, swinging isn't correct. We barely touched it. We maybe, *maybe*, got some shavings off."

He smoothed the faded brown fur back on the monkey's head, frowning slightly. "Luca was distraught. As the man of the house, I didn't want to disappoint him. I went into town and begged every man I could find to help us. I had to do petty jobs around town to earn their time, but we spent an entire summer building that treehouse with a handful of men. Every night after our studies, we would stay out there well after bedtime."

"What would you play?"

"Everything. Knights, mostly. I carved some wooden swords out of branches. Sometimes we'd read. I taught him how." There was endearing pride in his voice. "I liked history books; he liked folktales. Every night, we'd trade off. We had an expensive tutor, but Luca struggled to listen to anyone other than me. He wasn't slow but took his time. That's how he's always been, and it would frustrate our tutors. And I would get pissed at their lack of patience with him, so I ended up teaching him myself."

"Have you two always remained close?"

His jaw contracted for only a second before he loosened with a deep sigh. "Until I became angry with the world around me. I would be gone for long periods, but he'd be waiting at the dock for me every time my ship came in. Mira knew he was my best friend. I had alienated everyone else except for him and Edmund."

"What happened to the treehouse?"

He dropped the monkey back into my lap. "I'm sure it's still there. Scraps by now, probably. It wasn't that big. It seemed huge to us then, but I doubt even you'd be able to fit."

"I accept your challenge and would like to see it."

"I'll take you to it someday. Maybe when the forest is safe again, I can restore it for our children...."

And just like that, we were reminded.

I looked away from him. He would've restored it. He would've taken our son or daughter into the forest every day until it was the treehouse of their dreams.

His hands rested on my thighs as he went to his knees before me. He looked raw, swallowing thickly as he stared into my eyes. "When John left us, I became the man of our household. It was my responsibility to protect my family. And I failed at that, Raven. I became someone I am not proud of, and my decisions and recklessness led to the last two years of my life. It is because of me that my family was locked away."

"That's not true," I tried to say, but he shook his head.

"It is," he continued, "I wasn't there to protect them. Since the day she took them, I made a vow to myself to always put the ones I love first. Every decision I have made since then was to protect and defend."

His voice wavered as he said, "When I found out about the miscarriage, I didn't... I dealt with it the only way I knew how. I protected you. It was the wrong choice. I thought that giving you time to heal from Cade would make the loss of our child more bearable. I didn't want you to suffer through too much agony, Raven. I made a decision for you that I had no right to make."

Despair encroached as tears fell down my cheeks.

"Raven, I am truly sorry. I do not expect forgiveness, but I beg you to believe how regretful I am for making you doubt me or damaging the trust you have gifted me with. I know how difficult it is for you to let others in, Raven, and I have never taken that for granted."

He was laid bare and vulnerable on his knees, allowing tears to fall freely, and kept his touches on me feather-light.

"If you want to leave me, if you want to annul our marriage..."— he could barely get the words out but wouldn't allow me to speak before continuing—"I will honor and respect your wishes, but all I ask is to be allowed to stay. Please don't ask me to return to Reales without you. I won't bother you. I'll stare at you from a distance, but I can't... I can't live without you, I can't...."

"Zeke," I finally said over him, cradling his face between my hands, "I never wanted to leave you. I never thought about sending you away or annulling anything." I felt as if my ribs would collapse into my lungs any second from the heaviness of our combined heartbreak.

I slid down into his lap and rested my palms against his chest. "I am your partner, and what you did was wrong. I will not excuse you from that, but I will never leave you."

He palmed the nape of my neck. His attempts to hold back his cries were useless as they came out in strangled breaths. "Raven, what I did was inexcusable."

"Zeke, I love you. It is an imperfect love because that's what we are. We have always been a string of bad decisions thrown together, but there will never be anything you do that cannot be forgiven." It took an effort to lift his head so he'd look at me, and I nearly fell apart entirely at his tear-soaked cheeks. "I am upset, but it is not only with you. I lost our dream."

With one arm wrapped around my waist while his other gripped my chin, his shadowed eyes searched mine. "*You* are my dream, Raven. I have no dreams that do not revolve wholly around you. You must release yourself from this burden, Raven. I will not allow you to blame yourself for this."

"But I lost our child," I squeaked. "I wasn't strong enough. I didn't do enough."

He stood with me in his arms and turned to sit on the chaise with me in his lap. He struggled to speak, constantly clearing his throat or sitting with me in the strangling silence. I practically bathed in my tears, choking on the hair matted to my face but drowning in my regret.

"Raven, you are not at fault for any of this."

I didn't believe him. I couldn't.

"We will mourn our child, Raven."

"I need it to stand for something," I cried against his chest. "I need the loss of our child to mean something. It feels empty and worthless."

"Raven, it does mean something," he murmured, tugging me gently until I looked at him. "It does stand for something. It stands for everything. It stood for us. Our love created that. This loss" — he kissed my forehead — "we will always carry with us. The revenge you seek will not bring our child back, baby."

He peeled the hair from my face until it was tucked behind my ears. "I need you to forgive yourself. More than anything, I need you to understand that this was not because of you. Promise me that, Raven. Promise me you'll try."

It would take time—time I was tired of giving, but I would try for him and for us.

"I forgive *you*," I whispered, shoulders sagging from the release of that weight. "I forgive you. And I need you, and I don't hate you. I didn't mean that. Sometimes I think I love you entirely too much."

"Gods, Raven. I do not deserve you." He pulled me down to lie against his chest and kissed the top of my head.

"The gods seemed to disagree."

He smiled against my hair. "Fools. The lot of them."

"YOU ARE MY DREAM, RAVEN. I HAVE NO DREAMS THAT DO NOT REVOLVE WHOLLY AROUND YOU."

16

RAVEN

We returned to our chambers to bathe but stood awkwardly on either side of the room. I hadn't been naked in front of him since waking up in Perosan, and things since then had been rather unpleasant. My body no longer showed signs of bruising and had healed externally, yet I still felt broken and unworthy of him. Another man had touched me, and I had lost our child.

That, and I was married to a god.

At least as Blaze, I had slightly more confidence.

Wordless and just as uncomfortable as me, he turned the water

159

on and stared at it for way too long. I would eventually look back on this moment as amusing, since bashfulness wasn't a normal reaction from either of us, but right now, it was just thorny.

Digging my nails into my palms so hard that I drew blood, I winced in apology when his nostrils flared from the scent filling the room. Once the tub was halfway full, he removed his shirt and immediately sent warmth across my cheeks. I looked away instinctively—as if this man didn't belong to me.

And maybe he didn't. Perhaps he belonged to the person I used to be instead of the cracked and deranged woman I was now—the one who still itched for revenge on those who hurt us.

"Are you sore?" he asked quietly. "Do you need me to help you undress?"

That was the absolute last thing I wanted him to do. I would be okay to watch him bathe and cower in the corner. "No," I whispered, casting my eyes to the floor. "I am just struggling with"—I motioned toward the empty air—"all of this."

He seemed genuinely confused when I peeked at him as the silence dragged out, furthering my resolve to burrow into the floor. "All of what? Bathing with me? Is it because you're upset with me?"

"No," I answered quickly, cursing silently for reverting back to my incredibly infuriating habit of overthinking everything. "I'm just, you know, I..." Stuttering, I inhaled a deep breath. "I don't want you to see me."

"Raven," he said in disbelief.

Shame nestled itself directly in my chest. Cold sweats pushed through the heat on my skin as I took myself back to those moments with Cade, as fear infiltrated my every movement. "We haven't talked about it, and I don't want to describe every detail to you, but I am ashamed that he touched me. I betrayed you, and I don't feel... clean. Worthy."

I twisted my fingers nervously. "I stopped him each time, but I would understand if you no longer desire me. I am tainted and soiled and would not ask you to look past any of that."

"You think I no longer desire you?"

His voice wasn't gentle or soothing but held a sliver of anger. I wasn't sure what to do with my limbs, so I continued to move them to shield myself in whatever way I could.

"You've hardly touched me since then," I murmured, tugging at my nightshirt.

"Raven, I have lived in a constant state of agony since I found you." He shut off the water and stepped toward me. "All I want is to touch, feel, and kiss you. I have felt anguished that I couldn't do anything."

"I can barely look at you without feeling embarrassed." Tears stung my eyes, my throat welled, and I loathed how insecure I had become because of someone else's actions. "I feel I have broken your heart."

"Raven, all I do is want you."

Palming my eyes to cover my shame, I turned away from him to face the wall. "I want to believe you, Zeke, but I feel numb and dirty."

"My desire for you is stronger than it's ever been, Raven. When have I ever given you a reason to doubt?" He placed his hands on my waist to turn me around. "How could you ever believe I don't want you? I've thought of nothing but you since the night we met."

He kissed the tip of my nose. "You are all I want to look at. You are all I think about." He leaned in and pressed his lips against my ear. "There is nothing that would ever change that."

I sighed softly as he kissed along the shell of my ear, sucking gently on the skin beneath it. When he bunched my nightshirt in his hands, I was pulled from my daze and pushed against his hands to stop him.

"Raven, you're not going to stop me from seeing you unless you truly do not want it."

I wanted him; that hadn't changed. It never would, but my need for physical touch hadn't been satisfied in days, and I felt misplaced without it. I promised him I would try to forgive and move on from what happened, and the first step was allowing normalcy to return between us.

Not only because fate demanded our pairing, but because I loved him so intensely, I needed our balance restored before facing everything else.

Hesitantly, I removed my hands to allow him to continue until my nightshirt dropped to the ground. I brought my arms down to cover my body, but he pinned my wrists to the wall above my head. "Do you honestly feel like I don't want you?"

The emotions that swelled within me were the answer he sought. He could ask me thousands of questions and receive every response he needed just by sensing me.

His erection pulsed against my hip. "This is how my body reacts every time I see you. I don't even have to touch you to come apart, Raven."

Releasing my wrists, he wrapped my arms around his neck and lifted me until I curled around him. Our intimate embrace, which I had missed so much, made my bottom lip pucker out into a pout.

The touching of our bare chests was the most contact I'd had with him since all of this happened. It overwhelmed me to tears, the amount I had shed lately surely enough to fill an ocean.

"We still have fiery, unbridled passion, Raven. That isn't something that goes away, especially with us." He carried me back to our bedroom. "It will never go away. Look at what we do to one another like this."

Climbing into our bed, he rested on top of me. "I will never stop wanting you, but you are an addiction. Once I relinquish control, you won't be able to keep me off."

"I never wanted you off," I admitted. "Even while I was angry with you, I needed you near me. You're my safe place, Zeke. You're the only place where I feel the world won't hurt me."

"Before I lose control," he said hoarsely, "allow me just to touch you."

I remained utterly still underneath him. There was hesitation in how he looked at me, his fingers making light strokes down my cheeks and across my lips.

It was as if he were touching me for the very first time.

Our lovemaking was always passionate, but the way he was memorizing every inch of me with his hands brought another level of intimacy between us.

His hands brushed down my arms and hips while his lips slid across my collarbone. He lifted to his knees and drew lazy circles on my stomach with his fingertips, smiling at the way goosebumps trailed his touch.

"Let me see you, Raven." His eyes slowly slid up my body until they rested on mine. "It's time to give her back."

I had become so reliant on Blaze's warmth that pushing her down made me shiver, but I was ready to be vulnerable with him again.

Closing my eyes, I had to focus harder than usual on shifting into myself. Until recently, I had been comfortable in my own skin, but now I felt like a stranger trapped within myself.

His weight returned on top of me as he kissed away the tears from my cheeks. "It will get easier, my love."

I wanted to believe that—I *needed* to believe that the gnawing ache inside me would disappear one day.

Opening my eyes, I could barely see him through the blurriness of my tears. "I love you," I whispered earnestly. "You are the constant that always makes sense."

Butterflies fluttered in my stomach as he leaned in slowly, inch by inch, until his lips pressed tenderly against mine.

I could spend days like this.

Wrapping my arms around his neck, my hand slid into his hair and tugged the strands between my fingers. I was desperate for more, but he was moving frustratingly slowly.

Hooking my legs around his waist, I pushed my hips against his and whined when he pulled up to smile at me. "Hungry, my love?" he asked with a haughty smirk.

Scowling, I tilted my head to the side to expose my throat. "Hungry, my love?"

His gaze fell on the bite on my neck. The tip of his tongue slid over his bottom lip. If he would just bite me, he wouldn't be able to resist the rest. And perhaps he would stop treating me as if I could break at any moment.

"You've been thirsty," I said, lowering my shoulder to tempt him. "Drink."

I had expected hesitancy. Arguing.

Not how he moved so quickly that I couldn't take a breath before his teeth sank in. I pulled in cold air through clenched teeth as I tried to adjust to the pinch of my skin. "Zeke," I rasped, unsure if it was from pain or pleasure.

Using his tongue to suck out blood, he groaned the second the first drop hit his tongue. A hand rested against my neck to prevent me from moving an inch as he took so much so quickly that I became lightheaded.

His free hand pounded against the headboard, his hips thrusting against mine. I was too dizzy for logical thoughts, but I matched his thrust, at least aware that I needed him inside me.

"Zeke," I warned, "baby. Dizzy."

It seemed painful for him to release me. His fingers dug into the skin of my shoulders as he slowly pulled up. My blood dribbled down from the corner of his mouth, but his eyes struck fear into me.

The black shadows had wholly overtaken his irises, and the veins in his arms were darkened and pulsing.

Moving.

"Zeke, what is that?"

He kissed me like that was an answer. I tasted my blood on his tongue and his lips, and when he bit my bottom lip, it was only so he could take more from me.

As he sucked droplets from my lip, I tugged at his hair until he had to release me long enough to look at me. His eyes remained black but full of lust, and when he bared his teeth to me before growling, "I want you," I cared about nothing else.

"You send me into a frenzy," he said as if it weren't already obvious. "You belong to me, Raven."

Huffing impatiently, I nodded before raising up to kiss him. He stopped me with a hand around my throat, guiding me back to the pillow. "Say it," he snarled.

Snarled. Like a rabid beast.

"I'm yours," I promised.

I cried out his name when he gave me exactly what I wanted, filling me completely with a single twitch of his hips.

It was an explosion of colors painting our bodies.

For the first time since I was taken, the dark grays of our world were revitalized and awakened as he began a slow drive into me, exploring every inch like it had been a lifetime since the last time we touched one another.

He kept me cocooned in his hold, and I felt whole again. I didn't feel out of place or separated from my flame; I felt reconnected to him.

The emotions hit me all at once. When I whimpered, he slowed to a stop and looked at me with concern. "Did I hurt you?"

"The opposite," I said with a breath. "It feels like my heart is trying to fit back together."

"Raven." He kissed every inch of my face—my cheeks, eyelids, forehead, and the tip of my nose. "I am so sorry that I waited this long."

We were both in pain and mourned our loss, but it had never been clearer that we needed each other. "Please don't hold back," I pleaded. "I need to feel something. I need to feel you."

He flipped us over quickly, to my surprise, until I rested on top of him, his hands digging into my thighs. "Take what you need from me, Raven. Take it all."

So, I did.

I bared down until my clit was at the base of his cock, my nails digging into his arms. I took him until I felt nothing but him everywhere—until his hands and lips had touched every part of me, until the parts of my body that Cade had touched were replaced by only his.

His fingers dug into my waist as he sat up against the headboard, guiding me faster against him. "Fuck, you are a goddess." His eyes were molten lava as his stare raked across my body. "I would live and breathe only to fuck you, Raven."

Gods, the way his mouth could unravel me.

He held me still so he could thrust into me, each stroke carrying his anger from my doubt and how long it had been since he'd touched me. "Come, Raven. Scream. I want to hear you."

His hand wrapped around my throat and squeezed as I reached my peak, my cry of pleasure vibrating against his palm and triggering his release into me, but his thrusts didn't slow.

The high from coming had tension rolling off my body, and I

chased it. I held onto it for as long as I could. He would be what brought me back if only he realized.

He said my name repeatedly as he slowed before he groaned, fisting my hair and yanking my head to the side to sink his teeth into my shoulder. His lips closed over the bite as he sucked, his entire body shuddering as he drank from me, immediately hard for me again.

His mate. I was his mate and he needed my blood. I didn't know why; I didn't care, because as long as it was only mine that he wanted, he could have as much as he wanted. "I love you, you maddening, bloodthirsty—"

He kissed me to shut me up.

And as I clawed down his back with my nails, he took me to all the places only he could.

"RAVEN, I HAVE LIVED IN A CONSTANT STATE OF AGONY SINCE I FOUND YOU."

17

ZEKE

Watching Raven sleep on my chest while I ran my fingers through her hair, I sighed. I hadn't realized what my lack of touch was doing to her, but I never imagined she would conclude that I no longer desired her.

I had been uneasy touching her because of my guilt. I didn't believe I deserved her anymore. She admitted to hating me for giving her a future to dream of, one that was taken from us with a breath. I wanted to take her pain away, but somehow always created more.

There were still things I hadn't shared in full with her yet—the creatures I saw in The Forest Beyond, the skeletal army guarding it, the magic dwelling within. And without searching her memories, I couldn't experience what she did when Blaze came to life or when River saved her.

I was unsure of how to move on from something we wanted yet weren't ready for. We would have loved our child, and part of me always would, but our time would come. Though our plan with Mira was outed, the journey we were about to embark on still posed too significant a risk for a child. Mira would not go down without a fight. All we had managed to do was further irritate her. Not only would she want the realm, but she would also want revenge on Raven.

Raven had shifted back into Blaze before falling asleep. I wanted her to trust me enough to protect her. My little demon didn't need to come out to play all the time. I still wasn't keen on sharing this part of her.

My fingertips slowly moved down her arms, around her ribs, and across her stomach. After everything we had been through together, it was maddening that she believed the desire between us could dissipate so easily.

I would claw my way into her and live there permanently.

No bruising remained, and no evidence nor physical memory carried what had happened to her, but a heaviness pushed back as I moved to the outer edges of her mind. Her elements lingered like snakes, ready to attack and pounce on any threat.

No remnants left of the gentleness she was known for.

"I love you," I whispered before kissing her shoulder. "Don't break yet, Raven. We still have more to go."

She inhaled against my chest and exhaled through parted lips, her body warming at my voice, reacting to the bond between us — the one that grew more apparent every day. I wondered how intense mating used to be before it disappeared, and if it was similar to ours.

And why pairings restarted with us.

But you are not her mate, I heard echo in my mind.

The six words that haunted every second I spent with her.

The power in her petite body clung heavily to my chest, reaching for the magic, growing tired of remaining idle—the one that hungered for her blood.

The one she feared.

She never had any reason to fear me, no matter how threatening it might seem. Whatever this was inside me wanted her as much as I did. Every time I bit her, it was as if I could *hear* the blood racing through her. I tasted the uptick in her pulse from the pain and pleasure it sent barreling through her.

It was a sweetness I craved more than anything else.

I pushed feathery kisses along her neck and collarbone, and her body hummed. Kissing down her chest and across her breasts, I lingered on her nipples.

Her eyes fluttered open, and she sighed, wrapping her fingers around my shoulders. "Am I dreaming?" she asked in a playfully raspy voice, her ribcage bowing as she stretched her arms above her head. "I can never tell anymore when something feels this good."

Grinning, I nipped across her ribs and relished the whimper that escaped her. I loved when she screamed for me, but her soft noises made me yearn for her.

Falling to my knees, I dragged her with me until I could press my nose to her clit and drew in her scent. Her fingers tangled in my hair, and I grabbed her wrists, pinning them to the bed. "I do not need assistance to make you come, my love."

Her back arched at my words.

Gasping, she took the bedsheets between her fingers as I licked up her clit. Chuckling as I recalled the exact reaction from her our first night in the spring, I pulled away and grinned at her groan. "Miss me?"

Her head popped up with a smile, but then she glared as I teased her, holding her leg up while I kissed her along her inner thigh. "I want to come," she bit out in frustration.

"I am going to worship you, Raven. I will take my time, and you will not make demands of me."

She intended to argue, but I moved too quickly for her to try. Putting my arms under her legs, I flipped her over to her stomach and leaned in to bite into the flesh of her thigh.

She twisted enough to watch me, her gaze locked on mine while I drank just enough to temporarily satisfy my thirst. But who was I kidding? It would never be enough.

Releasing her with a disappointed sigh, I tugged the skin of her ass between my teeth while my fingers kneaded into the apex of her thighs, my fingertips teasing her clit.

She jerked at the touch, dramatically burying her face into the pillow as she cursed at me. I couldn't help but laugh at her desperation as I kissed along the lower half of her spine, sliding one finger into her core and moving at a leisurely pace.

Greedily, she wiggled lower, but I kept one hand pressed against her ass to stop her. "Don't, Raven."

She was nearly half off the bed and trying to fall into my lap, but adding another finger stopped her long enough for me to shove her back onto the bed.

"Zeke," she whined, attempting to look at me, but her face was covered by strands of red hair. "You're taking too long."

"I haven't had you in weeks, Raven." I took my fingers out and slid them into my mouth, squeezing her hip at the taste.

She fought me hard enough to twist to her back again, spreading her legs and baring herself to me. My eyes darkened on her, my hands wrapping around her waist to pull her back and give in, but before I could move, she closed her thighs hard enough to earn my glare. "Raven," I warned.

"Am I your queen, Zeke?"

Quirking a brow with an amused grin, I stared at the demon on our bed. "Technically? No."

Rolling her eyes, she shifted into herself.

"Yes, Raven, you are my queen."

"Do you want to make your queen come?"

I swallowed harshly. I had never wanted anything more.

"Then be a good prince and fuck me with your tongue."

It took a lot of self-control to keep myself from fucking her right here. "Fuck, Raven."

"Queen Raven," she corrected me. "Do as I say."

Not once had I ever wanted to be told what to do by anyone, no matter their position. And I had never heard her use her title to demand something from anyone, but gods almighty, I wanted nothing more than to do exactly as she said, like I was nothing more than a lowly subject. "Forgive me," I whispered, kissing beneath her navel, "Queen Raven."

Wrapping my lips around her clit, I sucked while sliding two fingers into her. She was soaking wet around my fingers, clenching tightly at the anticipation of coming. And the release she always found so quickly from me made me the cockiest bastard alive.

She writhed on the bed, her arms reaching above her to grab something, anything, and all I could think about was how much I wanted to serve her. Please her.

My cock was painfully swollen. I wrapped my hand around it and pumped as I replaced my fingers inside her with my tongue.

"Zeke," she cried, rolling her hips against my tongue. "I want to come, I want to come," she repeated like a chant as if she had any other choice.

She tightened around my tongue, giving me one final thrust before she released, the taste of her mixed with our earlier fuck.

Groaning from the combination of us on my tongue, I found my release seconds later and came on the floor at her feet.

I rested my forehead against her stomach as we panted, and my hands shook from how satisfied I felt with myself and how odd that feeling was. Being pleased with anything I did was a foreign concept, but completing what she asked of me gave me a sense of worth.

I wanted to do it again, but she grabbed me and pulled my hands to join her. "I'm sorry," she said.

I jerked back at her apology. "For what?"

"Making you call me that."

I rose from the floor and crawled over her, my hands resting on either side of her head. "Why are you apologizing for that? You are my queen."

"I'm your partner. We are equal."

"In marriage, yes. Position-wise? No."

"I don't give a fuck about position." She grabbed my face between her hands and forced me down, pushing her tongue between my lips.

I pulled away from her. "No, Raven, I earned your taste."

Her eyes narrowed. "Are you saying I need to earn the right to taste you?"

Shaking my head, I lay on my side and trailed a finger down her stomach. "I am saying that I'm selfish and do not share what is right-fully mine, even with you."

"And you're not saying that only to dispel my doubt?"

Before this moment, I had never wanted to simultaneously choke someone and love them. "Enough, Raven. We will stay in this bed and fuck until you quit feeling as if I do not want you." I placed her hand on my cock. "I just came from tasting you and want you again. It never stops, Raven."

Fuck me, she was made of all things divine.

I looked her naked body up and down, licking across my lips. "I want to pin you against a wall, my love. You are a goddamn master-piece." Perhaps I should've taken Edmund up on his offer to commission portraits of her. I would hang them up all over the castle.

She snorted. "You're a bit cheesy, you know that?"

I gaped but then smiled. "Never thought I'd be okay with that, but I am. For you, I would be the cheesiest."

She climbed on top of me and kissed down my chest. "Where else would you fuck me?"

I balanced my hands on her thighs. "Anywhere, Raven, I would fuck you everywhere."

"In front of people?"

I tried shoving her down my body so I could slip into her. "You know the answer to that."

She scooted down, kissing my stomach and licking the indentions of my abs. As she ground her wetness against my thigh, I was quickly pushed to the edge of desperation. "On a bed of bones?"

The idea intrigued me, but the flare inside my chest seemed to enjoy it more. And when she looked at me from under her lashes, I saw a look in her eyes that I did not recognize. "Would you fuck me on a bed of bones made from the men we're going to kill?"

I blinked in confusion. "Raven, what are you talking about?"

Her answer was her mouth around my cock.

And I stopped asking questions.

She had collapsed on top of me after fucking again. Her body was slick, sweaty, and my favorite smell. The room was full of a musky craze, the balcony doors fogged, and our blankets which had been thrown or kicked from the bed were strung across random pieces of furniture.

She was in my arms, yet distant. Something was on her mind, but it was buried so deep that I couldn't feel what it could be. Her magic had never felt stronger; it was as if I could taste it. It wanted to mingle with mine.

Dragging her up by her arms until I could kiss her, I nibbled on her bottom lip until she smiled. "Where's your mind, baby? I can't feel you."

She kissed me again and again until I needed to breathe. And when she came at me for another round, I stopped her with a gentle tug on her hair. "You won't let me bury things with fucking. You can't either."

She rested her hand on my chest and perched her chin upon it. Whatever she had to say, she didn't want to. "You will be king soon."

We had successfully avoided the subject of this since leaving Reales. I didn't want to be king. I never wanted to be king. The title would be forced upon me without my permission, but it would happen regardless once we defeated Mira.

I shifted her off and sat up, running a hand through my hair. This was a conversation I didn't want to have, and I was still perturbed that she had nearly changed our plan by attempting to kill Mira outright.

She sat up and pulled the only remaining pillow to cover herself. "I know you don't want to talk about it—"

"I don't," I interrupted and stood from the bed. "I don't want to fucking think about it, Raven."

I slid on a pair of pants. Having this conversation with her naked and painted my favorite color wouldn't work.

I tossed her nightshirt to her, turning from her as she dressed.

I wanted to be her husband, not her ally or political equal. I didn't want our nights of making love and living together as husband and wife to turn into business meetings and arguments about how to best rule two kingdoms.

She shuffled behind me. I turned to find her sitting on the edge of the bed. All my favorite parts of her were covered, which only added to my frustration.

I wanted to fuck the stubbornness and impulsiveness right out of her.

"We can't stay locked away in here pretending like the moment we walk out the door, everything won't change. I nearly killed Mira. We're about to kill her army right outside these walls. There are decisions we have to make before time runs out."

"Elric informed me that this war with Mira is bigger than our realm," I said, leaning against the table. "I had no chance to ask more questions before we were interrupted. I have no idea what will be left of Reales in her and River's hands, or if there will even be a kingdom to rule."

Her brows knitted together. "Why didn't you tell me that before?"

"Before what, Raven? Before you nearly burned Mira alive? I didn't exactly have time between you waking up for the first time and bathing. I didn't expect you to set the realm's future on fire so quickly."

Her eyes narrowed as she stood from the bed. "You're clearly still upset with me, so I'm not sure this is the right time to have this conversation."

"We need to have it," I said. "Because you're right. I will be king soon, and we have no plan in place. Am I moving? Am I leaving you to go back to Reales?"

"No," she huffed. "I never asked that of you, and I wasn't planning on it."

"Then what, Raven? What are we supposed to do now?"

She threw her arms up in the air, pacing the length of the bed. "I don't know!" she shouted. "I don't know what to do! I didn't realize that I would be kidnapped, nor did I realize that you planned on telling Elric of Mira's threats. That was a decision *you* made on *your* own."

"Because you're not suited for this!" I snapped, regretfully catching my outburst with a sigh.

She stopped pacing to face me, her lips parted in surprise.

I ran a hand down my face before hooking it around my shoulder.

"I'm sorry. I meant that you weren't raised to know protocols and how to accurately respond to issues like these."

I sank to sit on the edge of the table. "I cannot run another kingdom from here. There will be a lengthy time of transition. Reales was damaged before I left, and there is no telling what it's turned into since Mira welcomed in these friends of River's. I will need to work on a restoration plan, hire an entirely new court of advisers, and regain the people's trust, which will not be simple.

Not to mention dealing with the deaths of hundreds of men I captured and threatened. Melik was the first of many to find loved ones roped into fighting for Reales. It will be dangerous and will take time."

She listened in silence, which was a rarity for her. I worried I had hurt her feelings but sensed no emotion confirming it. She showed interest and intent, bobbing her head every few seconds.

And maybe I hadn't hurt her with my words, but what I said was still untrue. "Raven, you are capable of being a great queen. Your people respect and admire you. Sometimes, though, I feel you might not truly want it."

She opened her mouth to say something but stopped and looked toward the balcony. I followed her as she opened the doors, shivering from the breeze that wafted through and cleaned the fog. We walked onto the terrace, her arms spread wide as she leaned over to look down at the village below.

The village was brimming with life in the daylight. I had met nearly everyone who lived here and recognized each person moving beneath us. Raven needed to appear soon to assure everyone she was alive and explain why she tried to kill Mira. She needed to promise them that she wasn't the monster the rumors wanted to make it seem she was.

Hanging her head, she frowned, but I felt nothing but resolve in her. "I don't want it," she admitted. And once she said it, she seemed... relieved.

I drew in an unsteady breath, blinking a few times as I stared at her. She loved Seolia. That much was evident since the night I met her. Hearing that she didn't want her throne was somewhat shocking. "Raven, the throne belongs to you. With the news of your heritage, I hoped you'd feel more connected to it."

Though, even I had slight doubts about that. Gisela had informed me once that she didn't trust that Raven was indeed the heir of Leonidas.

"I wanted to," she spoke softly. "I love taking care of my people. I am proud that Seolia has remained untouched for so long, but I realized not long ago that it was only because Mira had planned to use me. It was because of John and..." She trailed off, casting her eyes to the ground. "Cade."

His name alone had me curling my hands into fists.

"When you took me to the basement, that was the first time I had seen it." She sighed deeply. "I went where I was told. I did what I was supposed to, but never more than what was needed." She looked toward the village again with a frown. "My people might respect and admire me, but not as their queen."

"Raven," I said her name, but I had nothing else behind it.

"I am not naive enough to believe that I would do well without you. It might weaken me, but I cannot live days away from you."

"It doesn't make you weak," I interjected. "We're bonded, Raven. We're not created to survive without each other. Even if you wanted to, it would be difficult. I read enough about twin flames to know that we would be driven to madness without one another."

She wiped a tear from her cheek with the back of her hand. I understood how difficult this was for her. She had only relied on one person for most of her life and made every effort not to need anyone else. Admitting that she needed me was knocking against every wall she had built around her heart.

"Then," she said, finally meeting my eyes, "I will go with you to Reales. You will become king, and I will abdicate my throne in Seolia. Not that there's much of a throne left to abdicate," she added with a slight grin.

I shook my head. "Raven, I would never ask that of you. Seolia needs you; the realm needs your heart."

"My heart will be in Reales. Without it, I will not be of much use. I will not be of *any* use." She came to me, wrapping her arms around my waist and kissing my chest before looking up at me. "Reales

176

needs *you*. You love your kingdom, despite your grumbling to the contrary. Seolia has survived well without me many times."

"Raven, I can't let...."

"You don't *let* me do anything," she said too quickly. "This is my decision, Zeke. And my decision is to be with you. I will be abdicating my throne after we defeat Mira. I will no longer be Queen of Seolia."

"WOULD YOU FUCK ME ON A BED OF BONES MADE FROM THE MEN WE'RE GOING TO KILL?"

18

ZEKE

I stared at her as she abruptly walked away from me and back into our bedchambers. I felt frozen to the ground and unable to comprehend how easily she could give up her kingdom after finally confirming it was hers.

"This is not up for debate," she said after I followed her inside. "I will not argue about this. My mind is made up, and you know better than anyone that it's impossible to change my mind once I've made a decision."

Well, she had me there.

"It will not prevent me from trying," I said, grabbing her wrist and tugging her to me. "Baby, you can't abandon Seolia."

"I am not abandoning anything," she argued, prying her wrist free and going to our wardrobe. "I will ensure it's left in capable hands."

I stayed on her and grabbed her hands, bringing them to my lips. "These capable hands, Raven. You cannot leave your people behind."

"If you're not careful, Zeke, I will begin to think that you do not want me in Reales with you."

Groaning, I released her to run a hand through my hair. "There has to be another solution, Raven—one that does not involve you giving up your title."

"I will still hold a title, Zeke. I'll be queen consort in Reales. I'll have a say in matters regarding the realm, and I know you'll respect my opinion. Let's not lie to ourselves and pretend I was made to rule a kingdom."

I grabbed the dress she pulled out and held it above my head, yanking it out of her reach every time she tried to take it back. "Is this because of what I said? You can learn the ways of royal life, baby. You are an excellent ruler."

She growled, pausing her small lunges to thread her fingers through her hair. "Zeke, we are married. You made me promise we would never be separated. This is the only way! One of us has to give up our throne, and while the martyr in you would love for that to be you, it will be me instead.

You were right. I am not suited for this. I never have been. You think you weren't given a choice? I was a child when this was forced upon me. You were taught politics and protocols, while I couldn't care less."

I dropped her dress to the table and grabbed her shoulders. "Raven, this isn't you."

She drew a deep breath through her nose, and I knew I was trying her patience. "This is me, Zeke. For my entire life, I have been told who I am and what I want, and I have learned that I can no longer live like that. I want to be free, Zeke. I want to travel and explore, not feel guilty whenever I leave my kingdom."

Backing away, I sat on the edge of the bed with my elbows on my knees. She gave me a slight shrug and stood between my legs, brushing her thumb across my bottom lip. "You wanted us to be together. You should be ecstatic."

"I will never be ecstatic when you give something up for me," I explained. "I wish I could make you realize why this shouldn't be an option."

Wordlessly, she sighed and backed away. I dropped my head, staring at the floor as I racked my brain for ways to convince her that Seolia needed her. She might not be the same gentle creature from that night at the Festival of Dreams, but goodness still lingered inside her, even if it was buried right now. Seolia was a small kingdom and would benefit from having Raven as its queen.

My eyes immediately narrowed when I looked up and braced myself for round two. She had abandoned her chosen dress and pulled out the outfit from the night we met. She refused to look at me as she tied the laces of her bustier tight enough for her cleavage to look sinful. And when she shimmied the leather pants over her hips, I stood up from the bed. "Are you trying to piss me off?"

Ignoring me, she braided her hair down her back before sliding on her thigh-high boots.

"Raven, you're not wearing that."

"I have work to do," she stated nonchalantly. "I need to find Jeanine so she can update me on everything that's happened since we've been gone, and I need to deal with the remaining men on the island."

"I don't have time to kill the army today, Raven, and I will have to if you meander outside wearing that."

She shrugged again, then left the bedchambers. I watched her in surprise. I knew she was punishing me for disagreeing with her and, knowing her, she most likely believed that I was finding excuses to not let her follow me to Reales, but her stubbornness was getting a bit out of control.

When the door slammed shut, I growled.

When I followed her into the hallway, she was already down the stairs. She was moving quickly, but my strides doubled hers and I caught her before she could get very far.

I pulled her back and slammed her against the wall. Her gasp was quickly replaced with a whimper as I wrapped her braid around my wrist and pulled until her throat was exposed to me. "I wasn't finished with you, Raven." I untied the laces of her bustier, freeing her breasts from their constraints. "You're not allowed to wear this. You belong to me."

I picked her up and lifted her high enough to wrap my lips around her nipple. She whispered my name as I carried her back upstairs and into our chambers.

"We are going to work this out. You're not going anywhere."

"I don't like being told what to do," she snapped.

"I don't give a fuck," I replied, tossing her down to the bed. "You will not walk around wearing that."

Ever the defiant one, she rose to her knees and started tying the laces together again. But I quickly stopped her with my lips on hers while pinning her hands behind her back. With my free hand, I yanked on the bustier until it was around her elbows. "I don't like repeating myself, Raven."

I released her wrists and threw the bustier to the floor. "You will not wear that." She was left in her leather pants and boots, and I was salivating as I stared at her. "Lie down."

"No," she replied stubbornly.

I pushed her until she toppled backward on the bed and straddled her waist. "I know what you're trying to do, Raven. You're trying to punish me."

"Maybe a little," she replied with a sweet smile.

I, however, did not feel sweet. I was unreasonably angry about the events the last few weeks had brought, the constant decisions she made without my input and the doubt I could never seem to dispel no matter how hard I tried.

When she caught my glare, she frowned. "You're upset."

"You're punishing me," I repeated. "You're being unfair."

She sighed dramatically. "I am tired of the tension between us. I miss when your attention wasn't so... angry and direct."

"You always have my goddamn attention, Raven. I know every breath you take, every thought you have. Every feeling. You can't move an inch without me noticing." I sat up, unable to stop staring at the exposed parts of her, which only added to my irritation. "I just need some fucking time to digest the things you say, and you punish me for it. Sometimes I have to be angry and direct with you because you're so fucking stubborn, Raven. It doesn't mean you get to pick fights with me and prey on my need to possess you."

"I wanted you," she whispered sheepishly. "I wanted you to touch and kiss me instead of fighting with me. I missed your obsession with me; I came to rely on it too much...."

Shaking my head, I grabbed her wrists and pinned them above her head. "It is never too much to want me, Raven, or rely on me, but you shouldn't have done that. I would never do something that makes you uncomfortable for your attention."

She gnawed on the inside of her cheek as guilt overcame her. "I'm sorry. I know you wouldn't. I just can't stop thinking about what Morana said, and it worries me..." She quickly clamped her mouth shut.

My hold on her loosened. "What are you talking about?"

"I... nothing. It's nothing. It doesn't matter."

My jaw tightened at her lie. "Tell me, Raven."

"I can't," she whispered. "It will hurt you."

I shoved into her mind. She yelled my name, squeezing her eyes shut to try and prevent me from searching her memories. I settled on the memory of us trying to rid her body of Morana, watching the moment when it was just the two of them.

And then released her wrists.

Everything in me felt like ice.

I couldn't move. I couldn't think.

This was the confirmation I needed. I hadn't dreamt what I heard the forest. It was true.

Fuck me, I wasn't her mate.

SHE SAT up quickly and cradled my face between her hands. "It doesn't matter, Zeke. It doesn't." Tears fell down her cheeks, her voice frantic. "I promise, Zeke, I promise it doesn't matter to me. I don't care who it is."

I didn't know what to say other than, "I'm not your mate."

"It doesn't matter!" she yelled. "It doesn't matter! You are my twin flame. I am *your* mate. That is all that matters. I don't want to know who my mate is or how it's even possible."

Sinking back on the bed, I stared at the scarred bite on her neck. "I am not your mate," I repeated. And then I laughed but cried, fisting my hair in my hands. And here I thought that impending war was our biggest problem. "I am not your mate."

She threw her arms around my neck and kissed me, but I couldn't return it. Everything felt numb. "Zeke, I belong to you. No one else has a claim on me, and no one ever will. You can kill him, Zeke. If he ever finds me, I want you to kill him. I promise you that I do. Can't you feel it? Feel me."

She put my hand against her heart. "This is yours. My heart only beats in tune with yours. That is the most important. We are the rarest pairing, Zeke. You have my heart."

"But you don't feel for me what I feel for you. The mating. You can't feel it."

She didn't deny it. "I love you as much as you love me. I want only you. I will never feel a pull to anyone else like I do to you." She was blubbering and trying to pull me closer. "Please, Zeke, you have to believe me. You have to believe that I only want you."

"I do believe you," I whispered. "I do, Raven, but fuck, I thought this was over. I presumed Cade would be it, but someone else will come looking for you."

"Kill him."

"Oh, I fucking will. The moment I realize who he is, I will kill him." I pushed her down again and covered her body with mine. "You will not stop me."

It wasn't a question, but she repeated it to me, "I will not stop you." She wrapped her legs around my waist. "Please mark me. Anywhere you want. Everywhere."

I stared into her eyes, wanting to believe this wasn't true, but it made sense. Raven hadn't verbalized it to me, but I could tell my reactions were more potent than hers regarding claiming. She loved me, but the primal need wasn't as evident in her as it was in me. My need for her blood wasn't mirrored. She didn't thirst for me the same way I did for her. I had initially chalked it up to my obsession with her, but it was more than that. Fate had given part of her to someone else.

"You're worrying me with your silence."

Sighing, I kissed her. This wasn't her fault. She would've chosen me if she could. She wouldn't have wished this for herself or for us. She wanted her future to be with me.

And maybe he wouldn't find her.

Maybe, for once, this wouldn't be a problem.

"Nova," I said as I broke from her. "We will learn more in Nova. Melik will have answers for this. And I could ask for his help with the war. I need to go to Nova—"

"Zeke, I don't want answers. Please, Zeke."

"Raven, I need to know what I'm up against. If you start to feel a pull toward someone else—"

"I won't!" she cried. "I never will! I didn't want to tell you because I knew I would never want anyone like I want you."

"Baby, I know, but it might not be something you can prevent. I need to be prepared." She opened her mouth to argue, but I put my finger against her lips. "Raven, please imagine if this were reversed."

Her jealousy flared at the thought of me having someone else.

Releasing her lips, I nodded. "Multiply that times thousands. That's how intense this mating is, Raven. I know you love me. I do not doubt you would turn him away or let me kill him, but I must be prepared if that day ever comes. We have been putting off finding answers about our bond for too long. I will not lose you, Raven."

"I will always be yours," she promised in a quiet, broken voice. "I'm so sorry, Zeke."

"Raven, I do not blame you for this. The universe seems to like fucking with us."

I wanted that to make her smile, but she still looked so broken. "I am fearful that we're running out of time."

I stroked her cheek with the back of my hand. "Time for what, my love?"

"Blissful unawareness."

I pressed my forehead against hers. "Let's live in this moment together for as long as possible."

AT THE TABLE in our bedchambers, we had a productive conversation yet found no real solution. She agreed to sleep on her decision to abdicate, but one thing was for certain: we refused to live apart and knew we would need to decide which one was going to give up their throne soon.

And as much as we wanted to, we couldn't continue hiding in our bedchambers. We had stayed in our chambers most of the morning —making love, bathing, and trying to come up with ideas. We were becoming reacquainted after weeks of pain. Two broken souls scarred with wounds from their demons were playing a dangerous game of trust, and it was something we needed to rebuild together.

But we had given one another reasons to doubt.

She doubted my need for her.

I doubted she'd ever truly be mine.

With the revealed revelation of her... *mate*, Raven took my requests seriously and dressed modestly in one of my shirts that she knotted at the waist with a looser pair of leather tights.

Her body belonged to her; if she had continued to protest, I wouldn't have argued about choosing what she wanted to wear, but she was *my* mate. And the more magic seemed to reawaken in our realm, the more our bond strengthened. It was slowly taking precedence over our marriage. Not only was she legally mine, but she was fated *for* me. I had to protect that and her.

I would not continue making the same mistakes.

I was biased, yes, but she was unlike anyone I had ever seen. Her beauty was unmatched, and I wasn't the only person who felt that way. Anyone who looked at her seemed shocked that someone could seem so unworldly and possess such an unfair beauty.

I knew that her... mate, fuck. Fuck.

She had a mate. And it wasn't me.

I knew that when her mate inevitably came to seek her out, he would be just as enamored with her as everyone else seemed to be. It was only a matter of time before we'd face that.

We had lived multiple lives together, and there were most likely many things we didn't realize. But of this, I was sure: she was the only one I had ever loved. I was grateful that we didn't have to worry about someone coming to claim me.

Luca had somehow managed to keep Jeanine from breaking down our door, which I appreciated, but she deserved to see Raven.

But even still, Raven clung to me. I tasted her guilt and anxiety. If she wasn't touching me, her eyes would fill with tears and I would pull her over to me, attempting to comfort her and promise that she wasn't to blame for our loss.

On rare occasions, she would touch her stomach like she could feel our child. Her face would twist, her body would shrivel, and we would stop until she recomposed herself.

She would tell me repeatedly how silly she felt for missing something that never felt like hers, but I would remind her that I felt the same.

Before we reached the library doors, she paused and turned to face me. She gnawed on her bottom lip as she looked up at me, twisting her fingers nervously in front of her. I wished she'd stop doing that. She shouldn't ever be anxious about talking to me.

I tilted my head and pulled her lip from between her teeth, brushing my thumb across it.

That seemed to calm her enough to take a breath.

"Before we run out of time, I wanted to say thank you."

I tilted my head curiously. "For what?"

"Saving me," she replied in a whisper, putting her palm up as I tried to stop her from continuing. "I know you did it willingly because you love me, but I never expect anything from you. You didn't have to, but you always do. You always save me no matter how I treat you or what happens."

"Raven..."

"Please let me get this out." She rocked on her heels before she found her steadiness. "Before you, even with... him, I always felt alone. I never felt I was worth saving or didn't feel like anyone else saw me. I would fall asleep at night wondering why. I would fill my time with whatever, whoever I could because I needed to feel something. Anything."

I nodded because I understood.

"And I know how often we say how much we love each other, even when people get completely sick of us...."

I couldn't help but smile.

"But I need you to know that I am grateful for your persistence and unyielding devotion to me. Sometimes I don't think you realize how important it is to me, how much I've grown to rely on it."

"Please let me touch you."

"Zeke, I am wildly and madly in love with you. I am stubborn, flirtatious, and maddening, but you must know that you are my rock. You are what I look for when I feel lost. The thought of you kept me from breaking when he had me."

I had to turn away from her, placing my palms against the wall. I ran my tongue over the roof of my mouth to keep from completely breaking down in front of her. "Please don't thank me, Raven. I nearly collapsed that day. I was the weakest I had ever been."

She popped up between me at the wall, staying caged between my arms. "But you were there. His actions are not because of you. You could not predict the kind of man he was. He fooled us both, Zeke."

"If I had never come here, Raven—"

"Do not do that," she snapped. "If you had never come here, we would still be half-living our lives."

"I could've saved you from him, Raven, but I kept hesitating every time."

"You did save me, Zeke." She slid her hands underneath my shirt and rested them against my chest. "You saved me in every way. He would've kept me here forever. You freed me from him, Zeke, and from a life of feeling unwanted and unseen."

I took her face between my hands. "You are everything but that, Raven."

"I know you want answers, and I understand why. I am willing to help you look for them but promise me, Zeke—promise me that during this next phase we're about to enter, you will not doubt how much you mean to me. I need you to promise me that whatever we find, you will not doubt me."

I had to clear my throat to keep my voice steady. "I promise, Raven. I promise that I will never stop looking for you. I promise that all you will ever have from me is unyielding devotion. You will always be my favorite thing to catch."

"I love you."

She said it so simply and earnestly that all I could respond with was a kiss so deep and loving that it was painful. It hurt my chest.

We were about to enter uncharted territory together.

"I love you," she repeated, throwing her arms around my neck. "Gods, I love you. I love you, I love you. You are all I will ever want."

"I know," I replied truthfully, kissing her again. And again, again. "I know I am."

"I would leave everything behind for you."

I kissed her forehead. Her cheeks. Her chin. "I know you would."

"I don't want to live a life without you."

"Oh, my love." I held her tightly against my chest. "You won't."

"I WILL ALWAYS BE YOURS," SHE PROMISED IN A QUIET, BROKEN VOICE. "I'M SO SORRY, ZEKE."

19

ZEKE

"We can check the library off our list," I said with a wink, kissing the top of her head as I led her down the hall.

We intended to find Grace in the library, but when we realized she wasn't there, I took Raven behind a shelf and made love to her. I couldn't hold off after she declared her love and gratitude; if I had dragged her back to our chambers, days would pass before I'd let her out again.

We discussed leaving everything and everyone behind, but we loved our family too much to abandon them. We did make one final promise to each other: if, or when, the time came when we no longer wanted to face any more of this, we would honor the other's request to leave.

If she ever asked me to give this up, I readily would do it for her.

And she promised to do the same for me.

It wasn't a solution, but we needed to know we had a way to be together without the threat of losing one another again. It was something we would never ask of the other, but having the guarantee between us was comforting.

But now I couldn't stop staring at her like the obsessed man I was. When all was said and done, we were all that mattered.

Whenever she caught me staring at her, she would give me the cheesiest smile. I would laugh and chase her down the hall, relishing her squeal each time I caught her.

It was the lightest we had felt in weeks.

But when we came across Godfrey walking down the hall, our memories from that fateful night rushed back.

I set her down as our expressions of joy turned stoic.

Quite the opposite of us, Godfrey flashed us a full-blown smile. I was relieved to find him alive and well, looking like new. Raven was a blubbering mess as she covered her face with her hands, jerking slightly when he put his arms around her but relaxing once she felt safe.

I grabbed Godfrey's shoulder with a smile. "I have never been happier to see another man hugging my wife."

"I will not become used to the permission," Godfrey responded with a wink.

Raven's eyes widened as she looked at me, returning to my arms. "He knew already," I assured her. "He learned about us the night Cade attacked you in the village."

She wrinkled her nose with a breathy laugh. "I suppose it doesn't matter anymore now. We don't have to hide it." She frowned at Godfrey. "How are you, Godfrey? Truly?"

"Permanently scarred," he answered, holding his side where the wound was. "Jeanine checked on me multiple times a day. She frequently reminded me that you would not be happy with me if I died, and I must ensure my queen remains so."

"You succeeded," she said sweetly.

He put a hand on her shoulder. "And how is my queen?"

"Permanently scarred," she whispered. "We both are, but we've grown from it. The two guards...."

Godfrey's smile disappeared. "Did not make it, I'm afraid." He gave me a sorrowful grin as Raven began crying again. "They knew the risks when joining the guard, Raven."

It was the first time he had addressed her by only her name. She didn't flinch or feel anything besides regret. Maybe I wasn't listening intently enough to her needs. Her habit of not wanting to be referred to by her title perhaps meant she would be happier by my side in Reales.

"There used be no risks," she murmured.

I squeezed Godfrey's arm out of respect for the men he lost, men he had most likely trained himself. "I am sorry for your loss, Godfrey."

Raven wrapped her arms around my waist and burrowed her face against my chest. I kept a hand against her head and shook Godfrey's hand. "Thank you for protecting her and telling me what happened while you were in grave pain, even if you were yammering about sun faeries."

His brows furrowed together for only a second before he dipped his chin in a tight nod. "Raven's safety will always be my top priority," he said. "I am on my way to meet two new guards to stand at the gate. You will need to meet them and give me your approval."

"I will. I'll find you this evening." I kissed the top of Raven's head. "We need to find Jeanine first."

Godfrey bowed slightly. "My prince."

I blinked. No one in Seolia had addressed me like that. All I could return it with was a bow of my head as he continued down the hall. I wasn't their prince, but I had earned enough of his respect to be addressed as such.

"*My* prince," Raven mumbled against my chest, causing me to laugh. She rose up and peered at me with sad eyes. "They stood at the gate all my life and kept my secrets. Kept your secrets."

My secrets? I wasn't sure what she meant by that until she added, "I would sneak out of the castle often to meet you or try to find you when I knew you were lurking. They never told Cade.

Well, they did once, but they soon regretted it when I scolded them."

Gods, I wanted the people who had sacrificed so much to ensure we ended up together to stop being harmed.

"I thought they hated me," I admitted. Tangling my fingers in her hair, I drew her head back to kiss the tip of her nose. "Adjusting to our new normal will be difficult. We need to award ourselves grace for the emotions we'll feel."

She climbed me. "Sew us together."

I kept her balanced on one arm while wrapping a hand around her throat to brush my thumb across her jawline. "We'll find my mother after speaking to Jeanine and ask her to do it."

"I am surprised no one sought us out after returning. It's been days."

My grin was one of guilt. "I asked John and Luca to allow us time together. John stopped by after you had fallen asleep the night we returned. They were tasked with keeping everyone away. Jeanine fought but understood."

She smiled while rolling her eyes. "Why am I not surprised?"

Honestly, I wasn't looking forward to seeing Jeanine after refusing to let her join me after Raven was taken. "We have a lot of people to see, my queen. Are you ready?"

She stuck out her tongue. "Stop calling me that."

Walking outside with her in my arms, I grinned. "You didn't mind earlier."

"I'll make you a deal." Her grin was rotten, and I was already anticipating what she was about to say. "I'll allow you to call me that once you become king."

"Oh, Mrs. Audovera." I kissed her softly. "You do know how to bargain. I'll give you that."

ON THE LONG walk from the castle to behind the mountain where the soldiers were stationed, she asked if I would share more stories from my childhood with her. I began with a story about the first time John took me fishing and how patient he was with me. I was four years old and had already watched him fish several times at a pond near our manor.

"Shadow drank from that pond when Jeanine took me to your manor," she said with a smile.

"John went fishing in his spare time when he wasn't by Rudolf's side at the castle. And one day, he came home with a rod just big enough for me. It took hours before I finally caught my first fish, and I was so proud that John camped with me outside so we could cook it."

Raven listened with a smile but then pulled her cheek in, contemplating something. "Did you"—she paused, wrinkling her nose—"did you ever try to find your birth father?"

"No," I sighed. "I contemplated it but didn't know where to look. Mother told me the bare minimum about him. John left shortly after informing me that he wasn't my father."

When I quieted, she squeezed my hand. "I'm sorry," she whispered. "I shouldn't have brought it up."

I dragged her toward me with an arm around her shoulders and kissed her temple. "I'm not upset, Raven. I haven't thought about my birth father in a long time."

"John loves you," she said gently.

I nodded. I knew that. And I knew he felt guilty for leaving us behind all those years ago. Being with him nearly every day since meeting Raven had helped with forgiving him, but it still bothered me to remember watching him leave us in Reales.

"Thank you," she said, pulling me from my thoughts long enough to look at her. "If we hadn't lost this child, I know I wouldn't have needed to worry about you leaving us. It says a great deal about the man you are, Zeke."

Warmth spread across me. "John is a good man. He protected you. It does make my relationship with him more complex, but I will always be grateful to him for that."

"If you ever wanted to find your father—"

"I don't," I interrupted, "that's the biggest difference between him and John." I looked at her with a shrug. "John always came back. He never did."

As we rounded the corner of the mountain, Raven lingered behind me, hidden behind some trees while I fetched Jeanine. Part of me hoped that she had sent the army back to Mira to let her deal with them, but then she would've had too many numbers against us. I was not looking forward to shattering the minds of two-hundred men, but I would do whatever it took to ensure Raven's safety.

Luca saw me coming first and looked behind me for Raven, but she must've hidden herself well because he looked confused at seeing me alone. I glanced over my shoulder and panicked for a second before I spotted her green eyes as she laughed and stuck her tongue out at me.

Jeanine turned upon hearing me and ran toward me, her head bobbing wildly to each side while looking for Raven. "Where is she? Is she okay?"

I hooked a thumb behind me, and she took off. I didn't need to look to know that they had reunited as their mangled sobs and incoherent words were evidence enough. "I needed to speak with Jeanine," I said as Luca approached me. "But I guess that can wait."

"She's been unbearable," he grumbled. "She asked no less than fifteen times a day to see Raven, but she kept her distance."

I watched Raven and Jeanine's embrace with a grateful heaviness. "She had every right to be unbearable. As much as I don't want to admit it, Raven needs more than just me. She needs someone like Jeanine to remind her that she'll see the light again."

The grief emanating from Jeanine made me turn away from them. Raven informed her of our loss, and I could only stomach the reminder so many times before the numbness started all over again. And when Jeanine called to me that they'd be right back, I only acknowledged with a slight nod before she dragged Raven away.

Men from both armies stood, waiting for orders. I wasn't sure who they were, but Mira had spies somewhere within her ranks here. It was only a matter of time before they learned that we had plans for them that no longer included war. Even being secluded on an island didn't prevent Mira from somehow getting letters to her spies.

"It needs to happen tonight," I muttered, eyeing the heathens I had broken and brought here. "Every day we keep them alive on the island is another day closer to them revolting against us. The island will suffer for it if they learn they aren't needed anymore."

Luca called a drill for them as a distraction, keeping his eyes ahead and not on me. "Does Raven know about this? How will you leave her?"

"She'll be at Isla's," I said. "I'll insist she visits alone. We'll line the village with our soldiers in case something goes wrong, but Raven will be safe in the cottage. If everything goes smoothly, I can shatter each mind while they sleep."

"And then what?"

Sighing, I looked at the faces of the men who had committed horrific and vile acts, contemplating if shattering their minds would be enough—the men who had been sent here under the direction to destroy our home if we did not obey Mira's orders. But the body still had to pay for the crime committed, and I couldn't be responsible for freeing men who might return to their perverse ways.

So when I turned from the men and looked at my brother, it was with no hesitancy or second-guessing as I said, "And then I kill them."

～

I STOOD with Raven on the hill above the mossy bank, watching as she kicked rocks around with the toe of her boot. I hadn't divulged my plan to her, and I wasn't going to—not to keep a secret, but to protect her. Raven would want to fight; I needed to do this without her fiery need for blood.

"We will still train our soldiers?" she asked, reading my mind. "After we decide what to do with Mira's army. Our army is small but will be useful. And I know you mentioned taking them to Thoya to train with Edmund, but how would we protect the island from an attack if our army isn't here?"

I nodded, unable to stop smiling. It was endearing to watch her think like a leader. She had every ability to rule a kingdom; if only she could realize how truly brilliant she was.

She rolled her eyes when she caught me. "I do have the capability to think like a queen sometimes."

"Oh, baby, I know you do." I brought her to me for a kiss. "You *are* a queen, Raven. I've never doubted that. And to answer your question, yes. I am positive Godfrey would appreciate more men at his disposal for your protection. He could utilize the open area between the Black Forest and the castle for daily drills. We wouldn't need to confine them to this area since they are Seolian men."

She nodded while she listened, dancing on her tiptoes around rocks. For a moment, I saw my joyful, youthful wife. "And you think it's necessary?"

"It is not about what I think, Raven." I watched her with a broadened grin. She looked so effortless in the delicate way she moved. "This is your kingdom, my love."

She remained quiet, buried in her thoughtfulness. Finally, she stopped dancing and looked at me with a shrug. "They can continue training. We'll inform Godfrey when we meet the two newest guards."

"Very well, then. Our soldiers will stay here in case you're wrong about River and he decides to drown the island."

"He won't." She looked at the peaceful, calm water, hardly moving in the breezeless air. "I am not fearful of River, Zeke. I wish I could help you understand."

"He tried to drown you," I reminded her. "Twice. Forgive me if I don't believe he is entirely sunshine and rainbows."

She threw her head back in a laugh. "And you believe I am?"

"No, my love, you are a star in the dark sky. You light the way for lost souls like me. I cannot say the same for your twin."

"You don't know him," she said gently. "He saved me, Zeke. That has to mean something."

"He did not save you, Raven. *I* did."

She frowned deeply and took my hand. "Of course you did. I only meant that because of him, I had time to run away from Cade. He didn't have to wake me up, but he did."

"Baby," I sighed and tucked a strand of hair behind your ear, "I want this for you. I want you to have a brother who loves and admires you, but I need you to be cautious and remember that if you had died that day, he would've lost something, too. Your death would bring the loss of his element."

"You're right," she whispered, palming her eyes for only a second before she laughed. "It would just be refreshing if I could find a family member who didn't want to kill me."

I laughed with her. "There is always your father."

I realized what I had said when she stilled and slowly lowered her hands from her eyes, blinking in confusion. At the slip, I closed my eyes and tilted my chin toward the sky.

"My... my what?"

"I DON'T BELIEVE HE IS ENTIRELY SUNSHINE AND RAINBOWS." "HE TRIED TO DROWN YOU. FORGIVE ME IF

20

ZEKE

Gods, she might kill me where I stand.

Running a hand down my face until my fingers wrapped around my shoulder, I very much blocked my heart from the possibility of an icicle stabbing right through it. "Gisela doesn't believe you belong to Leonidas. She said she's dined with Leonidas, and you look nothing like him."

She shifted into Blaze. I took a step back.

I wasn't sure when I had grown fearful of my wife, but she had been a little unhinged lately. "There's no basis for her musings. I didn't want to share this with you until she had something more solid."

"How long have you known about this?"

I cleared my throat. "Uh, well, a few weeks. Maybe longer. She mentioned it in passing when I commissioned portraits for our manor."

She stepped away, but I pulled her back. "Baby, don't do this. I wasn't keeping this from you. As far as we know, you are his daughter. Gisela just thinks you're too beautiful to belong to him."

"Is there anything else you'd like to tell me?" she snapped, shaking free. "Any other conversations you've had about me with women you've slept with?"

My blood went cold. "That's unfair."

"Is it?" she shouted, taking another step away. "First, it was the miscarriage, and now you're telling me that I might not know who my father is *again*? You clearly believe her, or else you wouldn't have said it." She laughed in annoyance. "This is fucking unbelievable, Zeke. Does everyone wake up every day and decide what they're not going to share with me? Is it something about me that makes all of you believe I can't handle things?"

I nodded towards her palms, which illuminated with flames the angrier she became. She followed my gaze and curled her fingers, suffocating the fire. And then she turned, leaving me on the hillside while she stomped toward the water.

"What did you do this time?" Jeanine asked, coming to stand beside me.

"I keep hurting her. And in turn, she hurts me back." My shoulders slumped. "Shouldn't we be better at this?"

We both watched as Raven paced the shore's edge. "No," Jeanine answered with a slight shrug. "You're essentially still strangers. You've only known one another for a few months, and you spent two minutes together before you married her." She gave me a warm, albeit amused grin. "Her life is unraveling daily with secrets that would bring down even the strongest person, which Raven is. She's strong but broken. And you... well, you're as fucked up as they come."

"I admire your honesty," I grumbled, lying.

"Fate wouldn't have paired you if it wasn't going to work between you, but growth takes time, Zeke. Trust walks a fine line with doubt."

"And I have given her plenty of that," I sighed.

Raven paused her pacing and glared at me as she kicked off her shoes and dove into the water. I stepped toward her, but Jeanine grabbed my arm and held me back. "See what she does first."

"She's trying to prove me wrong," I growled, fists curled at my sides. "She's trying to show me that River won't hurt her."

Raven resurfaced, lit the water's surface with flames, and then screamed. And the more she screamed, the brighter her flames fought against the water.

Crouching, I lowered my head and felt the pain radiating from her body. This was more than just about River. She was lost and broken, and I continued to amplify her pain. "Gods, Jeanine, what am I doing to her?"

Jeanine placed her hand on my shoulder. "It's not you, Zeke. It's not. The universe won't give her a break. We have expectations that Raven will always remain... Raven. But it's unfair of us to assume that. I fear she can't handle much more."

Raven screamed until her voice went hoarse. She covered her face and cried before disappearing under the water and reemerging a moment later.

Like she was trying to wash it all away.

Jeanine cried for her friend, lowering to sit beside me as we watched the happiest and the most effervescent person we'd ever known struggle for her next breath. Raven screamed again, irritated by the flames that kept drowning in the water.

"I can't bring either of them back. I can't undo what Cade did. I can't turn back time for her. I can't heal her. She can't heal herself from this. She won't allow me to shatter her memories of it. She won't even let me watch them. She longs for our child, that piece of us, because something finally belonged to her without secrecy. And I can't fix this."

She was a mess of red and fire in the clear blue.

Raven locked gazes with me for only a second before she was forcefully pulled underwater.

≈

BOOK THREE

River found her.

And as I sprinted down the hill, I worried Raven wanted to be proven wrong so she wouldn't have to resurface. She had already attempted to escape life by the water once, and maybe she thought if her brother was the one to end her life, she could remain blameless for giving in to the pain.

But the logical side of me said that Raven was far too ornery for that—no matter how upset she was or how much she might want to give up, she wouldn't abandon us.

But logic and illogic warred as I tried to locate her, kicking off my boots and diving into the water. Jeanine shouted her name when I resurfaced, panic threatening to drown me if I didn't hold it together. "I can't find her!" I yelled, pushing under the water again.

I kicked well beneath the surface but saw no sign of her anywhere. Jeanine's shouts turned into screams as she waded into the water.

Kicking low, so low that it was nearly black, a vortex of water spun around Raven's body as she tried to ice it, preventing it from dragging her deeper.

Her hands... were clear.

Her hands were *iced*.

She found me through the chaos and shot out enough ice to kick herself free, swimming to me and putting her ice-cold hands around my neck, but just like her flames, the chilliness was bearable and didn't feel uncomfortable against my skin. Her wide eyes mirrored mine.

I took her hands gently between mine, fearful of breaking them, but though they looked like glass, whatever substance they were made of was stronger and thicker and unbreakable—like ice didn't inhabit her; she became *it*.

I brought her face to mine, pressed my lips to hers, transferred the air I had left, and pushed her away. She grinned, closing her eyes as the blue glacier spread to her wrists. And when she opened her eyes again, her irises were nothing more than blue snowflakes, the white surrounding them as bright as snow.

I parted my lips and immediately regretted it as I had to kick to the surface to breathe more air. She followed me up and wrapped herself around me.

The veins in her neck and forehead slowly morphed into blue, her lips turning the color of frostbite. I felt as if I held a snowflake in my arms, unable to look anywhere but at her eyes. "Raven, I don't understand."

Her blue lips pressed against mine, and I jerked at the cold contact, but the shadows in my chest wanted nothing more than to keep her close, pulsing at the power she emitted.

"Do you feel it, Zeke?" she asked in a deeper tremor than I had become used to hearing. The airiness of her voice was replaced with confidence as she shivered in my arms. "Do you feel what happens when I use my fear?"

She placed her hands on my chest and slowly raised her eyes. "I feel them," she whispered, the fabric of my shirt scrunching between her fingers. "Your darkness wants to play with mine."

Those words sounded too familiar.

I shook my head slightly, keeping her still as she tried to push off to return underwater. "Raven..."

Before I could take a breath, the water vortex circled around my legs and pulled us both under. The ice in her eyes melted as she saw me struggle and flames returned, her hands shoving into the water to break it apart and allow me to return to the surface.

But she didn't return with me.

Jeanine swam over to me, and we watched an eruption of orange and blue collide underwater. "This isn't good," was all I could say as Raven resurfaced twenty feet away from us and shifted back into Frost. "She feels like I've been threatened now."

Raven placed her palms on the water's surface and shot ice out in every direction, jagged lines forming each time the water tried to break through the planes.

Frustration grew in her at the water tearing apart her ice. She shifted into Terra and held a palm toward the sky before bringing it down swiftly. Jeanine's hair flew back from the sudden wind that hit the water.

Terrified, we swam backward as a waterspout formed between Raven and us. Raven screamed as she twisted her hands in a circular motion, spinning the spout strong enough to cast water droplets down on us.

"She's in too much pain for this!" I shouted. "She's going to crave this feeling all the time!"

"Raven!" Jeanine shouted to no avail, covering her face as the water droplets turned into shards of ice.

I had never seen her so... powerful. It emitted from her like lightning during a storm. Uncontrollable and dangerous.

With eyes so gold they glowed, she clenched her teeth and used so much wind that I couldn't swim to her. The water around us began to groan from the force of it, and I worried we would drown trying to reach her.

Raven, you have to stop.

She found me amidst the havoc.

Do not let it overcome you, Raven.

Raven had finally broken. Years of doubt, pain, unanswered questions, and losing our child and her friend had become too much for her. And I felt nothing but heavy regret in her. Guilt. Grief.

Her hair was a combination of her elements, the strands mixing into each color, and there was a pull in her to keep going. To destroy.

When she didn't let up, when my voice in her mind did nothing to deter her, I looked at Jeanine. "I have to go to her. Find Luca if I go under and don't come back up."

"Zeke, no! It will pull you under!"

I had no other choice. I promised Raven I would always find her, and right now, she seemed more lost than she had ever been before.

Taking a deep breath, I dove under and tried to find my way around the vortex of water that the waterspout was creating under the surface.

The water was strong, and I was no match.

I fought against it, putting all effort into finding my wife and bringing her back to me. I kicked and bared my teeth as my air supply drained and my chest burned. And as I thought it was a lost cause, a force from underneath my feet propelled me to the surface.

River.

I resurfaced a few feet in front of Raven, cursing as one of the icy shards falling from the sky cut my cheek. Blood dripped down my face, and her expression of anger turned to despair as she realized it was because of her. She dropped her hands, crying my name, but the waterspout had to go somewhere, and we were in its direct path.

The disintegration of it pushed us back under. The weight of it hit me everywhere, pushing me down so deep underwater that all I saw was darkness surrounding me.

I covered my head as ice shards pierced the water, nicking my arms and tearing my shirt. Nothing but mayhem surrounded me, and for a moment, I wondered if I'd ever see the light of day again.

But then, flames.

Flames shot through the water above me before she followed, reaching out her hand as she came down to me. Purple flames grew between our locked fingers, sending enough energy through my body to kick my way to the surface with her.

I would never take breathing for granted again.

Gasping as I resurfaced, I barely had time to breathe before she clung to me, wrapping her arms so tightly around my neck that I wondered why I tried to breathe at all.

I put an arm around her waist and tried to stay above the water as I swam back toward the shore with her, but she was kissing me and crying through apologies, her body trembling in my arms.

Over a year of training nearly every day was nothing compared to the mere moments in the water with her, almost passing out from the exertion of strength I was using to get her to safety. "Baby," I rasped, trying to calm her. "I know you're hurting."

"It's never going to stop!" she wailed. "I am a twin born of darkness, and misery will follow me all my life."

"Raven, it will stop." Fuck, we were far from the land. "You are not this person. That was not you."

"I want to destroy everything, Zeke. I want people to hurt as much as I do."

Clenching my jaw, as I was almost positive hypothermia was setting in, I shook my head. "You don't, Raven. You have to fight through this. You are not the villain, baby. You're not." I kissed her as best as I could while her hands on my face healed the cuts from the ice.

"You have such a kind heart, Raven. It's just broken right now.

You are everything good, Raven. I promise that you are everything joyful and light."

"I am a mother without her child," she said through a sob. "That is a pain I cannot heal from."

"It's a pain you have to grow from," I said, pausing to catch my breath. I wouldn't let her go, but it was getting difficult to keep us both above water. "I will give you the future you want, Raven, all the tiny little demons you want, but we can't do this."

"No one will expect it from me," she whispered. "I could set the world on fire."

"Raven, please listen to me." I was losing her to her grief. "I am hurting, too, but I cannot lose you. I can't lose you because of this." I put her hand against my heart. "Feel this, Raven. It beats because of you. If this is the path you want to take, I will follow you into hell, but I don't believe it is. Heal with me, baby. Please."

"It hurts, Zeke."

"Fuck, Raven, I know it does, but you have me. Our life will be so wonderful, Raven, I promise. Do you trust me?"

She drew in a shuddering breath but nodded. "I'm sorry I hurt you, Zeke. I didn't mean to. I would never hurt you, never you."

"You didn't hurt me, Raven. Let me take you home." I returned to the shore with her in my arms, my knees nearly buckling, but I held steady. Looking at Jeanine, I shook my head to keep her silent but pushed into her mind.

She wasn't ready for this. Meet me with John in an hour.

"NO ONE WILL EXPECT IT FROM ME," SHE WHISPERED. "I COULD SET THE WORLD ON FIRE.

21

ZEKE

The reunion with my mother was bittersweet. John and Luca had informed her of everything that had transpired during our absence. I was heartbroken enough on my own, but feeling my mother's grief raised it to another level. I was her oldest son and had just lost my own child.

She said everything she needed to with her eyes before she pulled my face to hers and pressed our foreheads together.

Being as independent as I was and determined to provide for my family, there was still something about my mother's care that took me back to my adolescence, when everything had made more sense with her as the one in charge.

John, Luca, Godfrey, and Jeanine were gathered around the table in the sitting room, waiting patiently and quietly for us to join them. But before we did, my mother whispered only for me to hear, "Do not lose hope, my boy."

I wrapped my arms around her, nodding against her head because I had run out of words. And I was growing weary of trying to make sense of all the pain we constantly endured.

Raven had fallen asleep in my arms before we even set foot in our chambers. She remained as Blaze to warm herself and dry her body, curling into a ball under the blankets. I stayed by her side for a few moments after changing her into dry clothing, wondering if the consequences of her trauma would always come upon her so quickly —if she'd always switch from happiness to panic at a moment's notice.

The cuts in my arms burned, and I still wore my torn shirt and the damp pants which clung to my legs, but I felt I had no time to do anything other than worry about my mate.

My mother looked upon me with concern, cleaning the blood from my arms with a rag and leaving the room only to return shortly after with one of John's shirts.

I felt a bit warmer after changing into it, though nothing would compare to the comfort I always felt from Raven's warmth. And she had been Blaze so often lately that I had become dependent on her constant heat.

Balling up my soaked shirt, I tossed it into the fireplace and watched as the flames engulfed it. The fire overcame it quickly as Jeanine recounted the terror of Raven's moments in the water and how distant she became while yielding immeasurable amounts of power.

"This doesn't sound like Raven," my mother said, dabbing the dried blood from my arm.

"Doesn't it, though?" I asked quietly, sinking back against my chair. "When I met her, something was already growing inside her— something she didn't know how to control." I looked at John curiously. "Did you know? Were you aware of her need to kill?"

He, too, stared at the fire and continued to do so for a moment longer before he looked at me with a slight nod. "I knew she needed a way to get aggression out. More people were aware of her magic than she realized. I, Godfrey, and the two guards Cade killed at her gate, knew where she was at all times. I would be alerted each time she was in the forest, or anywhere for that matter."

That didn't surprise me. Alice informed me that John had been more involved than I realized.

"Petra and Damiana knew of Raven's magic," Jeanine said, looking at my mother. "Why?"

"Damiana knew Celestina," I said. "She informed us of that when we visited Thoya. She knew of River, though I am not clear how. It was something about Raven's thread with him." Questions arose, but I waved my hand dismissively in the air. "I can't explain Damiana's magic." Nor did I have the energy to try.

I looked at John again, leaning forward enough to put my elbows on the table. "Petra and Elric have magic. Do you know what they possess?"

John shook his head slowly. "I know they do, but they've never shared that information with me. They've always had an interest in Raven and frequently sent letters to check on how she was growing, even before she became queen. I figured it had something to do with Petra and Celestina being friends."

"Were they?" Luca asked. "Friends?"

Alice answered, "Celestina kept to herself, especially at the end. When she became pregnant with Raven, she was reclusive. And Rudolf was too passive to find out why that might be."

"When she became pregnant with *Raven*," I repeated. "We keep pretending as if River doesn't exist."

"Because he didn't exist until weeks ago," John said, rubbing the creases on his forehead. "I was there that night, son. I heard cries from"—he held up one finger—"one child. Unless the wet nurse immediately took River away..."

"There is no doubt that they're twins," Jeanine said. "They are identical, which shouldn't be allowed. Their beauty is..." she trailed off. "There is not even a word."

"Exquisite," I said with a slight grin, recalling Edmund's nickname for Raven. "And are we positive Raven belongs to Leonidas? Gisela seems to believe not."

At that, John shrugged. "I only know what Celestina told me. She asked that I protect her from Leonidas. He did not take the ending of their affair well."

I sat up straighter, my curiosity piqued. "*Protect* her from him? But did she ever say that Raven belonged to Leonidas?"

"Of course not," John said, "she died. It was assumed because of their affair. And Raven's memories, of course."

Right. Raven's memories. That was always where I kept getting stuck, because I had seen her memories. Leonidas and Celestina had said that Raven belonged to him, right? It had been so long since I had watched the memories that my recollection was fuzzy.

"We need to find a solution for Raven," Luca said, ever the protective brother. "We don't have time for a history lesson."

I nodded because he was right, though it didn't eliminate my interest in Gisela's musings about Raven. "Raven is heartbroken," I said. "She's lost our child and her best friend. She won't let me touch her memories, but from what she's told me, he admitted to manipulating her during their years together."

John asked, "What can we do for her?"

"I don't know," I answered honestly. "The deeper we dig into her pain, the darker she gets." I could barely get the words out, as it still seemed so out-of-character for my wife and her usual tenderness. "She wants to give up her title," I continued. "She doesn't want to be queen anymore, but I don't know if she's just projecting the blame onto Seolia for the pain she's endured."

"I can't say I blame her for any of it," Jeanine said. "Mira has put her through hell, and Raven never wanted the throne."

"She loves her kingdom," I added quietly.

"Then she needs to feel normalcy here again," Luca said. "We can open mom's shoppe. She's been looking forward to that for weeks."

I felt uncomfortable making plans for my mate without her here to speak for herself.

"She's been pulled in so many directions that she isn't sure where she's supposed to be," John said. "Let her decide when she wants to be queen again."

If she wants to be queen again.

I wasn't sure if it was from exhaustion or concern, but I allowed myself to feel weak and helpless for a moment. "She has a mate. I'm not her mate."

Gasps followed my words, coupled with questions I had no answers for. "She doesn't want to know who it is or how it's possible, but I need to. She's *my* mate, and I need to protect that bond. There are kingdoms outside of ours that might be able to help us."

"You want to go to Nova," Jeanine said. "Do you have time before we bring the war to Reales?"

Shrugging, I sighed. "It would take nearly two weeks to get there, but I can't live every day knowing if someone else is going to take her again. I need answers for her magic, for...." Not the blood. I wouldn't mention the blood. My mother was already worried about enough. "...everything. And Melik has become..." Friend was too strong of a word. "...an acquaintance. I would like to enlist his help for the war."

I moved my gaze to Godfrey. "We need to continue training the Seolian men. Tonight, I plan to eliminate Mira's army, but Raven must be distracted. With Mira's men gone, that barely gives us two hundred of our own. Thoya and Perosan's armies are substantial, but we need numbers. I know nothing of these men River brought to Reales, but we have been informed that they most likely possess their own magic."

"I will accompany Raven to Isla's," John said. "Your mother and I both will. We can keep her distracted long enough for you to do what needs to be done."

"I will line the village with soldiers," Godfrey said. "We will be available if it comes to a fight."

"You can't travel with Raven to Nova," John said. "It would be too much for her right now."

"I know," I responded, staring at the flames as they slowly began to flicker out. "If..." Trailing off, I looked at Luca. "If I wanted to go to Nova on my own..."

"Yes," Luca said. "I would go with you."

The thought of leaving her made me nauseous, but delaying could result in her mate coming to find her before I had any answers. It sounded plausible in theory, but could we survive nearly a month without one another?

But if I did travel to Nova, I could also enlist Melik's help with defeating Mira and taking Reales as her own. Surely he had his own army and, if they were willing to help, war might not be necessary at all.

"I would have no way of communicating with her," I said, shaking my head slightly. "It would be a risk to leave her. She's a little... unpredictable."

"That's one way of putting it," Jeanine muttered.

"And with River nearby..."

"I could prevent merchant ships from entering the harbor," John interrupted. "Unless we're expecting them, and if we are, each ship would be thoroughly checked before being allowed to offload."

"I would be here," Jeanine said softly, squeezing my hand. "You know I would protect her with my life."

Being without her blood for that long made my mouth dry. I wasn't sure I was strong enough to live every day not seeing her. "I would worry constantly." I looked at Luca. "I would be a nightmare to be around."

"No different from usual," Luca said with a smirk.

Rolling my eyes, I hit the table twice with my fist. "It's just an idea for now. I need to speak with Raven about it, but we'd need to leave as soon as possible. I want to spend some time here before traveling to Reales. I'll need time to speak with Edmund upon my return."

"King of Reales," Alice said, resting her hand on my arm. "You will be King of Reales." There was pride in her voice, but also concern.

I opened my mouth to argue since no decision had been made, but Luisa ran into the room, breathless, as she said my name. "There is screaming...."

Standing from my chair, I bolted out of the room and took the stairs two at a time to our hallway. Raven's screams echoed off the walls, chills racing down my spine as I threw open our door and ran into our bedchambers.

Raven thrashed in our bed, sweat covering her entire body as she screamed Cade's name repeatedly while begging him to stop.

Climbing in the bed beside her, I pulled her into my arms and shoved into her mind to shatter the nightmare. Her eyes flew open and she gasped, her skin clammy and cold. With her body curled into mine, her chest heaved as her heart pounded. Sleep was unkind to her and caused her to fall further into her pain.

I leaned against the wall as I panted. "My love," I whispered. "You are safe in my arms."

"It is the only place I am safe," she replied sorrowfully. "I am safe nowhere else."

"Then I will hold you for as long as you need."

Her thick eyelashes were wet and darkened with tears, and when she peered up at me, I glimpsed the fearful orphan from her memories—the girl who felt so misplaced and unloved.

She placed her palm against my cheek and brushed her thumb across my brow. "I wish you could free your shadows so they could destroy the world with me."

I wished I could free them just so I could understand what everyone else was talking about.

"Raven, we are not going to destroy anything."

"We are," she whispered, "I will seek retribution for the pain we have been caused."

My beautiful, kind wife was beginning to terrify me a little.

I shifted her until she straddled my lap and kissed her long and hard. I kissed her until the only thing I felt coming out of her was lust because it was where she would listen to me. Her dizzying passion for me was something I could control—it was the place she allowed me to dominate her every thought.

"Fuck, Raven," I murmured against her lips, "I can never have enough of you."

That was truthful, at least.

But when she started raising her nightgown, I stopped her hands. She looked at me in confusion and shame, but I quickly kissed her again. "Believe me, I want you. But I need you to talk to me first, Raven."

Ducking her head, she kissed along my jaw, down my neck, and back to my lips. I didn't notice that she'd pulled her nightgown off, and I watched with a sigh as she dropped it to the floor.

It took everything not to give in.

"Talk to me, Raven. We don't use sex like this."

"You have fucked me as a distraction hundreds of times," she argued, rolling her hips against mine.

"I am asking you as your partner."

She frowned at my words. "What do you want to talk about?"

"Your need for revenge."

She rolled her shoulders back. "I am powerful, Zeke. I will not have my power taken from me ever again. I will not be weak and feeble."

"You were never weak and feeble, Raven. Not once since I met you did I ever think you were anything but strong. What you went through proved that, Raven. No one has looked at you any differently."

"I have not even made a ripple in what I can do with my magic, Zeke. I felt it. I feel it now. There is so much hidden beneath the surface, and I can fix this for us."

"Raven, you can never fix this for us."

Her lips parted, but then her eyes narrowed as she climbed off me and walked toward the balcony. I jumped up quickly and grabbed her to stop her from walking outside naked. She tried to shove my arms off, but I spun her and lifted her up. "Raven, nothing will bring our child back."

"Stop," she said, turning her head away from mine.

"I love you, Raven, with every breath. And I know you're doing this because you love me."

Her eyes fell to the floor as she nodded. "I want to find him, Zeke. I want to find him and kill him, so you never have to worry." She looked at me then and coiled her limbs tightly around me. "That's how much I love you. You know that, don't you? You know I could never love another?"

Gods, all I wanted to do was make love to her into the next lifetime, and I would be lying if I said this darker part of her didn't intrigue me.

I carried her back to the bed and laid her down, staying on top of her. "I do." I kissed the tip of her nose. "I would kill for you. I would set the world aflame if I had your power. I wouldn't have the control you do to stop myself, but that's because you are not me, Raven."

"I could be like you," she whispered. "I *could* set the world on fire,

Zeke, but the flames would never touch you. We could rule everything together." She kissed me wildly. "Imagine how powerful we could be."

The need for control clearly ran in her family.

"Baby, we are." I discarded my pants and entered her, waiting for her to moan name before catching her lips in another kiss. "I feel your magic each time we touch. No one else can. That's the power we hold between us—the power only we share. But Raven, you cannot fix losing our child."

She puckered out her bottom lip as a tear escaped from her eye and slid down her cheek. "I feel so guilty, Zeke. I would've been a bad mother for being relieved." She took in a stuttering breath as her bottom lip quivered. "I would've loved the baby, but I would've been so scared..."

"I know," I promised her. "Raven, I feel the same. It's so hard, little witch, it is." I kissed away each falling tear. "Our tiny little demon will be so loved when that day comes, but you cannot bring our child back, my love, and you cannot hurt others by trying."

"I'm so sorry," she cried in a tiny, broken voice. "I'm so sorry I hurt you with my ice. I was so angry. I'm still angry at Cade and the universe for mating me to someone else. I want to hide somewhere with you, Zeke. I don't want him to ever find me."

"You did not harm me, Raven." I pressed the tip of my nose to hers. "My little demon can't ever hurt me." I drew out to the tip and slowly pushed in again, grinning as her eyes rolled back. "As for your mate..."

She stuck her tongue out in disgust. "Please don't call him that."

Chuckling, I twisted us until she straddled me again. I tucked one arm behind my head while another rested on her thigh. "I can promise you I will not allow him to ever see what is mine."

"Mm," she hummed, spreading her thighs wide enough to press her clit against the base of my cock. "Are you saying you would never share me?"

I bared my teeth at the taunt. "Don't, Raven."

She dragged a finger across her nipples and down her chest, leading down to her core. "You wouldn't want another man touching me?"

I dug my fingers into her thigh, my nails cutting into her skin at the thought of another man ever seeing what belonged to me. "Stop, Raven. I don't want to hurt you."

Tilting her head, she pulled in the corner of her bottom lip and rolled her hips again, earning a deep thrust from me. "Another man tasting my blood?"

My eyes snapped to hers. A cold sweat came over me as I imagined it. She gathered her hair in her hands and exposed her throat to me. "Feeling our pulse," she continued in a whisper, "Touching every beat with the tip of his tongue..."

Sitting up quickly, I placed a hand behind her head and brought her throat down to my lips. I sank my teeth into her flesh, digging deep enough to scar her again, and sucked her blood.

She cried my name as she came from the pressure, but I couldn't stop. No man would ever touch her again. No man would ever taste how sweet her blood was. No one would ever feel how warm her cum was. Every part of her was reserved for me and me alone.

"Dizzy," she breathed.

I released her throat and licked across my lips, but she pushed her breast against them. "Here."

I looked at her while biting into the soft flesh, creating another permanent mark. She watched with as much heat as I felt for her. "Scar me everywhere," she offered. "Because no one, Zeke, no one else will ever have me."

I came from her words, the promise, the taste of her, and the ability to claim her in any way I wanted to because this enticing, stubborn, beautiful witch belonged to me.

"We will kill him," she promised. "The second he finds me, we will kill him."

I decided this side of her evil would be one I allowed.

"I WISH YOU COULD FREE YOUR SHADOWS SO THEY COULD DESTROY THE WORLD WITH ME."

22

RAVEN

After spending the afternoon in our chambers, I finally convinced him that I felt more like myself and wanted to leave the castle. He had dropped to his knees and used his mouth to make me come before leaving another bite mark on my thigh.

I wanted more. I wanted scars everywhere.

I needed to be branded by him.

I had stopped counting how many he'd left on me, but I wanted to ensure that no man would ever want to look upon my body again. It belonged to Zeke, and I would never be used again for anyone else's satisfaction.

Those moments with Cade on the ship made me realize that being a woman would always put me at a disadvantage. No matter how much I fought or begged, men would always look at me as nothing more than something to possess.

It was up to me to prove that I was more; I was a weapon that would fight back. My heart and its need to trust everyone would no longer be a weakness. People would have to prove themselves if they wanted to be in my life.

If having bites from my husband across my body deterred them, then I wanted the scars. They weren't battle scars, but reminders of what I went through. No matter how hard someone might try to have me for themselves, I was already claimed.

If I ever found my mate, I would set him ablaze with the flick of my wrist. I would punish the universe for the sick joke of mating me to someone else.

Zeke grunted while sorting through our wardrobe for something to wear. I was perched naked on the table in the middle of our bedroom, waiting for him to stop dramatically brooding about still sharing a wardrobe. "You can remain naked with me," I offered, grinning as he stopped shuffling to look at me.

"You said you wanted to leave."

"I haven't had you nearly enough. I could be persuaded to change my mind."

"Raven, if I fuck you again, it'll be morning before I'm finished. It's nearing nightfall. Everyone must think I've consumed you. Your scars are becoming visible. It's only a matter of time before they realize that I sustain myself on your blood."

"No one knows you drink from me. They have no idea how vile you truly are."

"How vile *I* am?" He turned away from me again, his fingers whitening from his grip on the wardrobe doors as he tried to deny the temptation to have me again. "You did something extremely vile with your mouth earlier."

I pressed my tongue into the roof of my mouth at the reminder of his taste. "Are you complaining?"

He barked out a laugh. "You're so fucking infuriating sometimes."

He pulled out a shirt and gave up on finding pants, instead picking up a pair from the floor he had discarded days ago.

I traced the scarred bite on my thigh with the tip of my finger. "What does it taste like?" I didn't mind drinking his blood, but it didn't send me into ecstasy as mine did for him. I still hungered for food and basic necessities, but he seemed to survive on fucking and blood alone—especially since meeting me.

He used to eat, right? I had witnessed it a time or two at least.

He followed my finger with a darkened stare. "Heaven," he whispered hoarsely. "It is what I imagine the tides of heavens to be."

"And what do you feel when you do it?"

"Euphoria. Strength." He pulled his shirt over his head, stroking his bulging erection as he continued to watch me, his tongue sweeping across his lips. "The thought of tasting your blood sends me into a state of... I feel like I'm one with you and need you to keep me breathing."

I watched him with curiosity. Something permanently changed in him when the mention of my blood was brought up. A feral possessiveness seemed to inhabit him each time. "Is it addicting?"

"Yes," he answered gruffly. And like so many others had told me before, I could smell the intensity of our scent. "I would drink from you all day. Your blood, your cum. It is not a common desire. It grows daily. The need I have for you...." His head shook slightly as he brought his eyes up to mine. "I want to carve myself into every piece of you until the beat of your heart spells my name."

"The beat of my heart already does, my love."

He closed the distance between us so quickly that I flinched before he sank his teeth into my shoulder, drawing more blood. It didn't take more than three thrusts against my thigh before he came, groaning my name as he released my shoulder to press his forehead against mine. "I need answers for this, Raven."

"We are the answer, Zeke. We are the beginning and the end of every world."

I quickly drew in the breath he exhaled. He rested his hands gently on my thighs while mine dragged up and down his biceps. "Everything you say makes me doubt my need for finding solutions to our problems," he said. "You make it seem so effortless, so unimportant."

"It is. No matter what anyone tells us, it will not change our desire or love for one another. Our history or how we came to be does not matter." I wrapped my legs around his waist. "All that matters is that we are together when we leave this world. I am tired of wondering why our lust is so endless. Why question something that makes so much sense to us?"

"Because I want to drink from you until only your blood pumps through me. I want you living in me."

Smiling, I pressed myself against him and wiggled as if trying to enter him. "I am trying."

He laughed and attacked my face with kisses, his fingers kneading into my ass until I was pulled from the table and carried to the wardrobe. "Please wear something that makes me crazy. I want to drag you back here shortly and tear it from your body."

I fingered the dresses in my wardrobe. No matter what I wore, the result would be the same. "I am growing tired of you destroying all of my clothes. I will have none left soon."

"I know a seamstress."

"Are we going to talk about it?"

He dragged a finger down the length of my spine. "Talk about what?"

He had successfully kept me too distracted to bring this up since it happened. "Your blackened veins and how they moved when you drank too much blood."

Sighing, he ran a hand down his face and stepped back. "I don't understand why or how, Raven. There's nothing to talk about."

"What does it feel like? Have you always felt it?"

His hands went to my hair, and he brushed through it with his fingers. "It's hard to explain, and it's always more prominent when you're threatened or—"

"When you drink my blood," I finished for him.

His silence confirmed it.

When his hands dropped, I moved the braid he had woven over my shoulder and grinned at how far he had come since learning how to braid my hair only months ago. "Are they shadows, Zeke?"

"What the fuck does that even mean?" He took my hand and put it against his chest, where his heart beat soundly against my palm. "I am a mortal man. Other than my dream-walking and empath abilities, I possess nothing that would imply otherwise."

"*Zeke*," I drawled. "Your fucking eyes turn *black*. Your veins... moved. That doesn't scream mortal."

"I age," he argued. "I bleed. I fuck, I eat, I sleep."

"So do I." I said. "But I possess the universe's elements. Magic doesn't necessarily mean you're immortal. There is obviously something there. Why aren't you curious?"

"I think we have bigger things to be concerned about right now." He kissed my temple. "Let me kill your mate first, kill Mira, take Reales, and then I'll let you cut me open and explore. Deal?"

Rolling my eyes, I faced the wardrobe once more and muttered an agreement. Sighing, I chose one of my least favorite dresses. Sliding the dress on, I turned to wrinkle my nose at myself in the mirror. "I do not feel like this person anymore." I wore one of my lighter velvet dresses. It was dark magenta and tight around all his favorite parts of me, but the version of myself that used to wear this dress no longer existed.

That girl was naive and excited about trivial things like festivals and meeting strangers after spending months locked away in her castle, never knowing the full extent of what life could offer.

Zeke slid his arms around my waist and kissed my neck, meeting my eyes in the mirror. "You are mine, Raven. No matter what you wear, you are *my* Raven. The Raven I fell in love with wore these dresses, and those memories are some of my most treasured."

He went to the wardrobe and returned with a simple gold diadem, placing it upon my head. "Find your fire again for this kingdom, my love. This is our home, and you are their queen."

I stared at myself in the mirror, feeling years older than I was when I last looked at myself in this dress and diadem. "The brightness of that woman is gone," I whispered. "Will you still love who I am now?"

He kissed my temple. "She lives in me, Raven. I will always carry any version of you that you wish to be. I will always have your memories. I will love, worship, and admire you every day, every moment."

"Every second?"

He smiled the bright and charming smile that I had created for him. "Every second, Raven." He pushed memories of us into my mind —of us laughing or rolling my eyes, us dancing at the Feast Day banquet, our first kiss from the festival, our wedding. They flashed, and seconds flew by as he replayed our entire love story.

Tears fell down my cheeks as all the goodness and lightness from our time together warmed my body. As the joy collided with our pain, it crafted a new version of us that would grow together.

As we stood together and created a new chapter of our life, I was grateful and sure of one thing: we would face any and all of it together.

As one, like it always should have been.

As it always would be.

SINCE MY MELTDOWN in the water had delayed Zeke from meeting the newest guards, we needed to do it before nightfall. It was evening, and though the village was awake, Zeke feared that if I were bombarded, I might genuinely set something on fire.

It was hard to control right now.

The grief rolled in like a thunderstorm at the most inconvenient times. I would be fine — happy, even — before the most minuscule thing would trigger it. A smell, a thought, a breath. Grief didn't need a reason to exist. Once it had a hold of you, it would remain as long as it pleased.

Zeke kept his arm around me while walking through our hidden corridors, nodding to the right as we passed by the door that led into the dungeon. "Can I request another tour soon?"

Grinning, I shrugged. "I keep those reserved for only truly handsome men." I looked him up and down with my eyes, sighing. "You'll be aging out soon."

Gasping, he turned me until I walked backward and suddenly

pressed into the door. "Keep talking like that, and you'll earn some punishments."

I lifted one leg, and he held it against his hip as I ran a hand through his hair. "I'm waiting for this to turn gray."

His face twisted in disgust. "Stop. I won't allow that to happen."

"You can control many things, Zeke, but not the coloring of your hair."

He picked me up but then grunted and tipped over as if his back were breaking. "Oh no, I think it's already starting."

Squealing, I locked my legs around his waist and held onto his neck to keep from falling to the ground. "You're not funny!"

He raised me so fast that my hair whipped us in the face. We erupted into laughter as he pried strands from his mouth. "I'll choke on this one day."

"Just another way for me to kill you."

Huffing, he carried me through the door into the barn, nodding toward the loft with a grin. "I knew I was in love with you that night."

"That quick, huh? I wish I could say the same."

"You loved me before that," he said with a roguish smile. "I felt it on you."

I attacked his face with my tongue and laughed as he tried to yank his head away. "It took me some time to realize it because you were so distant," I said.

"If only you knew how close I truly wanted to be."

I looked at the lack of space between our bodies. "Making up for lost time?"

"There will never be enough time with you, little demon." He kissed me softly. "Are you ready? I will hide you the best I can, but you're very noticeable."

"Stop your flattery, Ezekiel. You can't hide me forever. I have to face the day eventually."

He slid me down his body and set me on the ground, cradling my neck with his hands. "Eventually, yes, but not before you're ready."

"Whatever this next phase is, you can't keep me locked away, and I have to be strong enough to handle it."

He brushed his thumb across my bottom lip. "I know, baby."

"Last chance," I whispered. "Last chance to ask me to leave with you."

"Raven." Leaning down, he pressed his forehead against mine. "Don't tempt me."

"Make me another promise. Anything you want."

He hummed to himself for a moment, and then a sweet smile spread across his mouth. "I promise to continue sharing a wardrobe with you until I die."

Something so simple and frivolous made me feel warm all over. It felt as if my heart was stuck in my throat, wanting to spill into his hands. "Even if none of your clothes fit?"

"I will stack them on top if I have to."

I inhaled a deep, steady breath and gave him a slight nod. "I'm ready."

Pulling open the door, I took my first step. Instead of turning to walk into the village, we made an immediate left and stayed close to the castle's wall. Isla's cottage was dark, so she was most likely in the village, gathering pastries for breakfast. John had informed her that I was alive and recovering, but I hadn't been able to make myself go to her yet.

Zeke put an arm around my shoulders. "I think you should spend time with her tonight. Alice and John planned on bringing dinner. You should go with them."

"Without you?" I asked, kissing his hand. "What will you do?"

"Miss you terribly," he replied, "But ever since bringing me back with you from Reales, you haven't spent much time with her. I'll eat dinner with Jeanine and Luca."

"And bore them with declarations of love for me?"

His smile was broad. "Absolutely. Maybe we can meet you at Duck's afterward. Stay with her as long as you'd like, little demon, but not *too* long."

I snorted. "Demons, angels, gods, heavens...." I glanced up at him. "Do you believe in any of it?"

"I'd be lying if I said I didn't." He avoided my gaze, instead watching a butterfly with gray and black wings fluttering in front of us. "I prayed to find you, Raven. I prayed for the first time in my life. I didn't know if I believed in it then, but I think something divine led me to you."

I was speechless, shocked by the answer, which was the complete opposite of what I expected. "You prayed to find me," I said in a squeaky whisper, tugging his shirt.

"I did," he confirmed, finally looking at me. "I would've done anything to have you in my arms again, Raven. Even if they did abandon us and had nothing to do with it, I will always wonder and be grateful that I did."

My spirit dampened as we turned the corner to enter the courtyard. Nausea rolled through me as that night came back to me like a harsh wave. I pressed my nails into my palms and squeezed my eyes shut as I recalled the sounds and smells, the memory of finding dead bodies at my feet when I fell.

My chest heaved. "No, no, no," I muttered, as my favorite wine now tasted bitter.

I felt Zeke's hands on my waist and heard the soothing sound of his voice as he said my name, whispering for me to breathe. He gently pushed into my mind and calmed it by seemingly squeezing me from the inside out. My eyes fluttered open from the unfamiliar sensation, and he seemed just as surprised while remaining nestled in my mind. "What was that?"

"I don't know," he replied in a raspy whisper. "I felt... you. I mean, I always feel you, but that was different."

"The bond?"

"I don't know if it's that or my ability that helped calm you."

"Queen Raven, Prince Ezekiel."

Godfrey came up behind Zeke and bowed to us before motioning with his arm toward the wall. "Your two newest guards are ready for their first night."

I followed where he pointed and smiled. "Abraham, Thomas." I took Zeke's hand and brought him to the two men waiting to meet him. "We had the same tutor as children. I grew up around these two men."

We were all the same age, and they were two of the boys I would blind with ice flecks, but now was not the time to share that with them. Abraham had blond hair and hazel eyes, and his skin was tanned from working at the docks; Thomas had a boyish charm with his dirty blond locks and light brown eyes.

They bowed to me before turning to Zeke. "We are eager to serve our queen and prince," Abraham said.

While I enjoyed the respect Zeke had earned from our people, one look at him would show anyone he needed to be *more*. He was working hard to convince me that I needed to be here, but Reales needed his mind and determination.

Zeke, fearful that any man was now his enemy, sized Thomas and Abraham up. Nearly as tall as him, they didn't cower, but they did shift uncomfortably at his attention.

Zeke looked at me, his eyes dropping down my body and back up, trying to sense any connection in me to either of them. Each man we came across would be subjected to this from now on.

When he seemed satisfied enough, he nodded once and took a step forward. "I appreciate you volunteering to protect my wife."

I no longer flinched from fear when he called me that in public.

"Her safety is of utmost importance to me. If anything alarms you, you must find Godfrey or me immediately. Report to your training every day and hone your skills. Unfortunately, training lapsed and we lost two guards."

"I have implemented a new system, Prince Ezekiel." Godfrey took a step forward. "We run things tightly now. That will not happen again."

"I appreciate the assurance and confidence, but"—he put an arm around my shoulder and tugged me toward him, kissing the top of my head—"the time of someone wanting her is not behind us yet."

"We're going to continue training the Seolian soldiers. They'll be under your command, Godfrey," I said as I looked around the empty courtyard. The shards of glass from my broken bottle of wine had been cleared away, and no one would ever know anything had happened here. "Every gate and doorway needs to be covered."

"And they will be," Godfrey assured us.

A slight grin appeared at the corner of Zeke's mouth as he stared at Abraham and Thomas. "I possess my own set of skills. Not as dark as our queen's, but I can sense what you're feeling. While she is beautiful, and you are free to think so, I need your thoughts to remain on protecting her and nothing else."

Their cheeks reddened as they stopped looking at me and mumbled their confirmation to Zeke. I rolled my eyes as Godfrey bellowed out a laugh. "He takes the no-bullshit approach, I see."

"In all matters," I confirmed with a sigh. "But especially when it has anything to do with me."

"And it will remain so." Zeke extended his hand to the newest recruits and held eye contact as he shook their hands. "If you'll excuse us, Raven has dinner plans."

"Thank you," I said to Abraham and Thomas, giving them a half-apologetic, half-genuine smile.

As Zeke dragged me away, I heard my name called and turned to see Abraham take a small step closer.

"*Queen* Raven," Godfrey abruptly corrected him.

Zeke held me against him, but I held a palm toward Godfrey. "Old habits, Godfrey." I looked at Abraham and waited to hear what he had to say, but he nervously stared at my husband. "He only bites when provoked, darling. What did you want to say?"

"We are relieved to see you're alive," he said with a small smile. "It is good to see you again."

I dipped my chin in gratitude. "Thank you, Abraham."

Zeke grabbed my hand to kiss it while pulling me out of the courtyard and back into his arms. "Can you stop calling men 'darling'?"

"Jealous, my love?"

"Of any man who looks upon you, little witch."

"For you, yes. I will."

"You could call me that instead."

I gave him one of my cheesiest smiles. "Why would I call you that when 'buffoon' works so much better?"

This time, he rolled his eyes. "So endearing."

"YOU DID SOMETHING EXTREMELY VILE WITH YOUR MOUTH EARLIER."

23

Raven

Standing outside Isla's cottage, I asked Zeke to reconsider leaving me alone. John and Alice were carrying a kettle of soup, the delicious smell wafting into my nose as they climbed the porch. I asked the latter to wave it around in front of Zeke's nose to entice him, but he insisted I spend time with Isla without him.

We had returned to the castle after meeting Abraham and Thomas so I could change into something more comfortable, but Zeke remained distant, as if something were on his mind. When I asked about it, he told me that the last few weeks had worn on him, and it was taking him some time to readjust.

Upon my return to the castle after dinner, he promised to be his normally jolly self, which I had scoffed at, since I had never once described him as jolly. As I stood on the tallest step of Isla's porch, I was still too short to be at eye level with him, but it did give me a better angle to kiss him. "Stay," I begged once more. "Don't you love me?"

He groaned at my puckered bottom lip before he nipped at it. "More than fudge, but Luca is waiting on me. I'd prefer if you waited until I returned to walk back to the castle."

I dramatically looked behind him at the castle, close enough to hit with a stone if I threw it hard. "Yes, it's such a long distance. How would I ever manage that all by myself?"

"You can get into quite a bit of trouble by yourself, little demon. Do this one thing for me. Please?"

I rolled my eyes at the overprotectiveness but shrugged. "Fine, I guess, though I don't understand why all of you couldn't have come here for dinner."

It was his turn to look behind me. "Luca and I couldn't fit through the door, Raven."

I snickered. "I give up. Just go." I pushed him off of me, only for him to return immediately.

"I'm not supposed to walk away without telling you something very important."

I waited with arms crossed over my chest, and my eyes flickered toward the sky as I ignored him. "Oh?"

Putting my chin between his fingers, he dragged my head down until I was forced to look into his eyes. "I am wildly, madly, passionately in love with you."

"I might feel the same."

He grinned. "Oh?"

I leaned in close, our lips only inches apart, but before he could kiss me, I whispered, "I'll let you know for sure after you come back to me."

He gaped, his jaw slack as I shimmied out of his grip and spun on my heels, sauntering away from him and only glancing at him over my shoulder right before I shut the door to say, "Enjoy your dinner."

He glared but grinned, remaining still until I was safely tucked inside Isla's cottage. I watched him walk away through the window, tilting my head curiously at his sudden need for distance.

I smelled her first before I felt her hand on the small of my back, staring out the window with me. "He is a handsome young man," Isla said.

"Handsome and mysterious," I muttered, waiting until he disappeared behind a castle wall before I turned and threw my arms around Isla. She smelled like home and thawed my heart. "Hello, Aunt Isla."

And in typical Isla fashion, she put my face between her hands and smushed our noses together. "Tell me all about it."

HOURS PASSED, and I barely noticed how dark it had gotten outside as I listened to even more stories from Zeke and Luca's childhoods— only these painted Zeke in a completely different light. Unlike his stories, where he was always the protector of Luca, I had to cover my mouth multiple times from laughing so hard at the torture they put one another through as children, instigated mainly by my husband.

"Zeke would pour a bucket of ice into Luca's bathwater," Alice said with a dramatic roll of her eyes. "He would stuff rocks into his pillows."

"Tried to drown him a couple of times," John added. "Claimed he was teaching him how to swim."

"I did hear about that one," I said with a laugh. "Poor Luca."

John bellowed out a laugh. "Poor Luca? Luca would throw all of Zeke's clothes into piles of mud and tell Alice it was Zeke's fault."

"He would say Zeke liked rolling around in the mud outside and pretending he was a pig."

I choked on my cup of tea, pinching my nostrils together as the liquid burned. "Gods. I wanted a boy someday, but I'm rethinking that."

Alice laughed and smiled warmly, placing her cup of tea down on the small table in the center of the quaint sitting room. "They had their moments, but my boys were also charming. When Luca had nightmares, his brother was always there to handle them. He'd let Luca sleep in his bed with him until they were both too big to fit."

Smiling, I pulled my knees up to my chest and rested my chin on one of them. I wanted Zeke to show me more of his memories. We had portraits of him as a young boy in John's office, but I wanted to see him protecting Luca. "Was Luca a heartbreaker like Zeke?"

John leaned back in the chair, his smile as wide as mine as he recounted memories of his sons. Even though he had left them at an early age, he always returned to make as many new memories as possible before returning to Seolia to protect me. "Zeke was not a heartbreaker, only because he never got close enough to anyone to let that happen."

"He wouldn't give anyone time to attach to him," Alice said. "There was a long time when I believed he'd never marry. I feared he'd given up on the entire idea of it. But, Luca was always the dreamer. He wanted a family, a wife, and kids."

John's smile dampened. "I worried that, due to my absence, Zeke would stop believing that he could be a husband or father."

"He knows you love him," I said gently. "He considers you his father and has come to terms with why you left. He told me this morning that he knows you always come back. It will take some time to repair your relationship, but he does love you, John."

John nodded and swallowed, staring into his empty teacup. "My biggest regret is making him feel like I didn't love him."

"There is always time to right wrongs," Isla said. "He is young. It is not too late for the two of you."

"It is not too late for any of us," I whispered.

Isla rubbed my back and a heavy silence filled the room. I looked toward the door, wanting Zeke to walk in and promise me precisely that, but he didn't. And with it getting so late, I wondered what was taking him so long. "Maybe I should go make sure he's okay," I said. "It's not like him to leave me for so long."

But when I moved to stand, John sat up quickly and clapped his hands together. "Let's have another cup of tea. Isla mentioned peppermint earlier, a flavor I have never tried."

Alice looked everywhere but at me. I quirked an eyebrow and placed my hands on my hips. "What aren't you telling me?"

John shook his head and blinked so quickly that it gave way to his lack of excuses. My breathing quickened slightly as I looked between him and Alice. "Where is he, John?"

"Now, Raven..."

I clenched my teeth together. "Where *is* he?"

Isla, in her innocence, looked confused. "Is he not at dinner?"

"No," I bit out. "He lied to me. And John knows where he is and isn't telling me, which is dangerous since you know I will find out for myself if you don't start talking." At John's continued silence, I threw my arms up. "Goddamnit, John, I am still your queen, and I demand you tell me where he is!"

John winced at the weight of duty versus fatherly trust. Alice finally sighed and took the choice from him. "He's shattering the minds of Mira's army."

"Fucking..." I turned and jogged out the cottage's front door, only to freeze at the line of soldiers guarding the castle and the village. "What the hell is this?!"

John came to stand beside me. "Precaution."

"I will deal with you tomorrow," I snapped, shifting into Blaze and running toward the pathway that led the back way around the castle into the forest. Seething, I held myself back from setting trees on fire solely to focus on the thought of throwing flames at Zeke instead. "No more secrets, Raven," I said mockingly, growling in frustration. "He clearly does not understand the definition of a secret."

I looked down at my leather leggings and loose top. *Wear something comfortable*, he had said while I changed. Because he fucking wanted me to be able to run if something went wrong.

"I am going to burn you alive!" I shouted into the emptiness of the forest, stomping closer to the grassy hillside that led into the empty field where we had been training the armies.

As I rounded the corner, expecting to hear only the waves sloshing onto the shore, sounds of steel on steel filled the open air. Fear rushed through me.

I should've stayed still. I had absolutely no experience in combat, especially against men much more trained than me, but was that what I did?

Of course not.

Instead, I bolted toward the noises and grunts of men, climbing up the hillside on my hands and knees to reach the top faster. And while some walked around, dazed and confused amongst the chaos and clattering, most had swords drawn and were battling men from my army.

A miniature war had broken out.

And standing in the middle of them, taking on two men all on his own, was my fucking husband.

≈

JEANINE SPOTTED ME FIRST.

Shit, she mouthed, piercing through a man's abdomen before yanking her sword out. "I told him to tell you!" she shouted at me.

Glaring at her, I trudged through the army and lit ablaze a man that was overpowering Luca. He looked around for me and tried to stop me from continuing, but at the sight of my flame-filled palm, he backed away and quickly found someone else to engage with.

There weren't many men left, but I recognized some of my own on the ground, either dead or close to it. I was too angry to cry or think of the families I would have to tell.

One of Mira's men charged at me with a sword raised, but I shifted into Frost and formed a long icicle in my hand, driving it through his throat and twisting for good measure. Blood splattered across my forehead and cheeks, and Blaze swiftly came to the forefront again. "Blood," I whispered, brushing my fingertips across my cheek.

I needed more.

I wanted to collect droplets like prizes.

So, I did. I fought my way through, using my elements as a distraction before plunging icicles into whatever body part I could reach. And I loved it; it was a feeling I would never not be addicted to, but no matter how angry I became, I could not manifest my powers as fully as I had in the forest or channel. They seemed stowed away in a locked box, buried deep within me.

I did not remain unscathed, cursing as the tip of a sword nicked my ribs and tore a hole through my shirt, drops of blood slipping down my skin. Shifting into Frost, I wrapped my fingers around his blade and encased it in ice. The sudden increase in weight brought the sword to the ground, leaving him weaponless and shocked.

Smiling, I shifted into Blaze and started at his legs, coaxing flames up slowly. Cruelly. I left him there to wail in pain and agony, resuming my trek toward Zeke. As Terra, I stomped a foot on the ground and a sliver of land cracked between Zeke and one of the men he was fighting.

As they both stumbled to the side, I shifted into Blaze and shot flames toward his opponent. It fastened to his arms and freed Zeke from the fight, but as he turned to find me, his expression showed guilt and fear. "Raven..." he started but stopped. His face and arms were covered in blood, his hair falling into his eyes, and he looked every bit the soldier Mira had turned him into.

Panting and chest heaving from fury and bloodlust, I held my arm to the side and released a flame, setting a man's face on fire as he launched toward me.

Zeke's eyes never left mine.

In the one look shared between us, it was evident that the dynamic in our relationship had changed. In our desperation to always protect the other, we had forsaken the one promise we swore to uphold through all else: partnership.

And nothing in this moment, or any future one to come, could change this one second where the realization dawned on us both— that at the end of all the turmoil and war and threats against us, the one factor that could cause us to crumble and break into pieces, was ourselves.

And that broke my heart more than anything else ever could.

A cry of pain had me whirling around to find Luca staggering, clutching his side. Blood covered his fingers, and his opponent raised his sword for one last blow, but that wasn't going to happen.

Zeke ran after me, blocking the sword with his own before the man could stab Luca. I fell to my knees at Luca's side and replaced his hand with my own. "It's not deep," I assured him, pushing healing into it. "Breathe, Luca."

I looked around the field from the ground, ears numbing from the sounds of groans, steel against steel, and dying men. Only two handfuls remained upright and fighting, but the casualties were equal. It was a harsh realization that if we were going to battle Mira and her legion of unbreakable men, it would take more than what I could provide.

"He needs stitches!" I shouted above the noise. "I have to get him to the infirmary!"

I needed to heal all of my men on the ground, but Luca was my highest priority. Shakily, I stood with him and kept one hand pressed against his side. Zeke finished off his opponent quickly in order to guide us closer toward the pathway to the castle, but I wanted none of his help right now.

With my free hand, I created two long pathways of fire, daring any of these men to try crossing through the flames to reach us. "Finish what you started," I ordered Zeke, enclosing the fire behind us to keep him from following.

Luca limped and leaned against me, trying to reason away Zeke's actions, but I didn't want to hear them. "Shut up, Luca. I'm upset with you, too."

We made it to the pathway through the mountains untouched, but Luca was heavy and I stumbled while trying to hold him up. The wound was closing under my hand, but his exhaustion didn't aid in keeping him upright. "Luca," I groaned, trying to readjust him against my shoulder.

"He shattered over fifty minds," Luca said breathily, still trying to defend his brother from my impending wrath. "Fifty minds, Raven, before one woke up and alerted the rest."

"Great, I'll make sure he gets a medal," I grumbled, my arm going numb from his weight. "Stop talking and preserve your energy."

I didn't see the silhouette cowering in the bushes, nor did I have time to defend either one of us before he lunged for me and stabbed a dagger through my side. Gasping, I stumbled sideways and clutched the hilt. Luca fell to the ground and tried to recover quickly enough to help me, but we were both wounded.

My vision blurred from the pain, my flames spitting out chaotically and missing him each time. "Zeke," I rasped, trying to call for him, but I couldn't focus on anything other than the pain.

Through the flickering and dying flames, I could've sworn I saw someone familiar staring back at me from behind the trees. But as the scorned soldier launched for me again, I barely missed his tackle, instead tripping over Luca and falling back to the ground.

And the only thought I could detangle in my mind was that at least this dagger wasn't laced with poison.

The man circled us, kicking Luca back down as he tried to stand. "This is for the threats he made against me," the man spat, "for the months of training under the guise he'd kill everyone I know."

He kneeled before me and grabbed my hair, yanking me up and twisting the dagger into my side. "It is too bad I didn't taste this fiery side of yours."

Gods, the pain was immeasurable, but I was sick and tired of men saying crude things to me like I was nothing more than a snack for them to devour.

I gasped and panted my way through a pathetic laugh. "Fuck you." Lifting my arm with considerable effort, I wrapped my fingers around his throat and lit my palm, screaming against his fight and squeezing until the flesh melted in my hand.

And then I dropped him, his body falling across my legs and pinning me to the ground. The familiar face crept out between the trees until he stood above me, his head cocked to the side and fading in my vision.

He sighed deeply. "You're going to need to do better than that, Raven," was the last thing I heard.

WE HAD FORSAKEN THE ONE PROMISE WE SWORE TO UPHOLD THROUGH ALL ELSE: PARTNERSHIP.

24

Raven

T wasn't in the meadow. Instead, I spun in a slow circle in a place made of red skies, where a black castle stood with towers so high that they disappeared into clouds of maroon. Wrapping my arms around my middle, I jerked at the raw wound on my side and dried blood on my skin.

"Zeke!" I called, but he did not reply.

In all of our memories, in every one of my nightmares, I always felt him near, but not here. Here, I felt out of sorts and alone. The sky, while vast and alarming, did not stretch as far as the eye could see.

In the distance, maybe hundreds of miles away, a sky of blue anchored against the red. Again, I spun. No trees surrounded me, no forests, just open fields of rivers and ponds, and no soul dwelled within this blood-red kingdom's confines.

"Zeke!" I whisper-shouted. "I don't like this place!" I took two steps forward but suddenly stopped. I did not want to walk into a castle made of black steel, spiky, barbed archways, and wide and doors weighing a ton each.

Heart-catching and stomach-dropping, I stilled out the figure behind one of the towers, gesturing grandly toward the castle. "Unique, no?"

I blinked in confusion and shock. "What are you doing here?" I looked around for Zeke. "How did you find me in here?"

River stopped in front of me, far enough away for me not to fear him but close enough for him to look real and not like something I imagined in one of my dreams. "Does Zeke know you're here?"

"No," River replied. "He is desperate to find you, though. But he cannot reach you here."

"Why? Where is here? How am I here?"

"Your dreams have always tried to tell you something," River answered. His responses were always like some kind of riddle for me to untangle. "Have you never wondered why they are so vivid?"

Not at this particular moment as I stood surrounded by blood-red everything. "You can dream-walk like Zeke?"

"We have a thread, Raven. I cannot dream-walk into anyone's dreams, only yours. And it's not so much a dream, just a projection of my memories into your subconscious."

That was comforting. I wasn't fond of having anyone but Zeke access the innermost parts of my mind, though I was curious if River had other magic besides his element if he could do something like this.

"Where are we?"

"Where I grew up."

I lifted an eyebrow, my eyes flickering to the dark castle and bloody skies before turning back to him. "Quaint."

The corner of his mouth twitched. "Something is coming, Raven. Someone."

As always, whenever my body tried to wake up, the surroundings of my dreams began to fade. "Who? How are you in Seolia?"

"I need you to come to Reales."

I snorted. Even asleep, I knew that Zeke would never allow that to happen. He would swim across the channel to physically pull me back if I ever tried to visit Reales alone. "I don't see that happening."

"Make it happen," he said. "I have already risked too much by not keeping my distance. We need this to end, Raven."

The castle warped into a smoky haze behind him, signaling our time running out. "Need what to end?"

"Come to Reales, Raven."

When he turned back toward the castle, I tried to follow him but was stopped by a force I could not push through. "River! I can't just go to Reales!"

"Wake up, Raven."

"River!" I shoved against the force, but the harder I pushed, the more everything around me faded.

Levels—I went through levels of dreams and memories as Zeke dug his claws into my mind to yank me free from whatever cage River had trapped me in. The harder he pulled, the faster I climbed, until I landed in the black room identical to the one Morana always locked me in.

I must've been badly hurt if it was taking Zeke this long to find me. Blowing out an annoyed sigh, I walked around the endless, bleak room until I stumbled directly into the glass pane that always held heartbreak behind it.

A child came toward me from the other side, tiny and unbalanced. Tears immediately filled my eyes as I clutched my stomach, watching as he waddled and swayed closer until he knocked against the glass and tumbled backward.

He. He. A boy.

Lowering to my knees, I placed my palms against the glass pane. "Little one," I whispered, desperate to see his face and eyes.

I fought against the tug in my mind. Not yet.

The small boy grunted as he rolled over to all fours, struggling to stand again. I laughed through my tears, desperate to find my way through the glass, but that wasn't how it ever worked.

The glass always stood between me and what I wanted, or

between me and what I feared. And a family with Zeke was both, making the pane between us even more indestructible.

Knocking on the glass gently, I encouraged the tot to turn around. To find me. And when he finally did, when he managed to stand and waddle toward the glass, banging on it with his palms and squealing, my lips parted at what stared back at me.

The child, with thick, black hair and eyes of dark green and ashy gray, was a combination of us. His skin was golden, just like Zeke's, but he looked like me, with his wrinkled nose. He looked like an ordinary, healthy boy with flushed red cheeks and pink puckered lips until you noticed his ears.

Pointed at the ends like tiny, sharp triangles, they stuck out above his wild hair.

I blinked, unsure of why or how. But when he babbled incoherently, it didn't matter what he looked like. He was mine. And my heart and stomach felt like lead at the realization that no matter how hard I tried, I would not be able to get to him.

"I'm so sorry," I whispered, pressing my forehead against the glass to be closer. I just wanted to smell him, touch him, hold him. "I'm so sorry I wasn't strong enough for you," I cried, tears smearing against the glass.

"I love you," I repeatedly said, trying to shove Zeke away from my mind to give me more time with our son. "I could stay here with you, I could be with you...."

"It's not real, Raven."

I crumbled against the glass, banging on it with my fists as Zeke found me, weaving his arms around me. "Baby, it's not real. This is where your fear and regret live. This is where your mind goes when it's broken."

"He is real," I rasped, clawing and scraping against the glass with my hands. "He is real! Look at him!"

Zeke refused, keeping his head lowered and eyes on me. "Raven, I need you to come back with me."

"I can't!" I shook my head wildly, coughing and blubbering from my cries. "I can't leave him, Zeke. He's our son!"

"Then he'll come back to us," Zeke whispered, trying to coerce my flailing arms into submission. "Baby, he'll come back to us."

"I can't leave him." My voice was like sandpaper. "Look at him, Zeke, and you'll want to stay, too."

"I can't," he whispered. "Because I have to get you out of here, baby. I can't look at him."

"I'm so sorry," I repeated.

The child locked eyes with me for a few seconds before turning away. I shook my head, banging on the glass and screaming as he waddled away from me. Zeke's tears fell on top of my head, wetting my hair as he tried to pull me to my feet. I fought, thrashed, cried, and begged for him to let me stay, to help me find a way through the glass.

But he dragged me backward and tried to calm my cries with promises I did not know if he could keep about fixing this for us, assuring me that I'd see him again. "Baby, breathe," he said. "I need you to breathe. I can't leave you in here."

I hit his chest with my fists. I tried to shove him off, but he only held me tighter. If I relented and relaxed, he would throw us out of there, and I wasn't ready. I had already come back to life once for him only to prove Morana right—we were cursed.

"I love you," he said against my temple, palming my head in his hand. "Gods, Raven, I love you. Please come back with me."

"He needs me," I argued.

"And he'll have you," he countered, "but right now, I need you more."

It wasn't until I looked over my shoulder to see nothing behind the glass pane that I finally stopped fighting Zeke, my body numb and empty. And he didn't give me time to second-guess it before scattering the room around us until it was nothing but a memory.

A TEAR FELL to the pillow under my head when I opened my eyes. The dimly lit candles did not aid in bringing the room into focus, but I knew I was alone with Zeke.

I heard his sigh of relief. His weary exhale of exhaustion. When I rolled my head to look at him, I saw an expression of guilt. But when he opened his mouth, I stopped him with, "Do not give me another empty apology."

He retreated into silence.

I touched my wound; the flesh puckered under my fingers but healing. "Luca?" I inquired.

"Good as new," he whispered, leaning forward to rest his elbows on his knees. "I found both of you right after you killed your attacker. I saw the flames."

"How many men did I lose?"

He hung his head. "Forty-four men. John has tended to the families. The wounded are in the infirmary."

I covered my eyes, my chest shaking with deep and painful sobs. Forty-four men who had pledged to fight for me against Mira died because of a fight I didn't know was happening. Men that I knew, men I had spoken to and trained with, men whose families would be devastated to learn that they had left their homes under the guise of protecting the village as a precaution, only to not return. "You lied to me."

He did not answer. Did not argue.

Clutching my side, I sat up and grimaced from the pain as I adjusted to lean against the wall. "You lied to me *again*," I repeated. "You promised me there would be no more secrets, Zeke. You said you wanted my trust back. How could you do this?"

Judging by the look of him, he hadn't moved from that spot since finding me. He was covered head-to-toe in blood and dirt, with cuts along his arms and neck and his hair wet and matted from sweat.

"I thought I could handle it on my own," he murmured, lacing his fingers together between his spread knees. "I took Luca, Jeanine, and Godfrey with me to watch for men who woke. I shattered over fifty minds before the subconscious of a man fought back. He woke up and alerted the rest."

He refused to look at me. His shame was apparent. "Godfrey, thankfully and on his own, informed the Seolian men to linger close by. When they heard his call, they arrived with drawn weapons. Fifty men stayed in the village in case the fight was brought to the people."

"And you all knew. All of you planned this without informing me, sending me off to Isla's cottage to sit around and fucking drink tea while *my* men died." I swallowed, irritated by his silence. "Because they are my men, Zeke. They are men I have known my entire life, and you risked their lives tonight for what?"

"Our protection, Raven. I warned you that war is dirty. These things are going to happen—"

"This did not have to be a war!" I shouted. "Instead of walking around like some fucking martyr all the godsdamn time, Zeke, you should've planned this better! You could've included me! We could've at least given our army a warning so that they could say goodbye to their families!"

"War is not planned, Raven." He maintained his calm tone, attempting to placate me. "If you make plans, you risk a leak. We had to eliminate Mira's army quickly before word got to them that they were no longer needed."

"You should've told me."

He raised his head and looked straight into my eyes as he said, "No, Raven. I will not apologize for this. I did what I needed to do to protect you."

Fuming, bewildered, and speechless would be what I was remembered for when I died someday. It was my constant state. "I am the queen, Zeke. Regarding matters of this kingdom, you do not get to act like my husband—"

"*Act* like your husband?" he interjected, curling his fingers. "I am your husband. More than that, you are my mate—"

"Gods!" I bellowed, fisting my hair in my hands. "Enough! You don't get to use that every time you fuck up! And you fucked up, Zeke! There is no excuse for what you did!"

"If I had told you, Raven, you would've wanted to fight with me. You would've been there, waiting and ready to draw first blood. And I could not have you there. I would've constantly been wondering if you were okay, if you were alive, hurt, or bleeding. It would've been riskier for us if you were there."

"So, instead, you hid me away. You used your parents to distract me. Did you even think about what would happen to me if something had happened to *you*?" I swallowed my groan and stood from the bed, as I could no longer wallow in my anger while sitting still. "Did you even think for one-second about the guilt and anguish I would feel if you were hurt?"

His silence told me that he hadn't considered it.

"You make all of these grand gestures under the pretense that I don't feel for you what you feel for me, that I do not need you like you need me, that because of some fucking bond with someone else that I don't even want, I wouldn't be as destroyed if you were hurt." I wrapped a hand around my throat as it burned from rising cries. "I watched you bleed at my feet in Reales, Zeke. I felt you nearly die, I watched you bleed out in my arms, and there wasn't anything I could do about it. And yet you sit there, brooding about how I can't understand why you chose the wrong path."

I was fatigued and bone-tired of the constant tug and pull between us. "I love you," I whispered, "I love you, but you fucked up. I could forgive the secrecy of the miscarriage. I could forgive you for hiding from me that Leonidas might not be my father. I have forgiven you many times, but I cannot move on from this right now. I cannot forgive you for *this*."

"I'm going to Nova," wasn't even on the list of things I thought he would say. "I am going to Nova to enlist Melik's help with the war. I am taking Luca with me, and we'll leave at dawn."

"That is not why you're leaving. Even after all of this, you are still determined to find him. Killing whoever he is will not fix us, Zeke."

"We are not broken, Raven."

"You are in denial."

"Are you going to leave me?"

The directness of his question felt like a dagger to my heart. I would've been lying if I had said it hadn't crossed my mind since waking up from my nightmare within a nightmare, but despite everything, all the poor decisions and secrecy, I still longed for the splintered and damaged man before me. Mostly, I longed for what we could be if we could push past the discourse and failure to communicate.

He didn't need a verbal answer from me. He could feel it on me the second he asked, but he still deserved to know that no matter what mud he dragged me through, he was still someone worth forgiving. "I am really fucking angry."

He stood from the chair, and I immediately backed away. I had learned his tricks, how easily he could ensnare me with his proximity. And it wouldn't work this time. "Are you," he repeated, "going to leave me?"

"No..."

"Then I am not in denial."

"But you owe me an apology."

His jaw ticked. "I won't ever apologize for protecting you, Raven."

"You made a decision for me. *Again*. And now you're leaving me to deal with the ramifications while you go gallivanting across kingdoms."

"Gallivanting?" he asked. "I don't believe seeking answers for our future is gallivanting, Raven."

"You are leaving me so easily after swearing to never leave my side again, Zeke. Excuse me if I'm having trouble comprehending this change of heart so quickly."

"Is that why you are so angry with me?"

I scowled. "There are many reasons why I am angry with you, but that is the most recent."

"It is not as if I want to leave you...."

"I am doubting your infatuation with me."

He blinked. "You are not."

"Aren't I?" I placed my hands on my hips. "You have stopped treating me as your equal. You are keeping me in the dark. You speak of me with others like I have no opinion, no say in any of it. What you are showing me is not love, Zeke. It is control."

I stung him. He faltered a step, clutching his chest, but then narrowed his eyes. "You're wrong, Raven. I make these decisions for you, for us. I am your husband. It is my sole purpose to protect you."

"I will not be controlled, Zeke, not by you, not by anyone. I might not want to be queen anymore, but that does not give you the right to decide what is best for my kingdom while I hold the throne."

I gestured over my body with both hands before resting a hand against my heart. "I have given you all of me, inside and out. I have promised you that you are my partner, but you cannot give me the same respect. So, while I did not ask for it and do not particularly agree that it is in our best interest, you should go to Nova."

He sank back down onto the chair. "You're telling me to leave."

It was taking everything I had left not to give in, not to fall into his arms and beg him to love me the way I wanted to be loved, but I was tired of begging to be respected. I was tired of being protected and treated like glass. "You want answers. It has become obvious that no matter how many promises I make, you cannot believe that my heart only belongs to you. So, go. Go to Nova and seek your answers there. Leave me here with my nightmares and dead bodies. It is quite a fitting end."

THE CHILD, WITH THICK, BLACK HAIR AND EYES OF DARK GREEN AND ASHY GRAY, WAS A COMBINATION OF US.

25

RAVEN

H e followed me out of the room, repeating the same word over and over. "End? What end?" He grabbed my hand, only to growl when I yanked away. "Raven, we have no ending."

Silently, I walked to our chambers, fighting back the tears of frustration and begging the ache in my chest to disperse elsewhere. I tried to slam the door shut on him after entering the room, but he barreled right through. "You are not fucking leaving me, Raven," he snapped, grabbing my wrist. "I did not lie to you. We had dinner."

Scowling, I iced my wrist. The chilly bite made him release me.

"You are not getting out of this on a technicality. You did not tell me that dessert would be risking the lives of my men!"

"I could smell your goddamn blood!" he shouted, pushing his hand through his hair. "That field had gallons of blood, Raven, but the second you were nicked by a sword, I *smelled* it. I thirsted for it. I couldn't fucking think straight. I might've lost if you hadn't set fire to the men I fought. I was *that* distracted. That is why I could not have you near me! You are a risk!"

I opened and closed my mouth, unable to speak.

"That is one of the reasons why I need to go to Nova, Raven. Melik spoke of mates. He knows more than we do. I need to know why I want to drink your blood like a fucking monster, I need to know how my mate could be mated to someone else, and I need his army to assist in protection because I cannot have you out there with me, Raven.

I do not doubt how strong you are, how powerful, and how much better off we would be if you fought with us, but until I know how to control this, I cannot have you near me while fighting them."

I slowly walked into our chambers and he followed so closely behind me that he bumped into me, as if fearing I may bolt away. "But you are not leaving me," he continued. "I do not make these choices to hurt you. The last thing I ever want to do is make you doubt my utter and complete obsession with your every breath, and I am sickened with the thought that we have reached that point."

As I turned to lean against the table, he placed his hands on either side of me and caged me in. My only route of escaping would be if I back-rolled across the tabletop. "Say it, Raven. Tell me you're not leaving me. Please give me a little more time. A tiny handful of grace. I love you so entirely, so unfathomably, that my actions come off the opposite."

I raised my brows as if to say, *really?*

He tucked a strand of stray hair behind my ear. "You look beautiful covered in blood, my love."

I rolled my eyes. "Do not be poetic with me right now. My love for you is very much sharing a border with hatred."

"I do not mind your hatred, Raven. As long as you feel something toward me, I'll take it all."

"If I asked you to stay, would you?"

"Yes," he answered quicker than a heartbeat. "If you asked me to stay here, I would not go, but I would slowly be driven to madness. I do not want to continue feeling helpless, Raven."

"You did not ask me to come," I whispered. "That is what hurt most of all."

"Raven, I will travel the world with you someday." He wrapped my thighs around his waist and lifted me, carrying me to the bed and sitting down with me in his lap. "And I want to take you with me, and if you want to go, I will gladly put you into my bag and bring you. But here, tucked away on our island, I know you are safe. Godfrey will watch over you with what remains of our army, John is closing the harbor to ships, Jeanine will move in here, and I can sleep well at night knowing that you can handle yourself."

"What about Reales?"

"I intend on being back here before then. It will be close, but I do not want you to be there the next time I see you. Godfrey will communicate with Edmund in my absence if that does happen. We have a plan in place, and I am more than willing to share that plan with you."

"I do not wish to spend my last few hours with you discussing war strategies," I admitted. "Godfrey can fill me in later."

"Raven, you are the queen. I am a soldier. It is what I want to be until we solve this. And as your soldier, my purpose is to protect you. Your purpose is to be there for your people."

"I'm powerful, Zeke. You don't have to do this alone."

"Baby, I know you are. And I promise that if I can figure out how to be near you without wanting to consume you, you will be beside me on the battlefield."

I frowned. "I need you to keep your promises."

"I do, Raven, even if you don't see it immediately." He searched my face for a moment until he settled on my eyes. "Tell me about the dream I could not pull you from."

"How did you know?"

"I have spent months familiarizing myself with your mind, Raven. I have never been shielded from one of your dreams."

If I said what I was thinking aloud, it would have been that I did not feel like sharing something with him when he couldn't deign to include me in his plans for my kingdom. Instead, I closed my eyes to recall as much as possible from the time spent with River. "It was in a kingdom of black and red, and River was there. He tried to warn me of something but never came out and said what it was." Upon opening my eyes, I shrugged a shoulder. "That's all I can remember."

"When I pulled you out, I shattered a dream you had. I did not break it into so many pieces that it couldn't come back together, but it'll stay buried until you're ready."

I did not ask what it was nor did I want to know. On top of everything else that had transpired since this morning, remaining ignorant seemed the best choice. "I'd like to visit the wounded men," I said, "and Luca. Is Jeanine okay?"

He nodded with a slight grin. "Jeanine killed as many men as I did. She was assisting in burning the bodies when I last checked."

"I could've at least done that," I grumbled, feeling utterly useless. "There is nothing left for me to do."

"There is, Raven. Be there for the living."

I spent a quarter of a century never stepping foot into the infirmary. After just a few months with Zeke, I had been in here too many times. It wasn't big enough to hold many men, but there weren't many wounded during the fight. It seemed like it was either all or nothing with them — they either died or survived.

Theodore tended to the wounded, and I breathed a sigh of relief to learn that he was not among those we lost. His wife, Evangeline, assisted in bandaging but when she saw me, she immediately stopped to bow. I shook my hands out in front of me, begging the others who began to follow her lead to please... not.

While, yes, history books on our realm depicted queens staying inside the castle during battles, I was not a typical queen; I was a weapon, and one that desperately wanted to be used. I would not sit idly by while men fought for me and our kingdom. I needed to be on the battlefield with them, bleeding for my people.

"Do not harbor guilt, Raven," Zeke said behind me. "It changes nothing."

Forgiveness would not come easily between us, but I nodded because he was correct. Guilt would not heal these men, but I could.

One by one, I went to each man and placed my hand against their wounds, distributing enough healing into each one equally to numb the pain and quicken the process. They uttered their thanks and I returned them with my own.

And when the groans of pain died down and silence enclosed around us, Evangeline took a wet rag and cleaned the blood from my hands. "Thank you," I murmured. "Where is Eva?"

Evangeline smiled warmly. "With Arthur. He is Eva and Teddy's godfather."

I tried to smile but could not even force one. "I am sorry this is happening and taking time away from your family."

Gently, Evangeline dabbed at my cheeks with the rag. "It was inevitable, Queen Raven. We are lucky peace lasted as long as it did. And now, we fight for our families. We fight for our home. We fight for you."

"Evangeline, I have done nothing to earn your life. Theodore's life. Any of the men's lives we lost tonight." I glanced around the room. "We will lose more in Reales."

"Then we will lose more," she stated simply. "Raven, people need something to fight for. Everyone needs something to believe in, whether for you or for this kingdom. Without the gods, we've lost the ability to believe. I would rather live my days knowing that Theodore and I placed everything we had into ensuring a good life for our children rather than sit idly by while evil tries to take it away."

I admired her perseverance and loyalty and noticed the constant looks shared between her and Theodore, even as she spoke to me. It was endearing, and I was envious. Their marriage reflected what I hoped mine would look like one day.

Evangeline's eyes flickered behind me for only a second. "He looks miserable," she muttered to me.

I knew precisely which *he* she was referring to, and I had no doubt that guilt was eating away at him, despite his dramatic arguing to the contrary. Standing and sighing, I thanked her before grabbing a satchel from the wall. While sifting through our medicinal cabinets, I filled the bag full of tonics and gauze.

Since disease and illness were uncommon in our kingdom, we overstocked medicines. Though I didn't know what any of these were for, I placed two of each in the satchel before fetching four empty vials that were as long as my hand.

I did not need to tell him to follow me as I left the infirmary, not stopping or speaking until we reached the empty throne room. The pool of gold remained in the center of the room as a reminder of just how much I rejected my title.

Zeke closed the doors behind us, his expression inquisitive as I held out the satchel for him. "I will not be there to heal you. Most of your trip will be by foot, and while you believe yourself invincible, you're not."

Most of the vials were made from herbs Keaton had put together from his garden. I never needed them, but I trusted that the plant expert knew what he was doing. "I'm assuming the labels on these will tell you what they're for," I said through a forced laugh, shaking the bag in front of me for him to grab.

"Raven," he murmured, taking the bag and placing it on the floor. "We're going to be fine. I've traveled often. We'll find horses to make the trip quicker."

I was angry and irritated with him, but I did not want him to leave. I did not want to imagine what the weeks without him would be like. The last time we attempted it, we almost drove ourselves insane from longing. But we deserved to know what lived outside our realm, and while I would've loved the chance to go with him, I was needed here.

And I would be fine. With Cade and Mira's soldiers gone from my island, our only threat lived days away by ship. And despite what Zeke believed, River wouldn't harm me. Not physically, anyway.

And Zeke... well, just the sight of him was enough to send anyone scurrying. It seemed the more blood he drank, the stronger he became. He had changed since meeting me. His muscles were more defined, his reflexes sharper, and even his canines were more distinctive.

If I didn't know any better, I would believe he wasn't mortal, but something else entirely.

Something terrifying.

And I dared anyone to try their hand against him.

"You have the gift of knowing where I am while you're gone," I explained. "I, however, will have no idea where you are or when you'll be back. Please allow me this."

He said nothing, dropping to his knees before me. I stepped away, but he grabbed my hips and pulled me back. "Raven," he began, clutching me tightly. "I am so sorry."

That could cover any number of missteps.

"Raven, despite what you think, I am the villain. Every decision I've made thus far has been for you. It has not been for the people or for the continuation of this kingdom." His eyes held no guilt as he looked up at me. "I care about nothing but the guarantee that it'll be the two of us in the end. You believe me to be better than I am, Raven, but I am selfish."

"A man possessed is dangerous," I whispered.

"And I am," he agreed. "Possessed and dangerous. Raven, I do not hesitate when murdering. I don't think twice about it. I lose no sleep. When I act alone, it is to preserve what is left of your soul. You speak of burning the world for me, but Raven, I would fucking rip it apart for you. I would bathe in oceans of blood if it meant you were safe in my arms every night. I don't know how else to convince you that this is who I am. I am the villain, but only for you."

I did not need convincing, because the most feared man in our realm was on his knees for me.

"I do not apologize for protecting you," he reiterated. "But I am sorry for making decisions without you. I am sorry for making you doubt me or my love for you. I wish for nothing more than the day when doubt will cease to exist between us."

"Wouldn't that be something?"

He grinned. "Do you forgive me?"

"No," I said. "Not yet. I will, but I expect things to change. I am not your pet, Zeke. I am your wife. You will seek your answers, but then you will drop this. After we defeat Mira, I want to live our life happily and without tension."

He nodded, but when I asked, "Can you give me that?" I genuinely needed the answer. Because I could not, *would* not, continue living in constant fear of something else unraveling between us.

He pressed his forehead against my stomach, his arms wrapping tightly around my waist. "Yes, Raven."

In the past, our disagreements would have been solved with apologies. He would have lowered me to the floor and kissed away my anger, but I couldn't find it in myself to forgive him so quickly this time. Understanding why he kept the secret about the miscarriage was something entirely different from trying to reconcile how he could handle losing the lives of my men without warning me first.

And when he pulled away to raise his head, staring into my eyes, he didn't need verbal confirmation to know I was still wary around him. The dynamic between us had shifted. It was no longer just my doubts about him wanting me—I couldn't trust that we worked as partners. I would always wonder if he was planning something without my knowledge. His promises were not enough. I needed more.

But instead of informing him of this, I pointed toward the satchel beside us. "There are four empty vials in there. Hand them to me."

Studying me, curious about the words I wasn't saying, he released me to pull the four empty bottles from the bag. Pressing my palm against his lips, I waited for him to break the skin with his teeth and *tsked* when he tried to suck the blood through his lips, instead pulling my hand away and holding it over each bottle until they were all filled.

"I cannot supply you with four weeks' worth, but I can give you one a week." Though angry and confused, I still needed to take care of him. Whether or not we would make it through this distrust unscathed, I doubted I'd ever truly leave him, though he certainly wasn't making it easy on me.

Once the fourth was filled, he took my hand and sucked from the cut until the wound closed. I secured lids on the vials and pulled a string of worn leather from the satchel, sliding each bottle across it. "Don't need you accidentally mixing these up with tonics. Luca wouldn't appreciate it the same."

He forced a laugh, standing and throwing the bag over his shoulder. "How are you so calm about this? *Why* are you so calm?"

I knew from the weariness in his eyes that his questions needed answers and the reassurance that he would come home to me still being his wife, but I couldn't find it in myself to make him promises yet. Instead, I lifted a shoulder in a slight shrug. "I barely am, but I know you're doing it for us."

"I am," he confirmed and leaned in for a kiss, which I allowed. "That is my only driving force for leaving. Melik will allow us to stay in his castle. I'll gather all the answers I can."

The fact that he was obsessed with finding answers about my supposed mate when we had other things to worry about made me more bitter than I was willing to admit.

"And then you'll come back to me."

"And then I'll come back to you," he repeated.

"YOU LOOK BEAUTIFUL COVERED IN BLOOD, MY LOVE."

26

RAVEN

We should've spent the night tangled up in each other. Our way of communicating had always been with our bodies, and this should've been no different. But, that wasn't how we spent our night. After returning to our chambers, we fought. I struggled to understand his decisions, the ramifications of his actions that I would be dealing with alone, and his ability to leave me so easily. And when not defending himself, he was questioning how easily I could forget how much he loved me—how everything he did was for me, how I should understand.

We argued often, but most times, it was only to make up.

This time... was different.

No matter what I said, no matter how many times I promised him that I didn't care about my mate, no matter how hard I tried to convince him that we needed to focus on taking Reales, he was adamant that the most important and treasured thing in his life was me. And it was the look in his eyes, the movement of his chest as he panted from that admission, the way his fists clenched and veins blackened from frustration, that made me realize I was no longer speaking with my husband.

I was fighting the darkness within him—the one that was so desperate to have me as its own. And when Luca knocked on our door to drag him away to prepare their ship to leave, he didn't hesitate to leave me standing alone.

Because he was nothing if not an excellent master of masking his pain. Appearing indifferent toward me was the only way he could leave me here. And that was exactly what I had conveyed to him, causing him to pause in the doorway before he followed Luca out.

And in true fashion, I could not remain still with my thoughts, allowing them to consume my mind, which was how I ended up in the Black Forest alone for the first time since Cade had drugged me and dragged me through it.

Struggling to keep my breathing even, I continued stomping through the trees as stubbornness prevailed. I refused to be afraid in my kingdom, and becoming familiar with my forest again felt a little like healing. Whether or not The Forest Beyond had any ties to mine, the Black Forest still felt like a sister to the jungle where Blaze had come alive.

That brought me a small sense of safety as I called Shadow's name to no avail. It had been weeks since I'd last seen him, and I wasn't sure what he was surviving on. "He wouldn't drink the salt water," I muttered to myself. "Where else would he go?"

Before Zeke, I believed I had explored the entirety of the forest, but he was the one who taught me about the thermal spring. That gave me doubts that I truly knew every inch of the forest and I wondered if more secrets lay somewhere within.

Frowning, I stopped to pull a handful of pink daisies from the ground. Finding color within the Black Forest was a rarity, and it surprised me to find such a vivid bunch at my feet against the grays and blacks of the leaves and trunks.

I spun the stem of one between my fingers, the soft earthy scent making me shift into Terra without calling upon her. Blinking my golden eyes, my lips parted as the pinkish hues of the petals brightened for only seconds before they dimmed once more. A whinny from between the trees made my head snap up. I quickly tucked the flower behind my ear. "Shadow!" I scolded with my hands on my hips. "Where have you been? I didn't invite you to my island for you to disappear."

Shadow guiltily hung his head while he trotted toward me, knocking his gargantuan head against mine. I hissed from the pressure, rubbing my forehead. "Okay, I forgive you." Running my hands through the tufts of his mane, I sighed. "Shadow, I need you to accompany Zeke on a trip."

Shadow responded as I expected him to, backing away from me to turn his head and huffing through his nostrils. I had learned quickly that Zeke was not Shadow's favorite person. They were both annoyingly possessive over me and tended to butt heads when it came to sharing.

"Does every male in my life have to be so goddamn pigheaded?" I grabbed Shadow's muzzle and turned it back toward me with substantial force. He clearly hadn't starved during his absence. "Shadow, I need you to go with him. I will be safe here."

Shadow side-eyed me as if to say, *are you joking?*

I glowered at him, putting my hands on his cheeks and trying to draw his head down to mind. His black eyes shined in the moonlight, his silky hair reflecting the spring water. "Shadow, please. I know he's... difficult, but I need you to keep him safe."

Sighing loudly and somewhat dramatically for a horse, he dipped his head to rest his forehead against mine. He could crush me easily from this alone, but I stood with him for a moment before kissing his nose. "Thank you, Shadow."

～

JEANINE WAS SITTING on the dock watching Zeke and Luca load the ship when I arrived with Shadow. She immediately stood and came to fawn over my horse while Zeke paused, placing his hands on the railing of the ship and raising a curious brow. Shadow didn't need instruction from me as he left Jeanine's embrace to climb the ramp of the ship, staring my husband down before trotting to the very opposite end of the ship.

I puffed out my cheeks and released the air slowly at the tension between them, in slight disbelief at how human he acted at times. Zeke simply rolled his eyes at Shadow's snarky dismissal, descending the ramp to take the bag of apples from my hand. "Why, Raven?"

I snorted. "Because he loves me, which means he won't let anything happen to you."

"I feel like this is more of a punishment," he muttered, tossing the bag to Luca from the dock.

"Consider it both," I replied.

There was more than a foot between us, but when his eyes focused on mine, the heat was palpable and made me shift. One look from him had the power to completely unravel me and tempt me to beg him to stay, which I knew he was waiting for me to do, but I held my ground. I did so weakly and with hesitation, but holding him here could be what tore us apart. "Luca is waiting for you," I whispered.

Frowning, he turned away from me to continue assisting Luca in moving the last two trunks onto the ship, but not before he plucked the pink daisy from behind my ear to place it behind his, twisting a strand of my violet hair between his fingers. "You do know how to wound me, my love," he murmured.

I closed my eyes as a tear slipped down my cheek. Jeanine slipped her arms around my waist, whispering promises of understanding and pulling me down to sit beside her.

They would be on one of our smallest ships, and I noticed that Zeke had removed the Seolian flag from the stern. Since they would be docking on land that didn't technically belong to any kingdom in the realm, he didn't want anyone to know where they had come from. It would come at a risk to me — not that there was a soul left in our realm who wasn't aware of our meaning to one another.

They would sail to the land between Thoya and Reales, hopefully

258

stumbling across another horse. Until then, they could take turns riding Shadow.

Sitting on the dock with Jeanine, I laughed while she explained to me that she had tried to help, but after accidentally dropping one of their trunks into the water while lugging it up the ramp, she was banished to the dock while John and Alice prepared another one for them.

It hadn't set in yet that he would be gone for weeks.

I worried that without enough of my blood for that long, he would weaken.

Boots thudding against the dock had me turning my head to see Arthur approaching, holding a wicker basket in his hands. At the sound of Jeanine's whoops and hollers, Luca and Zeke popped their heads over the ship's side.

Jeanine was up and bounding toward Arthur to grab the basket, but Luca yelled, "Stop!" making me laugh as Jeanine cursed from afar. Zeke descended the ramp to take the basket from Arthur instead, mussing Jeanine's hair with his hand while she swatted him away. "Go sit back down with the other troublemaker," he said, dipping his chin toward me with a wink.

I smiled, but the ache in my chest made it hard to breathe. He was so devastating to look at, and he belonged wholly to me. I owned his heart and wasn't looking forward to letting him go. I suddenly wished I wasn't so stubborn.

Jeanine sat in my lap, and I wrapped my arms around her waist. I rested my forehead against her back and wondered if she'd let us sit here for a month until they returned.

"I slept with Luca," she whispered.

She kept my arms locked around her waist when I tried to shove her off to hammer her for details.

"Last night," she continued. "Do you want my comparison notes?"

I threw my head back in a laugh, nearly toppling both of us backward on the dock. "What does this mean?"

She shrugged a shoulder. "I already told you. I'm not looking for anything serious, and neither is he. We agreed to fuck without pressure to make it anything more. I guess him nearly dying from a stab wound made us realize that life is too short not to try."

I looked at Zeke after she said that. Zeke ensured I was his the second we locked eyes. "They're complete opposites," I said, listening to Zeke bossing Luca around.

"They're not," Jeanine said, "not really. Zeke is in love with you. That is the only difference between them. He wouldn't have committed to anyone else."

I gnawed on her shoulder. She shoved my face away before rubbing the bite mark. "Does that not bother you?" I asked.

"A little," she snapped, looking at the reddened skin.

I giggled, kissing her shoulder. "No, you and Luca."

"Oh." She shook her head. "We're not in love. I love him, but it isn't near anything you feel for Zeke. I would be okay if he found someone else and vice-versa. I told him not to hold back while he's gone and that I'd try to seduce you."

"Gods, he's going to share that with Zeke on their trip, and he's going to have a meltdown."

"I know," Jeanine said through a laugh. "That is the plan."

Arthur returned to the dock from the ship, grabbing our hands to pull us up. "They're well-stocked with rum. I figured Zeke would need the distraction."

"Did you leave any for us?" Jeanine hooked a thumb in my direction. "It's not like she'll be a bed of roses."

"Roses," I whined, covering my face with my hands.

Sighing, Jeanine twisted and wrapped her arms around me. "This damn bond," she muttered aloud what I was positive everyone else was thinking.

"Leave her be," Arthur said, putting his hand around the back of my head. "She can't help it. It's reflexive. The bond between twin flames is like life itself. Be patient with her while he's gone." He tugged on my hair gently until I pulled up from Jeanine's shoulder to look at him. "What you're feeling is normal, Raven. I left my wife's books with Godfrey. Reading about your bond while you were apart last time helped Zeke. It might help you, too."

"Thank you," I whispered, squeezing his hand. "I'm sure I'll visit you often while he's away."

"You are always welcome, but you already knew that." He winked at me and waved before walking back toward the village, passing Alice and John along the way

Zeke and Luca came to take the trunk from their hands. It was the last piece of Seolia to load. When Zeke and Luca returned to the dock to say goodbye to Alice and John, I ran my tongue along the roof of my mouth to keep from crying while the boys exchanged goodbyes with their parents.

While Zeke was my heart, the boys were Alice's *entire* heart. She was tearful during her goodbyes, insisting that they write to us whenever possible. We didn't know much of the places beyond our realm, but the world was vast, and they would stumble upon villages from time to time. Our biggest fear was that the people might be unfriendly, since both boys were intimidating walls of muscle. Add in Zeke's rage, and you would be face-to-face with a threat.

John gave them several maps and explained as much as possible about other kingdoms. He had researched some after learning that Mira was working with another army, but no place bred "unbreakable" men that we knew, so they truly were going in blind.

Now, John was nothing more than a father concerned for his two boys. It was twice in a matter of weeks that John and Alice were telling their sons goodbye, each adventure more dangerous than the last.

And that had me seeing our loss in a new light.

Zeke and I were still newlywed and getting to know one another. It was enough of a stomach-clenching heartbreak not to be around him. As soon-to-be royals of two kingdoms, there would have been many times of having to separate from our child, and as I watched Alice and John, I knew we wouldn't have been prepared for that.

Did it make it less sorrowful? No.

But it eased some of the weight.

Alice dabbed her face with a handkerchief as John led her back down the dock and toward the castle. At least after decades apart, they had each other.

Jeanine and Zeke exchanged a hug before she looked at me. "I'll say goodbye to Luca on the ship, and then I'll walk with you back to the castle, okay?"

I nodded the best I could before hugging Luca goodbye. "Take care of him," I whispered in his ear, "and yourself."

He cradled my face in his hands and kissed my forehead. "I promise, Raven. Keep Jeanine out of trouble."

I forced a smile as he pressed his forehead against mine lightly before releasing me altogether and taking Jeanine's hand to pull her up the ramp.

Zeke immediately wrapped himself around me. "Tell me to stay, Raven," he said hoarsely, pressing his lips to the top of my head. "I'll do it, Raven, I swear."

"I know you will," I squeaked. "That's why I can't."

I did want to ask him to stay. I did want to beg him to focus on defeating Mira once and for all. I wanted to give him my forgiveness and promise him that there was nothing he could ever do to damage us, but then I thought of the devastated families in my village on the other side of the grassy hillside behind me, and didn't say any of that.

"I don't want to leave you." He tipped my chin up, kissing me repeatedly. "Fuck, Raven, I can't leave you for four weeks. I don't know what I was thinking. Anything could happen. Tell me to stay."

I bunched his shirt between my fingers, wishing I could. I wanted to beg him to forget everything and stay with me until our next lifetime. More than anything, I wanted to tell him to leave with me so we could live on an uninhabited island where the threat of another mate wouldn't exist. I wanted his mind back—I selfishly wanted his attention focused solely on me and no one else.

But we needed distance.

Gods, and that was what hurt most of all.

Taking his hands in mine, I put them between our chests and kissed my name across his knuckles. "You're doing this for us, Zeke. When the distance becomes too much, tell yourself that." I forced myself to look into his eyes. "Nothing will happen. I will be safe with Jeanine."

"*If* anything happens...."

"I'll go to Thoya," I finished for him. It was the plan we had come up with last night in-between arguments. If any threat arose, I had strict instruction to hop on a ship and sail to Thoya where Edmund would find a way to alert Zeke.

"Zeke!" Luca called from the ship.

Zeke flicked his eyes toward him before narrowing them.

"Zeke." There was a gentle warning in my voice. "Be nice to Luca, please. He's doing this as a favor to us."

"Yeah, yeah," he mumbled before resting his gaze back on me. "Four weeks, Raven, and you'll be back in my arms."

"Yes," I whispered. "Four weeks. But Zeke..." I held his gaze with determination. "When you return, I expect your thoughts to be consumed with only me again."

He stilled. "Raven, they are—"

"No more lies," I interrupted. "Say nothing else. I do not want our final moment together to be an argument. Just kiss me like that's all we'll ever do again."

He kissed me long and hard, cupping my head in his palm to keep me pressed tightly against him. Our comforting familiarity with one another was the only thing keeping me from crumbling in his arms. And when he pulled away, it was only for a few seconds before he was back, kissing me until my lips were raw and swollen.

I felt a hand on my shoulder, and his eyes closed, sighing deeply through his nose. "I have her, Zeke," Jeanine said softly. "Nothing will happen to her."

If it weren't for Luca and Jeanine, we would never leave this dock.

I would fight with him again if it kept him here.

He nodded before kissing my forehead. "I have to walk away from you now, little demon."

I couldn't speak. I fought the urge to reach for him while he transferred me from his arms to Jeanine's. She kept her arm around my waist, allowing me to lean entirely on her while he took one last look at me before ascending the ramp to his ship.

I blew out my cheeks and sniffled, putting an icy hand around my throat to soothe the burning. "I love you!" I called out with raspy emotion. If he couldn't believe anything else I said, I needed him to believe that. Through it all—the fights, the turmoil, the doubts—I loved him fiercely.

He paused and clenched his fists, warring with himself to board the ship. Inhaling a deep breath, he continued until he reached the deck. It wasn't until then that he gripped the railing and looked at me from aboard. Shadow appeared at his side, whipping his head in the way of goodbye.

"Take care of him!" I shouted to my horse, wiping tears from my eyes with the back of my hand.

It was an agreement between the three of them that I wouldn't watch him leave. But when Jeanine started tugging me to go, I shook my head wildly and planted my feet.

"Raven," Jeanine warned. "Don't make this harder for him."

Shifting into Blaze as a defense for my heart, I coughed out a mangled cry and turned away. It wasn't until I began walking away that I heard the groan of the ship as it pulled away from the dock.

I could stop them if I asked. All I had to do was ask, all I needed was to say the words, and he would stay here with me.

But when I was too far away to run back and beg him to stay, I heard him deep in my subconscious, in the corner of my mind where he had taken up permanent residence.

Baby, all I do is love you.

I WORRIED THAT WITHOUT ENOUGH OF MY BLOOD FOR THAT LONG, HE WOULD WEAKEN.

27

RAVEN

Arthur had left the books with Godfrey under the impression that I would read them at the castle, but I ended up right back at his bar the next night with the books sprawled out in front of me.

With the wounded cared for and the rest of the soldiers either guarding the castle or in their cottages, I had given into Jeanine's request to grab some drinks at Arthur's and detox from the unimaginably difficult few days I'd had since returning home.

I honored her request, but only if we could find Grace and invite her along. Jeanine and I could very easily pass out from drinking

265

between the two of us, and Grace would, at the very least, find Godfrey to get us home.

Jeanine hovered on my right, shoving drinks down my throat whenever I whined or came close to it. I would be drunk often these next four weeks, if she had any say.

Even now, the words blurred together as I tried to read, but Arthur said these books helped Zeke. It wouldn't hurt for me to read up on bonds between pairings, if you could have a separate twin flame *and* mate, and how I was both of Zeke's.

Grace hadn't found anything on River. Since our history books on magic had been destroyed, it didn't leave us with much hope that we would ever learn anything about the elemental water twin that had hidden in a neighboring kingdom for all of his life until deciding it was time to come out and torture his sister, who could barely hold it together to begin with.

But I digressed.

Everything in Arthur's book contained most of what Zeke had already told me about twin flames. Multiple passages—not just a couple—highlighted that once flames paired, separating them would bring discomfort. It didn't exactly make me look forward to the next month.

Jeanine pressed the glass against my lips, tipping it back to pour the cool, amber liquid on my tongue before I had a chance to decline.

"Jeanine," I said upon swallowing. "No matter how drunk you get me, I am not fucking you."

She snorted. "I wouldn't need to get you drunk to fuck me, Raven." The confidence in her voice told me that was too true. "This is purely for numbing the pain until I'm convinced you won't set something on fire or create another tornado in the middle of the channel."

I wanted to insist that I would never do that, but I had already proved that theory wrong on more than one occasion.

"You're allowed to wallow for a couple of days, and then we'll discuss strategy with Godfrey." She took a draw from her own glass.

"Strategy," I said with some difficulty. "My only strategy is killing Mira once and for all, though I'm wondering if Zeke doesn't want me to since we refuse to rule kingdoms that would separate us."

"You're apart now," Grace slurred.

I glanced over at her, convinced this was the first time she'd ever drank anything stronger than milk. Arthur slowly slid Grace's glass away from her and to the counter behind him. She didn't seem to notice.

"Right," I said with an amused grin. "We are, but I'm discussing a more permanent separation."

Jeanine snickered at Grace, bobbing her head in either agreement or disagreement; there was no way to tell. "Mira must die, whether Zeke wants her to or not. We'll decide on the rest later."

"I think opening the Under the Stars shoppe is an excellent disguise," I said, nearly toppling backward off of the stool as I finished my drink. "Mira will believe we are planning to attend a ball."

When Jeanine asked for another drink, Arthur shook his head and removed our glasses from our hands. "I don't believe there is a person on this island that Zeke did not give strict instructions to about the wellbeing of our queen."

I rolled my eyes. "He drabs on about me being the queen, yet he is the one everyone obeys. It hardly seems fair."

"Welcome to the last three years of my life," Jeanine muttered. "Ever since he became unbearable to be around with his brooding and demands, no one has ever bucked against what he wanted."

"Until Raven," Grace mumbled, her eyes closed. "My mother has to make sure you remain fed."

"Gods!" I shouted, hopping down from the stool. "I am a grown woman. It wasn't like I was a homeless kitten when he found me. I do know how to take care of myself."

Arthur tapped my wrist and motioned with his chin toward Grace. I twisted in my chair to see her passed out against the bar, cheek squished against the counter. The freckles that were splattered across her nose and cheeks made her look much younger than nineteen.

"We've corrupted her," Jeanine said with a sigh.

I giggled, moving the fluff of Grace's bright red hair off her face so she wouldn't choke on it while trying to breathe. "We should get her home."

I realized I wasn't entirely sure where she lived. I had met her in the bakery and had only spoken to her mother there, too. I looked at Arthur, and without needing to ask, he dragged his fingers down his chin in a contemplative manner. "I'm not sure which cottage it is, but it's behind the gardens. I've passed her mother a time or two over there."

"We'll find it," Jeanine said, hopping off the stool. She grabbed Grace's arm and hauled her up until she was sitting, wrapping it around her shoulders. "I've been craving some strawberries anyway."

Appreciating the numbness from the alcohol that was drowning the pain of Zeke's absence, I took Grace's other arm and slung it around my shoulders while maneuvering her off the stool. She whimpered in protest, which caused us to erupt into a fit of giggles. "Grace, darling, you can't sleep at Duck's. Your mother most likely already detests me for how long you stay in the libraries every night."

"Nu-uh," Grace mumbled, at least putting one foot in front of the other as we guided her out of the bar.

Jeanine could barely contain her laughter, which only aided in adding to mine.

Even Grace was beginning to giggle as we bypassed the main road through the village to walk between the rows of shops and cottages.

We passed by the fruits and vegetable gardens, and when Jeanine leaned over to pluck a few strawberries for herself, Grace stumbled, and we all landed in a heap on the ground.

"Do you see what happens when you're impatient?" I snapped at Jeanine, wiping the dirt from my hands on her shirt.

"I was hungry!" she chided back, swatting my hands away.

"He can see the same sky, you know."

We twisted to look at Grace as she stared up at the sky from her back. She didn't look at me, but I knew who she was talking about, and even the alcohol didn't help at the mention of him.

However, Grace tugged on my arm to get me to lay beside her and pointed toward the sky. I followed her finger to the mass of stars above us, twinkling and staring back.

Her voice was a little steadier when she said, "Twin flames and stars go hand-in-hand. It's an ancient science…."

I was highly impressed by how sober she sounded.

"The stars decide how compatible you are," she continued, lowering her hand to rest on her stomach. She hadn't been pointing to any star in particular, but I found myself staring at two that seemed so close they nearly touched.

Grace, laughing at the irony while she grabbed my hand with her other, said, "It's typically decided by earth's elements."

I grinned, my smile broadening when Jeanine lay beside me and rested her head on my shoulder. "Why do we need books when we have her?" she asked.

"But the gods used the elements when deciding compatibility," Grace said softly, "along with the sun and the moon. Each journey of a twin flame pairing is detailed among the stars."

If this were coming from anyone else, I would chalk it up to drunken rambles, but aside from Zeke, Grace was the most intelligent person I knew. And I believed she wasn't only telling me this to console me in his absence.

"He said we fell in love under the stars...."

"Under the stars, because of the stars, your story with him is written *in* the stars, Raven." Grace waved a hand across the sky. Stars seemed to follow in her wake. "Each piece of your journey was carefully crafted by the goddess of love." She turned her head against the ground to look at me, her hand squeezing mine. "That is not a privilege given to anyone else, even your mate."

≈

AFTER NEARLY FALLING asleep on the ground, we had eventually gotten Grace to her cottage. Lara had enticed us to come in by promising hot cocoa, and there we remained, bundled up on the floor under mountains of blankets.

The crackling of the dying fire in the hearth beside me had me peeling my eyes open, forgetting where I was for a few seconds and trying to find my husband's scent.

I dropped my head back to the floor harder than necessary when I realized he wasn't there. But a very sweaty and sticky Jeanine was clinging to me, her breathing steady and smelling of rum and cocoa.

Grace was on my other side, sprawled in an awkward and undoubtedly uncomfortable position, her hair matching the colors of the dying flames.

As much as I would have loved to fall asleep and stay like that for the next month, I needed to check in with Godfrey.

A gangly teenage boy peeked over our makeshift loft and found my eyes. He had hair like Grace's and nearly identical freckles, but he was at the stage where his boyish features were falling away and growing into a man.

He looked bewildered as he stared at me. "Queen Raven, your hair is red."

Prying my hand from Jeanine's sweaty grasp, I touched my hair. It ended at my jaw, and I sighed. I was shifting into Blaze even when I didn't realize it.

No wonder it was so fucking hot in here.

I worried shifting into myself might frighten him, so I remained as Blaze. "It is," I whispered. "Who are you?"

"Franklin," he answered, "Grace's brother."

I had to stop meeting subjects like this. I was the queen of a kingdom, not the resident drunkard of the village.

"Hello, Franklin." I maneuvered my way out of Jeanine's tight hold and scooted backward until I was free from the blankets. My head pounded from either sleeping on the floor or drinking too much rum, and considering the only release I ever found from a hangover was from my husband's tongue, I was on my own.

For the life of me, I couldn't remember how I used to function before him. One of the only negative side effects of being bonded to someone else, I guessed.

I could only hope he was faring better.

"My mom baked biscuits," Franklin said, hooking a thumb toward the kitchen.

By the sunlight streaming in through the singular window in the next room, I assumed it was mid-morning. I was sure John was worried about why Jeanine and I didn't return home last night, and I wouldn't be surprised if our soldiers were scouring the village in fear of Zeke's wrath.

Being in a baker's home had its charm. The cottage smelled like cinnamon and peppermint, and remnants of flour were speckled across the floorboards.

Palming my eyes, I drew deep breaths through my nose and released them through my mouth to cease the throbbing in my head. As tempting as drinking away the next four weeks was, I couldn't survive like this.

Franklin continued to stare at me. I dropped a hand to squint an eye at him. "Shouldn't you be at tutoring?" Spring months would be ending soon, which meant that children would be given a break for a few weeks, but not yet. And him being here mid-morning meant that he was missing some of his.

He winced as if not wanting to answer, which made me raise an eyebrow. "What?"

"My mom wanted me to stay and ensure you didn't..."

"Light anything on fire," I finished for him with a sigh. News had apparently spread that I was having trouble controlling my elements, and now I couldn't even be trusted in a cottage. "I won't," I assured him. "You should go."

He rocked awkwardly on his heels as he continued to look at me. "Can I... can I see?"

Flicking my eyes up toward the low-bearing ceiling, I contemplated that. Could I light my fingertips anymore without it spreading across my hands and wrists? If I thought about Zeke and how much I missed him, I might set this entire place on fire.

But Franklin looked genuinely curious, and I wanted to give him something to brag about in front of his equally gangly friends, so I nodded and raised my hand.

Focusing on keeping my emotions in check, I lit the tips of my fingers upon release. He gasped in awe and intrigue, coming close enough to wave his hand over the flames. They swayed with the movement of his hand, growing brighter from someone new being so close.

The tips of my fingers grew a coat of flaky snow and suffocated the flames until they looked like nothing more than glass. And I hadn't even shifted into Frost.

Franklin looked downright dumbfounded.

"I upheld my end of the bargain." I nodded toward the wooden front door of the cottage. "Go learn something."

He made a sound between a huff and a curse as he straightened and grabbed a canvas satchel from a wooden chair in the corner, slinging it over his chest.

Once he left out the front door, I stretched my arms over my head and rolled my neck. Cracks and pops shot up my spine, warning me to stop sleeping on hard floors. My body had grown so used to sleeping only on Zeke that even the idea of a bed sounded uncomfortable.

I trudged toward the kitchen, where sunlight streamed in from a small window. The biscuits Lara had made were cold but doughy and soft. I withheld from using my heat to warm them because, like Lara, I also worried that I could quickly become unmanageable.

I needed to hold an audience or gather the village around the bridge to assure them that I had no plans to set the island ablaze, turn it into a frozen tundra, or break it apart.

I promised Zeke he would have a home to return to.

It wasn't long until Grace entered the kitchen, much like I had. Her hair was frizzier than usual, and one side of her face had the indention of the floor carved into it.

I couldn't help but smile at her. She only had one glass of rum, and I doubted she would ever drink again.

Holding a biscuit out to her, I took a bite when she refused with a wave of her hand. Instead, she plopped onto the wooden stool beside mine and planted her face on the counter. "Head hurts," she grumbled.

I rubbed her back. "It will for a few hours."

"No remedy?"

"Water and reminders that there are consequences when drinking the devil's juice."

Grace snorted, holding her forehead as she sat up. "My mother would kick you out for talking about the devil in her home."

"Religious?"

Grace nodded, perching an elbow on the countertop and leaning against it. "She believes in gods and the underworld and..." She waved a hand dismissively in the air as if to say *all of that*. "I've read so many books that I'm not sure there is only one thing to believe in. Gods and the underworld, sure, but also karma and creatures beyond."

This conversation was too intense so early in the... mid-after-noon?... but the latter half piqued my interest. Damiana had mentioned other creatures before, too, though I paid it little mind. "What kind of other creatures?"

"All sorts," Grace said through a yawn. "Some with wings, some with pointed ears and magic even you could only dream about. Our world has been home to many of them, though I am not sure they exist anymore."

"Demon spirits?"

Grace nodded, her eyes blinking heavily as if she might fall asleep right where she sat. "Spirits of death is the better term for it," she said as if it were political. "Spirits of life, stars...."

"What happened to all of these creatures?"

A shrug of her shoulder had her nearly slipping off the counter, but she caught herself. "No one really knows. They just... disappeared."

Plaguing her with questions was my plan until Jeanine stumbled into the kitchen, eyes wild as she reconciled where we were. "Out of all of us, you're the alcoholic," I lamented, laughing at her. "You shouldn't be so... disheveled."

Her hair was a tangled mess that stuck up in all directions, and she had the faintest pink lipstick smeared across her face, which was painted red from the heat and being buried against me all night.

She flipped me off and took the biscuit from my hand, taking a bite and climbing into my lap. The stool wobbled underneath us, but I grabbed the counter quickly to keep it from falling. "Is it your main objective to remain stuck to me like this the entire time he's gone?"

Her mouth was full of biscuit as she answered, "You are less likely to get into trouble if I'm close."

I highly doubted that, but I didn't argue with her. Knowing Zeke, he gave her strict instructions on how to handle me during his absence, and since I craved touch from those I loved and trusted, he knew I would need it from her.

"I need to return to the castle and bathe," I said, tugging at

Jeanine's hair. "I would like to do that alone if that's all right with you."

She sighed dramatically. "I suppose." But then she twisted enough to look me up and down. "You can't leave the cottage like this. You still have an image to uphold."

I glanced down at my dirt-and-dust-covered clothing, running a hand through my bob. I was about to say that Zeke never told me what to wear, but then I clamped my mouth shut because that would be a lie. "Fine," I sighed. "Gracey..."

She pointed a finger toward a dark hallway. "In there."

I RETURNED to the castle in a dress much more youthful than I was used to. It was a bright yellow color, not one I usually would've chosen for myself. Jeanine had braided my hair after I shifted back into myself, but when I asked why she didn't have to change, she replied with a snarky remark about being nothing more than a lowly adviser to the shifter queen.

I called her out on her nonsense and she responded with a smack to my ass before we went our separate ways to bathe.

I stood at the entrance of my chambers, talking myself into entering. Was I hoping that Zeke would be in here waiting for me? Absolutely. Had I lost the childish nature that still believed in dreams? Absolutely twice.

Pushing open the door to my silent chambers, I groaned. Our scent was everywhere. It *lived* in here. If anyone but us ever took residence in these chambers, they would have to demolish the entire castle to rid it of our unmistakable combination of pear and pine.

I dragged my feet into our bedchambers to grab a dress to wear after my bath but stopped short.

Sitting on my table was a bouquet of red roses in an intricate clay vase. I placed my hand over my heart to prevent it from bursting out of my chest. I hadn't thought of anything nearly this romantic for him, instead supplying him with weird herbal tonics and blood.

Perched on the table and sitting against the vase was a hand-written note from my love. I had to prepare myself and blink away my tears before I read it aloud to myself, "Keaton was unsure where to find roses for every day I would be gone, so don't be surprised if these are far and few between, but consider each rose an apology."

I smiled as I touched a delicate petal of one of the twelve roses before walking to the bed and falling onto it while I held his note up in the air to continue reading, "If you're reading this, it means it's day two of my departure, and I can guarantee you that I am dying inside."

"Me too," I said to him, wishing I could hear his voice.

"In case you've forgotten," the note continued, "I love you more with each breath, Raven. If I could, I would hold you every day for the rest of time, but even then, it wouldn't be enough." I flipped over to my stomach and balanced the note on his pillow. "I yearn for your forgiveness, Raven. Your gorgeous green eyes will be in my dreams each night we are apart. Hold me close, my love."

His name was signed in cursive that only a prince would be taught — delicate curves, but bold like him. I felt like a giddy young woman in love as I held the note to my chest, tears running down my cheeks.

And then I read it over and over.

Each time sweeter than the last.

"EACH PIECE OF YOUR JOURNEY WAS CAREFULLY CRAFTED BY THE GODDESS OF LOVE."

28

RAVEN

I walked on air as I went to Jeanine's door. I hated corsets more than anything else, but I wore one only to have a safe place for his note, since I planned to reread it multiple times throughout the day. I had contemplated carrying the roses around but didn't want to explain each time I was asked about them.

No one needed another reason for me to bore them with stories of how wonderful I found Zeke to be when he *wasn't* irritating me.

Before I could knock on the door, Jeanine swung it open and lifted an eyebrow at the smile on my face. "That wasn't an expression I planned to see for a while," she said.

Jeanine was such an oxymoron in herself. She had bathed and

was wearing the colors of the Seolia. Her tunic was light blue, which only accentuated the dark blue of her irises, and her pants were made of shiny gold fabric—loose, but close enough to reveal her solid yet slender frame. She looked dainty and pristine but could kill you with her finger. And I could understand why both women and men were threatened by her.

I remained envious of her beauty, even with her being my best friend.

I grabbed her arm and pulled her out the door, sliding my arm through hers. "I was greeted by a dozen roses and a handwritten note from Zeke. I'll be smiling for a while."

"Look at that bastard being all romantic. He's come a very long way since meeting you. There were talks in Reales of him never settling down." She nudged her shoulder with mine. "It's nice seeing both of you so happy."

I couldn't help but laugh. "Please. You're so fucking sick of us. I think everyone is."

She laughed along with me, slightly nodding in agreement. "That doesn't mean we're not overjoyed for the two of you. Plus, it's not your fault you're so disgusting."

I shrugged a shoulder as we strolled down the hall toward the throne room. "I don't know. I mean, the bond... *enhances* our feelings, but even without it, I would still be just as crazy about him. I was before the bond snapped in place for me."

"Do you wish it didn't?"

I glanced over at her, unsure of what she meant by her question. She met my gaze, sighing before she elaborated, "I mean... that intense tie to someone. Do you wish it wasn't *so* intense? It seems as if the two of you can't breathe without the other. I'm not sure if I would like that."

I mulled over her words carefully before I answered, "Before him, the idea of it may have seemed suffocating. And yes, it does over-whelm me sometimes. And I can't lie to you and say that recent events haven't made me question everything." I played with the end of my braid against my chest. "I've always been about the freedom to make your own choices in life, and I take solace in the fact that I chose him before I knew about the bond or what it entails."

She listened intently, perhaps wondering if finding a mate would result in the exact expectations we had of one another.

"At the end of each day, I ask myself to imagine life without him, especially on the hard days. Before the bond solidified, we decided to be partners, both in life and everything in between," I continued. "And while that has been strained lately, I wouldn't change anything about us or the intensity of our love. Zeke might have needed saving from himself, but he's also saved me in more ways than I could ever verbalize, though I am sorry our scent is so strong."

She smiled at that, nudging me in the ribs with her elbow. "I've become used to it. I'm envious of your love but also frightened by it. If pairings truly return to the realm, I wonder what it'll be like if I ever find mine."

"Wonderful," I assured her. "I promise you'll wish you had never lived without them."

WALKING to the throne room in the morning was a habit, but then I was reminded that I had no throne. John wasn't sure what I wanted to do about the melted pool of gold on the dais, but it certainly wasn't leaving it there as a reminder of my meltdown.

We agreed to order a new one, and when he asked me if I wanted two thrones, I wasn't sure how to answer. If I remained Queen of Seolia, I would like a second throne for Zeke. But I was still leaning toward following him to Reales so he could become king.

Instead of answering, we agreed to shut the throne room down until a decision had been made. I wasn't sure when Zeke informed John that I wasn't sure what I wanted to do regarding Seolia, but he didn't push for a decision, nor did he pry on whether or not I had thought about it.

Because truthfully, I hadn't.

Jeanine had talked me into visiting the village instead of returning to my chambers to reread Zeke's note until eventually passing out and sleeping another day away. We needed to maintain the trust of our people, especially after losing so many. Black ribbons had been placed on every door in honor of lives lost, and I stopped to speak with each family who wouldn't have a loved one returning to them.

I listened to their stories, cried with them, and reminded them of how grateful I was for their sacrifice in keeping our kingdom protected. And when the hard questions were asked, like how we would prevent something like this from happening again, Jeanine stepped in and detailed the precautions we were taking, the daily training our soldiers would maintain to strengthen our army, and the backing of Thoya and Perosan's armies should anything go awry.

Support in providing meals for the grieving families in the weeks to come would be brought to them daily, and they had the freedom to ask for anything they could possibly need while they healed from their losses.

Their doubt in me was evident on their faces. Their fear *of* me was apparent in how hesitant they were to get close to me, tentatively grabbing my hands if I reached out to comfort them. It was in those moments that I realized Zeke was right—I had become nothing more than the horror stories of what magic was capable of.

I wished I could provide more to calm their fears. Our island was primarily self-sufficient, but there was only so much I could offer while awaiting shipments of goods from Thoya and Perosan. And with each ship that entered being strenuously checked, it slowed the process down. I couldn't help but wonder if this was our future—always fearing the unknown—or if it would end with Mira.

Eva's smile was one thing I could always count on through the grief.

Grunting as she lunged for me, I caught her with all the grace of a newborn fawn, nearly losing my footing. She had grown at least a foot since I'd last seen her, barely more than a month ago. "Eva!" I scolded playfully, pinching her ribs. "You are not supposed to grow."

She wore one of the bright dresses I had brought back from Reales, which made the yellow of her hair nearly blend in with the high sun. "That's what my pop keeps saying." She tilted back, her arms stretching wide in an overly dramatic shrug. "I cannot help it!"

Jeanine caught her head as her weight had me leaning forward from her sudden theatrics. Eva broke into a fit of giggles as she pulled back up, throwing her arms around my neck. "Where is Mr. Caterpillar?"

I smiled but then rolled my eyes, spinning us around quickly toward the harbor and pointing. "Out there somewhere. He is on a great adventure with his brother."

She gasped in her tiny, darling way. "I hope he finds mermaids!"

I mirrored her gasp while shaking my head. "He better not. He would be in huge trouble."

"They're just fish!" she shouted at me.

"Just fish!" I repeated. "Just fish, she says! They are fish with glimmering tails and long, beautiful hair. They lure sailors in with their songs and drag them underwater until they can no longer breathe."

"They wouldn't do that to Mr. Caterpillar." She sighed dreamily, tucking her hands under her chin and looking longingly toward the sea. "He's too handsome."

Jeanine laughed loudly while my jaw dropped, and I began tickling Eva again until she gasped for air. "Are you going to steal Mr. Caterpillar's heart away from me?"

Her cheeks bloomed red, but the rotten, darling girl nodded at me. "I love him, I love him!"

I clicked my tongue. "You might be the one girl I'd *consider* sharing him with, but don't tell anyone."

She darted her eyes around slyly before whispering, "I promise." And then she wiggled free from my grasp, running toward a group of girls her age that danced in the middle of the cobblestone road.

Jeanine hooked her arm through mine as we watched them spin and giggle together, her head leaning against my shoulder. "To be that free again."

Frowning deeply as I watched mothers notice me and pull their children off the street to follow them home, I lowered my eyes. "Mm," I hummed. "To be that free."

∽

WE PLANNED to finally open the Under the Stars shoppe the following day. All part of the *Returning Raven to Normalcy* plan my family had cooked up, according to Jeanine. "Not that I had anything to do with it," she had said.

"You're a fucking liar," I had responded.

Contrary to what I had feared, no one in the village asked a single thing about me nearly burning Mira alive — either out of fear, or they had been instructed not to by someone. I felt it was the perky blonde hanging off of me as she dragged me to the shoppe. She had grown quite used to the power given to her as an adviser and was obviously using it to her advantage to keep me calm.

But that didn't stop the looks. The whispers. The sidelong glances when we walk pass by shoppes and cottages, everyone waiting for their queen to set fire to something.

I had woken up to another bouquet of roses, courtesy of my husband. Another handwritten note had been laid beside it, but I did not read it aloud. Instead, I blushed an obscene amount while he detailed exactly what he'd rather be doing to me.

Even in a drawn out fight, he still knew how to make me weak.

And then I fretted at the idea of Keaton reading each note Zeke had left for me, though the thought only thrilled me more. My depraved deviant had made me as twisted as he was regarding our desires for each other.

Jeanine had tried taking the note from me multiple times to be annoying, and finally, I started reading it aloud to her with my lips twisted in a foul grin. She listened to the first line and scowled in disgust, and said, "Ew, gods, okay. Either I remove my ears or your tongue, but one has to go because I will not listen to that." That didn't stop her from stealing my roses, though. Two of them were currently looped through her thick braid.

Zeke had been gone for three days, which most likely meant he was still sailing, and I had a feeling they were quickly making their way through the alcohol Arthur had gifted them. I only hoped he hadn't done the same with my blood vials.

It wasn't a fluke that Jeanine had practically slept on me at Grace's cottage. That girl was fond of cuddling. I had woken up many times last night, sticky from her curled up beside me as if we were spoons. I wasn't sure if it was more comforting for her or me to sleep in the same bed in place of the boys' absence.

"Do you miss Luca?" I asked aloud as she practically dragged me toward the shoppe.

She laughed and then sighed at my question. "Not in the way you're hoping, Raven. I know it's difficult for you to understand, but we're not in a relationship."

I gasped, utterly offended. "It is not *difficult*. I was merely curious."

"Mhm," she hummed. "I know you're hoping we'll fall madly in love, but I can guarantee it won't happen."

I pouted. "But we could be sisters if you two marry."

She pulled me to a stop and whipped me around to face her, shaking my shoulders until I smiled. "We are sisters, Raven. You are my best friend, and I love you. Marrying Luca wouldn't change a damn thing between you and me."

"Mean it?"

"Swear it."

My smile broadened as I linked my arm through hers again. "Fine, I'll stop asking. But as your sister, friend, *and* queen, you'll have to get my permission for whoever you marry, and I will not give you away to just anyone."

"Oh, you're my queen now?"

I pinched her arm so hard that she yelped, flicking my nose in return. "Would you come back with us to Reales?" I asked.

"Of course I would, Raven. As would John, Alice, and Luca." She nudged my shoulder with hers. "Which is why I need you to think long and hard about this decision."

I hadn't considered that, either. If I abdicated my throne in Seolia, our family would follow us. Seolia would be left without the leaders it had come to know so well and thrust into the hands of someone different.

"Reales needs Zeke," I said quietly, frowning. "It would benefit from his knowledge of its history. And he is much better suited to be a leader than me."

Jeanine nodded while I spoke. "Just because you lead differently does not make you any less a leader than him, Raven. You are compassionate and lead with heart. Zeke is..." She laughed lightly. "Zeke leads with his mind. What he lacks in compassion, he makes up for in agility. He adapts. However, that does not mean your leadership skills are any less imperative, Raven. You two are a perfect balance. Both kingdoms need you."

"We won't be apart, Jeanine. And while that might be selfish, we have already sacrificed so much. Neither of us asked for titles, yet we were both handed kingdoms. It is past time that one of us gets what we want."

Before anything else could be said, we both stopped and dropped our jaws. A line weaved around the shoppe, full of women, girls, men, and boys, all waiting for the doors to open. And once they spotted us, girls squealed and women looked ready to pounce. Some men looked positively stressed at the coins about to be spent, but this was already beginning as a very successful launch.

John peeked out from the small window inside the shoppe, beckoning us forward with a wave of his hand. Once inside, we found Alice pacing across the shoppe.

"I did not expect such a turnout," I said, looking around. Dresses lined the walls in every shape, size, and color one could imagine, and it still didn't seem as if it would be enough for the line outside.

"With the announcement of the upcoming faux-ball, it seems every person in the village wants something unique," John said, anxiously watching Alice pace. "She is worried she did not prepare enough."

Jeanine was already looking through the dresses, pulling a black and gray one from the wall. She shrugged her shoulders as I rolled my eyes. "What? I want to get one for myself before they're gone."

"Jeanine, there isn't going to be an actual ball. Alice, it's going to be fine," I assured her. "If you run out, only take on what you can manage. People will understand."

"You weren't in Reales," Jeanine said with a snort. "Girls used to show up at their manor begging for a dress. You can imagine how Zeke felt answering the door to an onslaught of gawking girls. Luca didn't mind."

That didn't surprise me. Once I found out that Alice's partner was the one who made the red dress for my birthday ball, I was positive I would've been one of the girls at her doorstep, pleading for her to make me something.

I winced, squeezing an eye shut while I tried to think of something else soothing to say. "Once the women find out there won't be a ball, the pressure on Alice will lax."

"But there will be one," Alice said.

"Alice!" John scolded.

I looked between them. "What are you talking about?"

John sighed. Jeanine looked everywhere but at me. But it was Alice who clapped her hands together before grabbing mine. "He wanted it to be a surprise, but with the tension between the two of you lately, I feel you should know." She pulled me to the back room and tore away an ivory cloth from a wooden dress form. "Before you go to Reales, we will have a ball for the kingdom."

And when I saw the dress, I gasped.

So navy it was almost black, the dress *glittered* like stars in the night sky. The skirt was made of layers of tulle in different shades of dark blue with silver glitter everywhere. The sleeveless bodice was made of gauzy blue fabric that changed from dark to light, leading from waist to shoulder with crisscrossed straps that never touched the same shade of blue. Intricate patterns of constellations woven in glitter spiraled up the waist.

It was downright sinful, and I had no doubt that once Zeke saw me in it, he wouldn't bother with dancing.

Upon closer look, I saw a small, star-shaped broach pinned to one of the gauzy straps and nearly swooned.

"He wanted it to be special," Alice said beside me. "His suit will match. He said the dress should represent all that the two of you are."

"How did he plan all of this before leaving?" I couldn't tear my eyes away from the dress. "The roses, the notes, this. He planned all of it in a day's time."

She touched my shoulder. "Never underestimate a man in love, especially him."

That had many meanings behind it.

"He honestly did have dinner with Luca and Jeanine that night, Raven, but then he did all of this. Luca helped, as did Jeanine. We all see the magic between you two, even if you can't right now."

I never felt his absence too heavily. He lingered everywhere from here, to our chambers, to Duck's. He was always so adamant that he was the blessed one for being mated to me, but if anyone should be grateful, it was me.

"No one else will ever love me like this," I whispered, touching the bodice of my dress. "How could he ever worry, Alice?" I sniffled, fingering the small broach. "No answer he finds will ever change how we feel for one another."

"He is a man possessed, darling." She stroked my hair, brushing her fingers through it. "He will not rest until you are his in the end."

"I will always be his. That is the most maddening thing of all." I turned to face her, wiping away tears with my wrist. "Not being away from him, not the ache living in my chest, but the simple fact that it is not something he will ever accept. The only possession that should plague him is me."

I grabbed her hand and held it between mine. Her eyes shined like the glitter of my dress. "Tell me you understand, Alice. I need someone to understand me. I just need someone to tell me that they understand I could never care for another—that I could live my life every day, never wondering about my... mate."

It was the first time I had claimed him like that.

And the word tasted so sour.

Him. The stranger who lurked somewhere beyond, who believed he had a claim on me that Zeke had already staked.

And that was when it hit me. At this moment, the depth and truth of it all rained upon me. There was someone else in this universe that was fated to me. Another man wanted my heart, my soul, my body.

Another being had a bond with me that I would feel if we ever met—a tug in the deep trenches of my soul that should only be given to one man. "I do not want this," I repeated over and over. "I do not want this, Alice. I did not ask for this." I stammered and stuttered, each word heavier than the last. "I will not love another. I *cannot* love another."

She held me as I cried, her arms squeezing tightly around me as I sobbed and repeated the exact words to her so many times that they sounded foreign. And she cried with me.

She mourned for her son, for the heartbreak we both knew he was experiencing as he grappled the idea and fear of my bond with another man. And that was when I understood why—why he had been going mad and desperate in his decisions and felt the need to leave me.

She held me as I cried from the losses we kept experiencing. I explained to her that I believed our child was a boy; even though I realized it too late, I felt the magic our love had created in our manor. And that it was a boy—a boy who would've stolen my heart just as his father had.

And when I promised her that I would one day provide a grandchild for her, she took my face between her hands and said through her grief and sorrow, "You have given me a daughter, Raven. You have given my son happiness. You have given a mother everything she could ever want."

"But I'm a mother, too," I whispered, crestfallen and crushed that I did not have the evidence of the soul that once grew inside me. "And I do not know how to wash away this pain. He won't let me help or lift a finger, and I cannot fix this, Alice. I cannot fix any of this."

She wiped my tears away with her thumbs. "My dear girl." Her forehead pressed against mine. "No one would ever ask that you do."

"JUST FISH, SHE SAYS! THEY ARE FISH WITH GLIMMERING TAILS AND LONG, BEAUTIFUL HAIR."

T he opening was a success.

We let groups of five in at a time, limiting each person to only one item of clothing. And we sold out before the line even ended. Alice took more custom orders than she could handle, but I couldn't scold her for that. I would've done the same. And I got to listen as some of the older women talked about how their friends in Reales would always brag about the dresses they had, and now we had the very seamstress who made them. I could only imagine their disappointment if our family returned to Reales.

Now, I sat at the dining table with Jeanine, John, and Godfrey while Thomas and Abraham stood in each doorway, pretending to mind their own business. "This is absurd," I grumbled. "I don't need to be watched like this. Zeke said so himself that our island was safe now. I have my own weapons."

John chuckled. "Godfrey is following his orders."

"Tell them to leave," I ordered, "no offense."

"None taken," Abraham responded, but then winced as Godfrey scolded him for speaking out of turn.

Godfrey looked hesitant until I curled my fingers over my fist, created a ball of fire, and threw it into the fireplace. The wood flickered to life, crackling from the sudden burst of heat. It was only then that Godfrey excused Thomas and Abraham to resume their duty outside the courtyard gates.

"I am your queen," I reminded him. "Zeke is not royalty in our kingdom. You do not have to listen to him every time."

Godfrey gave me an apologetic grin. "It is not only because of him that I am cautious, Raven. It is my lapse that allowed Cade into the kingdom that evening. I do not want harm to befall you because of me again."

My perspective changed after that. I could hear the guilt in his voice, though I didn't blame him in the slightest for the choices Cade made. But Godfrey was not the type of man who needed validation, so I simply responded with, "I understand," and dropped it. "Tell me what plans you have."

Spread across the middle of the table was a map of our realm. It had been hanging in Leonidas's office until I moved into his chambers, when John moved it into his. "Admittedly, we did not have too much time to speak of it," John said. "But Zeke is most knowledgeable about the layout of Reales and believes we should not dock in the main harbor."

Godfrey pointed to the cliffs. "He believes we should sail behind the cliffs and station at the shores. Edmund and Elric will travel to Reales with their armies by horseback. It will take Edmund the longest to get there, so he will leave two days sooner than Elric's army."

"If all goes according to plan, the three kingdoms will arrive the same day."

I bobbed my head as I listened, studying the map. Our island seemed so small compared to the other kingdoms that spanned miles. "And what are we to do? Are we to pretend we are arriving there for a ball?"

"No," Jeanine answered. "We arrive at Reales in the middle of the night to eliminate as many soldiers as possible before we begin battle the next morning."

I leaned back against the chair, twiddling the end of my braid in my fingers. "How many men do we have?"

John sighed deeply and rubbed his chin. "We have just over one-hundred men left. Thoya and Perosan might have eight hundred combined. I am unaware of the size of Melik's army."

I chewed on my bottom lip. "Under a thousand?"

"Maybe more, depending on Zeke's success in Nova. If Melik does not agree to help us, then yes," John confirmed.

With Zeke's charm, I did not doubt he would be successful. "With the soldiers left over in Reales, Mira has two-hundred and fifty. I do not know how many men River brought with him or if they intended to fight. If they do not, it will be a quick battle."

Jeanine ran a hand through her hair. "But if they do intend to fight...."

"Then we could be faced with a war," Godfrey finished. "In the end, it is not the numbers that matter. It is the determination of both sides."

"But why would they fight for her?" I asked.

"It depends on what she promised them," Jeanine said. "Mira bargains for what she wants. If our realm has something they need or want, she will use that to her advantage."

I looked at John, and the second he recognized the look on my face, he shook his head. "Do not even think about it, Raven."

"John, I could learn of her army. I could go under the pretense of wanting a truce. I could... I don't know, lie about an alliance for a split leadership."

"She'll know," Jeanine interrupted. "Mira will know you are lying. She knows you stand for peace, Raven. It would be a wasted trip and a great risk to you."

"She won't harm me," I said. "I am too valuable to her. She enjoys the idea of my elements too much. And knowing what we're up against would help us."

"She's right," Godfrey agreed. "Otherwise, we'll be walking into Reales unaware of who will be waiting for us."

"No," John and Jeanine said in unison.

I slumped. "I would turn right back around and come home. I wouldn't spend more than a day there. I'll take Jeanine with me. Godfrey needs to stay here to protect the island."

"Zeke..." John started to say.

"Zeke isn't here," I said before he could finish. "And I cannot sit idly by while Zeke performs *useful* tasks. Twiddling my thumbs and promising our people that nothing like this will ever happen again is untruthful. Something will happen if I continue to do nothing."

Jeanine, the more logical thinker between her and my husband, listened intently. While a trip to Reales might come at a risk, that was the consequence of war, as Zeke continued to remind me. War is dirty, he had said, and I liked to fight filthy.

"I will be back before Zeke returns," I continued. "Will he be angry? Yes. But he will understand. Eventually." I forced a carefree smile.

"I would like to go on record saying that I advised you against this," John grumbled with a sigh.

I looked at Godfrey. "If anything happens while I'm away, Edmund will take in our people. Send everyone to Thoya and he will not stop you." Tapping my fingers on the tabletop, I eyed the map. "Why hasn't she already attacked?"

"Conquering one kingdom at a time is too risky," Godfrey explained. "If she attacked and won Seolia, Thoya and Perosan would be here instantly to take it back. Her decision to lure each kingdom to Reales is wise, but invading Reales earlier than expected gives us the advantage."

John asked, "When will you leave, Raven?"

If I answered honestly, it would be that I wasn't sure. Hidden deep in my memories, River lingered. He had asked me to come to Reales. He had been on the island the night I was stabbed. And I didn't believe I needed a ship to travel to Reales, but explaining all that to them would lead to further questions.

"In the next couple of days," I said. "Zeke has only been gone for a few days. I can make it back before he returns, even if I wait."

"Take Abraham or Thomas," John pleaded.

Jeanine snorted. "It would be more of a risk to take someone. Mira could use them against us. We'll be fine on our own."

"And you can't honestly believe that traveling with other men wouldn't incur even more of Zeke's wrath," I added. Not wanting to discuss this any further, I stood from the table. "I will inform you of my departure soon, John."

Jeanine came around the table and grabbed my hand. "We'll be in the Black Forest. Raven cannot remain in this castle for too long before she begins to pace and look longingly over the balcony for her prince to return to her."

I scowled at her. "Do not belittle me into some damsel from a fairytale. I don't look *longingly*."

Jeanine widened her eyes and puckered her lips, resembling a doe with her head turned toward the door, her hands tucked underneath her chin. John and Godfrey laughed, but I shoved her and she stumbled sideways. "I do not do that!"

"You don't *not* do that," Jeanine taunted.

Feeling one of Zeke's notes against my breast, tucked underneath my corset and mocking me in proof that maybe I did miss him *too* much, I rolled my eyes and came up with what I believed was the only way to end the teasing. "Whatever."

JEANINE HELD my hand as we walked through the Black Forest with no particular plan in mind. Per usual, the forest was utterly void of anyone but us, and it piqued her curiosity as she looked around. At first, I expected her to be fearful of traipsing through here, but I quickly remembered that she had spent three months with Zeke while they both stalked me daily.

"I am confused by the fear," she said finally. "Nothing ever bothered us here. Or me, anyway."

I side-eyed her.

"The caves," she reminded me. "Zeke was adamant that they

talked to him or something. It almost drove him crazy." She laughed, not from humor, but from remembering her time with him while he undoubtedly drove her mad. "He started talking back."

I had never asked him about it, nor had he offered any information of what he'd heard. Like the forest in Perosan, we treated things as if they were better left unsaid.

"Those caves have been empty for over a century," I explained. "Years ago, when Leonidas was king, he sent soldiers in the forest to find out exactly what those caves held."

"And?"

The corner of my mouth lifted in amusement, since I had never witnessed anything to be feared here, yet the rumors were strong enough to scare a century's worth of people. "No one returned."

"Odd, right? That we practically lived in the forest for months but saw nothing? Except for the bodies you burned."

I laughed at that, looking in the direction of where the corpses remained. Shrugging, I pulled in the corner of my bottom lip and contemplated silently before glancing at her. "In Perosan, I ran into the forest there."

Her eyes widened, and her hold on my hand tightened. "That forest has long been rumored to be haunted. I don't know by what, but there is a reason Petra and Elric keep it locked down. It's believed that the jagged rocks on their shores were man-made to prevent anyone from entering."

"Something happened to me there," I continued quietly. "I felt... something. Power that I had never felt before, twice the amount I felt in the water. And Blaze... she came to life. She was the one who attacked Cade. It wasn't me."

"Came to life," she repeated slowly. "Came to life how?"

I held out my hand in front of us and lit my palm. "I could... wield her outside of my body. She formed into a fox with a scorpion's tail and fangs." I stared at the flames. "She was beautiful."

"Just when I thought you couldn't get any more terrifying," she muttered.

"I haven't been able to do it since. Though lately, it feels like my magic is growing stronger, even here on the island—as if being in that forest... unlocked something."

292

"Unlocked something." She grimaced and refused to meet my eyes. "John mentioned in Reales that you were the key to something. Something to be unlocked."

My flames seeped back into my hand as I pulled her to stop. "What?"

"I don't know," she answered. "He knows things, Raven, but never enough for us to question. Damiana and Petra have known about your magic your entire life, but he doesn't know how or why."

I wasn't sure how to respond. Damiana had asked me if the rumors about my magic were true—why would she ask if she already knew the answer? "She asked me about my past," I murmured, trying to remember our conversation. "She asked how much I knew about where I came from."

Jeanine seemed just as bewildered. "But she knows you came from Reales...."

"Unless I didn't," I interrupted. "If Leonidas isn't my father, then we don't really know where I came from, do we?"

We retreated into silence until she asked, "Any more notes?" in an attempt to lighten the subject.

Smiling, I pulled the most recent note from my corset and twisted it between my fingers. "This one is much sweeter," I said, offering it to her. "Since you're so curious."

Jeanine grinned as she unfolded the note, shrugging slightly. "It's just nice. I spent months with him being very dark and hopeless, Raven. We give the two of you a hard time, but I am genuinely happy you've found one another." She held the note out in front of her. "And it is nice to see another side of him."

Looping my arm through hers, I rested my head against her shoulder as she read his note aloud, "My darling Raven, if you are reading this, I am somewhat surprised I have not turned around and returned to you by now."

"Aren't we all?" I asked.

Jeanine continued with a smile, "But it only shows my determination in guaranteeing that your dreams of lounging amongst the wildflowers behind our manor come to fruition. I promised myself not too long ago that I would give you nothing less than the entire world someday, my love, and I intend to keep every promise I've made to you. I will make you one right now, as you read this: Every time you hear the wind whisper through the trees in our forest, it means I have fallen deeper in love with you. Only yours."

As she folded the note after finishing, I wiped a tear falling from the corner of her eye. "Are you growing sappy in your old age, Jeanine?"

She threw her head back in laughter, wiping her eyes with the back of her hand. "I so desperately want the future the two of you envision for all of us." She bit her bottom lip as she glanced at me. "Will you forgive him?"

Frowning while tucking the note back into my corset, I mulled over her question. "I am very hurt by what he did, Jeanine, but I do know that the way he learned to love isn't conventional. It is hard to remember that when I am on the receiving end of his questionable decisions. However"—I nudged her arm with mine—"my love and forgiveness for him knows no bounds. All will be well, I promise."

She dipped her chin in a defiant nod. "Want to go to the caves?"

I nodded. "Lead the way."

THREE CAVES, yet only one Zeke seemed to yell at the most. I took her into the first two and showed her that nothing lurked inside. Entering the third, I wiggled my fingers at her. "Ooh, I'm going to get you!"

She rolled her eyes, spinning in a slow circle. "I don't know what he was so upset about every time he passed by here. It grew worse as time went on."

I shrugged. "I've slept in this cave many times. I haven't been here since I met him, but I doubt anything has changed since he arrived on the island."

We both shrieked as we turned toward the entrance of the cave. I covered my heart with my hand as I panted. Jeanine covered her eyes while doing the same. "It has his stealth; I'll give it that," she said with a breath.

Standing in the center of the entrance, nearly invisible in the night, sat Zeke's cat. I hadn't seen it in months and wasn't sure it was still alive, half-surprised it hadn't sought him out.

"He's rather fond of it," I said, lowering into a crouch and beckoning it forward with my hand. "I had never seen it before. It seemed to arrive the same time you did, unless it was hiding."

The cat made no move to come closer. Instead, it tilted its head enough to creep me out as I stood. "It clearly prefers him."

But as its bright green eyes brightened in the moonlight, we locked gazes, and it pinned me.

Screams—the same screams I'd heard when Zeke bit me pierced my ears, causing me to sway and stumble to the side, knocking against the cave wall.

"Raven! What's wrong?"

I couldn't break my stare with the damned cat as the screaming amplified, but it wasn't only sounds anymore. It was flashes of black trees and darkened skies, this cave with silhouettes standing within, but I couldn't recognize them. Each image lasted only seconds, but blood—I saw so much blood that I covered my ears, hoping it would stop the cries of pain and utter agony from wherever I was.

Clutching my side where a ghost of pain swept through me, I was convinced I was bleeding. Everything but the cat's eyes blurred around me, slitting and resembling a wafer-thin moon. I tried to fixate on the visions and chase them, but the more I saw, the more pain I felt.

My name.

I heard my name called from so many different voices in multiple directions that I couldn't pinpoint any of them. I clutched my chest because I recognized one of the voices.

It was the faintest—raspy and strained, but I knew it.

It was him. Dying.

Zeke.

∾

"RAVEN!"

Jeanine's shout pulled from me wherever—whatever—I had just

traveled to. The cat left the cave, but my legs felt like stone and I couldn't reconcile anything.

Those visions weren't from this lifetime, and the trees in the forest looked younger, nor did the stone archway of the caves look as aged as they did now.

She shook my shoulders and said my name repeatedly, but my eyes were closed as I chased the screams and the visions… the memories. Because that was what they had to be—memories of one of our lives, but why was I seeing it?

Why was he in pain?

All the blood.

I shoved her out of the way and fell to my knees, vomiting on the ground as I relived it. Nausea rolled through my stomach and down my spine, cold sweats dampening my entire body. His screams still rippled through me as if he were bleeding out beside me.

Jeanine held back my hair as I vomited again, unable to stomach even a memory of him in pain where I was unable to help.

"What is going on?" she asked frantically.

The weight of this secret we'd held between us for so long was becoming unbearable. There were no books with answers, and he wasn't here to decipher the memories or try to find where they could've come from.

Sitting up, I removed my shirt. I no longer owned any sort of undergarments, since Zeke continued to destroy them all, so I kneeled bare before her. She lifted an eyebrow, speechless and most likely convinced I had lost it.

Until she saw them.

The various bite marks across my body, scarred from his need to drink my blood. She touched one on my collarbone first, her brows knitted together before moving to the one on my neck and the newest ones across my breasts.

Heat bloomed across my cheeks, not from shame but from reasons I could not understand—from the look in his eyes every time he drank from me, how each drop seemed to strengthen him, and how it was changing him.

Before I could say anything, she put a finger against my lips. "Were they done with your permission?"

I nodded quickly, taking her wrist to lower her hand from my lips. "Of course. He wouldn't have done it otherwise. Something is happening, Jeanine. He drinks my blood but doesn't want to. He does, but he's ashamed of it, yet needs it. The black in his eyes? It's because of this. It happened after he'd bitten me for the first time soon after we met."

I was rushing through the words, but she didn't seem to struggle to keep up. Instead, she kept touching the bites, the confusion on her face a mirror of how we'd both felt since it started.

"And when he bites me sometimes, I... hear things. I can never see them, but they're awful. Screams..." Tears fell down my cheeks as the panic returned. "And they're always his, but I don't know why or how to help him."

She handed me my shirt. "Why haven't you told anyone?"

Sliding it on, I sank back on my shins and sniffled as I shrugged. "We didn't know how any of you would react. It isn't exactly something you bring up in conversation on a whim. It's partially why he wanted to go to Nova. He needs answers to why he craves my blood."

She took my hand, kissed it, and squeezed until I yelped. "You two are so incredibly... ugh!" She put my face between her hands and wiped the tears away with her thumbs. "We are your *family*, Raven. You can always come to us with anything, even cannibalism."

I coughed out a tearful laugh. "What do we do?"

"We do what we always do, Raven." She pulled me to my feet. "We will find answers for you."

"SHE FORMED INTO A FOX WITH A SCORPION'S TAIL AND FANGS."

30

ZEKE

I growled from the boot that repeatedly pressed into my ribs. The blinding light prevented me from opening my eyes as I failed to shove the foot away.

"Get up, Zeke."

That was the last thing I wanted to do. I had been apart from Raven for four days, maybe five, and it hadn't gotten easier. I had difficulty remembering the last few days and wondered how I had made it three months without her last time, though I at least had the pleasure of stalking her daily.

But now, I couldn't even see her. Couldn't feel her. I remained unsure if she would ever forgive me... *could* ever forgive me.

When the boot nudged me again, I cursed and peeled my eyes open. Nearly blinded by the sunlight, I groaned and covered my eyes with my arm.

"We're docking today," Luca said. "Get up."

I wanted her. I hungered for her on my tongue, on my cock, on my face. I wouldn't be picky. I had sought solace in the bottles of rum Arthur provided before we left Seolia.

Contrary to my current paralysis from longing and a pounding headache, I had spent every night at the helm while Luca slept. The days away from her were the hardest because she wasn't the sun or blue skies. She was the stars that surrounded me.

I had spent each night combing through memories with her, even the unpleasant ones, because it kept us connected. That and our heartbeat, which fluttered yesterday evening, meaning she had found another bouquet of roses.

Every morning when dawn hit, we drank rum.

I wasn't thrilled that Luca woke me up while the sun was high, but if we were docking soon, the next part of our journey wouldn't be safe aboard our ship. We would camp under trees or hopefully stumble across villages with rooms available at inns.

Shadow stared at me while I sat up, disapproving.

I would never understand how she managed to talk him into joining us on this trip, but here he was, judging me every day. "You know she's mine," I continued to remind him. He would only huff, unamused.

The liquor basket beside me was lighter than usual when I flipped the lid off to begin my day drinking. When I peered into it, I was disappointed to find it empty.

"It's gone," Luca said, equally depressed.

"We went through eight bottles in four days? How are we still alive?"

"*We?*" He shook his head but kept his eyes on the water ahead. "I had *maybe* two bottles. You tried to *swim* to her when I woke up this morning, Zeke. It's good that it's gone."

"I did not try to swim to her," I argued, though I did remember falling asleep with my clothes wet.

299

"You did, and rather sloppily, too. If I hadn't jumped in after you, you would've drowned, and then she would've burned me alive."

I rolled my eyes, but a grin peeked at the corner of my mouth. It did sound like something I would do during my drunken desperation to return to her. "She would've died with me. I would be doing you a favor."

"Get our shit ready," Luca demanded. I found his bossiness rather annoying. "We'll dock within the hour."

"You know I'm above you, right? Title and every other way possible."

"I know you're an asshole," he responded. "And that I've kept you alive. I'm not dragging you on land, so sober up and saddle Shadow."

"If I wanted to be bossed around, I could've brought Jeanine instead." I stood slowly, running a hand down my face, well aware that I looked like shit.

Passing out from alcohol consumption was not the same as sleeping. It never revitalized me the same as a decent night's sleep would or... I glanced over at the canvas satchel Raven had packed for us. I hadn't yet touched the vials of blood she'd given me.

I was more fatigued than usual, but I needed to make it last. I worried that once I tasted it again, I would drink every vial at once.

Luca snapped his fingers, drawing my attention away from the temptation of her blood. "*What?*"

"Your eyes were doing that weird thing again."

Rolling them, I turned to throw the clothes we'd cycled through and washed into our bags. We traveled light, only bringing what we absolutely needed. The trunk of food supplied by our parents wasn't feasible to carry with us, so I would have to ration enough to keep us from starving before we reached Nova.

Shadow had his saddlebags full of apples, courtesy of his over-protective owner.

"We're not having this conversation again," I said.

"Maybe Morana was right."

"Luca," I sighed, shoving his clothes into his canvas backpack and contemplating throwing it overboard to make him play fetch. "I have no shadows. Morana was a demented demon."

"Exactly," he continued, testing my patience. "If anyone would know, it would be her. Your eyes turn *black*, Zeke."

"You sound like Raven," I muttered. After stuffing it full of his least favorite fruits, I closed his bag and stood facing him with my arms crossed. "Drop it. Everyone needs to stop obsessing over this."

"What does Raven say about it?"

Ignoring him, I leaned over to grab one of the apples from Shadow's saddlebag. I extended my hand to him, and he turned his head away. "Shadow," I warned. "You have to eat. We'll be back to her soon."

Shadow side-eyed me with one of his shiny black eyes, menacing and far too beastly for my liking. Between him and that elusive cat, I considered myself to not be an animal person. Finally, he took the apple from my hand and trotted to the opposite end of the ship.

I took one of the maps from my bag, unrolling it. If we could find another horse quickly, it would only take five days to get to Nova. Otherwise, it would nearly double our trek, putting us at the two weeks I told Raven it would take to get there.

I wanted to surprise her and return sooner.

Stretching the map across the helm, I pointed to three separate villages that stood between us and the kingdom of Nova. "I know nothing about people outside of our realm, only that many of the inhabitants are those who've fled other kingdoms. That doesn't bode well for us since I don't know what we're up against."

"Fucking fantastic," Luca grumbled. "You know, I always wanted to travel on one of your grand adventures, but now I'm regretting it slightly."

"My adventures were never grand, Luca. We need another horse." I pointed to the village in the middle, circling my finger. "This is most likely our best chance of finding one. The first village looks small. The third village is close enough to Nova that getting a horse there would be pointless."

Luca nodded while he listened. As irritating as I found him, he trusted my travel instincts. He would come in handy for schmoozing over any people we came across, since he was apparently nicer than me, but he understood that since I had traveled more than he had, I should be the navigator.

Rolling the map up and sliding it back into my bag, I pulled out a dagger and tossed it to him. "We stay strapped at all times. Do not sleep or take a breath without this on you. Melik knew who I was when he came to Reales, which means others might, too. From my understanding, I'm not exactly respected outside of our realm."

He didn't seem shocked by that.

"If you don't want to kill anyone, I understand. Just render them useless long enough for me to do it."

"I can do it," he said quietly, sliding the dagger into the waistband of his pants. "You can rely on me, you know."

I paused my instructions, my brows knitting together. "I know that, Luca. That's not what I meant."

Luca wasn't one to back down from an argument with me, but he said nothing else about it, instead raising an eyebrow at me. "Anything else?"

"Yeah," I said. "Trust no one."

∾

The Village of Reine

Our first night was uneventful. We made camp in a meadow, unlike where my soul collided with Raven's. This meadow was brown and dry, with no nearby water source for Shadow, who both of us had refused to ride until we found another horse. We didn't want to leave one of us at a disadvantage should an attack occur.

We approached a small village of no more than ten cobblestone cottages, but unlike the meadow, these were surrounded by lush green grass that snaked around the walls into leafy vines. There was only one dirt road through town, trees sprouting from both sides like a makeshift fence.

Altogether, the town couldn't have been more than two miles long. I paused and looked around. There was silence up ahead and no one around us, which seemed odd for a small town. Typically, men or women would be tending to crops or gathering pails of water to bring back.

Luca looked at me, hooking his arm on Shadow's back to take a breather. We had walked miles. We wouldn't make it much longer without dehydrating. I had taken a sip of Raven's blood from the first vial after struggling to fall asleep, too cautious of what might be lurking around us.

It had given me a slight energy boost, but I needed more. And Luca was looking worse for the wear. The amount of rum we had ingested over the last few days did nothing to conserve the natural water in our bodies.

We each had a dagger stashed in our waistband, but my bow was hanging from Shadow's saddle. I could nock the arrow quickly if I needed to.

"It's too quiet," I muttered to him, taking a small step forward. "Even with its size, we should see someone."

"Maybe you're too paranoid," Luca responded.

His eyes were hollow, and his color drained from the sun overhead. I needed to find him some water quickly. His wound had healed externally, but from the look of him, it seemed as if it hadn't wholly mended internally.

"Keep in mind that magic exists outside our realm," I explained to him. "I might be paranoid, but I'm also correct."

Luca sighed, shaking his empty canteen before tipping it up to drink the remaining drops. "Do we need to go around it?"

If I were alone, I would've. I was more experienced at living without necessities for longer than needed, but Luca wasn't. He had been in an underground dungeon for over a year without being exposed to the outside elements. Luca and my mother always had what they needed, except for sunlight and basic necessities like freedom.

Even while training on the island, Raven had doted on Luca more than the other soldiers, ensuring he was adjusting well to being free again.

Though he balked at the idea, I needed to protect him. He wanted me to believe I could rely on him, and I could, but I wasn't about to risk his life for his pride.

"No," I answered, putting my hand on Shadow's flank. He eyed me as if understanding my silent plea to prevent any harm from coming to my brother. "We'll walk through but keep your eyes open."

Our walk was slow toward the road covered by shadows of the

trees with only slivers of sunlight peeking through. I sensed Luca's unease but said nothing of it.

Rolling my neck, I straightened my shoulders and attempted to appear as the threat Raven believed me to be with others. Luca put his hand on the hilt of his dagger and I shook my head, keeping my eyes straight. "Never give away the location of your weapon," I whispered.

He quickly dropped his hand and hung his arms loosely at his sides, attempting to mirror my stance. Shadow neighed softly between us, halting his slow trot and whipping his head to the side to tell us to stop.

I looked ahead. A woman stood at the tree line. She looked a little younger than Damiana, wearing a full skirt and corseted top, her hair long and hanging over her shoulder in a stringy braid.

Luca glanced at me, but I continued to stare at her, cocking my head to the side. A troublesome grin spread across her lips as she slowly raised one arm from her side. I blinked, watching in anticipation for something. The eerie way she moved her limbs reminded me of something—something I had hoped I would never face again.

"No," Luca said with a breath. "It can't be."

"Fuck," I said, watching as three more women appeared behind the one still holding her arm toward us. This quaint and quiet village was being protected by something, and we were about to get our first introduction to the magic others had long feared.

"This is a coven of witches," I said.

And from the woman's fingers came black ribbons, heading straight toward us.

⁓

"Fucking death ribbons!" I shouted, taking steps backward as they skated across the ground toward us. We knew Morana wasn't gone. She had just taken up residence with another witch.

"What do we do?" Luca shouted back. "How did she know we'd be here?"

I had to think quickly, which didn't always work out in my favor. Morana always wanted me. She had used Raven to get closer to these godforsaken shadows of mine. I could get Luca out of here and safely away from the village while I dealt with this.

"Luca, climb on Shadow."

"You're fucking insane if you think I'm going to leave you here!" he yelled at me, shaking his head. "I promised Raven nothing would happen to you...."

"Nothing is going to happen to me." I took Shadow's lead rope and shoved it against Luca's chest. "Get away from the village, Luca. I'll meet you on the other side."

He opened his mouth to protest, but I was already gone, running toward the ribbons instead of away from them. If Morana wanted the shadows, she'd have to work for them.

Luca shouted my name in terror, in frustration. I wasn't quite at a point to decipher it, but I didn't stop. The witch who had loosened the ribbons stared at me in shock and bewilderment while they inched closer to me.

"Come on, Morana," I goaded. "I still won't choose you."

The ribbons flew faster toward me at my provocation, and when they were less than two feet away from touching me, I jumped over them. Landing on my feet, I ran again but glanced over my shoulder. The ribbons had done exactly as I wanted, turning around to chase me instead of continuing toward Luca.

Luca, however, threw his hands up from where he stood and climbed onto Shadow.

The witch possessed by Morana narrowed her eyes at me as I began closing the distance between us. The three witches behind her had stepped back and were staring at me in awe and concern. I only hoped a witch in this coven could heal or conjure up something.

Because what I was about to do would require it.

Around my neck was the leather string with a vial of Raven's blood. I uncapped it as quickly as possible and downed the rest, dropping the vial back to my chest and closing my eyes as the small amount of her blood intertwined with mine, giving me the kick I needed.

The witch braced but smiled — the ribbons were catching up to me quickly. Grabbing the hilt of my dagger from my waistband, I pulled it out and slid on my knees, dragging the tip of my blade across her abdomen.

The ribbons behind me screeched and curled into themselves as the witch fell into my waiting arms, bleeding. A burst of hazy smoke shot from her wound just as she had done to Raven's, but aimed straight for me.

I hadn't thought this far ahead.

The haze closed in on my chest, but Morana wailed a hollow shriek as the cloud touched the empty vial of Raven's blood. Twisting into a spiral of black and gray, the smoke shot itself far enough into the distance that it was nothing more than a speck.

I looked at the drying, blood-coated vial around my neck.

Was Morana afraid of Raven's blood?

"She needs help!" I called out to one of the waiting witches while the other bled out in my arms. Upon closer look, I was correct in the assumption of her age. Her hair was graying at the roots, but there was still such youthfulness in her eyes that it physically pained me to watch her life slip away in my arms.

Two women appeared on either side of me, one tearing a hole big enough in the bleeding witch's top for the other to rub a clouded white balm across her open wound.

And then they begin to chant in harmony.

I didn't know what language this was, and I couldn't even guess what they were saying, but it was entrancing. More surrounding voices joined as a chorus repeated the same three phrases.

Anima tua avolabit.

Anima tua liberabit te.

Anima tua ad me redeat.

Over and over, chanting, holding hands. The leaves from the trees above us rustled, and I thought of Raven, wondering if she could decipher any of this—if she would join in to sing with women like her.

I felt out of place in the middle of such an intimate moment between a coven, yet strangely welcomed.

And when the witch in my arms gasped, color returning to her lips and cheeks, I laughed from relief. Whatever the balm was made of had created a barrier and stopped the bleeding.

"Let us take her," the witch on my right said, moving her head from my arms into her hands. The witch on my left cradled her body and stood with her, walking quickly toward one of the cottages hidden between trees.

Luca appeared on the other side of the road, waving me forward. I stepped toward him, but another elderly witch blocked my path, bending at the waist in a slight bow. "You are the prince," she said. "We have been expecting you."

I tensed, unsure of how or why that could be.

"You are mated to the Dark Half-Witch."

"YOU ARE MATED TO THE DARK HALF-WITCH."

31

ZEKE

L uca and I sat around a wooden table in an ill-lit cottage, watching as the elderly witch brewed us some tea. Shadow was outside, drinking from a pail of water and peeking through the foggy window.

Bottles of herbs and ointments were placed on the counter with labels written in the same language they had chanted. Luca seemed nervous but was anxiously awaiting something to drink. In the quiet, while the witch's back was turned, I pushed into his mind.

They know Raven.

He flinched at my voice, even after years of me intruding on his subconscious.

I don't know how, nor do I understand how Morana ended up here. I don't feel threatened, but let me smell the tea before you ingest anything.

I didn't need his acknowledgment to know that he would wait for me to tell him it was okay. I wasn't particularly well-versed in poisons and how to identify them by scent, being that our realm had been relatively peaceful for most of my life and war was always the last thing on Rudolf's mind, but I had enough basic knowledge.

I hoped.

While we waited, I peered out the foggy window. The cottages across the road and through the trees looked warped from the glass, but a handful of witches were gathered around one. "Is she going to live?" I asked quietly.

I ensured I sliced only deep enough to give her a chance of survival, though that didn't lighten the guilt.

"That is up to her," the witch responded as she poured the tea from a brassy kettle into tiny teacups.

"I didn't mean to harm her," I said honestly. "I have some experience with Morana. It was the only way I knew to purge her."

Her movements were wobbly at best as she turned from the counter to bring us our cups. Her features showed years of wisdom; she looked like she had spent every day of her life in the sun, though her hair didn't reflect it. Instead of a bright blonde, it was an ashy white that braided down her back, not unlike how Raven wore hers.

"We know this," she answered, setting down the teacups in front of us. "You are mated to the Half-Witch. You would not harm her kind."

I didn't know if that was necessarily true. Though Raven was a witch, I didn't show favoritism toward anyone until I could be sure they were not a threat to her.

But I nodded, taking the teacup in my hands and bringing it up to my nose to take a deep breath. I smiled broadly before looking at her as she sat across the table. "Jasmine?"

"And honey," she answered. "It'll improve your friend's health."

I glanced over at Luca. He looked even wearier in the dim light. He was waiting for my permission to drink, so when I nodded, he practically inhaled the tea before politely asking for more. I slid him my cup as she stood to pour more into his. He drank from mine just as greedily.

She returned to the table and handed me Luca's cup. I took a sip, closing my eyes as Raven's partial scent flooded me from the jasmine leaves. I wondered where she was, what she was doing, and if she missed me as much as I ached for her.

"There is a basin in the back room," she said, looking at Luca. "If you want to wash up or clean your clothes, there are oatmeal soap bars. And," she added with a small smile, "a bed for you to rest."

Luca looked at me. We needed to continue to Nova sooner rather than later, but aside from training with the army for the past few weeks, this was the most activity Luca had experienced in nearly two years. I worried if I pushed him too hard, he wouldn't make it to Nova in one piece.

I tipped my head toward the back room. "Go on, Luca. I'll wake you before sundown."

"I can keep going," he argued halfheartedly.

Reaching over, I squeezed his shoulder. "Rest, Luca. We're going to talk about Raven."

He hesitated, but his exhaustion soon took precedence, and he nodded once before standing from the table and heading straight for the back room. I waited until he was out of sight before focusing on the witch. "What's your name? You know Raven? How did Morana get here?"

She looked amused, the corner of her mouth twitching. "You have many questions."

"And I need many answers," I responded. "That is why I've taken this journey. It's for Raven's benefit."

"My name is Larinda, and I am the eldest witch in our coven. I do not know the Half-Witch in the way you might think. Morana entered our Seer fourteen moons ago."

Fourteen moons. Two weeks.

"Your... Seer?" My knowledge of witches did not extend past covens. Until Raven, I wasn't aware they still existed. While I had studied some history of magic, I did not expect it to come back so quickly after meeting her.

"There was a prophecy...."

I sighed, running a hand through my hair. "Yes, I know of the prophecy. Twins born of darkness to restore magic to creatures across the lands."

She poured more tea into my cup—so much that steam rose and wafted into my nose, causing me to draw in a slow and steady breath. Calmness washed over me, and I cocked an eyebrow. "You did that on purpose."

"There was a prophecy," she started again, ignoring me. "Magic began dying over a century ago. It has been slow but painful. The more time that passes, the quicker it leaves."

"And you think Raven is your solution to that?"

"Our Seer sees glimpses of coming days, though not always distinct. She saw a glimpse of the prince coming and pieces of your life with the Half-Witch."

I wasn't sure why she kept referring to Raven in that way. "And what pieces did she see of my life with Raven?"

Her fingers curled around my wrist and a brisk chill raced down my spine at the look in her eyes. "Blood," she hissed in a whisper, "blood and death."

That was when I felt the effect of the tea.

I hadn't taken my own advice and had let my guard down. *While you believe yourself invincible...* Raven's words echoed through my mind.

"Luca!" I called out, but there was no answer. I wrangled my wrist free from her grip and stood, jogging into the back room where she had sent Luca. Larinda did not rise from the table or even move. She simply watched me.

Panic arose when I saw his body in a heap on the floor.

Falling to my knees, I flipped him over and pressed my fingers against the pulse in his neck. It was weak but still beating against my fingers. "Luca," I said hoarsely, reaching for him. I needed to get us out of here.

I was growing dizzy but dragged him over my shoulder, using the doorframe to guide me to my feet. The floor seemed to be moving underneath my boots, the walls closing in on me quickly. A few more steps would get us to the front door, and Shadow could do the rest.

"Shadow," I whispered, falling first to one knee. "Shadow," I repeated as Luca fell back to the floor from my shoulder.

"Raven," was my last word.

GROANING, I blinked my eyes open. My head throbbed and my throat felt like a pound of sand had been poured down it. I moved to touch my forehead but couldn't move either of my arms. Squinting an eye, I turned my chin upward. Chained to an iron headboard, the cuffs around my wrists prevented me from moving anything but my legs.

"Luca," I whispered, then coughed. I desperately needed water, but more than that, I needed to get us out. "Fucking witches," I grumbled, shaking the chains to gauge how tight they were around my wrists.

The tea must've had some kind of sedative disguised by the jasmine leaves. If I could free myself, locating and unlocking Luca would be another challenge.

What did they need us for?

I tried remembering the details of our conversation.

Half-Witch. Raven. Prophecy.

What did Raven have to do with sedating me? Unless they planned to use me as collateral to lure her here.

That wasn't an option. I needed to free us and leave before word got back to Seolia that we were captured. Raven was strong, but could she take on an entire coven alone?

I didn't want to find out, especially if they wanted her for their own reasons.

Rattling the chains, I tried to use the leverage of my legs to break them from the headboard but stopped quickly. It was too loud. I didn't want them to know I was awake.

Underneath me, a groan sounded.

"Luca!" I whisper-shouted.

Another groan in response, and I sighed.

"Luca," I said again. "Are you chained?"

"I have no shirt on," he said in response, confusion wafting out of him. "What happened?"

"The witch poisoned our tea. The jasmine leaves reminded me of Raven and I let my guard down." I dropped my head back to the bed, and guilt set in. I had gotten him trapped again. "It was brilliant on her part. I don't know how she knew it would distract me."

"There's a reason witches were burned," Luca snapped, the sound of his chains clanking. "I'm cuffed by my wrist to the foot of the bed. How do they know Raven?"

"I don't fucking know," I said with a snarl. "But they want her badly enough to sedate us. We need to get out of here."

"No shit," he grumbled in reply. "How?"

The squeaking of the door handle quieted us immediately until I whispered very quickly, "Close your eyes."

With my eyes closed, I picked out each sound I could. Feet shuffling, chains underneath me shaking. She was ensuring Luca was still trapped. The scent of musk and betrayal told me that it was Larinda.

I felt her beside me, leaning close enough for my breath to hit her face. I remained utterly still, feigning sleep. I didn't have much tea, and I wasn't sure how long she assumed I would be out, but I felt she expected me to wake up soon.

Ripping my shirt open, she slapped a slab of gooey balm across my chest. I nearly jumped out of my skin. Whatever it was, it smelled rotten. None of the herbs Raven sent with me smelled like this, nor were they thick like paste.

These were witches from history books that dwelled in covens and cast spells. No one believed they still existed, but I had spotted at least ten of them outside when we arrived.

Obumbratio, she kept repeating as she slathered more balm across my chest. *Obumbratio opus est tenebris Half-Witch sanguine.*

Half-Witch. Something about Raven was tied to this shit she was spreading across me.

Her hands left me, and her feet shuffled across the floor, followed by the door closing. My eyes flew open, and I lifted my head to look at what lay across my chest.

"Shadows," Luca said beneath me. "She said something about shadows. That shit stinks, by the way."

I lifted an eyebrow. "You understood her?"

"Barely." He shifted, his chain gliding up one of the iron rails until his head popped up beside me. He sat awkwardly, but it relieved me to see him. "We were tutored in ancient languages, Zeke. Did you pay any attention at all?"

"Evidently not." I knew full well that I hadn't. I didn't think I would possibly need to know about languages that hadn't been heard in over a century. "Whatever she spread on me has to do with Raven and shadows."

With his unchained hand, he swiped a finger across my chest. "It's balmy." A grin spread across his lips as he took a fistful and disappeared underneath me.

"Luca, what the fuck are you doing?"

His chain rattled, and he grunted as he pushed with his feet, the bed slightly creaking as it moved a few inches away. I rocked against the mattress, the chain from my cuffs biting into my skin. He tumbled backward and cursed. "Fuck, I think I broke my thumb."

He popped back up but with both hands freed.

I was impressed.

He stood, and I tracked him around the room as he located his shirt and our satchels, throwing them across his chest. He moved stealthily and quickly through the room. Maybe I hadn't given him enough credit.

I wanted to protect him. I was desperate to prevent anything from happening to him again, but he was the one who had found a way out while I remained chained to a bed.

Returning to my side, he scooped up another handful of the balm. I was suddenly grateful that she had left so much on my chest. Spreading it across my wrists, he held the headboard against the wall with one hand while I began freeing one of my hands.

The pain in his expression gave away that he had broken his thumb, which was tucked against his chest.

"I'm fine," he said when he caught me looking.

I said nothing about it. I tucked my thumb into my palm as much as possible to prevent the same thing from happening to me and yanked until my hand finally slipped from its constraints. "Fuck!" I whisper-shouted.

The skin around my wrist was inflamed, indicating that we had been chained for a while. I wondered if Shadow was okay or if they had sacrificed him.

The door flew open, and Luca whipped around. With one of my hands still bound and his thumb broken, we were at quite a disadvantage.

Larinda cursed at us in the old language, disappearing from the doorway. Her quick footsteps meant she was fetching help to wrangle us back into a catatonic state.

"Go, Luca!" I shouted. "Go find Shadow!"

"I am not leaving you here!" He pulled at my arm as we tried to free my wrist.

"Find Shadow, Luca," I growled as the raw skin of my wrist tore from the steel. "Fucking Reales and all their steel!" I had no doubt that my own kingdom had crafted these cuffs.

Voices came from outside, drawing nearer by the second. "Luca, go! Find Shadow and meet me at the edge of town. I will be there."

"Zeke..."

"Luca. Go."

He hesitated for a few seconds before he nodded, disappearing out the door. As my fingers and arm numbed from the pressure, I closed my eyes and thought of Raven.

Raven, Raven, Raven.

I needed to free myself for her.

Groaning in pain, I pulled at the chain on the bed and wished I had asked Luca for one of her blood vials. Instead, I went off the memory of how it tasted, the strength I felt from each drop, the way the shadows...

Shadows. Dark Half-Witch.

They wanted to free my shadows.

How would the Dark Half-Witch free them?

I didn't have time to analyze it right now. Luca was alone, and I needed to find him before they did.

One last hard tug and my hand slipped free, though not without consequence. The skin around my wrist had ripped to the bone. Hopefully, one of the mystery herbs Raven packed for us would stave off infection.

Ripping a scrap of a sheet from the bed, I wrapped it around my wrist and hurriedly located my boots, running out of the room before I had entirely slipped them on.

The cottage was empty and the voices outside had quieted. I stole a moment to glance at the bottles on the counter. Though I couldn't read them, they might come in handy. If not, Keaton could analyze them upon our return home.

I grabbed an armful and looked out the fogged window. I couldn't see anything but the trees in the darkness, yet I heard nothing either. No voices. No thundering footsteps to trap us.

It was now or never.

Opening the front door, I prepared to run.

But I didn't have to.

I looked up and down the village to see the bodies of witches strewn across the ground. I crouched and put a finger against the pulse of the one nearest. It was faint but still beating, yet no witch moved. The only sound was Shadow neighing from the end of the road and Luca calling my name.

I was utterly bewildered. They hadn't all fainted.

Luca couldn't have taken them down on his own.

I walked to the center of the road. To my left, Luca waited with Shadow and a silhouette of... another horse?

Someone else stood to my right at the very end of the road. Even with the moonlight shining directly behind them, I couldn't make out anything about them other than they were male. I squinted, and he tilted his head.

Whoever it was, he saved our lives.

And just like that, he was gone.

Vanishing in the blink of an eye.

Luca couldn't explain.

The other horse had been tied to a tree with Shadow. The witches had already begun fainting when he ran out of the cottage, though some of them had put up a fight. He didn't mention seeing the vanishing man and didn't have time to question what had happened. His only concern had been grabbing the horses and waiting for me.

316

I rode Shadow while Luca rode the other horse—a dark brown one that reminded me of the fudge from Thoya. And when that thought crossed my mind, I sighed.

I only had three vials left, but I craved her blood. She had instructed me to drink one a week, but that seemed implausible as my energy waned and my wrist burned. We didn't want to stop at another village in fear of running into more witches or other magical creatures, which meant we would arrive in Nova starved and unclean.

I could survive from only her blood. I had done it before. Drinking it assuaged my hunger for food and replenished my stamina, giving me more strength.

She would want that.

Or at least that was what I convinced myself when I asked Luca for my satchel. And he had watched as I fished out a vial and uncapped it, tipping it against my lips.

And was still watching with disgust when I slipped it back into the satchel. "What the fuck?"

I chuckled stiffly. "I drink her blood. Daily, if I can help it."

He stared at me, partially in horror, half in bafflement. "But... but why?"

"We don't know," I answered honestly.

"Do you..."—he looked genuinely unsure of what to ask—"drink others? Like... Jeanine's?"

The idea of drinking anyone else's blood but Raven's made me want to gag. It seemed odd to need it, but hers was the only one I craved. I didn't believe my body would react the same way to other blood. "No. Only Raven's. Ever."

He nodded but still didn't understand. I didn't, either. I did, however, want to change the subject. "How is your hand?"

He still held it against his chest. "Fucking hurts."

I sifted through the satchel and began pulling random bottles of herbs and tonics. "Raven supplied us with medicines." I pulled out a bottle labeled '*Numbing*' and handed it to him. "Might help with the pain. Keaton made these."

Uncapping it, he brought it to his nose and inhaled whatever was inside. "Blueberry," he said after a moment before drinking half of the bottle and handing it back to me. "Take the rest. Mine will heal. Yours could get infected."

I would've argued had my wound not been burning, but when I unraveled the bloodied sheet from around my wrist, I stared in surprise. The skin was slowly closing in front of my eyes, puckering and pink, but healing.

Luca leaned over, his eyes wide as he grabbed my wrist to study it. I grimaced, pain shooting through my arm. Shadow huffed in frustration as Luca's horse knocked into him from Luca's sudden movement. "How?"

I started to say I didn't know, but then stopped. "Her blood."

Her gift of healing lived in her blood.

Could that be why it restored strength?

Why it made me stronger?

Why I craved the power I felt from consuming it?

Luca released my wrist and straightened, but he continued to stare at the skin of my wrist as it closed. It would be healed by the time we arrived in Nova.

"Shadows," Luca repeated. "Half Dark-Witch and shadows were all I could make out from what she said, but I wonder if they want Raven for that reason." He nodded toward my satchel. "Her blood, Zeke."

I clenched my jaw at the idea of someone else wanting the blood that belonged solely to me. The minuscule amount she had given me in each vial was enough to heal an open wound on my wrist. All of the blood in her body could heal an entire kingdom, and that information in the hands of the wrong person...

As he looked from the satchel to me, Luca understood, his brows knitted. "Raven's blood is like gold. But that's not the biggest question."

I glanced at him.

"What does that have to do with your shadows?"

THEY WANTED TO FREE MY SHADOWS. HOW WOULD THE DARK HALF-WITCH FREE THEM?

32

RAVEN

Dusting the spines of old books along the shelves, I half-listened to Jeanine as she introduced herself to the newest owners of the bookshoppe in the village. Sria and Vivianne had moved here from one of the many outside kingdoms not long before Cade took me, though the way they spoke about it, it had been more like a small village where royalty kept away, uncaring of the people.

Since they were the parents of four young children, they wanted to move to a kingdom where their children would be well-fed and would have access to daily tutoring sessions, which is where they were now, giving us a perfect chance to meet the newest residents of Seolia.

Or it sounded something like that.

It had been five days since Zeke left, and I spent every one of them with Jeanine beside me. We would always end up at Duck's every night, but would read instead of drinking ourselves into a stupor. And talked about Arthur's wife.

Arthur believed his wife was his mate, though he didn't recall any official bonding or *snap* like there had been for me. The way he talked about her was endearing. They spent nearly forty years together before she passed away from an illness, before I became queen.

They almost sounded *too* perfect together. Her name was Abigail, and they met when Arthur was working at the docks. She had been delivering food to the dock workers that day when he stumbled across her, nearly knocking her down. He caught her and the basket simultaneously, and when they locked eyes, that, he'd said, was that.

He smiled at me then, squeezing my hand as he admitted that was why he understood the obsession Zeke and I had with one another. Arthur couldn't stand to be away from Abigail. She worked for her father in a tavern that no longer existed on the island but would sneak out to spend time watching Arthur offload ships that came into the harbor. He would become so distracted by her that he'd be shouted at, so instead of pulling it together, he quit.

They were wed within two weeks of meeting.

It was because of Abigail that Arthur opened Duck's. They wanted to be together, and Abigail had experience working at a tavern, though being in competition with her father didn't bode well for family dynamics. That was when Arthur decided to only supply alcohol instead of food.

"Why Duck's?" Jeanine had asked.

Arthur chuckled and explained that ducks used to play in the harbor during their courtship. One had even plucked the sandwich she made him right from his hand.

Not once had I ever seen ducks on the island. The romantic in me wanted to believe that when Abigail passed on, they left with her.

Abigail would spend her days reading her books at his counter, which was how they lived for forty years.

Until the morning she didn't wake up.

Life had at least given Zeke and me the guarantee that one would accompany the other when we died. I didn't share that with Arthur, though. It seemed unfair that I possessed such a gift while he had to live the rest of his life without Abigail.

I had been staring at the spine of one book when I heard Jeanine mention my name, drawing my attention back to her and the newest residents.

Sria and Vivianne looked to be in their early forties and, physically, complete opposites. Sria's hair was cut short, not falling past her ears and so black it appeared blue when she walked through streams of sunlight. Vivianne had a blonde brighter than Jeanine's and stood at least a foot over Sria, similar to how Zeke towered over me.

Their clothes were unique—heavy skirts and corseted vests made of beige and black and faded from age.

Sria caught me staring and dipped into a curtsy, which I quickly dismissed with my hand. I had never been comfortable with anyone bowing to me unless a man had pissed me off. And then it was a fringe benefit of being a royal.

"We heard about what happened...." Sria began.

I quickly stopped her again with my hand. "Please, don't feel the need to apologize for it. It is no one's fault but his for touching things that did not belong to him."

"I wasn't going to apologize," Sria continued with an upward grin. "I was going to say that we have been anxiously awaiting to meet you."

I lifted a brow as I lowered my hand from the books. "Oh? Why's that?"

We walked to a large, waist-high glass table in the middle of the room with open books sprawled across the top. I touched a page with my fingertip while trying to silently sound out words from a language I didn't recognize.

"Yes," she continued, trying to hold my attention. "Since we learned that you had returned to Reales, which is only days away by foot from our village."

I hadn't realized news of my return had spread. I always found it shocking that people outside our realm knew of me. Zeke had told me of Melik hearing my story, and while I didn't particularly enjoy being talked about, I supposed it came with the territory of possessing something that had been banished long ago from our realm.

I couldn't stop staring at the words written on the page. They seemed familiar somehow, yet I couldn't untangle them in my mind. "My husband is on his way to Nova. Maybe he'll pass through your village. Friendly, I hope." Not that I was too worried if it wasn't. Zeke could undoubtedly handle himself.

I realized we were alone when I no longer heard Jeanine's voice. I called for her, but she didn't return the beckoning. The silence made me uncomfortable. I glanced at Sria from the corner of my eye. "Where are Jeanine and Vivianne?"

Instead of answering, she gestured with her chin to the book I was touching. "Do you recognize this?"

I continued to look around the small shoppe for Jeanine, shaking my head slightly. "Not really."

"*Tenebris Dimidium-Witch.*"

All I gathered from that was the word *witch*, which had me pausing my need for Jeanine's location to look at Sria. The book suddenly closed on my fingers by itself. I winced, shooting ice through my fingers to cool the pain from the snap.

That could've only been done by magic. "Where did you say you were from again?"

Sria circled the table slowly, and I stepped backward, feeling chased around the round table.

"I didn't," she answered. "Though, you will find out soon enough."

Vivianne reappeared without Jeanine. My eyes immediately narrowed as I looked back and forth between them. This shoppe was full of books which I did not want to set ablaze, but I would if I had no other choice.

"It was almost too easy moving into this kingdom," Vivianne cooed, brandishing what looked like a letter opener in her palm. "We had expected more of a fight."

"I can give you a fight," I offered.

"When word spread that the *Tenebris Dimidium-Witch* dwelled here, we were overjoyed," Sria said. "We have been waiting a very long time."

"I have no fucking idea what that means." I lit my palms, slowly backing toward the back of the shoppe and closer to Vivianne. I needed to find Jeanine.

"It is really quite selfish of you, Half-Witch." Vivianne's voice had turned silky. "To not uphold the prophecy for you and your twin."

My eyes flared only slightly. I was not going to admit I had a twin, though I was curious about how they knew of River. And what made me a *Half*-Witch? My mortal father? Or was Gisela correct, and my father was something else entirely?

"We waited patiently to find you alone, yet he never left your side."

We had switched to Zeke now. "And you believe you have the chance now to what? Harm me? You will be disappointed."

Sria maliciously grinned. "We have him, Half-Witch."

Sweat immediately pooled at the base of my neck at her words, the way her eyes gleamed with joy at the threat in her voice.

Him. Him. They had *him*.

"And with your blood," Vivianne tacked on, her silky voice deepening, "Magic will freely flow once more."

"Him," I said with a choked breath. "By him, you mean...."

"Him," Sria repeated, "the prince."

It was small at first, the way the flames shot from my hands, but then they grew until the bookshelves were engulfed in a mixture of orange and purple, desperate to defend the man who held my heart.

I didn't expect them to fight back.

Sria shrank the flames with her hands as she crouched, putting her palms against the floor. Vivianne stared at me, her pupils dilated while sweat beaded across her brow.

"We need her blood!" Sria breathily shouted from the exertion of energy to lessen my flames. "Do it!"

Do *it*, do what?

A high-pitched sound rang in my ears. I had to cover them with my hands, shrinking my flames back into my palms and screaming so loudly that the glass windows of the shoppe cracked.

Ringing, so much ringing that my brain felt it might implode.

Stomping my foot, ice shot across the shoppe floor, knocking Vivianne to her back and breaking her concentration long enough for the ringing in my ears to stop.

"Raven!"

I turned my head toward the door just as John ran in, his eyes widening at the damage to the bookshelves and the blood dripping from my ears. He ran to me, putting my face between his hands. His mouth opened to say something, but in a breath, his eyes widened and filled with tears.

Standing behind him, her hand around the handle of the letter opener, was Sria, twisting it farther into his side.

"No!" I screamed, trying to hold him as he fell to the ground. "John, no, stay with me, stay...."

Jeanine crawled out from the back archway of the shop, the crown of her head covered in dried blood.

Why was this happening?

Who were these women?

Vivianne followed my gaze to Jeanine, and seconds later, Jeanine was screaming, covering her ears and balling into a fetal position on the melting ice.

Chaos surrounded me.

John was on the floor bleeding from his side, Jeanine was wailing in pain, books were burning, shelves crumbling, and my husband was at the mercy of strangers far away.

Standing on shaky legs, I pulled the letter opener from John's side and sliced my arm open. Sria and Vivianne's attention snapped toward me again as my blood dripped onto the floor beside John.

"You want it?" I growled, my teeth clenched, "Come and get it."

Sria foolishly lunged first.

I wrapped a hand around her throat and lit my palm, using my other to form a sharp icicle and jamming it into her side. She couldn't make a sound as I quickly burned through the flesh of her throat.

I did not let go. I did not give in. Even as my arm burned from the gash and the loss of blood dizzied me, I burned until I felt cartilage and bone in my hand, and it was only then that I dropped her to the ground.

Jeanine stood on wobbly legs and pounced on Vivianne, breaking her focus long enough for me to crouch and press my palm against John's side. His eyes were closed, his pulse barely beating, but I would not let the boys return to their father dead because of me.

"Stay with me, John. You cannot leave him." My bottom lip trembled, my voice unsteady. "He will never forgive himself if you do not make it through this."

Just as his wound began to close under my palm, the ringing returned, and Jeanine was tossed across the room, her head knocking against a splintering shelf.

"Why are you doing this?" I shouted across the room, though I couldn't hear my voice through the ringing, nor did I expect any response from her.

I couldn't focus and tell myself to use any of my magic because it felt like my brain was seizing.

The three of us would die in this shoppe.

Luca would return to everyone but his mother dead.

All because I wasn't strong enough.

I was never strong enough.

Over my dying flames and the pool of blood at my feet, courtesy of three different bodies, I painfully and soul-crushingly cursed the universe for gifting elements to the wrong person, because no matter what happened to me, no matter how much I wanted to fight, it wasn't ever enough.

Whatever I had left, I gave it to John. I pushed all the healing I could into his open wound. I took Zeke's newest letter from my bodice and held it against my heart, closing my eyes as I remembered how he described what marrying me felt like – the elation he felt when I accepted his proposal. And I hated myself for not forgiving him sooner.

Because this might be it.

As Vivianne drew nearer, the ringing increased, as if she were torturing me with each step. My body shook, pressure built in my head, and I worked my damndest to ensure I had some kind of memory of Zeke at the forefront of my mind.

With the letter opener dangling from her hand, I braced, preparing for the inevitable.

And then I felt him.

The ringing stopped all at once, and my eyes flew open, watching as Vivianne's hand froze mid-air, her eyes widened, and her lips turned blue.

And standing in the doorway, unmoving, his head cocked to one side and emotionless...

...stood River.

STANDING IN THE DOORWAY, UNMOVING, HIS HEAD COCKED TO ONE SIDE AND EMOTIONLESS STOOD RIVER.

RAVEN

I fell backward, watching in shock and awe as Vivianne kept utterly still in front of me. The only part of her that moved was her eyes as she frantically looked around, but all she could see was me on the ground, mirroring my terror with her own.

River leaned against the doorframe, almost bored, as he focused on her. This wasn't an element he was fighting with. This was entirely different—a power so strong that it took up the entire room. I could feel it surrounding us, suffocating the embers of my flames.

And then, clear as day, Vivianne just... evaporated.

Droplets of blood showered everything in the room aside from

327

him as he stood in the doorway, lifting his head and straightening the sleeves of his jacket.

I blinked, my mouth agape and an intense headache pounding at the base of my skull. The last half hour hit me all at once, and I fell backward against the scorched bookshelf, keeping my hand pressed against John's side even though I wasn't sure I had anything left to give him.

Jeanine had woken up and looked as terrified as I felt. She stared at River in the doorway before crawling over to me. Blood dripped from the crown of her skull, bruises forming across her face and arms. She cradled my neck and started saying something, but I couldn't make out any of it. I couldn't even utter a word in return.

My arm still dripped blood, slow in its healing since I had given as much as possible to John instead. But everything and nothing hurt simultaneously, and I couldn't fathom why...

Why *anything*.

"Zeke," was what I said first. "They have Zeke."

It was then that River finally moved from the doorway, his stride slow and nonchalant until he was crouching in front of me and studying my face.

"Zeke," I repeated. "I have to go to him; I need—"

"He is alive," River interrupted, plucking Zeke's letter from my hand. "I ensured that."

Nothing about this made sense, and everything around me began to blur the way it always did when the strain on my body became too much. "Who *are* you?"

His irritating half-grin was the last thing I saw.

A SPLASH of cold water on my face woke me up. I didn't believe it was meant to be annoying, but I found it all the same as I hissed and swiped at him.

I missed.

Gasping, I shot up from wherever I had been lying, and before I could take another breath, I said, "Zeke."

"Is alive," River repeated from earlier.

My temple throbbed, I couldn't open my eyes, and the faint ringing in my ears told me that I hadn't dreamt everything up. We had been attacked by two strangers in a bookshoppe who wanted my blood and nearly killed me to get it. "John, Jeanine..."

"Are alive," he said with a sigh, seemingly irritated that he kept repeating himself.

Finally, I looked around. I was in my bedchambers, sitting on my bed, and River was casually sitting at my table like we weren't enemies, his ankle propped up on his knee. He didn't look disheveled in the slightest. He was in a black suit, per usual, his black hair slicked back, and his expression one of pure boredom.

Like always.

I found myself glaring at him. "How are you here? Who are you? Why do you possess so much magic? Where is Zeke?" I looked down at my clean skin and raised my eyebrow at my nightshirt. "Did you... bathe me?"

He lowered his foot to the floor and looked unamused by my line of questioning. "Zeke's mother cleaned you up, as well as the feisty blonde one who shouted at me until she, too, passed out. John is recovering in his chambers."

"That answered only one question," I snapped, holding a palm against my clammy forehead. "How do I know Zeke is actually alive? I don't trust you."

"You're alive, aren't you?"

I was positive I hated him, though his answer made sense. If I were alive, it meant Zeke was, too. "Who were they?"

"Sria and Vivianne came from a coven outside of Reales—the Village of Reine," he explained.

"That tells me nothing." I wanted to stand. I needed to check on Jeanine and John, but every limb felt like lead. I froze. "They have children here."

The corner of his mouth twitched. "Did you actually see the children, Raven?"

"I..." Clamping my mouth shut, I sighed through my nose. No, I hadn't. I hadn't even bothered to inquire more about them before waltzing into their shoppe like we were old friends. "There weren't any children."

"There might've been children when they arrived." He adjusted the collar of his shirt beneath his jacket. Every movement of his seemed calculated. "But I can guarantee there are not any now."

I wrinkled my nose, confused by what that could possibly mean. "I don't understand. Did they leave?"

"Sparing you the gory details, that particular coven has found ways of preserving their youth when magic wanes."

I held up my palm toward him, stomach lurching from the implication. "I don't want to know anymore." Quickly changing the subject, I scooted to the edge of the bed. "I would like to see him. Take me to him in whatever way you can travel so quickly."

"I cannot do that."

"Like hell, you cannot do that!" I shouted, setting fire to my fists and burning the sheets of my bed. "I need to know he's alive! I will not simply take your word for it."

His eyes darted to the flames in my fists before returning to gaze at me. "I have a proposition for you."

"Fuck your proposition," I bristled, shakily rising to my feet. "I will find him myself." The last thing I would do was trust River, the twin who tried to drown me on multiple occasions. I wasn't even going to try to dissect why he had saved me just as many times. "Why do you only show up when I'm near death?"

I wobbled to my wardrobe, throwing open the doors and sifting through to find my traveling clothes. River stayed at the table, perching his elbow on it while he watched me. "Raven, I am not deceiving you. I have saved your life on multiple occasions. If you would listen...."

"No!" I barked, pulling out a top. "He is not something I am willing to bargain for. I need to see him."

River contemplated something, his eyes churning with the words he wasn't saying. "I will take you to him," he offered, but I knew better than to accept immediately. "But only after you come with me to Reales."

I blinked. "It wasn't a dream, then."

"It wasn't *not* a dream," he countered.

The fact that the tone of his voice hadn't wavered in the slightest irked me even more. He was always so reserved, even when I was surely irritating him. We were such opposites in every way except for appearance. Even adding that in, he was still taller than me like everyone was, and his beauty was more elegant while mine was pure chaos at all times.

"You will risk your people if you stay here."

That had me pausing my resolve to get him out of my chambers, my shoulders slumping at the possibility that I might be at fault for the future demise of my people.

"The news of your existence is traveling beyond this realm. It is no secret that you possess something others need. Sria and Vivianne were only the beginning, Raven."

He took a small step closer to me, his confidence almost charming in how he appeared disarmed while speaking so cordially. "I have the answers you need and am offering them to you"—he held up one finger when I tried to interrupt—"but only after you travel with me to Reales. Your absence here will guarantee the safety of everyone on the island until you are reunited with Zeke."

He said his name like they were old friends.

I crossed my arms over my chest, my brows knitted. "Why can't you tell me now? Why does it require me to travel with you? How did you infiltrate my mind?"

His nostrils flaring was the only proof that I was finally wearing on his nerves. "Some of your answers lie there."

Why did everything always revert back to that dying kingdom?

I gnawed on the skin of my cheek. "I want Jeanine to come with me."

His eyes rolled.

Rolled.

It was the most emotion I had ever seen from him, which made an uncontrollable smile cross over my lips.

"I do not understand why you insist on being friends with such an insufferable woman, but if it entices you to agree, then fine. She may come, too, but that is all."

I weighed my options, though it didn't seem like I had any. If I decided to go with him, I might find out why my blood was being sought after. If I stayed, I might subject my people to more attacks, and lives could be lost.

"I want an answer to one question before I give you mine." When he didn't object, a mixture of shame and embarrassment heated my cheeks. "Why is your magic so controlled while mine... isn't?"

"Out of all the questions you could've asked me, that is what you chose." He tilted his head ever so slightly. Maybe he didn't know the answer to that question. Perhaps my magic was bound to be forever out of control, but if one twin could remain calm and steadfast, surely the other could, too.

"You have not been taught that casting your feelings aside is the most important aspect of controlling your magic, Raven." From his fingers, droplets of water appeared as if invisibly falling from the sky, but we remained under the roof of my chambers. "You do not react with magic from anger or pain or hurt. You wield magic; it does not wield you."

A breathy laugh came from my nose. "Try telling that to Blaze then."

He flinched. And then he turned from me enough so that I could only see his profile. "How do you know her name?"

I had been asked that before by Jeanine. And just like then, I still didn't have an answer. I knew the names of my elements before my own. "I don't know," I answered honestly. "I just always have."

He studied my wall intensely, and his jaw ticked once.

"Does yours? Have a name?"

A beat of silence. And another. "I answered your question," he said quietly. "It is time for you to answer mine."

I sighed, fidgeting with the top still in my hands. "You will take me to him afterward?"

"I have kept my word so far, Raven."

I could tell he didn't like repeating himself. I knew another stubborn man like that. "Then I don't suppose I have a choice."

I stood inside John and Alice's chambers for the first time in my reign. John was awake and arguing with Alice about resting. Though they were not biologically related, Zeke inherited a lot of his stubbornness from his father.

332

My panic and refusal to let him die had closed the wound in his side, and now it was up to him to remain still long enough for the raw scar to heal. Having given up entirely from frustration, Alice excused herself to fetch him a bowl of soup.

I smiled while watching her leave, envisioning a future where I begged Zeke to rest while he refused. And then I looked at John, wagging my finger at him. "She's right, you know."

"I am perfectly well," he grumbled, grimacing as he pushed himself to a sitting position in his bed. "Now, tell me about what River said."

Shrugging, I sat in a velvet chair beside his bed. His chambers were nearly as large as mine, and rightfully so. Due to my naïveté, I hadn't realized that John was more involved in the kingdom's decisions than I thought. I was so busy worrying about my own loneliness that I never really had a conversation with him without Cade present.

His chambers had a split view of the mountainside and the water, and from his balcony you could see the Black Forest. I thought about what Jeanine said before we went into the caves and how John always seemed to know exactly where I was at all times. His view of the Black Forest all but confirmed it.

"John, why did you tell Jeanine I was the key to something?"

"For reasons like what happened today." He grabbed a pillow and set it behind him so he could sit taller. "The mystery surrounding you has plagued me for many years, Raven. Leonidas was adamant about who came into this kingdom. Fearful, almost."

"I regret not inquiring more about the relationship between Leonidas and Celestina," I said. "How long were they together?"

His smile was sorrowful. "Do you really want to know all of this, Raven?"

I nodded. Alice returned with his bowl of soup on a tray, placing it over his lap before sitting in the chair beside me. John took a sip from his bowl to appease her and rested his head against the headboard. "It went on for years. Leonidas was quite taken with your mother."

"Until the end?" I asked.

"It was quick," he answered. "Their courtship ended so abruptly. She stopped agreeing to see him just months before you were born."

"Wait." I looked between him and Alice. "*She* wanted to stop seeing *him*?"

When he nodded, I shook my head slightly. "That's not what his letter said. His letter said that he was the one to end things because her magic frightened him. He believed it would get out of control."

"That is untrue," Alice said. "It was Celestina's decision. Leonidas took it terribly. We had to halt shipments to Seolia for months. John had to prevent him from traveling to Reales."

"Then why would he tell me the complete opposite?"

"I don't know," John said. "Leonidas would've married your mother if not for Rudolf. Living without her tore him apart day by day."

He'd stated in his letter that he needed to leave Celestina because of her darkness, and that murdering her was the only way the realm would be safe.

John asked, "Raven, what did River say?"

I blinked out of my trance. "He didn't say much, to be honest. He promised to take me to Zeke if I traveled to Reales with him."

His frown was deep. "And you believe him?"

That was a loaded question. I hardly believed anything anyone said anymore, but I wanted answers as to why witches had infiltrated my island for my blood. And how River was able to travel so swiftly to wherever I was.

"I believe I want to see my husband," I said quietly. "I have questions about River that only he can answer. Grace found nothing about him, and I burned the books in the bookshoppe. He said if I stay here, more attacks will occur."

John looked as torn as I felt. We would be risking Seolia either way, whether I stayed or went. "Godfrey is here and has continued to train the army," I added. "If something happens, Seolia has a defense."

"At the end of the day, Raven, that is not my concern."

Warmth crept up my spine. He was concerned about my safety, the way a father should be. And though he wasn't my father, he loved me as his own. He would have none of his children here if I left.

"I remember once when you were a young girl, you ran through the cottages and giggled, and every person was so taken with your gleeful nature. I have shielded you from many things, Raven, much like Zeke tends to do, but it was to preserve that for as long as I could." He smiled at the memory, at the resemblance between himself and Zeke. "I knew who you were. I knew you were fated to marry my son." He took my hand and sandwiched it between both of his. "I loved you then as I love you now. I trust your decision, but I implore you to be careful. You may learn things about who you are that will be shocking."

I had learned over recent months that there was never any correct way to prepare for something like that—learning secrets about myself and attempting to piece them together to make a whole picture.

He squeezed my hand. "You are the daughter Alice always wanted. We are both very proud of your resilience, Raven."

"Thank you," I whispered. "And thank you for your sacrifice in keeping me safe. It couldn't have been easy leaving your family, but my life would've been much different had you not."

He swallowed, his eyes gleaming. "You have made it worth it, my girl. Now, go see my boys. Bring them home."

"JOHN, WHY DID YOU TELL JEANINE I WAS THE KEY TO SOMETHING?"

34

RAVEN

S tanding in the sitting room with River, I looked around to
avoid making awkward eye contact. I offered to let Jeanine
stay in Seolia, but she wouldn't hear of it. I would have felt
better if she had let herself recover from the concussion Vivianne had
given her, but it earned me a glare when I expressed that.

River stared at the portrait of Leonidas on the wall above the fireplace. Now more than ever, I wanted to know where River came from,
and if he knew who our father was. "Did you ever meet Leonidas?" I
asked him, taking small, airy steps closer.

River's sidelong glance had me studying his expression. "Why
would I?"

I looked from him to the portrait of the man I never knew yet supposedly shared half my life's blood with. "Because he is our father?"

His eyebrows lowered even more, creating a deep V on his forehead. "Who told you that?"

Jeanine strode in, dragging a large satchel behind her and looking more annoyed than usual. "Let's get this over with," she grumbled.

River sighed through his nose, not even looking at her when he asked, "And what is that?"

"I didn't peg you for dense," she responded, groaning as she lifted the satchel to rest across her chest. I had healed most of the bruising on her face, though her eyes still showed faint signs of purple. "I assume we'll need basic necessities like fresh clothing." She looked around the floor. "Where is yours?"

I shrugged. "He told me not to bring one. We won't be gone that long."

"Everything you need will be provided for you. I am not carrying that with us."

"Carrying?" Jeanine asked. "I can carry it to the docks."

He turned from the fireplace to face us, tugging at the cuffs of his jacket. "We're not traveling to Reales by ship."

I stayed silent, scratching my nose at the anticipation of River trying to explain his ability to travel to Jeanine. "There is no way to travel to Reales from here," Jeanine explained, "Everywhere we go is by water. Is that... are we traveling by water somehow? Like... like fish?"

I snorted. River looked utterly exasperated. "Is that how you believe I travel? By swimming underwater? I am not a merman."

"More like a shark," Jeanine muttered under her breath.

He clasped his hands behind his back. "I walk through what is referred to as the Time-Antre. It is called shadow-walking. It is very strenuous and exerts much of the mind."

Jeanine stared at him in disbelief. "You travel through time? Through what, exactly? A dark cave of betrayal and lies?"

If I had a knife, I could have sliced right through the tension between them. "Jeanine..."

River gave me a slight shake of his head. "It's fine, Raven.

Shadow-walking allows me the ability to manifest fully or by vision only. I found Raven in Perosan the day I left Reales. It allows me to travel quicker and bypass the time it takes to travel by foot or ship. It is not my favored mode of transportation, but it is the only way I can carry both of you simultaneously."

"Then why didn't you save her?" Jeanine asked. "If you knew where Raven was, why didn't you save her from Cade before he could harm her?" She stepped toward him but was held back by my arm wrapped around her waist. "You found her," she seethed, "And you did nothing!"

"I did not know he had taken her until the letter arrived in Reales." He glanced over at me with a slight frown. "I would have..." But he stopped and collected himself before showing any emotion. "I cannot step into the Time-Antre blindly. I must know where I am going or feel her elements to locate her. I can travel to places I've been to before. Otherwise, there is no map. With our connection to one another...."

Unexpected tears sprang to my eyes. We had no emotional connection, but our elements kept us tied together. I wished it meant more to him than that. As I stood beside him, I felt I was staring at a stranger, not my brother.

River didn't seem to notice my sudden posture change as I leaned into Jeanine. "I can locate her quicker when her elements call to me," he continued. "They did that morning when I found her in Perosan. I located her as soon as I felt her elements."

"But you wouldn't help me," I whispered.

He remained unmoving though I could've sworn I saw the slightest look of guilt cross his features. "I couldn't."

"Why?" Jeanine asked. "You are making massive demands of us, yet we know nothing about you. I promised Zeke I would protect Raven at all costs, and now you're asking me to trust that she will remain safe in Reales. Why do *you* need us in Reales? Are those men still there? What will Mira do when she sees Raven?"

Four questions, yet the only one River would answer was, "Raven will remain safe. I assure you."

"Your assurance holds no weight with me." Jeanine turned to face me. "Raven, we don't have to do this. We should wait for Zeke."

Sighing, I ran a hand through my hair and winced once I remembered it was braided. Jeanine untangled my fingers from the wisps of hair that wrapped around them. "Jeanine, we decided we must see what we're up against. And River said he would take me to Zeke afterward."

"A dinner," River said. "All I request is a simple dinner."

Jeanine's eyes closed briefly, sighing through her nose. "Nothing is ever simple with you," she muttered.

The last time I forced her to do something against Zeke's wishes, one of Zeke's soldiers punched me so hard that it released poison into my bloodstream. I understood that this decision was not one to take lightly.

"I want a guarantee." Jeanine pulled me to stand behind her. "I want you to make an oath. A promise. In magic, in blood, however you want to do it. Promise me Raven will leave Reales alive. There is a reason you need her, and it's not brotherly love. I will not betray her or my friend by sending her into an enemy kingdom without your promise that she will not be touched."

Zeke had taught her well.

River's eyes narrowed slightly on Jeanine. "Is my word not enough? I have already promised—"

"You have tried to drown her. You watched Zeke get stabbed in Reales and nearly die. You paired with your bitch of a sister to threaten Raven." Her laugh was not one of amusement but rather utter disdain. "Your word doesn't mean shit, River."

He bared his teeth for only a second, but it was long enough to notice the bright white of his perfectly straight teeth and the sharpened ends of what appeared like fangs. It was enough to send me a small step back.

He noticed that.

Blinking, he clenched his jaw shut and flared his nostrils. "I cannot make promises in blood, but I will swear an oath. It requires your hand."

Jeanine didn't hesitate. She left me, extending her hand to shake his, but he grabbed it and flipped it over, exposing her wrist. Placing his index finger against the soft flesh, he held her still while she flinched and cursed, staring intently at her wrist.

Yanking her hand away from his, she held her wrist up. Placed on her skin, in dark ink that matched the one River revealed on his wrist, laid a raised wave with two sharp crests.

It looked oddly familiar to the flame on Zeke's chest, yet distinct in the controlled movement compared to the chaos of my fire. River's eyes gleamed with amusement when he caught my gaze of confusion. I didn't ask how they were so similar because he wouldn't have answered me anyway.

"If any harm befalls Raven, it will be inflicted upon me." He lowered his arm and adjusted his sleeve, covering the mark. "The bond will break when she is safely removed from Reales."

Jeanine looked at the wave in disgust. "And this will be gone, too?"

"Yes," he said through clenched teeth. "I will not entertain any more demands. You have already wasted my time."

"With charm like that," Jeanine grumbled, returning to me. "Fine. We will accompany you to Reales in your strange time hallway. We need to be back on the island soon. Godfrey will inform Edmund if we're not back within three days."

With yet another demand, River looked ready to annihilate her. Before anything else could be said, I stood between them. "Okay, enough. What do we need to do?"

"Drop the satchel."

Jeanine barked out a laugh. "No. It has things."

"The extra weight will prevent us from walking," River countered. "Leave your *clothes* here." By *clothes*, he meant *weapons*.

A headache formed from their constant arguing. "Can we just..."

"Promise or not, I need to protect her."

"She will be fine!" he shouted.

We both silenced, staring at him in surprise. It was the most emotion we had conjured from him, and he looked ready to abandon the plan if it meant he wouldn't have to be near Jeanine.

I, however, needed to see my husband.

Cradling Jeanine's face between my hands, I pressed the tips of our noses together. "I love you, but I will be fine. I have my own set of weapons, remember? You don't have to like him, but can we *try* to trust him and see where it gets us?"

340

"Fine," she grumbled, then flashed him the fakest smile I had ever seen from anyone. "Let's go, waterboy."

I covered my mouth to hold in my laughter as she dropped her satchel to the ground, but not before sliding a small dagger into the waist of her pants. He watched her with an irritated scowl and reached his hand out to me.

Hesitating on instinct, I sighed before resigning to take my own advice. He had saved me multiple times. I wanted to believe that not every person I met harbored evil within, and it would be especially lovely if that included my twin.

I took his hand. The glower remained as he extended his other hand toward Jeanine. She looked equally repulsed but took it in hers. "Do we chant something?" she asked.

A breathy laugh escaped me before I took my top lip between my teeth when I caught his glare moving to me. "Stay beside me," he said. "Do not let go of my hand. It is easy to become lost in the Time-Antre if you don't know where you're going."

I was excited. I hadn't experienced much magic outside my own, and his vault impressed me. He was proving to be full of surprises, and I wondered if the magic he had attained could be learned.

If he could do it, so could I.

Before we grew bored of waiting for something to happen, the room around us slowly faded and my eyes widened. The colors weren't as bright as the grayish hue that engulfed us. Jeanine's head whipped back and forth. River remained still and calm, effortless in his stance and posture.

It wasn't smoke surrounding us; it was shadows. Wispy tendrils of it wrapped around us, covering our bodies from head to toe. I touched it but felt nothing, not even the faintest hint of anything abnormal.

One-second, we were in the sitting room, but the next... my lips parted as I looked around, convinced it wasn't real, that maybe River had crafted some sort of illusion.

Stone archways lined on our left and right, far as the eye could see, fading into pitch black. Within each archway, colors and sounds whizzed so quickly that I couldn't tell what they were or where they were coming from. I touched a stone brick, aged and cold from the chilliness of the hallway, and peered into the colorful scene unfolding before me.

Jeanine grabbed my elbow and tugged me over to her as if I might fall through one, and rightfully so. A step would be all it would take for me to jump into the colors underneath the arch. "What is this place?" I whispered in awe.

Jeanine, refusing to heed River's advice, held onto me instead of him. He pulled me along with him, using his free hand to point to the multiple archways on either side. "Time," he answered simply, like it should explain everything.

"And you can feel me here?"

"I can feel your elements," he corrected. "I could not feel you as death or yourself. It requires much concentration to find you when you're shifted or lighting something on fire, which has been more often as of late."

"But how?"

The corner of his mouth lifted to reveal a sliver of emotion. "They call to mine. Elements are partners."

I returned his admission with a grin of my own. There was a mystery surrounding him but also protectiveness regarding my safety. I didn't feel like a pawn used for war anymore, so what else could there be if not genuine... not love. I wasn't naive enough to believe he loved me, but concern for my wellbeing, perhaps.

"How long is this hallway?" Jeanine asked. "What are these things passing by us?"

"Moments in time," River answered. "Each archway represents a period of time, but only the ones worth visiting, or revisiting, are passing by us. Most of these moments belong to me." He nodded ahead. "There are some that do not."

I bit the corner of my bottom lip. "Could I... could you..." I drew in a deep breath. "Could we change what happened with Cade?"

His frown reappeared as his head shook slightly. "Moments that shape a being cannot be changed, even as painful as that moment might've been. Timelines cannot be altered; if you tried to change something, you would be thrown from the moment."

That wasn't the answer I wanted, but I understood. I wished I could go back and stop it from ever happening. Maybe we would still have our child if I did, but changing the moment might've led to other unwanted things, like Cade's survival.

"Do I have moments here? Or just you? And what of the others you alluded to?"

He looked nowhere but straight ahead, his mask of boredom returning, and I was learning that it was a defensive measure he took from revealing information he didn't want to. "Some things about the Time-Antre are better left unknown, Raven. This is still magic, and magic is soulless."

That was ominous and stopped me from saying anything else. Jeanine, however, sighed impatiently. "How long do we walk through this? There's no end."

"There isn't an end," he said with slight amusement. "It's time. Time doesn't end."

The glare she shot at his back made me snort.

We stopped between two archways. I looked into both while Jeanine stared at one, taking steps forward to watch the moments passing. River caught her by the elbow and pulled her backward, ignoring her protests. "I cannot allow you to accidentally fall into random moments. Raven would make me look for you, which could take days."

"I am surprised you aren't shoving me into one," Jeanine responded, yanking her elbow free from his grasp.

"Me too," River mumbled before extending his hand to her.

Jeanine crossed her arms over her chest.

His fingers curled into a loose fist. "We cannot stay here longer than needed. It's unsafe."

Jeanine looked around the empty hallway dramatically, her hair whipping back and forth. "Looks fine to me."

I sighed.

"I am not the only one with access to the Time-Antre. If we stay here too long, we might encounter beings desperate to change the story time has already told."

Eerie. And could make for some awkward encounters.

Jeanine took his hand. Barely. I wasn't convinced their hands were touching, but when she grabbed mine, I felt better knowing she'd travel with me — if that was even how it worked.

"Do not wander," was River's only warning before the archways became a smoky haze and began morphing into a small room.

Wherever he was putting us, it was definitely not Zeke's spacious chambers. And as the smoke around us began dissipating, I looked around, recognizing exactly where we were. Jeanine, however, looked bewildered.

She hadn't been with us when we discovered River holed up in this room within the cathedral. And the fact he had placed us in here immediately raised my suspicion. "Why aren't we in the castle?"

"My visitors still linger," he said, releasing our hands once we stood on solid ground. We hadn't moved an inch from the Time-Antre, yet we had just traveled five days away from Seolia. It only took minutes.

Sailing would seem like such a drag now.

"There are clothes for you in the wardrobe and food in the basket by the bed. I will come back to get you for dinner."

Jeanine tensed beside me. "What kind of dinner?"

River didn't look at her but continued to stare at me. "Lively conversation with my friends, of course. A grand dinner. Champagne fountains, flutes"—he waved his hand dismissively—"the works."

"Why would *your* friends want to welcome Raven?" She threw open the doors of the wardrobe to reveal two dresses. "You said nothing of a grand dinner, River. Grand is not simple. You've said nothing about anything, actually. Why are we here?"

River turned to leave, ignoring Jeanine, but left us with these parting words, "Do not leave this room. I will collect you in two hours. Your questions will be answered then."

As calm and relaxed as ever, he glided out of the room and closed the door behind him. Jeanine looked at me, and I suddenly regretted trusting him.

We were now left alone in enemy territory.

WE WERE NOW LEFT ALONE IN ENEMY TERRITORY.

35

NOVA

Standing on the outer edge of the kingdom of Nova, I looked over at Luca. We hadn't stopped at any other village before arriving here, only pausing our journey to set up camp for the night before rising again at dawn to continue riding.

Luca would never admit it, but he was exhausted. I would've been lying if I said I wasn't. This journey had been much longer than anticipated, even by horseback. We'd lost the lead we had before arriving at Reine. The witches stole an entire day from us, which only meant more time away from my wife. The temptation to abandon this trek and return home to her was strong, but we'd made it this far.

I glanced down at my ragged and worn clothing, the dirt on our hands and faces from sleeping on the ground. We looked the part of weary travelers, but I wasn't sure that would get us an invitation into the castle, which we could see from standing on one of the surrounding cliffs.

Nova reminded me of Thoya.

From my vantage point, I saw that roofs of manors and cottages spanned miles. Cobblestone roads weaved throughout the kingdom, littered with carriages, wagons of peddlers, and shoppe owners.

It was abundant. There was no mistaking that.

It confused me slightly. As a realm, we'd been told multiple times that the surrounding kingdoms were less than kind to their inhabitants, which was how many of them ended up in one of our four kingdoms.

Staring at Nova in front of me, I doubted the validity of those stories.

The castle sat in the center of town. It had multiple access points through tall, golden arches. The beige coloring of Melik's castle itself matched ours in Seolia, but it looked brighter with the grand windows wrapped around its entirety.

To the left of the castle were so many stables that I couldn't count them at first glance. Horses freely cantered, led by stablehands, in grass that was nearly too green.

Nova looked almost *too* plentiful.

Why would anyone flee from here?

Luca didn't look at me as he asked, "Now what?"

I wasn't afraid to enter Nova, but I was hesitant. While Melik had left the offer open to visit, Raven had burned his arm. I wasn't sure how long he could remain so forgiving.

"We need to get to the castle," I answered briefly. "We are at a disadvantage here. Melik and Alfie are the only royals I'm acquainted with, and Raven didn't leave a good impression." I chuckled despite it. I missed that fiery little witch more with each breath I took.

"I don't want to be here long," I continued. "Two days tops. I want to find out what kind of magic lives outside our realm and how I can acquire knowledge of Raven's mate and how it's possible she has one other than myself."

"That's a lot to learn in two days," Luca said. "Especially since it'll take at least a day to get you looking presentable."

I grinned, looking down at my clothes again. I would care if the only person I ever wanted to impress wasn't days away from me. Everyone else would just have to deal with it.

"If you don't need me, maybe I can see what kind of women Nova offers."

I rolled my eyes. "What about Jeanine?"

I followed behind him as we began our descent down the rocky ridge. Despite Shadow's elusive behavior, he must've been bred for travel. He didn't balk or fight me, no matter what kind of terrain we were on. Luca's horse, however, was more timid, and we had to stop often while it got its bearings. Shadow would huff impatiently every time.

"We're not together," Luca shouted to me over his shoulder as small rocks tumbled down the cliff. Each one spooked his horse, and he cursed aloud every time they came to a stop. "We agreed to keep it strictly sexual."

I couldn't judge. That was my philosophy for every woman I met until Raven came along. Now I wished to be strictly sexual with her several times a day.

I didn't pry any further. It wasn't my business; and honestly, I couldn't care less. They were both adults. If they wanted to keep feelings out of it, I admired them. Between strangers, that was easy. It was entirely different between friends, but after seeing them together daily for weeks on end, it somewhat surprised me that they didn't want to pursue anything further than *strictly sex*.

Or maybe I was too in love to understand.

"How are you holding up?"

I lifted an eyebrow at his question. I wasn't sure what kind of answer he wanted. How was I holding up without Raven? Without my daily intake of her blood? Or how was I holding up while maneuvering this steep pathway of imminent death?

"I just want to get this over with," I answered, covering all sides.

Jeanine had promised that she would keep Raven out of trouble, but no one could swear that and uphold the promise when it came to her. Raven seemed to *like* seeking out trouble. She was adventurous and curious and sometimes chose the most dangerous choice possible, and while Jeanine was stubborn, all Raven would have to do was flutter her eyelashes for even the most stubborn of people to give in to her.

"Can you feel her heartbeat from this distance?"

That was an excellent question. Mine had remained calm, even when I woke up chained to a bed. I hadn't wanted to frighten Raven, so I kept my breathing even and my adrenaline down so I could avoid sending my heart into a frenzy.

I hadn't felt anything unusual. There was a slight uptick a couple of days ago, but it ended quickly. "I don't know," I answered. "I like to believe I can."

"I'm envious of you."

I waited for more. I wasn't one to pry, nor was I going to remark that everyone should be envious of what I had with Raven. Honestly, I wanted my little brother to find as much happiness as I had. He was the one who deserved it.

But more never came. And those four words were enough.

THE REST of our ride was silent until we found ourselves standing behind trees beside the cobblestone road leading through the center of town and straight to the main archway of the castle.

I watched people move back and forth across the road, exchanging pleasantries and goods. They certainly looked like mortals. I wasn't sure what I expected, but Melik had made it sound like magic was something tangible in his kingdom. I was hoping it would be more apparent.

Their clothing was... different. Women wore brighter colors than I was used to seeing in our realm, even on Gisela. I had seen her wear dresses of many different colors, and the ones in my mother's shoppe from Reales had been colorful, but these were made of every color imaginable.

Men walked around in looser clothing of mostly blues and grays. The tops were tied together at the clavicles by leather strings, and while looking at their leather boots, I decided to pick some up for myself before we left.

Everyone here seemed relaxed—as if war wasn't looming over their realm. They seemed genuinely joyous. I could pick out multiple languages, which didn't tell me which originated in this kingdom, yet every person seemed to know each language spoken.

I slid off Shadow and reached into my satchel, pulling out two black masks and tossing one at Luca. I tied mine around my neck while he stared at his. "Why do we need these?"

"Two reasons," I answered. "One, I don't know what others might know about us. Melik mentioned something about knowing me. Two, I am quite terrified of my wife. If another woman approaches me, she might appear out of thin air and burn her alive. This deters them from trying."

"What if I want them to approach *me*?"

"Put the goddamn mask on, Luca. You can whore yourself out after I've been allowed into the castle."

He tied the mask around his neck and pulled it over his mouth. "I wonder if Raven is being this mean to Jeanine."

Chuckling, I pulled my mask up. "I doubt it."

∾

It was obvious to everyone who looked at us that we were outsiders. I didn't hold anyone's gaze for longer than a few seconds, but Luca waved at any woman he found attractive.

This quickly earned him a punch on the arm.

People stopped us every so often to offer random goods and food, which was tempting, but we didn't take any of it after being poisoned only days prior. I hoped Melik would take pity on us and offer food and beds for the night.

Otherwise, I would return to Raven starving and frustrated from embarking on a pointless excursion.

I had only two blood vials left, and I was trying my damndest to save them. They called to me, though, like a siren. I could continue without food if I drank them. I ran my tongue along the roof of my mouth while I fought the temptation, squeezing the lead rope between my fingers until the leather burned.

I hadn't realized we had stopped until Luca stood before me, shaking my shoulder. "Zeke."

Her blood. I wanted her blood. The pulsing in my chest *needed* her blood. It craved the sweetness of it.

"Zeke," Luca warned in a hushed tone. "Your eyes."

"Blood," I snarled. "Give it to me."

Luca shook his head, tightening his hold on the satchel strapped across his chest. I had stupidly given him possession of the vials to prevent me from using the last two before leaving Nova. "Not yet. Two days, Zeke."

My nostrils flared as I bared my teeth to him, clenching my fist to prevent tearing the satchel off him.

Luca's eyes darted around. "You're drawing attention."

I didn't give a fuck. This was the mad chaos Arthur had warned us about. It had been days since I had last tasted her. Her blood was the only way I knew she was safe. "Give me her blood, Luca. Now."

"Think of your wedding!" he blurted out. "Of watching her try and catch fish in Seolia—how ridiculous she looked."

"What are you—"

"You always make her think of happier memories when the darkness comes, Zeke. I might not have your ability, but I can remind you of them. You have to keep going for her. You cannot have the vials. Not yet."

Oddly enough, his words calmed the raging pulse in my chest as I thought of her laugh and smile. He was right. If I drank them too soon, I might wholly consume her on sight from thirst after returning. I was keeping her safe by holding myself back.

I drew deep breaths through my nose and slowly released through parted lips. A hint of need lingered, but the relief that crossed Luca's face told me that my eyes had returned to their usual gray.

It was becoming more difficult to doubt that I did possess some kind of shadow deep within that was as obsessed with Raven as I was. And it was a war within myself over how much of her I was willing to share with this creature.

Once composed, I gave Luca a nod. He studied me for a moment longer before he continued down the road toward the castle. I would be lying to myself if I said I could go on like this without reprieve soon. It was unnatural for twin flames to be apart once paired.

Every inch of our bond was strung tight.

I tried to feel her mind from where I was, desperate to talk to her. If I could just hear her voice and be guaranteed that she was safe...

"Well, well, well."

I looked behind me, whistling for Luca to stop. Melik stood in an obscene amount of royal garb — a crown atop his head, an intricate woven top, a jacket that hit his knees, and, unlike the other men walking around, his pants were tight.

"You look ridiculous," I said.

"Still a pleasure, I see." Melik looked behind me. "Did the universe curse us with two of you?"

The corner of my mouth twitched. "Not quite. This is my brother, Luca. We're not twins, though we're often mistaken as such." There were no guards or other members of royalty with him. "Still walking around alone?"

"I have yet to witness you and Raven together. I might believe you lied about her and that she can't stand you."

"Only on the good days," I said with a chuckle. "How is your arm?"

"I am reminded of her every day."

My grin widened. "She knows how to make a mark on people."

He smiled then and extended his hand to me. "What can I do for you, Prince Ezekiel?"

I took his hand, my grin faltering. "I need your help."

HER BLOOD. I WANTED HER BLOOD. THE PULSING IN MY CHEST NEEDED HER BLOOD.

36

Zeke

The castle of Nova was similar to Edmund's in terms of gold, but that was where the similarities ceased. Melik's castle was over-the-top, much like the clothes he wore. Plush velvet chairs lined the walls underneath portraits that had to be taller than Raven. The frames were made of gold so heavy that one had to wonder how they had even managed to hang them. I knew nothing of the history of Nova, so I didn't know who these portraits were portraying, but one of them looked like an older version of Melik that I assumed was his father. A picture of an older woman with a demure smile was beside it.

"My mother," Melik said once he caught me staring.

"She's beautiful," I complimented him, squeezing his shoulder. His mother. He had told me about the adviser that raped her, and why his brother had murdered the man in retaliation.

"She is alive and well," he explained further.

I nodded, immensely grateful that it hadn't gotten that far between Raven and Cade. She had barely recovered from the ways he touched her. Melik's mother must have immeasurable strength to continue on living day-to-day after being violated against her will, and Alfie was the man the world needed for killing her rapist.

I would repeat killing Cade every day if I had the chance.

Servants walked around—some holding trays, others exchanging linens—but avoided looking at us as we meandered through the golden corridors.

I watched as a maid scurried in front of us before glancing at Melik to ask, "Are you having a party?"

His confusion told me that, no, they weren't having a gathering. This was their day-to-day. "No, Ezekiel. I didn't know you were coming. If I had, I could've thrown together a soiree."

Luca snorted behind me. I rolled my eyes. "Not for me, Melik, though I appreciate the bare minimum. Your kingdom is livelier than mine or any other kingdom in our realm, even one as abundant as Thoya."

"Thoya?" He brushed his fingers across his chin. "I have not heard of Thoya. It is in your realm?"

That was odd. I assumed there would at least be a map of our realm somewhere that showed each kingdom. Arguing with Melik would be pointless as he yammered about the castle's history, who built what, and so on.

I looked at Luca over my shoulder every so often to find him as unamused as I was, shrugging a shoulder as we both remained silent and asked no questions for fear it would extend the history lesson.

Perhaps, I should've been paying attention. Maybe some of my answers lay within the palace's history, but I couldn't find it in myself to care when I had dirt in every crevice of my body and the thought of Raven's blood at the forefront of my mind. It made it difficult to concentrate on anything else.

We came to a stop as we entered another corridor. We had taken

353

so many lefts and rights that I was not optimistic I would be able to find the front door again. Melik gestured to side-by-side doors made of heavy steel but painted to disguise them as gold. "Adjoining rooms. Clean yourselves up. There are fruits and cheeses available in your rooms. I will fetch you for dinner. Rest."

Luca looked at me. "Better than witches."

"Ah," Melik said with an amused grin. "You made the mistake of going through Reine, then?"

I gritted my teeth in annoyance. "Yes. You know them?"

"They are part of our kingdom," Melik answered. "We leave them alone but provide protection if necessary in exchange for them leaving the inhabitants of our dwellings alone. Did they harm you?"

"They tried," Luca answered. "They wanted Raven's blood and kept referring to her as—"

"Luca," I snapped. I wasn't planning on giving information about my mate so freely. Though I believed I could trust Melik, as I sensed no ill-intention from him, Raven was not something I would ever gamble.

Melik held up his palms. "I do not pry, Ezekiel. Only tell me what you're comfortable with." He looked around the hallway. It was empty aside from a couple of servants. "But please, remember my warning. I trust my people, but you never know the lengths someone will go for such information."

I remembered his warning well. No one was to know of the bond between Raven and me, and I intended to keep it that way. "Thank you, Melik, for your hospitality."

"It is the least I could do for my brother's return." He dipped his chin and waved once as a goodbye before disappearing down the corridor.

"Do not speak of Raven again," I demanded. "She is wanted outside of our realm. If anyone were to know that we are close to her, it could bring our deaths or capture. The only one who knows of her is Melik."

Guilt poured from Luca as he ran a hand through his hair, clumps of dirt falling to the floor. "I'm sorry, Zeke. She's my sister. I'm used to speaking of her freely."

Sighing, I rested my hands loosely on my hips. "I know. It's different now. The witches wanted her for a reason, which means others will, too. We can't make the same mistakes as before. I trust Melik, but I can only extend that trust so far. He is the only one allowed to speak of her while we're here."

I nodded toward his door. "Now, let's check your room."

"Check my room?"

"For anyone unwanted, Luca. Spies, assassins, hunters, anyone who could know us or why we're here. I haven't made many friends while procuring soldiers for Mira's army."

"Why would they be in *my* room?"

"Because you are my brother!" I whisper-shouted, annoyed with his line of questioning. "It is my responsibility to protect you. Just open the goddamn door, Luca."

With a hint of amusement in his voice, he twisted the handle and said, "If you don't start being nicer, I will feed your blood vials to wolves."

~

AFTER CHECKING HIS ROOM, I used the adjoining door to enter mine. Luca stood by a table while I searched every corner, popping strawberries into his mouth and peppering me with questions again about why I needed Raven's blood.

Closing the door behind me, I leaned against it and exhaled slowly. I had been with him for nearly two weeks, and while I thought I would be grateful for the silence, it only reminded me that I wasn't with Raven.

I would have to sleep alone.

I couldn't remember the last time I had slept alone.

Having Luca beside me had kept me distracted enough to not realize it, but tonight would be the first night I would sleep in a bed without my wife.

Small things, yet they felt so large and suffocating.

I should've gone to wash off, rest, and put on clothes that didn't smell like mud and horse. Instead, I walked around the room and studied the pictures on the walls.

These were not of royals. These featured oddly shaped creatures with scales and bones sticking out of their skin, like something from the nightmares of children. However, the pictures hanging next to my bed were of different creatures. Some had wings, some didn't, but all of their ears were pointed. One picture depicted them in a land of red, while the others stood in snow-covered banks.

And as I looked down the line of pictures, I realized they told a story. The nightmarish beings had been obliterated by the winged ones. Between the two was an intricately painted image of war. There was fire and smoke, ice and frozen tundras, all blended into magic and chaos while the winged creatures stood above the bodies of the others.

But on the other side of the bed—substantial in size and topped with far too many pillows—were portraits of men that looked mortal, yet there was something eerie that struck me. The paint had begun to chip and gave me little indication of who these men could be. All that remained were their eyes.

Red. Their eyes were red.

A loud knock on the door made me jump and clutch my chest as adrenaline shot through me. I exhaled an annoyed breath and stomped toward the door, throwing it open to see a timid maid holding a bucket with a bottle inside.

I softened my stare and greeted her. She didn't appear to hold any magical abilities. Perhaps Melik had overcompensated with his explanation of Nova and the magic it held.

"Prince Melik wanted you to have this." She thrust the bucket out toward me awkwardly and then began apologizing. "It is a bottle of his favorite whiskey, and he said he promises it is not poisoned."

I took it from her with a slight grin. "Thank you."

It was almost as if I could hear Raven saying, *stop smiling at her.*

She extracted a pair of gloves from the pocket of her waisted apron. "He also said that her name is unique."

It took me a second to reconcile what that could mean, but then I looked down at my hand holding the bucket. Raven's name was boldly printed across my skin. I didn't like the idea of hiding her or that I belonged to her, but Melik seemed concerned.

I took the gloves from her with a slight nod. "Express my gratitude to him, please."

She dipped into a curtsy before scurrying back down the hallway. I closed the door and tossed the gloves on a small table nearby before twisting off the lid of the bottle of whiskey. Hating that I needed to, I sniffed around the rim.

Sweet caramel wafted into my nose. Tipping the bottle back, the buttery and smooth liquor pooled on my tongue, and the tension I had been holding in for days loosened.

Undressing, I drank until the bottle was half empty and placed it on the floor next to the grand tub in the lavish washroom. The water was scalding, but I welcomed it as my sore muscles slackened.

Two days until I could leave and return to Seolia.

Two weeks until I would see her in the dress my mother sewed for her, until I could dance with her all night in our castle and worship her until the sun rose the next day.

I watched memories of us as I sank lower into the tub, my eyes closing and body relaxing until it was numb.

Two weeks, Raven.

∾

RUNNING through the castle hallways in Reales, I laughed as her giggles echoed against the walls. Her long hair whipped around the corners as she darted from room to room. Each time I nearly caught her, she ended up farther away.

"Raven!" I called out to her, following her voice.

No reply.

I stopped short as I entered one of the sitting rooms where my tutoring lessons were held as a boy. Raven stood in the center, pale-faced and wide-eyed. She was in a white dress, the same one she was wearing when I found her in Perosan, her skin muddy and her hair disheveled and swaying as she clutched the fabric of her dress between her fingers. I looked down at her stomach, stumbling back a step as blood began soaking through her dress. "He's gone," she whispered.

Tears wet my cheeks as I ran to her, but as I lunged for her, I caught nothing but air. I looked around for her, calling her name, panicking. I didn't feel her anywhere.

A dark presence looming behind me made me whip around to find a man standing in the tall door archway. Faint recognition lingered between us. I hadn't met him before, but he knew me. I sensed it in him. He knew me, and he hated me.

All I felt was anger and envy from him as he observed me from where he stood, but this wasn't a memory. This wasn't a dream I'd had before. The portraits hanging on the walls differed from when I was a boy. The castle seemed even darker than before, and the eerie feeling of death was everywhere.

The hair on the back of my neck stood. "Where *is* she?"

He stepped out from the doorway, his hands loosely shoved into the pocket of his fitted pants. "With me."

He lifted his eyes.

Red.

I WOKE UP WITH A GASP. Water sloshed around in the tub and splashed onto the floor with enough force to knock the half-drank whiskey bottle over. The aroma of it quickly filled the room as I panted, my chest heaving. I swiped a hand down my face and tried to chase the dream.

It was a nightmare. It was only a nightmare.

Raven was safe on the island. The man was from the picture in my room. No one had red eyes, and Jeanine wouldn't allow someone to take her again without getting word to me. Edmund knew where I was headed.

Raven was safe.

But that still didn't calm the gnawing feeling in my gut that the dream felt too real. *He's gone*, she had said. She had been clutching the dress at her stomach. Bleeding. There had been so much blood.

He's gone, he's gone.

Tears sprang to my eyes. Our son. Her nightmare I had shattered many nights ago, had taunted her with our child. She had begged me to look at him, to let us stay there where we could all be together, and now he haunted my nightmares.

The water in the tub had gone cold, but it was nothing compared to the iciness of my heart, to the cold sweat pooling at the base of my spine from the idea that we had lost a son. And that I was reliving it through nightmares. I hadn't had a nightmare since before meeting her.

Why was I dreaming of our son?

The pain from our loss lingered, but I had grown used to it. Like always, Raven repaired the holes caused by my pain. I swore each time she laughed, it mended a piece of me.

Two days was too long. I needed to gather as much information as possible and be gone by tomorrow evening.

Standing from the tub, I didn't bother drying off as I walked back into the bedchambers. I sifted through my satchel only to find that it was empty except for the herbs and medicines Raven had sent.

All of my clothes were gone.

I tied a blanket around my waist and banged on the adjoining door to Luca's chambers, waiting impatiently for him to open it. He answered it with a yawn, his eyes heavy with sleep. And naked. I assumed his clothes were gone, too. "Is it your life's mission to wake me up every time I've fallen asleep?"

"My shit is gone," I snapped, "all of my clothes."

"Calm down," he said with a groan. "The maids took them to wash. They waited at my door while I grabbed yours. You slept for hours. No one stole anything, Zeke. Who would want those, anyway? They reek of your mixed scent."

Bypassing the fact that my brother was willing to let me drown in a tub while I slumbered instead of waking me, I punched him on the shoulder. "I know," I growled. "That's why I didn't want them cleaned. I wanted to smell her."

He cursed. "You smell *of* her, Zeke. Isn't that how it's supposed to work?"

I opened my mouth to speak but stopped myself. He was right. Our scent was permanent. It wasn't something that could be cleaned from me, which meant my clothes would smell like her every time I wore them.

"And," he continued, "if their kingdom believes in magic and pairings, they'll know you're mated. You're very dramatic, you know. It's okay to not believe the worst in everyone you meet."

"How long until I can have another vial?"

Luca sighed and looked into his room, presumably at the satchel, which I was positive I could wrestle away from him. "I'll give you one when we leave here."

That only strengthened my resolve.

"Get dressed. There are clothes in the wardrobes."

He groaned, pressing his head against the doorframe. "And where exactly are we going now?"

"Wear your mask. Don't leave her blood here."

"IF YOU DON'T START BEING NICER, I WILL FEED YOUR BLOOD VIALS TO WOLVES."

37

ZEKE

I
t was late afternoon when we made it out of the castle. We took many wrong turns but somehow ended up at the front gate. The clothes we wore were almost as ridiculous as what Melik had been dressed in, but we didn't have another choice.

Luca was wearing an intricately woven pattern of floral embellishments on a knee-length, dark-purple tunic over a pair of black pants that may as well have been tights. He continuously cursed while adjusting himself, waddling in front of me and throwing glares at me whenever I snickered.

It wasn't like I received the better end of the deal.

I rarely wore anything but black, with the rare exception of gray.

Even choosing a navy suit for my mother to design to match Raven's surprise ball dress was a stretch.

My... light blue garment reached my thighs; it couldn't even be described as a shirt. I had a couple of inches on Luca, so it didn't fall quite as far, but still longer than anything else I had ever worn. It was embellished with silhouettes of horses.

At the bottom of the stacks of tights were a looser pair of brown pants. They clenched at my ankle, so I ripped out the thread binding them to loosen the cuffs.

At least the maids had left our boots alone.

"I would like to officially declare that I never wish to return here," Luca said while he waddled past the front gate.

The satchel containing my vials kept bouncing against his hip, and I worried they would break if he didn't stop fidgeting. Grabbing his shoulder, I held him in place long enough for him to stop and look at me. "Relax. And stop walking like that, or your chances of fucking someone will be nonexistent."

He tugged at the bottom of his tunic and shrieked, "Does it look like I will be fucking someone in this?"

I couldn't help but laugh. "You never know, Luca. The women here might go for the overdressed-and-masked type."

"Easy for you to say," he grumbled. "You could show up to Seolia wearing that and Raven would still fall to her knees."

As tempting as that sounded, I would not subject myself to the mockery this outfit would undoubtedly bring from Raven and Jeanine.

We walked along the stone pathway toward a cobblestone road we hadn't explored. I doubted we would cover all we needed to in the time we were here. From the cliff, I saw dozens of streets. I didn't care enough to explore the entirety of the kingdom. I wanted to see what kind of creatures dwelled here, but was praying we wouldn't run into more witches.

We certainly weren't alone. Unlike Reales and the tiny kingdom of Seolia, people were scattered... everywhere, carrying more goods than I had ever seen. Some greeted us as they walked by, and some raised an eyebrow at the masks we wore, but mostly, they seemed friendly.

Luca tilted his head when a woman with a wicker basket full of bar soaps passed us. "Thia's father orders soaps from outside kingdoms, right? Did we ever import from Nova?"

I shrugged a shoulder. "Not that I'm aware of. I don't recall where he imported from, but I didn't know Nova existed until I met Melik."

"Thia," he sighed. "Maybe we can stop by Reales on the way home, yeah?"

I scowled. "Raven would burn her alive if she even looked at me. You would be taking that trip alone."

"You're going to be king. You'll have to interact with all of your... conquests."

I hadn't thought about that—not that it mattered. I had blurred all of my memories with other women. "We don't know if I'll be king yet, Luca. I haven't made a decision. I don't want Raven to give up her throne for me."

Luca scoffed. "Raven would give up the sun for you. She would throw all of us into eternal darkness for you."

I grinned at the truth of that. "Just because she would doesn't mean I expect her to. Raven is a strong leader... or she could be if she stops doubting herself."

"She doesn't have to with you around."

I stopped. "What does that mean?"

He glanced at me over his shoulder and frowned, sighing as he turned to face me. "I love Raven, Zeke. She's my sister. But you're more experienced. You were taught how to rule a kingdom. As smart as she is and as kind as her heart remains, she wasn't. She will always feel inferior to you because Cade weaponized her goodness."

"She's not inferior to me. She's equal."

"I know she is. We all know she is. But it's something you need to ask yourself. Do you want Raven to remain on the throne of Seolia, and have her constantly wonder if you'd do things differently, or would you rather her rule beside you in Reales while having the freedom to be with the people?" He gave his shoulder a slight shrug. "That's where her heart is, Zeke. It's with the people. Not being doted on."

He left me to ponder as he walked away, readjusting himself for the hundredth time. Seolia loved Raven. It started thriving after

Raven was put on the throne, but was that because she was a good leader or because she spent nights roaming her kingdom in disguise and knew it by heart?

I jogged after Luca as he turned a corner onto the road. Open-faced shoppes, canvas tents, and stone dwellings with no doors left little to the imagination when looking for available goods.

It reminded me of the trader's market in Thoya, but it also made for many awkward social interactions. And despite our masks, we were often stopped to ask if we were looking for something in particular.

I turned everything down, aside from a new pair of boots. Luca had already purchased multiple items to have delivered to the castle. It would be refreshing if Luca were yelled at for spending too much money instead of Raven and me.

So far, no one had stood out to me. Everyone looked mortal and ordinary. Of course, I looked the part, too, yet I could kill every person in this marketplace by simply entering their minds. Women would stare and gawk, and I would've been lying if I said I wasn't silently wishing Raven would show up. Her jealousy had become one of my favorite characteristics. It always ended in some earth-shattering fucking.

Gods, more than anything, I hoped she would allow me to love her like that again. In my time away from her, I had slowly become more aware of the missteps I'd taken in our marriage, and I was desperate to rectify them.

"Zeke!"

I stood outside one of the booths while waiting for Luca. Sighing from impatience, I irritably glanced at him. He held up a golden necklace and pointed to the dangling charm. "For Raven!"

Squinting an eye, I tried to make out what the charm was. I had already bought her a crescent moon necklace she wore often, and she wasn't fond of being spoiled.

I shook my head, but it didn't matter. Luca was already purchasing it. Shadow wouldn't be too excited about carrying all of this home.

As Luca explained that it needed to be sent back to the castle, I returned to studying the people surrounding us. It wasn't until I looked down the road a little further that my curiosity was piqued.

Still as death, and staring at my brother, was a man. Only, he didn't look completely... human. He looked as if he were made of stone. With his hair bright blond and his skin nearly translucent, I wondered if it was safe for him to be in the sunlight.

But he wasn't just staring at Luca.

He was leering at the satchel.

"Luca!" I shouted.

Luca continued to speak animatedly with the merchant. The man moved slowly at first, the tip of his tongue darting out to touch the point of one of his canines, which looked too sharp to belong to a human.

In the blink of an eye, so fast that I stumbled back a step, the man suddenly stood only feet away from me. And seconds later, he grabbed the satchel's strap at Luca's side.

I attempted to push into his mind but was met with a stone wall. Fuck, I really didn't want to have to fight anyone on this journey.

I lunged forward in two steps, grabbing the wrist of the man while Luca tried to pry the strap away from his fingers. "You have a treat," he hissed. "I can smell it."

The same rage that had built when Cade's skull was in my hands returned at the threat in his voice—at the idea that he could scent *my* mate from her blood.

The bone of his wrist cracked between my fingers.

He howled in pain and removed his hand from the satchel long enough for Luca to stumble back and move behind me. I didn't release him. I called for whatever lurked inside me to free itself, but nothing came.

Only the rage remained.

"You cannot have her," I snarled.

He bared his teeth, showing off his canines. They looked like sharpened blades, the tips no thicker than the point of a needle. "You possess the Dark Half-Witch. I recognize her... *scent*." The rumble in his throat was low, and his nostrils flared as he continued to scent the vials of blood.

"Yes," I confirmed, though I was positive he scented our bond and did not need my confirmation. "And her blood belongs to me."

Though his wrist was in pieces between my fingers, his smile was malicious. "It belongs to *him*."

I blinked. Him.

Her mate. This man knew who her mate was. "Who?"

He opened his mouth to answer when his eyes suddenly widened. They turned from gold to the red from my nightmares. The veins in his forehead and arms were strained, and nothing but a croak came from his throat before he just...

...vanished into tiny droplets of blood.

BLOOD SPLATTERED across the canvas walls of the tent, my ridiculous clothes, and the face of the merchant as she screamed in horror. Luca grabbed me by the collar and pulled me out of the tent, shaking me as I stared into the tent in shock. "What did you do?"

"That wasn't me," I rasped.

"How do we know?" he continued to shout. "How do we know your anger didn't somehow—"

"It wasn't me!" I repeated, coming to. "Luca, that was not me." I shook free of his grasp and looked around the marketplace. Upon first glance, all I saw were the terrified faces of the others who had seen what happened.

Until a flash of green eyes met mine.

I moved a foot to run toward him as he turned from me, but I was caught by my arm and held back. Thinking it was Luca, I yanked my arm free, only to be grabbed again. "Ezekiel, this is not the place."

The sharp voice was one I recognized—not because it was Melik pulling at me, but because I had used the same voice when commanding my own people as the prince.

I swiped at my cheeks as the dried blood on my skin, tearing my arm free from his hand. "Who *was* that?"

Melik looked around us. It was evident we had drawn a crowd. And the concern coming from him told me that whoever they were, it was a problem that one of them had exploded right in front of me.

Melik plastered on a fake smile and held his hands up before shushing the growing voices. "My people! What you have witnessed was merely an accident. He did not know how to control his magic. You are safe!"

The sweat beading on his temple told me that wasn't true. That, and the fact that I could smell his lie. And since he knew my abilities, he glanced at me quickly. "Go back to the castle. I will find you and explain."

I hesitated. I wouldn't have agreed so quickly if I couldn't sense truth and deceit, and I wanted this blood off of me. The idea of someone else's blood repulsed me. It felt like fire against my skin, as if it were reminding me that I belonged to someone else—that her blood was the only one I could ingest.

It belongs to him.

Her mate, whoever he was, wanted her blood.

I paced the length of my room. Our clothes had been returned to us, and we had both changed while waiting for Melik. To drown my nerves, I requested another bottle of whiskey, which was promptly delivered to me.

I drank half. Luca finished the rest.

He kept asking me to explain, but I had no explanation. I couldn't stop thinking of how that man had just... evaporated. It was as if he never existed. The way his eyes changed from gold to red, the way his veins bulged and pulsed in those last few seconds, was something I could not explain.

"And you're sure it wasn't you?"

I stopped moving and glowered at Luca.

"Okay, it wasn't you."

I possessed power. I understood that. But it was a power that I hadn't realized yet. I was angry, but not in a controllable way where I could make someone explode. My way of handling things was rarely measured and surprisingly messier. I enjoyed seeing bruises on skin and blood pouring.

Whatever happened to him was too easy.

A man should have to work for his kills.

Melik didn't bother knocking. He breezed right in and slammed the door shut behind him, his hand raised to his forehead as he used his other to motion toward me. "That was not how I envisioned your visit going, Ezekiel."

"Who are they, Melik?"

Before he answered, he shut the adjoining door to Luca's room until we were secluded in mine. With apparent paranoia, he pulled back my curtains to peek outside, but my room was several floors up from the ground.

"They infiltrated my kingdom not long after I met you." He turned away from the window and crossed his arms over his chest. "The numbers were small at first and then began to grow. Every day, more came. It stopped for a very long time, years even, but now they have returned."

I pointed to the picture beside my bed. "They have red eyes, Melik. I had a nightmare that one of them had taken Raven. And then one just happens to be in your marketplace and knows who she is?" I curled my fingers. "Who *are* they?"

Melik's shoulders slumped, and he sat in one of the velvet chairs by the window. "All we have are rumors. They've made no demands because we have not met their leader. We aren't aware of who it could be, or if he still even exists. But my people have begun disappearing. There is no trail or reason as to how it could be happening. The timing is too coincidental."

"He knew Raven," I repeated. "He said I possessed the Dark Half-Witch. It's what your witches called her."

Luca asked, "What rumors have you heard of these men?"

"They are not men," Melik answered. "They are…" He looked uncomfortable, shifting in the chair. "We believe they are Undead."

Luca laughed, but his eyes widened when Melik didn't admit to telling a joke. "Undead?"

I looked between them. "What the fuck are Undead?"

"Many years ago—over a century ago, to be precise—it is said that creatures of blood would move through the night to feed from mortals," Melik explained. "Their eyes would glow red once satisfied.

Villages never stood a chance. They were too powerful. Too beautiful. No one could resist them."

I raised an eyebrow. "What happened to them?"

He was lost in thought, his voice distant as his head shook slightly. "We don't know. They disappeared, but no one believed they were truly gone. We would hear stories as children about The Great."

"The Great?" Luca asked.

"The Great is where it's said they congregated. I don't know where it is or if the rumors are true. I didn't believe in their existence until men who fit their description came to my kingdom, and my people began dying. It is like history is repeating itself. This was a problem for my ancestors, it is why—"

"It's why villagers flee," Luca finished for him. "Fear."

"You said your kingdom has magic, Melik. I came here to see it. Why aren't you defending yourselves?"

Melik chuckled. "What kind of magic were you expecting, Ezekiel? I told you that no one here possesses what Raven does. You met our witches. Within the kingdom, we have pairings and abilities like chlorokinesis, thaumaturgy..."

"I have no idea what that means," I said.

"Magic exists here, Ezekiel. Isn't that what you wanted to know?" He tilted his head slightly. "Or is there something else?"

I drew in a deep breath through my nose and blinked. "Raven has a mate. She is mine, but I am not hers. And..." I hesitated, still uncomfortable sharing this about myself. "I crave her blood. I need to know why."

Melik's genuine confusion summed up how I felt daily. "But you are twin flames."

I wasn't going to confirm the obvious.

He stood. "Come. I have someone you can talk to."

"RAVEN WOULD GIVE UP THE SUN FOR YOU. SHE WOULD THROW ALL OF US INTO ETERNAL DARKNESS FOR YOU."

ZEKE

We followed Melik through hallways and down several staircases to the basement. It looked like a mixed space, where cots rested against the walls lined with cabinets in between, full of medicinal bottles.

Tables with open books littered the other half of the room. It was dusty but maintained well. Luca looked through the medicine cabinets, picking up each bottle to read the label. Compared to the two handfuls Raven sent with us, Melik's inventory could aid his entire kingdom.

I had forgotten what it was like living in a kingdom where the queen wasn't a healer. Though Raven kept her abilities hidden, our minute infirmary in the castle proved that our people had remained healthy enough to not need more. The villagers grew the island's food, and none was imported from other kingdoms. Since people within our realm didn't travel often, the transfer of diseases wasn't ever an issue.

In Reales, Mira never allowed anyone to leave. Even with the influx of men I brought in from outliers, we never faced anything more severe than the occasional flu.

Here in Nova, they seemed prepared for any kind of illness.

It seemed odd now that I thought about it. I hadn't realized how secluded our realm was until I traveled outside it. Even though I considered myself well-traveled, I realized how little I knew of the world the longer I stayed in a kingdom outside our domains.

"Oh!"

A surprised squeal from the entrance of the basement made me turn. Melik had been flipping through the open books on the table when he stopped to smile at the woman standing in the doorway.

She looked to be Raven's age, but her timidness reminded me of Grace. Her hair was brown and wild, and she wore the same type of frilly garments I'd seen in the village. The skirt cinched at her waist and fell to the floor, and her top was intricately detailed with moons and stars. It covered every inch of her, and I grinned. "Where can I find a top like yours for my wife?"

I would buy the entire stock so no man could see any part of Raven.

Luca snorted behind me.

The woman looked at her top and tugged at the cuffs of her sleeves. "Um..."

She was nervous around us, but I promised Raven I wouldn't make any woman too comfortable around me. I smiled awkwardly while trying to gauge the amount of pleasantry Raven would allow. Melik and Luca looked at me as if I was having a stroke. I certainly felt like it. Raven terrified me.

"From a shoppe in the village," she finally answered. "It's the one nearest to the right gate."

I dipped my chin once in gratitude and decided to stop talking to people.

"Right, then. If Ezekiel is finished asking for fashion tips...." Melik moved from behind the table while I glared at him. "Avalie, we require your brilliant assistance. Zeke is from the kingdom of Reales and has traveled far to ask some questions about his mate."

He looked at me and grandly gestured toward the woman standing in the doorway. "Avalie is our most brilliant scholar. She has studied the ways and laws of magic for many years. I guarantee she knows or can find the answer to any question you might have. Her power is that of Enhanced Reading. Anything she reads, she obtains as knowledge."

"Your mate smells delightful," Avalie said with a smile, nostrils flaring at the evidence of our bond. "Sweet, yet..."

"Feisty?" Luca asked with a chuckle.

I cocked my head. "Does it not repulse you? Everyone who comes around us can't stand the smell."

"I am mated," she said. "When one is already mated, the smell of another bond is not bothersome. What questions do you have for me?"

What questions *didn't* I have for her?

"My mate is... well, mine," I explained. "However, I am not hers. She is mated to someone else. We wanted to know how that was possible."

Avalie tapped her chin. "It's not. The mating bond is only given to two people. It is implausible that she would have another. It would take a very strong being to change the bond between mates. Even then, it would never be completely gone."

I couldn't tell if that was bad or good news. I wanted to believe we were just being paranoid, and that Raven didn't have a mate, but my more cynical side knew that, with our luck, it was because of someone else.

"She has one," I continued. "It was confirmed by a spirit that knew us from past lives." And a forest full of living skeletal guards and whispering trees, but I was positive I was already appearing crazy enough without adding that.

I looked at Melik. It would be helpful if I could give Avalie more information, but I wasn't sure who I could trust with the full scope of our bond. "Raven and I share more than a mating bond."

After I said it, I sensed what Melik felt. There was no trepidation or anxiousness. And when he nodded, I felt at ease enough to share more.

This was a risk, but if I left here without something to tell Raven, it might add to her hopelessness of finding a happy ending with me. "We are twin flames. We have seen the golden strand between us. I can feel it, even now. And I feel everything a mate should toward her. Raven, however, cannot. Something is holding her back."

"Twin flames are rare," she said with slightly widened eyes. "It would not make sense that she is mated to another when you share that bond. Can you speak to her?"

"Speak to her?" I quirked a brow. "Like..."

"Mind-to-mind," she answered with a small smile. "Do you speak to one another?"

I blinked. "I speak to her, but I can do that with everyone. Should she be able to speak to me?"

Avalie looked as if she was questioning everything I said. "All mates can speak to one another through mind bridges. I can hear my mate now. He's a cook in the castle. He's telling me of the dinner course." She looked at Melik. "Roasted pig, by the way."

"Excellent!" Melik boomed. "My favorite."

That all but confirmed that I was not her mate, and envy swelled at her sharing something like that with another man.

"We do not have that," I murmured sorrowfully.

Melik frowned at the look of irritation on my face, not with Avalie, but because I could not find reasons for why or how Raven would belong to another.

"He drinks her blood," Luca added.

I sighed.

He shrugged. "You're taking too long."

Avalie didn't look repulsed as I expected her to. Instead, she said, "Bloodlust. It is not uncommon for those who were bloodmated to desire their mate's blood. There are variations in mating. Mine was decided by fate, just as twin flames are. Bloodmating, though, is an ancient tradition. I didn't realize there were still kingdoms that practiced it."

I exchanged a look with Luca. "We don't practice it," I said. "I don't even know what bloodmating is. Until I found Raven, pairings were nonexistent in our realm. I didn't crave blood until I met her and tasted hers for the first time."

Avalie puckered her lips in thought and went to one of the tables covered in books, pulling one closer to her. "Bloodmating spans centuries, but it was only between creatures of magic. Do you not possess magic?"

"I do," I answered. "Empathic and dream-walking."

"Mind-shattering," Luca said.

"Would you *shut up*?"

Avalie didn't look hesitant as she asked, "Can you elaborate? Perhaps show me?"

"I do not want to shatter your mind, as it's irreversible," I said. "But I can bring a memory forth."

She nodded and closed her eyes, which was unnecessary. I could enter minds without even looking at a person; hers was easy to find. It was gentlest of all the minds in this room.

I grabbed one of the first memories I could find: of her and her mate eating a picnic in one of the castle's courtyards. Joy spread across her as she watched the memory, and I smiled. It was nice to be reminded that I could use this gift for good.

The memory faded, and her eyelids fluttered open. "That is a unique gift. I have not yet met someone who can do that."

"You're lucky he likes you," Luca muttered. He was one remark away from being kicked out of the room.

Avalie giggled while flipping to one of the pages in her book. "There was a man like you once. He was said to be the strongest magical being this universe had ever seen, but he was killed by the leader of the Undead."

Concerned, Melik lifted a brow. "The Undead?"

We exchanged a look. The Undead were making too many appearances for it to be coincidental. They had something to do with Raven.

Avalie nodded and pointed to faded pencil sketches of a group of people. It contained no color, but their fangs were evident. "They used to roam these lands. Their leader was ruthless and obsessed with a woman. It drove him to madness when she chose another. The Undead used bloodmating to find their mates. He wanted to be hers, and since the Undead were viewed as demons, fate didn't gift them with fated bonds."

I asked, "And the other she chose was...."

"The Phantom Prince," Avalie answered, turning the page. "He wasn't Undead, nor anything pinpointed, really. He showed no allegiance to any other being until he met her. The magic he possessed was envied by all, yet no one ever questioned him or tried to acquire it for themselves. It would've been pointless. His shadows performed most of the work for him and could move without being seen."

"The Phantom Prince," I repeated. "Why the name?"

"The Phantom Prince moved as swiftly as death and like a thief in the night," Avalie answered. "His shadows lurked behind him, disappearing in the dark."

Luca cleared his throat. "Is there... Do you have a picture in there of the Phantom Prince?"

I wasn't sure why he wanted to see it, but when she nodded, he stood beside her. She flipped through more pages until landing on one and pointed to the picture in the middle.

Luca's color drained. His entire face paled as he took the book from her and brought it closer. He looked from the page to me and back again. Before I could say a word, he asked Avalie with an unsteady voice, "Avalie, who was the woman?"

Avalie looked bewildered as she tilted her head at his concern, but she rose to her toes to flip another page for Luca. Luca landed in a chair, lips parted, his emotions filtering between disbelief and shock. "It's not possible," he whispered.

"Who?" Melik asked. "Who was it?"

Avalie shrugged a shoulder and calmly stated, "The Dark Half-Witch, of course."

～

I COULDN'T MOVE.

My chest was tight with short breaths. Luca swallowed as he stared at the page in front of him. Melik leaned over to look at the picture before repeatedly blinking, expecting the image in front of him to change into something more believable. He took the book from Luca's hands and brought it to me, but I couldn't lift a hand.

Everything felt paralyzed.

That name—the Dark Half-Witch.

Raven's blood. Bloodmating.

Shadows.

"Ezekiel, you need to look."

Nothing but my eyes moved to the book he held in front of me. On the page, in a faded sketch, was a portrait of a face I dreamed about every night. Her full lips, undeniable profile, and the quirk of her lips. Her long black hair hadn't changed and was styled similarly to how it was now—braided over her shoulder.

I stared at my wife on the page.

"This doesn't make sense," I whispered, staring into her uncolored eyes. "Raven is twenty-five years old. This cannot be her. John was there the night she was born...."

"Raven as in..." Avalie inquired, "the missing princess? Celestina's daughter?"

I clenched my jaw, refusing to answer. I had already divulged too much information.

"Celestina was a powerful grey witch," Avalie continued. "She was used for breeding by a king, and she stopped using her magic for the greater good."

Luca asked, "Was the king's name Leonidas?"

Avalie wrinkled her nose in confusion. "Who is Leonidas?"

I wasn't in the mood to give a history lesson. "Avalie, I need you to tell me about the rebirth of souls. Is it possible?"

"Of course, it's possible," she answered. "Reincarnation is still very prominent. If souls leave their earthly bodies too soon, they will be reborn in another physical entity."

"How many times?"

"I don't understand...."

"How many times can a soul be reincarnated?"

"Oh," she pondered, flicking her eyes up to the ceiling. "As many times as needed, I suppose. Why?"

"What happened to the leader of the Undead?"

She shrugged her shoulders slightly. "No one knows. After the Dark Half-Witch's death, the Undead disappeared. Obviously, they don't die, so I'm not sure how they've survived this long without blood. The leader can survive on blood other than his mate's, but it won't replenish his power as quickly. Without her, it is only a matter of time before it empties completely."

"That would lead to desperation," Luca said with warning as he looked at me.

Melik stood from where he leaned against the table and looked toward the door. His people died after rumors of the Undead arrived in his kingdom. No one in his kingdom was safe if they needed blood to survive.

And if the Undead had returned, it meant no one was safe anywhere.

Luca asked before I could, "How long ago did the Dark Half-Witch die?"

Avalie gestured toward the book. "It's on that page, but if I remember correctly, around one hundred and fifty years ago."

One-hundred and fifty years.

Our realm was created only a short time after. That had to be a coincidence. This woman on the page couldn't be my wife because crazier things *hadn't* happened. This was impossible.

I asked, "Can bloodmates survive off blood alone?"

She nodded. "Of their mates? Yes. Blood and"—she cleared her throat, her cheeks reddening—"other things."

"Fuck," I muttered. I took the book from Melik and flipped a few pages back until I saw the picture of the Phantom Prince. "How? It can't be."

The picture of Raven could be a coincidence if I wasn't staring at a picture of myself now. It was evident by my clothing—shaded to all-black, as was my hair on the drawing. And behind me, lingering like snakes, were two shadows.

"How did the Phantom Prince die?"

Avalie looked between the three of us. "Why are you so curious about this? Does it have anything to do with Raven?"

I glanced up from the book. "Why are *you* so curious about Raven?"

"Because of the rumors," she answered defensively. "Raven was rumored to have died as a baby. If Raven belongs to Celestina, her magic would be unstoppable."

"But she's half-mortal," Luca said. "Wouldn't that lessen her power?"

"Half-mortal?" Avalie shook her head. "A witch as powerful as Celestina wouldn't have chosen to breed with a mortal. It would've dampened the child's powers."

"But Leonidas was mortal...." Luca looked at me. "Right? And Mira is mortal."

Gisela's warning came flooding back to me. She didn't believe Raven belonged to Leonidas, but who else would that leave? Rudolf possessed no magic. We only knew of her marriage and affair. Did Mira not belong to Celestina? This was too much.

I ended up in a chair next to Luca's while I flipped through the pages of the book. "Avalie, did the Dark Half-Witch have a twin?"

"Oh!" she exclaimed, slapping her forehead. "I forgot to mention him. The Prince of One."

"Prince of One..." I repeated until it clicked. "Prince of One. One element?"

"Water," she confirmed. "The Dark Half-Witch possessed three, though they didn't strictly come from her being a witch."

I felt my brain would explode from all of this information. "Not from her being a witch? How else..."

"Her father," Avalie answered, exasperated. "Raven would only be a full elemental witch if Celestina possessed the elements."

Luca rubbed his forehead in confusion. "Raven *isn't* an elemental witch?"

"That's not what I said. You know shockingly little about her," Avalie muttered.

"How do you know so much?!" I shouted in frustration. "How do you know so much about Celestina and her history?"

"Because it's *history*," Avalie answered. "I have books on the history of magic, and Celestina played a large part in that. It was rumored that she still existed, but no one could find her until she became Queen of Reales. It's odd she wasn't sought out after that. In fact, it's strange that your entire realm has remained quiet...."

The cabin in the forest of Reales. She remained hidden there, but why? What would she need to hide from? Or... who? "The Prince of One, was he an enemy of the Dark Half-Witch?"

Avalie shook her head with a smile. "From what I've read, they were very close until she died."

"And how did he die?" I interrupted, looking for his name on any of the pages.

"River?"

She knew his name.

She knew his name.

The Prince of One was River, and River was in this book. River was in this history book that contained people who looked a lot like Raven and me, and Avalie didn't know the Dark Half-Witch was Raven, nor did she realize I might've been the Phantom Prince, which could only mean...

"He didn't. River never died."

PART TWO

"HE DIDN'T. RIVER NEVER DIED."

39

ZEKE

Slamming the book shut, I tossed it to Luca and jogged toward the door. "We have to go, Luca. I have to get back to her immediately. We may have eliminated the danger from the island, but I left the biggest threat alive."

Luca turned to follow me, but Avalie's question made me pause. "It's her, isn't it? Raven is the Dark Half-Witch. Her name... it's in that book."

I contemplated shattering her mind. That wouldn't be necessary. Instead of answering, I pushed into her mind and grabbed the most recent memory—this one.

I broke it into pieces.

385

Avalie blinked, her eyes glazing as we became unrecognizable. She put her palm to her forehead and swayed before looking at Melik. "I apologize. I can't remember if I introduced myself to your guests."

Melik looked at me with a half-annoyed, half-amused grin. "If you weren't a mate protecting his own, I would be more upset about this."

We said our quick goodbyes to Avalie, ran out of the room, down the hallways, and weaved through the corridors until we were back at our doors. "Get your shit as quickly as possible," I said to Luca before turning to Melik. "Will you ready our horses?"

Melik nodded and said nothing as he left us. Luca disappeared into his room while I entered mine, stuffing my bag full of clothes and random vials as fast as possible.

I knew there was a reason I couldn't see River in Mira's memories. He wasn't born the night Raven was—but they were twins once upon a time. He was alive before the creation of our realm, so what could he want with her now?

Luca entered my room with the bag slung over his chest and a vial in his hand. "I understand why you need this now."

I lunged for it, unscrewing the cap so quickly that I nearly dropped the vial and threw it back like a shot. "Shadows," I said, licking my lips. "Something about my shadows is tied to her blood."

Luca patted his satchel. "Hopefully, this book can help us."

I slung my bag over my back and tucked the empty vial into one of the pockets. "The blood vial is what prohibited Morana from harming me in Reine. It was empty but still enough to keep her away."

"Raven isn't mortal," Luca said, looking down at his satchel while recalling everything Avalie had shared. "She can't be if her parents weren't. What else could she be? She doesn't drink blood. She can't be Undead. What else is there?"

"I don't know," I answered. "But it's up to us to find out before whoever her father is comes for her. Celestina hid for a reason. Our realm has remained off maps. Leonidas prevented unknown ships from coming to Seolia. He told John not to let anyone see Raven… whoever her father is, I have a feeling we won't want to meet him."

"What about Leonidas? Why would he take Raven?"

I ran a hand through my hair. "All great questions, Luca, but I don't have time to find the answers right now. We need to return to Raven before River does."

Luca followed me toward the door but then grabbed my arm. "Wait... if Raven didn't inherit her elemental magic from Celestina, what *did* she get?"

I thought of Raven's fury, her thirst for blood, and shivered. "I don't know," I whispered. "But whatever it is, I don't want to find out."

~

WE WERE ALMOST at the castle's front doors when Melik called our names. He held a basket of food in his hands and a bag over his shoulder. He handed the basket to me and the load to Luca. "All of the items you purchased from the village," Melik explained. "I will have some of the requested tops delivered to Seolia, Ezekiel."

That was no longer a high priority, but I nodded. "Thank you for your hospitality and for helping me find answers. I have more questions, but at least I'm returning to her with... well, something."

"I would call it more than something," Melik said with a chuckle. "I always knew there was something different about her. It seems like you have a history of your own."

I couldn't care less about my history. My only concern was returning to my wife, but as we were about to bid farewell, the front doors flew open. And standing in the entry, pissed off and seething, was the elderly witch from Reine.

"Ah, fuck," Luca muttered.

"YOU!" Larinda shouted while pointing at me. "You have brought death to my witches!"

I had no patience left for this woman. "I did nothing to your witches. You were all passed out when I escaped your torture cottage."

"Larinda, I can assure you that Ezekiel is not at fault for any deaths," Melik said, standing in front of Luca and me.

"The Dark Half-Witch!" she exclaimed. "When she learned of

your capture, she murdered them! She burned Sria! She burned her own kind!"

"Why was Sria on our island?" I growled, stepping around Melik. "Where is Raven? What did you do to her?"

She cackled, an evil sound that sent goosebumps racing across my skin. "Her blood, Phantom Prince. We need the Dark Half-Witch's blood before *he* finds her."

I couldn't say I cared for the nickname.

"Why do you need her blood?" Luca asked, throwing his hands up in the air. "What is the obsession with Raven's blood, and why does everyone want it?"

She stepped forward, and we all stepped back. She was only one woman against three trained men, but something about her was making us eerily uncomfortable, and I remained unsure of what kind of magic she had.

"We have waited so long," Larinda said, pushing her sleeves up. Her arms were covered in markings that were written in the same language they chanted in Reine. "Her blood will restore everything. Her blood is the life of our universe."

"Her blood belongs to *me*," I rumbled. "Her blood will not be used for anything else."

"I am too mortal for this conversation," Luca muttered. "Does no one else find this disgusting?"

"A tad," Melik answered, giving me an apologetic grin.

It was abnormal, but was that only because we hadn't been exposed to magic in our realm like others had?

Were we the abnormal ones?

I asked, "Why haven't you come to claim her sooner?"

"The shield," Larinda hissed. "The astral witch projected a shield around your kingdoms, hiding the Dark Half-Witch behind it."

Damiana, the only astral witch I was aware of.

Damiana knew of Raven's magic. Had she been protecting her this entire time from being found?

Who were we hiding her from?

Luca asked, "And there isn't a shield now?"

If there wasn't a shield around our realm now, anyone could find Raven. The men. The unbreakable men from the letter. We were warned that they knew of Raven. Why was everything coming together while I was away from her?

"The shield began to crack the night you met her," Larinda said, looking at me. "Our seer foresaw it. We waited for your shadows and her blood to merge again, but nothing came."

The night I met her at the Festival of Dreams broke the shield. I would ask how, but that wasn't getting me anywhere.

"Morana," Larinda drawled, "Morana told us that you would not free your shadows for the Dark Half-Witch."

Refusing to free them and not knowing how to do so were two completely different things.

"He has her," she continued with a sneer. "It is too late for you, Phantom Prince. He has her now in your kingdom. And now"—she touched one of the words on her arm—"It is time to seek retribution for my witches."

I bared my teeth at her, moving toward the door. I was tired of people preventing me from seeing my wife.

Raven was in Reales. Why was Raven in Reales? I gave Jeanine strict instructions to only go to Thoya if there was trouble...

"Your nightmare," Melik breathed. "Your nightmare... tell me again what you saw."

"The man with red eyes had her...." I started before trailing off, my gut seizing. "The man in my nightmare—"

"Was a warning," Melik finished.

"*Arescet et labe.*"

"This can't be good," Luca said, backing away from Larinda.

She repeated that phrase over and over, staring directly at me. For a moment, nothing happened. I moved to step around her, but then my chest began to hurt as breathing became difficult. I clutched my heart and shook my head, holding on to Melik's shoulder to remain standing.

He yelled for her to stop. He threatened to pull protection from her coven, but she only got louder. The words echoed off the walls of the grand entryway and back to my ears, my body aching and sluggish as I fell to a knee.

This was some kind of death spell. Larinda was going to kill me on the floor of this castle, and I would never be able to protect Raven from the men who sought her.

"Vial," I rasped. "Luca, vial!"

Luca fumbled through his bag for the last vial and threw the cap to the ground, pouring the remainder of Raven's blood into my mouth.

It only took seconds for the pain to lessen enough for me to stand, much to Larinda's surprise.

Okay, but now what?

I looked at my hands. The double dose of her blood made the veins in my arms darken, but that was the extent of it. The shadows swam through my arms and pounded on my chest, but I couldn't free them.

"Zeke!" Luca whisper-shouted. "Now would be a great time to figure it out!"

"I can't!" I recoiled, shaking my hands in front of me as if I could throw the shadows out. "I don't know what to do!"

Because I wasn't the goddamn Phantom Prince.

I was a mortal man with only a faded sketch to go off from. I didn't know how the shadows came to be or if I could even physically wield them. For all I knew, the shadows hadn't fully reformed when my soul reincarnated.

Larinda laughed. "How rich! The Phantom Prince cannot even defend himself with his shadows!" she taunted. "He will never stop the Dark Half-Witch's mate without magic!"

"Enough!" I shouted, pushing into her mind and squeezing her subconscious. "I have had enough of you! You poisoned my brother and me." I took a step forward. "You tried to take my mate!"

She screeched, putting her hands against her temple as I pinched her mind so tightly that my pulse drummed in my ears. "Tell me where she is! Tell me who has her!"

Blood dripped from the corner of her eyes as I tore apart her mind piece by piece. Raven's blood moved through me rapidly, strengthening my abilities.

"He will destroy you!" Larinda squalled. "He will destroy all of us if he gets her first!"

"Who?" I bellowed. "Who has Raven?"

"He! The leader of the Undead!"

I released her mind and stumbled back a step at the dreaded confirmation. Melik stepped forward as Larinda fell to her knees, sneering at us with her blood-soaked eyes. "He has waited over a century for her to return. He has preyed on the weak, sustaining himself on mortal and immortal blood until he could reunite with his bloodmate."

Somewhere amidst the chaos, Melik's guards and servants stopped to watch and listen. Everyone nearby would now know that Raven was only days away from the kingdom.

"The Undead have returned," a servant girl behind us whispered. "We are unsafe!"

Melik was left speechless as the murmurs grew, unable to look anywhere but at me.

"Once he has his bloodmate, he will hold the key," she continued. "He will control all beings with the enticement of a drop of her blood. The healing! The strength!" She wailed and pressed her face against the cold tile, her blood smearing. "The magic she possesses! We have waited so long."

"I will spare your life," I said, clenching my fists to my sides. "As much as I do not want to. You will leave our realm alone. You will prepare to fight the Undead."

"You stupid boy," she spat. "No one can fight the Undead." She tilted her head up to look at me. "The Phantom Prince no longer lives. You cannot win this."

"The Phantom Prince might be gone, but I am not. I will not let anyone take her from me. That is a promise I will keep, no matter what or who waits for her."

"He already has," she said, wiping the blood away from her eyes. "He has her in Reales with your queen."

As I stared at Larinda, I tasted the truth. I couldn't decipher which part was the truth, but I had to get to Reales and find out. From right outside, Shadow neighed.

I broke my gaze from Larinda and turned to Melik. "Here." I dug into my bag and retrieved a map of our realm with all four kingdoms drawn on it. "Your maps do not show Thoya or Perosan. I did not understand why until now. Damiana has kept it that way for a reason."

I pointed to Thoya. "If you feel unsafe here, move your people to this kingdom. It will be a journey, but you can get there by land. Tell Edmund that I sent you. We will prepare to fight. Ready your forces. I shoved the map against his chest. "Keep the witches out of my realm."

He took the map and conveyed gratitude with his eyes, unable to utter a word. All of this shocked me, too, but I needed to save Raven before I could think about it.

"Tell me what kind of magic to look for," I said, turning again to Larinda, who remained on the floor in a heap.

Shadow, impatient as ever, trotted into the castle and neighed at me again. I ignored him and crouched to face Larinda. "What kind of magic does he possess?"

"All magic." She looked weary and hopeless on the floor. "He has collected all magic."

I didn't know how that could be if magic had waned while he waited for Raven, but I was wasting time. Without a word, I nodded for Luca to follow me. "We will not stop," I said. "I am riding until Reales. It could be dangerous once we're there. If you want to stay...."

"Fuck off," Luca muttered, slinging his bag over Shadow's back.

"WHO HAS RAVEN?" "HE! THE LEADER OF THE UNDEAD!"

40

RAVEN

J eanine and I were lying on the bed, bored. River left us over an
hour ago, but we hadn't been brave enough to find out what
lurked outside the cathedral. We had already risked too much
by coming here. I half-expected Zeke to bust through those
doors and save us, but the other half of me hoped he would never
find out about this. My decision to test boundaries annoyed him.

"We should've stayed in Seolia," Jeanine said, finally breaking the
silence. "How do you know River meant what he said about our
people remaining safe without you there? It could be a decoy to take
the island while we're here."

I rolled my head against the pillow to look at her. "Do you think he'd go to all this trouble just to take our island?"

She rolled to her side and played with the ends of my hair. "I don't know what he would do, Raven. I don't know River, and he doesn't give me the best feeling. John doesn't believe he was there the night you were born."

"I love how you all openly share this information with me long after I need it," I snapped, crossing my arms over my stomach. "That would've been great to know before I agreed to come here, but it also doesn't make sense. We're twins."

She shrugged and fell dramatically to her stomach. "I don't know!" Her voice was muffled in the pillow. "Does anyone ever really know what's happening? We go into all of these adventures blindly."

I laughed at the truth of that. "Maybe we should stop."

"Are we truly going to stay in this room until he fetches us?"

Shaking my head, I rose from the bed and extended a hand to her. "That doesn't sound like something we would do, does it?"

She took my hand. "Absolutely not. That would be far too responsible of us."

ONE OF THE cathedral's front doors still showed evidence of the night I burned through it. Crouching down, I peered through the hole into the courtyard. "I don't see anyone," I whispered. "Where's the closest entrance to the forest?"

"Right outside," she whispered back, shoving me to the side so she could look through the hole. "Directly to the left. If we walk along the wall, we'll end up at Zeke's manor."

Inhaling a deep breath, I held it until she opened the door just enough for us to slip out. She laced our fingers tightly together as we ran silently toward the hidden door in the wall, not uttering a sound while she unlatched it and held it open for me to sneak through. I eyed our surroundings in the forest, worried that since Zeke was gone, no one had prevented men from sneaking through the woods.

Adjusting the dagger in her waistband, she swept my body dramatically with her hand. "Are you going to shift or what?"

I blinked. "Are you... are you actually asking me to shift into Blaze?"

When she nodded, her brows drawn in from confusion, I ignored the tears pooling in my eyes and shifted into Blaze. "No one has ever asked me to shift into her for their protection." I cleared my throat. "Aside from Zeke, she scares everyone."

She resumed holding my hand. "I'm not scared of any part of you, Raven. I love you and all of your personalities."

My warm smile was the only response I could conjure up at the moment, relishing the feeling of someone calling on my fury to feel safe instead of asking me to bury it.

"Zeke told me," I said, swinging our hands between us. "About Gisela's musings."

"He doubts the validity of it," she replied with a shrug. "He watched your memories. He saw it all unfold. Celestina admitted that you belonged to Leonidas."

"I have doubts, too, but not about the validity. Ever since I read Leonidas's letter, I had high hopes that I would feel... I don't know if *better* is the right word, but I hoped to feel a connection to Seolia. I thought it might help me be a better queen, but I feel as misplaced as ever."

She squeezed my hand. "Raven, you can be a wonderful queen, even if you aren't the true heir."

"But do I want to be? No one ever asked me."

"*Do* you want to be?"

The question I had asked myself hundreds of times but never felt I had an answer to. It was the question I would stay up late pondering, unable to sleep from the weight of a kingdom's future on my shoulders. And with only a letter from a man I'd never met, I wondered if maybe he lied, like everyone else in my life had at some point.

Finally, I shook my head with a frown. "I don't think I do. I never have. I did it because I didn't believe I had a choice. I want Zeke to help Reales. After everything your people have been through with Mira as queen, they deserve to be taken care of. Zeke can do that, and with Mira gone...."

"It works out perfectly," Jeanine finished for me.

"I can see myself being truly happy here, Jeanine. I want to restore it. I want to help people and learn about Zeke's past. I want to see him be the leader I know he can be."

She nodded while listening, quiet for a moment afterward. Until finally, she tugged at my hands. "Then, let's move back to Reales."

"Jeanine, you don't have to come back with us. I understand that your past here is painful..."

Pulling me to a stop, she put her hands on either side of my face and pressed our foreheads together. "I shared with Zeke long ago that I want to be where you are, Raven. You are my sister. And after a lifetime of feeling like I would never find a friend, I cannot let you go now."

I threw my arms around her neck and pulled her to me so quickly that we stumbled into the wall. We both groaned from the pain, her hand rubbing the back of my head from knocking against the stone. "We truly are very uncoordinated," she said with a wince.

~

We saw no one.

Not a soul. Aside from us and the trees, the forest was empty. Standing at the edge of the wall, I stood on Jeanine's shoulders as I peered over the edge, looking at the backside of Zeke's manor. Since it rested on the top of a hill, I couldn't see anything else but high grass. "It's clear," I said.

Without warning, she took my feet off her shoulders and shoved me up, nearly causing me to tumble over the wall and to my head. "Jeanine!" I hissed, holding on for dear life as I dangled halfway over, taking a moment to readjust myself and straddle the wall. "That would've been an effortless way to kill me. Imagine me having to explain that to Zeke."

She snorted from down below. "How does that work, by the way?" She took my extended hand and grunted as she climbed the wall to sit in front of me, looking for anyone who might have spotted our graceful attempts at getting over.

I shrugged a shoulder. "When one of us dies, the other follows, and we meet in a meadow. It's beautiful. It's what I imagine the heavens to look like."

"Maybe that's what it is," she countered. "Maybe each pairing gets their own version of the heavens."

I frowned. "Maybe, but Zeke doesn't seem to think our souls will be presented with rebirth after this life. He believes this is it for us because I saw glimpses of our future."

Her head cocked. "What did you see?"

I twisted the tail of my shirt between my fingers as something deep in my mind clawed at her question. "Our son," I whispered. "At least, I believe it to be a boy. The baby was swaddled in a blanket in my arms."

Taking my fingers, she squeezed until my eyes focused back on her instead of chasing whatever was trying to break through. "Did he look like me?"

I threw my head back in a laugh. "Absolutely, because that would make all the sense."

"If he knows what's good for him, it would." She slapped my thigh hard enough to make me yelp before throwing her leg over and dropping to the ground. "Do I need to catch you, Queen Raven? I know how fragile you can be."

I rolled my eyes. "You sound like Zeke." I pulled my leg over and slid down the wall, immediately rolling both ankles after landing.

She watched me with an amused grin. I stuck my tongue out at her and gestured for her to lead the way. The grass was taller than us, dull and dying from the sun and lack of care. "We have our work cut out for us," I muttered.

"Reales was beautiful once." She hit the grass out of the way, keeping one of my hands in hers. "Rudolf took care of the kingdom. Zeke will restore it."

"I was hoping we'd pass his tree house in the forest."

"We didn't go far enough into the forest." She pointed backward as if that would've told me exactly where it was. "My dad was one of the men who helped Zeke build it. He made Zeke move steel in exchange for his time."

I smiled at the shared history between the three of them. "Did you ever play in it?"

She scoffed. "No. I was told to stay away from the Audovera boys. Despite their royal status, they were far too charming. Mothers loved them, and fathers feared them. I wasn't allowed to be near them." She laughed to herself. "I shared some tutors with them. Zeke rarely showed up to lessons, but when he did, he'd argue with the tutors and pull Luca out to take him into the forest."

"Zeke showed me a memory of one of the balls from when he was younger. It looked grand."

"Balls *were* grand. Rudolf took great pride in our kingdom. He was aware of Celestina's affairs, so I believe he distracted himself with putting together events. He was surrounded by a large court of advisers who would keep him busy."

"What would Mira do?"

"Follow Celestina around," she said with a sigh. "Their relationship was... odd. Celestina didn't seem close with Mira, but Mira wanted to be right by her side at all times. Strangely, Mira is so obsessed with avenging her, even though Celestina rarely gave her the time of day."

I was about to pry into Zeke's father when Jeanine froze and placed her hand over my mouth. She looked around the grass with wide eyes and dragged us down until we were crouched. I didn't hear anything, but she refused to release my mouth.

"We can *smell* you," a male voice sing-songed from the distance.

"There's no use in hiding," another male added.

I wrapped my fingers around Jeanine's wrist. Their voices sent a distinct discomfort down my spine. With her free hand, she pointed behind us and then put her finger against her lips.

Nodding, I released her wrist and kept low against the ground, awkwardly crawling through the high grass as quietly as I could. She remained behind me, touching my leg every few steps to let me know she was still there.

Was this why River didn't want us to leave the cathedral? The men I always ran into in the forest never claimed they could smell me unless you counted Melik, but that was because of my shared scent with Zeke. Could they smell my bond?

When a pair of shoes appeared directly in front of me like a silent bolt of lightning, I fell backward, heart pounding in my ears. Jeanine grabbed me and shoved me to the side, keeping us hidden from the shoes behind a tall clump of weeds.

Her nails dug so deep into my wrist that she drew blood. I pried her fingers from my skin and covered the tear in my skin with my palm, trying to heal it quickly. If it was my blood they could smell, it would only add to Zeke's anger of us leaving Seolia and again placing our safety at risk.

Looking from my wrist to between the blades of grass, I met a pair of red eyes staring back at me and shrieked. Without thinking, I released a burst of flames from my hand and grabbed Jeanine, pulling her up into a run.

We ran fast enough that my chest burned from the lack of air and increased panic. "Red eyes," I said with a shuddering breath. "His eyes were red!"

"We have to get someplace safe!" she yelled back.

I didn't want to look behind us, instead releasing more fire to set the grass ablaze. Jeanine braved a glance over her shoulder and cursed loudly. "They're fucking fast! Two of them!"

I could hear them gaining on us, their footsteps thundering against the ground. Staring at my hands, I shifted into Terra and leaned over to drag my fingertips against the ground. When a divide shot out between Jeanine and me, she grabbed my hand and leaped, nearly knocking me down as she landed beside me. "We have to get better at this!" I cried.

Out of breath, she nodded but then screamed as a man's hand grabbed her arm and yanked her away. Quickly, I shifted into Frost and created an icicle, telling Jeanine to duck as I hurled it toward him. It sliced across his cheek, giving Jeanine a second to pry herself away. A strong arm wrapped around my waist right before she grabbed my hand and tugged me backward.

Jeanine lunged, but it was useless.

Within seconds, we were trapped in the arms of our captors. Thrashing, I jammed another icicle into the thigh of the man holding me, but he simply... pulled it out and sighed. I tried to turn my head to look at him, but he grabbed my chin and kept me still. "I don't enjoy playing with my food," he taunted, his voice silky soft like the strings of a harp.

Jeanine was fighting and kicking while trying to free herself, but the man holding her barely moved. His red eyes stared directly at my icy-blue irises, pinning me with his gaze. He was... beautiful, but alarming.

He said nothing, but when Jeanine whimpered, I shook my head. "Stop!" I shouted, watching as his arms tightened around her. "Stop!" I repeatedly screamed, trying to wrangle myself free. "Stop! I'll give you whatever you want! Let her go!"

"You have nothing we want," the man holding me stated calmly.

"I would disagree," a familiar voice said between the trees. "I believe they hold more power than you think." River casually leaned against a tree, his arms crossed. "And if you harm them, he will not be pleased."

The man holding Jeanine loosened his arms enough to allow her to draw in a breath, her eyes rolling back for a second. "Who are they?" he inquired, his voice similar to the man holding me.

"His guests," River responded, nodding toward me, "Especially that one. Raven, please shift into yourself."

I shook my head slowly, jaw tight, distrusting. River simply lifted an eyebrow. "Shift or they have no reason to believe me."

"And you do smell divine," my captor taunted, pressing his nose against the pulse in my throat.

I jerked at the contact and jammed another icicle into his arm, gasping as the ice cracked at the touch. It was as if the ice was meeting stone. "I trusted you!" I shouted at River.

"Shift, Raven."

"Don't do it!" Jeanine shouted, groaning as his arms tightened around her again. Her eyelids fluttered, her head rolling to the side.

Crying her name, I gave in and shifted to myself. "Let her go," I pleaded. "Please, please, let her go."

Both men immediately released us. Jeanine fell to her knees, and I ran to her, hoisting her up to rest against me. Shifting back into Blaze, I created a circle of fire around us. "I am returning home!" I shouted, fanning the flames with a gust of wind as I shifted into Terra.

I silently begged Blaze to come out or for my hands to glass over and turn these men into ice, but without touching them, I couldn't protect us with anything more than flames.

A gush of water suffocated my flames.

Exerting a frustrated cry, I created another circle, only for River to drown it again. Jeanine was in no position to try outrunning them again, but I would stand here all day and fight if I had to.

"Raven, it's time for dinner," River said calmly.

"Fuck off!" I yelled in return.

Sighing, River straightened from the tree and adjusted the sleeves of his jacket. All three men were dressed in immaculate fitted suits. I couldn't get a good glimpse of the two strangers through the haziness of the leftover smoke from my flames, but I didn't care to. We should've never come here.

"Raven," River tried again, stepping toward us.

"Do not," Jeanine rasped, sitting up, "Come near her. You're disgusting, River. How could you do this to your own sister?"

He stilled, his fingers curling before his hands flexed. "Dinner," he repeated. "Just as we discussed, Raven." He stared into my eyes as if I had forgotten about our bargain.

I hoped my heart was beating fast enough to alert Zeke that something was terribly wrong—that I had not stayed in Seolia, that I was stuck in Reales with River and his creepy friends, and that I needed him.

The only guarantee we had that I wouldn't die while here was the oath he made with Jeanine. And when I touched the small wave on her wrist as a reminder, she sighed and dropped her forehead against my shoulder. "I can't let the next time Zeke sees you be in the meadow," she murmured.

Disheveled and dirty, we held tightly to one another as we stood. I eyed the men on either side of River, unease wafting over me at the scarlet red of their eyes and the beauty they possessed. "Dinner," I said. "That is all. And we require bathing in Zeke's chambers, or you do not have a deal."

River slid his hands into his pockets and tilted his head to the side, but I held firm. It would be on my terms if we were forced into dinner. "Take it or leave it, River. You've learned by now that I will stubbornly fight you to the end."

401

Finally, he dipped his chin in the most defiant nod I had ever witnessed from a man, including my husband. "Fine. You may bathe and dress in Zeke's chambers, but if you try to run, Raven, I will not be able to defend your actions again."

I dismissed his threat with a wave of my hand. "Well, I suppose it's good that someone wants to meet me so damn bad, then."

"I CAN'T LET THE NEXT TIME ZEKE SEES YOU BE IN THE MEADOW," SHE MURMURED.

41

RAVEN

River returned with us to the castle. The other two men disappeared back into the forest, but I couldn't find the words to ask River who or what they were. I wouldn't trust a word he said anyway. And when he left us in Zeke's chambers with instructions to again stay put until he came for us, I didn't acknowledge him with even a nod.

Jeanine collapsed onto the bed while I drew her a bath. Zeke's chambers still smelled exactly like him, and while looking around, I was relieved to find them untouched. The bedsheets remained ruffled from nights we previously spent here; and that was proven by a pair of my panties that were still there, ripped to shreds.

I snorted, unable to control myself. Jeanine didn't raise her head from the bed but asked me, "What?" in a muffled voice.

"Zeke has an obsession with tearing my clothes," I said. "There are still remnants of that."

She muttered something about her discomfort of sharing a bed where he had fucked me, but I promptly reminded her that she had been sharing our marriage bed for weeks. She gagged dramatically.

Throwing a ball of fire into the water to warm it quicker, I smiled at the soaps Zeke had picked out for us that were still on his ledge. "Come on, Jeanine. You can bathe first. I want to look around and see if there's anything I should try and take back to Seolia for him."

Undressing, she gave his chambers a quick look. "He won't want any of this. He didn't even want to move in here. While he was with you, it was the longest I'd ever seen him in this castle wing. Most of the time, he'd fall asleep in the forest. I would find him there nearly every morning."

It saddened me to hear about his life here in recent years. He was so lonely, so isolated without his family, and didn't know that there was someone just like him a kingdom over, waiting for him to come and sweep her off her feet.

"Did he and Mira ever speak before she locked away Luca and Alice?"

Jeanine hissed as she lowered herself into the hot water, resting her head against the rim. "Not often. He avoided her when he could. Most of their interactions happened while Rudolf was still alive. Zeke would eat breakfast with him almost every morning, and Mira would be there. I believe it was Zeke's closeness with Rudolf that truly cemented her disdain for him."

"Would you eat with them?"

Grabbing a soap bar, she disappeared under the water and reappeared with bubbles in her hair. "Yes." She swiped a hand down her face to clear off the water. "In the beginning, I stayed close to Mira because I believed what we had between us was love. Zeke encouraged me to train with him one day, way before... well, you know."

Hearing about their *time* together didn't make me as uncomfortable as it used to, so I encouraged her to continue with a wave of my hand.

"Once I started spending time away from Mira and more time in the kingdom around the men she had forced Zeke to enlist, I began to see the monster she had become. I started spending more time in the dungeon with Luca and Alice, apologizing for my blindness. But I didn't know how far it went."

"I'm just trying to understand her intentions," I sighed. "If she doesn't respect her own kingdom, what will dominating all of them look like?"

"Our realm will die." She stood from the tub and grabbed a towel, wrapping it around herself before draining the water to run it fresh for me. "And maybe that's what she wants. In some way, I believe she wants to prove she can do better than Zeke."

"I might be biased, but"—I stripped out of my clothes and warmed the water with my hands before stepping into the tub—"Zeke and Edmund are exactly what this realm needs. It will thrive between them."

"Have you given any thought to maybe combining our kingdoms?"

I ran soap through my hair, silently waiting for her to elaborate.

"I realize with the distance, it might not be possible, but it would allow both of you to rule the kingdoms as one. You could reside in Reales with Zeke but the two of you would still be the rulers of Seolia."

I mulled over the suggestion, pursing my lips. It wasn't something we had thought about, and it could be a viable solution to our problems. But before I could answer, a solitary knock whipped our heads whipped toward the door. Jeanine tightened the towel around herself and called out to inquire who it could be, but only silence answered.

After I sank lower into the tub to cover every inch of my body except my face, Jeanine pulled open the door, only a sliver, then sighed. Reaching up, she unhooked our dresses from Zeke's door and returned with them slung over her arm. "I guess we have no choice but to be formal this evening."

Glancing at our clothes in a pile on the floor and seeing how dirty they were from the chase in the forest, I wrinkled my nose. "It's better than arriving in those."

She laid the dresses on the bed and stared at them. "Something is going to happen tonight, Raven. I can feel it. Those men"—her head shook—"they're different. The pressure he emitted just by putting his arms around me..."

Unbreakable suddenly sounded much more ominous now than when we first learned of the men who had infiltrated Reales. "We can't let them near us," I said. "We have to keep our distance. With River near me, my fire is useless. He will drown the flames every time. The icicle did nothing to deter the one holding me. Terra is powerful, but unless we want to split the castle floor, I am not sure what I can accomplish with only her."

She sank onto the bed. "Raven, I feel like your magic is trapped. In Seolia, when you created the vortex, you showed so much power, but it only happens when something tragic has happened and it never lasts. There has to be a reason."

"Jeanine, my magic has been a mystery my entire life." Standing from the tub, I caught the towel she tossed to me. "The only place I have ever somewhat received answers was The Forest Beyond, and I don't anticipate returning to it any time soon."

"Maybe we should've gone there instead."

"Hindsight," I grumbled.

THE DRESSES WERE INDEED FORMAL.

Not fancy enough to be worn to a ball, but too dressy for any meeting we ever attended in Seolia or Thoya. The leaders had become so familiar with one another that overdressing wasn't required, but River's friends were clearly more traditional.

Jeanine's dress was simple and black, floor-length with capped sleeves and a jeweled bodice. The dagger tucked between her breasts didn't come with the dress but was rather her chosen accessory for the evening. And with her hair brushed and curled at the ends against her shoulders, she looked every inch an innocent and harmless woman.

It was the best disguise.

My dress, however, was more detailed. The corseted bodice was tied in ribbons across my chest, reaching a point at my hips before blossoming into a full skirt. The color of crimson—how it matched the eyes of our captors in the forest—made the dress nearly unbearable to be in.

Between that and my anxiety over meeting these men, my palms were sweaty and cold chills came in waves across my skin. Jeanine was back to holding my hand, even as River led us through the dark corridors of the castle, which still seemed just as intimidating as before. And without the protection of my husband this time, my hatred for this castle grew.

River remained silent, and we didn't ask questions. We passed by the dining hall where we regularly attended breakfast, and I glanced at Jeanine. "We have a more formal dining room," she explained. "It hasn't been used in years, but I guess River's friends expected more than what Mira normally provides to guests."

River sighed but did not invalidate her claims.

With my braid resting against my ribcage, I nervously twisted the ends of my hair with my fingers. Everything about this dinner made me tense, as if we were walking into a lion's den and serving ourselves as the main dish.

Before we entered the formal dining hall, Jeanine tugged my free hand between hers. I put on a brave face but felt anything but brave. "We can do this," she whispered. "One dinner, Raven, and he'll take you to Zeke."

From the corner of my eye, River stood with his hands clasped behind his back. "Is that true, River? One dinner, and you'll bring me to Zeke?"

A subtle nod was his only reply, and a knot twisted in my stomach at the sudden belief that he was lying about that, too. Extending his arm, he gestured toward the entrance of the dining hall. "After you," he said cordially.

"Prick," Jeanine muttered, leading me inside.

Our only advantage so far was Jeanine's familiarity with the castle. If we needed to escape or hide, she would know where to go. Much like the less formal dining room, this one reflected the grays of the castle, the only light coming from hundreds of candles placed sporadically throughout the room and in three striking, golden chandeliers.

Mira sat at the head of the table, pointing to two chairs on either side of her for us to sit. Jeanine immediately shook her head. "I will sit by Raven and preferably not next to you."

I bit my upper lip to keep from smiling but squealed on the inside at Jeanine's defiance against the woman who had used her for nothing more than pleasure. And Jeanine didn't give Mira time to retort before pulling out my chair beside Mira and taking the spot next to me. River took the chair across from me, leaning back casually and maintaining a locked gaze.

"Where are your guests?" I asked.

"They like to make fashionable entrances," Mira answered with a hint of annoyance. "And only Felix is joining us this evening."

"Felix," I repeated, hoping to unclog a memory of meeting him before since they claimed to know me, but his name rang no bells.

I jumped at a loud clap from the entrance of the room, covering my heart with my hand as my pulse drummed in my ears. Mira sighed, but River acted as if it were a regular occurrence.

Blond, tall, and the color of snow, a man strode into the room with more confidence than I had ever witnessed from anyone. Everything about his presence irked me, down to the superior grin on his face. His tailored black suit curved to every inch of him, his hair nearly blinding in the candlelight, and his eyes so golden that I could've sworn I saw the room reflected back in them.

But like the men in the forest, his beauty was evident.

With glossy and smooth skin, he moved like porcelain. Graceful and swift but domineering in stature. And his voice... fuck, his voice was more serene than the sound of soothing rain.

He dipped into a dramatic bow but never dropped his gaze from mine. "Raven," he said as if tasting my name for the first time, drawing out each syllable like a long, harmonic tune. "We have been awaiting your arrival with such elation."

"I can't say we've felt the same," Jeanine said.

His eyes flickered to her. "River warned us of you."

Jeanine grinned like a feline. "He talks about me? How obsessively unattractive of him."

River scowled but remained quiet.

The man I presumed to be Felix refocused his attention on me. And as demure as his greeting was, I wasn't in the mood for proper acquaintances and small talk. "What do you require of me? It is no secret that I am no longer in an alliance with Mira. I would be of no help to you."

He slowly began to circle the table, and the closer he got to me, the harder Jeanine squeezed my hand.

"Will you not allow me to introduce myself to you, Queen Raven? I would love for you to call me by my name."

"I don't care to know your name," I responded, though I already did. Something about how he moved told me he could kill me instantly, but I didn't care. I might've earned it for walking in here. "What is it that you need?"

Clearly undeterred of my disinterest in aligning myself with him, he halted beside my chair and took my hand. I jerked at the cold contact of his hand, the smoothness of it being the complete opposite of Zeke's rough and calloused hands, which I highly preferred over this.

And I avoided eye contact like the plague. His eyes of gold reminded me of mine when I shifted into Terra, and I wanted no connection between us.

He first touched the diamond of my wedding ring, pinching it between his fingers with a catlike grin. "Where is your keeper, dear one?"

"Her *keeper*?" Jeanine repeated in disgust.

"My *partner*," I emphasized, "is on his way back to me. And he would prefer you not sniff his mate," I added with a bite, taking my hand from his after he brought it to his nose. "Let us at least act civilly and not as dogs, unlike your men who chased us through the forest."

Felix looked at River, who sighed. "Renauld and Pol found them in the forest before dinner. They were visiting a friend's childhood home."

I was about to dispute that when River's eyes snapped to mine, causing me to close my mouth. Felix was clearly unaware of Zeke's manor being nearby, but I didn't see why it would matter.

"They called us food," Jeanine added. "If all of you are that disrespectful, I do not anticipate Raven having any partnership with you."

"I apologize on behalf of our members," Felix said, leaving my side to stand behind the chair opposite Mira.

Members, Jeanine mouthed to me. I shrugged my shoulders slightly.

"But we are not looking for a partnership with Raven," he continued, pulling out his chair to sit. "When your former adviser came to Reales and informed us of your rebellion against your sister's demands, we decided that we needed to meet you before our alliance with Mira came to fruition."

I looked from Felix to Mira. "You have allied with Mira to dominate our realm. For what purpose?" I sat up and leaned over the table, inching closer to Mira. "What did you promise them, Mira?"

I hadn't realized before how... tired she looked. With sunken eyes and stringy hair, Mira seemed more unkempt than usual, as if even the idea of war now tired her. And when she didn't answer my question, I glanced next at River. The subtle shake of his head told me that he wouldn't respond, either.

I was suddenly freezing as the reasons why I was brought here started making sense. "Mira," I repeated. "Mira, what did you promise them for their alliance?"

It was Felix who answered with, "Our original oath..."

I closed my eyes. Oath. Mira bound herself to them with magic. I searched her wrists for markings of any kind.

"...entailed us waiting patiently while you trained an army in your kingdom and persuaded the royals to attend your wedding in Reales."

"Raven, I think we should go," Jeanine whispered, but I knew we would not make it out of this room if we tried.

"When your adviser informed us of your plan to not uphold your end, we needed to form a new agreement. Instead of you building an army, we decided to create our own."

River hung his head. I couldn't form a complete thought.

"We came to Reales with large numbers already, but with the expectation of three armies against us, we needed to secure our victory." Crimson poured into the gold of his eyes like drops of blood.

"Mira, what did you do?" I asked again, imploring her to look at me.

"And once we learned that you were no longer on Mira's side," Felix continued.

"We were never on Mira's side," Jeanine corrected him. "Despite what she might have told you, we were forced into an agreement with her under the threat of your resident waterboy drowning our kingdom if we didn't play along."

"Waterboy!" Felix repeated with a booming laugh, pointing his finger at River. "Waterboy is going to stick. That's quite clever." He looked at Jeanine. "I don't believe I learned your name."

"You don't need to," she responded.

"Ah, they both have a bite to them." He peeled his upper lip back to reveal two sharp fangs, his tongue swiping across the point of one. "I would love just a little taste..."

"Felix," River warned.

Felix bared his teeth at River, revealing the entire top row. His two perfectly pointed fangs were accompanied by the straightest teeth I'd ever seen. Every inch of these people was perfect. I couldn't pick out one singular flaw about any of them. They all stood straight and tall, their hair shiny and effortless, and each outfit looked individually made for them.

They didn't even look like they breathed.

Felix sighed deeply and adjusted the lapels of his jacket. He was dragging this on much longer than necessary. I wanted to find out what he wanted with me so I could return home and again think of a plan to bring down Mira. "Our agreement with Mira was simple: assist her in becoming the leader of your realm."

That seemed simple enough. Only what did they get out of it? They didn't appear as people who needed the assistance of our realm. They looked healthy and strong on their own. What could they possibly need from us?

Jeanine asked, "And what is that she agreed to give you?"

Felix showed his bright, gleaming smile, looking nowhere but right at me. And before he could say it, I knew the answer, and my gut felt like a pound of lead had just been poured into it.

"Raven, of course."

❦

JEANINE LAUGHED MANIACALLY, pulling me to stand from my chair and shoving me behind her. "That is not going to happen."

I couldn't speak. I stared at Mira. Her demands of bringing our realm down were harsh and unnecessary, but she had at least given me the option to be with Zeke, even if it was under her rule.

But now, she had bargained me away.

She had sold me to these people.

Was I truly that disposable that my sister would agree to hand me over to people I had never met before? "You have made a mistake, Mira."

I bravely stepped in front of Jeanine and didn't cower as I stood directly beside Mira. She didn't flinch or even look at me, continuing to stare at the empty plate in front of her. "You hate me for what Leonidas did to our mother." I didn't have to wait for her words of confirmation before I continued, "But I am not his daughter."

Was that true? I wasn't sure, but all signs pointed to yes.

And when her eyes flared, and her lips thinned as her head slowly turned toward me, I wondered if she already knew that. Or maybe, a small piece of her would realize she had been loathing the wrong person.

"Using me to seek retribution for her has gotten you nowhere." I stood taller, tipping my chin upward in defiance. "Because you will not win this war, Mira. No matter what you do to me, what you threaten me with, or who you sell me to, you will wake up every morning knowing that no single person in this universe loves you."

I blinked back tears. "I, however, get to live every second of my life knowing I have someone who would stop breathing if it meant I still could. I have a sister who would bleed on the ground at my feet if it meant I could live."

I inched one step closer and held her gaze. "You do not. And the worst part about it is I could have loved you. I was willing to give you a chance and be the sister you pretended to want. We would've held power over two kingdoms, which could have been enough. But now..."

I leaned forward, satisfied when she flinched, finally showing a sliver of emotion. "Now, Mira, I can promise you, you wretched woman, that I will kill you. I will bleed you dry and feed your body to the fish. I will relish your screams and cries for help, and I will ignore them."

She had no response, and I didn't want one. I wanted it to end there. I would not be taken again. But when I heard a male voice from the doorway say, "My, little poppet. That was delicious," the comfort that slid over me from the silky sound of his voice alarmed me.

"Silas," River said, standing from his chair. "We weren't expecting you this evening."

No one said a word as I sidestepped around Jeanine to find the source of the voice that seemed to call to me like a siren.

Stepping into the room was a man, similar to everyone else, yet somehow different. He was nearly as tall as Zeke but boasted the same bright blond hair and pale skin as Felix. His hair fell to the middle of his neck, but it was smoothed back without a strand out of place.

Like Felix, this man's allure was undeniable. There were black markings across his neck, but I couldn't tell what they were under his suit.

And he was solid—bigger than Felix and the men from the forest, but not built like a soldier. The build of him just... *was.*

Gracefully, he stepped toward me.

He stared at me, our gazes entwined as he pulled air from my lungs, breath by breath. I felt uncomfortable, yet I could not tear my eyes away from his—from the scarlet irises with flecks of gold and black, like tainted rubies. His lips, the same crimson as my dress, revealed the points of fangs, his tongue stroking over the tip of one after catching the way I was gaping. His cheeks reflected a slight bloom of red. I blinked. He appeared so human, yet the draw of his allure was inhuman. With pale, flawless skin, my heart fluttered.

Not from lust, not from desire, but from fear.

Pure terror and unease.

Because this man before me, the man who shared the same longing gaze as my husband every time he looked upon my face, this man with an undeniable and elegant refinement, was my mate.

413

THIS MAN WITH AN UNDENIABLE AND ELEGANT REFINEMENT, WAS MY MATE.

42

RAVEN

I should've panicked or run away. I could've grabbed Jeanine and given everything I had to escape this castle of horrors, but I didn't. This was a man I promised to kill on sight, yet I remained frozen in place. "You," was all I managed to say.

Silas' eyes swept across my body, never hiding the sharpened points of his canines. He looked at me as if I were a ghost standing before him and not a woman made of flesh and blood. There was familiarity between us, but not one that I could recognize. He gazed at me with the same longing I had seen from many men, but he resembled Zeke's in the way he settled on my lips for a long moment before raising his eyes to mine.

And I... could not move. I couldn't do anything other than stare back at him the same way he stared at me. I couldn't place the unsettling feeling of knowing him, but not in the way I knew everyone else. This was... deeper. I had never met this man before, but it was as if his eyes told a story written before about us.

"You," I said again, weaker than before.

The man Zeke had left me to search for—the one I promised him I would kill if we ever met. Yet my curiosity outweighed the promise. At least, momentarily.

"Raven," Silas drawled twice, as if tasting my name for the very first time. "I have been waiting a very long time to gaze upon your face once more."

I swallowed. "I don't recall ever meeting you."

Unlike Felix, he did not bow to me or refer to me as royalty. He formally introduced himself with a slight dip of his chin. "I am Silas."

Silas. Silas. *Silas.*

I repeated the name over and over in my head—so much, so quickly, that I started to laugh. I laughed loudly, covering my mouth quickly as the sound echoed through the large ballroom.

Because unlike when I heard Zeke's name for the first time, there was no recognition. I did not yearn to hear it again—I did not ache for his touch on me.

And I laughed from the absurdity of all of this. Because fated or not, *mated* or not, this man would never own me. I preferred night over day, dark over light, which was everything Zeke was made of.

And despite how Silas looked like he was formed from women's wildest dreams, there wasn't a man alive that could compare to my husband. My heart had been snatched and locked away months ago, and only one man held the key—a man I hoped would bust through the doors any second.

Silas appeared bewildered, and somewhat annoyed, at my sudden joy, his eyes flicking to River before back to me. "Do I amuse you, little poppet?"

I recomposed myself, clearing my throat and resting my hands against my waist gingerly. "No, no... I just hate being a disappointment." I brought my left hand up between us. "Felix greatly admired the ring of my *keeper*, and Zeke is not the sharing type. Unfortunately, you are too late."

"That's an understatement," Jeanine chimed in.

Silas gripped my wrist before I could even blink, my amusement fading completely as I winced from the pressure. "You will dance with me, Raven."

I shoved his chest and tried to light my wrist with fire, but nothing came. Panic flooded through me at the silence of my elements, the sudden reminder of how weak I was without them, and the fear of not having my own weapon. "Give them back to me!" I shouted, trying to look at River over my shoulder as Silas dragged me closer. "River!" I pleaded, trying to wrangle my wrist free. "You knew about this! You knew he could take my elements!"

River didn't move a muscle, but his jaw flared at the proximity between Silas and me.

Jeanine lunged, but Felix caught her quickly. She fought against him with everything she had, dropping curse words and screaming for him to free her.

Silas didn't release me, nor did he look anywhere else when Jeanine began screaming—not from frustration, but in pain. And he held me in place as I tried to move toward her. Felix held her up while she wailed in agony, the veins in her neck strained, tears streaming down her cheeks.

"Silas," River finally said. "Silas, this is not the way."

"Stop!" I shouted, desperate to free myself, but the bone of my wrist felt as if it might crack from the pressure each time I moved. "Whatever you're doing, stop! Let her go!"

Immediately, her screaming ceased and was followed by short breaths as she gasped for air. To her dismay, she had to lean against Felix while she caught her breath.

Silas pulled me so close to him that I had to lean my head back to keep our lips from touching. "Dance with me," he demanded again, his lips twisting in a humorless grin.

"There is no music," I rasped, my teeth clenched tightly. I needed to find every excuse to get his hands off me.

"We do not need music, little poppet." He wrapped an arm

around my waist and pulled me flush against him, no inches spared between our bodies. "Felix can sing. Felix!"

A deep tremor preceded words that were sung in a language I did not recognize—smooth, flowing, and elegant, and sang with an arrogance that fit their personalities perfectly.

"The language of my clan," Silas boasted, spinning me around the room. "It has been spoken for centuries. I will teach you."

"No one has ever been able to teach me anything," I muttered, my neck straining uncomfortably to keep distance between our faces. "Evidenced by my trip here."

Mira hadn't moved from her seat, watching Silas move me around the room in this fever dream. She looked to be somewhat in a trance herself.

"Do I frighten you, little poppet?"

"No," I whispered my lie.

"You are not curious about our history?" he asked me as his fingers curled into the ruffled fabric of my skirt.

"No," I repeated. "You believe yourself to be my mate."

"I *am* your mate." The smoothness of his voice deepened from frustration at the insinuation that he wasn't.

Silas practically carried me around the room, moving too quickly for me to ever catch my balance without him. The heavy dress I wore no longer felt beautiful, and the dark red fabric made me think of blood. I wondered if I would be spilling any tonight and how it would look dripping down their pale skin, across the gold tablecloth and white lilies in the center of the table. The thought of blood steadied me. And when the visions of pools of my blood in my mind slowly changed from on their skin to being smeared across my lips, I gasped.

I could taste it on my tongue—bitter yet sweet.

"I could provide you with life," Silas murmured, the room darkening around us as he spoke.

And suddenly, we weren't in the grand ballroom of Mira's castle, but within the walls of the black castle River shown me in a dream.

And our feet glided across the floor as if we were floating, the sound of Felix's voice distant. "The life you need," Silas continued, the tone of his voice smooth and crisp. "We would be powerful together, little poppet."

I didn't know which part of me his offer was calling to—but something within me reacted to it. The idea of consuming life intrigued me, the thought of being so powerful, and the promise of blood... It was nearly too much to bear. "Blood," I repeated.

"All you could ever want," he replied, his chin dipping slightly to stare at my throat.

But even deeper within me, more prominent and embedded, lay the golden strand gifted to me from the gods, promising my life to someone else—a man who had already sworn to give me everything I could ever need. It was a bond that would always trump the one Silas claimed to have with me.

And that was why I waited. Through wherever he had taken me, and however it was possible, I waited until his eyes fell to the spot between my neck and shoulder where a scar awaited like a branding.

And when he saw it, the red of his eyes darkened into maroon. His irises swirled with anger and envy. His mouth twisted into a sneer and covered his fangs as he saw Zeke's bite scarred into my skin.

A reminder that would live there forever—it was as if his name was tattooed across every inch of me. I didn't know my history with Silas, nor did I understand why he wanted to bite me—why anyone did—but my blood belonged to Ezekiel Audovera.

"Do you feel it now?" I whispered with a smile.

And the look in his eyes told me he did. As the room fell away from us harshly, volumizing Felix's voice once more as we left the disarming vision Silas stuck me in, he glared at me as if I had burned him.

But it wasn't me—it was the bond within me, the one fate had bestowed upon Zeke and me. He reacted to the revelation just as I had hoped he would. "I will never belong to you," I stated, the silky confidence returning to my voice.

"Fate has already decided my future. And it is not with you. It is with Zeke, my twin flame. The rarest and most cherished bond between any being, magical or not, lives within our very bones. It is a strand that can never be broken, so even if you did plan on taking me, it is useless. Once I die, I will reunite with him."

Mira watched us intently from the table as if her life depended on it. And maybe it did. Maybe Mira had gotten so deep with these creatures that I didn't leave with them, she would suffer.

It added to my determination to leave.

"And she knew," I added, partially hoping he would finish her off to eliminate me having to find a way. "Mira knew of my bond to him."

I expected him to be more upset. I hoped the revelation would make him kill Mira for holding such a secret from him. I did not expect him to chuckle so lowly in his chest that it was as if I could hear it rattle against the emptiness behind his ribcage.

"Ah, that *minor* detail. Oh, beloved. That is most unfortunate for you." It was his smile now that contained the self-assurance I had before. "Bloodmates can bring their mate back to life." He leaned in close—so close that my breath touched his lips. "With a drop of my blood on your tongue, you will never die, nor will you ever see your *twin flame* again."

"Bloodmate," I repeated. "What the fuck is a bloodmate?"

"Many moons ago, little poppet, you and I bloodmated. We exchanged blood and swore to be at each other's side for our entire lives, and that we would always bring the other back to life should anything happen to us."

I shook my head, wholly convinced he was lying. "Fate bonded me to Zeke. It wouldn't have done that if I had sworn myself to another. Your eyes deceive you, Silas. I am a witch, lest you forget, and while elements may be my power, I am in love with a man who can smell lies, and he has taught me a thing or two about how to detect them."

"It is the sweat on your brow," I continued. "The way it has begun to bead at the threat you feel from me being bound to another. And it is how you are one stitch away from ripping my dress with your fingers every time I mention his name. If I didn't know any better, *Silas*," I drawled his name the same way he had mine, "I would say you are the one who is frightened."

I had yet to learn if he even breathed, but his chest stiffened underneath the palm he kept pressed against it. And while I was having the *grandest* time, I would need to make my exit soon.

"It is time I remind you," he said, peeling back my dress around my shoulder. "One bite, little poppet, and you will remember everything."

I didn't have the chance to fight him.

Because River was beside me instantaneously, placing his arm around my stomach and tossing me backward as if I weighed nothing before delivering a kick to Silas's chest that had him flying across the room. And in the corner of my eye, Jeanine unsheathed the dagger from between her breasts and thrust it into Felix's thigh.

From the floor, I watched as Silas landed on all fours, sliding against the sleek tile, cracks following his weight. Blinking, my lips parted when I noticed just how little damage he took as he slowly rose to his feet and clenched his fists.

The shock from River's betrayal made Silas' veil fall away from my elements, flooding my body with power once more. And as Jeanine staggered over to me, having bought us a moment of reprieve, I shifted into Terra and placed my hands against the floor.

The tiles shook and cracked, the legs of the table landing lopsidedly, forcing Mira to jump up from her chair. But Silas and Felix recovered too quickly, looking between the three of us.

Silas zeroed in on me, and River yelled, "Go!"

A crack widened between Felix and us as he pulled the dagger from his thigh and threw it to the floor, snarling at Jeanine. I shifted into Blaze and hastily stood up, grabbing her hand and running toward the door. Creating a half-circle of tall flames around us, I guarded us between the fire and the wall until we could slip out of the ballroom and into the hallway. "We have to hide!" I shouted to her over the crackling of the fire.

From the other side of the flames, Silas paced the length of them, trying to find his way around—but I could not see River. And part of me wanted to turn around and help him, to ensure he was alive.

But Jeanine gave me no time.

Taking my hand, she pulled me around many corners and up so many stairs that I constantly tripped over my dress. It was only when we reached the top step that I recognized where we were going. "Jeanine," I hissed. "If they find us, I'll have to burn the entire library down!"

"I can't get us outside safely! There are no places to hide for miles, and he clearly has more friends. The doors to the library lock!"

After witnessing Silas' ability to trap me in a vision, I hoped locks would be enough.

～

ONCE INSIDE THE LIBRARY, I helped Jeanine lock the doors and pile chairs in front of them. We ran to the farthest back corner and crouched, keeping the doors in sight from where we hid. Her hands trembled in mine, and I pulled her closer to me. "We're going to be okay," I promised, not thoroughly convinced of what I said. "We'll find a way out of this."

"Silas and Felix..." her voice quivered, fear in her eyes. "They weren't..."

"Human," I finished for her. "I know. Silas wanted to bite me and didn't... breathe. We have a history, though I can't understand how. I have never met him before."

"In this life," she said aloud, the thought that had crossed my mind, too. "Those memories you had in the caves could've been from a lifetime with him."

"I had no life with him." Of that, I was confident. I couldn't imagine any version of me loving anyone but Zeke. There was a reason fate chose us to respawn in each lifetime. "He might've been there, but I didn't love him. The faint memories I have are with Zeke — he's the one I'm crying for. I fear his pain was because of Silas, but I can't understand it."

"Do you think he's on his way? Do you think he's going to save us?" She curled into me and put her head on my shoulder, and I could feel her tears wetting my skin. The fact that she was afraid added to my own fear. Jeanine was the strongest person I knew and nearly as stubborn as me. Her fear and hopelessness didn't exactly give me hope that we could find a way out.

"I love you," I whispered, because if I had learned anything from the many instances of nearly losing my life or the lives of people I loved, it was that I should never take these moments for granted.

"I love you," she replied, barely loud enough for me to hear.

I squeezed her hands. "We're going to make it out of here, and then we'll come up with a new plan to eliminate Mira once and for all."

From the other side of the library, past the rows of shelves and tables, a voice echoed loudly and made my heart catapult into my throat, "My, my. Your fear smells delightful."

"BLOODMATE," I REPEATED. "WHAT THE FUCK IS A BLOODMATE?"

43

RAVEN

Our chairs hadn't moved, and the doors didn't open. Felix had found his way into the library another way and was searching for us, taunting us with our scents and the way he could hear our hearts pounding against our chests.

What the fuck were these creatures?

So far, they showed unfathomable magic, more than I had ever seen before.

Quietly, we stood from our spot in the corner, and no sound carried with us as we tiptoed through the shelves. Though, if he genuinely could hear our heartbeats, he would locate us quickly.

"That was quite the party trick," he shouted, and his voice was too near for comfort. "It is quite a shame for you that you failed. We cannot be killed as easily as that."

I needed to gauge his location. Unfortunately, while trying to lock them out, we locked ourselves in. Our only option was for me to find a way to kill him, or bring enough harm forth that it would give us time to find an alternative.

I slid a book from a shelf and tossed it across the library. It thudded loudly against another shelf before falling to the floor. He was there instantly, laughing as he bent to pick the book up from the floor. "Clever." He held the front and back cover in each hand and quickly tore through it before dropping the pieces back to the ground.

Strength. Bloodthirstiness. The ability to enter rooms without opening doors. They moved quickly and couldn't be killed by daggers or icicles to the legs or arms. And Silas had the ability to trap me within visions, to infiltrate my thoughts and replace them with his own.

I silently cursed the leaders of this realm who banned books on magic. I had no idea what these creatures were, which gave me no indication of how to kill them. Stabbing wouldn't work—not that we had any more weapons hidden.

We couldn't hide from him forever.

I bit my lip as I looked at Jeanine, who immediately shook her head at me. *Don't you dare*, she mouthed.

"All they want is me," I whispered. "I can save you."

"Don't you fucking dare," she whispered with her teeth clenched and her fingers dug so hard into my hand that tears filled my eyes. "We do this together."

"I'm really sorry about this."

I warmed my hand enough for it to sting hers. She released instinctually, but before she could grab me again, I shifted into Frost and trapped her between a wall of ice and a bookshelf.

She screamed in frustration as I ran toward the middle of the library and was quickly met by Felix. All that stood between us was a long table. "You have many forms," he said, motioning to my white hair.

"Tell me what you are," I demanded, shifting into Blaze. Stabbing him or the others didn't work—they seemed to heal as quickly as me.

But raising fire against them in the ballroom at least delayed them from following us. It gave me hope they couldn't touch flames, which left Blaze as my only defense against him.

"We are what others fear," he replied, which made me roll my eyes. "We are why your astral witch cast a shield over your realm." He stepped around the table, and I backed away.

Our astral witch. Damiana had referred to herself as an astral witch, but why? What reason could she have had for shielding us?

"We are why your mother took you away from your father and feared the power you possessed."

I paused. The power *I* possessed?

Why was my backstory constantly changing, and why could no one ever just answer my questions without involving some kind of riddle?

Delay, delay, delay. It was my only weapon right now while I was trying to think of a way out.

"My husband will kill you," I promised. "Simply for looking at me, he will torture you and wish you had never come to Reales."

Felix took small steps closer. "There is no man who can kill us."

"Zeke isn't a man," I whispered, keeping my voice steady to sound convincing because I wholly believed there was more to Zeke than that a simple mortal life. Like Silas and Felix, Zeke ached for my blood. The commonalities could not be a coincidence. "He has darkness within him. He was with me in another lifetime, multiple lifetimes, because the gods promised our union in life and death."

Felix stilled. Something was churning in his mind as he stared at me, blinking once. If they knew me in another lifetime, it meant they had to know Zeke, too. We had been following one another since the beginning—the reasoning was a mystery we had not yet figured out. But if River did not want them to know of Zeke's manor nearby, there was a reason.

When actual fear flooded Felix's eyes, it confirmed something I always wondered about my husband—the answer I desperately sought. The blood he craved, the black that flooded his eyes, and the constant anger he held for anyone that wasn't me. "Is it because of his shadows?"

Felix sneered, his voice spiteful and full of malice, the same type I felt toward him. "He no longer possesses his shadows."

I grinned. "Doesn't he?"

He *lunged*.

He closed the little distance between us in one jump, taking my throat in his hand and tossing me clear across the room. My back hit the shelves, and I fell to the floor as books tumbled on top of me. Jeanine screamed my name from her icy cage, her fists pummeling against the wall as she begged me to let her out.

"He will kill you for that!" I yelled, lighting my palms while I stood. Blood dripped from a cut on my cheek, and I didn't miss how he bared his fangs. "Silas believes I belong to him. I do not believe you should touch me."

"Do not speak of what you do not know, witch."

"I know that you are beneath Silas," I taunted. "I know that you have to do everything he says. You even listened to River when he told you not to touch us. Silas veiled my elements. You are fearful of my husband. I believe your kind is weaker than you let on."

I continued to bait him while he snarled, his chest heaving and his fingers gripping the table's edge as if he was trying to hold himself back. The cut on my cheek healed, but the blood remained. "Can you smell it? It is the sweetness that Zeke craves." I stepped toward him. "Does it anger you, Felix? That Silas wants me all to himself?" I touched my cheek, letting some of the blood coat my fingertips. "How awful that must be for you to be held back from something so delicious..."

That was all it took.

Felix flung himself across the room, throwing tables and chairs out of the way. I braced, spreading the fire to my wrists and ready to fight him with everything I had, when I was suddenly jerked back and knocked into the bookshelf. River appeared before me out of thin air.

He grabbed my wrists, and we were gone.

∿

HE DID NOT TAKE me through the Time-Antre.

426

This method was much quicker.

We were surrounded by pitch black for seconds, moving so quickly through whatever this was—time, space, I didn't know— before we were standing on a lush, grassy hillside that was so clearly not in Reales.

I immediately vomited while he put an arm around my waist to prevent me from keeling over. "What the fu—"

"Walk straight, Raven." He pushed me forward, not giving me time to collect myself or ask what had happened.

"River!" I shouted, pushing his hands off of me. "What the fuck is going on?"

It was the first time I had ever seen him look concerned. "We're standing outside of Thoya, Raven. I don't have time to explain."

"*Make* time! Who are they?"

"Follow the path into Thoya, Raven. You'll be safe there. Tell Damiana I sent you. Tell her Silas knows."

I threaded my fingers in my hair. "Knows *what*?! River, you have to tell me something!"

"She will explain everything to you, Raven. I cannot stand here with you and try to do so myself, or he will find us. You have to go." He turned to leave, but I caught his wrist.

"Zeke will know something is wrong, River, and he needs my blood. Take me to him—"

"He's fed from you?"

I wrinkled my nose. "*Fed* from me? It's a little repulsive when you say it like that, but I suppose—"

"Finding him would take too long. He is no longer in Nova."

I looked toward what I assumed was the direction of the channel. "I can find him. Put me in the forest of Reales—" I clamped my mouth shut when his words registered. "How did *you* know he was in Nova?"

It was refreshing to see him uncomfortable for once. "I have been following him. I prevented one of Silas's members from harming him."

I raised an eyebrow. "How have you been following him? *Why* have you been following him?"

I learned long ago that he hated when I peppered him with questions, and now was no different. "You are both integral to the downfall of Silas. I cannot tell you more right now because you need to leave."

"Take me to the forest."

"No!" he shouted, but sighed afterward. "No," he repeated calmly. "This ensures your safety."

I was still dizzy from how we landed here from the library, and I was nauseous from worry and confusion. "River, I can't leave Jeanine there! I won't! You have to take me back!"

"I will save Jeanine, Raven, but you have to go, or I won't have time. Felix will have already informed Silas that I've taken you, and they'll take Jeanine next."

"River!" I wailed as tears filled my eyes. "River, you have to save her. She's my best friend; I can't lose her; you must understand…"

"I do." He sputtered without reprieve, "You will get your answers in Thoya, but you must go. Jeanine only has moments left."

Without a word, he shifted.

He *shifted*.

I watched with widened eyes as his black hair lightened to a dark blue, the colors of his eyes changed from our green to the color of pure, untouched saltwater, and his ears…

"I am just like you, Raven. Silas wasn't supposed to touch you. You weren't supposed to see him tonight. He only needed to be assured you were alive and that I wasn't lying to him. But the temptation proved to be too great for him."

Waves appeared behind his irises in the same way snowflakes and flames danced in mine. I stared, enamored and shocked, and honestly only half-listening.

He grabbed my shoulder gently. "There is a war coming, Raven, but not for the realm. It's a war that's been a long time in the making. Damiana will tell you, but you must go."

"You're not my enemy," I said with tremors of hope in my voice. The idea that was on my side was too comforting. It gave me too much to long for.

"I have never been your enemy, Raven, but I am not without fault. I have taken too many risks lately, and bringing you here was another."

"Why can't you take me to the castle? Why are we standing on the outskirts of Thoya?"

"Damiana took extra measures to ensure Thoya's safety. Any magical being that crosses into Thoya without permission will lose their magic."

"But I have magic and Zeke——"

"Zeke will not be able to reenter Thoya since he left the realm," River said with a frown. "Not unless Damiana brings down her shield, which she cannot do with Silas so close."

The thought of Zeke never coming to Thoya again was heartbreaking. We wanted a future here—we dreamed of our children running through the field behind our manor.

"He cannot retrieve me here," I said, wiping tears away with the back of my hand. "When will I see him again?"

"When it's safe, Raven."

I held out my wrist. "Promise me, River. Promise me you'll find him before he gets to Reales. Promise me I'll see him again."

He stared at my wrist before he placed his finger against it, applying pressure to my pulse. And slowly, a gray ink mark in the shape of a wave appeared on my wrist, matching the one he had made with Jeanine. He showed me his wrist then—the one with Jeanine had faded, but ours was fresh.

"I promise to reunite you with your flame, Raven."

That was when I broke down, covering my face with my hands. If I had stayed in Seolia, I would've seen Zeke in just a few days. But now, I didn't know when I would see him or any of my family again. "Can I return home? Are my people safe?"

"Yes, Raven," he whispered. "Your people are safe. Silas has sworn to Mira that he will not touch anyone outside of Reales, otherwise she will not have a realm to rule. Once they have taken the realm, Silas will come for you. We have to be prepared for that moment."

"Outside of Reales?" I blinked back tears as I peered up at him. "What about the people *in* Reales?"

His silence answered for him, yet I did not ask for the details because I couldn't stomach anything else. "And why haven't they done anything sooner? They seem strong enough——"

"They're not," he interrupted. "That is why..." Sighing, he tilted his chin toward the sky, clearly uncomfortable with sharing something with me. "They will be strong enough soon, Raven. I really should go help Jeanine. I will not be allowed back in the castle. I have to move quickly."

"Take me with you. Please, River. I can't live without her, it would be too unbearable."

He shook his head, taking steps backward. "I can't, Raven."

"Then promise me again!" I flung my wrist out. "Promise me you'll save her, River."

Unexpectedly, he put his arms around me and held me close for a moment. "I am sorry to have disappointed you. I will make it up to you, but I cannot swear another oath. I will send word for you to return home. Until then, stay with Damiana."

I nodded as he stepped back. I had a hundred more questions, however Jeanine's life was more important. But as he began to fade, I asked one more, "What is your shift's name?"

His face lit up with a broad smile—the first of his I had ever seen. I couldn't help but mirror it with a smile of my own. "I have always been River," he answered.

I scowled. "That hardly seems fair."

He laughed, then disappeared.

I FELT he could've dropped me somewhere closer to the kingdom, but maybe Thoya was more extensive than I realized.

I was sick with worry for Jeanine. I kept hoping River would drop her somewhere near me, but nothing of the sort ever happened. And as I walked, I kept my arms wrapped around my waist. It had been a very long time since the last time I was alone—truly alone—and I didn't care much for it.

Solitude used to be normal, but now I had a family. I was surrounded by people who loved me every day, and once you had that, it became hard to live without it.

I thought of John and Alice, wondered how my kingdom was faring, and if River was telling the truth. It seemed that wherever I went, people were put at risk. If Silas could not deny himself the temptation of touching me, then what could guarantee he wouldn't seek me out wherever I was?

And why had it taken him so long to find me?

But mostly, I thought about Zeke. I ached for him. I needed to tell him all of this—I needed to show him my memories of Silas and rottenly say, *I told you so*, after he felt the nothingness between us. I needed him to promise me that we would figure this out together and that spending weeks apart would never happen again.

Mira *sold* me.

Every time I forgot about it, the confession returned to haunt me. This entire time, Mira had been bartering my life away, and I was fretting about whether we should move to Reales.

It all seemed so trivial now.

Mira was terrified of Silas, and if she believed him and his followers to be dangerous, I couldn't begin to imagine what that meant for the rest of us.

Frowning as I descended one last hillside, I watched Edmund sparring with another man in the broad fields behind the castle. He looked just as skilled as Zeke, only maybe a touch more graceful, which wasn't surprising. Zeke went for the kill; Edmund liked to taunt.

I was a sweaty, disheveled mess in my red dress, dragging my bare feet from exhaustion and plagued with worry. Edmund stopped swinging his sword when his counterpart motioned toward me with the point of his blade.

He turned and, as soon as he saw me, Edmund threw his sword to the ground and ran toward me. The comfort of seeing someone so dear to me and knowing I was once again safe made me cry his name as I met him step for step.

His arms enveloped me as we met, and I pressed my face against his chest so close I could hear his heart thundering against my forehead. And I wept. I clawed at his shirt and cried for Jeanine, trembling as I relived the moments in Reales, and I held him as close as I could. He didn't press or attempt to find out why I was here alone, emerging from the back hills of his kingdom.

All he asked was, "Are you hurt?"

I shook my head, unable to stop shaking, unable to believe that what I just lived through wasn't a nightmare.

And with even more concern, he asked, "Is Ezekiel?"

"No," I mumbled against his chest, "At least, I don't think so..." But not knowing if that was true, a fresh set of tears fell down my cheeks. "Oh, Edmund, so many bad things are coming..."

He lifted my chin, his eyes frantically searched mine, and his arm wrapped around my waist as if maybe I wasn't as safe as I claimed. "Raven, I don't understand. Ezekiel would never let you wander..." But then he stopped until the realization crossed his face. "He does not know you are here. He is still in Nova."

I shrugged a shoulder, sniffling. "I don't know where he is. I went to Reales with Jeanine, Edmund..."

"Raven," he said, accompanied by a long sigh. "You were supposed to stay in Seolia or come here. You were not supposed to visit any other kingdom."

"I know!" I covered my face with my hands. Guilt nearly strangled me. "River said I had to go to Reales, or my people would be unsafe. I was attacked in Seolia, Edmund, by witches who wanted my blood. River saved me. We went with him to Reales through a time hallway."

He removed my hands from my face and stared at me in disbelief. "A time hallway?"

I nodded but didn't even begin trying to explain that one. "He has... so much magic, Edmund. And Mira offered me to these... men, these creatures."

"Who?"

"My mate." I felt like vomiting after referring to him like that. "His name is Silas, and he's.... well, creepy. He's working with Mira to go to war with our realm, and they have more magic than I have ever seen, and Jeanine is still there..."

He placed his fingers against my lips and waited until I mimicked his deep breath before speaking. "Take a breath, love. Come. Let's clean you up, and then you can tell me all about it."

RIVER APPEARED BEFORE ME OUT OF THIN AIR. HE GRABBED MY WRISTS, AND WE WERE GONE.

44

RAVEN

Edmund did not take me to my manor, knowing it would've been too painful to visit it without Zeke. Instead, we rode to the castle on one of the many horses he owned that grazed the peaceful hillsides of Thoya. And the entire time, I was imagining a future where Shadow could be with wild horses while watching my children enjoy the simplicities of life—chasing butterflies, rolling down the hillsides, running from their father to avoid bedtime.

I so desperately wanted that life with Zeke.

We halted at the front doors of the castle. I was so tired, yet wide awake. I feared I wouldn't sleep peacefully again, especially if I continued to spend time away from the only person who kept my nightmares away.

Edmund slid off his horse first before assisting me. He hadn't asked yet about my outfit, but the curiosity in his expression made me explain. "River didn't inform us until we arrived at Reales that there would be a formal dinner in my honor. This dress was much more elegant before... well, everything." I glanced down at the slightly singed skirt and ripped ends of my bodice.

"I am not looking forward to explaining this to Ezekiel," he mumbled, taking my hand to rest in the crook of his arm. "It is only fun to torture him when he is here. He will not be pleased that I have seen you so... revealed."

"He will be fine," I promised. "He knows you only flirt to drive him mad. He loves you like a brother, Edmund."

"You are his mate," he countered. "He can only extend patience so far before it becomes unbearable for him. I've been speaking with my mother about bonds."

"Your mother knows more than she led me to believe. Silas knows your mother, Edmund. He knows Zeke and me, but I don't know how. I don't remember meeting him. River says your mother will tell me why."

Edmund led me to the room where Zeke and I stayed during our last visit, but did not open the door. Instead, he placed a hand on my shoulder and kissed my forehead. "My mother loves you, Raven. We all do. Whatever she knows but didn't share, it was for a reason. Do not believe her to be an enemy, love."

"I don't," I assured him. "I am just tired of the secrets. I deserve to know who I am and where I came from, and I intend to find out."

He opened the door for me and motioned inside with his chin. "Bathe. Rest. I will tell Gisela to fetch you some new clothes, and then we will all dine together."

"Edmund, I..." I was too embarrassed to ask. Ashamed, even. But he had insisted many times that I could request anything of him. "Ever since... Cade"—I still had trouble saying his name, reliving those moments—"I haven't been able to sleep alone. I have nightmares about him and about the child we lost. If it's not too much to ask...."

434

"Gisela will stay with you, love. She would be delighted."

I ignored the red that was blossoming on my cheeks from the need to sleep with someone like a child, but reminded myself that healing from trauma didn't have a time limit. I was allowed to ask for help.

"Thank you, Edmund. For everything."

Playfully, he shoved me inside and winked. "Anything for you, exquisite creature. Go before I am forced to flirt with you more and put my life in Ezekiel's hands."

～

I STOOD at the end of the steep road that led to the castle in Reales. I had been here before—lived within this moment. This was so familiar to me, and it was during a time when I lived without Zeke. When I couldn't find out how or why our connection was so strong after only knowing one another for days and why everything always hurt when he was gone.

The path was steeper than usual; I crawled on my hands and knees to reach the top. Instead of the cobblestone rocks typically scattered across the pavement, this path was made out of bones. I kicked and pushed them to the side when I slipped, and could hear as they shattered into pieces at the bottom of the incline.

The higher I climbed, the more bones I found. Fingers grasped for me and wrapped around my wrist, but I pried them off as I screamed for them to stop.

If I could just reach him, if I could just make it to the door, Zeke would save me.

He called my name from the top of the road, extending his arm, but I could not reach him no matter how high I climbed. I cried his name, I crawled faster, but someone's hands wrapped around my ankles to tug me down.

"Come on, baby," he said, encouraging me not to give up.

But I was so weary—so exhausted of always having mountains to climb, of always being pulled away from him.

He jerked his head back, his eyes glazing over as he seemed to lose focus for a moment before blinking. "This is it," he murmured.

"This is how we speak to one another."

I didn't know what he meant. This was a nightmare; I could never wake up from a bad dream until he threw me out.

"Baby, stop moving. You're not going to reach me."

I shook my head, continuing my ascent. "They're going to pull me down, Zeke. I can't leave until you throw me."

"I'll throw you," he said. "Baby, where are you?"

I motioned dramatically around myself. "Are you blind?"

He grinned. "Where are you, little demon?"

"I..." I paused. Blinked. And remembered I was outside of this dark nightmare. "Thoya. I'm in Thoya with Edmund."

"Did you go to Reales?"

I kicked off more bones, cursing as they seemed to multiply. "Zeke, I'm scared. I can't... I can't remember what happened, I..." I stammered while trying to push through my subconscious. "*Him.* Zeke, he's there. I met him, he's there in Reales, he has foul, twisted magic that makes me see things that aren't there, and he tried to bite me..."

I winced at the growl he emitted, at the teeth he bared. "Stay in Thoya, Raven. Stay there until I find you."

"Zeke, you can't. River said you can't come here." Vivid memories poured through my mind, and a cold sweat overcame me. "Jeanine! Jeanine is in Reales! River said he would save her, but I don't know if he did. And they're strong, Zeke, they're powerful."

When my feet started slipping, I held onto the road with my fingers for dear life and made the mistake of looking down. The road had grown since I started, leaving me dangling. "Throw me before I fall!"

"Baby, look at me."

I whipped my head toward him, my hands sweating and beginning to slip as I lost grip on the rocks.

"I love you."

My entire chest hurt. I didn't know if any of this was real, but I wanted to believe I was really speaking to him and that he wasn't harmed somewhere. "What is this?"

"I can't explain it. We're supposed to be able to speak to one another mind mind-to-mind, but we can't. I think this is our stubborn way of trying anyway."

One of my hands slipped. I had seconds left with him. "Promise me I'll see you again."

Lying down on his stomach, he extended his arm as far as he could, his fingers straight and flexed as he reached for me. "I promise, Raven. Now, come here, little witch. Let me touch you."

Groaning, I dug my toes into the road, stretched until my ribcage felt as if it might break, and swung my arm up toward his. Before he could touch me and throw me out from wherever this was, I held his gaze and whispered, "I love you."

The tip of his finger touched mine, and energy shot through my body. His body hummed in response. Even my subconscious knew that no other pairing could have what we had as our magic reached for one another. When he smiled at me, I knew he realized it, too.

"Come back to me, Zeke."

"I will always come back to you, Raven."

Before I could fall, before the hands could pull me down into oblivion, he threw me.

And I prayed it wouldn't be the last time I ever saw him.

I woke up with a gasp. Disoriented, I placed my palm over my forehead and tried to take steady breaths. The comfort I felt from waking felt misplaced and confusing. It was the first time I had slept without anyone beside me since Cade's death, and while it the bones made it seem like a nightmare, it also felt like a gift when remembering how I really seemed to have spoken with my husband.

Mind-to-mind, he had said. He spoke to me in my mind all the time. I did not possess the ability to talk to him like that, and not understanding what he meant added to my already steep frustration.

Closing my eyes, I laid back down again and begged myself to fall asleep. He promised to always find me in my dreams, and it seemed he could do so even without being near.

I needed more information. I needed him to tell me where he was. Why didn't I ask any important questions or brag to him about how I felt nothing for Silas?

Why didn't I reassure him?

I wholly blamed my subconscious. It could never be trusted while I was panicking. But for the first time in months, I did not dread going to sleep. In fact, I was looking forward to it.

Stretching my arms above my head, I leaned forward to look out the window. Dusk had fallen, and Edmund would soon be knocking on my door for me to accompany him to dinner.

It was finally my opportunity to ask questions.

Sitting on my table, tied with a pretty pink bow, were at least three days' worth of outfits. Gisela must've snuck them in while I was napping. I meandered toward them, calmer than I had been in a long time. Even if the dream wasn't real and I hadn't really talked to him, his presence gave me hope that he was safe.

If only I could be sure Jeanine was, too.

Untying the ribbons, I picked up the first set. Like always, Gisela had chosen something for me in a style I had never seen before. It seemed Seolia was always the last kingdom to see the newest trends. I never inquired where Perosan ordered their textiles and fabrics, but Petra always found the most vibrant colors.

Unlike the old style of the gown I had worn when meeting Silas, this violet set was airy and loose. The pants bunched around my ankles and cinched at my waist but ballooned around my legs. The top, with its quaint V-neckline, hung loosely around my chest and stomach but cuffed around my arms. I felt as if I was wearing the comfiest set of pajamas ever, only these were much more elegant.

I opened the door at the knock, my smile broad as I saw Gisela standing on the other side in a similar outfit. She threw her arms around my neck while mine closed around her waist, and we stayed like that for a while. We didn't exchange pleasantries, nor did she apologize to me the same way everyone else had since learning of my abduction; Gisela spoke through the way she held me, through her pressing her forehead against mine and wiping my tears away with her fingertips.

"Whoever they were, they would've been beautiful."

"A boy," I whispered, closing my eyes. "It was a boy. I feel I've dreamt of him before. I never see him, but I know he's there."

"My, what a gift from the gods that is."

My eyes burned as I stared into hers.

"To love your child even when he cannot be with you physically. He is waiting until he can return to you, love. Hold that with you when it all seems hopeless."

I laughed through my tears. For the first time, I laughed as she put our loss into an entirely different perspective— ne that did not focus on the grief of it, but on the promise of his return. And she smiled with me, pecking me on the lips before she pulled me out into the hallway. "Everyone is waiting for you, love. I am just as anxious as you to hear what my mother has to say. I have always suspected she held secrets."

I was nervous. The last time I visited, Damiana made no indication that she knew River, yet River told me to tell her he sent me. Felix insinuated that she had been protecting me from them.

I walked in with no idea what to expect.

As we entered the dining room, Damiana, Baldwin, and Edmund stood from their chairs. Edmund and Baldwin bowed their heads to me, but Damiana came straight toward me with wide open arms. I walked straight into them.

Nothing about her seemed disloyal.

"You must be angry with me," she said against my hair while playing with its ends.

"I am not angry," I replied. "I am desperate."

Taking my hand, she led me to a chair beside hers and across from Gisela and Edmund's seats. We waited in silence while the food was brought to the table. I wasn't hungry, but Zeke would insist I needed to eat. And it did not surprise me that Atticus didn't make an appearance. I hoped they hadn't dismissed him from his position, but that wouldn't have shocked me either, considering how much Edmund loved my husband.

After inhaling water like I hadn't had a drink for days, I rested my elbows on the table and looked at Damiana. "Excuse me for jumping right into it, but River said you would tell me about Silas."

Damiana exchanged a look with Baldwin before sighing. "I had hoped that he would give up after lifetimes of never finding you again, but he did not."

"Lifetimes," I repeated. "So, he wasn't lying about knowing me before... this lifetime." That still seemed so... impossible. I had no memories of him, but he had many of me. It was oddly unsettling and intrusive.

"He was not lying," Baldwin answered. "Silas knew you, and he knew us."

I blinked. Even Gisela and Edmund looked bewildered.

"Is Leonidas my father?"

Damiana shook her head, and I jumped when Gisela slapped the table and exclaimed, "I knew it!"

"That, I will leave to River. He is your brother, and it is his place to tell you where you came from. I can, however, share with you what Silas wants with you and how I've been protecting you for as long as I could."

I remained silent, waiting.

"Silas has been alive for a very long time. I do not know how long, nor does it matter. You are Celestina's daughter in this lifetime and one more before."

I should've requested a stronger drink.

"Long ago, you were born for the sole purpose of continuing a bloodline. Your father needed the power of Celestina's magic to entwine with his. And he received it, not only with you but also with River. But you were more than he bargained for."

Edmund had moved around the table without me noticing and took my hand between his. It was then that I realized I was breathing entirely too fast.

"You have always possessed the elements, Raven, but your blood makes you untouchable and very sought after."

"My blood," I repeated. I couldn't feel my tongue. Not only had I been used in this lifetime, but it sounded like it was the same in lives before.

"Your healing," she specified. "The way you can heal others is only a sliver of the magic your blood truly holds. You restore strength, you bring back life, and a single drop can elevate someone's magic.

Silas learned of this. Though he was powerful, your father agreed to ally with the Undead by marriage—Silas' marriage to you."

"Undead," I repeated, rolling my eyes. "Clever."

"Celestina did not stand for that," Damiana continued. "She took you and River and hid." She took a sip of her water, and I couldn't help but wonder if she was delaying while deciding how much to share with me. "She hid you in Seolia."

"I don't understand," I said. "Seolia did not exist until the realm was created. How could she have taken us there?" But Damiana did not need to answer that question, because I had studied the history of our island. "Witches," I said. "The island belonged to witches."

"Our coven," Damiana said.

"Your coven?" Gisela asked, looking between her parents. "That would mean..."

"That I am very old," Damiana stated. "We hoped Silas would not find us there, but your mother feared that your father would come and take you away. He did not realize that agreeing to give you to Silas was the worst choice he could've made for his species."

"Species," I repeated.

"Witches can breed with mortals," Baldwin said. "But not Celestina. Her power was too great to waste on mortal bloodlines. You are a Half-Witch, Raven."

"The Dark Half-Witch," Damiana interjected. "You grew to be the most powerful witch in existence because of your bloodline. You were highly sought after when you were taken away from your home. We managed to keep you hidden until"—she smiled and her voice softened—"until the Phantom Prince found you."

She didn't have to tell me who that was. I sat up straighter at the mention of him, nearly falling out of my chair as I leaned forward, desperate to hear more.

"He did not come to the island for you, but that is why he stayed. And the two of you fell into an all-consuming love. The Phantom Prince was also born of two bloodlines, and when he asked you to be his bloodmate, you agreed."

Edmund wiped away my tears, his own eyes glistening as he smiled with me. Even in a different lifetime, Zeke and I had fallen in

love. He did not need me for my blood or magic the way others did —
he loved me then, just as he did now. "What was his name?" I asked.

Baldwin chuckled. "No one knew of him by any other name. He
only revealed it to you."

How I wish I could remember that instead of hearing the cries
from his death.

Damiana continued, "The Phantom Prince was the most
powerful creature, equal to you. Your union would've threatened
every magical being, and when a witch in our coven betrayed us, Silas
found you."

I suddenly froze because now the screaming I heard made sense.
And when I held my hand up and shook my head, Damiana paused.
"I do not want to hear about our deaths," I whispered. "Not without
him here."

Gisela asked, "What was Celestina's power? What made Raven so
strong?"

"Celestina was a grey witch," Damiana answered. "She could use
her power for good or evil with blood charms. That is why we believe
her power passed to your blood. She could use her charms to heal,
hex, or harm. Toward the end of her life, your mother became very
bitter."

"I thirst for blood," I said. "And you knew that."

Damiana nodded. "After you died, magic began to wane. That
was when other beings learned that it had been tied to your blood.
Your blood was what restored strength. When a seer prophesied your
rebirth, we waited. When mortals began to move away to the
surrounding lands, we needed a plan. When Seolia was infiltrated by
men, we were cast out, and many were burned. Your mother and I
were the only ones who remained."

I asked, "How did you rise to power?"

"Petra," she answered. "Petra is not a witch, but I cannot tell her
story. Petra's magic was great enough to slowly erase memories of
magic and the witches who once dwelled in our realm until hardly
anyone could remember. It was then that we worked our way onto
courts and eventually, the thrones."

"And then," Baldwin added, "Your father found Celestina again.

She tried to move on, took many lovers over the years, including Leonidas, but he lied to her to force her into agreeing to once again carry his child."

"Me," I said.

"After she became pregnant, she learned of his trickery. She came to me and informed me of who she was carrying, and that was when I cast a shield around our realm to protect you from not only your father, but also from Silas to prevent him from coming back and claiming his bloodmate."

"He never took another," Baldwin said. "He has waited for your soul to rebirth by using River."

Damiana *tsked* and shook her head. "We do not tell his story. He will be the one to tell Raven of his past."

I became lightheaded from the information I was taking in. "River said you cast a second shield around Thoya, and that Zeke cannot find me here since he left this realm."

"He is correct," Damiana confirmed. "Once I had my own children, I needed extra assurance that my family would be safe. I created another layer around Thoya to keep those with magic out, and if they cross the barrier, they lose their magic unless I have given permission for them to enter."

I sank back in my chair, unsure of what else to ask. My head swam with all the new information, and I wasn't entirely sure I believed all of it. I still felt like there were so many missing pieces that only River could fill in. Gisela looked utterly dumbfounded and had somehow ended up on my other side, almost in my lap.

"So, you and father are... old," Gisela said again. "You have been alive for how long?"

"Over a century," Damiana said gently. "We will answer any questions you and your brother may have, Gisela, but let us speak after Raven settles."

Edmund took hold of the conversation. "How do we defeat Silas? How can we prevent him from taking Raven?"

"Raven is only one key," Damiana said. I felt her stare, but I couldn't find the energy to look anywhere but at the untouched plate of food in front of me.

"And the other key *is*?" Gisela asked, exasperated.

"Zeke's shadows," Damiana replied. "And Zeke's shadows can only be released with Raven's blood."

"WHAT A GIFT FROM THE GODS TO LOVE YOUR CHILD EVEN WHEN HE CANNOT BE WITH YOU PHYSICALLY."

45

ZEKE

"You're doing it again."

We had been riding for nearly three days. We had stopped thrice to sleep and let the horses drink water from whatever source we could find nearby. I was beginning to recognize our surroundings, which meant we were close to Reales, but Raven wasn't there anymore.

And how did I know that?

Because I started dreaming while awake.

Somewhere in my mind, deep and buried, I felt her. A tug pulled on my subconscious and I followed it, unsure what to look for. But after Avalie mentioned something about a mind bridge and being able to speak with your mate through it, I stopped questioning things that seemed unrealistic. None of this was normal. At least, not to us. We seemed to be the only ones who didn't know every avenue magic could take.

Luca shoved my shoulder. My legs clenched around Shadow to keep myself from falling to the ground. "Fuck, Luca."

"You can't ride the rest of the way to Reales with your eyes closed in hopes of finding her again."

I grumbled something inaudible about how I could do whatever the fuck I wanted, but I knew he was worried about me. I hadn't tasted her blood in three days, and I was going a bit mad. My irises changed colors without reason, my chest tightened with a feeling of unprovoked anger, and pain shot my arms from the lack of... well, release.

The longer I went without drinking her blood or fucking her until I felt nothing but love and lust, the more dangerous I felt. I became unhinged, but not in the wildly happy way Raven wanted me to be.

I wanted to kill.

Her mate was in Reales. He had touched her—tried to bite her. And while Luca continued to question whether I had really talked to her, I knew I had. It took time to realize it once I saw her climbing toward me and could not reach her, but I knew that only mirrored the distance between us.

I wasn't sure what the skeletal remains meant, but unlike the ones in The Forest Beyond, these weren't guarding something. They seemed to want her, which only added to my desperation to end her mate before it got any further.

When I looked ahead at the border of the forest of Reales, I cocked my head at the silhouette pacing the edge—one that looked similar to the one I saw in Nova when the man exploded in front of me.

"River," I said aloud, nodding toward him.

Almost like he could hear me, he stopped moving and turned to face us. I would not be meeting him like the man he saw in Perosan. I was armed with the knowledge that he had been lying to all of us, or at least withholding some crucial information. His so-called friends he brought to Reales included Raven's mate—a man that had mated himself to her against fate, using her blood the same way everyone else seemed to want to use it.

A demon unworthy of her.

And when we neared River and I slid off Shadow to take my aggression out on him, he just... vanished. I spun around and found him ten feet behind me, holding his palms up and trying to keep me from lunging.

It didn't work.

But again, he disappeared, and I growled, looking for him as Luca rode beside me. "What the fuck is happening?" he yelled from frustration, disbelief, and the way our lives had drastically changed in the last few days.

Magic that we had been told all our lives no longer existed was still extremely prominent and very dangerous.

"River!" I shouted, running toward the forest and stumbling back as he appeared in front of me.

"I need to speak with you about Raven," he said calmly.

"Or about how you're fucking...." I couldn't think of the number right now since I was drained of energy and confident I might pass out soon from exhaustion. "Old?!"

Luca ran up beside me, leaving the horses behind us to graze the green grass that was slowly fading to brown the closer we got to the border of Reales.

The corner of River's mouth twitched. "You learned a bit on your excursion, did you?"

I pounced. He vanished. I cursed.

He appeared in front of me again and raised his eyebrows, sighing through his nose. "You're wasting time."

"You brought *him* here to my fucking kingdom, River. You tried to drown my mate multiple times, you lied to all of us..."

"I did not try to drown her," he countered. "I taught her how to fight back, or at least that's what I am trying to do. It's taking a bit of time. She's quite stubborn."

Every single one of my muscles became rigid. "Don't speak of her as if you know her."

He appeared utterly unbothered. "But I do. I have known her longer than you have, Zeke. Maybe not in this lifetime, but her soul is tied to mine as much as it is to yours. And I can answer some of your questions if you stop trying to attack me."

"I need to kill her mate, and then I'll consider it."

"You cannot," River said. "You do not yet possess the power to bring him down. You need her blood."

I stilled. Luca's face continued to twist in disgust every time it was mentioned. But River continued, "Raven informed me you have fed from her. And when you do, what do you feel?"

I didn't answer. Trust would not come easy between us. Instead, I asked, "Where is Jeanine? Is she with Raven in Thoya?"

Now, he looked bewildered and contemplative before more confusion skated across his face. "You can't have the mind bridge. Silas's bond to her prohibits it."

"I don't," I muttered, still bitter. "I found her while she was dreaming. I talked to her. She did not mention trusting you, but she did say that Jeanine was still in Reales. Is she alive?"

I didn't miss the hopefulness in Luca as we waited for River's answer. Like Petra and Elric, I couldn't sense what River felt. And his silence made me uneasy.

"She's..." he teetered, pausing. "I'll take you to her soon."

Luca stepped forward. "Take me to her *now*."

"I cannot. Not yet. Have you learned what Silas is?"

"Undead," Luca answered. "Are you?"

"No," River said. "I am not. I have lived in their kingdom for a very long time. And I am not the enemy." He held up a hand to stop me from speaking. "Yes, I lied. But I did it for a greater purpose. I am no longer welcome with the Undead. After saving Jeanine from their feast, Silas learned of my true intentions."

I crossed my arms over my chest, disbelieving. "Which *are*?"

"*Feast*?" Luca asked.

River clasped his hands behind his back and looked over his shoulder toward the castle of Reales, only visible by the tallest towers. "When Raven died," he started, his voice distant and surprisingly full of sorrow, "He could've brought her back to life. Bloodmates are tied by their blood, and hers was considered sacred. She sacrificed herself." He looked at me, his gaze penetrating. "For you."

I blinked, my throat constricting from the implication or idea that Raven would continue to sacrifice herself for me, even now. "Why?"

"I am not going to speak of your deaths without her," he said... almost in defense of his twin. "But when Raven died, he could've brought her back. However, her body was saved before he could. Instead, he took me."

The look on his face was one I knew well — as his eyes glazed, I knew he was remembering something he didn't want to. "Since we were... *are* twins, my blood was nearly identical to Raven's. It didn't supply the same power as hers, but it has been enough to sustain him."

"He fed from you," Luca breathed.

I couldn't help but pity him.

As he continued, he seemed to brush it off. "I was truthful about our elements. When Raven died, I lost mine. My life seemed hopeless, and I felt more alone than I had ever been." He lowered his chin slightly as a frown crossed his face. "Despite what you might believe, I loved my sister."

"I know," I admitted. "We learned that."

"One day, my element returned to me. I was so shocked and confused that I did not consider hiding it from Silas. It had been rumored that Raven would be reborn, but years passed, and the memory of that rumor began fading." From his fingers, water droplets hovered about his palm.

I wasn't as impressed with his element as with Raven's, but that might've been because I was obsessed with only her. However, I couldn't deny that watching water appear out of thin air was mesmerizing.

"He hadn't taken another bloodmate since her death, hoping she would return, not because of love but pure obsession. Raven's blood was the *lifeblood* of our universe. Before our mother took us to hide from our father, creatures would travel long distances for just a drop of her blood."

I rolled my neck at the thought of anyone but me ever having her blood as my stomach clenched from envy.

"When he learned that my element had returned, the obsession to find her tripled. Each time I lost my element, we knew she had died. And it was a pattern that repeated every twenty-five years."

Luca whipped his head toward me. I shook mine, unable to understand. "Raven is twenty-five..." I panicked, turning to call for Shadow. I would ride to Thoya if I had to.

In each life, we only had a quarter of a century to find one another and fall in love. If her life was truly that short, if I was going to lose her soon, I certainly wasn't going to waste it with a history lesson. We would leave this place and live our remaining days together.

"She will not die!" he called, waiting until I looked at him over my shoulder. "Raven died at twenty-five in each lifetime because it was the age she sacrificed herself. Her soul has been waiting to return to *this* timeline."

Luca asked, "Why? Why now?"

"Because it is where she belongs," River answered simply. "Raven is the Dark-Half Witch. She is immortal."

I balked. "Raven has been aging," I argued. "She has celebrated her birthday every year."

"Raven only ages to the year she died," River said. "She will not age anymore. The Raven you see now will be the Raven you'll see years from now."

The idea that Raven would be beautiful for the entirety of our life did not surprise me, but it also saddened me. While I never wanted this life with her to end, I had been looking forward to us growing old together—to having a long bloodline... "I am mortal," I said as my throat burned from the realization.

River said nothing, but his silence said everything. Luca turned from me, his chin tipping toward the sky as torment flooded his body.

I fell to my knees and threaded my fingers in my hair, my entire body shaking and heavy. "I am not immortal, am I? I will age while she will not."

River crouched until he was at eye-level with me. "I have been around for a long time, but there are things I still do not understand. We do not yet know what unleashing your shadows will do, but you cannot lose hope."

He touched my shoulder. I didn't move or prevent him from doing so, but I still remained cautious, even when his eyes conveyed genuine sorrow. "Let us kill Silas, Zeke, and then we will seek answers. You, too, have a bloodline made of magical beings. It is not impossible that you could be immortal once your magic is unbound."

I did not care about myself or who I used to be. I did, though, remain curious about Raven. "You were not in Raven's memories," I said, staying on my knees. If I tried to stand, I would be back on the ground shortly after. "But Leonidas and Celestina were. Celestina told Leonidas that Raven belonged to him—"

"That is not what happened," River interrupted. "I do not know how or why Raven's memories appear as such, but I can show you what really happened. It does require quite a bit of trust on your part, though."

I raised an eyebrow.

"I took Raven into the Time-Antre," he explained. "I can travel through moments in time. It is the slowest method of traveling I can use, but Raven insisted that Jeanine accompany us to Reales. I cannot travel with two through... well, that's a story for another time. I can show you the moment of Celestina's death, but I can only take you."

I looked at Luca. He did not trust River and that was very apparent when he threw his arms up and shook his head. "No. No way. We don't know if any of what he's saying is true. He could be taking you to Silas, for all we know. Where is Jeanine? I want to see her. I want to see my sister. I want to know what the fuck is happening, why everyone wants Raven's blood, and how we can defeat these... *Undead*."

He said it with such disgust that I couldn't help but grin at him. River remained focused on me, giving me the space to consider his offer. "Will the memory unveil who your father is?" I asked.

"No," he answered. "And that is not information I would share with you before I share it with Raven."

That was fair. It was her history, and while I wanted to know every inch of her life, she deserved answers first. "Will Luca be safe here alone?"

"Yes," River said, ignoring Luca's protests. "I have not allowed Silas to feed from me since I found Raven on the shores of Perosan."

I waited for an explanation of why that mattered.

He sighed. "Silas has blood bonds with each member of the Undead. He never allowed anyone to feed from him so he would stay tied to Raven, but instead fed from others to form more bonds. With those bonds, he can detect where each of his members is, but the bonds fade as time passes without blood. We still have one, but it is not as easy for him to find me now. The longer he goes without feeding from me, the weaker our bond grows."

Luca asked eagerly, "And his power?"

"Blood sustains his power," River explained. "While my blood is the closest to Raven's and strengthens his magic, any blood will keep him strong."

"I will go with you," I said, holding my palm up toward Luca to prevent him from arguing. "But then you will take us to Jeanine."

He nodded and stood, waiting on me.

The risks I took for my girl.

Sighing, I stood and looked at Luca. "Stay here. Do not seek out Jeanine on your own. If you see anyone coming, even if you know them, take Shadow and leave."

Luca's expression was filled with tension, his shoulders slumped forward in worry. He shifted his gaze from me to River and narrowed his eyes. "I may not possess abilities like my brother, but I can promise you that if harm befalls him, I will find a way to kill you."

My eyebrows raised to my hairline. I didn't believe Luca had ever threatened someone in his life and truly meant it, but there was no doubt or hint of remorse in his voice.

Contrary to the amusement River typically portrayed when threatened, he nodded in complete understanding. Wordlessly, he put his fingers around my wrist and looked at me. "When we enter the Time-Antre, do not loiter or wander. There are creatures with access to it who will plead with you to change a moment in their history. They are persuasive."

Before I could acknowledge or pry, we faded.

EVERY SINGLE ONE OF MY MUSCLES BECAME RIGID. "DON'T SPEAK OF HER AS IF YOU KNOW HER."

46

ZEKE

Nothing should surprise me anymore.

But that didn't stop my eyes from widening, unsure of where to look as Luca and the field we were standing in changed into something else entirely. I spun around when River dropped my wrist. I gaped at the sight of a long hallway with arches lined on both sides, full of blurring colors that flew past us faster than I could blink.

River chuckled while watching me. "Raven had the same reaction." He pointed to the left, down a black and empty void. "Future." He pointed to the right, which seemed even eerier. "Past. That's where we're going."

I found my voice. "And present?"

"Here, where we stand. The farther you walk toward the future, the more your reality becomes distorted. It's where many beings have become lost, searching for answers they won't ever find."

I had many questions, but "Why?" seemed the simplest.

"Because the future is subjective," he explained. "It changes based on decisions. The future you might imagine you'll have now will be different tomorrow. If I were to take you ten years ahead, it would not accurately represent what lies ahead."

I looked down the opposite side of the hallway. "And the past?"

"Is full of regret," he said quietly. "We will come across many who want to change choices they have made, but they cannot. You cannot alter the past as much as you might want to. Doing so would result in confusion and alternate realities. The moment would throw you out, much like your dream-walking."

"Alternate realities?"

The corner of his mouth tilted upward in a slight grin. "I think you have learned enough shocking information today. Let's focus on the memory first and see if you're still curious about realities outside of ours."

Nodding, I stayed beside him as we walked down the dark hall-way. I wasn't sure where to look as a burst of moments passed by us. None ever formed enough to catch what they could be, but I did find it curious how something with so much power could exist for people to walk through. "How was this created?"

"By a witch," he said. "Very long ago. A very powerful one and only those who have been able to decipher her charm have been let in."

"But you made the wanderers seem so..."

"Dense?" he asked. "They did not start that way. Some of the most brilliant minds have come here, only to be bewitched by the idea of changing their choices."

"Could I..."

"No," he answered before I barely got the words out. "Raven already asked. It doesn't matter how strong a person might be. No amount of magic can change things that have already happened." His gentle expression seemed genuine.

"I want to believe you truly care for her, River, but you have not given us much proof."

"I mean no disrespect when I say that you are not the one to whom I need to prove my loyalty. I know that you could kill me once your power is realized. I am willing to assist you in realizing that power, but I have nothing to prove to you."

His self-assurance was annoying me to no end.

I stopped him with a hand on his arm. "She is my mate and my wife. You have *much* to prove to me. I have made the mistake of letting people into her life that did not deserve to be there. I respect that you are her brother, but the loyalty stops there until you prove you are trustworthy."

He was a champion at feigning boredom, and it was a mask I knew well. The fact that he felt he needed to wear one proved that he heard what I said, but instead of acknowledging any of it, he said, "We cannot linger."

I released him with a look of warning. While my power may not be realized yet, a glorified hallway would not be enough to keep from her if he tried to leave me here.

As we neared an older woman in ragged clothes that had to be from another century, River did not slow or say anything. I followed his lead but was alarmed when she grabbed my shirt as we passed by, promising me pounds of gold if I assisted her in changing a moment.

I ignored the woman, per River's demand, but watched her over my shoulder as she stared into an archway, talking to herself in a language I could not understand.

"Why did you take Raven to Thoya?"

We passed by another woman whom River instructed me to ignore. He waited until we had put a good measure of distance between us before he answered, "I have known Damiana for a very long time. She was in our mother's coven."

I stopped mid-stride, unable to keep from laughing from a mixture of exhaustion and suspicion. "Damiana is old, too?"

"I won't tell her you said that," he replied, motioning for me to continue following him. "She is the reason Raven has remained untouched. When Celestina became pregnant with Raven, she was fearful of Raven being hunted again. Damiana created a shield around the realm, hiding it from anyone who possesses magic, but Silas in particular. And when she had her own children, she took extra precautions and cast another shield around Thoya. Anyone with magic who crossed into Thoya would lose their magic and any memory of ever possessing it."

"But I have entered Thoya many times. As has Raven."

River grinned. "You were in Thoya when she created the second shield. As was Raven."

My brows knitted together. "On our most recent trip?"

"No." He pointed ahead at the nothingness. "We're almost there." He glanced at me, sighing at my inquisitive expression. "Raven traveled to Thoya as a child, shortly after becoming queen. She was eleven."

I nodded, already aware.

"You were sixteen. Edmund had invited you to Thoya so the two of you could meet. It was Damiana's idea. She needed you and Raven to be in Thoya simultaneously."

"Wait..." I ran a hand through my hair as a headache began to form. "I've met Raven before?"

"No. Once Damiana saw how fearful Raven was of being queen and how"—he smiled and laughed—"clumsy she was with her magic, they decided that you and Raven should not meet yet. Raven stayed in her room while you spent your days with Edmund."

I remembered that trip well. It was the first time I felt I could have a true friend apart from my brother. "But if I had met her, I could've prevented Cade from ever..." I stammered through the words, attempting to keep my anger from shoving River into a moment. "I could've helped her. I could've prevented all of it."

"Raven was too young. She was already struggling with who she was. It was too risky to introduce the two of you to each other and have her realize that she was part of a pairing. She already felt out of place. Your father promised to keep her safe on the island until she matured, but we feared she would pass through another lifetime once she turned twenty-four."

"You speak of this like you were part of the entire thing."

"Petra sent me letters when she could, keeping me updated on

Raven. Silas would intercept most of my letters, so they had to be far and few between. When the two of you finally met in Seolia the night of the festival, your bond was strong enough to alter the shield around the realm. That is when Silas felt her."

I smiled at the idea that our love was so strong that it could break apart magic. I made a mental note to inquire more about Petra later. "And that is when you came to Reales?"

"I tried to hide it as long as I could, but when Raven traveled to Reales, the pull became stronger, as did my element. I have always possessed powers, but none quite as potent as my element. That is when he forced me to find her."

"And you have been held hostage in his kingdom?"

"The Great," he corrected me. "Yes. I have not been allowed to return home, and even if I tried, he would've found me through the bond. I did not want to subject my people to that. That is why I could not assist Raven on the shores of Perosan. I helped her as much as possible, but it would've risked an entire species if I had used my powers."

He stopped me before I could inquire as to what this species might be by saying, "She must learn first."

We stopped in front of a tall archway. The moment between the columns was dark and gray, like what I imagined the death of a witch to look like. "Please remember that you cannot change anything. You cannot help Raven or attempt to try."

I looked into the void, trying to convince myself I could do this. I had watched her memory once. I could do it again. "Will they see us?"

"No," he answered sorrowfully. "I have revisited this moment often."

"You've tried to help her," I whispered.

"She is my mother."

Nothing else was said as he grabbed my wrist and stepped into the bleakness.

$\sim$

WE STOOD inside the cabin from Raven's memories — the one in the forest of Reales that I was unable to see. Celestina was sleeping peacefully in the bed while coos were coming from a cradle in the middle of the room.

Smiling, I looked down into the cradle to see the baby from my mother's memory. Her black hair was wild and rumpled from sleep, her green eyes bright, and her lips puckered into a slight pout. Raven was only days old, but her eyes showed curiosity as they moved across the ceiling above her until, finally... they settled on me.

I froze, as did River beside me.

"I thought you said they couldn't see us," I whispered.

"They cannot," he said with a smile. "But Raven has always been the most headstrong."

My smile melted into a frown as I thought about what she was about to experience. Raven was about to be part of her mother's murder, and there wasn't anything I could do to stop it. "I thought I could do this," I said. "But I can't."

"It's too late," River said, nodding toward the cabin door.

I watched as a young Mira rushed inside, peering over the cradle and leaning over to grab Raven, but before she could, Celestina sat up and called for her daughter to hide under the bed. Mira crawled underneath just as Leonidas walked through the door.

TWENTY-FIVE YEARS Prior

Leonidas

Leonidas stepped into the quaint cabin, unsure why Celestina had decided to stay here instead of the castle, or why she still allowed him in. He was angry, rightfully so, after she had ended things between them.

He looked at the baby in the cradle, scowling. The child's beauty was evident, even so young, and it only made him loathe her more. Because of her, his mate denied him, driving him into anguish and desperation.

Celestina rose from the bed, and Leonidas hated that he still felt such a soul-wrenching love for her. She was beautiful and dark, which only added to her aura of intrigue. She was much older than him, but her spirit still seemed so young. And while he remained a mortal, he would have happily grown old beside her until his last breath.

But she loved another—a man that wasn't him, nor her husband. Celestina loved someone from her past, a man that had rejected and used her repeatedly, the father of her child—the child that seemed to stare into his soul with her eyes made of pine needles and snow.

Celestina stood from the bed and, with concern on her face, she scooped up the child from the cradle and held her close to her chest. "What are you doing here, Leonidas?" she asked with a tremor of anger. "I told you not to come back here."

Her words were like a shot of venom straight down his throat and into his heart. "You are not leaving me," he answered with equal viciousness. "You are my mate and belong to me, not him. He doesn't even want you, nor has he come to claim his own child after using you for breeding."

"I have hidden her!" she shouted, cradling the back of the child's head. "He will never find her!"

"You stupid woman!" Leonidas scolded, walking around the cradle as she backed to the other side of the room and away from the bed. "He possesses more power than you, and a hidden cabin in the woods will not slow him down."

"I have to protect her!" she cried, kissing the baby's head. "I have already lost one; I will not lose another."

She was referring to the other child, the one that Leonidas believed to not exist. He was the boy Celestina spoke about in her dreams, the one she cried for when performing the most trivial tasks, and the one who took up so much space in her heart that there was hardly any room for him.

She did not seem to care for the daughter she shared with Rudolf —the heir to the throne of Reales.

"I wish Rudolf's ancestors had found your beloved king long ago when invading Perosan. I long for the days when they'll find his realm and burn it to the ground. Maybe you will realize you have made a mistake in choosing him instead of your own mate."

"You are not my mate! You lay no claim over me!" Celestina held the child so tightly against her chest that it made him sick. It became clear to him that the woman he loved had new priorities—this child that had stolen away his entire life due to some godsdamned prophecy.

"Give her to me, Celestina."

She sneered and turned her body away from his. "I do not love you, you horrid man. You infiltrated my island! Your ancestors burned my coven!"

Leonidas neared her with giant steps, backing her into the corner of the room. "I am tired of hearing about your coven! Seolia is my kingdom. Your witches were burned for their evilness. You are blessed because I chose to spare your life, and now I will take your daughter and let you live with the reminder of what it's like to lose the one you love."

"You will not touch my daughter!" she screamed, lifting her hand to reveal the tips of black ribbons coming from her fingers. "I have been too patient with your threats, Leonidas. Raven will take Seolia back one day. She will fulfill the prophecy to restore magic and be protected by what is left of my coven. She will be protected by her aunt."

"Your wretched half-breed daughter will live with peasants and be treated as such," he spat, knocking Celestina's hand to the side as he reached for the child. "She will be burned for her magic and will join the witches in hell!"

He unsheathed the dagger covered in poison from the waist of his pants and drove it into Celestina's side. Her eyes filled with horror as the baby screamed in her arms. Blood pooled and seeped through her nightshirt as she fell to her knees, clutching the child in her arms and whispering her name as death neared.

"Mates do not deny bonds," he seethed, tearing the child away from Celestina's arms.

But as he did, strands of gold and black weaved together as they left Celestina's dying body to seep into Raven's. He felt the weight of the magic enter her and watched with widened eyes as Raven's eyes filled with terror and pain.

And she screamed and screamed for the warmth of her mother — the comfort that Leonidas had just stolen from her. He sat with guilt and regret as he watched the woman he loved so fiercely bleed out at his feet. The daughter she had been protecting during her entire pregnancy was now his responsibility.

Because, even as the monster Celestina's denial had made him, he could not bring himself to bestow the same fate to the baby in his arms. He would hide her in Seolia and task August with finding a peasant capable of raising her and preventing her father from ever seeking her.

The magic she possessed would be of benefit to him when she aged. He could use her as collateral and bargain with the great king that was hiding his realm in The Forest Beyond. Celestina's death would be payment for how she broke his heart; now, her daughter would become his most significant interest.

"MATES DO NOT DENY BONDS," HE SEETHED, TEARING THE CHILD AWAY FROM CELESTINA'S ARMS.

47

Zeke

River prevented me from chasing after Leonidas as he carried Raven out of the cabin. Mira was screaming and crying for her mother from underneath the bed, even for the sister she would not see again.

"She denied the mating bond," I said, looking at Celestina's lifeless body. "That is why he killed her. It wasn't because of her magic."

"No," River said. "Leonidas was prideful because he was one of Celestina's lovers. They were not mated, though he desperately wished it to be true. He was cruel when bragging about it to those closest to Rudolf."

I felt sick. I desperately wanted to change this moment for Raven

—prevent Morana from ever entering her body. "That is why Raven's memories are different. Morana inhabited her and wanted Raven to be spiteful. Celestina loved Raven. She did not want to use her for war."

"Celestina only cared about protecting Raven."

I watched as Mira ran out of the cabin, leaving Celestina alone. "Mira wanted revenge," I whispered, feeling pity for the child that had to witness her mother's murder.

"Mira wanted revenge for herself, not for Celestina," he corrected, continuing to stare at his mother on the floor even when I stared at him in confusion. "Mira is not Celestina's, Zeke."

My mouth slackened, convinced I had misheard him.

"My mother was powerful. When creatures of magic breed with mortals, it sullies bloodlines. Celestina married Rudolf to maintain power over the realm with Damiana and Petra, but she did not love him."

I stared at Mira as a child underneath the bed, seemingly frozen in time. "I don't understand. She looks like Celestina."

"Rudolf took a lover that favored Celestina. He needed an heir but was displeased that Mira was a female."

His closeness to me suddenly made sense. "He chose me."

"Yes," River confirmed. "He wanted you to take his place in death. Mira did not take it well. She desperately tried to become close to Celestina in hopes that she'd take pity on her and convinced Rudolf to allow her to become queen, but then Raven was born."

"Did Celestina know who I was?"

"She had her suspicions. There were rumors you two were paired after Raven's birth, making both of you a threat to Mira's crown. Mira's bitterness birthed her need for revenge, but not for Celestina's sake. She wanted to prove Rudolf wrong, and controlling you to assist her in realm domination was the best kind of revenge. Harming and threatening Raven was the best way to weaken you, and it nearly worked. It probably would have had it not been for Raven's love for you."

I sank against the wall. "What happened to Mira's mother?"

"Rudolf had her killed once Mira was born so that no one could ever contest her right to the throne if a son wasn't born."

I had viewed Rudolf as a kind and loyal king for my entire life, when all along, he'd been no different from Leonidas. "That is why Mira has so easily dismissed Raven and hurt her. Mira and Raven are not related."

River shook his head slightly. "No. It was a story I played along with to gain Mira's trust. I needed her to allow me to bring the Undead to Reales."

"Take me to Mira," I said. "I can kill her."

"I cannot," River said with a sigh. "Silas and Mira swore an oath. Silas has to help Mira dominate the realm before he can have Raven. If we kill Mira beforehand, the bond will break, and Silas will be free to take Raven."

"Fuck this," I muttered, shoving the door open and walking into the forest, which was much more alive than it had been in recent years. The leaves on the trees were green instead of brown, and the cliffs weren't the gray, jagged stones of promised death they were today.

River followed me outside. "Zeke, we will need to fight the Undead. It is the only way this can end. It will not be simple. They possess more power than you could imagine, but it is not impossible. Silas needs to die. He has tortured too many for too long."

I turned to face him with my hands loosely on my hips, my stance wide, and my body wound tight with rage and frustration. "You have more magic than I've ever seen and are apparently a descendant of some great king. Why can't your people fight Silas and the Undead? You ask me to enlist my mortal friends and my family and put Raven at risk."

"My people are dying. It is slow, but it is happening. Without Raven's blood, it is only a matter of time. They are weak. Mortals do not need her blood to survive."

"Even if we kill Silas, I am not freely giving Raven's blood to anyone," I snarled. "She is mine. That is not going to change because of some fucking bloodsucker."

"You are one of them."

My mouth dried as I breathed through my nose too quickly to release.

"You are a descendant of a variation of the Undead and one of my people. Before your death, you could survive on food or blood. You bloodmated with Raven before your death, but she could not take your blood before Silas found her. That is why she is your mate, but you are not hers."

"I am Undead... or was."

He nodded with a shrug. "Partially."

I balled my fists. "Can you ever give straight answers?"

"There was a spring in our realm," he said. "Three drops of Raven's blood would supply our entire species with magic for months. That was all that was required of her. When Celestina took her to the island, Raven kept the coven supplied with the spring."

The spring on the island. Our spring. Our thermal spring was part of Raven's history—part of *our* history.

"No one drank from her," he continued. "That was something she only allowed you to do. It would be the same now. Beings only need mere drops of her blood to survive. It is why she is being sought out by the Reine coven. We have all waited a long time for her rebirth into this universe. But if Silas is the one to find her, he will lock her away and use her as leverage to remain the most powerful. Species will have to fall at his feet and do as he says for the promise of a drop of her blood."

"She feels nothing for him. There was nothing but anger in her at the mention of his name," I said. "How can that be if they are mates?"

"Because Raven has no memories of him. Once he bites her, their bond will be restored. We cannot let that happen."

No. I *wouldn't* let that happen.

"Take me back to my brother and then Jeanine." I was more determined than ever to end this, but I wouldn't do so impulsively. We needed a plan that Raven would agree to, and not one that she only kind of said yes to but would change her mind at the last minute. "And then I need to see my wife."

But when he stepped toward me to take us back into the Time-Antre, I was reminded of something Celestina once said to Leonidas. "Her aunt," I repeated to River, tilting my head to the side.

River sighed and hung his head. "I was hoping you had not caught that."

My eyebrow quirked. I had been patient with his lack of direct information so far, but I needed to be aware of anyone who claimed to know my mate. I did not move, except for my hand, when I knocked his hand away to prevent him from transporting us anywhere. "I will not ask where you're from or what species you keep referring to, but I demand that you tell me who her aunt is and if she's still alive."

"She's still alive," River muttered, and though I couldn't feel his emotions, I was fully aware that I irritated him. Finally, he looked at me, his invisible mask of aloofness falling away to reveal a hint of apprehension at the information he now had to reveal.

"Petra is our father's sister."

HE PULLED us into the Time-Antre before I could pry. Petra was Raven's aunt—her biological aunt. And when I asked why Petra hadn't raised Raven, or why she hid this secret for so many years, or even what kind of magic she could possibly possess, River only answered with, "Petra is not a witch."

I disliked him immensely.

But I understood. Raven deserved to know these things before me, regardless of how irritated I was about that.

When we returned to the field outside Reales, neither Luca nor Shadow were anywhere in sight. I called his name but was quickly silenced by River. He stepped forward, his eyes cast to the ground and his nostrils flaring, and I wondered for a moment what kind of creature he was. And when he pointed to drops of blood sprinkled on the ground, I silently questioned if he was an Undead.

"This isn't Luca's," he said.

I raised an eyebrow. "How do you know?"

I wasn't surprised to not receive an answer. I was, however, beginning to panic at the idea that something had happened to my brother—if maybe Mira had found him again and was planning to use him to draw me back in.

I ran toward the forest, but River caught me, grabbed my arm, and we vanished into thin air, reappearing beside the cliffs. I stumbled backward until my back hit the ridge, and I pressed a palm against my forehead to calm myself from the dizziness that accompanied the jump. "What the fu—" I didn't finish before I vomited on the ground.

"You and Raven," River mumbled, waiting until I recomposed myself before answering, "It's how I took her to Thoya so quickly. It's how I watched her in Seolia those nights you thought I was drowning her..."

"You were on the island," I interrupted. "You weren't controlling water from thousands of miles away."

He looked *amused*. "It's flattering that you believed I could."

"What was that? Can Raven do it?"

"With time, perhaps. We refer to it as Arrowing."

"I don't like it," I grumbled, pushing off the cliffside.

He grinned. "It's ironic you do not like the things you yourself used to perform. It is... difficult for me to remember that you are now mortal and not the..."

"Phantom Prince?"

He looked surprised but nodded. "You do not seem very curious about who you were then."

"I'm not." As we walked, I stayed close to the cliff, looking for any sign of snapped twigs on the ground that would indicate Luca's trail. "I am more concerned about Raven and how we can keep her safe. It does not matter who I used to be..."

Suddenly, Shadow bolted out from an entrance of a hollowed cave between the split of two cliffs, pulling up to his rear legs to guide us backward. River vanished and reappeared at the cave entrance, leaving me to deal with Raven's overdramatic horse. "Shadow," I scolded, reaching up to thread my hands into the tufts of his hair. "It's me. Calm down."

He calmed down slightly, landing on all fours and knocking his head against mine. I couldn't tell whether that was from frustration or relief, but it hurt all the same.

I rubbed my forehead as I peered into the cave to see Luca sitting on the ground, knees propped up and glaring at me. He retrieved a bloodied dagger from the ground and tossed it to me. "One of River's friends found me. Blond, pale as fucking snow, and tried to *bite* me."

"Felix," River said, sighing. "He is trying to find Jeanine."

At that, Luca stood. I did not miss the envy and concern that simultaneously flooded his body. "What would he want with Jeanine?"

"They are bonded," River stated.

"Bonded," Luca repeated, his jaw tense and fists balled. "As in mated?"

"No," I replied, sighing as I looked at River. "Remember what Avalie told us? Undead are viewed as demons by fate and are not given mates. Undead claim mates as their own by blood against fate."

That also meant that Raven had once been forced into a mating bond. Even if it was lifetimes ago, it was returning to haunt us now.

"I don't understand," Luca said. "How can Jeanine have a bond with an Undead then?"

My blood went cold. "He would've had to bite her. Silas creates bonds with each member by ingesting their blood, which means if Felix bit Jeanine..."

River met my gaze, guilt heavily in his expression. "I saved her, but it came at a cost."

I shook my head slightly, not wanting to believe I could be right. "Say the words, River."

He hesitated, looking deep into the forest before returning to me. "Jeanine is Undead."

Luca lunged, catching River by surprise. They landed on the ground, and Luca straddled him, getting in two punches before I pulled him off and held my arms around his chest to prevent him from further attacking.

"Raven trusted you to save her!" Luca shouted, trying to shove my arms off. "And now she has turned into..." He couldn't even get the words out, the pain in his voice evident.

River stood, wiping the blood from the corner of his mouth with his arm before straightening his jacket. He tried to appear unbothered, but it was apparent that the idea of disappointing Raven was distressing him. "I tried to get there in time." He spoke quietly and carefully. "I left her in the library when I took Raven. Raven had built a dome of ice around Jeanine to prevent her from escaping. I thought it would give me enough time."

I tightened my jaw. My wife had attempted to sacrifice herself again, despite my pleas for her not to.

River turned, and we had no choice but to follow him in hopes of him leading us to Jeanine. Luca leaned over to take his dagger from the waistband of my pants, but I quickly stopped him. "You cannot kill him. We need him."

"He has brought nothing but misery!" Luca shouted. "Raven nearly died multiple times because of him! The Undead are here because of him!"

"Luca, it's more complicated than that," I tried to explain, grabbing his shoulder only for him to pull away. "He is her brother."

"*I* am her brother!" he bellowed.

River stopped and turned at that.

"It was me who went with you to Perosan to save her, I watched over her when you disappeared, and I took care of her after Cade attacked her in Seolia!" He ignored the tears falling from his eyes. "I am her brother! And now, Jeanine is... *gone*, Zeke. Jeanine is never going to be the same. She is going to want blood, *need* blood, and you want to keep him alive?"

He was right about everything, but that didn't make it any less complex. River knew Silas and the way he moved and thought. He had a bond with him, which gave us an advantage in eliminating him.

And while Luca was Raven's brother through me, River was Raven's *twin*. While our bond was rare and cherished, Raven possessed a link with him that no one else could ever claim. It was a bond that could never be duplicated or denied.

And despite my disbelief in River's intentions, he did genuinely seem to care for her in his own fucked up way. If he could give her answers about where they came from, I would not take that away from her.

Instead of answering Luca, I faced River. "Is Jeanine unharmed? Does she know what happened?"

"She is stronger than she's ever been," River answered, watching

Luca as he turned to slam his fist against a tree and immediately curse.

I sighed. "Luca, your thumb is still broken."

"Fuck off," he muttered.

River continued, "She is aware and outraged, especially after I locked her in the cabin."

"The cabin," I repeated. "The cabin from the memory? The one in which Celestina hid? I tried to find Raven there once. How were you able to get in?"

"Celestina protected it by blood. Only those with permission or our same bloodline could enter."

Now it all made sense. Raven could enter the cabin because of their connection, but didn't know how to make it visible and accessible to others. "How do you possess so much magic while Raven has so little?"

"Raven's magic hasn't been unbound yet. She has as much magic as I do, maybe even more. We don't know yet."

"And how—"

"Can we focus on Jeanine?" Luca interrupted, shouting at us. "I am just as curious about Raven, but I want to see Jeanine. I want proof that she is... I can't say alive. I just want to see her. She will want to know all of this, too."

"You're completely right." I touched Luca's shoulder. "I'm sorry. Of course, you're right. We need to check on her. Is it safe for Luca to be around her?"

Was it safe for *any* of us to be around her?

River shrugged a shoulder. "We won't know until we try. I must warn you, though, she will look different. The same, but different. The Undead cannot kill beings that possess magic with a bite, but they can harm mortals. And mortals want to be bitten by the Undead once they see them; it's part of their magic. *You* are safe, whether immortal or not, because of the magic you have. Luca must resist."

"I won't let him near her." I looked at Luca. "You have to stay away from her, Luca. Not only for your protection but also for hers. She wouldn't be able to live with herself if she harmed you."

Luca wiped his face with the collar on his shirt. The heartbreak in him caused my chest to tighten. They had become close, and though he didn't want anyone to believe it was serious between them, he was acting as if it were the opposite.

Finally, he swallowed and nodded. "I won't touch her."

I tasted his lie but said nothing. I would hold him back if needed. "Take us to her."

I TASTED HIS LIE BUT SAID NOTHING. I WOULD HOLD HIM BACK IF NEEDED. "TAKE US TO HER."

48

Standing at the door of the cabin, we paused. River warned us again that Luca must stay away from her and that she would look like herself, yet different. I wasn't sure what we were about to walk into, but I made Luca stay behind me.

River opened the door, immediately holding up his palms toward the person hissing inside. I told Luca to wait a moment so I could gauge how she was before exposing him to her. He lingered on the ground while I ascended the porch, peering inside.

Jeanine was in the corner of the dimly lit cabin, glowering at River. But then her gaze quickly snapped to me, and her entire face crumpled.

I stepped inside, intending to go to her, but she was across the room in an instant, slamming against me, unaware of how fast she moved. Her body felt like stone against my chest and I nearly fell back against the wall from the impact. Jeanine had always been strong, especially after training the armies in Seolia, but now she felt like nothing but muscle.

I put an arm around her, ignoring the goosebumps on my skin from her chill. Like Raven when she shifted into Frost, Jeanine felt like ice. And I couldn't sense her like I used to.

Tears filled my eyes as I held my friend, putting my lips against her hair as she cried against my chest, her grip around my waist making it difficult to breathe. My ribs could easily collapse from the pressure, but I didn't make her move.

I wasn't sure what to say. There wasn't anything I *could* say to make this better. I didn't believe being Undead was reversible. I hadn't seen her face yet, but River's warning was correct. Her hair was a brighter blonde and softer. It wasn't her typical tangled mess from our days of training. I hadn't ever seen Jeanine hold a brush, but it looked combed and longer than before.

"I'm so sorry, Zeke." Her words were a jumbled mess against my chest, but there wasn't anything she should be sorry for. "You told me to keep Raven on the island, and I didn't. Is she okay?"

She lifted her head as I was about to respond, but her nostrils immediately flared, and before I could utter a word, she returned to her corner in an instant, pressing her back against the wall as Luca came in behind me. The walls of the old cabin shook.

His body immediately filled with lust as he stared at her.

Her skin had paled and appeared almost translucent, but there was a glow about her. Her blue eyes lightened and gleamed in the candlelight of the cabin. Though pale, her cheeks showed a hint of red as if they naturally blushed, and her frame was deceiving from a distance. Instead of the strength I had just felt, she looked almost... fragile.

And I wondered if that was part of the allure the Undead possessed—to make you believe they couldn't harm you before attacking. "Her eyes aren't red," I said.

"No," River said, crossing his arms over his chest. "Undead who are unwillingly turned keep their natural eye color unless they refuse to feed. Her eyes will turn gold or red with time."

Luca stepped toward her, but I stopped him with an arm across his stomach. "No, Luca."

"I can smell you," Jeanine whispered, her voice an octave lower and much softer than what we were used to.

River was right. She looked like herself, yet different. And since I was immune to the beauty of others now that I was mated to Raven, Luca's emotions alerted me to how mesmerizing she was now.

"So sweet," Jeanine murmured, tilting her head to the side. "I hear your blood swimming through your veins." Her upper lip peeled back to reveal fresh fangs.

"Jeanine," I said softly. "How do you feel?"

"So thirsty," she replied, pressing herself further into the wall. "And so angry." Her eyes shifted to River and narrowed. "He took Raven from me. He left me there for Felix."

"I saved your life," River countered.

"You ended my life!" The pain and intolerance of what she had become were evident in how her voice hitched. "I would've died for her! It would have been a worthy cause. Now, I am no more than a monster who will need to feed from humans to survive."

"Jeanine, Raven wouldn't have wanted you to die for her," I said. "This isn't ideal, and you have every right to be angry, but Raven needs you in her life."

She covered her face with her hands. "I am a monster."

I looked at Luca. "I swear to the gods, if you move, I will kill you myself." I lowered my arm from his stomach and went to Jeanine, removing her hands from her face. It took much more force than I expected. "Jeanine, you are not a monster. You are our friend, and that will not change. You're part of our family."

"I want to drink his blood!" she cried. "I will want Raven's just as they all do! I will need it because he"—she pointed at River—"says I will have magic once I feed!"

I glanced over my shoulder at River, who nodded. "The more she feeds, the stronger her magic will become. I do not know what she possesses, but she will have something. All Undead do."

Jeanine fell into me. I wrapped my arms around her. "Listen to me, Jeanine. Raven is immortal, and so are you. You two will be by each other's side for the rest of time."

She peered up at me, sniffling. "Raven is immortal?"

I shrugged a shoulder. "Apparently."

"Is she okay?"

I nodded with a small smile. "She's safe in Thoya with Edmund. We'll see her soon. Once we return home, we'll send for her, and she will love you just as much as she always has."

She shook her head quickly and stepped away from me. "I cannot return to Seolia. I will not put our people at risk.

"Jeanine, you can't stay here," Luca said. "You need to be home with us. You don't belong here with them."

"You have a bond with Felix," River said. "Because of his bite, you have created a bond. If we go to war with them, that might help us. It would help Raven."

Jeanine remained silent, crossing her arms over her stomach. I touched her shoulder gently. "I will not force you into anything, Jeanine. This will take adjusting, but I believe you can do it. I believe you can return home with us and not hurt anyone." I looked at River. "Can she feed from animals?"

He nodded but frowned. "Yes. It will not be as potent as human blood, but it will suffice. She can survive off of blood alone."

Jeanine asked, "Food?"

River shook his head slightly. "You can consume food, but it will not restore energy or replenish strength. It is more or less for appearances or pleasantries."

Jeanine fell into a heap on the floor, curling up into a ball. "I hate what I've become, Zeke. I do not want to be like this."

I lowered to sit in front of her. "I am so sorry, Jeanine."

Jeanine had quickly become one of my closest friends after meeting Raven. We had tackled so much together and lived through so much, but our loyalty to one another never wavered. It broke my heart to see her in so much pain, to know that this was something she would have to live with for eternity.

Luca sat on the bed, keeping a safe distance from her. "What is going to change for her?"

River's frown deepened as he sat in one of the chairs around the small wooden table. "Everything. Everything will change. She cannot be mated by fate. Her strength and speed will be immeasurable, and she will thirst for blood. A good feed will sustain her for a few weeks, but animal feedings will leave her longing for more."

Jeanine rested her head against the wall, looking absolutely defeated.

I took her hand between mine. "And she can't feed from us?"

"She could," he answered. "But not mortals. If she fed from you or Raven, she would have to be able to stop. A single bite cannot kill you, but consistency will. Undead bites contain venom that even magical beings cannot fight off if too much is injected into their bloodstream."

Luca cleared his throat. "And what about..." He shifted on the bed, drawing a deep breath through his nose.

"No," River answered, sparing Luca from needing to ask. "Not with mortals. During intercourse, Undead have to bite when..." River cleared his throat, "Finishing. The euphoria is unlike that of mortals. It's stronger, and Undead can only come down from the high by biting. It would kill a mortal."

Jeanine's eyes closed as a tear slipped down her cheek. Luca sank into the bed, his eyes falling to the floor. Whatever they had between them ended quicker than it had begun. And I felt nothing but sorrow for both of them.

My eyebrows knitted together. "Are you saying Silas hasn't slept with anyone since Raven died?"

"He has," River answered. "He bites whoever he's with but has another male or female in the room for his partner to feed from. Bloodmating is done by ceremony, but he's never taken the risk."

I scowled. I couldn't imagine ever being with anyone but Raven, even if we were apart for a century. It only proved that Silas wasn't after Raven because of genuine love or desire; he only wanted her for her blood and the power it would bring him.

"Since Felix and Jeanine have a bond, can he discover where we are if we return home?" I asked.

River shook his head. "Felix can feel the bond, but he didn't consume enough. It will fade, and he will try to find her before that happens."

I tugged at Jeanine's hand. "Please come home with us, Jeanine. We can't do this without you. Do it for Raven."

Her eyes fluttered open, meeting mine. "I will if you promise me something," she whispered.

I braced, already anticipating.

"If I become a monster, if I get out of control, you will be the one to kill me."

"Jeanine..." I shook my head, choked.

"Zeke, I would do it for you."

And that was true. To prevent me from harming others, she would be the one to kill me if she had to.

So, I nodded, as much as I didn't want to. "I promise."

Luca stood from the bed. "Do we sail home?"

"No," Jeanine answered. "River can take us."

"Arrowing," I answered Luca. "He can take one at a time. Will you bring Raven home today?"

"I can't," River said. "I can't enter Thoya. We'll have to write to her. Meanwhile, I can work with both of you until she returns. I can teach Jeanine how to Arrow. Without Raven's blood, Zeke, we can't work on freeing your shadows."

I rolled my eyes. "I can't free them. I tried."

"Time," River said. "Patience. We'll make this transition as easy as possible for Jeanine."

"Do not think we will be friends," Jeanine said, baring her fangs at him ever so slightly. "You will remain my enemy. I am only tolerating you for Raven."

Living in peace with these three would not be simple.

"I understand," River said quietly. "I am genuinely sorry, Jeanine. I would not wish this upon anyone."

I had to believe him. He had been fed from against his will by Silas for over a century. And now, Jeanine was turned because of his obsession with my mate.

Killing Silas would be highly fulfilling.

I pulled Jeanine to her feet. She swayed, still not used to her newfound strength. "Take Luca first," I demanded. "Jeanine will be last, so we can be there when she arrives."

River stood from the chair and took Luca's arm. "Brace," was his only warning before they disappeared.

I looked at Jeanine and gave her the most encouraging smile I could manage, which she didn't return, but the attempt was there. "Nothing will change between us," I promised. "You're still my biggest annoyance, aside from Luca, of course."

"And most formidable threat," she added, trying to sound cheerful. "Do you forgive me for bringing Raven here?"

"Jeanine, no one can refuse that little demon." I grabbed her shoulders and looked her straight in the eye. "I promise that I am not upset with you. Please forgive yourself. The price you paid..." Trailing off, I sighed and hugged her once more. "I'm the one who's sorry. For everything."

I WASN'T ASLEEP, but I smiled when I found Raven. I couldn't sleep until I held her in my arms, not through a dream.

Leaning against a tree, I watched her stomp through the Black Forest with an amused grin. I couldn't create dreams for us since she was too far, but when I felt her tug in my subconscious, I cast an image of the forest in the forefront of my mind, hoping she would find me there.

It was better than her being pulled at by skeletal remains.

When she walked between two trees, she saw me and beamed. And then she flashed me the most flirtatious smirk, and her determined walk turned into a saunter.

She wore a short nightshirt, revealing almost every inch of her legs, and I never before realized it was possible to salivate in a dream. "Did you wear that for my benefit, little witch?"

She shrugged a shoulder, biting on the corner of the bottom lip and taking too long to make her way to me. She looked gorgeous, even as a dream.

My heart swelled, surely about to burst as I watched her, just as enamored as always any time she was near. And when she was within arm's reach, I grabbed her quickly and lifted her to wrap around me. "Gods, my love." It hurt my chest not to smell her, but feeling her was overwhelming.

She kissed me. Long and hard and frantically.

I held a hand against her head, keeping her pressed against me. I would've been content to stay like this until the dream ended, but Raven liked to talk. "How long do we have?" she asked, pulling away from me.

"Not long enough," I answered with a frown. "I can't control these dreams, Raven. I don't even understand how they're possible."

She ran her hands through my hair. "Where are you?"

"Home," I said with a smile. "I am home and anxiously awaiting your return."

"We're leaving at dawn." She practically squealed from excitement. "I'll see you in three days, though I am quite angry with you."

I tucked a strand of hair behind her ear. "What did I do to upset my little demon?"

"You said four weeks," she said with a sigh. "It has been longer than that."

I raised an unimpressed brow. "And whose fault is that *really*?"

She rolled her eyes but then frowned. "How is Jeanine?"

I mirrored her frown. "Missing you. I'll explain everything when you're home, baby. We have a lot to talk about." I didn't want to discuss the heavy things in this place with her. "Has Edmund flirted with you?"

She threw her head back, laughing. "He is frightened by you! He won't flirt with me, even when I beg him to. He has been training me."

"Training you?"

She nodded, kissing me again. "Silas veiled my elements. I have learned that I am not a very coordinated fighter without them. He's been teaching me things when I'm not lounging with Gisela. They're both distracting me." She pressed her wrist against my lips. "Can you taste me here?"

The temptation was too great not to try.

I broke the skin easily and pulled, but nothing came. She sighed and dropped her wrist from my lips. "It's been days, hasn't it? How are you feeling?"

"Lost," I answered honestly. "Thirsty. Fatigued. You are quite an addiction, little demon, but I will have you again soon."

She wiggled against me. "You *could* have me now."

I chuckled. "Not here. A dream will not allow me enough time for everything I plan to do to you. I want to be able to smell you, taste you, truly feel you."

She traced my jaw with her fingertips. "Is this real, Zeke? Are we really speaking to each other?"

I shrugged. "I don't know, Raven."

"You promised you'd always find me in my dreams," she whispered tearfully. "Fate is allowing you to keep your promise."

I pressed her forehead against mine. "I love you, Raven. There is so much about our past that I don't understand yet, but I want to learn about it with you."

The ground beneath us shook, which was enough to tell me we were running out of time. "I have to throw you, baby. Promise me you will return to me in three days. No more adventures."

She nodded, holding me tightly. "I promise, Zeke. I am so sorry." Her voice hitched. "I am so sorry for leaving. I am so sorry for not forgiving you."

"Baby, I am not upset with you. You didn't know what was waiting for you. And as for forgiving me..." I sighed. "I am sorry for ever doing anything that needed your forgiveness. But baby, it's okay."

"I was scared for our people, Zeke. I didn't want the witches to return, and River told me we'd be unsafe on the island if I stayed..." She stuttered her way through her words, and I put a finger against her lips.

"Baby, I know. The fact that you exist is a risk, but we'll discuss it when you get home." My hold on her tightened when I stumbled to the side from the ground splitting. "Baby, I love you. Say it, Raven. That's all I need."

She kissed me deeply, her hands cupping my neck before she whispered against my lips, "Baby, all I do is love you."

"THIRSTY. FATIGUED. YOU ARE QUITE AN ADDICTION, LITTLE DEMON, BUT I WILL HAVE YOU AGAIN SOON."

Zeke

Luca hadn't left John's side since we returned.

John was on the mend, but even with Raven's healing and my mother taking care of him every moment, he hadn't left his bed. He recounted everything that had happened to me, explaining how River was the one to save them all. River had carried Raven into the castle and assisted in getting John to the infirmary while Alice had tended to Raven.

Was River my favorite person? No. But would I be eternally grateful for his help in saving my family? Yes.

But even knowing what he did, Luca still didn't trust him. I didn't believe he ever would. Luca had been through too much with Raven to allow anyone else to stake the 'brother' title claim. And I wouldn't force him to try. He had rightfully earned that spot.

Jeanine hadn't entered the castle once. She had stayed within the caves of the Black Forest, fearful of being too near anyone. Since River and I were the only ones around who possessed any magic, we were the only people she allowed to come near her. And all she did was ask about Raven.

I informed her that I could find Raven when she slept, and every time I did, Jeanine would find me to ask how she was. She blamed herself for their trip to Reales, but it wasn't her fault. It wasn't anyone's fault—not really.

Raven feared for her people, as she always did. She didn't want to be responsible for lives lost if someone else came looking for her.

Jeanine was tasked with protecting her and she knew Raven well enough to know that if she didn't go with her, Raven would go alone. She would've sacrificed herself in the library that day if Raven hadn't trapped her.

And River.... Well, I was still figuring River out. He acted like he wanted to eliminate Silas, but I had yet to feel any emotion in him to prove that. He had answered all of my questions aside from where Raven came from, and he had assisted me in trying to find a way to finish this once and for all.

He informed me that this had always been the plan—that Petra had written him very few letters over the last twenty-five years to update him on Raven's wellbeing. And that John hadn't been aware of how deep this went, but Raven's safety was of the utmost importance.

There wasn't a set date that they wanted me and Raven to finally meet, but as her twenty-fifth birthday neared, Damiana told John to make it happen. River wouldn't divulge details about that interaction and told me to ask Damiana. The letter he wrote to her after returning to Seolia asked that she accompany Raven when returning.

Now, all I could do was wait.

Anxiously. As they would be arriving today.

Jeanine had refused to eat since returning. While she needed blood and craved it, the idea of it repulsed her. She had asked me what it was like, and when I asked what she meant, she told me that Raven had shown her the bites.

"I can't explain it," was all I could say to her. "Raven's blood is unlike anything I've ever tasted. It's sweet like honey but thicker. It is not what you imagine blood to be when you see it drip. It's like molasses on my tongue but smooth."

But instead of allowing me to hunt food for her after that, she cowered in the corner of the cave and sat there, unmoving. I expected her to still be there as I walked toward the caves, holding a dead squirrel by the tail at my side.

I leaned against the cave entrance and dangled the squirrel in front of me, only seeing the white of her eyes from the back of the cave.

Jeanine was a predator now. There was no mistaking it. Her entire demeanor, build, and speed proved it. She was a threat before, but now she was untouchable.

"Have you spoken to Raven?"

Her voice carried like a song through the caves, and I understood what River meant about the enticement of the Undead. She sounded angelic. I felt sympathetic toward any mortal man who would come upon her.

"Not yet," I answered, somewhat sorrowfully. I hadn't found her in her dreams since the dawn she left Thoya. "I haven't felt her, but she's safe. River has trouble finding her when she's sailing since she's constantly moving, but he's felt her elements through the Time *hallway*, as he says you call it."

"Do not speak of him," she hissed.

"He wants to help you," I said gently. "You have powers now, Jeanine. We should find out what they are."

"I am a monster," she repeated for the hundredth time since we found her. "I wish to die."

"Jeanine." I placed the squirrel on the ground and walked into the cave until I could see her, frowning. It looked as if she hadn't moved an inch. "You are not a monster. You're my friend. You're Raven's sister. I drink blood, too."

Her bright blue eyes rose to mine. "What were you?"

"Undead." I lowered to sit in front of her. "I think. River won't tell me anything else until Raven and Damiana arrive. I crave Raven's blood because she was my bloodmate. We weren't chosen by fate, yet the gods created a strand for us to follow one another into each life." I gave her an encouraging smile. "I would like you to be there when we learn why."

"When you left," she whispered, resting her chin on her knees, "I asked Raven what it was like to have a bond like yours. She promised I would find one." Her eyes shimmered. "Now I am viewed as a demon by fate. I will never be bonded to anyone unless forced by blood."

"I doubt fate would curse someone like you," I assured her. "We don't know what the future holds, Jeanine." I nodded toward the entrance of the cave. "But I do know that you need to feed. Can you try it? Please?"

She eyed the squirrel before shaking her head slightly. Sighing, I was about to offer to find a different animal for her when River appeared at the cave entrance.

"Zeke," he said, unable to hide the slight grin. "Raven."

We both stood and jogged out of the cave, though Jeanine was much faster and had to stop herself frequently while waiting for us to catch up. She stopped at the border of the forest before I reached it and covered her face with her hands. I touched her shoulder as I followed her gaze to the middle of the town.

"She's okay," Jeanine cried. "She's okay."

I smiled. That she was.

Raven strolled through the center of the town, immediately crowded by our people as they greeted her. She flashed her brightest smile at each of them. And similar to what we did all those months ago, we watched her from afar.

Only now, with her twin.

The irony of standing where it all began so long ago was not lost on me; only now, I had made her mine. So much had changed since that night when I first saw her, but my love for her made for the most remarkable difference. It continued to grow daily, enveloping my every breath.

I wanted to hold her, kiss her, smell her, taste her, but my feet were frozen to the ground as I watched her move, completely awestruck by everything she made me feel.

My heart swelled. My tongue dried.

And I was certain I wasn't breathing.

Raven's eyes kept darting around the crowd, searching for me, but I remained still. I wanted to admire her for a moment. I wanted to be convinced that this wasn't another dream where she would disappear.

Damiana lingered behind her, introducing herself to everyone who seemed awestruck by her elegance, while Edmund stayed beside Raven. I chuckled as I noticed them holding hands, but I felt no jealousy, nor did I feel anything but concern in him, even from where I stood.

Each time someone got too near to Raven, he would pull her close as if worried she would be snatched away from him.

And Raven was even better than a dream.

The evidence of her training with Edmund was in the mold of her body. Her waist was slimmer, but I was grateful that the curve of her hips hadn't changed. I wasn't, however, enjoying what she was wearing—at least, not in front of others.

The outfit reeked of Gisela.

Sighing, I took her in inch-by-inch. Oddly cut pants ballooned around her legs, accentuating her waist and hips. Two too many inches of her stomach were exposed before disappearing under an airy top that showed her spine every time she lifted her arms to hug someone. Rather, side-hug them since Edmund wouldn't let her go.

Her hair looked longer, her twin braids falling to the bottom of her ribcage. And her skin was tanned from lounging on the hillsides with Gisela.

"Your species posses beauty, don't they?" I said to River. "The Undead are undoubtedly alluring, but Raven is..."

"Different," Jeanine finished for me.

"Yes," River stated simply, giving me nothing else.

"Go to her," Jeanine said. "I want her to be happy before everything else. Tell her I'm napping."

Sleep. Another simple comfort that had been stolen from Jeanine. She no longer required rest and would spend nights by the water until I began to nod off. Only then would she insist I sleep while she returned to her cave.

River slept. It was proof enough that he wasn't Undead. Yet every time he spoke or grinned, I noticed the sharpened ends of his canines. He wasn't Undead, but his species still drank blood. Combined with the magic I had witnessed from him, I wondered if his species was as intimidating as the Undead.

Before I could argue with Jeanine, she was gone, running back into the forest. River looked at me with a shrug. "Go. I'll try to speak with Jeanine. We'll see you this evening."

Yeah, like I would give Raven up that soon.

I took a step forward, and Raven's head snapped toward me. We locked eyes and held our gaze briefly as if we both feared a dream shattering. One shared look between us held so much longing.

Her face twisted and she pulled her hand from Edmund's to run. He chased after her until he saw me, smiling as he pulled back. My feet flew underneath me as I met her step for step, opening my arms just in time for her to jump and wrap herself around me.

We didn't speak. We didn't greet one another with anything but a kiss—a kiss so deep, so meaningful, so full of unspoken words, fear, and yearning that it was like I was kissing her for the first time.

I was overwhelmed by her touch, her smell, how her body felt different yet the same, and the feeling that I had nearly lost her once again. I wove my arms so tightly around her that she groaned through our kiss but didn't break from me, instead matching my fervor with how her legs squeezed my waist.

I still wasn't convinced she was real.

That anything could feel this good, this right.

The fear of her living an immortal life without me gripped my stomach and heart. I could not let Silas find her. If he could genuinely bring her back to life with his blood like River told me, I couldn't leave her side. I couldn't risk not finding her in our meadow if one of us died before the other.

"My love," she whispered against my lips.

I said nothing. I couldn't. Instead, I carried her into our castle courtyard and up the stairs until we stood at our door. I was a master of walking with her lips against mine, since this was how we always traveled together. I'd memorized every inch of each pathway that led to our chambers.

She twisted the handle and I kicked the door open and shut with my boot, carrying her to the bed and laying her down. We didn't break our kiss, even as I laid on top of her and pinned her hands above her head to prevent her from removing her clothes.

I didn't want that—not yet.

Right now, I just wanted to feel her.

And she didn't try to fight me. She kept her legs locked around my waist and allowed me to kiss her until her lips were raw and swollen, until she needed a breath, and then I was right back against her.

But when I did pull away, her first question was exactly what I expected. "How is Jeanine?"

I brushed my thumb across her reddened pout, unsure how to answer that question without lying. "She has missed you," I whispered, kissing her again. "We'll see her this evening, apparently, though I can't be expected to allow you to leave this room for at least a few weeks."

Her green eyes held a hint of amusement until they slowly changed into unease. "Did you miss me?" she asked in the smallest murmur.

"Gods, Raven." I kissed every inch of her face. "I have not felt whole since I left you. I am so madly, catatonically, in love with you."

She closed her eyes. "Say more."

"The need I have for you is paralyzing, Raven." My fingertips grazed across her cheekbones and forehead, smiling at how her body warmed. "I am proud of you, little demon."

Her eyes fluttered open as confusion flooded through her. "Proud of me for what? I nearly ruined everything. John was hurt because I couldn't control my elements, Jeanine was left in the library, Silas found me."

"But you fought," I interrupted. "Your magic is bound, Raven. That's why you have trouble freeing it. John is alive and bossing everyone around from his bed. It's good that he's resting. Jeanine was left in the library because of River, not you. You were trying to protect her."

487

Her eyes rolled. "Do you ever tire of defending every bad choice I make?"

I laughed loudly, dipping my head to rest my forehead against her collarbone. "I did not say you don't irritate me, Raven, but I understand your actions, as dangerous as they were."

She blew out a deep breath and pulled my face back up to hers, kissing me again. "I am sorry, Zeke. I promised I would stay put on the island, but I felt nothing for Silas, and now we know who he is."

"I dreamed of him," I admitted, sighing as I sat up and pulled her into my lap. "In Nova. I had a nightmare that he had you in Reales. I didn't want to believe it until I learned who the Undead were... what they *are*."

"Mira sold me," she whispered with tears in her eyes.

"Raven, I know. Baby, I know." I adjusted her in my lap until she straddled me, wiping tears from her cheeks. "Baby, there's something else I need to tell you. There's a lot I need to tell you, actually." Envy flooded her body, and I scowled. "Gods, Raven. Really? You believe I was unfaithful?"

"No," she said, her teeth clenched. "I am just preparing to hear that someone touched you."

I found the irony amusing since she had a mate, and I obsessed over no one but her, yet she was sitting in my arms with the audacity to be jealous. "No one touched me," I assured her. "Baby, you're immortal. And I... I might not be."

Her nose wrinkled. "What? Immortal?"

Right. Our line of communication was basically non-existent since we'd been apart. I had learned much more than she had. "We'll learn more tonight, but there is a chance you will have to live without me someday."

"I don't believe that." She attempted to move off my lap, but I held her still. "I don't want to hear that. Don't tell me that."

"Raven—"

"No," she snapped, flames flaring behind her irises. "We are bound together by a thread, Zeke. If I'm immortal, you have to be, too. Do not tell me we do not have a future together after weeks apart."

The tension between us made me ill. "I'm sorry. You're right. I should've waited until we spoke with River."

She turned her head away from me. I gently took her chin between my fingers and pulled her back. "Baby, I love you. I didn't feel right having you again before I told you. I promised you no more secrets."

She opened her mouth to respond, but a knock on the door had me growling. There was no way in hell that I would be giving her up yet, especially not when things were tense between us. We needed a release and some normalcy before I let her leave this room.

"Stay here," I demanded, shifting her from my lap to the bed. I hated the despair coming from her and needed to rectify my mistake of bringing in such heaviness so soon after reuniting. But when I opened the door, I was surprised to find Damiana on the other side.

"Ezekiel, I need to see both of you immediately."

I shook my head slightly. "Not yet, Damiana. I haven't seen her in weeks."

"Ezekiel."

"No, Damiana. Not yet. We'll see you this evening or tomorrow. Maybe a couple of days."

"Ezekiel, I really must insist—"

"No!" I sighed, running a hand through my hair. "I apologize, but I need time alone with her before we can speak."

"Ezekiel, your thread has been cursed!"

"THE NEED I HAVE FOR YOU IS PARALYZING, RAVEN."

50

RAVEN

Upon hearing what Damiana said, I stood and hesitantly walked to the door. Zeke must've gone into shock. He didn't respond or move; he only stared at her.

"Zeke," I said gently, touching his hand.

He stepped back and allowed Damiana to enter our chambers. I followed her into the office, but Zeke remained at the door, staring into the empty hallway.

"I noticed your strand looked strange when you reunited," Damiana said after calling for Zeke to come in, but he remained firmly in place. "There was gold, but also black. I am sorry for interrupting, but I needed to tell you immediately."

"Of course you did," I reassured her. "Give us a moment."

I left her in the office and closed the door until nothing but a crack remained. Zeke hadn't moved an inch, and I wished I could feel him the same way he always felt me.

I was sure I'd feel nothing but heartache.

"My love." I took his hand between mine and kissed my name across his knuckles. "This changes nothing."

"It will never stop." His voice was distant, and I didn't feel he was speaking to me. "We are followed by misery, Raven. The more magic reawakens, the more targeted we become. If I had never come to Seolia, if I had stayed in Reales, if Leonidas had never taken you...."

"Don't do that," I scolded, dropping his hand. "Do not wish to erase us or our history. It's hurtful."

He said nothing. No reassuring words, no promises that everything would be all right. Instead, he pushed the office door open and took my hand. "Show us."

Damiana clasped her hands together and pulled them apart slowly. And just like before in Thoya, our strand followed. Gold weaved around our arms, glowing as brightly as the last time. And for a moment, I was hopeful she had been mistaken. But then, as the ends curled around her shoulders, I covered my mouth with my hand.

Black covered the tips of the strand. It suffocated the gold, drowning it and causing the ends to fall limp. Wordlessly, Zeke touched the end of the strand on his shoulder before looking at its twin around mine. "How?" he asked.

"I do not know," Damiana answered. "Your strand was crafted by the gods. It would take a strong being to cast a curse potent enough to kill it."

"You said our strand could never be broken," I whispered, attempting to flick the dying strand off my shoulder.

"It cannot be broken," she reassured. "But it can be deadened until you barely feel a pull between you. The stronger this strain grows, the more you will feel it."

The tension between us was a result of this. Our reunion

should've been a joyous event. I was expecting him to whisk me away to make love to me until tomorrow, but instead, he dropped heart-breaking news. Nothing between us felt normal, and I had attributed it to our time apart.

But it was because of this.

Zeke refused to look at me, so I looked at Damiana. "Can we restore it?"

Damiana sighed deeply. "I do not know, Raven. That can only be answered by the one who cursed it. You must resist disagreements or anything that could strengthen the curse. It will feed off your anger."

We were two of the angriest people I had ever met. Most of the time, we fought so we could make up. This would change our entire dynamic.

"Leave us," Zeke rasped. "Please."

Damiana nodded sympathetically as the strand faded, but stopped before she reached the door to glance over her shoulder at Zeke. "Ezekiel, the love I have witnessed between you and Raven is immeasurable. It is rare and apparent. Do not lose hope. We can find a solution."

His only acknowledgement was the dip of his chin.

Silently, I escorted her out of our chambers, but when I turned, I gasped. Zeke, the strongest man I'd ever known, the most feared man in our realm, fell to his knees and broke.

The weight continuously cast upon us had cracked under pressure and pushed him down until his palms rested on the floor, tears streaming down his face and falling onto his thighs. I ran to him and lowered, trying to push on his shoulders for him to raise, but his strength always overpowered mine.

"Zeke," I cried. "My love, please." My body became numb with sorrow, and his pain made me feel like I was being shoved underwater with no reprieve. "Zeke, I love you! Please look at me, my love, please."

"I will lose you," he murmured through his cries. "Everyone stands against us, Raven. They are determined to separate us, and I will constantly be running." He sank back to his shins and palmed his eyes, his voice hoarse. "I chase, Raven. All I do is chase. I search for answers, for help. I plead with the gods to let me have you, but nothing works."

I tried to pry his hands from his face. "You will not lose me. I love you." I placed a palm against his heart. "This changes nothing. My love for you has never been stronger, Zeke. Fuck the curse, fuck all of it, because they cannot break us apart. We were not blessed with a bond only to lose one another."

He said nothing, reverting back to his ways of silence as a defense. It only made me seethe. I shoved at his chest and spat his name like a curse. "Zeke! Do not make me doubt you!"

He lowered his hands with narrowed eyes. "Do not make *you* doubt *me*?" He grabbed my wrists and yanked me toward him. "I have done nothing to make you ever doubt me!" His tone carried heavy frustration. "I have done wretched things for you, Raven, for us. I have shattered minds and memories to protect you, and you are threatening me with doubts?"

I pried my wrists from him and shoved his hands away when he tried to pull me back. "Every word you do not say is like a twist of a dagger in my heart, Zeke." I moved to the other side of the room, turning away from him when he stood. "You feed me lies about how we would've been better off if you had never found me and how we cannot get past this. If that is how you feel—"

"Do not," he growled, "finish that sentence, you infuriating little witch. I am not going anywhere and not giving up on us, but I did not say I would've been better off if I didn't find you. You didn't let me finish my godsdamn sentence before you made assumptions!"

I crossed my arms over my chest. The air between us felt like lead and stuck to me like molasses. My throat burned from the cry I was burying, and I desperately needed his arms around me.

"What I was going to say" —his voice softened— "what I *meant* to say was that if all of those things had never happened, Raven, I would've never known what it was like to want to fight for something. I never would have known a love so heart-wrenching and palpable that it makes me unbearable to be around."

I felt his presence creeping up behind me.

"Not once did I say I was not going to fight for us, Raven. I will always fight for us. All I ever *do* is fight for us. But, like always, you do not give me the time to absorb the information before demanding a plan from me."

He put his hands on my shoulders, pressing his thumbs into my neck. "I am weary, Raven. I am tired and hungry for you. I need you more than my next breath, and it hurts me that you could ever believe otherwise."

"You said you would lose me," I whispered, my groan strained as he applied pressure around the top of my spine. "You are not supposed to say things like that."

His raspy chuckle washed over me as he wrapped one of my braids around his wrist and tugged my head back until the skin around my throat was stretched tight. "You threaten to leave me." He pressed a kiss to my temple. "You threaten to walk away at every slight inconvenience."

I scoffed, but he pulled tighter. "And you disagree with me too often." A feathery kiss on my shoulder. "Yet I say one thing in a state of panic and despair, and suddenly you doubt my devotion to you."

With his free hand, he cradled my neck and licked my skin. I braced for his bite, closing my eyes and waiting, but when it didn't come, I cursed at him and tried to pull away.

The turn of my head was exactly what he wanted.

His lips found my ear, and he nipped at my earlobe before he whispered, "Now, be a good girl and remain still." It was my only warning before his canines sank into my flesh, not edging gently but wholly consuming.

The skin pinched, and tears flooded my eyes from the pain, but I clamored for more. I did not want him to stop. I wanted him to drink enough to free the shadows he had kept buried. I wanted to see if Damiana had been correct in assuming that my blood was the key.

When he moved to raise up, I pushed his head back down. His teeth returned, his tongue stroking as he pulled more. I pushed through the dizziness and the tingling of lightheadedness, but I wasn't strong enough to disguise it.

The weakness of my limbs wasn't a match for him as he pulled away long enough to spin me. My eyes widened in shock at the thick blackness of the veins in his neck, the way they pulsed and disappeared underneath his shirt. And the way he looked at me like a feral, untethered animal.

His head jerked, his chest heaved, and he pinned me to the wall with his hips. The way he blinked rapidly and the strain of his neck as he tried to calm down had me shaking my head. "You're shoving it down," I said. "That's what you've been doing. You've been pushing it down!"

"I do not want to be like this!" Even his voice had changed into a coarse growl, the standard gray of his eyes replacing the black.

"You are what will save us, you bastard!" I shoved at his chest with my fists, but he didn't budge. "Everyone has been waiting for *you*. You have to free them, Zeke!"

"There has to be another way," he argued, watching the mark on my throat heal. "I just need time, Raven. I can come up with something. I can think of a way—"

"No!" I shouted. "This is why you need my blood! We cannot win this if you don't free them!"

"I do not want to be this!" he repeated, finally releasing me and stalking toward the opposite side of the room. "I have murdered too many, Raven. I have been a monster for too long. I do not want to crave any of it anymore." He stared at his hands. "I do not want to wish for their blood on my hands. I don't want to see the light leave their eyes. I want to be your husband and your mate, Raven. That is all I *need* to be."

Arguing with him was pointless.

Instead, I walked past him. He called for me, but I ignored him and left our chambers, knowing he would follow me into hell if that was my chosen route.

"I cannot believe this is how we spend our first day together!" I shouted over my shoulder, not caring that we were passing by soldiers while they trained and drew their attention. "I have done nothing but miss you and long for you, and this is what you are making me do!"

"Raven!" he roared, reaching for my wrist. "Get your ass back here and talk to me!"

"River!" I called, stomping toward the forest. I wasn't sure why I believed he was in here, but we were twins. Surely that gave me some kind of connection with him.

I shifted into Blaze and lit my palms. "River!" I called again, swatting Zeke's hands away. "I swear to the gods I will find a way to burn you," I seethed, mirroring his glare.

River appeared in front of me out of nothing and leaned against a tree, watching in amusement as I shoved Zeke off. "He won't free them," I said. "He nearly did, but he keeps shoving them down, and now, our strand is cursed."

"One is not because of the other, you demon." He stepped toward River. "Take me to Silas," Zeke demanded. "Take me to him, and I'll finish this."

"You will die," River stated simply, crossing one foot over the other. "Silas has immeasurable strength, Zeke. And without your shadows, we cannot eliminate him."

"I do not need fucking shadows," Zeke barked. "I have other abilities. It doesn't have to be all or nothing."

"It does," River argued. "The Undead possess power that you wouldn't believe, even if I told you. Silas has stayed strong from the blood and bonds he's created with others. I am the one who turned the Undead male into dust in Nova. If I could do that to Silas, don't you think I would have by now? The members of his clan have fed from villages for over a century. It has not been as strong as Raven's blood, but it has sustained their strength. If I take you to him, we will both die."

I shrugged dramatically as I turned to face my pigheaded husband. "Will you listen now? You want to live a long, happy life with me? You can't unless we learn whether you're immortal or not. Right now, I could probably jam an icicle into your side and you'd bleed out."

He bared his teeth. "I fucking dare you, Raven."

I screeched from frustration and tempted to flick ice in his eyes the same way I did to the boys when I was a child. But then, my gaze softened slightly as I remembered that my sudden annoyance with him was because of an entity that was out of our reach. "I have felt you die before. I do not want to live through that again, nor do I want to live a life without you. Why can't you work with River on freeing them? All you need is my blood."

"You say that like it's normal."

I rolled my eyes. "None of this is normal. Until a couple weeks ago, I didn't believe creatures like this existed, and then I danced with one."

I realized I had made a mistake when River hung his head with a deep sigh and Zeke clenched his fists. "You did *what*?"

"I, uh... well, I, you know..."

Zeke pointed toward the castle. "Moments ago, you were ready to light me on fire at the mere idea of someone *touching* me, and you're standing there telling me that you danced with your *mate*?"

"Don't call him that!" I snapped.

"She did it to save me."

I whipped around at the voice that sounded familiar yet oddly different. Melodic, almost like a soft song being hummed. And through the trees, I spotted her, and I beamed. But when I stepped in her direction, she stopped and stepped back. "Jeanine, what's wrong?"

Though he was angry with me, Zeke came behind me and stroked my hair. "Baby, something happened in Reales. Jeanine, she needs to see you."

"I don't understand," I said. I wasn't sure what to prepare for but waited impatiently as Jeanine slowly took a few steps closer.

She had always been beautiful, annoyingly so. I spent many weeks envious of her, but now, I was staring at an angel. Her hair was effortlessly wavy and glossy, her skin so pale that it looked like porcelain, and her lips naturally blood-red. But her eyes locked me into place as she stared into mine. They were a brighter blue than before, with hints of gold that lingered in her irises.

Gasping, I covered my mouth. My heart fell into my stomach as my chest cracked into two. Zeke caught me before I could fall to my knees and held me up, trying to shush the cries that I couldn't seem to stop.

I left her in Reales. She had been turned because of me. Zeke turned around and pressed me tightly against his chest, keeping his lips against my head while I cried.

"She doesn't blame you," he repeated over and over until the words lost all meaning, because how could she not?

I had let her down. It was my idea to go to Reales, my innate need to disobey every demand made to me. I had spent days pining for my husband while in Thoya, surrounded by people who doted on me while my best friend had lost her life, only to be reawakened as something unnatural.

I wanted to know how it was possible or if it was reversible and why everything seemed to never work out for any of us.

Zeke tensed, his arms tightening around me for a second before they loosened. I lifted my head curiously, my vision blurry as I wiped the tears from my eyes. He looked down at me but nodded toward...

I peered over my shoulder to see Jeanine standing right behind me. Her nostrils flared, and the hint of fangs vanished as quickly as they had appeared. Zeke seemed hesitant to release me but allowed me to turn enough to face her.

"You do smell good," she whispered.

River barked out a laugh.

"I am so sorry," I rasped. "Jeanine, I'm so sorry I left you there. I didn't know this was possible."

"It isn't," River said. "Not usually. I threw Felix off her before he could inject too much venom. Your barricade of ice prevented him from getting to her quickly."

"I am not angry with you, Raven." Her voice was enticing and soft. I wanted to hear more of it. "I am the one who's sorry. I shouldn't have agreed to go to Reales. I risked your life."

"Do not apologize to me." I tried to wiggle out of Zeke's grasp, but he wouldn't let go of me. "Am I not allowed to touch you? I just want to hug you, Jeanine."

She looked at Zeke. Before, I could read her expressions easily, but now, she resembled the statuesque demeanor of Silas and Felix. "I have not fed," she explained. "It would be a risk."

"Feed from me," I offered, holding up my wrist.

Zeke *snarled*. I winced.

"Three drops of blood would hold her over for weeks." River moved to stand beside her. "Drops of Raven's blood would prevent Jeanine from having to feed from animals."

Zeke pulled me tighter. Jeanine shook her head.

But River sighed. "Jeanine needs to feed. I need to learn what kind of magic she possesses and teach all of you how to Arrow. It takes time and patience to learn these things, which we cannot afford."

We all looked at River, fully aware that it held a deeper meaning. "What are you talking about?" Zeke asked.

"Mira made a deal with Silas," River said.

"We know," Zeke said with a sigh. "Realm domination in exchange for Raven. But you said he cannot reach her here because of your weakened bond with him."

"He can't," River said. "But Mira can tell him how to get here, as well as Perosan. Thoya is still protected."

"Then what is he waiting for?" Jeanine asked. "If Mira can tell him where we are, why hasn't he already tried?"

"Mira has burned every map except one," River explained. "It is hidden well because I am the one who hid it. The promise of Raven was not the only bargain Mira made with Silas and his clan."

We waited. River seemed hesitant to continue. "For years, the Undead have ransacked villages for blood, but never had they come across a kingdom with so many people and such few illnesses. The blood is strong amongst your people."

I wrinkled my nose. "I don't understand."

"We are running out of time because Reales is running out of people," River said quietly.

"No," Zeke said, catching on before I could.

River frowned. "The Undead have been restoring their strength and preparing for war by feeding from the people of Reales."

"YOU SAID OUR STRAND COULD NEVER BE BROKEN," I WHISPERED.

51

RAVEN

Z eke released me so he could back away, his hands threaded through his hair as he shook his head in disbelief. Jeanine stared blankly at River for only a moment before she launched toward him. She was quick, but he was prepared as he vanished and reappeared behind me. I scowled at the fact he was using me as a shield.

"How could you let this happen?" Jeanine shouted at him. "You sat by and did nothing while Silas killed our people!"

"I did not have a choice," River explained calmly. "Each step of this plan has been meticulously planned. If I had asked them not to, they would have known I planned to turn against them. I did not spend over a century being used only to ruin everything now."

"You have already ruined everything!" Jeanine spat. "We could've defeated Mira had it not been for you showing up in Reales! All of this could've been over if you had never informed Silas that you found Raven."

"And instead allow Silas and his clan to continue murdering thousands of innocents?" It was the first time I had ever heard River raise his voice. "He never would've given up on finding Raven whether he had me or not. It was only a matter of time, and despite what you think, I am *not* your enemy!"

"Silas has been to Seolia before."

We all turned around to look at Zeke.

"It is where he murdered me and took Raven," Zeke continued. "Why has he not returned here?"

"Memories fade," River answered. "Silas has stayed strong through my blood and the blood of others, but even he is not immune to waning magic. With Damiana's shield around the realm, it was invisible to him, and with time, the location of the island faded from memory. It is how my people have remained protected and how Raven has been able to live her life untouched by those who seek her."

"The shield around our realm protected *your* people," Zeke said with a slight grin. He clearly caught something that I didn't. "Are you saying that your people live within this realm?"

River sighed behind me and put his hands on my shoulders, much to my surprise. We rarely touched, but this felt familial. "The day I found Raven on the shore of Perosan, I told her that I could not use my magic there."

Zeke looked at me, and I nodded in confirmation.

"My bond with Silas had begun fading, but it was risky for me to go there. As I believe you learned on your own, the forest is guarding something."

Zeke had yet to share with me what he experienced in the forest aside from some terrifying guards, but he nodded with a tight jaw.

"It is guarding a realm outside ours—a realm only accessible by magic. When the royals of Reales first attacked Perosan all those years ago, it was not for domination of the realm."

"It was for what the forest guarded," Jeanine said from behind us, coming to stand beside River. "Perosan has something that Reales wanted, doesn't it?"

I wanted to reach for her, but she shook her head at me with a sorrowful grin. I was not fearful of her, yet Zeke called my name in warning when I moved to try.

I rolled my eyes but stayed put.

"The Forest Beyond harbors my realm. If I had used my magic to save Raven, it would have risked the lives of every being there. I knew the forest would protect her."

Zeke asked, "And who are your people?"

I tipped my head back to look up at River, also wanting to know the answer. I hadn't been told much about my history—only that Celestina had protected me from someone.

River held Zeke's stare. "I will tell you when Jeanine feeds. Until then, my secrets remain my own."

Sighing, I dipped my chin once more to look at Zeke. He beckoned me toward him, but I still wasn't fond of his behavior, so I crossed my arms over my chest and did not move. He narrowed his eyes at me but asked River, "How did our strand become cursed? Was it Silas? It is causing unnecessary tension between my wife and me."

"Only witches cast curses," River said. "Silas would've needed to find a witch willing to curse a strand crafted by the gods, or maybe he threatened one of them."

"Or promised them something," I mumbled. "It seems to be how the Undead make all their bargains."

Zeke's shoulders slumped. "The Reine coven?"

"It would be the closest coven," River said. "And if Silas promised them a drop of Raven's blood, they would be desperate enough to do anything he asked."

Jeanine and Zeke exchanged a glance. "We can't leave our people in their hands," Zeke said. "We're going to need to rescue them. And the less blood Silas has access to, the easier it will be to kill him." He then looked at River. "And you can teach us Arrowing?"

"Yes," River replied. "I can teach it to all of you."

"We will meet tomorrow," Zeke said with a sigh. "I require a night with my wife before our life changes again."

"I would suggest we start today," River started to say.

"No," Zeke growled. "I have been without her for weeks. I am not willing to sacrifice another evening with her. If you want my obedience, you do not have a choice."

I bit my upper lip to keep from smiling. I still found his need to possess me charming, even if he did annoy me endlessly. And his coinciding grin told me he sensed every emotion running through me.

River released me. "Tomorrow, then. We will begin."

We returned to our chambers in silence.

I loathed the discomfort between Zeke and me but understood it wasn't because of us. The curse made the air so tight between us, strangling the love we wanted to share.

He sat on the table in our bedchambers and rested his feet on a chair, his arms hanging loosely from his knees. The expression on his face was a mixture of emotions—sorrow, desire, longing, desperation, all of the ways he usually looked at me, only with a new fear of losing me.

"I would like to apologize to you." He spoke, his voice soft and raspy from the lingering unknown between us. "I should not have mentioned the possible inability to grow old with you so soon. It was only because of how badly I broke your heart when hiding the miscarriage."

I nodded in understanding.

"It should come as no surprise that I am terrified, Raven. I know you believe me to be unshakeable, but these last few weeks without you have proven otherwise. I lived in daily dread at the thought of any harm befalling you. I learned much more than I bargained for in Nova and nearly lost my life twice at the hands of witches."

I stepped toward him, but he held a palm up. "Let me get all this out first because once I touch you, I will not stop."

I was growing impatient but still halted.

He chuckled, but it was not from amusement. "When I learned that Jeanine was Undead, River warned us of her beauty. He said that ignoring her appeal would be impossible." His eyes bore into me. "But it was not for me. And do you know why?"

"I have a slight idea," I whispered, only because I had experienced something similar when seeing Silas.

"Because if it is not you who is in front of me, Raven, I am blind. I am ignorant of beauty and charm. No one, not a mortal or creature of any kind, could ever entice me the way you do."

"Zeke..."

"I am not finished," he interrupted. "My people are dying. They are in the hands of the Undead, and I can do nothing to stop it, yet instead of finding an immediate solution, I am here with you. Because at the end of each day, Raven, as the moon rises and stars surround us, I am reminded of one thing: that none of it matters without you."

He stood from the table and continued his words of affirmation with each step toward me, saying things I already knew but needed to be reminded of. "I will fight Silas, Raven. I will become the monster again if it means spending a lifetime with you. What I will not do, however, is spend our days in turmoil. Curse or not, you are mine. If you want me to chase you through the castle and the forest, I will. And I will always catch you."

He cradled my face between his palms. "We began and ended on this island once already, Raven. I intend to continue that tradition with you, no matter the cost or lives I have to take. You will be standing with me at the end."

"Yes," I confirmed, but he didn't need it. He wouldn't have accepted any other answer.

"Now, I promised you something, and I am going to keep that promise," he said with a smile. "I am going to ask that you stay in our chambers until told otherwise."

"I'm sorry, what?" I tightly wrapped my fingers around his wrist when he tried to step away. "It has been weeks since I last felt you, Zeke. You're truly walking away from me? I need you. You said all sorts of things in your letter to me, and you're not going to do any of them?"

He brushed his lips across mine. "Oh, I will perform all of them, Raven. You will be screaming my name this evening and well into the morning, but only after I prove how much I love you."

"I know how much you love me," I argued, raising on my toes to try and kiss him. "Truly, I do, so let's skip whatever you have planned and make me scream *now*."

"Delayed gratification, my love. Please trust me and allow me to do this for you." He pried my hands off. "Please stay here. Promise me."

"For how long?" I whined.

"Not too long. Promise me you'll stay."

Blowing out an irritated sigh, I rested my hands on my hips. "Fine, but do not think I am not highly offended that you are leaving me again after weeks apart."

"If you weren't, you would not be the infuriating witch I love." He pecked me on the lips and denied me a long kiss before flashing an irritatingly charming smile. "Stay."

"Sometimes I loathe you, Ezekiel Audovera!" I shouted as he walked away from me.

He laughed in response and closed the door behind him.

When I wasn't pacing and leaning over the balcony to try and spot him somewhere in the village, I was throwing his clothes around the room in frustration. We had been apart for weeks, and I was spending my first day home alone and desperate for him.

Whatever he was planning, it better be good.

After our wardrobe had been completely emptied of his clothing, I sighed and sifted through my own. I had cleared half my dresses out to donate to the village and returned all of his clothing to the wardrobe, smiling since they finally fit.

But night had fallen, and he still hadn't returned.

I looked longingly toward the office. While separated, dreaming of our future was one of the only things that kept me from falling apart. I had planned to someday turn the office into a nursery, but now I wondered if we would ever get the chance.

I wished he hadn't told me about his possible inability to live immortally with me, which was ironic since I demanded no more secrecy between us. I could kind of understand why I drove him to madness sometimes.

I wanted to keep a promise to him. I wanted to stay here and not search for him, but a crazed Undead was on the loose and looking for me, and Zeke was the type to try and fight him alone without telling me.

I wished I could say I debated with myself, but that would've been a lie.

Throwing our door open, my look of determination quickly withered into surprise at the person huddled in the corner of our small entryway. "Jeanine," I whispered.

Only her eyes moved as they raised to meet mine. "I've been here since shortly after he left, but I didn't want to come in." She paused then said, "That's not true. I did want to come in, but I couldn't."

I frowned. "Did he tell you not to?"

She shook her head slightly. "No, but I know that's what he would want. He asked me to look after you while he was out, though I don't understand how he could ever trust me with you again."

This was so unlike Jeanine. Aside from myself, she was the most confident person I knew and never second-guessed herself. But she had been changed into something against her will and couldn't trust herself to be around the smell of blood. "He loves you, Jeanine, as do I."

I stepped out into the hall, and she cowered even more. "Though, I am quite frustrated with you."

She nodded, probably incorrectly assuming the reason. Smiling, I lowered myself but maintained a comfortable distance between us. I honestly did not believe she'd lose control around me, but I did not want to add to her anxiety. "I believe you might be more beautiful than me now. You know how vain I can be."

She scoffed. "Please. The moment he saw you return this afternoon, he fucking melted. So did I."

"I will need you to remind me of that every day. It needs to be the *most* important. Pretend there is no impending war or Undead lingering in the shadows. You must always put *my* needs first."

She snorted, and the sound made me smile. "I would believe you if you weren't the most selfless person I know."

"I have grown rather tired of that." I sat on the floor and scooted a tiny bit closer. "I think I shall change into the most conceited. It's always good to change things up."

She looked so flawless before me, yet it was as if I could see the darkness she felt inside through the way her smile slowly changed back into a frown. "I am sorry, Jeanine. I did not know they could change someone into one of them. I never would've taken the risk if I did."

"We both made mistakes."

She did not say it to be cruel or unforgiving. She said it because it was true. We had each made mistakes, and someone always ended up hurt because of the choices we continued to make. "We need to be a team," I said. "We need to stop acting independently."

"I don't believe we have another choice." She tipped her head back against the wall to stare at the ceiling. "I want to believe we can win this, Raven, but I was there with you. All we have is River, and he's not even fully reliable."

"I believe he wants to help us," I said gently. "I just don't think he knows how to act around anyone. He's been with Silas for over a century. We were only around Silas for a few moments, and I found him unbearable. I can't imagine what a century would be like."

"You'll find out." She dipped her chin. "If we do not beat him, you will find out exactly what it's like."

"Then you need to feed. You must, Jeanine. I cannot lose you." I rose to my knees and inched closer. "We can start small." I extended a hand to her. "Hold my hand."

Her nostrils flared, but I remained patient and entirely still. "You can do this, Jeanine. If anyone can overcome this, it's you. You will not harm me."

Flexing her fingers, she blinked a few times, and then almost painfully slowly, our palms touched. Her eyes closed as her body relaxed, her fingers intertwined with mine. My laugh was breathy as relief flooded through me. I would never again take something as simple as touching my best friend for granted.

We had gone from her practically sleeping on top of me to us barely holding hands, but I took it gladly. "See?" I whispered. "Baby steps. We can do this."

Hope shone in her eyes. "We can do this."

"SOMETIMES I LOATHE YOU, EZEKIEL AUDOVERA!"

52

RAVEN

We had mastered holding both hands before I heard someone coming up the stairs. I hoped it was Zeke, but Edmund and Alice appeared. Edmund's jaw dropped —*dropped*—upon seeing Jeanine. She stood from where she had been cowering, slowly relaxing the more time we spent together without her biting me, but she stilled again at Edmund's noticeable interest while gawking at her.

I stood in front of her, blocking her before Edmund could ask questions about how someone so physically flawless could exist. "I

509

am returning to the forest," Jeanine whispered behind me. "Enjoy your evening, and I'll see you tomorrow."

Before she could step around me, I grabbed her hand with mine and squeezed. "I love you. Maybe Shadow..." I trailed off, panic rising. "Shadow. Where is Shadow? I'm assuming River did not bring him back."

"River said Shadow can find his way home," Jeanine interrupted. "He did not say why or how, but that he would be safe."

Edmund cleared his throat. "I do not believe we have been introduced." He extended his hand toward Jeanine. "I am Edmund, the Prince of Thoya and Ezekiel's biggest threat," he joked, winking at me.

I looked him up and down, quirking a brow. He was overly dressed for a visit in a fitted suit with embellishments of gold.

Jeanine snorted. I grinned. If anyone was a threat to any of us, it was her. "Men," was all she said before descending the stairs.

Edmund curled his fingers as she left him standing there, his cheeks blossoming from her rejection. Alice let out a small laugh behind him while I patted his shoulder. "Don't feel too bad, Edmund. No one impresses her."

"Right, well." He dropped his arm and rolled his shoulders back. "I am here to formally escort you downstairs, Queen Raven."

I wrinkled my nose. "Please don't call me that. Escort me to where? Where's my husband?"

Alice came from behind Edmund. In her arms was the dress she had sewn me to wear to the ball Zeke had planned. The glitter shined so brightly that it added light to this dark hallway. "To the ball, of course. Edmund will wait patiently while I help you dress and do your hair."

I began asking questions, but Edmund shook his head with a chuckle. "We have been instructed not to tell you a single thing."

Alice beamed at me. "Let's go, darling. He's waiting."

～

I stood with Edmund at the gate of the courtyard, confused. And nervous, but I was unsure why. Well, that was partially untrue. I never knew what to expect from Zeke and his grand gestures. I had only been back for a day, and I wondered if he had been planning this since returning home.

My wavy hair, brushed and silky, rested against my chest. Alice had chosen a simple silver diadem with a sapphire diamond in the center to rest on my head, and even with heels on, the skirt of my dress still grazed the ground whenever I moved.

Edmund took my hand and rested it in the crook of his arm. "You look devastating, love."

I pulled at my skirt anxiously. "I suppose you have become used to the simple outfits Gisela has been dressing me in. If I am being honest, Edmund, I feel out of sorts in dresses after what happened with Silas."

"Look at me, love." He waited until I did and gave me an encouraging smile. "I believe that is partially why Ezekiel has put this together. Between"—he shifted uncomfortably—"*Cade*"—the look on his face told me that saying his name disgusted him—"and Silas, Ezekiel wants to give you back a piece of your life. He said that celebrations like these brought you two together in the past."

Nodding with a slight frown, I peeked around the corner of the courtyard wall only to be promptly tugged back. "Each ball we've attended has reminded us how much we love one another."

"I should not tell you this, Raven, but I spent all evening with him while we prepared for this. He is frightened by what we might encounter and worried about his people in Reales, but you are still his top priority."

My eyes lowered to the ground. "Do you believe we are being selfish by not preparing right now?"

"No, Raven." He gently placed his palm on my cheek and turned my face toward him. "I believe restoring what the two of you have will give us a better chance of defeating Silas. And don't we deserve one last night together before it all changes?"

"Well, when you phrase it like that," I responded with a smile, "I suppose we do. But why are we outside?"

Luisa rounded the corner and nodded to Edmund before extending her hands to me. I was taken back to the night of my birthday celebration when she did this exact thing, only moments before Zeke waltzed in and changed my life forever. "He is waiting for you, Queen Raven."

She dropped my hands and stood to the side, but when Edmund tried to encourage me to move, I couldn't. "Deep breaths, love," he said. "I don't want to carry you in and explain to Ezekiel that you fainted."

With a breathy laugh, I bit down on the corner of my bottom lip and nodded. I first believed we were going into the village, but was surprised when he turned me toward the forest instead. "Edmund," I warned, looking over my shoulder toward the town. "I know you've never been here before."

"Originally, the ball was to be in one of your ballrooms," Edmund started, giving me a gentle tug to keep going toward the forest. "But after seeing you this morning, Ezekiel changed the location to the forest. I'll be honest, Raven, a ball in a forest seemed strange, but I've learned not to question my friend."

Following his nod, I gasped.

Weaved through the trees, hanging off branches by strings, were long and brightly lit ivory candles. Accompanying them were exact cut-outs of stars and moons from the Festival of Dreams, and the ground was covered in the same purple and blue glitter. Tables from Duck's had been brought in and covered in arrangements of red roses.

Bottles of our favored rum sat open at each table next to plates of fudge, which made me laugh through my shock. Ribbons of gold mirroring our strand entwined through the backs of chairs, and pink and yellow flowers made of airy paper and tissue were placed sporadically across tabletops and chairs.

Pieces of our relationship and time together blended into the trees in color and chaos, perfectly mimicking who we were as a couple.

Edmund bowed before dropping my arm from his and joining Damiana beside one of the tables. I stood at the border of the tree line and couldn't stop smiling. All my favorite people were here— including some of the villagers who had always been too afraid to enter the forest.

I was highly impressed that Zeke had managed to persuade them to come. Even if it was just at the border, it was more than I had ever been able to do.

Isla, Arthur, Luca, Grace, Godfrey, Luisa, Theodore, Eva, and Keaton waved and smiled at me—each person a vital fragment of our story. John leaned on a cane with one hand and held Alice's hand with the other, attempting a slight bow to me. I wanted to go to him, but Alice instructed me to remain still, tipping her head sideways toward the trees.

Always with the perfect timing, a tall silhouette sauntered out of the shadows. "Gods," I whispered, watching as he straightened the sleeves of his jacket and flashed his catlike, cocky grin at me.

The effect he had on me needed to be studied.

All the tension, frustration, and anger, everything I had been feeling since our reunion, dissipated. And it wasn't because of the carefully constructed makeshift outdoor ballroom I was standing in, nor was it because we were about to spend our night dancing together under the moonlight.

As I stood alone, watching him walk toward me with charming confidence and longing in his eyes, I remembered fate wasn't the reason I was so madly in love with him. It was a choice I had made long ago, before the confirmation of our pairing, before the complications that accompanied it; a choice that was sealed that one fateful night at a festival when we locked eyes for the first time, and every moment before that one no longer mattered.

When he ran his hand through his hair with a wink, I threw my head back in laughter. "Sex, sleeves, and his hair," I repeated from the night of our wedding.

He stopped before me and bowed, trying to hold in his laughter at my scowl when he referred to me as "Queen Raven." He extended his hand to me and asked, "Would you honor me with a dance?"

Heat bloomed across my cheeks as I took his hand, grateful that the butterflies in my stomach returned with full force. He pulled me flush against him and placed both hands on my waist. "I need to be the last man you dance with," he whispered, leaning in and kissing me so tenderly that my heart nearly burst.

"You are the only man I ever want to dance with," I assured him after putting my arms around his neck. "You are the only man I ever want anything with."

"I would ask if I could get that guaranteed in blood"—he brushed his fingers across the scar on my neck—"but I already have it."

"Dance with me, Ezekiel Audovera."

He flicked his wrist once, and music filled the forest from a trio of three men from our village. "Mrs. Audovera, it would be my pleasure."

And then, we danced.

He spun me around and kissed me repeatedly, saying nothing aloud but telling me everything he needed to with the way he held me and stared into my eyes.

Everyone else soon joined us, but all I wanted to see was him. "You included our entire love story," I whispered to him, tipping my head back to stare at the moons and stars above us.

"This is not our entire love story, Raven." He followed my gaze before bringing my chin down. "This is only the beginning. Our story doesn't have an ending. It has moments. These moments were important, yes, but we will have many more. Tonight is just about appreciating how far we've come together, baby. Tomorrow, we'll face reality."

He kissed me again. "But tonight, my love, just dream with me." He touched the crescent moon charm on the necklace that was resting against my chest. "You put the stars in my sky."

My heart fluttered at the familiarity of his words. "And you, you wonderful, unyielding man, make me so wildly unhinged."

THAT WAS ALL the magic I had expected—the swooningly romantic act of piecing together our love story within the forest where it all started, but I needed to stop underestimating him. After we danced together, Zeke led me through the trees to greet everyone, then promptly dragged me to the center again and winked before shushing the guests for their attention.

I glanced around the crowd, my gaze resting on Edmund longer than on anyone else as he seemed to be masking his grin with boredom, which I immediately knew was faux as Edmund was never bored. And when he caught me staring at him with a raised brow, he quickly flicked his eyes up toward one of the moon cut-outs, suddenly extremely interested in it.

Taking my chin between his fingers, Zeke dragged my focus back to him and smiled. He smiled so broadly that my own smile mirrored it, though I was unsure what could possibly be making him so joyous at this particular moment.

"I'm going to do this right, Raven. I'm going to do this because I want to—not because we're being forced or threatened to do it." I didn't have time to ask questions before he dropped to one knee before me and pulled out a small box from the inner pocket of his navy jacket.

My lips parted, my heart thundering. "Proposing has become a habit of yours," I murmured, though I still felt as giddy about it as the last time.

Taking my left hand in his, he cleared his throat. "I want to bind myself to you, Raven, in every way possible. I want to see the sun rise and set each day with you by my side. I want the guarantee that you're mine, and only mine, for all eternity." Opening the lid on the small box, he balanced his elbow on his drawn knee while he presented it to me.

"Zeke," I whispered.

Inside the box, perched on a delicate pouch, was a silver band, cut to perfectly fit the pear-shaped diamond on my ring. It wasn't simple, since nothing ever was with him. Instead, in a cursive resembling his penmanship, the phrase 'under the stars' was engraved. "We fell in love under the stars," he said softly.

I was completely speechless, the only sounds coming for my unsteady breathing and hammering heartbeat. He removed the ring from the box and slowly slid it up my finger, perfectly aligning the band with my ring. "When this is over, and when we can breathe freely again, I want a mating ceremony with you, Raven. I want a wedding in front of all our family and friends. The entire realm. Every kingdom known to man, Raven, I want them all here." He kissed the back of my hand. "I will be held accountable by every person in existence, Raven. I will be the husband and mate you deserve."

As his equal, I didn't answer until I was on my knees before him. "You already are," I assured him tearfully, tearing my eyes away from the band to stare into his eyes. "But yes, Zeke, I will tie myself to you in however many ways you can think of." Which I had no doubt would be plentiful. "We will make a new beginning."

He cradled my neck between his hands. "Say it again."

I threw my arms around his neck and kissed him repeatedly, laughing and smiling through each one. "Yes!" I squealed. "Yes, always yes."

With one of his arms around my waist, he waved the other one around dramatically. "She said yes! Again!"

I buried my face against his chest while our loved ones cheered and clapped, and I wondered if anything he did would ever not embarrass me, but I never wanted it to stop. Zeke always ensured that I could never question his love for me for too long, and doubting that he would spend his entire life proving his devotion to me was not something I was capable of. If there was ever one thing I could be sure of, it was the very simple fact that Ezekiel Audovera, mysterious and brooding and perfectly broken to fit my own splintered pieces, admired me in a way that no other being ever could.

⁓

THE BALL HAD TURNED into a celebration. I danced with everyone, as did Zeke. It was incredibly endearing when he offered to dance with Grace. Her cheeks had turned as red as her hair, and she couldn't look him in the eye while he spun her around, even going so far as to dip her, causing her to erupt into girlish giggles.

And even more heartwarming, while also holding a levee of grief, was watching him carry Eva through the trees in a unique mixture of dancing and playing with her on his back while he trotted around like a horse.

While I knew our child was a boy, Zeke dreamed of a girl. And after all of the dreams he'd made come true for me, I wanted to give that one to him. Someday.

I danced with Arthur, Theodore, and Godfrey. Even Isla tried her best to spin me around, but mostly, I watched my family and subjects interact and felt nothing but gratefulness and admiration for the fight all of us kept choosing to endure for this kingdom.

Guards stood across the treeline to keep watch, but I did sneakily supply them with fudge every so often, only to be whisked away again by Zeke. Before he could dance with me again, Eva demanded his attention once more. I waved them off with a playful roll of my eyes.

River appeared in my line of vision and bowed. As he approached, I huffed in response, placing my hands on my hips. "Did Zeke tell everyone to do that?"

"More like demanded," he replied.

"Mm," I hummed. "He likes to annoy me. Where did you run off to? I worried you had already grown tired of us."

He gave me a guilty grin. "I tried to get Jeanine to feed. I thought maybe if she did, she could make an appearance."

I frowned. "And I'm guessing she didn't."

"No, but she didn't try to kill me this time. I consider that progress."

I swallowed my laughter of disbelief. "Maybe. You seem to like her now."

"I pity her." He took my hand and spun me. "I know what it's like to have no way out, to feel helpless and hopeless. I don't particularly care for her, but I understand."

"Whatever it is, I appreciate your help."

Alice appeared beside me to take my hand and squeezed it. "John is tired, Raven. We will return to our chambers, but I am so over the moon for the two of you."

I wrapped my arms around her tightly. "You raised two wonderful boys, and I am blessed with the devotion and love of one of them."

She kissed my cheek. "You have the devotion of all of us, dear girl, particularly the youngest."

Luca's arms wrapped around my waist from behind, and he kissed the top of my head. "I will be in the forest tomorrow. Jeanine hasn't let me come near her, but she needs to see that we're not going anywhere."

"I agree. Having all of us there might persuade her to at least attempt feeding."

"Bright and early," River said. "Dawn."

"Fuck," Luca muttered, releasing me. "He might be stricter than *your* husband."

"Believe me," I assured, "*Your* brother cannot be topped."

"I heard that," Zeke said, transferring a sleepy Eva to my arms. She whined slightly, and he laughed as I scoffed.

"I think she likes you better than me now." I pouted and tucked her hair behind her ear as her eyes fluttered closed.

"He said I was the prettiest girl with blonde hair here," Eva sighed dreamily, her voice scratchy from exhaustion.

My eyes lit up with amusement as I moved her into Theodore's arms. "You better take your daughter before I feed her to the mermaids, Theodore."

Eva giggled, opening her eyes to place her tiny palm against my cheek. "You will always be my butterfly."

I leaned into her touch. "And you will always be pure magic, Eva, the brightest spot in our days."

As everyone slowly bid their farewells, I watched them filter out of the forest with a whole heart. Zeke kissed my temple and held me against his chest until we were left alone.

He turned me around and pressed his lips against mine, locking his arms around my waist and swaying with me in the silence. "Thank you," I whispered against his lips.

He rested his forehead against mine. "I just wanted to remind you, Raven. We have already overcome so much, and I think we lose sight of that sometimes."

"It is easy to forget," I said with a sigh.

"Dance with me."

I smiled. "There is no music."

"We do not need music for our kind of dancing." His hands slid down my ribs, smiling as goosebumps rose on my arms. "I have missed you in more ways than one, Raven."

I feigned innocence with my eyes. "Do tell."

The deep, rumbling growl in his throat made the hairs on my neck stand. "Why tell you when I can show you, my love?" he asked.

He didn't need my verbal permission; my overzealous nod was answer enough.

"Come with me."

~

UNSURPRISINGLY, we were standing in front of our spring.

He left me to slowly circle the outer edges of it, his hands clasped behind his back. "I learned, Raven, that this spring played a part in our story from the beginning."

"Oh?" I asked breathily, watching him with a craving so deep that the tips of my fingers tingled. I didn't care to know how or why at this particular moment, and he didn't divulge anything else.

After removing his jacket, he untucked his shirt, fully aware that I was watching every movement with heady anticipation. "Tell me, baby. Did you touch yourself during our time apart?"

I wondered where all my words had gone as I shook my head in answer, biting my lip as he discarded his shirt. The lack of daily training had done nothing to change his physique — he was still very much built like a soldier. And while he was gone, living like a wanderer with his brother, he grew a shadow of a beard, and I wondered how the rough texture would feel against my skin.

And when a piece of hair fell into his eyes, I muttered, "Gods."

"Oh, Raven." He pushed the hair back and took a step closer. "They will not be joining us tonight. In fact, I've come to believe they left us because of the vile, *ungodly* things I fantasize about doing to your body daily."

His mouth would be what killed me one day—the absolute way his words could rearrange my insides would be my demise.

"Tell me why you didn't touch yourself."

"Because." The word tumbled out of my mouth like rushed, broken syllables. Clearing my throat, I tried to recompose myself though it was pointless around him. "Because only you bring me pleasure."

I closed my eyes when his palms cradled my face, a mewling whimper escaping me at the return of his rough, calloused skin against mine. And when he brushed his thumb across my bottom lip,

519

I shuddered. "That is the perfect answer, Raven. Now, tell me what you want."

"You," I whispered, unsure how I could still be timid around him after all this time.

Taking my hands, he placed them against his chest. "You have me, Raven. Tell me what you *want*."

Opening my eyes, I stared into his gray ones with a look of disapproval. "I want you to stop looking like you were crafted *by* the gods," I mumbled.

His laugh echoed off the empty, hollow cave of the spring. "And I want to burn every outfit Gisela gave you, but we cannot all have what we want, Raven."

I ran my tongue along the roof of my mouth to stifle a grin. "Oh, did you notice those outfits?"

He began backing me toward the cave wall, caging me in his arms. "Did I notice that the parts of you which are only allowed for me were exposed? How your spine bowed and curved each time you lifted your arms?" He dragged his fingertips across my stomach, making me worry that he would rip through my dress. "Your fucking delicious navel that followed peeks of your hip bones? Yes, Raven, I noticed that."

My fingers trembled while I unbuttoned his pants and pushed them down. "Only a little bit," I reasoned. "I wore it for your benefit."

"Like the nightshirt you were wearing in your dream?"

Silver lined my eyes, and I blinked. "That was real?"

His lips danced down my throat. "Yes, baby. It was. It was real each time I found you in a dream." And when he kissed me, it lasted much longer than I believed he meant. As much as he enjoyed teasing and taunting me with how badly I wanted him, it was just as tortuous for him.

"I would only benefit if I could keep you hidden," he whispered against my lips when he finally broke from me. He stood bare in front of me, already swollen and desperate. But when I tried to lower, he held me up by my elbow. "No, Raven, no more delaying."

"Just let me taste you," I begged. "Please."

When he shook his head, I wrapped my fingers around his cock and smiled as he groaned. "Imagine if this was my mouth, Zeke." I squeezed down his length once. "Just a little taste, and then you can have me."

"Remove your dress first."

He took a step back as I shimmied out of my dress until I stood in the pool of glittery tulle. His eyes raked slowly down my body and back up, his breathing elevated and uneven. "Fuck, Raven, how have you become more breathtaking?"

My body had changed since training with Edmund. I felt stronger and more capable of defeating enemies, but I felt like a goddess under Zeke's heated gaze. The air around us was tight and hot, and sweat was already beading across our bodies from nothing but the exchanged glances of longing between us. "Forget the taste. I need you now."

He was on me instantly, lifting and wrapping me around him. And before I could take another breath, he quickly thrust into me. Gasping, my legs tightened around his waist while I tried to adjust to him after weeks of absence. He didn't care about the pain it caused, only muttering, "Good," when I expressed to him that I would be too sore to walk after this, driving deeper until I felt I could take no more of him.

"Raven," he muttered in time with each stroke, his forehead against my collarbone while watching himself drive into me. "My love, my mate." He sucked one nipple between his lips, groaning when I clenched around him from the sensation. "Fuck, Raven, the way you own me."

Each word out of his mouth dripped with honesty. And the way he held me so close to him, never allowing any inches to come between us, meant more than anything he could say. His words were always lyrical, but the way our bodies moved together was like poetry.

Endless, divine, and always different, yet you could always rely on the narrator because of the comforting familiarity between us. Beginnings and ending simply held no weight when it came to the story he was determined to write for us. We were made of middles and in-betweens, highs and lows, and heartbreak.

Determined to not let this end so quickly, I barely managed to say, "Water."

At first, I didn't think he would relinquish control so quickly, but after a few more deep thrusts, he lowered us into the heated water. Steam surrounded us, and it took considerable effort to remain myself and not shift into Blaze from the heat his touch ignited.

Leaning against the spring wall, he kept me wrapped around him but allowed me to rock my hips against his, our gazes locked.

With our heartbeat raging and bodies connected like this, a curse against us seemed impossible. Wasteful, even. There wasn't a force in this world that could prevent us from spending our nights like this. And the thought was laughable. It caused a single tear to slip down my cheek and made me *angry*.

And when his eyebrows knitted together at the mixture of emotions running through me, I kissed him. I wrapped my hands around his throat and kissed him with every ounce of passion, obsession, and love I could without completely shattering around him.

He matched everything I gave him. His fingers pressed into my waist deep enough to leave bruises as he kept me still, remaining so buried inside me that I would be sore for days. The constant doubt was draining, and I would not let it win anymore. I would not allow it to ruin what we had.

Zeke loved me with an intensity that would never be matched or replicated. A curse on our strand would not change that—it couldn't. He didn't love me because of it; he loved me despite it. Fate might have played a role in bringing us together, but it wasn't why we woke up every morning choosing one another.

Reaching up, I removed the diadem from my head and tossed it to the ground. He pulled away at the noise, but my hands returned to his throat. "I am nothing if not wholly yours, my love. When I am in your arms, I do not want to be anything but your Raven."

"*My* Raven," he replied gruffly, beginning to push and pull my hips, guiding me closer to release. "You will always be my Raven. Nothing else."

"Nothing else," I promised.

As we came together in this spring full of our memories and beginnings, as he bit me at the point of his climax, I was never more certain of one thing than in this moment: We would live this life together, or not at all.

"AND YOU, YOU WONDERFUL, UNYIELDING MAN, MAKE ME SO WILDLY UNHINGED."

53

RAVEN

W e spent the rest of the night in our chambers, reconnecting and laughing with one another for the first time in weeks. He would throw grapes into my mouth from across the room, only to end up crawling back to me and having me for his snack. And then he'd hold me against his chest after each round, begging me to tell him about every moment we spent apart.

I shared with him how Edmund and Gisela argued over how I spent my time in Thoya, and he told me about the predicament he and Luca had gotten themselves into in Reine.

While it would be nice to interact and meet more witches, the coven in Reine had tried to kill us both. Seeking them out was not high on my list of priorities, though we couldn't help but wonder if one of the witches was the one who assisted Silas in cursing our strand.

And when he shared with me that Mira was not my sister, that she had lied about everything, and that her actual need for vengeance was against Zeke and her father, I wanted to be more surprised.

But seeing how easily she had traded me, that was not something I wanted to believe could be done by family. I had struggled to connect with Mira, and now I knew why. She wanted my mother as her own, and loathed me for being the true daughter of Celestina. And knowing that her revenge was directly related to my husband made the idea of her impending death even sweeter.

And learning how betrayed Zeke felt by his former king, the king he had trusted and admired so greatly, ended up with me giving him so much of my blood that I remained on the floor, dizzy and begging him to reconsider releasing his shadows.

He walked away every time the taste of my blood became too tempting for him, and distracted me by sharing the story of how my wedding band came to be.

Before he'd left for Nova, and in-between writing all the love notes to me, he wrote to Edmund, informing him of how badly he'd screwed up with me and asked if he could have the band inscribed with a message for me, leaving the three words messily scrawled along the parchment. It was Gisela who handled the ring—politely threatening the jeweler in Thoya that they simply must find a way or else the loads of coins she drops at that particular establishment would find a new home.

Gisela was supposed to attend the ball with Edmund as another surprise for me, but my hasty drop-off in Thoya and introduction to Silas changed the plans slightly.

But as dawn neared and someone knocked on our door, the mixture of arguing, laughter, and lightheartedness ceased. We wanted the entire night to ourselves before meeting River in the

524

forest, but with death on the horizon, we couldn't stay hidden anymore. We had lives to save and a war to fight, and despite Zeke's threats of torturing anyone who dared to bother us, my brother simply did not care.

My entire body was sore in all the right places, and Zeke kept kissing my neck and temple while we dressed. "I love you," he repeatedly said, securing a permanent smile on my face. "We could ignore him."

"We could," I agreed. "But I believe River has proven that a door is merely a formality for him."

He nipped at my earlobe. "I am not finished with you, Raven Audovera."

"You will never be finished with me." I turned in his arms after slipping a robe on. "That is the greatest guarantee of our bond. We will always have this."

As he was about to lift me up, kissing me so deeply that it almost enticed me to change my mind, River knocked again, and Zeke growled in frustration. "I miss the times when you didn't have a sibling."

"At this moment, I feel the same." I tightened the straps of my robe, sighing as I walked to the door. "River," I said upon opening the door. Damiana lingered behind him. "And Damiana. Come in."

Zeke was muttering obscenities from the bedchambers, loud enough to make Damiana laugh. Sadly, he pulled a shirt over his head as he came out, his eyes narrowed on River for the interruption. "Didn't I tell you to give us until morning?"

"It is my fault, Ezekiel," Damiana said. "I have not been away from Baldwin for many years. I would like to return to him today, but I owe you and Raven an explanation." She looked at River. "We both do."

Part of me didn't want to hear what they had to say, which was ironic since I had spent most of my life begging everyone to be truthful with me about where I came from. But I couldn't delay Damiana's return to her mate since I understood what that separation felt like.

Zeke palmed the nape of my neck and squeezed. "You make the

decision, my love. I would prefer to ravage you until morning, but I am also curious."

River's face twisted in disgust—the exact way a brother's would when hearing something alluding to his sister's *activities*, and it made me laugh. I was becoming used to him showing more emotion.

"I would apologize, but I am not sorry," Zeke said.

I slapped his stomach with my hand and motioned for Damiana and River to enter my office. "Damiana is used to your crassness, but River is not."

His hand slid over my backside and squeezed. "If he thinks that's offensive..."

"Ezekiel Audovera!" I hissed, but followed it with a laugh. "Behave just for a little while, and then you can defile me as much as you'd like."

He mocked me playfully as he led me inside by his hand on the small of my back. River and Damiana sat in two chairs in front of my desk while Zeke brought in an extra two seats from the table in our bedchambers, positioning us in a wide circle. Well, somewhat. Our chairs were practically on top of one another, and he had one of my hands between both of his. I doubted he would ever put space between us again.

"We told each of you pieces of your story but never the entirety," Damiana started, "There are multiple beginnings, and I am not sure where to start."

"Let's start with Raven," Zeke offered. "River has alluded to being from a species's been in hiding since Raven's death. Who are they?"

River nodded and shifted in his chair. He had been keeping this secret for a very long time, and now he would have to lay it all down. "Celestina is our mother, but our father is a High King. Celestina was in love with him and believed him to feel the same for her. Their union was respected. It was apparent that any child they bore would be powerful."

"But, what our father did not share with Celestina was that he was in love with a mortal. Bearing children with a mortal woman would have caused his subjects to question his entire reign. He is powerful, but there was no proof that his children would be if he did not breed with another magical being." River's tone held a hint of defensiveness as he added, "He tricked Celestina into believing that he would make her his queen if she gave him children, and she did."

"He used her," I whispered.

"He used her," River confirmed. "And he waited until after we were born before admitting the truth to her. He knew if he told her while she was pregnant, she would leave his realm and return to her coven."

"Your coven," Zeke said, looking at Damiana.

Sorrowfully, she nodded. "Celestina was my sister. Not by blood but by love. We tried to warn her about the king, but she was blinded by love and empty promises."

River continued, "As we grew, it was evident that Raven was the one who had received the bulk of our parents' magic. Not only did she have three elements, but it was learned quickly that her blood supplied healing and strength to those who consumed it. And similarly to Silas, our father bartered her blood for favors."

Zeke squeezed my hand, his jaw ticking. I held up a hand to River to stop him from speaking and nudged Zeke with my arm. "This was a very long time ago, my love. You cannot be angry about a lifetime we don't remember."

"I have loved you through those lifetimes, Raven," he replied hoarsely. "I can be as angry as I please."

"Okay, but please do not break my hand in the process."

He relieved the pressure on my hand with a slight grin and brought it to his lips. "I apologize."

I rolled my eyes with a smile. "Go ahead, River."

"Celestina was angry that he was using you in the exact same way he used her. Our mother was a gray witch, meaning her ability to manipulate blood somehow transferred to you."

"What makes Raven the Dark Half-Witch?" Zeke asked. "It sounds like that title should belong to Celestina."

"We were born from lies," River said. "Deceit. Darkness carries over. Raven was light, but there was no mistaking the similarities both her and our mother had, and their draw to blood. Raven could not manipulate it like Celestina, but she was wanted for hers. The thirst she has for drawing blood was inherited."

"Celestina returned to our coven on this very island," Damiana said, "And brought the twins with her. It is where they grew. There is a spring in the forest where Raven would supply us with drops of her blood to sustain our magic. And their father never learned where to find them."

Ah, the history of our spring. Zeke squeezed my hand when it clicked in my head what he meant earlier.

"But Silas found her," Zeke said.

River sighed. "Silas struck a trade with our father. He offered to be an ally in exchange for a bloodmating ceremony with Raven, and our father accepted as long as Raven returned to resupply the fountain in our realm with blood. Celestina did not want her daughter bloodmated to a demon. She believed Raven deserved more."

Zeke chuckled. "She bloodmated with me."

"Almost," River replied sadly. "You came to the island in search of Celestina. You wanted to end your life and had heard rumors of Celestina accepting trades of life for blood. You were willing to sacrifice yours if it meant finding a way to die since you were unable."

Tears pooled at the idea of Zeke wanting to end his life in any of our lifetimes. "Why was he unable to die?"

"While you were undoubtedly powerful, Raven, Zeke was your male equivalent. He did not want to die at anyone else's hand unless it was on his own terms, and his shadows, though controlled by him, sometimes acted on their own in his defense. They prevented him from dying. He came to the island to find Celestina but instead found you." River leaned back in his chair with a slight shake of his head. "It took one look between you for everyone to realize that fate had brought you together."

"We could not pry the two of you apart," Damiana added with a wide smile. "It was only days before Zeke asked to bloodmate with you, Raven, and Celestina could not deny you of it after seeing how happy he made you."

Some things never changed.

"But bloodmating is done by ceremony," River stated. "It is performed without magic. And when your defenses were down, Silas and his clan infiltrated the island. You had given Zeke your blood, but you did not have a chance to take his before Silas drove a stake through his heart."

Zeke wrapped an arm around my waist and pulled me into his lap at my raspy cry. "I do not want to hear anymore. Please. Not of his death."

"Refusing to live without him," Damiana said, "You sacrificed yourself by driving the same stake through your stomach. Before you could take your last breath and as you lay dying across Zeke's body, Silas exchanged blood with you."

"It was done without ceremony and against the will of your coven," River said, his voice laced with anger. "When you died, he planned on bringing you back to life with a drop of his blood, but you were saved." River exchanged a quick glance with Zeke. "By Petra."

"Petra is your aunt," Damiana said before I could raise questions. "She is your father's sister and took your body back to your kingdom, but a strand was created between you and Ezekiel before she could. Your sacrifice for one another was blessed."

"Elric is my uncle?"

Damiana shook her head. "Petra and Elric are not married. They have mates of their own, but that is not a story relevant to this right now."

Zeke leaned forward slightly. "We've always been told that they wed."

"Many stories were created, Ezekiel, to protect the realm," Damiana explained. "I do not have time to speak of each one, but more will be revealed as the days go on. We do not want to overwhelm you too much in one night."

"I lost my element when Raven died," River said, not allowing Zeke to argue more. "That much was true. If one of us dies, the other loses their elements. That is how we are bound as twins. And since we are twins, Silas hoped my blood would bring the same strength to him as Raven's would have."

My head was spinning. "Petra... is our aunt? I don't understand. Why didn't she raise me? Why did she let Leonidas keep me in the dark for my entire life?"

"It would've risked everything," River answered, though that didn't satisfy me. "Perosan guards our realm. Having you so close would've been a risk against your life if anyone ever discovered who you truly were."

"That doesn't make sense," Zeke said. "If magic has waned with your people, why wouldn't they have wanted Raven back for her blood?"

"They did. Celestina fell for our father's charms again," River answered. "He found her right before she became pregnant with Raven again. He wanted Raven back and was told by a seer that she would return if he seduced Celestina again."

"When Celestina learned he lied to her again, she wanted revenge. She asked that I protect Reales from Raven's father ever finding her again, so I created a shield." Damiana sighed deeply. "But it did not prevent Morana from finding Celestina."

"When Petra learned that the spirit of death had transferred to Raven upon Celestina's death, she did not want to risk our people," River explained. "We had no proof that Raven's blood still held the same magic as before and no way of knowing how to purge her of Morana."

"But what we did know," River continued, "Is that Silas was still looking for Raven. He would use me. Every time my element returned, he knew she had been reborn into a lifetime, but we never knew how to find you. He fed from me daily, since our blood is nearly identical, and it only aided in his continued obsession with Raven."

"We had to protect you while also protecting The Forest Beyond from an invasion," Damiana said.

I stood up to pace the length of the room. How could any of this be possible? This was a plan over a century in the making for something as simple as my blood.

"There were Undead in Nova. Why did they not seek Raven?" Zeke asked.

"Certain members of the Undead refused to allow Silas to feed from them to prevent bonds from forming, and he banished them from his clan, which is the worst punishment you could give an Undead. They have no protection, no guarantee of blood," River answered. "Banished members of the Undead have no direct link to Silas and therefore did not know where Raven was. When he smelled her blood in your satchel, he would've told you of Silas before searching for Raven himself, which is why I sent her to Thoya. Every Undead male and female wants her."

"Upon Celestina's death," Damiana took over. "I had to cast a shield around our entire realm. River knew you were alive and in Seolia, but he did not tell Silas. We had no plan in place and no way of knowing if we could protect this realm forever, but then" — she looked at Zeke — "John informed me of your tie to Raven. That is when we learned that you were twin flames, and that the Phantom Prince had followed her back into this lifetime."

Zeke leaned forward with his elbows on his knees. "I am not the Phantom Prince. I cannot free them nor want to free them."

"You must," Damiana said. "We wanted you and Raven to meet as adults but were unaware of the torment Mira was putting you through. John informed us of Mira's intentions, and we were prepared, but we did not realize how deep it went until Jeanine came with you to Seolia."

"Full fucking circle," I groaned, pressing my palm against my forehead as a headache started forming. "You're telling me that you could've introduced me to Zeke sooner and possibly spared us from Mira being involved?"

"Mistakes were made," was Damiana's only reply.

"Mistakes that nearly cost my mother and brother their lives!" Zeke shouted. "You have been waiting a quarter of a century for this plan of yours to come to fruition, and because of it, I murdered hundreds of men for Mira! I nearly lost Raven and spent most of my life without her, and all you can say is mistakes were made?!"

"Ezekiel, this is bigger than any of us!" Damiana scolded. "We knew you two would be together in the end, but we did not anticipate the night you met would crack the shield I had been holding in place since Celestina's death. Many decisions had to be made very quickly, and the longer you went without freeing your shadows, the harder the decisions became!"

"Raven, we did not know what you were capable of," River interjected. "We had to be certain that Morana did not outweigh your elements. We needed to see that your blood still possessed healing and strength."

Zeke stood and wiped tears from my cheeks, holding me tightly against his chest. "You made the wrong decisions," he growled. "Raven nearly died that day in The Forest Beyond. She was raised around a man who groomed her and secluded her while I fought for the lives of my family. I visited your kingdom and was friends with your son. How could you hide this from us for so long?"

"We were frightened." Damiana's tone was gentle yet stern. "We were safe within my shields. Raven was protected. We did not want to rush her growth nor force her to spill her blood for every dying species. Our decisions were made from love, and the longer we went without incident, the more appealing it was to stay this way. Once I had Edmund and Gisela, I did not ever want to break the shields. I did not want to fight a war I had already fought."

"But we believe you've both returned to finish this war," River said. "We believe you can defeat Silas."

"Once I met Raven as an adult the day you two visited Thoya, I told Petra it was time, but Raven admitted to possessing Morana. We needed to wait until she was gone." Damiana stepped toward us from her chair, but Zeke pulled me back. "Our intentions were to protect her for as long as possible. John said she struggled with her magic."

"Because she was alone! Raven had family here," Zeke argued, uncaring about the war or why we were brought back. He only ever cared about my well-being. "Petra should've taken her in. She should've taken care of her instead of letting her feel alone. She could've helped her. Raven should have been warned. She should've been given a choice to decide what to do—not cast aside while the rest of you decided what to do with her life."

"Yes," River agreed in a whisper. "She should have. I agree with you on that point. We do regret it, Raven."

"Fuck your regrets," Zeke snarled. "If I was believed to be the savior of our realm with my shadows, why were Petra and Elric unkind during my visits to Perosan?"

River blinked, his nostrils flaring as he drew in a deep breath. I raised my head from Zeke's chest and tilted my head to the side. "River, who are our people?"

"Enemies of the Undead," River said. "And Zeke was not an enemy, but they feared him because of his heritage. Petra and Elric feared the rumors of Zeke's abilities and the darkness that accompanied him before his bond to you snapped in place."

He was trying to change the subject but was unsuccessful.

"River," I repeated. "Who are our people?"

"Raven..."

"Answer her!" Zeke bellowed.

River recoiled before holding my gaze. "The Fae."

He nipped at my earlobe. "I AM NOT FINISHED WITH YOU, RAVEN AUDOVERA."

54

RAVEN

I misheard him. Surely. The Fae were from storybooks. They were rumored to once have roamed the earth but had disappeared long ago, never to be seen again. Not even *rumored* to have been seen again. But like he had done in Thoya the day he took me there, River shifted. And just like before, his ears changed from looking like mine to having pointed ends. "We are Fae royalty, Raven."

I touched my ears. "I do not have those," was all I could say through my shock.

He shrugged a shoulder. "You look like Celestina."

"We're identical," I challenged. "How can you...." I felt nauseous, bewildered, and betrayed. Again. No matter what kind of information I learned about myself, it always led to betrayal. "How can you look like me but different?"

"I don't know," River stated, sighing. "I don't know why I look like the Fae and you don't."

"She has their beauty," Damiana answered. "But Celestina was beautiful, too. Raven received both."

"You." Zeke pointed at River. "You are one of the creatures pictured in my room in Nova, but you do not have wings."

"Only warriors have wings," River said. "I am a prince. Raven is the Fae princess."

"Does your father know Raven is alive?" Zeke asked. "Does he know she's here? Or did Damiana successfully prevent him from finding her?"

"He does not know she's alive, though that could've changed once Raven entered the forest," River answered quietly. "We decided to keep the Fae realm safe by keeping them clueless. Petra has maintained contact by using The Forest Beyond for messages. Raven's entry into the forest the day I found her in Perosan was the first contact the Fae has had from anyone in a long time."

"Those were sun faeries that day," Zeke said. "The ones that burned me. Who is Godfrey, truly? He knew of them. He told me to take Raven to the snow-covered roses and sun faeries. How did he know about those, River?"

I was beyond lost now.

River ran a hand through his hair. "These are questions I do not want to answer yet—"

"I do not," Zeke snarled, "give a fuck what you want to answer. I *demand* answers. How does Godfrey know Petra?"

"He is her mate," River answered with a sigh. "Petra sent Godfrey to Seolia to protect Raven."

The room suddenly felt stuffy, and I was dizzy from too much information.

Zeke was crushing my ribs underneath his arm as if trying to shove me into his body for protection. "If Raven was in The Forest Beyond, won't they know she's alive now? Why haven't they come for her? Nothing about your story makes sense, River."

"The forest is charmed," River explained. "The Fae cannot leave their realm until the charm is broken."

Zeke's eyes narrowed on River. I looked between them. River looked guilty and weary, rising from his chair to stand behind it as if he was using it as a shield against my husband. "Blood charms," Zeke said, releasing me only to move me behind him. "Celestina charmed the forest and prevented the Fae from leaving unless blood opened it."

Zeke stepped toward River slowly, his fingers curled into loose fists. "That is why you're here, isn't it? You are not here for Raven or to finish the Undead."

"Zeke," I said. I wanted to protect River from his wrath because there was something Zeke knew that I hadn't realized yet.

"He used you, Raven." His head shook slightly. "When we were in Reales, River explained that the cabin was protected by a blood charm, and only those with Celestina's bloodline could cross it unless given permission."

That made sense now, though I wanted to know how you could grant permission to others.

"I am not using her," River argued. "But I do need her."

"Need her." Zeke chuckled, and I sighed. It was not from amusement, and this kind of laugh usually prefaced an attack. "You need her *blood*. You will ask that she free your realm—that your father find her again and use her the way he did before her death."

"Ezekiel," Damiana said gently. "River is not the enemy."

"He is the enemy if he wants to use my wife," Zeke responded. "He is using all of us to defeat Silas and his clan while his people remain untouched. That is why he hasn't asked that they be freed. He wants his twin to sacrifice herself and her people for the sake of his."

"They are hers, too." River nodded toward me. "Her elements are the result of her Fae blood. She is an elemental *Fae*-Witch. I am not asking that she sacrifice herself, but I am requesting that we use our people as a last resort. They have been through enough."

Zeke *lunged*.

River was quick but not quick enough to dodge the beast Zeke became when unleashed. I yelled for him to stop, but he shoved River against the wall, ignoring my pleas. "They've been through enough?!" he shouted at River, pointing backward toward me. "Your sister has been through enough! While you've been planning her entire life, she has lived hers alone! She was surrounded by rulers who knew who she was and where she belonged, yet no one told her a damn thing until they could be certain she wasn't dangerous!"

Zeke was visibly shaking from anger. "Cade was despicable, but none of you are any better. You left her in his hands." He looked at Damiana. "I trusted you. I trusted your family. I thought of you as my own, and you have let me down so greatly."

"Ezekiel, we didn't know what kind of man Cade was," Damiana said, but he wanted nothing to do with her words.

He returned to me and took my hand, pulling me out of the office and away from them. "We're done here. I am not willing to bargain away her safety anymore."

River chased us out. "Zeke, we have to kill Silas. We have to end this, not only for the Fae but for beings everywhere. He will continue to feast on mortals, Zeke, innocent people who do not deserve to die because of him. He will stay preserved, and if we do not fight him, we are sentencing everyone to death."

Zeke spun, placing himself between River and me. "I am not sacrificing my mate, River! What can you not understand? She will not be used for her blood, nor will she be manipulated by you or your conniving Fae father."

"Zeke," I whispered, squeezing his hand. "Zeke, I can't allow more people to die because of me. If River believes we can beat Silas, then we must try."

Zeke hung his head because, whether or not he wanted to admit it, I was right. Our realm had stayed unharmed because of Damiana's shields. We couldn't continue living in this protective bubble while everyone else suffered. "You're friends with Melik," I reminded him. "You have made acquaintances outside our realm. We cannot leave them without our help, my love."

"None of it matters without you." He turned to face me and leaned in, pressing his forehead against mine. "Baby, I can't risk you again. And fighting Silas would be a risk. Freeing the Fae would be a risk."

"I never agreed to free the Fae."

He stared into my eyes, searching for the answer.

"I will help defeat Silas," I said, sliding my arms around Zeke's waist, but I pulled my head away from his to look at River. "But I will not be used by a father I never met. You have hidden secrets from me for too long, River. I am no longer disrespecting myself or my husband because of what people expect of me, especially those who have refused to tell me who I am until they needed me."

I continued, "If beings want my blood, it will be under our conditions. The decision will rest with Zeke, who will bloodmate with me upon Silas's death. I read enough of Arthur's books to know that pairings were once respected. You will respect my mate's decisions if we help you."

River wanted to argue. I recognized the look on his face because it was the same one I always got when I disagreed with something. But before he could utter a word, Damiana stood behind him and nodded. "Of course, Raven. I will perform the bloodmating ceremony myself."

Zeke kissed my temple. "Tell us how to defeat them. The Undead are vampires, right? I have a book from Nova, and while skimming it, I noticed a section about the history of vampires."

"They are not vampires," River said. "Vampires are extinct."

"The Undead were born from vampires and mortals," Damiana said. "Many years ago, vampires bred with mortals. The Undead have beating hearts. Blood runs through their veins. That is why they are so powerful."

I wrinkled my nose. "But... they're dead."

"They're not. Not really." River looked toward our bedchambers. "Is the book in there?"

When Zeke nodded, we followed River and gathered around our table, where the book was placed in the center. I hadn't looked through it yet, but Zeke had explained that it contained information about our history, both together and apart.

River opened the book and flipped through pages until he landed on one, pointing toward pencil sketches of a vampire and mortal side-by-side. "Undead survives off blood alone, similar to their vampire ancestors, but the blood in their veins and arteries results from their mortal parents. Because of it, they are stronger than vampires and nearly untouchable."

I looked toward the door. "So, Jeanine still has her own blood moving through her?"

"Yes," River answered. "And she will never die. Undead are immortal. No one understands why or how that's possible, but once other beings learned of these creatures, they killed the ones responsible."

"The Fae," Zeke said. "In Nova, I had pictures in my room of a war. I saw creatures with ears like yours warring with men with red eyes."

"The Fae succeeded in eliminating vampires but could not defend themselves against the Undead. Each species possesses unfathomable magic, and it was like fighting against oneself." River flipped to the back of the book. "Fae take blood, but only from their mates. They can survive off food."

On the page was a picture of a man who looked like River with pointed ears and sharp fangs. River peeled back his top lip to reveal a matching set, brilliant and terrifying.

"But magic needs balance—dark versus light," Damiana continued. "And since the Undead survive off blood alone, the Fae wanted to protect mortals. The Fae can mate with mortals by fate and view the consumption of their blood by the Undead as a threat."

"You," River said, looking at me, "were considered a solution. If you mated with Silas, it would've allied the Fae and Undead. Silas agreed to provide his clan with drops of your blood while keeping the Fae supplied. I later learned that he did not intend to keep that promise. While forcefully feeding from me one night, he said that he planned on letting the Fae starve if he found you again."

Frowning, I grabbed his hand instinctively. He stiffened at the touch, staring at our linked hands before he cleared his throat. "They are not simple to kill, and the more blood they consume in Reales, the more impossible it will be. Their chests are like plates of steel, and they only can only be killed by blades through their hearts."

"Then why do you need Zeke's shadows?" I asked.

Zeke sighed behind me. "I am good with swords and arrows. I can train others to be, too."

River ignored him. "The Phantom Prince's shadows killed members of the Undead much like Morana's ribbons. They were the only weapon Silas was ever fearful of. He couldn't see them coming, nor could he touch them."

I couldn't help but grin. "A nightmare come to life."

"The Phantom Prince also possessed powers of both the Undead and the Fae," Damiana said. "You were a Fae-Witch, and he was the last living Fae-Vampire."

Both of our heads whipped toward her.

"Your mother was a vampire, which was unheard of. Male vampires could sire children with most beings, mortal or immortal. Female vampires, however, could not have children. And since vampires were considered demons from the deepest pits of hell, it was said that your shadows were crafted by Hades himself," Damiana said, looking at Zeke. "Your father was a Fae. And with both species in your bloodline, you were untouchable."

"What happened to his mother?" I asked.

Damiana frowned. "She was murdered after childbirth."

Despite never having known her, Zeke still hung his head at the idea his birth could've caused the end of someone else's life. I wanted to ask about his father but stopped. That was a decision he needed to make for himself.

"Your bloodmating ceremony was Silas's only way to defeat you," River continued.

Immense guilt sat on my shoulders, which Zeke immediately addressed, "No, Raven. Do not blame yourself for my death, especially one that happened so long ago."

"If Zeke was a vampire, why were we blessed with a bond? He was a demon."

"Because of the sacrifice you made for each other," Damiana explained. "You made the ultimate sacrifice to be with one another in death."

Zeke kissed the top of my head. It was a sacrifice we would both gladly make for one another again.

"I wish we could see how they fight and what they're capable of," I whispered, leaning against Zeke's chest. "I don't know what to prepare for."

"He could show us," Zeke said. "In the Time-Antre. You could take us back to that day and allow us to see how they fight. We might understand a little better if we could watch what happened. I must admit that I am having difficulty wrapping my mind around this."

River shook his head. "I would not recommend that."

"I can't watch you die, Zeke. River said you can't change moments, but I feel like I am the type of person to try anyway."

Zeke chuckled. "You are, but I'll be there with you. I will be living and breathing beside you, Raven. My death then brought us together now."

"I can't take both of you at once," River said. "One of you would have to wait alone while I returned to the present to carry the other."

"You will take me first," Damiana offered. "I have lived in that moment before. Bring Raven second, and then Ezekiel."

My gut twisted into tight knots. "Have you been in the Time-Antre, Damiana?"

"No, love. I do not believe in revisiting moments of regret and being tempted to try and change them. While moments cannot be changed, I possess a skill that can shield those I love." She winked at me. "I have never wanted to risk changing time."

"River visits often," Zeke said, resting his hands on my shoulders. "He will safely guide us in and out."

I raised an eyebrow. "You visit often?"

River's glower was pinned to Zeke. "Not often. There are just some moments in time I wish I could change." Not wanting to offer more information, he motioned toward my body. "Change into something else, and we'll go to the caves. You will need a jacket."

"Why do we need jackets?" Zeke asked. "It's nearing autumn and still warm."

"Because," River sighed. "You died at the end of winter."

"The end of winter," I repeated.

With a frown, River nodded. "You died on our twenty-fifth birthday, Raven."

"YOU DIED AT THE END OF WINTER." "THE END OF WINTER," I REPEATED.

55

RAVEN

River hadn't shifted back yet from his Fae form. I couldn't stop staring at his ears as I walked between him and Zeke toward the caves. They were long and slanted, more prominent than most rounded ears. When he caught me staring, he grinned. "You get used to them," he said. "I've been glamoured for so long that I've forgotten how alarming it can be for others."

"Glamoured? This isn't a shift?"

He shook his head. "No, this is... *was* my form until Silas took me. Undead look down upon Fae. I did not need another reason for them to treat me differently. They know I am a Fae, but my life in The Great was much simpler when I looked like them."

Zeke asked, "Where is The Great?"

"Veiled," River answered. "I cannot find it on my own. My bond with Silas is nearly gone. I couldn't return there unless I bit an Undead or allowed Silas to feed from me again, which I do not want to do."

Damiana trailed only a few steps behind us. "What is The Great like?" she asked.

"Dark," River replied quietly, the strain of his voice full of discomfort. And I remembered it vividly from the shared memory. It looked as if it were painted with blood. "The sun rarely comes out unless you leave the veil, which Silas does not allow unless it's time for feeding."

"You can't survive off of blood," I said. "What would you do?"

"Go with them to villages."

He didn't say anything else, and I didn't pry. I could only imagine the things he had witnessed while living with the Undead for over a century and having to find a way to feed himself while the Undead around him fed from mortals.

"The Undead in Reales moved like statues," I stated.

"Silas's bonds are tight in the minds of his clan. If he tells you to move, you move. If he tells you to be still, you remain so until he says otherwise. He can control each male and female with his bonds. He lets them wander in The Great, but when he needs them, they are at his disposal."

"If someone were to feed from him, could they also control him?" Zeke asked, grabbing my hand. "That's not a suggestion, little demon."

I rolled my eyes, disgusted at the idea of ever feeding from Silas. Consuming anyone's blood other than Zeke's repulsed me. If I was being honest, taking blood of any kind was still something I hadn't become used to.

River shrugged. "We don't know. No one ever got close enough to him to try. Someone would need to consume liters of his blood with the amount of power he holds."

"And if he bites me..."

"Yes," River said before I could finish. "You will feel your bond then. He will be able to control everything you do or try."

Zeke chuckled. "My bond with Raven isn't like that, yet I mated with her. I wouldn't mind controlling her sometimes."

Scowling, I raised his hand to my mouth to bite his finger hard enough to draw blood. He yelped and tried to pry his hand free, but I ran my tongue across it to heal the bite. "Be nice, Vampy."

River and Damiana laughed loudly, causing a broad smile to spread across my face as Zeke muttered obscenities. "You wanted a different nickname," I reminded him.

Scooping me up, he wrapped me around him and kissed me all over my face until I laughed. I caught Damiana smiling at us before she said, "It is strange to see someone who was once so feared be so gentle with you. To me now, he is Ezekiel, the annoying boy who raced horses with Edmund. But back then, he was the Phantom Prince. He showed no allegiance to any species, even his own. Until you."

I was overwhelmingly pleased that every version of him had chosen to love me. "History is repeating itself, I'm afraid." I kissed him twice, throwing my arms around his neck. "He will fight for me because I asked. After this war, expect him to revert to his antisocial and brooding self while keeping me stowed away somewhere."

The caves were just ahead, but Zeke stopped and nodded for them to continue. "We'll meet you there in a moment."

Sliding me down his body, he turned me around while he braided my hair to rest down my back. "Stay with Damiana until I get there. Do not wander, Raven. She's been there before. You'll have to trust she knows what she's doing."

"It's my forest," I argued. "I'll know where I am."

He tugged on my braid, and I hissed, swatting his hand away. "It's not your forest. We're traveling back in time, Raven. It's not going to look the same, and we're going to see things that will alter us. Can you please do what I ask?"

"Do you trust River?"

"No," he said too quickly. "I don't. I was starting to until I learned he needed you to free the Fae. The Fae were feared just as much as the Undead, Raven. Like you did with me, they would entice mortals with their beauty."

I gasped, shoving his chest as I turned. "Are you saying it was not my natural charm and flirting that drew you in?"

He shook his head with an amused smirk. "I wanted to fuck you because of your looks, Raven. I was shallow, but you're unearthly. Now I know why. I've wondered how a person can possess so much beauty, and now I know it's because you are not human. Not only do I have to worry about how sweet your blood is, but how easily you can ensnare someone without trying."

Blush bloomed across my cheeks as his endless compliments. "I have already ensnared the man I want. And if you do not stop flirting with me, Ezekiel Audovera, we will never make it to the caves."

"Oh yeah?" He stepped toward me, and I stepped back. "You know how much I love a challenge."

I wagged a finger. "No, Ezekiel."

"Come on, little demon. We can play a game of cat and mouse." He caught me in two swift strides, pulling me up again. "Promise me you won't wander, or I'll kiss you until you forget where we are."

I pouted, puckering out my bottom lip, which he nipped at. "I promise to not wander *if* you kiss me until I forget everything when we return."

"I like your bargain much better." He kissed me anyway, placing his hand on the nape of my neck to keep me still long enough to sink his teeth into my bottom lip.

I whimpered from the break of the sensitive flesh. I had become used to him focusing on my throat. He didn't pull nearly enough to awaken the shadows swimming through his veins, but it was enough to keep him connected to me.

When he released my lip, I ran my tongue across it to heal the bite. He pressed my forehead against his and took a deep inhale of my skin. "Please stay safe until I get there, Raven."

"I will," I promised. "Everything will be fine."

$\approx$

JEANINE WAS PACING the cave as we entered. I wished she would move back into the castle instead of staying in the caves alone. River was leaning against the cave wall with his arms crossed, and I looked between them. "What?"

"Why do you continue to trust him?" she shouted. "You've been in the Time-Antre, Raven. You know how easily someone can get stuck. And he said there are wanderers. What if this is his way of taking you to Silas?"

"It's not," I assured her. "He's taking Damiana first. She wouldn't let anything happen to me. We're going to return to the day of our deaths. We need to see what the Undead are capable of, and then we'll return."

"Why the caves?" Jeanine asked. "Why did you bring them here? Afraid others would see you take them? And why are your ears like that?"

River rolled his eyes. "You're here, aren't you? You'd warn someone if we didn't return. No one else knows how deep this goes, Jeanine. We're all immortal." He glanced at Zeke. "For the most part. I didn't want to ask Luca."

I followed his gaze to Zeke. "How do we know he's not immortal?"

"Because he won't release his shadows," River mumbled.

"Enough," Zeke said, pulling me closer to him. "Before we go anywhere, lower whatever is blocking me from feeling your emotions."

River startled, straightening from the wall. "Am I going to have to prove myself every time we go somewhere?"

"This is the first time I am requiring this of you," Zeke argued. "And I wouldn't be doing so if you hadn't admitted you need Raven for her blood. Until I can trust you again, yes. You will have to do this."

The tension between them was sticky, and I shifted uncomfortably from one foot to the other. I wanted to believe River was being honest about not using me, but I had just made a speech about trusting Zeke's decisions as my future mate. With the curse on our strand, I couldn't blame him for taking extra precautions.

Zeke drew in a deep breath through his nose. I was envious of his ability to sniff out lies and deceit. My life could've been much easier if

I had his gift instead of my constant inability to control Blaze and her fury.

When Zeke nodded, River extended his hand to Damiana. "I'll see you in the past," she said with a wink before shadows and smoke engulfed them.

"How long do I give you before I tell John?" Jeanine asked, crossing her arms. "Not like we could find you if I did. River could trap you in there for an eternity."

"He won't," Zeke said. "There wasn't any hint of concern or deception in him. I've traveled with him to a moment before." He ran a hand down my braid. "He took me to watch your mother's death."

Cold chills swept across me. "He... he what?"

"Your memories were incorrect, Raven. Morana changed them into what she wanted you to see. Leonidas claimed Celestina was his mate and that she denied the bond. He killed her for it. He took you with him out of revenge, though I'm still uncertain why he made you queen. But River said fate wouldn't have mated someone as powerful as Celestina to a mortal. "

"Only the Undead are viewed as demons," Jeanine said with venom laced in her words. "And only *we* are denied bonds."

"You are not a demon, Jeanine." I wiggled free of Zeke's grasp and stepped toward her, extending my hand. "You are my sister and so very loved. Please return with us to the castle tonight."

She took my hand, lacing our fingers together. "Someday," she responded woefully. "Maybe someday."

"No more than an hour," Zeke responded to her question. "If we do not return after an hour, inform John and tell him to find Petra. He'll know exactly what that means."

"I'm part Fae. Apparently. As is Petra."

Jeanine's lips parted. "Do your ears..."

"No," I said, accompanied by a breathy laugh. "That is the difference between River and me. I look more like Celestina."

River returned, clearing the shadowy fog surrounding him with a swipe of his hand. Pointless since we'd create more. "Damiana is waiting for you."

I dropped Jeanine's hand only to be spun around to face Zeke. He kissed me twice, brushing his fingers down my ribs. "Whatever you see, Raven, you must remember that it's not real. These moments happened long ago, and we cannot change them."

Frowning, I nodded slightly. "I know."

"Baby, you forget that I can feel your every thought. Our deaths were in sacrifice for each other, and we were gifted our strand because of it. We have lived lifetimes together. There is nothing sorrowful about what we're about to witness."

"I'll behave," I muttered half-heartedly.

"Are you sure you can't take both of us?" Zeke asked River, holding me against him.

"Positive. Carrying Raven and Jeanine was a strain, and they're both light. It takes a lot of willpower to carry someone into the Time-Antre, but we won't have to search for the moment by walking down the *hallway*." He glanced at Jeanine in amusement. "It is not far from the present since these are the caves where you died."

"That's ominous," Zeke grumbled, sighing. "I'll be right behind you, little demon. Let's get this over with."

River was truthful. Unlike when we traveled from Seolia to Reales, the archway containing the moment of our deaths wasn't far. I didn't understand how the Time-Antre worked, but I had no space left in my head for any more shocking information, so I didn't ask.

And knowing Zeke was most likely annoying Jeanine with his anxious pacing while waiting to join me, I didn't make River travel into the moment with me, but instead stepped through the archway alone so he could return to Zeke faster.

Blinking as my eyes adjusted to the sun setting in the forest, I looked around. Zeke was correct. The forest looked the same, yet different. The trees weren't gray, like they were in the dark and dreary present, and they seemed to have more life. A butterfly flew across my line of sight, and I smiled in surprise. The wings contained so many colors and seemed out of place here in the forest where I had grown up.

"It happened because of your death," Damiana said, coming out from behind a tree as if she was reading my mind. "Once you died, the forest did, too. The universe lost a bright soul that day, Raven, and it has never recovered."

"I cannot be that important," I responded, watching the butterfly until it faded from view.

Damiana's laughter still comforted me in a way not many could. "We have proven otherwise, yet you still don't believe it."

I shrugged a shoulder, coming out from the entrance of the cave. "Would you believe it if someone told you that your blood is the key to solving all the world's problems? Months ago, I was just a woman forced to hide her dark magic during the day and traipse through the forest at nightfall. I have since learned that I am a Fae-Witch whose powers are still bound and that my husband was once a vampire who might have living shadows within him."

"It is quite a lot," Damiana replied, wiggling her fingers at me. "Come. I have something to show you."

"I promised not to wander."

"It is not wandering if I am with you. We will be back in time to watch your deaths."

"You say that so lightly," I took her hand, "And not as if I am about to watch my husband's murder. I do have a question for you, though."

"I do not believe I ever have the right to turn down another question of yours again, love."

"You and Baldwin have alluded to living in this time together, which would mean he is as..." Trailing off, I grinned, "I do not want to say *old*, but... well, as *wise* as you."

Her smile was broad. "He will never be as wise, and that was not a question."

"What is he?"

"Undead," she replied simply as if telling me how she liked her eggs. "Witches are encouraged not to mate with mortals, and I desperately wanted a life with him. Your mother persuaded an Undead male long before your birth to turn Baldwin so we could be together for eternity. The male gave him immortality in exchange for a blood charm from your mother."

"Then you bloodmated," I said. "And Baldwin only feeds from you."

Her usual joyful demeanor dampened slightly. "Yes, until long after your death. We were not lying when we said that bonds started losing their intensity as magic waned. He began thirsting for blood other than mine as the pull between us weakened. He never fed from any other female, but he occasionally hunted for male blood."

The sadness in her voice made me frown. "I am sorry, Damiana. I can't imagine how that must've felt."

"He could not help it. It is not something you will ever need to worry about with Ezekiel, but if Silas manages to bite you, he will become obsessed with bloodlust."

"Bloodlust?"

We stopped between two trees. "Bloodlust is the result of pairings. Once you mate, you have a frenzy of needing the other's blood. I believe it is why Ezekiel has been able to control himself thus far. If his powers are ever unbound, he might be unable to continue doing so."

"And here I believed he was already out of control."

"We have not touched the mountain of power between the two of you. It is why your bloodmating was so feared by other species."

A slight tremor of voices had me whipping my head toward the left. I peered over one of the tree trunks, took a small step toward the sounds, and covered my mouth.

Standing mere feet away was my mother and... me.

I couldn't fathom it, couldn't believe that I was staring at a version of myself from long ago—a version that had her mother with her. Celestina was standing behind me and braiding my hair in the same style I was wearing now.

Then, I wore a long, black dress made of velvet with an ivory corset. The sleeves were hidden by a matching black cloak that I hadn't fully pulled on yet as it rested around my lower back, the fabric wrinkling at my arms. It looked odd compared to the casual dresses I wore now.

"Can I touch Celestina?" I whispered.

"Do not touch, but you can get closer to her." Damiana put her hand on the small of my back and gently pushed me forward. I trembled as I neared my mother, tears filling my eyes at how delicately she braided my hair. The only version I had ever seen of her was the one Morana had conjured in my nightmares, not the gentle woman before me.

"Mother." My voice wavered as I watched in awe, slowly circling the two of us.

I toyed with the sleeves of my cloak while she finished braiding my hair, my eyes darting around the forest as I undoubtedly searched for Zeke.

"You will never change," I informed my former self, laughing as tears fell from my cheeks, but there was an immense sadness as I stared at myself with the knowledge that I was about to give my life to be with him in death.

"He is waiting for you, my darling."

The sound of my mother's voice had me covering my face. Damiana's arms around me were the only thing that kept me from buckling. "She loved you, Raven, so very much. Watch, love. This is your last moment together."

Hesitantly, I lowered my hands to watch as my mother turned me around to face her and adjusted my cloak to sit daintily around me, pulling the thick hood over my head. She reached into the hood to pull the braid through to rest against my chest, her eyes shimmering with tears.

It was as if she was speaking directly to me, saying, *"I have loved fiercely, darling, so please understand that I know what you feel when you look at him. As your mother, I have to remind you that while he is powerful, you are special. Don't ever let anyone dim the magic in your eyes, Raven. You were born for greatness."*

"He will not dim my light," I had assured her.

"He has not dimmed my light," I assured her now.

"Thank you for allowing me a bloodmating ceremony, mother," I had said. *"I do understand how you feel about them."*

"Your happiness is always the most important, my darling."

And when Celestina's eyes flickered to me, I froze. It was as if she stared right through me, pinning me in place.

But then I jerked to the side as River appeared at our side in his Fae form, an airy lightness about him that he did not possess now. *"He demanded I inquire what was taking the two of you so long."*

I snorted as Damiana laughed. "Always the impatient one."

Celestina rolled her eyes just as I did now, making me smile. *"Stay in your witch form, Raven. Your elements cannot attend the ceremony."*

The three of them linked hands and left toward the caves.

Damiana and I stayed behind them while I fought the urge to try and warn my mother about what would happen in only a few moments. I wished to touch her. Hug her. Smell her, feel her. I longed for my mother's warmth; here she was, only inches away, yet I couldn't touch her.

As the caves came into view, I looked around. "Where are River and Zeke?" I whispered to Damiana. "They should be here by now."

"River planned on taking Zeke to the shore where the Undead infiltrated the island. He wanted to show him they moved as one to give an idea of how it'll be when we fight them," Damiana explained, looking behind us toward the shore. "They should be here soon."

Movement in the cave caught my attention. I turned my head just in time to see my husband step out, only it wasn't my husband.

It was the Phantom Prince.

"ONLY THE UNDEAD ARE VIEWED AS DEMONS," JEANINE SAID WITH VENOM LACED IN HER WORDS.

56

RAVEN

"Fuck," I whispered, stepping toward him only to be held back by Damiana.

Zeke now was delicious and unfairly attractive, but Zeke then... was like waves of a midnight ocean. Beautiful. Hypnotizing. He had maintained the same silky confidence, but the way he moved alluded to the power within him. There was no doubting who he was and what he could do, and the velvety lustful way he stared at me nearing him engrossed me then just as it did now.

He wore all black but had a long cape tied around his neck that swayed in tandem with his every movement. Glossy and thick, his black hair was slicked back and perfect. His eyes were not gray but black, yet bewitching. And his ears... were pointed.

Fae.

And I ached for him—envious of how my former body could press against him. "I want to touch him," I said, trying to free myself from Damiana's grasp. "I just want to touch him; he won't mind."

"Raven," she warned, "You cannot. We'll be thrown from the moment. Time does not take kindly to those who try to change what has already been written."

"I won't change it," I argued. "I just want to feel him."

I stilled as Celestina began to speak in the same language I'd read in the book in Seolia—the language that the witches of Reine asked if I recognized. And from the inner pockets of her cloak, she produced two separate vials of blood.

Pouring them over our entwined hands, the blood did not drip to the ground as I anticipated. Instead, it formed thick strings that weaved in tight bonds around our hands. And I watched as I had tilted my head to the side for the Phantom Prince to lean in and sink his teeth into my flesh.

A ghost of pain warmed the same spot on my neck, and I widened my eyes as I touched the scarred bite. "It is the same spot," I expressed in shock.

Damiana looked at me, bewilderment evident in her expression. "You can feel it?"

The Phantom Prince pulled up from my throat, the tips of his fangs glistening with my blood. And right as I was about to perform the same act on him, the sound of leaves rustled behind us.

I was about to witness our deaths and realized I could not stand here and do nothing. I shifted into Blaze, but as I was about to turn to face the Undead, my former self stopped and turned her head toward me as if feeling the awakening of our fire.

"Impossible," Damiana whispered. "She feels you."

Not only did she feel me—she *saw* me.

Our eyes connected, and both widened in surprise.

Run, I mouthed.

But it was too late.

I felt it first—the power behind me as it shot toward us and unraveled the blood bonds from our hands. The Phantom Prince had shoved me behind him and called for his shadows, but it was not enough. It happened in seconds—the wooden stake was thrown at him and pierced through his chest. Shock and heartache shot through his eyes. His raspy cries while he said my name were the same as what I'd heard in my memories.

And I screamed—both then and now—as I watched him fall to his knees. "Raven, you mustn't!" Damiana shouted as I lurched toward him, desperate to heal him.

I could do it—I could fix all of this.

On my knees in front of him, my hands about to pull out the stake from his chest, a strong arm wrapped around my stomach and yanked me backward. I expected to find Zeke or River behind me, but the voice in my ear froze my insides into stone. "Hello, little poppet."

He threw me to the ground, away from the Phantom Prince, away from myself, and I had to watch in horror as I grabbed the stake from Zeke's chest and plunged it into my stomach. "No!" I screamed, crawling backward from Silas, away from the deaths and calls of my mother and twin.

But the Silas that chased me was not the one from the moment—that one was crouching before the deaths he had just caused, studying the Phantom Prince to guarantee he was truly dead, then taking my hand in his to drink my blood, forcing me to become his bloodmate as he sliced open his palm to pour into my parted lips.

The one running toward me was real and now, peeling his lip back to reveal his primed fangs, ready to bite and revive our bond.

"Raven, run!" Damiana bellowed.

I staggered to my feet and tried to run, but I was no match for an Undead. He caught me swiftly and painfully, the strength of his arms nearly crushing my ribs as he yanked me toward him. "I hoped to find you here one day," he hissed, turning his head into my hair to take a draw on my scent. "And unprotected, no less."

Lighting my palms, I shoved them against his chin to turn his head away from me, but my arms shook from the difficulty. He truly did feel like he was made of steel and marble, yet the fire seemed to agitate him further as it burned against the coolness of his skin.

"You cannot stop this, beloved!" He squeezed me so tightly that breathing became a chore, as if aware of how easily I tended to faint.

And then, he pulled us into another one of his visions.

I whipped my head back and forth, trying to locate Damiana, Zeke, River... anyone. But it was only me and Silas. "Stop this!" I shouted, squeezing my eyes shut. We remained in the forest, yet the colors began to dull, alluding to a time after our deaths. "Let me out of here, you foul creature!"

Silas hissed in my ear, dropping me to the ground. I scrambled to my feet and tried to light my palms, but he had veiled my elements again. This power, this ability to alter realities, was intense and alarming, and my panic did not assist me in shattering it again as he paced around me. "You are a ravishing, wicked thing, aren't you?" he asked, not trying at all to hide his lustful sneer.

"And you are an awful thing," I shot back, wishing I could conjure up some kind of storm to break apart this vision but with Terra veiled and my magic still bound, I couldn't do anything other than stand here and hope River would break me out. "Eliminating the Phantom Prince during his bloodmating ceremony shows how weak you truly must've been against him."

"Bloodmating to my mate!" Silas shouted. "You were promised to me!"

"Women are not promised," I argued. "We are not prizes to be traded."

He appeared before me in an instant, no space left between us, one breath shared between two as he grabbed a chunk of my red hair and dragged my head back. "One bite, little puppet, and trading your blood for what I want is precisely what will happen."

I was about to fight, I was about to flail and thrash and use the training Edmund had instilled in me against him when, in my blurring vision, two black clouds shot toward us, and he instantly released me, stumbling back a step as he ducked before the shadows could touch him. "It is not possible!"

His surprise and fear broke the vision, releasing me from its confines.

River and Zeke appeared before me, breathless and panicked. "I did not feel him here," River said hurriedly. "He sometimes visits this moment to try and change it."

"That would've been great to know!" I shouted breathlessly, dizzy, loosening enough fire from my palms to put a wall between Silas and us. "He pulled me into another one of those... things!"

Zeke growled, stepping forward with the intention of fighting Silas, but I grabbed his hand quickly and pulled him back. He wouldn't survive if he tried. "We need to get back to Damiana. We can't stay here!" I exclaimed.

"We have to get back to the caves," River said. "It is the quickest way to return to the present."

Zeke grabbed my hand, and we ran.

We ran past my wall and back toward the caves, yelling for Damiana to follow us as we neared her. River glanced over his shoulder and cursed, causing me to follow his gaze back to Silas weaving around the trees to follow us.

"I cannot Arrow all of you to the caves," River said.

"Take Raven," Zeke demanded. "Take her first."

"No!" I shoved River's hands away when he tried to grab me. "I am not leaving you! This is our chance!"

"Raven, it's not," Damiana said. "Not yet, not without your magic unbound."

Before I could move or blink or argue, Damiana stopped and turned. She held her palms up and released a cry as a nearly invisible stiff plane of air shot out from her hands. "Go to the caves! I can hold him off long enough!"

Zeke tugged my hand just as Silas lunged at the shield, falling back to the ground from the impact. His usually untouched demeanor was disheveled from the security between us, and I saw how feral an Undead can be when kept away from their mate.

I didn't want to leave Damiana with him, but Zeke didn't give me a choice as we resumed our attempt to reach the caves. At the sound of her scream of pain, I whipped back around to see Damiana slowly falling to her knees and Silas standing completely still with a tilted head.

"He's hurting her!" I cried, pulling at Zeke's hand. "We cannot leave her! He will kill her!"

"Baby, I have to get you out first!" Zeke argued, trying again to keep me moving.

"Think of Edmund! We cannot leave her!"

"Raven," he tried to argue.

"She has a mate!" I placed a palm against his chest. "What if it were you and me?"

A booming crack sounded through the forest and we covered our ears, watching in shrouded agony as Damiana collapsed on the ground, unmoving.

"No!" I screamed and ran toward her, toward Silas, but I could not let her die, not after everything we had already been through together in such a short amount of time, not after the gifts she gave me of showing us our strand and the final moments with my mother.

"Raven, I've got her!"

River Arrowed from beside me to next to her, scooping her into his arms and vanishing, leaving us alone with Silas. The grin on his face told us that he believed he had already won this fight—that I would be his by the end of this.

But he did not realize that the shadows were not a fluke. Though the Phantom Prince lay dying, his soul remained in this moment while the gods created the strand between us. And I saw it from the corner of my eye—how the strand of gold wrapped around us as Silas hovered over my dying body to finish exchanging our blood.

He couldn't see it then, just as he did not see it now.

"I can... feel them," Zeke murmured. The Phantom Prince's shadows, and though they weren't the ones living within Zeke, they answered to him now just as they did then. Because somewhere buried deep within him, Zeke was still the Phantom Prince.

"Do what you can," I said to Zeke.

Zeke did not move, did not lift a finger or verbally call to anything, but two shadows wrapped around me in greeting. Somehow, I recognized them from somewhere deep within the fibers of my soul. And they clung to me, touching each part of me they could before I whispered, "Go fetch."

Zeke chuckled beside me and dipped his chin toward Silas, sending the shadows flying toward him. Silas evaded them; his eyes widened in genuine fear from the tendrils of smoke that chased him.

And I wanted it to be enough. I wanted the fear to strike enough hesitancy in him that he would give up.

But he knew—Silas understood that the Zeke beside me was mortal and that he did not possess the full strength of the Phantom Prince. And when a look of determination crossed his features, I realized our time was running out.

It all happened within a moment.

Silas focused on Zeke, and I shook my head, remembering the pain he had brought to Jeanine. And when Zeke's chest heaved and a choked cry escaped his lips, I shifted into Frost. Forming an icicle in my hand quickly, I chucked it toward Silas, guiding it closer with a gust of wind.

Silas lifted a hand, and the icicle shattered into pieces before reaching him. I cried out in frustration and crafted two more, but the results were the same. And when Zeke fell to his knees, I called for the Phantom Prince's shadows, but nothing came. They faded before my eyes as our souls left this moment, greeting one another in our meadow.

And without any shadows at all, I was Zeke's only defense.

I curled my fingers into loose fists as Silas took slow steps toward me, believing it was over. As my soul began to crack from Zeke's pain, it would've been easy to accept our fate. I could've stabbed myself the way I had before, and we could've died together, but I wouldn't have followed Zeke into another life this time. Silas would bring me back to life, and I had promised my husband that we would not live any life without one another.

When I shifted into Blaze, it was with the knowledge that, even though my magic was bound and not strong enough to defeat him yet, I would not go down without a fight. One way or another, I would live or die with my husband.

"You will never have me the way you want me," I taunted, placing my hand against Zeke's throat as I stared at Silas. The purple flames between our skin gave Zeke some reprieve as his fingers wrapped tightly around my shin.

"Many have tried," I continued, pushing everything I had into Zeke. "All have failed, and it's because of him."

"You cannot rewrite history," Silas said, his voice steady, smooth, and severely irritating. "You witnessed us become bloodmates, beloved."

Fighting against the immeasurable pain, Zeke feebly rose to his feet but moved my hand to his chest to continue pushing my flames into his skin. "She is not," he rasped weakly, "your beloved."

Zeke could not fight, but I knew he'd try. And unbeknownst to him, River had returned and was waiting behind us. So when I said, "Now, River," Zeke looked at me in confusion before he felt River's hand on his shoulder.

"Raven!" Zeke shouted but could say nothing else as River Arrowed him back to the caves and hopefully into the Time-Antre.

"That was brave, little poppet."

Words were my only weapon. "I feel nothing for you," I said. "Not even a hint of a pull. Even without your bite, bloodmates should feel *something* for one another."

With his teeth bared, I should've felt more intimidated, but I pitied him. Like Cade, he harbored an obsession for me, and it had eaten away at him for so long that he could not focus on anything else. But I was no longer the naive girl who believed in second chances and felt no allegiance toward him. "You forced me to be your bloodmate," I continued, motioning toward the empty caves through the trees. "The Phantom Prince had my heart then, just as he does now. Your bite will not change that."

He *tsked* while slowly circling around me. I turned with him, pausing to see the Phantom Prince's dead body on the ground, which only enabled my fury. Flames spread to my wrists. "I did think about that, little poppet, which is why the curse conjured against your strand is so imperative. The more time we spend together, the more it will rot, and we will see if your love for him still holds enough weight to deny me."

River had been correct in assuming it was Silas who cursed our strand.

Prick.

I hid my smile as River appeared from the shadows of the cave, holding a finger against his lips. As quickly as he came, he vanished. I needed to continue stalling.

Luckily, Silas enjoyed toying with me as much as I liked taunting him. I remained locked in place as he circled me like a vulture sizing up his prey. "I was stalked by your kind before. In fact, Felix nearly bit me. He did seem more impressive."

His laugh felt like ice against my skin. I tried to manifest Blaze into her physical form but couldn't. "Envy is unnatural for me, little poppet. If you believe Felix to be more impressive than I, then you are free to do so."

"You wouldn't know freedom if it bit you in the face," I hissed. "You are trying to force me into something against my will. *Again.* You speak of envy, yet you cannot stand the idea of me mating with someone else, and I never even loved you. I never wanted you."

"We never met." He stopped circling to stand directly before me. "Your wicked witch of a mother took you away before we could be formally introduced. She is the one who stole your choices away, not me. Your father wanted a different life for you."

"My father wanted to sell me like livestock to the highest bidder. Your promise of an alliance with the Fae won him over."

"River has filled your head with lies, beloved. He is angry with me for feeding from him for so long yet never wanting him as much as I needed you."

I rolled my eyes. "Do not feed me your lies, half-breed."

I hit a nerve. His nostrils flared, his fists clenched, and his impossibly pale skin flushed, giving a hint of the mortal blood that still lived within him. "River told me all about your kind. Half-vampire, half-mortal. Pathetic, if you ask me."

"No more pathetic than your mortal husband," he spat with venom laced in his words. "He could not even control the shadows that once lived within him. We could have a long life together, Raven."

It was the first time he had said my name so casually. I couldn't say I cared for it.

"Children," he continued, stepping closer. "You cannot have children with your mortal husband, but I could give them to you. Did River share that with you, beloved? You will be treated like a queen in my kingdom. I will provide you with everything you need." He was within arm's reach. "A son, beloved. We could have a son."

My heart hammered in my chest, my grief returning like a wave. "I will have children with him," I whispered.

He shook his head with a grin. "You will not. Cannot."

"You know what they say."

We both tipped our chins up to see River perched in a tree, his shoulder leaned against the trunk, his feet crossed, and a cocky grin across his lips. "Anything is possible. I managed to get away from you, Silas. I think you're losing your touch." River looked at me. "Chilly, yes?"

He turned his palm toward the sky and twisted it quickly, bringing down a pool of water. I shifted into Frost and iced it, staggering backward just as the plane of ice shattered over Silas's head.

The proof of his mortality pooled at the crown of his head as blood dripped down his cheeks. River appeared before me and winked before grabbing my hand and Arrowing to the caves. I stumbled backward, palming my forehead from the rush of dizziness. "Why didn't he fight back?"

"When our elements combine, I can manipulate them. The frozen water droplets iced his nerves when they fell on him. It's not a permanent fix, but it gives us time to return to the Time-Antre."

"Can I manipulate them? Why didn't you kill him?"

"You can do more than me, Raven. We have a lot to figure out." He retook my hand and moved us into the Time-Antre. "I wouldn't have had enough time to kill him. You're underestimating him, Raven. I had seconds to get you out before he fought through the paralysis."

"How is Zeke?"

"Really upset," he said, wincing. "I had to shove him out of the Time-Antre and back into the present. I imagine he wants to kill me."

"Why didn't Silas bite me when he had the chance?"

"Silas likes to be challenged."

I snorted, then sighed. "Delayed gratification."

"Something like that."

We jogged down the hallway toward the present, but when River cried out in pain and fell to the ground, I spun around to see Silas standing on the opposite end of the tunnel. River writhed at my feet, and my panic made me shift into Blaze and shoot a line of fire down the tight hallway. It spread across the ground and lined the archways, seeping into moments.

I pulled River up, putting his arm around my shoulder while I half-dragged him and half-jogged with him toward our moment. Sweat beaded on my brow from the heat of my flames, but when I looked behind me, I saw Silas moving toward us swiftly.

"River! What should I do?"

With jagged breaths, he shook his head. "We must make it to our moment before he catches us, Raven."

"No shit," I muttered, shoving River off and spinning. Shifting into Terra, I crouched and placed a palm against the ground. The archways cracked as an uneven line split the floor in half.

Silas stumbled to the side and put his palm against a crumbling archway to keep from falling into a moment. I stood and placed my palms against the wall, screaming while putting my energy into bringing down the walls around us.

"Raven!" River shouted, standing and lurching at me. "We cannot destroy the Time-Antre! Celestina created it!"

My eyebrows knitted together as I stared at him. He grabbed my hands away from the wall and ducked his head as part of the ceiling above us fell. "She created it after I was taken! She tried to use it to find me. We can't break it apart, Raven. It's how I visit her; how I see her again."

Tears welled in his eyes, and his voice shook with emotion as he pleaded with me. I cradled his face in my hands. "River, you don't need to revisit the past anymore. We're together now. She wouldn't want you to fill your time with regret."

"I have to see her, Raven. I can't..."

Silas had found his footing again, dodging falling stones and jumping over cracks. We were quickly running out of time. "River, you have to fight for the life we have now. We can make new memories, River. Together. It is what she would want. She would want us to be happy together."

He looked down the crumbling hallway, his hesitancy evident, but his eyes widened when the Antre began tearing apart on each side. "We're going to get stuck in here, Raven. It'll throw us into whatever is left before it crumbles."

Zeke. I had to get back to Zeke.

Shifting into Frost, I shot ice across the ground toward Silas, watching gleefully as he slipped. But the glee was short-lived as the ground leading into our present moment cracked and split. River kept me from falling into the crevice of the void, shouting at me to create a bridge.

"I don't have that kind of power, River!"

"Do it!" he shouted.

Swallowing, I held my hands out. Ice exploded from my palms but created a shelf that only reached halfway across the split. River didn't let me try again before he grabbed my hand and tugged me across the dissipating bridge. "Jump!"

Closing my eyes, I kept his hand in mine and leaped.

A few seconds felt like a lifetime before we painfully landed in a heap on the hard stone ground, skidding across the broken rock. Blood poured from my nose, and River couldn't even stand as he shot out a hand to turn my ice into water right before Silas could cross it.

Silas wobbled and stumbled backward to prevent himself from falling into the emptiness. Blood was dripping down my mouth and neck, but I held his savage gaze with my victorious one. Behind me, River was crawling toward our moment, but before I followed him in, I wiped the blood with the back of my sleeve and placed my hand against our archway.

Shifting into Terra, I glanced at Silas once more as the stones tumbled down and the entrance to our moment became smaller. "Do you want to know the difference between me then and me now?" I shouted across the void.

He paced the jagged ledge, his nostrils flaring at the scent of my blood only feet away from him.

When I was confident he could not reach our moment even if he managed to make it across the ledge, I removed my hand from the archway. "I fight back."

His growl of defeat echoing off the crumbling walls was the last thing I heard before I slid into our moment until it was nothing but rubble.

I ROLLED MY EYES. "DO NOT FEED ME YOUR LIES, HALF-BREED."

57

Zeke

The second I saw Raven appear through wisps of smoke, I lunged for her and threw my arms tightly around her. The pressure made her cry out, but I didn't care. I wanted to strangle her for what she did but never let her go again, and when I saw her face covered in blood, I wanted to return to the Time-Antre and kill Silas.

"Broken," she rasped, placing her hand over her nose—her beautiful, perfect nose that was bleeding so much it soaked through my shirt.

Jeanine was beside me in an instant, but when I tried to shield Raven from her out of fear that she only wanted her blood, Jeanine shoved me back a step with surprising force and held Raven's wrist still against her nose. "I can fix it, but it's going to hurt like a bitch. Zeke, stand behind her."

Grabbing Raven from behind, I pinned her arms by her side while Jeanine placed two fingers on the bridge of Raven's nose. And when Jeanine looked at me, I tightened my hold on Raven only a second before two cracks echoed through her skull.

Raven screamed and then fainted.

I cradled her in my arms and tried to shake her awake, but when I glanced up at Jeanine, she was staring at the blood covering her hands, her blue eyes showering with drops of red down her irises.

"River!" I shouted, backing away from Jeanine with Raven in my arms.

River, who had been beside Damiana on the ground, Arrowed in front of Jeanine and grabbed her shoulders. Jeanine shoved him hard enough that he flew backward and hit the stone wall of the cave.

With the wind knocked out of him and Raven passed out in my arms, I called for Jeanine to look at me. The red had almost wholly overtaken the blue in her eyes, and her focus on my wife made me uneasy.

"Jeanine, fight it! You have to fight it."

But as she was about to brush her fingertips across her lips, River leaped across the space between them and knocked her hand away. And I watched in awe and terror as their bodies blurred from their swift movements, as River fought to keep Jeanine from tasting Raven's blood under duress. I witnessed precisely what Damiana warned us about.

Their strength was a mirror of one another's.

Backing away, I gently laid Raven's body beside Damiana's. Damiana hadn't woken up yet, and I feared she was dying. Raven needed to wake and heal Damiana before we lost her.

I took a deep breath and braved getting between a Fae and an Undead as they battled each other, both too stubborn to stop. Their hatred for one another was palpable, and when Jeanine accidentally hit me instead of River, she exerted a frustrated scream at my interference. "You have to stop!" I shouted at them, holding a palm against River's chest.

To be honest, I was terrified of Jeanine's strength.

"Let him wash your hands off, Jeanine. Your intake of blood needs to be controlled and watched. Your first taste cannot be of Raven's blood."

Chest heaving, she looked at Raven unconscious on the ground and then at her hands, internally warring with herself. River shoved my hand off and took Jeanine's distraction to shoot a blast of water at her, most likely harder than needed.

I sighed, running a hand down my face. The blood from her hands was gone, but the glare on her face had returned as she balled her fists at her sides. I blocked River from getting to her, shaking my head. "Jeanine, we need him, as much as I hate to say it."

"He is *using* her!" she bellowed, her voice echoing off the cave walls.

I hung my head with a slight nod. "I know, Jeanine. I know. But we cannot defeat Silas without him. He can help you control your urges. You don't have to like him, but you do have to tolerate him until this is over. And you *have* to feed, Jeanine."

When Raven whimpered from where she was laying, I left them to either kill one another or temporarily call a truce while I returned to her side. With her palm against her forehead, she groaned from the pain. I sat on the ground beside her and pulled her into my lap. "Baby, breathe. I am growing tired of bruises on your body from other men."

I attempted to wipe the drying blood from her face with my shirt, but she weakly pushed my hands off. "Hurts," she muttered.

"I know, Raven, but if I don't get this off you, there's a good chance Jeanine will devour you."

River, having removed his shirt, handed it to me. It was doused with water and dripping onto her skin. Nodding with gratitude, I gently cleaned the blood from her face and neck. "Baby, I need you to heal Damiana."

Her eyes flew open. Dazed and cloudy, she looked around the cave for Damiana, crying her name, when she realized she was lying beside her. Crawling away from me, she placed her palms against Damiana's chest. And with eyes closed, we all waited with held breaths while Raven pushed healing into Damiana's body.

"I can't feel her!" Raven cried, sliding a hand up Damiana's neck to press two fingers against her pulse. "It's weak, Zeke, and she's not waking up!"

Placing my hand on the small of Raven's back to calm her, I focused on Damiana's mind and pushed in. It was dark, but I followed a silver strand and tugged. Damiana gasped, her eyes blinking open, but even after she woke up, her pulse didn't quicken.

"Damiana," Raven whispered, holding one of her hands between hers. "Damiana, we're back in Seolia. I destroyed the Time-Antre, Damiana. I bought us some more time, so I need you to return to the castle with me so we can get you home."

Damiana blinked, her shimmering eyes focusing on Raven. "Twins," Damiana sputtered, coughing.

Raven nodded and motioned for River to come over, but Damiana shook her head. Shakily, Damiana raised a hand and pointed toward me. "Twins."

"I don't understand," Raven said, shaking her head. "What do you mean?"

Damiana slid her hand out and pushed one of Raven's hands toward me. "Twins born of darkness," she scratched, the movements of her chest slowing.

Of course.

The twins born of darkness were assumed to be River and Raven, but we hadn't thought of the other possibility. "Raven," I said gently, grabbing her hand. "Baby, we are the twins born of darkness."

Raven whipped her head toward me, recognition ghosting across her eyes. "Our deaths. Our rebirth."

"You came back to this timeline for a reason," River said from behind me. "Your strand is what was prophesied. The two of you will be what restores magic to the lands."

"You knew," I said, not needing to look at River to know I was right. "You knew it wasn't about you and Raven."

"Baldwin," Damiana whispered, her eyes fluttering closed. "Ezekiel... Baldwin."

Raven shook her head, blubbering Damiana's name and begging her to stay, but as I felt Damiana's energy wane, I grabbed her hand

and nodded. "I will ensure you return to Baldwin, Damiana. I promise."

Raven shook her head wildly. "No!" she shouted, placing her palms against Damiana to shove more healing into her. "No! Edmund and Gisela cannot lose you!"

"Raven." I ran a hand down her hair. "Baby, stop. She's at peace, Raven, I promise. I feel her."

Raven crumbled, resting her head against Damiana's stomach while keeping her hands against her chest. "No," she squeaked, her body trembling. "No, we didn't lose her. She did not die trying to save me, Zeke. I can't tell Edmund that he lost his mother because of me."

"Raven, she died protecting someone she loves." I wiped my tears away with the back of my hand. Damiana had been like a mother to me; she had opened her home during some of my darkest days. And the more I thought about the profound loss of someone like her, the less encouraging words I could find.

River lowered to kneel on the other side of Damiana's body and placed his hands over Raven's. He said nothing because there weren't words that could convey the pain of losing her.

Jeanine crouched beside Raven and pulled her off Damiana's body to rest against her chest, holding her still as she sobbed and screamed. And it was Jeanine who looked at me and said, "I will stay here while you retrieve Edmund, Zeke. He is in my former chambers."

I looked at Raven in her arms, hesitant to leave her here with someone who thirsted for her blood. But Jeanine shook her head at me, kissing the top of Raven's head as tears fell from her eyes from the pain her best friend was experiencing. "She is safe here, Zeke. River will stop me. Go."

Heartbroken and woefully, I looked once more at Damiana and revisited the dozens of memories I had made with her over the years. The last words I exchanged with her were full of anger and frustration, and I silently prayed that wherever she was, she knew how much I truly admired her.

And now I had the task of telling my best friend that he would never have a chance to embrace his mother again. Gisela would have to live without her mother. And Baldwin. I clutched my chest at the realization that Baldwin would be without his mate.

Because she saved mine.

Swiping a hand down my face to clear the tears, I pulled whatever remnants of strength I had left and leaned over, kissing Raven's temple. "I'll be right back, my love."

She couldn't speak, her sobs mangled and raspy from having nothing left to give. And this was only the beginning of our losses. I looked at River, and he nodded in confirmation that he would protect his twin, which he assured me of when he lowered the shield blocking his emotions.

Concern. Sadness. And as he stared at Raven... love.

Genuine love. River loved his sister, and he gifted me with confirmation.

When I left the caves, I did not miss the cat sitting between the trees, the green eyes shining in the moonlight, and mewling as if in mourning. Nor did I miss the speckled owl with golden eyes flapping its wings as it landed on a branch above me.

"Thank you," I whispered.

In the end, both Celestina and Damiana returned to their island after all.

I STOOD outside Edmund's door, trying to convince myself that I could do this — I could inform him of Damiana's death. I could stand here while he broke down and tried to explain that she sacrificed herself for Raven. That, once again, the ones we loved continued giving their all for my bond.

But when Luca came down the hall and saw me covered in blood, he immediately rushed toward me and shook my shoulders, asking me what happened, if Raven was okay, and why I was covered in blood and shaking. "Damiana," I whispered, covering my mouth with my fist as the loss further cemented in my chest. "Caves."

Luca asked nothing else, leaving me to stand alone once more as he ran down the hallway and out the castle door. Clenching and unclenching my fists, I knocked twice on Edmund's door.

Edmund opened it quickly, dressed and ready to attend River's lesson on Arrowing. Though Edmund possessed no magic, he was always prepared to stand by and give us support. But when he saw me covered in blood, he sighed deeply. "Ezekiel, why am I always faced with the consequences of your fighting? I refuse to get my hands dirty, but I will assist you in finding a location for the body."

I tried to smile. Honestly, I tried to find the humor in his words from the countless memories of him seeing me in the village of Thoya, drunk and arguing with someone just so I could feel something. But right now, standing here and staring at the man who had kept me from completely losing myself before meeting Raven, I felt nothing but heartache.

"Edmund," I began, shaking my head slightly.

Concern flooded his body as he stepped out into the hallway and looked around. "Is it Raven? How can I help, Ezekiel? Where is she?"

"It's not Raven," I rasped, vision blurring from tears. "It's not Raven, Edmund."

Slowly, painstakingly, realization crossed his eyes. "No," he said, shaking his head. "No."

"Edmund," I grabbed his shoulder with one hand and drew in a deep breath to steady my stuttering, "Edmund, something happened. It is hard to explain, but your mother..." Trailing off, I had to recompose myself as tears immediately filled his eyes, "Edmund, she was protecting Raven from Silas, and..."

"Where is she?" he interrupted.

"Within the caves of the Black Forest."

THREE DAYS PASSED by in a blur.

We did not train. We did not beg Jeanine to feed. The night of Damiana's death, we bathed and boarded a ship with Edmund and Damiana's body and sailed back to Thoya. Edmund was inconsolable, staying beside his mother's body for the trip and only allowing Raven below deck to keep him fed. He would only allow himself to sleep with his head in her lap, and she would rest against my shoulder until he started to stir, which was when I would return above deck to allow him the space he needed to heal.

And now, as we were standing on the deck of our ship against a dock in Thoya, Edmund's task was to inform his father of the loss. Damiana's body was escorted from the ship, covered in a cloth of ivory and gold embellishments.

Damiana had remained on the throne of Thoya for decades, using a combination of Petra's magic and her own to keep her long reign without anyone asking questions. Without her, the people of Thoya would feel her loss for years to come. While she was once a witch in a coven on the island of Seolia, her heart had found a new home here with her mate and her children, protecting the kingdom from invaders.

And now, accompanied by her death, came the breakdown of the shields she had maintained for years. Thoya had lost its fiercest protector and would now be at risk of the Undead and other creatures finding this untouched kingdom.

But being mated, Baldwin had already felt her death. He had felt the snap of their bond as she took her last breath. After not being able to practice magic for so long, he had lost his ability to travel like Silas and River, having to wait until we sailed back with Damiana's body. It was immediately apparent that he hadn't rested. And when Gisela came running down the dock, it was straight into Raven's arms.

Raven held her tightly as Damiana's body was removed from the ship. She sank to the floor while Gisela sobbed in her arms, crying for her mother, and when Raven asked me to please carry Gisela back to the castle, I did not question her. I scooped Gisela up in my arms and followed my wife to the front gates of the castle, where black flags flew above mourning bystanders.

While preparations were made for saying goodbye to Damiana's body, I took solace in believing her soul lived on our island, joined once again by the witches of her coven. But as I stood in the courtyard of the castle, surrounded by the people of Thoya, as Damiana's casket was lowered into the ground, covered in the flags of Thoya and Seolia, I mourned.

⁓

WE SAT in silence around a table in Edmund's sitting room — the room Raven had fallen in love with the first time she entered the castle. It was mid-afternoon, the day after we said goodbye to Damiana, but unlike the ordinary sunny afternoons of Thoya, it was cloudy and gray outside, the gloomy weather casting a dark light in the room.

The silence was deafening because we didn't have time to mourn and revisit our great memories of Damiana. We had a war to plan, and now more than ever, we owed it to Damiana to finish this fight.

It was already personal for Edmund since Silas wanted Raven—he viewed Raven as part of his family—but now it had awoken vengeance in him for the loss of his mother.

River, who was now able to travel to Thoya without losing his magic, sat beside us. Raven rested against my chest in my lap, her face reflecting the dried tears that had not stopped falling since Damiana's death. Loss was becoming so prevalent in our lives that the numbness coursing through her body no longer frightened me.

We had not yet discussed Damiana's confession—that we were the twins born of darkness, but we were both highly aware that the misery that had been following us wasn't going anywhere anytime soon.

Gisela entered the room and sat in a chair next to Edmund, wiping the tears from her face with an ivory handkerchief. "He won't eat," she said to Edmund, sniffling. "I keep trying."

I pressed my lips against the crook of Raven's neck and closed my eyes. My chest felt heavy from the idea of losing her and the pain I knew Baldwin must be experiencing.

Edmund, now faced with avenging his mother and ruling a kingdom while his father mourned, rolled his head against the chair to look at his sister. "Time, Gisela. He just needs time."

But I knew from experience that time would never heal the hole left by losing his mate. Weeks away from Raven nearly ate me alive. There would never be a remedy for losing part of your soul.

"I can speak with him," I offered. "The two of us are similar in ways many others are not."

When Edmund nodded, Gisela rose from her chair and waited for me to kiss Raven before I followed her into the hallway. Feeling her warmth behind me, I looked over my shoulder to see Raven watching me from the doorway, and when she mouthed that she loved me, I pushed into her mind and returned the sentiment.

We did not break our gaze until Gisela turned into another corridor, leading me into her father's study. I had been in here before during one of my visits when Baldwin lectured Edmund and me on the correct way to bet on horse racing, which didn't include thousands of gold coins.

Baldwin sat in his leather chair, facing a wall that held a large portrait of Damiana. Gisela said his name, but he did not turn. I touched her shoulder gently and nodded toward the door, but she briefly hesitated. "Go, Gisela. Take Raven and eat. I'll find you in a little while."

I waited until she left before I sat in one of the chairs in front of Baldwin's desk. Moments passed before he finally broke his stare with Damiana's portrait and turned in his chair to face me. "I have many regrets, Ezekiel."

I silently waited for more. I had never loved anyone as I loved Raven. I had never mourned to the lengths of which Baldwin was now mourning his wife. My heart was never split apart the way his must've been when he felt the crack in their bond, so I could not fathom the grief he had been experiencing in the last few days.

But I did recognize the tormented expression on his face; it was the same as the one on my face when I had learned of Raven's abduction—the way fear and regret had gripped me so tightly that I wasn't sure I would ever breathe steadily again. Even now, sitting in a room away from her was strapping our bond so rigidly that the amount of strength I needed to muster to remain sitting still should be accompanied by a round of applause.

I pitied him for the loss he endured. It was one I hoped to never experience.

"Over a century with Damiana, and it still does not feel like we had enough time together." He rested his elbows against the top of his desk. "I am sure you have been made aware of what I am."

I nodded. "An Undead."

"I cannot die," he whispered, "even though I no longer have magic from being out of practice so long, I cannot die unless someone drives a stake through my heart." He covered his chest with his palm. "A heart that no longer serves a purpose without her."

I shook my head slightly. "I will not, Baldwin. I did not come in here to offer you a chance to leave."

He banged his fist on the desk. "She sacrificed herself for your mate! The least you could do is allow me to follow her in death."

"But you will not follow her in death, Baldwin. The Undead are viewed as demons. If I killed you, it would only eliminate your pain while Edmund and Gisela are left here to suffer."

"I am already in hell, Ezekiel."

"You will not do that to your children, Baldwin. You will honor Damiana's memory by finishing this war with us. If you wish to die, it will not be by my hand."

"I betrayed her!" The strain in his voice made me flinch slightly. "I betrayed her many times! I took the blood of others! I could not stop; without her blood, I will wither until I feed!"

All the meals I had watched him consume over the years had simply been for appearances. "Gisela needs to know what you are, Baldwin. Edmund has been made aware, but Gisela is struggling."

His features softened. "She is my girl. I cannot tell her about the monster I am. I cannot break her heart."

"Her heart is already broken. Becoming well for her will aid in mending it. Thrusting your death upon their grief will tear her apart."

He sank back against his chair, looking every part the broken and dismayed man. He did not possess the beauty of the Undead, having spent so many years within Damiana's shield without magic. "I knew you once, long ago."

I shifted uncomfortably in my chair.

"You speak of honoring Damiana's death, yet you won't do what we have been waiting for. It has been over a century, Ezekiel, over a century of waiting for you and Raven to return."

Resting my elbow on the arm of the chair, I placed my forehead against the palm of my hand. Nothing about hearing of my past in another lifetime would ever feel normal, and still none of it made sense to me. It seemed implausible that we had existed before—that

575

our realm depended on the magic we still could not recognize within ourselves.

"You want to make this right?" From the corner of my eye, Baldwin leaned forward. "Then you work on freeing your shadows. You have nothing left standing in the way with the loss of Damiana's shields. Your magic was directly tied to them."

I glanced up in confusion.

"She created the second shield the day you and Raven came to our kingdom many years ago. And because of it, your magic was bound within hers."

"Raven's magic is freed?" I asked, hopeful.

"Both of your magic is freed," he said, his voice low and full of frustration. "*Both*. You must stop denying this, Ezekiel. The prophecy cannot be fulfilled unless you both find a way to manifest your powers. Do you want to honor Damiana? That's how you can."

My jaw ticked at the idea of being forced to do anything—having to unbind something within myself that I did not want. I did not want to take on this persona that people expected of me. I did not want to risk my wife becoming something others would use simply because of her blood, and I did not like the power I felt while controlling those shadows when we revisited our deaths. The abilities I possessed now had made me arrogant enough. What would wielding shadows do?

But Baldwin hit me with the one factor, the one statement that would change everything. "If you want a chance at protecting your mate against Silas, you must once again become the Phantom Prince."

PART THREE

"YOU MUST ONCE AGAIN BECOME THE PHANTOM PRINCE."

58

ZEKE

"Zeke, you can do this."

I paced in small spurts, my hands hanging loosely on my hips, and my eyes narrowed on River. Raven's eyes gleamed with slight amusement while she watched me from the other side of the clearing. Jeanine was more apparent in her mockery, taunting me while sitting in a tree, her feet dangling idly off a branch.

Since returning from Thoya three days ago, we had been relentlessly working with River. Jeanine was the first one who mastered Arrowing after she finally fed from squirrels. She was slowly working toward eventually needing Raven's blood, which was a mental block for me. Jeanine needed it for strength, but the idea of sharing Raven with anyone had me struggling to push past the wall between me and magic.

And then, Raven mastered Arrowing.

But she was fucking light as a feather. Of course, it was simple for her. It was equivalent to moving a tiny lamb around. I was a lion who desperately wanted to consume the lamb, which led to River sticking Raven clear across the small field.

Whenever I'd try to walk to her, she'd Arrow back a few feet. She wasn't quite graceful yet and would end up falling backward because Raven was nothing if not clumsy. And my need to prevent even the most minor scratch distracted me from the task at hand.

"We're losing daylight," Jeanine taunted, hopping down and brushing her hands off. "I think it's time we try something different."

I knew this trick well and growled loudly from where I was standing as she marched her annoying Undead ass to stand behind my wife. Jeanine had become cockier since feeding, knowing she now possessed immeasurable strength and that I could no longer threaten her.

Because I could not free my shadows.

At least, not yet.

I tried to feed from Raven the night after we returned, but she passed out in my arms from how quickly I inhaled her blood. I did not try again.

And the reason she couldn't manifest Blaze in physical form or turn into a human icicle was apparent—our magic was bound. Damiana had created the shield around Thoya with both of us inside. Unless one of us freed our magic, the other's would remain trapped.

"Zeke, we need to try and move the prisoners tomorrow," River irritatingly reminded me. "If you don't want Raven to be the one to do it, then we need to figure this out."

"I can do it!" Raven argued for the hundredth time since we decided that she would not accompany us to Reales to free the remaining prisoners and prevent Silas and his clan from strengthening from the blood of my people.

I was about to say something when she Arrowed and appeared a few feet away, casually tripping over a rock and stumbling to the side. "Raven, your chaos cannot be controlled," I said, gesturing toward her legs as she tried to find her footing.

She glared at me but did not try to Arrow again. Instead, Jeanine Arrowed behind her and put her hands on Raven's arms. I took a step forward. "Jeanine, do not taunt me with her."

River shook his head. "Jeanine, I would advise against this. Zeke's bloodmating bond is getting out of control. When defending her, he might lose sight of who is on the receiving end."

That was something that *had* changed.

Because of the demolition of Damiana's shields, the veil over bonds in our realm faded away. And now, even just standing on the opposite end of a field from Raven was nearly too much to bear. I could smell her blood from where I stood, and my need for her seemed to strengthen by the day. And when I stepped toward them, Jeanine wrapped an arm around Raven's waist and Arrowed away with her.

River bristled. "She's two steps ahead. I didn't teach her how to Arrow with someone."

Wrapping my wife's braid around her wrist, Jeanine tugged Raven's head back. I bared my teeth. Raven closed her eyes to either brace herself for a bite or ignore my reaction. "Jeanine," I warned, clenching my fists. "Don't."

She peeled her top lip back, and from where I stood, I saw the tip of her tongue prime the glistening brightness of her fangs. And each time I moved toward them, she'd Arrow farther into the forest.

Inch by tortuous inch, Jeanine closed the gap between her canines and Raven's throat. Raven's face twisted at the breath against her neck, balling the bottom of her shirt in her hands from nerves. And the fear and tension in her body called to me, awakening the darkness in my chest that yearned for her.

Closing my eyes, I listened to River's instructions.

I held a picture in my mind of where I wanted to go. I had Raven in the center, I remained angry and jealous of the hands on her, and then I just...

Vanished.

It was quicker than falling asleep.

Everything blurred around me as if I were flying. And when I landed in front of Raven, it was much steadier than I could have hoped. Jeanine startled, especially when I placed my palm against her forehead to shove her head away from Raven's throat.

"Move," I spoke calmly but sternly.

Instead of making it easy, Jeanine tested me by placing a feathery kiss against Raven's throat. It happened in an instant — the way I pushed Raven behind me, black shrouding my vision until there was nothing but rage. Jeanine's smug smirk nearly sent me over before River Arrowed between us.

Still brimming with hatred for him, Jeanine stepped back to maintain enough distance between them while Raven moved in front of me and placed her palms against my chest. "You're pushing boundaries, Jeanine," I snarled, not missing the way Raven pressed the entire weight of her body against me as if her minuscule frame could stop me.

Jeanine shrugged her shoulders. "Don't I always?"

"We need a break," Raven said. "He needs to walk away."

"We don't have time for breaks," River argued. "Zeke needs to be confident enough in Arrowing by tomorrow night, Raven."

Raven turned but remained against me. "He needs a break," she repeated. "Even he can only tolerate so much before it becomes too much."

"He has to try feeding from you again," Jeanine reminded us, much to my dismay, and then looked at me. "You agreed to try tonight."

"You shouldn't speak to me right now," I growled.

"Okay," Raven intervened, shoving at my chest to get me to move. "I am going to feed Vampy, and then we'll reconvene tonight after we attempt... that."

I loathed that nickname, but it had spread through our family like wildfire, and now everyone used it when I was angry.

River sighed but nodded. "Jeanine needs to feed, too, to maintain her strength. She'll need a drop of your blood tomorrow night."

Before I could move, Raven lunged at me until I had to pick her up to keep her from falling. She placed her palms on my face and held my gaze. "Breathe," she said. "There are no enemies here."

The temptation to Arrow away with her to a secluded island for the rest of time was eating away at me. But as always, the tenderness of her kiss released some of the tension I was holding in my chest until I could focus on only her. "Duck's."

She slid down my body. "Duck's."

~

I DIDN'T NEED to eat.

I only hungered for her, but I did want the rum that Arthur poured into my glass while we piled around a table in the center of the room. We bumped into Luca on the way here. He, too, had attended some training sessions with River, but John still wasn't fully recovered, so Luca spent most of his time helping with John's regular duties.

"I need to speak with Godfrey," I said, taking a long sip from my glass. "I haven't been able to since Damiana shared with us that Petra is his mate."

"His secrecy does not make him an enemy," Raven reminded me. "They all felt they had reasons for hiding these things from us."

"These life-altering things?" I scoffed. "I will never understand that, Raven. Wanting you to grow up with some normalcy? I understand that. Hiding it for as long as they did? That I cannot."

"They needed to be sure I would live past my twenty-fifth birthday," she said softly. "We passed through so many lifetimes that they had the right to be weary, Zeke."

I brushed my fingers across her jawline. "Damiana's death does not excuse their actions, Raven."

Frowning, she leaned into my touch. "I know."

"He's right," Luca said. "Petra could've provided stability, Raven."

"She couldn't have taken me without question," Raven countered. "Leonidas wouldn't have simply given me over to anyone from what Zeke told me of my mother's death. He wanted to use me."

"You still deserve an apology, Raven." I pulled her into my lap and kissed her shoulder. "Am I upset by how things worked out? Of course not. Our love was strong enough to break shields. I wouldn't change anything about how we found one another, but I believe your life could've been much simpler if you had someone there who could help you with your magic. You wouldn't have felt so alone."

She finished my rum. "I wasn't alone, Zeke. Isla gave me a home and family. Godfrey kept me alive, and John ensured my place on the throne. I was always watched and protected. You're just upset because you would've done it differently."

"I am doing it differently." I took the glass from her hands after Arthur refilled it, tipped it back before she could, and nearly choked on a laugh when I saw her scowl. "If anyone wants you, they'll have to go through me."

She rolled her eyes. "So, I will return to being alone then?"

Leaning up, I tugged her earlobe between my teeth before whispering, "I am more than enough for you."

She shivered in my hold, and I grinned as the scent of her arousal filled my nostrils—another result of our pairing. It happened often and quickly became my favorite scent. No one mentioned anything about the change, so I hoped that meant this was something only I could pick up on.

But my joy was quickly dampened when Jeanine and River strode in. Arthur welcomed them in, but I tightened my arm around Raven's waist and pulled her down to rest against my chest.

Jeanine's eyes were glowing a bright blue, signaling that she had fed . When she hungered, drops of red or gold would cover her irises. Arthur hadn't asked why Jeanine looked different, but that was simply because he didn't care. To him, we would always be the misfits who drank too much and bled his bar dry. And even though the Undead didn't need anything other than blood, Jeanine still inhaled rum like it would be the last time she ever did—but she never became drunk.

I envied her.

River motioned for us to follow him outside, but I shook my head. "I'm done until Raven falls asleep. I'll work with you after she rests."

Raven huffed. "I still think it's unfair that I need sleep if I'm immortal. Jeanine has a beating heart, and she doesn't need sleep."

"Perks of the Undead," River said. "It's unexplainable. No one has ever figured out how the Undead can breathe and have beating hearts but survive off of only blood and retain strength."

Jeanine glared at him. "There are no perks to being Undead, River. I am a demon because of you."

"That never gets old," River muttered.

"Remember when we all used to get along?" Raven asked, looking around the table but then giving River an apologetic grin. "You probably don't."

Luca changed the subject. "What is your plan for tomorrow night?"

"We will Arrow to the dungeon of Reales," River explained. "Since all three of us have been inside, it shouldn't be an issue. We will Arrow back and forth to Seolia with prisoners."

"And if you get caught?" Raven asked.

"We shouldn't be," River explained. "I know their feasting hours. Louis will prepare bodies to be drained in the early hours of the morning."

I sensed Raven's anxiety and kissed her shoulder. "We'll be fine, Raven. I plan to work on Arrowing with River all night."

"I still think I should come with you," she said. "I could help. I can carry people back, too."

River shook his head even before I could. "You'll be too much of a distraction for Zeke. He needs keep his focus on rescuing, and not whether you've wandered off or been discovered by one of Silas's followers."

"What if I promise not to wander?" Raven asked hopefully. "Then could I go?"

"No," Jeanine and I answered in unison.

Raven's shoulders slumped.

"Stay here, baby. Help the ones we bring back understand what's happening. They'll be disoriented and most likely starved."

"Not starved," River interjected, wincing. "They've been keeping them well-fed. The healthier their bodies—"

"The healthier their blood," Jeanine muttered.

"And how many are left?" Luca asked.

River tipped his chin up, running numbers in his head. "The prisoners were spread throughout three dungeons. The one underneath the castle and two of the towers. The Undead moved so quickly that no one had a chance to escape the kingdom. Before I left, they had gone through maybe half the town."

"So... hundreds," Raven said, her body refilling with anxiousness. "Hundreds of people to be saved between only the three of you."

"Arrowing is the quickest method of traveling," River assured her. "If we each take two at a time, it will not take us long. However, once the Undead realize we've taken their food source, it will bring war forth much quicker. The blood is healthy in Reales, but they can only survive off of it for a few days before they hunger again. They're greedy and have become too comfortable with having blood at their disposal."

Luca's face twisted in disgust. "I never thought I'd miss when our conversations only consisted of Zeke's obsession with Raven."

I grinned. "I am more than happy to provide that for you, Luca. I never tire of speaking about how *delicious* I find her."

The three of them groaned while Raven placed her palm over my mouth. "I need to take him back to the castle to satisfy his, um, hunger," she stuttered, clearing her throat. "I won't keep him too long."

"Visualize them," River said to me. "It might help. And don't take your time."

I grabbed the half-empty bottle of rum from the center of the table and tucked Raven under my other arm, saying nothing else as we left Duck's. "I can't fucking stand that guy," I muttered.

Raven giggled, patting my stomach. "Take your hatred out on me, my love. I'll benefit greatly from it."

I NEVER THOUGHT I'D MISS WHEN OUR CONVERSATIONS ONLY CONSISTED OF ZEKE'S OBSESSION WITH RAVEN.

59

ZEKE

Raven and I were standing inside our chambers after bathing, staring at one another and contemplating how we could try this again. I had to try and drink enough from her to unbind our magic, but not so much that she would pass out.

Raven cleared her throat, and I smiled at the bashful way her cheeks filled with red. "I think this time shouldn't consist of you fucking me while trying it. Since the blood rushes to my head, it might kill me."

She was joking, but I frowned. She sighed, running a hand through her hair. "Zeke, you can do this. You Arrowed today! If we can both figure out how to do that, we can master this, too."

"Moving from one side of the clearing to the other is not the same as drinking blood from you, Raven." My mouth dried at just the mention of tasting her again. "I could very well kill you."

She rolled her eyes. "You won't kill me. I was being dramatic." Lighting her fingers with flames, she wiggled them back and forth. "We need to free Blaze again, and we don't have time to travel to The Forest Beyond to attempt it there."

I shook my head. "I don't want to go back there."

She quirked a brow. "You're going to have to tell me one day what happened to you in that forest."

"Let's just say if the Fae are anything like what guards them, I will encourage you not to unseal the forest."

"Noted," she said with a sweet smile. "Now, come here. Whether or not you unbind us tonight, you still need to drink." She gestured to the length of her body. "I'll even stay fully clothed to prevent you from fucking me."

I smirked, leaning against the doorframe with arms crossed. "Nothing could ever prevent me from fucking you, Raven."

She sat in one of the chairs around our table, hooking her finger to motion me over to her. "Come on, Vampy. Bite."

I scowled. "I wish you'd stop calling me that."

She stomped her foot. "Stop stalling."

I could've continued stalling. When protecting her, I had self-control and could stop myself from unraveling her. But that was before the shield broke, before I started to feel the depths of our bond. And the curse against our strand seemed to make my draw to her even stronger, as if consuming her blood convinced me that nothing would ever get between us. I owned her.

And when she tilted her head, straining her neck, I clenched my fists at the sound of her blood moving through her. Closing my eyes, I just listened for a moment. Her blood sounded like waves crashing through her body most of the time—a result of her constantly moving—but on nights like this, when it was just us, the sounds were that of a calm stream.

It had become my favorite sound.

These moments with her belonged to me.

Raven was chaos around everyone else.

But with me, she was always just my Raven.

Opening my eyes, I smiled at how the moonlight reflected in hers. We may not speak about it as often, but my obsession with her remained just as extreme as before. She was still the absolute center of every move I made and every breath I took.

And patiently, she waited while I concentrated solely on how much I loved her instead of the anxiousness of possibly harming her by doing this.

She believed in me. And for her, I would try.

Kneeling in front of her, I slid my hands up her thighs and contemplated how I could bargain with her to allow me to have her while drinking, but she was right. It might be safer this way.

She did, however, allow me to kiss her.

A deep, lasting kiss. An apology for what was about to happen, a promise that I'd try, and a reminder that no matter what happened, nothing would ever change between us.

"I love you," I whispered against her lips, drawing in the breath she released.

"I know," she promised, kissing me softly.

Snaking one arm around her waist, I brought her closer until her knees rested against either side of my hips. The proximity between us caused nothing but lust to fill her body, and I chuckled. "That isn't helping, Raven."

"Sorry," she squeaked, flicking her eyes toward the ceiling to keep them off me. "You could at least put a shirt on. I at least had the decency to dress—"

"Stop talking," I demanded, ignoring the need to *make* her stop. "You know I love nothing more than shutting you up." Bracing my hand against her neck, my thumb rested against her jaw and she leaned into my touch.

I ran my tongue across the roof of my mouth at the sound of the pulse drumming quickly in her throat, matching the one inside my chest. The anticipation alone was euphoric. And when her chest stopped moving, I whispered, "Breathe."

She released a tight breath.

I primed the spot between her shoulder and throat with a lick, and she shivered. I would have to ignore her body's reactions to mine if I was going to make it through this without burying myself inside her. I kissed her skin in a warning.

And then, I bit.

The first drop of blood sent me into a frenzy, a state of ecstasy—a universe where only she and I existed together, a binding so deep and vital that I felt it, felt her, everywhere. And I plummeted so deep within it, chasing the tie between us, that I wasn't aware of how quickly I was pulling blood from her.

And when blackness filled my veins, my shoulders and arms appeared as webs of interlaced shadows. They pulsed and moved, wanting her. They always swam directly toward wherever she was as if wanting to leave me and enter into her.

And gods, her whimpers. Her moans as I squeezed her hip in a nearly bone-shattering grip. I drank so much that her blood dripped down my chin and across her skin, the bitterness of the rum she drank mixed with her blood's sweet nectar. But no matter how much I pulled, no matter how much her pulse slowed, it was never enough.

I always wanted more.

And instead of asking me to stop or slow down, she rasped, "I need you."

We shouldn't. I knew that. Right at the very edges of my mind, I knew it would be dangerous for her, but I didn't stop her from shoving my pants down, nor did I prevent myself from raising her dress to rest around her waist and allow her to slide off the chair and onto my swollen cock.

Bloodlust.

This was the absolute definition of it. There would never be a feeling more fantastic than the one I felt while simultaneously consuming her blood and being so deep inside her that she groaned from the pain.

She rolled her hips against me repeatedly, and I drank more. I pulled so much so fast that even I became lightheaded, clawing at her shoulders as I bucked into her, meeting her thrust for thrust.

And the shadows, they shoved at my skin. They filled my fingers until they were nothing but black.

But when she breathily said my name as she shattered around me, spurring my own release, I realized what I had done as her head fell limp against my shoulder. Putting my fist against my lips as I released her from my bite, I shook her body slightly. "Raven," I rasped, cleaning the blood from my lips and grabbing her chin. "Baby, wake up, please, please."

Standing with her in my arms, I sloppily made it to our bed and laid her down. Blood covered her neck and shoulder, the bite mark deep and buried underneath a pool of blood.

And the shadows in my skin faded.

SHE WOKE up within moments to find me staring at her in shame and fatigue—not physically. Physically, I felt stronger than ever before. Mentally, however, I was exhausted. "It's not going to work, Raven."

She opened her mouth to argue, but I stopped her. "Raven, it's not going to work. With our bond as strong as it is, we can't resist our desires for one another, and it ends with you like this." I motioned toward her tired body, her neck still covered in dried blood. "For all we know, I'll need every drop in your body to free these godsdamn shadows, and that's not a theory I'm willing to test."

With considerable effort to appear as if the bite didn't sting as it healed, she raised up to her palm. "The prophecy said it's up to us to restore magic, Zeke, and we can't do that with Silas alive."

I nodded, looking out the open doors of our balcony. It was nightfall, and River would expect me in the forest soon to continue practicing for tomorrow night. "I know, baby, but we'll have to kill him without my shadows, without Blaze in her physical form. I can't continue drinking from you until you faint. Especially when there's no guarantee it'll work."

Shifting into Frost, she stared at her fingertips with a frown. Without powerful emotions, she couldn't will the ice past her fingertips. "Neither of us will ever reach our full potential." And then her eyes shimmered with tears. "We won't know if you're immortal."

"Hey," I whispered, grabbing her thighs and dragging her closer. "Raven, we will live a very long, blissfully miserable life together."

"But there will come a time when you're gone," she rasped,

burying her face against my throat. "And I can't live knowing that, Zeke. I won't."

I kissed her temple. "I promise to try again after this is all over, Raven. I won't give up spending an eternity with you so easily."

"He said we can't have children, Zeke." She sniffled and raised her head. "In the forest, Silas said we couldn't."

I brushed the tears away from her cheeks. "We have a son, Raven. He might not be with us right now, but he will return. I have no doubt about that, my love. Please believe me." I hesitated before I said, "I can show him to you if you'd like."

She blinked, her eyes searching mine. "How?"

"Your nightmare I shattered before I left for Nova was of him, Raven. You didn't want to leave him there, but it wasn't real, so I had to bring you back. I..." I cleared my throat to swallow the burning lump in my throat, "I didn't see him. I knew that if I looked at him, I would want to stay, too."

She smiled, wiping a tear away from my eye with the back of her hand. "Show him to me."

Moving to sit behind her, I rested against the headboard before I pulled her in to lay against my chest. She lazily drew shapes on my thighs with her fingers while I kept my lips pressed against her hair, bracing myself for who we were about to visit.

"It's not real," I reminded her. "I'll create the dream for us, Raven, but we cannot stay there." I nudged her head with my shoulder until she dropped it down to look at me. "Promise me you understand, Raven. I can't do this unless you promise."

I sensed the war within her and waited.

It took a moment for her to nod, her chest moving from the long breath she drew to steady herself. "I promise. But don't I need to be asleep?"

I grinned slightly. "You will be." Softly, I brushed my fingertips down her arms. "Close your eyes."

She did as I said, relaxing against me with her eyes closed. And she didn't even flinch as I pushed into her mind and soothed it with mine, slowly knitting them together. And then, I sang.

I hummed the melody mind to mind—the song I had always known yet didn't know why. And she gasped when she heard my voice in her mind, her hands squeezing my thighs. "That's so beautiful," she whispered.

Smiling, I shushed her until she relaxed again, her fingers loosening. And when it was nothing but the notes of the soft melody passing between our minds, the hushed whimper told me she had fallen asleep. "My love," I murmured, but she didn't stir.

Hesitating briefly, I silently reminded her of her promise she made before I cast forward the black room that haunted us in every one of her nightmares, stitching the one with our son back together piece by piece.

And I waited.

～

GRACEFULLY, Raven appeared from the darkness. Recognizing the room as the place Morana always found us in, she looked around fearfully until she noticed me waiting for her. Extending my hand to her, she grabbed it quickly and touched my chest with her other. "Real?" she asked in a whisper.

I shook my head. "Not real, baby."

"Why are we here?"

Brushing my fingertips across her jaw, I tilted my head toward the glass pane in the center of the room. "Relax and think, Raven. Who did I tell you we would see here?"

She closed her eyes for only seconds before she squeezed my hand. "Our son."

"And what did you promise me?"

She frowned. "That I wouldn't stay."

I nodded and gently tugged her toward the glass pane. "This is the place that shows your greatest desires and fears, Raven. He won't appear until you ask for him."

"When I was pierced by the arrow, I saw you here." She smiled and touched the glass with her fingertips. "You were my greatest desire then, and now I long for a miniature version of you."

Standing behind her, I locked my arms around her waist. "This will not be easy, Raven, but it is a gift. Just because it is a dream does not mean it won't ever happen. Remember that, and then tell me your heart's greatest desire, my love."

"You," she murmured, lifting one arm to place her hand on my neck. The other remained balanced delicately against the glass. "And a family of our own."

We heard him before we saw him.

Giggles and incoherent noises.

The sounds filled the dark room, spreading warmth across both of us. And if this was all we got, we would've been content with that. But when he came waddling out of the void toward the glass, Raven's hand flew to cover her mouth and tears pooled in my eyes.

He was the most beautiful boy.

And we both sank to the floor as he neared, touching the glass with tears falling down our cheeks. The boy spun in ungraceful circles, stumbling dizzily and blowing raspberries, his lips puckering in the same pout Raven always had.

"Our boy," she cried.

I tilted my head as he waddled closer, my eyebrows knitting together. "He has River's ears."

She laughed loudly and shook her head. "Yes, but also yours. You didn't see the Phantom Prince during our deaths, but your ears were once pointed, too."

Our son of Fae and Vampire heritage was flawless with his wild black hair, pointed ears, and golden skin. And when he made it to the glass pane and slammed his pudgy, tiny hands against it, I chuckled. I was uncontrollably happy at the sight of him—my boy, our son, the perfect combination of the two us.

And I loved him. I ached to hold him.

"Gods, Raven, look at him." I placed one of my hands against his. "Look at what we created."

"Why can't we touch him?"

I ran my other hand down her hair. "Because our minds know, Raven. We'd want to stay here."

She sniffled. "Is he lonely?"

"No, baby." I fully sat on the ground and pulled her to sit between my legs. "He's not real, Raven, not really. It's his soul that lingers within ours." I kissed her cheek. "And how could he ever be lonely with parents who love him so much? We honor his memory every single day, Raven."

"This is what we're fighting for," she breathed.

I nodded, placing my hand over hers against the pane. Our son pressed both of his against the same spot and babbled. "Yes, little demon. This is our future. He is our future. I will not give up."

"Promise me, Zeke. Promise me we'll break the curse and find a way to end this. Promise me we'll see him again, we will have our son in our reality instead of this dream."

"I promise you, Raven. No entity in this universe will ever stop me from having this life with you." I held my wife in my arms as we smiled at our son, my heart full. "This perfect life with our tiny little demon of Fae and Vampire."

"And a little witch someday," she reminded me.

My smile widened into a grin. "Yes, Raven. Anything you want, I'll give you. I promise."

"Now that we have that figured out, we need to work with you on how you can carry someone while Arrowing."

Nodding, I yawned, not from fatigue but from boredom. We had been at this for hours—long enough that dawn was peeking over the horizon. Godfrey had checked in with me once every hour after attending to Raven and reporting that Abraham and Thomas remained stationed outside our door at all times for her protection.

And since I doubted she'd ever try scaling the walls of the castle again, after nearly dying last time, I took his word for it. I trusted him with Raven's safety, and I was more than curious about his story with Petra, but I hadn't found a moment to inquire about it.

"I am going to Arrow to the docks," River continued, drawing me from my thoughts and my longing gaze at our balcony. I had spent too many nights lately apart from my wife while she slumbered.

I didn't need to sleep with a fresh intake of her blood, and if that didn't scream immortal, I didn't know how else to convince her that we would spend an eternity together.

"Why did Silas tell Raven we can't have children?" I asked, interrupting his instructions.

"Silas said what?" Jeanine asked from beside me.

Sighing, River stared at the ground like he was contemplating what information to divulge, and it irritated me that there was still so much he hadn't shared with us yet. "Long ago, it was rumored that Raven's body carried so much power that birthing a healthy child would be impossible. The power... sustains itself on life. Her blood."

"So," Jeanine said, taking a small step forward. "The magic in her body takes to give?"

River nodded with a shrug of his shoulder. "Simply put, yes. Her miscarriage may have been due to physical trauma and stress, as Petra's physician said. Or, it could've been from her body's inability to distribute life elsewhere."

I swiped a hand down my face. "It has nothing to do with me possibly being mortal?"

River shook his head. "No, witches can birth mortal children. All beings can, except for Undead females, even with their mortal blood."

"Is there a chart you can draw with all these rules and regulations for our lives?" Jeanine spat, turning from him. "I cannot have children. Ever?"

River answered with silence.

Reaching up, I squeezed her shoulder. "Jeanine, I..."

"Don't apologize," she whispered, shaking me off. "Don't pity me. Please. I've had enough of that for a lifetime. It's fine. I'm fine. Let's just continue."

I wasn't going to push her here in front of River, so I gestured for him to continue. "You want me to Arrow while carrying Jeanine?"

"Yes," he answered. "It'll be more difficult but not as strenuous as it will be carrying prisoners tonight. Once Raven is awake, I'll have you carry both."

When he vanished to the docks, I turned to Jeanine. She hung her head but showed no emotion, nor could I feel her. "River taught you how to shield your emotions," I said.

She nodded her head, then slowly lowered it. "He doesn't know anyone else with empathic magic, but just in case. You can shatter minds, but some creatures can read them. Raven will need to learn, too."

I frowned at the idea of being unable to feel my wife whenever I wanted, but Jeanine was right. Raven would have to learn to shield her mind and feelings.

She laughed breathily, not from amusement but from irony. "I never wanted children. Honestly, I never saw myself as a mother, but it feels like all of my decisions were just... ripped away from me." She turned to face me fully. "I apologize for upsetting you earlier, Zeke. I have been"—she ran a hand through her hair—"struggling with all of this. I have lost so much, including my life."

I moved to hug her, but she shook her head. "I cannot lose Raven, Zeke. Do not forget that we fell in love with her at the same time. We were a team trying to save her from Cade the first time, and then we kept her from completely falling apart together. I can't, Zeke, I can't lose her."

"I know," I whispered. "Jeanine, I know. I've always told myself that if there is anyone in this universe that I would allow to love her as much as I do, it would be you. I know what you're doing is for her. I know you are choosing to live this life for her."

"I am, Zeke. She is my best friend. You might have hundreds of bonds with her, but she's mine, too. I'm unwilling to step back because fate decided she's yours."

"And I am grateful you love her so much, Jeanine." I knocked her shoulder playfully with my fist. "If you continue to allow only me to benefit from the physical parts of her, I'll continue sharing her with you."

Snorting, she rolled her eyes. "She does smell *really* fucking good once you get past the pine," she returned my smile, "but I've never thought of her that way. I did offer a threesome once, though."

I rolled my neck. "I am laughing on the inside."

She threw her head back in laughter but then groaned as River reappeared in front of us. "Oh, I apologize," he declared loudly. "I did not realize it was chit-chat hour! I will stand here and wait while the two of you exchange pleasantries while the universe waits for us to save it!"

"A tad dramatic," Jeanine muttered. "Must be genetic."

601

Chuckling, I grabbed Jeanine's arm and pulled her over to me. "Go on, River. We'll be right behind you."

River disappeared just as Raven breezed onto the balcony, leaning over and beaming at us. Tipping her head to rest against my arm, Jeanine waved to her and said, "I'm not worried about your children, Zeke. Raven is the most stubborn person I know. She'll figure out a way if she wants children with you."

As Raven disappeared to undoubtedly dress herself and come join us, I wrapped an arm around Jeanine and replied with, "I refuse to believe otherwise," before we Arrowed away.

RAVEN WAS CHAOS AROUND EVERYONE ELSE. BUT WITH ME, SHE WAS ALWAYS JUST MY RAVEN.

60

RAVEN

S tanding at the border of the Black Forest, I anxiously listened to River instructing Zeke and Jeanine. The moon was high, and it was time to rescue the prisoners from the dungeons of Reales.

Godfrey, Theodore, Abraham, and Thomas lined the border alongside Evangeline and me so we could tend to any injuries. Grace and Luisa would assist in calming the rescues, who would most likely be disoriented upon arrival. Lara had baked muffins and scones and placed them on tables we had brought from Arthur's. Alice was pouring warm milk into mugs, and John was standing beside Zeke while Luca paced around them in a tight circle, much to River's annoyance.

"This could be a trap," Luca continued, repeatedly reminding Zeke of all River's betrayals thus far.

I couldn't lie and say there wasn't a tiny part of me that wondered whether Luca was onto something, but with Zeke and Jeanine's skillsets, I had no doubts that they would not go down without a fight.

Finally, Zeke had enough of Luca's pacing and punched him in the chest to keep him still. Groaning, Luca limped over to me as if Zeke had injured his leg instead of his chest. "I hope he gets caught," he grumbled. He rubbed his chest, then sighed. "I didn't mean that. I'm just worried."

I squeezed his arm. "I know, Luca, but River has been nothing but helpful. He didn't have to teach us how to defend ourselves, but he did."

Dispersing, they somehow all ended up in front of me. Zeke took my wrist and bit, placing it against his lips to drink. Abraham and Thomas blanched at the sight, their eyebrows raised to their hairlines as they watched Zeke inhale my blood. I couldn't help but smile at their disgusted bewilderment. Since we were running low on time, we chose to stop hiding it, and even explaining it.

"I have to give Jeanine a drop," I said, wincing when Zeke shook his head and pinched my skin. "Zeke, she needs it."

"Never suggest that while he feeds," River said. "The result could be... well, catastrophic. I suggest you take her away from him into the forest."

"Do you not need any?" I asked.

River shook his head. "Since we are twins, our blood is nearly identical. My blood does not strengthen like yours does, but it sustains. If your blood is considered gold, mine is silver. Therefore, I do not need yours."

"That's refreshing," I admitted, "to not be hunted by someone for my blood." I cried out when Zeke's canines dug deeper. "Gods, you monster. Off." I pushed at his forehead until he released me, covering the wound with my palm. "You have to try and control your jealousy while feeding, or you're going to rip me to shreds."

He grinned but then frowned at the look on my face. "I'm sorry. I didn't mean to hurt you."

I wiped the blood from the corner of his mouth. "I know, Zeke. Just try and remember that I don't willingly give my blood to anyone other than you. I do not wish for this."

Nodding, he leaned down and kissed me softly. "She fed," he whispered against my lips. "Why must you give her yours?"

I rolled my eyes. "Didn't you two make up?"

He scoffed. "Raven, I will never have an approved list of people who can have your blood, no matter how much I may tolerate them."

"It's just a drop, Zeke. You won't even know it's missing." I rose up and kissed his cheek. "We'll only be a moment, you overly possessive buffoon."

He gaped, grabbing for me when I sidestepped around him. River hopped between us. "Be quick," he warned, putting an arm against Zeke's chest to keep him away from me. "You might think he's being dramatic, Raven, but he's not."

Just as Zeke shoved River's arm off, Jeanine grabbed my hand and we Arrowed away.

~

Instead of the forest, she Arrowed us into Duck's. Arthur was with Lara, helping her bring in more platters of pastries to the forest. "He'll hop around until he finds us," I said. "We have to make this quick. Try and take only a few drops."

Nodding, she took my extended hand but hesitated. "Raven, if your blood tastes as good as you smell, I don't know if I'll be able to stop."

Sighing, I took my hand from hers and walked around the bar, searching for something sharp to cut my finger with. "I miss when I thirsted for blood instead of everyone else wanting mine."

"You thirst for blood because of that." She climbed onto a barstool. "You take to give. River explained it to us. Celestina's magic only worked by others giving blood to her. That passed along to you."

I raised an eyebrow. "How?"

"Your blood needs life," she said with a shrug. "Your bloodlust comes as retribution for the blood you give. Life for life, essentially."

I hated how much sense that made. "The more I give, the more I want to take."

"Sounds like it." Reaching over the bar, she uncapped a bottle of rum and took a swig. "Since Celestina's blood charms required the blood of others, it makes sense that your healing power does, too."

"That is why I began wanting to kill," I said. "Months ago, before you came to the island with Zeke, I had such strong and sudden urges to murder."

"Because you were nearing your twenty-fifth birthday." She passed the bottle to me. "Your magic was tired of lying dormant, I guess."

I took a small sip. "Nervous?"

"A little," she admitted. "We know the area we're going to well, and if River's memory is correct, we will not come across any of the Undead."

Hidden under the bar top, I sliced the very tip of my middle finger. Jeanine's nostrils immediately flared, her pupils dilating as the blood dribbled down my finger. "Gods, I understand his obsession now."

"You can do this," I assured her, "You won't harm me." Bringing my hand up, I rose to the tips of my toes to lean over the counter. "Tilt your head back. I'll let it fall into your mouth."

Doing as I said, she parted her lips in anticipation. I pinched the tip of my finger and waited until three drops had fallen to her tongue before I pulled back and curled my finger into my palm to heal the cut. And closing her eyes, her fingers wrapped around the counter and instantly splintered the wood.

"Jeanine, control it. Arthur will not be pleased if you tear apart his bar for more blood."

"Immeasurable," she whispered, her eyes fluttering open. "Three drops fed an entire species for months, and you just gave that to me. And I feel it, Raven, I feel the strength that's pushing through me. Gods, you taste splendid." She leaned up, licking across her lips. "I have ways to coerce you."

Her voice had dropped into a low, sultry tone, and I quirked a brow. "Are you honestly trying to seduce me right now?"

She shrugged slightly. "Is it working?"

It wasn't *not* working, but I put my hands behind my back when she saw the drying blood on my finger. "No more, Jeanine. I love you, but I have to respect Zeke."

And that was when he found us, Arrowing inside of Duck's and landing right beside me. Jeanine pinched her lips shut, her eyes widened in faux innocence. Zeke looked at the broken countertop before narrowing his eyes at her. "What did you do?"

"Controlled herself," I said quickly.

"River gave us ten minutes," Zeke informed her. "Go wait for me in the forest."

Jeanine saluted with an eye roll, but I grabbed her wrist with my clean hand before she could stand. "Be safe, Jeanine. I demand that you return to me alive."

"I am already dead," she said with a wink, kissing my hand before she vanished. It was evident that with my blood, she felt invincible, which only added to my worry, but with River's constant assurance that the Undead were hard to kill, I had to remember that she wasn't returning to Reales as a feeble human.

Jeanine was a lethal weapon.

"And as for you," I said, but before I could turn around, he pushed my pants down and kicked my feet apart. And before I could take another breath, he slid into me until I was completely filled.

Wrapping one hand around my throat, he kept my back arched against his chest with his lips against my ear. "You're mine, Raven," he growled. "And this will serve as a reminder whenever you willingly give away what's mine."

Coupled with pleasure, the drive of his thrusts sent aches through my entire body. "Zeke," I rasped, "I am yours, always yours." But the promise did nothing to slow him down, bending me over until my chest was fully flat against the bar with his hand threaded through my hair.

And I did not want him to stop.

The curse against our strand made each touch more intense, each stroke a harsh remembrance of what we had to lose. The tender moments were far and few between, making each one all the more delicate and remarkable, but the masochist in both of us clamored for the agonizing idea of ever losing this unnatural amount of lust and passion.

"I want your cum all over my cock when I enter those dungeons, Raven." He kneaded my hips, leaning down to suck the top of my spine. "If he shows up, I want your mate to smell you all over me."

"Don't call him that," I snapped, trying to pry myself free from his grasp in defiance.

He grunted from my fight, wrangling me until I was at his mercy again. "You can't escape me, little mouse. That's the real reason the gods gave you to me. I am the only one who can control your outbursts."

"I loathe you," I sort of lied, though it was true that I hated nothing more than when Silas was referred to as my mate.

Bottles fell to the ground and shattered as he cleared a space on the bar. Pulling out of me only long enough to twist and lift me up, he kissed me with so much passion that my breath caught in my chest, sliding into me again. And when he looked at me with a smirk, he said, "And fuck, Raven, I love the ways you hate me."

His tongue plied into my mouth, sweat beading along his brow, the thundering of his heart beating against my chest. And I wanted to slow him down, I wanted to freeze time, but I couldn't. There was absolutely nothing I could do to stop what was about to happen, and knowing me so very well, his tattooed hand returned to collar my throat. "Scream," he breathed against my lips, "scream my name, Raven."

He stopped me from shaking my head, wrapping his arm around my waist to drag me closer until I felt nothing but him across every inch of my body. "I love you," he promised, "I will live for you, Raven, but I need to hear you. I'll give you stars."

Squeezing so tightly around my throat that colors impeded my vision, I could not hold back one-second longer. His name left my lips in a strained and strangled scream as I came, trembling and quivering.

My name was a praise on his tongue, and he filled me thoroughly before he bit into my shoulder. Blood rushed to my head, but he continued to squeeze my throat. And when my pulse slowed too much for him, he released me and pulled me to rest against his chest. Heaving and breathless, he tried to inhale deeply through his nose. "I *am* a monster," he whispered, kissing my temple. "Your blood tastes much sweeter when you're dying, Raven."

I tried to laugh, but the odd mixture of pleasure and panic made me numb. "Leave with me."

He stilled. He completely stopped moving.

I raised my head from his chest. "I'm so frightened, Zeke. What if you don't come back? What if something happens?"

He pressed his forehead against mine. "Nothing will happen, Raven, but I made you a promise that I'd leave with you if you asked, so I need to be sure you mean it."

I started contemplating and hated myself for it. We could leave this all behind. We promised we would if one of us asked, and I knew he'd hold true if I told him I was serious. And partially, I was. At this moment, nothing sounded better than not risking his life.

"I mean it," I whispered, brushing my thumb across his bottom lip, "but not yet. However, I require a very long, passionate trip with you when this is over."

He kissed my fingertip. "You will hear no argument from me." Pulling me from the bar, he set me down and slid two fingers inside me.

I whimpered from the tender rawness of coming only moments before, but watched as he covered his already glistening cock with more of my release, proving he wasn't just bluffing.

"You're looking for a fight," I scolded. "Aren't you?"

"If he finds me and smells you, he'll be untethered. He'll be easier to fight if he can't focus, and your cum is very distracting."

I shoved him. "Your only task is freeing prisoners. I am not sending you there to fight Silas!"

He pinned my wrists to the bar. "I will not seek him out, Raven, but he will know you belong to me if he finds us. It might be barbaric, but the Undead survive off blood and fucking. I own both when it comes to you."

I tried to pry my wrists free. "Get off me. You used me."

"I did fucking use you, Raven. I do it multiple times a day for my benefit, but also yours." He grinned, freeing my wrists to slide his fingers into my mouth. I tasted both of us. "Taste how good it is when I use you, Raven."

"Fuck you," I muttered as I pulled away, but when he roughly grabbed my chin between his fingers, I threw my arms around his neck and kissed him. "It is unhealthy how badly I want to kill you."

"Likewise," he replied, readjusting my pants before doing the same to his. "Stay here, Raven. Don't watch me leave."

I shook my head. "No, I have to come."

He cradled my neck between his palms. "No, Raven. I won't be able to leave if you're there. Give us five minutes, baby. Please?" He gestured toward the floor with his chin. "Clean up this mess you made. It'll distract you."

"The mess *I* made?"

He winked, then kissed me. "I love you, little demon, and I will come back to you."

"Don't be a hero, Zeke, please."

"Raven, when have I ever been a hero?" He threaded his fingers through my hair and pulled, his eyes bearing into mine with such intensity that I nearly cowered. "I will destroy the world for you and only you."

It took longer than five minutes to clean up the mess we made, and while running toward the Black Forest, I forgot that I possessed the ability to Arrow now, which would have made the trip much shorter. But even in the time it had taken me to get there on foot, no one had returned. "Where are they?" I asked, grabbing Luca's arm as I stood between him and John. "John, where are they?"

Godfrey answered, "River briefed me on what they would face when they arrived at Reales, Raven. The prisoners are shackled to the walls. It will take some time to free each one and escape."

My head whipped toward the empty forest where they were supposed to Arrow to once finished. "They didn't tell me that! That gives Silas plenty of time to find them; I have to go to them...."

Luca grabbed me. "No, Raven. Zeke would be more at risk if you Arrow to him. He won't focus."

"I cannot stand here and do nothing!" I shouted, stepping away to Arrow, but from the corner of my eye, a blur of bodies appeared in my vision.

I locked eyes with Jeanine. "There are a lot of people to rescue!" she shouted, motioning toward the two vomiting on the ground from their first trip through space and time. "This might take longer than we thought!"

I hated saying what I did, but I still called back to her, "Your lives are the most important, Jeanine! Don't linger." If I lost any of them, not only would my soul split in two, but our chances of defeating Silas would dwindle significantly.

Even from where I stood, I could see her roll her eyes. "Yes, because that's exactly what I want to do."

And then, she was gone again.

Alice took my hand, pulling me toward the freed prisoners on the ground. I hadn't met many people in Reales and did not recognize the two in front of me, but they saw Alice and began sobbing, blubbering incoherently about the horrors they'd been through.

It was a factor I hadn't considered yet.

Alice, Zeke, Luca, John, Jeanine... they were all from Reales. The people they were rescuing had a history with each of them. And they were about to learn which of their friends had survived Silas's clan... and which ones didn't.

River returned next with two more, giving me a count of how many remained, the amount numbing me from anxiety. I just needed to see Zeke; I needed to know he could escape. But just as I was about to ask, River disappeared and I was faced with two more strangers. I tried to calm them, explaining where they were and that they were safe now.

Time blurred by as River and Jeanine continued to return with more bodies, all hands on deck as we fed them, wrapped them in blankets, and tried to figure out where they could rest for the night.

But with each new batch of people who came, it was never with Zeke.

And when River Arrowed back again, I lunged at him to stop him from leaving. "Where is he?" I growled, squeezing his arms. "Where is Zeke?"

"He's the strongest," River answered, breathless. "We couldn't find the keys to unlock the cuffs. He's pulling the chains from the wall one by one."

"He said he wouldn't be a hero!" I shouted. If they wouldn't let me Arrow with them, I had to try and help him from here. Grabbing River's hand, I gave him no choice but to follow me to one of the tables nearby. "Bite my palm," I demanded.

Sighing, he took my hand and pinched the skin between his sharp canines, pushing deep enough that blood poured quickly from the opening into a mug. And once it was halfway full, he grabbed it and vanished before I had a chance to say anything else.

Turning to assist Alice again, I froze as I stared directly into the eyes of a weary and hollow Thia. Her usually rosy cheeks were pale, her eyes red, and her frame frail. "Raven," she squeaked, falling to her knees before me.

I met her on the ground, wrapping my arms around her as she fell into me. I had no words to make this better—to heal what had happened to her. I couldn't even begin to imagine the things she had witnessed, the horrors she endured.

And when I looked around, the ones that had been saved did not come to check on her, nor did they look anything like her. "Your family," I whispered, stroking her hair. "He got to them, didn't he?"

Her strangled sobs answered for her.

And when I looked up, I met Zeke's eyes, standing between two prisoners. Relief flooded my body, but it was also drenched with substantial grief. And the look in his eyes told me that he felt the exact same — because even though he didn't want to be King of Reales, he loved the people he grew up with, the men who had helped build his treehouse in the forest, the women who had wanted to dance with him at balls — some of them were no longer alive.

And as I held Thia in my arms, a woman I had loathed for knowing his body like I did, it suddenly did not matter anymore. She was now someone I needed to help, heal, and show compassion to.

When Zeke dipped his chin once, I mirrored it.

Partners, we had promised each other, believing that only applied to our relationship. But this... this was a partnership. People needed us, and as much as we wanted to leave and start anew without any heartache and uncertainty, the prophecy chose *us* for a reason. Our love was strong enough to withstand anything; curses, death, mates, the Undead...

None of it mattered.

Because as I stared at the man who had taken up residence in my heart and soul, it was then that I realized that no matter what fate decided to throw at us, we would come out stronger. Better.

We were the twins born of the darkness, lovers torn apart in death, trailed closely by misery at every turn. And we would be the ones to save everyone.

Together, beyond the end.

"YOU HAVE TO TRY AND CONTROL YOUR JEALOUSY WHILE FEEDING, OR YOU'RE GOING TO RIP ME TO SHREDS."

61

RAVEN

I t felt like hours had passed, but it hadn't even been one. The three of them had saved hundreds, and before she left again, Jeanine said there weren't many left. I hadn't stopped moving, tending to injuries on each prisoner, mostly around their wrists and ankles from being chained to the walls. I didn't ask any of them what had transpired these last few months in Reales, and no one seemed ready to talk about it.

Like River said, most of them seemed well-fed. It was the ones like Thia who had lost their families that clearly hadn't been eating. John decided to take the weakest ones inside the castle, and put the multiple rooms in the basement to use—those that had fallen into disarray over the years. It would serve as a shelter while they healed and until we found a more permanent solution.

River returned with a man and a woman before vanishing again. I didn't recognize the woman, but Alice came over to take care of her. Luca rushed over to me and pulled me away from the man, and I jerked in surprise at his sudden need to protect me. "Luca, what are you—"

"Raven," the man said.

The voice sent chills across every inch of my body, and I was grateful for the safety of Luca's arms around me. August stood staring at me, his eyes jaundiced, his face twisted in anger.

"Where is my son?" he asked me, stumbling forward a few steps to reach me as Luca continued to pull me backward. "Where is Cade? What did you do to him?"

"You better back the fuck off," Luca shot back, pushing me behind him. "You are lucky Zeke did not know you were in that dungeon, or you never would've been brought back here."

"She poisoned his mind!" he shouted, drawing Godfrey's attention, who dropped everything he was doing and ran over. "Where is Cade?" he shouted repeatedly. "Where is my boy?"

"Your boy," Luca yelled, "tried to rape her! Your boy nearly killed her! He drugged her and dragged her across the realm! Your boy was a despicable excuse of a man!"

I had buried those memories.

Weeks had turned into months since he'd taken me, yet seeing August before me brought everything back. And I clutched my stomach, scrunching my shirt between my fingers as my chest heaved, and everything inside me became cold and heavy.

I had spent many nights in August's cottage with Cade. He was the one who gave me to Isla, the man who had hidden who I was from me just as everyone else had while his son groomed me to rely solely on him. And I thought I had moved on since the nightmares stopped, but as nausea rolled through me like tidal waves, I realized that there would always be something that could trigger the trauma again.

August continued to yell at me, backing me against a wall as Luca and Godfrey stood in front of me like a shield. I fell to my knees behind them, the exhaustion from the last hour melding with the rising panic, the memory of visiting my son in a dream rushing back and engulfing my heart with pain.

Because *his son* had stolen that from me. Even after learning of the possible inability to have children from the power in my body, it was *his son* who took away my chance to find out, *his son* that tore me away from my husband, who nearly killed me from obsession, and yet *I* couldn't find the strength to stand as *I* was the one left to face the consequences.

My face was cradled between two hands—solid and calloused hands. I couldn't hear him through the ringing in my ears, through the reminder of my grief and fear. And when he stood, Luca knelt down beside me and scooped me up, carrying me away from the man who continued to shout at me, blaming me for the loss of his son. The power that lingered in Zeke's chest collided with my own, trying to crawl to each other, desperate to find their escape.

Revenge, it murmured, vengeance.

And I didn't have to look to know what was happening under Zeke's hands; that even without his shadows, the strength that remained within him was enough to make a grown man scream.

Luca waited inside Duck's with me until Zeke Arrowed inside, instructing Luca to wait for Jeanine. Only a handful of prisoners remained in Reales, but that didn't matter to him as he came over and pulled me into his lap.

His hands were covered in blood from the rescues; I didn't ask for the details of what he did to August. "I'm sorry," Zeke said, kissing my temple. "I worked so quickly that I didn't recognize him. I never would've allowed him to be brought here."

I nodded because I knew that. River brought August back, unaware of who he was. "Do you need to return?"

"I am right where I need to be, Raven."

The right thing to do would've been insisting that he continue to help, but in his arms where we were both safe and sound, I didn't care about doing anything other than kissing him. "How are you?" I asked between kisses, brushing his sweat-soaked hair back. "What did you see?"

"Bodies," he answered tightly with a frown. "The bodies they drained were stacked in Luca and Alice's cell. The survivors had to smell the rotting corpses, Raven. Their road to recovery will be long."

"We will be here to aid in that," I assured him. "We will ensure they have everything they need, Zeke. I can promise you that."

He sank back in the chair, jaded, disgusted, and angry at the terror his people had endured. "I can't believe Mira allowed it to happen. She may be horrid, Raven, but this..." He shook his head slightly. "She sentenced our entire kingdom to death all because of her hatred for me."

"Hatred is a virus, Zeke. There is no antidote once it spreads, and I believe she received more than she bargained for with Silas." I grazed his eyebrow with my fingertips. "You, beautiful man, found your way back from the darkness. Mira is too lost."

"I am still in the darkness, Raven." He kissed me softly. "But you are my light guiding the way."

Death lingered outside, but I let him kiss me.

Until Jeanine ran inside, breathless. "River. Raven, it's River. Silas found him."

~

IT WASN'T until I saw River on the ground bleeding from a deep gash in his shoulder, that I realized I loved him. And I didn't care about the reason as Zeke threw his shirt to me to stop the bleeding before I could attempt to heal it. "I couldn't save the last two," he rasped, slumping. "I tried, but he found me."

I didn't miss the look that was exchanged between Zeke and Jeanine, and I quickly said, "Don't even think about it," before one of them tried to Arrow back to the dungeons. "That's an order."

Not once had I ever ordered them to do anything, but I would take the discomfort accompanying it if it kept them on the island. Zeke didn't have to listen to me as royalty of his kingdom, but his respect for me as his mate stopped him from trying to save the two remaining in Reales.

"He smelled your blood, Raven."

I focused my attention back on River. "How?"

"The mug I brought back," he explained, "he could smell it. He appeared behind me and bit me."

Removing the shirt from his shoulder, I gasped at the torn skin, quickly covering it with my hand.

He drew in a sharp breath through clenched teeth. "This happened because I pulled away."

"Your bond," Zeke said. "Did he get your blood? Can you feel him?"

River attempted a nod, but he was in too much pain to do more. "It's only a matter of time before he finds the island, Raven. It won't take him long."

"Fuck!" I shouted, looking at the rescues and then at my village, full of blissfully sleeping people.

"Will he bring all the Undead?" Jeanine asked.

"No," River breathed. "Only Felix. All he wants is Raven. He's tired of waiting for her. The only thing between him and finding her was the bargain he made with Mira. Now that he knows where Seolia is, he'll take Raven to Reales before he starts a war for the realm."

"We have to get everyone out," I said. "We have to get them to Thoya." I looked up at Zeke. "We can't leave them here. We just stole away the Undead's source of blood. If Silas sees how many people are here—"

"Raven, I can't take them to Thoya," River interrupted. "With the bond fresh, Silas will be able to locate Thoya. He didn't take much from me, but it was enough to feel me if I Arrow them to Thoya."

"The ships?" Jeanine asked. "Can you get as many on ships while we Arrow the rest?"

Shakily, River stood with a slight nod. "I can do it, but Raven has to go to Thoya. She can't be here when he arrives."

Zeke grabbed me, but I shook my head. "No! I will not leave my people here with only the three of you to save them. I can get some of them out!"

"Raven," Zeke growled.

"No, Zeke." I pointed toward the village. "There are children here.

Isla is here. Our family is here. You cannot ask me to leave them when I can help."

"Raven, I will not lose you—"

"You won't lose me," I interjected. "Get our family out, Zeke. Let me take Eva and Teddy to Thoya. I'll return and grab Isla and Arthur, and when Silas gets here, I'll leave, but I refuse to stand by idly again while you save everyone."

River and Zeke looked at one another like they could decide for me, but I didn't wait for them to tell me no again, instead I Arrowed into the heart of the village. But I was naive to believe he wouldn't follow me. "Raven," he tried again, "I can work quickly. I need you safe. I need you in Thoya...."

I placed my hand against his chest. "Zeke, there are children inside this cottage who believe we'll protect them. What if it were us, huh? What if they were our children?"

He looked at the cottage that housed a sleeping Eva and Teddy before squeezing his eyes shut. "You save only them and Isla, Raven, and then you leave. Let us handle the rest."

I nodded and moved to go inside, but he grabbed my elbow and pulled me back. He lifted me up and kissed me, giving me no warning before he jerked my head to the side and sank his teeth into my neck. With our limited time, he pulled blood quick enough to cause dizziness, but he needed as much as he could take if he had to transport our entire village to Thoya.

"Why is it that Jeanine can last off of three drops, but you must drink constantly?"

He stroked the spot with his tongue. "Because you are my mate. I am addicted, Raven. I am addicted to the power it gives me, to the connection it spawns between us..." He returned to pull more, never finishing his list of reasoning.

"We really need a quicker solution for this addiction then," I said once he released me. "This is time-consuming."

He lowered me to the ground and licked his lips clean. "Add it to our to-do list."

As he Arrowed back to the forest, I ran inside, searching for Eva and Teddy in the quaint cottage. Stopping once I stepped into their room, I breathed a sigh of relief at the sight of them peacefully asleep in their beds. I kneeled beside Eva and rubbed her back, forcing a smile as her eyes fluttered open. "Butterfly," she whispered sleepily, holding a stuffed bear against her chest.

"We're going on a trip, Eva. Do you trust me?"

"Mama and Papa?" she asked in a murmur, rubbing her eyes.

"Will be there," I promised. "It is a kingdom of gold and dreams, Eva." Scooping her up in my arms, she held her bear against her chest as I woke up Teddy next and grabbed his hand. I had never attempted to Arrow this far, and I wasn't entirely confident I could, but as I closed my eyes, I pictured the castle in Thoya clearly in my mind.

And jumped.

～

Gisela took a dazed Eva from my arms while Edmund picked up a crying Teddy. I had woken them both by shouting their names in the empty foyer, seeing how dawn hadn't even broken the horizon yet. "Expect many more," I said after explaining the link between River and Silas. "Jeanine and Zeke will save as many as possible and will bring them here directly. River is loading the ships with the rest. Godfrey and John will sail them here, but I must go—"

"Raven," Edmund interrupted, "shouldn't you stay? You are who he seeks."

"Edmund, I cannot remain idle. I owe it to my people and your mother to fight, not cower and hide." Leaning up, I kissed his cheek and then Gisela's. "These two children are very important to me. Treat them as if they were my own."

Whirling as the doors to the castle opened, Zeke strolled in with Evangeline, who ran to her children. "Theodore stayed behind to assist loading the ships," Zeke explained, grabbing my hand. "The quicker we move, the more you can save."

I smiled at him, appreciating how he understood my need to help. He winked at me before we returned to the village of Seolia.

I hoped that Arrowing quickly from kingdom to kingdom would eventually become easier on the stomach one day.

"I've got Luca and Alice," he said quickly, jogging with me toward

Isla's cottage. "Jeanine took care of Arthur and will meet me in the castle to start moving our people again."

"I'll help until he arrives," I said, kissing his hand. "If you start to worry, my love, remember that you can feel my heart. As long as it beats, I am safe."

"You're my greatest treasure, Raven. I will always worry." He kissed my temple. "Don't be a hero."

I snorted, watching as he disappeared before me, reappearing at the forest border to grab Luca and Alice. Since daylight was still hours away, I ran into Isla's cottage, knowing she'd still be asleep. And sure enough, as I ran into her bedroom, I found her huddled underneath blankets and snoring lightly.

"Isla," I whispered, swinging open the doors to her wardrobe to stuff clothing into a small canvas bag. "Isla, I have to take you to Thoya."

Isla stirred but must've thought she was dreaming as she rolled in her sleep, causing a blanket to fall to the floor. I picked it up and threw it over my arm before nudging her shoulder. "Isla, I'm on a tight schedule."

She swatted my hand away—the same way I always did when someone tried to wake me up. Smiling, I shoved her shoulder a little more forcefully. "Isla, Zeke will come in here and yell at me if I don't get you out quickly."

Finally, her eyes opened, and she squawked in surprise to find me beside her. "Gods almighty, Raven, I told you to stop doing that!"

I rolled my eyes. "Isla, I haven't lived here in over fifteen years. It's been a very long time since I last did that." I started pulling blankets off her, sighing impatiently as she pulled them back. "Isla, I have to get you to Thoya! It's a very long story, but a terrifying man is coming to take me, and I don't have much time...."

Sitting up, she swung her feet over the bed. "Where is he? I'll talk to him. I've had enough of these men stealing you away."

"He's not really the listening type, Isla." I took her hands and pulled her up. "I have to get you out of here. You'll be safe in Thoya."

"Raven, I am very old." She took the bag from my hands and ruffled through it to see what I had packed for her. "This is my home. How will I drink my tea?"

621

I took the bag back and slung it over my chest. "Isla, Thoya has tea and a very handsome prince who loves talking about me. You will have much in common with him. Now, can we please go?"

She wagged her finger at me and fetched a knitted cardigan from her wardrobe. "I think I need to speak with John about this. There is much to be desired for your protection around here."

Sighing, I followed her through the cottage and out the front door, reaching for her hand as she descended the porch. She would have to speak with John once he reached Thoya with the boats full of our people. Grabbing her hand, I was about to Arrow with her when I stilled, the hairs on my neck rising.

Slowly, I turned my head toward the courtyard of my castle. Stepping out from the shadows, his feline grin stretched across his lips, stood Felix.

And behind him, coming into view with his hands behind his back, cocky in stature from finally locating me after a century of searching, awaited Silas.

"I AM STILL IN THE DARKNESS, RAVEN. BUT YOU ARE MY LIGHT GUIDING THE WAY."

62

RAVEN

I quickly stepped in front of Isla, even though Silas and Felix were approaching slowly, as if they were mocking me. "You have a bargain with Mira!" I shouted to them, "You can't touch me!"

"Our agreement with Mira says we cannot bring you back to our kingdom yet, little poppet," Silas answered. "It says nothing about keeping you as our pet in Reales."

I curled my fingers into fists. "I am no one's pet."

Shifting into Blaze, I was prepared to fight them to the death, but Jeanine appeared beside me, sighing from boredom. "We really must stop meeting like this," she called to the invaders, but then lowered her voice to me. "Zeke is in Thoya. Baldwin insisted he was briefed about the plans. I can handle Felix, but you'll have to fight Silas until he returns."

I didn't have time to argue before she began taunting Felix, "Can you still taste my blood, demon?" She stepped forward, shoving my hand away when I moved to pull her back. "It's a shame you didn't finish the job when you had the chance. I have become untouchable with Raven's blood."

Silas snarled, revealing the tips of his fangs.

Felix was matching Jeanine step for step, his tongue darting out to swipe across his top lip. The bond from tasting her blood before River saved her had driven Felix to madness, according to River. Taking blood from an Undead but not enough to fully form a link between them would leave them constantly searching for the one whose blood they'd taken to complete it.

By Jeanine's looks alone, she would be a prize for any Undead to bond with. Her strength and yet-to-be-discovered powers only added to her enticement. And since Felix was the one to change her, he already viewed her as his possession. Jeanine knew that — she knew that mocking his inability to form an attachment with her was a reflection of his failure.

"Do not listen to her, cousin," Silas hissed. "She is trying to lure you in like bait."

Felix encroached like a predator.

Jeanine sneered. "I want nothing to do with him," she shot back. "I would not bond with such a weak male. I doubt he'd even be able to bite me again."

Though it was nerve-wracking listening to her insult him, it did buy us time for Zeke to return. But that didn't stop me from grasping for thin air when Jeanine disappeared, followed immediately by Felix.

Silas gave me no time to recover.

He pounced, clearing the distance between us within a breath, but it wasn't me that he sank his fangs into, puncturing deep in the throat.

Isla jumped in front of me quicker than I could stop. "No!" I screamed, lighting my palms and pushing them against Silas's face until he released her.

Isla sank to the ground, blood pouring from the wound, her eyes glazing and trying to focus on me. "Isla!" I cried, covering the puncture with my hand. "Isla, you must hold on!"

But the venom was too potent, and she was too old. Too weak. Too mortal. And couldn't utter a word before the last breath she'd ever take sputtered past her lips.

I panted. I heaved. I exerted a scream of pain and frustration at this creature who believed he held some kind of claim over me and had now stolen the only person that had loved me unconditionally as a child—the one person who didn't wait around to see if my magic was evil. She'd taken a baby wrapped in a blanket on her porch without question and had provided her with a normal childhood.

And when he came at me again, his skin black and charred from the flames but healing on its own, I shot more toward him, pushing him farther away from Isla's body. Immortal or not, Zeke was the only person ever immune to the searing pain from my fire. And Silas proved that as he darted back, trying to lessen the flames with whatever powers he could, but my fury was too powerful.

And I was too chaotic to be controlled.

I chased him, Arrowing closer and shifting each time, so he never knew what to expect. I fought with fire and ice, with Mother Nature as I split the ground beneath our feet, breaking apart cottages and land, covering my head as roofs shattered above us, and launching bricks and stones at him until I eventually pushed him into the castle.

Adrenaline shoved through the exhaustion that came from using too much power too quickly; my body had not yet adjusted to how much was lingering inside me, untouched and uncharted.

But Silas was wise and knew how to fight back—his only irritation came from the fact that he hadn't found a way to touch me; I kept covered in flames any time he got too close.

"I do not belong to you!" I screamed, shifting into Terra and placing my palms against the wall to tear apart the stones and hopefully crush him under rubble. "I am not your prize!"

He Arrowed within inches of me and I shifted into Frost, swiftly jamming an icicle through his hard-plated chest, missing his heart by a handbreadth.

Shifting back into Terra, I shot my hand up and clenched my fists, howling as I tore apart the ceiling above us and brought down chunks of brick. He dodged the falling rocks, but I crumbled the room around us. The castle floors groaned from the shift, walls around us rattled, portraits from over a century of royals fell and shattered against the ground.

River found me first.

He blasted water from his hands, which I iced and shot toward Silas. The first blast nicked his arms, but he was more prepared for the second one, flicking his wrist to the side and shattering the ice at his feet. River shifted into his Fae form and raised his hand toward Silas, his jaw clenched tightly as the powers I didn't yet understand between them collided.

I shot flames toward Silas's feet to distract him, naively believing that this was it—that it was *this* simple. But we had angered him, and when he raised a hand toward me, an invisible collar wrapped around my throat. I gasped for air, clawing but feeling nothing but my own skin.

River looked at me with fearful eyes, calling my name before Silas waved his arm and tossed him to the side of the room. His head and back knocked against a crumbling wall, his eyes closing from impact. The collar didn't tighten, but I still struggled to draw in breaths as he took steps closer.

"You cannot stop this, little poppet." He spoke too calmly for someone who endured the fight I had just given him. "I have waited too long, practiced and gathered magic from all kinds of creatures in exchange for a drop of your blood once I had you again."

I tried to rasp River's name.

Silas used his free hand to clear away the rubble that stood in his path to me, with the other still raised and pointed at my throat. "I'll admit that your strand was a shock, but I believe I have rectified that." He looked around with a grin. "It is why he has not found you yet, beloved. He cannot feel you as he once did."

I shook my head, tears falling down my cheeks from my silent cries. Zeke would always find me.

"And once we return to The Great, he'll never see you again," Silas continued. "My bite will restore our bond, and your memories of him will fade with time."

"I wouldn't count on it," a familiar voice drawled behind me. "She's quite obsessed with me."

The pressure around my throat loosened enough for me to take a full breath, and Zeke's voice slipped into my mind. *I can't enter his mind*, he whispered into mine, *when he releases you, Arrow to Thoya.*

I couldn't turn my head but saw a flash of silver whizz by and pierce straight through Silas's chest. I fell to the ground from the release around my neck, gasping for air. Zeke was instantly at my side, prepared to Arrow us to Thoya, but he groaned.

A groan of pain I recognized.

Feeling dizzy, I leaned over him to find the same stake that once ended the Phantom Prince's life hanging from his ribcage, and I watched as blood poured from the wound. "Foolish mortal," Silas hissed, resuming his advance toward me.

Shifting into Blaze, I created a wall of fire between Silas and us, trying to delay the inevitable. Zeke's skin paled, his hand holding the hilt of the dagger. I took his face between my hands and kissed him. "Stay with me," I cried, "Zeke, if he kills us, he can bring me back...."

I wailed in agony as a strong force enclosed my body. Zeke tried to lean over me, but the dagger was speared too deeply in his side. "Raven," he breathed, pulling the blade out from between his ribs and rising to his feet.

I cried out from the feeling of my bones crushing under an invisible weight, unable to move or do anything other than scream and beg for release. Zeke blocked my body, standing before me and dangling the dagger from his fingertips.

Ready to fight a war he would not win.

The flickering death of my flames was all I could see from the corner of my eye as I writhed on the ground. Fate be damned—it had cursed us both. How could a prophecy be so incorrect?

"The great Phantom Prince!" Silas bellowed, mockingly bowing at the waist. "How amusing it is to find you here, in mortal form— the exact way I killed you many moons ago."

I tried to say Zeke's name, but I couldn't produce anything besides screams of torment.

"Let her go," Zeke said weakly, undoubtedly in immense distress while bleeding from his side. "You might have the power, Silas, but I have her. There is no amount of time on this earth that will change what we are to one another."

We were both too weak to Arrow out of this maze of trial and torture. And with the force squeezed so tightly around me that it felt like my lungs were about to collapse, I would've gladly accepted death. Living anywhere with Silas while he could inflict so much pain without touching me frightened me more than my final goodbyes to this life.

"I am going to give you a kindness, mortal," Silas said. "Once I kill her, I will kill you. You will not have to live without her; she can live a long life within The Great after I resurrect her."

"No," I rasped, back arching off the ground.

"You will not," Zeke growled, "touch her."

"I will do as I please with what is mine."

Panicking, I grasped for rocks around me as my body started lifting from the ground, my back bowing and head dangling. Zeke threw the dagger at Silas's chest, but Silas knocked it away with a flick of his wrist.

I climbed higher and higher, trying to wrap my fingers around Zeke's as he grabbed for me and tried to hold onto me.

The bones in my left hand started to break, and I shrieked, clutching it against my chest. And Zeke calling my name over and over added to my woe—the pain of his cries echoing through my shambled castle, reminding me of the screams I heard from him in death all those years ago.

Helpless. We were utterly helpless.

History was repeating itself. I would be taken away from him, but also unable to die due to the bond between Silas and me, I would never again feel him, laugh with him, or see our son.

A dream. We were always just a dream.

And oh gods, the pain, the shattering of my bones and crushing of the spirit withered away any fight I had left in me. Zeke would be freed from this life, and I took solace in that alone.

The misery would follow only me.

But I could guarantee that no matter how many years passed, I would never find another love. I would sit under the stars every night and think of him, remembering the short time we had together before we lost it all. "I love you," I achingly whispered, tears falling down my cheeks, "I love you."

Over and over it, I repeated it because I needed it to be the last thing I said, the last words he heard.

But while hovering mid-air, my body fracturing and shredding as if it were nothing more than a vase made of clay, I had forgotten Zeke's promise— hat he would give me nothing less than the stars someday. *We fell in love under dark skies*, he had said the night we wed, but I was his light.

At our very core, we were an eclipse.

Fire and ice and earth, and him—the moon and night sky; we were what darkness was made of.

When the earth rattled, skies dimmed above us, and dark gray thunderstorm clouds rolled in, I felt a force greater than anything I had ever experienced. It was stronger than my elements and more substantial than my bloodthirsty fervor. It split the sky apart, giving way for lightning to strike and illuminate the remnants of the crumbled room.

Rain poured through the cracks in the roof, wetting my body and distracting Silas enough to loosen his hold enough for me to take a breath.

Cords of gold and silver weaved around me, my arms extending as electricity pulsed through me. The feeling, gods, the feeling replicated the one I always felt whenever Zeke touched me in our dreams; it was here. It was right at my fingertips.

The pulsating in my chest, spreading across every inch of me and wrapping itself tightly around each fiber within, was magic unbound.

Because Zeke finally gave me what I had been begging for since meeting him. He released the monster he did not want to be and gave me what I always wanted.

He gave me his shadows.

THE MOON AND NIGHT SKY; WE WERE WHAT DARKNESS WAS MADE OF.

63

Zeke

B lack tides poured from my fingers, forming two wispy shadows that pooled against the ground. Flinging out a hand, one of the shadows caught Raven as she fell from the sky, wrapping around her body like a silk cloth and remaining cradled around her to give her body time to heal.

Silas stared at me in horrified shock.

A shadow stood erect behind me, its head curved like a snake ready to bite, the body twisted like a tendril of smoke. I wasn't entirely confident I could control them yet, unfamiliar with the power tingling at my fingertips and unsure of what that meant.

But the look on his face told me it didn't matter—he didn't know that he would still be able to easily overpower me. "She is not yours," I said, "she is mine, and she will remain so."

"It is not possible," Silas muttered, looking from me to the shadow behind me to the one wrapped around Raven. "You are mortal! You were not supposed to rebirth in this form!"

Trying to grasp what was unfolding around her, Raven whipped her head around at the translucent shadow beneath her to the one behind me. And then, she stared at her hands.

Since my power was unbound, so was hers.

And it *called* to mine.

I felt them entwining, their desperation to mingle and burn the world down, which was admittedly unsettling. So much lingered between us that I wondered if the universe made a mistake, unknowing that her blood would one day free what others feared.

Scrambling to her feet while keeping her broken left hand against her chest, fire dripped from the fingers of her right hand but did not take the shape of flames. The pool of fire changed into something else entirely—a fox made of reds and yellows, its tail curved like a scorpion, its fangs primed for a fiery death.

Blaze.

And gods, it was beautiful. Deadly as it prowled closer to Silas, my shadow followed closely behind. Silas stumbled back, tripping over rubble as he stared at the fire and shadows in terror. His eyes flicked up as River came to stand beside Raven in his Fae form, his drops of water morphing into the shape of a wolf, its tail reminding me of a tadpole, its fangs curved like a beast. It followed behind its fiery sister.

It seemed River had not shared with us that his powers couldn't be completely unsealed without Raven's.

"You will not win this, Silas," River said. "The prophecy chose them for a reason. They will be what ends you once and for all."

Silas seemed speechless for once, his eyes darting around at the power between us. But then, he stared at my wife, his eyes narrowed on her. He wasn't going to let a century of seeking her go to waste that easily, and from the look in his eyes, I knew we were in for a fight. A fight I was determined to come out of as champion.

Tipping my head toward her, the remaining shadow slithered

over to her and wrapped around the length of her body as she swayed from exhaustion. River took a step closer, wrapping his hand around hers in a show of allegiance to his sister, but his eyes were weary as he stared at the way hers seemed to roll back.

"This is not over," Silas snarled, taking another step back when Blaze pounced, barely missing the claws protruding from her flaming paws. "Her blood will be mine once more whether it is spilled or drank."

"No," Raven breathed. "I will ensure you starve."

Felix appeared behind Silas, his eyes widening at Blaze and the shadow trailing her. He whispered something in Silas's ear, and I glanced at River.

He shook his head subtly, silently answering my question. Raven was too weak to try and fight them now, and I didn't know how to control the shadows to our advantage yet.

Felix vanished, but Silas lingered, his gaze pinned on my mate, who looked as if she was about to collapse. I stepped forward and clenched my fist, the shadow following behind Blaze, shooting across the ground toward him.

And when Jeanine appeared beside me, Silas realized he was significantly outnumbered. No amount of power could bring down four of us at once, and none of us would give up until he was dead. Right as my shadow reached his feet, he growled and disappeared.

I ran to Raven, uncurling my shadow from her body in time for her to fall into my arms. "Baby," I said, pushing her sweat-soaked hair from her face, "Raven, talk to me. Tell me what ails you."

"Everything," she whispered.

"The amount of power she holds in her body could kill her," River said quickly, placing the back of his hand against her forehead. "She needs rest. Her body needs to heal, but we cannot stay here."

"But your bond with Silas..."

River shook his head. "It was only potent enough for him to find us here. He did not take enough of my blood. Unless..." River looked at Jeanine. "Unless Felix bit you."

Jeanine smirked. "Felix did not touch me. I bit him." When we all looked at her in surprise, she shrugged a shoulder. "We needed to track their movements. The best way to do that was for one of us to control a bond with an Undead. I have a direct line to him, but he cannot find me."

River looked thoroughly impressed. "Clever."

She scowled. "I do not need your validation."

I swiped at the shadows that were enclosing Raven, annoyed already at their obsession with touching her. "River, I'm going to need your help with these."

Blaze bounded onto Raven's lap, the fire seeping back into her skin. Raven gasped from the added power, trembling. Bringing his wolf closer, River guided it to gently lay across Raven, the water cooling her skin. I felt the pain in her body and cradled her in my arms as I stood.

Jeanine touched the gash in my ribs, but I didn't flinch because there was no longer any pain. But then, her eyes widened, and she reached up, blinking with parted lips. "Your ears... they look like River's."

I didn't care right now. All I wanted to do was get Raven somewhere safe. "Stay with me, little demon."

"Your voice sounds like night-kissed waves," Raven whispered, her eyes fluttering closed.

"You are all I want to kiss," I replied softly, before we Arrowed out of Seolia together, leaving our kingdom for what might've been the final time.

≈

TWO DAYS HAD PASSED, and Raven still couldn't keep her eyes open longer than a few moments. After burying Isla in the open field behind our manor, she hadn't moved from the bed due to a combination of grief, sorrow, and exhaustion. We had yet to find even a moment alone together. While she slept, I stayed up with Jeanine to make plans, knowing Raven was safe with my shadows wrapped around her at all times.

We hadn't talked about them, mostly because I didn't want to, nor had anyone other than Jeanine brought up how my ears and canines looked different. All Raven had said before passing out the night prior was, "Looks like you're the demon now."

Most of the time, the shadows lingered beside Raven like two serpents. And though I had released them, I couldn't figure out how to wield them. River tried to help by returning to the castle in Seolia for the book from Nova, but even the history of the shadows told me nothing about how to control them. And after becoming exhausted from talking about myself, I began to inquire why Raven was having such a hard time moving.

Raven's head was in my lap as I ran my fingers through her hair, listening to River try and explain why this was happening to her.

"Imagine a dam," he said, "picture water being sealed with nowhere to go until one day, the gates open, and it floods through too quickly, weakening the structure that held it in place."

I looked down at Raven's fragile body.

"That is what she is right now," he continued. "She is harboring an uncontrollable amount of power. It is not only her elements. Her healing requires blood. It needs life to sate it, or else it'll continue to build."

"So..." Jeanine sighed, looking at me. "She needs to kill someone?"

"Life for life," River reminded us. "Raven gives only as much as she takes. Magic needs balance. And right now, her power is hungry. It has been buried for so long that it wants to be fed."

My shadows spiraled around her legs. I hadn't figured out how to keep them off her, and they didn't listen when I tried to pry them off. "I don't like these," I muttered.

River grinned. "They're responding to your bond with her, Zeke. They can feel her blood. That's why they attach to her like leeches."

"That won't come in handy when we're fighting the Undead. I'll need them to listen to me, not chase her."

"Feeding from her beforehand will help control their urges," River said, nodding toward Raven's wrist. "Try it, and you'll see."

I shook my head. "Not while she's unconscious."

Raven lifted her arm up. "I can hear you."

"Raven, you're too weak...."

"It might actually release some of the pressure that is building inside of her." River interrupted.

Jeanine stepped forward. "If you don't want to, I will."

I quickly pressed Raven's wrist against my lips and bit. The second her blood hit my tongue, her body relaxed, and the shadows around her legs loosened. The intake of her blood was directly connected to how I controlled them.

"You will need to be well-fed before we battle the Undead," River said. "It is the only way you can remain undistracted and focused."

The front door to our manor opened and closed downstairs. Jeanine's nostrils flared, then relaxed. "It's Luca and Edmund. And a scent I do not recognize."

I released Raven's wrist with a stroke of my tongue, tucking it between our bodies to allow it to heal. Luca glided in first and came to sit on the edge of our bed, staring at the shadows that seemed to study him right back but never left Raven's side.

Edmund breezed in, followed by Petra, who gaped at the shadows. "It is true then," she said, stepping closer, "You have released them."

Raven stiffened at the sound of Petra's voice.

"Not well," I admitted. "They seem to answer to someone else."

Luca timidly reached over to touch Raven's hand. The shadows inched toward his fingers, but I called them back. "I don't know how to teach them who they can trust around her."

"Time," Petra said. "But first, we need to teach you how to use them. It takes nearly two weeks by foot to reach the cliffs of Reales. We'll need to leave tomorrow evening and train along the way."

"Once we're a week away, we'll begin Arrowing," River added. "We need the element of surprise against them. Mira will assume we won't be there for another week."

"Only four of us can Arrow," I said. "Arrowing that many soldiers and weapons will take too much energy."

"There are seven," Petra replied. "Myself included. Godfrey and Elric can Arrow."

"Gisela, John, and Alice will stay behind with my father while we prepare for battle," Edmund said.

Jeanine crossed her arms. "We must kill Mira first to break the bargain between her and Silas. If we lose, we cannot risk her becoming the leader of whatever is left of this realm."

"We won't lose," I said, glancing at Petra. "Right? Isn't this what the prophecy said? I have my shadows. Raven's magic is unbound."

Petra frowned. "The prophecy said you will restore magic, Ezekiel. It did not say how or when."

I looked at Edmund. "How many men do we have?"

"Not as many as I'd like," he admitted. "Under a thousand. Mortal versus magic never works out well for the former."

One of my shadows weaved around Raven's left hand. She groaned from the ache of her broken fingers. "Fire and shadows," I whispered, my eyebrows knitting together. "We need more magic."

Raven's head popped up from my lap, sleep clearing from her eyes. "You're not seriously suggesting—"

"Balance," I said. "You need balance. Life versus death. It's not a permanent solution, but it could be temporary."

"We wouldn't know how to find her," Jeanine added. "She could be anywhere."

Edmund looked at each of us. "Who are we talking about?"

"A spirit," I answered.

River looked down at Raven's broken hand, recognition crossing his eyes. "Morana's song. It is an avenue I had not considered, but you are right."

Raven's nose wrinkled. "Morana's song?"

I shuddered at the memory. "I witnessed her song once, but that is not why I feel we need her. She can be Raven's solution to counter-acting her need for blood."

"She can be a solution in multiple ways," River said. "The Undead die by blades to their hearts, but there is another way. Along with your shadows' invisibility, Morana's ribbons entice beings to hand over their lives with her song promising them whatever they want in the afterlife."

"Morana promised me you," I said, tucking a strand of Raven's hair behind her ear. "In your nightmare when you saved me. Morana's ribbons hummed a melody that sounded like your name."

"You're suggesting we put that demonic spirit back into Raven?" Luca stood from the bed. "It nearly killed her last time!"

"Luca is right," Petra said. "You will need to offer her something in exchange for allowing Raven to control the ribbons."

Jeanine raised her eyebrows in confusion. "What can we offer a spirit of death?"

River chuckled. "Life. A physical body."

"Morana prefers bodies of witches," Petra explained, "but I am positive she could be persuaded to live within the body of an Undead."

Sighing, Raven sat up and shrugged a shoulder. "I'm willing to try, I guess. I would take anything over feeling this fatigued."

Jeanine gave her a sympathetic smile and came over to sit beside her on the bed, hissing at my shadows when they snapped at her. They recoiled.

"Of course, they listen to her," I grumbled.

River clapped his hands together once. "We need to bargain with Morana before we leave tomorrow. Where can we find her?"

Luca looked at me in annoyance before he said, "The Village of Reine was her last location."

SINCE MY POWER WAS UNBOUND, SO WAS HERS. AND IT CALLED TO MINE.

64

R*AVEN*

S tanding on the outskirts of Reine, I raised my eyebrow in doubt. "It doesn't appear frightening," I said, looking between Zeke and Luca. "Are you positive you did not embellish your story?"

Zeke, looking more devilishly handsome than ever, glowered at me. I hadn't allowed myself to thoroughly study him since we left Seolia, mostly because I had been too exhausted to do anything about how much I desired him since he released the shadows that were currently wrapped around my waist.

Even his ears, which he refused to talk about. I found them charming and now understood why our son, in my visions, had them, too. He looked just like his father. And now, I stood between two Fae males, and only one of them didn't want to be a Fae. He didn't want to be anything other than my husband.

And I would like to have just one afternoon to digest everything that had happened to us since meeting River. The more time we spent with him, the more information he divulged, and none of it was normal. I missed our shielded dome, where we remained blissfully unaware of what lingered outside our bubble.

Zeke's glare from my insult softened when he caught the longing in my gaze for him and a return to normalcy. Pulling me to him, he kissed my temple. "If you'd stop breaking, I am sure these shadows would love a chance to explore more of you," he whispered, sending shivers down my spine.

River scowled at him in disgust. "Can we focus on the task at hand, please? Your scent is undeniable."

"Even I can smell it," Luca muttered.

While attempting to unravel a shadow from around my waist, I sighed. "When I asked for these, I did not mean quite so literally."

"They sense danger," River said. "It might look quaint, but there is something that lingers within that they're protecting you from."

"Are we sure they are not just projecting Zeke's unnatural need to protect me from all things that aren't him?"

Zeke chuckled, nipping at my earlobe.

"I have to agree with Raven," Jeanine said, stepping forward. "I don't understand why this required all five of us. It's empty."

"Just wait," Luca said.

Zeke's shadows strapped around my chest, and I clawed at them but couldn't feel anything but my own clothes. "Zeke," I hissed, "loosen them!"

"I can't," he growled through clenched teeth. "Have you not been listening to me?" He flicked his wrists and arms, not appearing intimidating in the slightest, while trying to move his shadows.

"Is that some kind of mating dance?" Luca asked in amusement.

I snorted. "If it is, it's not working."

Zeke scowled and crossed his arms. "You're on your own with them then."

"We don't have time to wait." Jeanine took my hand and pulled me along, calling over her shoulder to the fearful men behind us, "We can handle it ourselves if you're all too chicken!"

Zeke called for us to wait, but Jeanine was basically invincible. It would take something of great power to bring her down. And when they realized she wouldn't stop, the men begrudgingly followed behind us, muttering something about a habit of surrounding themselves with such headstrong females.

"We're close to Reales," Jeanine reminded them. "The quicker we accomplish this, the sooner we can return to Thoya. Raven's close proximity to Silas is a risk."

Their grumbling stopped.

Walking along a cobblestone road hidden between tall trees, Jeanine left me with Zeke while she Arrowed door-to-door, knocking before she peered into the fogged windows. River followed her lead and repeated it on the opposite side of the road before the two of them met in the middle. "It doesn't appear as if anyone lives here anymore," River said.

A coven wouldn't abandon their village that easily; that much I had learned from Damiana.

Spinning, I grabbed the dagger hidden in Luca's waistband and dragged it across my palm, blood spilling onto the pavement. Zeke cursed at me and held my hand. "What are you doing?!" he asked frantically, licking across the wound to clot the blood.

"Just wait," I repeated.

The shadows tightened around my chest, so hard that I could barely breathe. "Zeke," I squeaked.

Sighing, he closed his eyes and inhaled deeply, much to my envy. And then, with a slight tilt of his head, the shadows loosened enough around me to where I gasped for air. "Off!" I shouted, shoving at the spirals of wispy smoke. "Now!"

The shadows slowly unraveled from my chest and slithered down my body until they lingered at my feet like spools, recoiling from my scolding. "I am having trouble believing these were once feared, Zeke."

He shrugged a shoulder. "They just love you like I do, baby."

I rolled my eyes, shoving down the need to smile. "Don't be cute with me right now."

One moment passed, then two, and I started to feel foolish, but then a woman appeared at the end of the road, dressed in clothing similar to what I had seen Celestina wear at the moment of our deaths. "Larinda," Zeke said, "she is the witch who chained me to a bed and then tried to kill me in Nova."

"Hello!" Jeanine shouted, grabbing my arm and shoving me forward. "We have the"—she paused and glanced over her shoulder—"what did they call her?"

"Dark Half-Witch," Zeke answered.

"We have the Dark Half-Witch!" She motioned dramatically over my body. "We need your help!"

Larinda did not move, so I stepped closer. "I have a proposition for you! My blood for your assistance!"

"Raven," Zeke snapped.

"Just a drop," I assured him. "Zeke, we need her help if we want a chance at finding Morana before tomorrow. I am tired of aching and don't have time to find people to kill to calm this..." I touched my stomach, the feeling of significant power pushing back. "Whatever this is. I feel I could explode at any moment and burn everything down."

Apparently finding my offer enticing and intriguing, Larinda walked toward us.

Jeanine took my wrist and pulled me to stand beside her, hip to hip. Larinda paused an arm's length away from us and studied me, her eyes bearing into mine, but I did not shrivel or look away. I held her stare, knowing that I owned something they tried to kill my husband for. "You want my blood," I stated.

She did not move or speak.

"And I am willing to bargain with you for it, but I need to speak with the witch possessing Morana."

"It's the least you could do for poisoning our strand," Zeke said, coming to my other side. "You placed a curse against a bond blessed by the gods."

"You killed two of my witches," Larinda shot back with venom in her words. "We are even."

"We are *not* even," Zeke snarled. "Your witches tried to kill my mate. You see my shadows. You know Raven's powers. Consider us not murdering your entire coven today a kindness."

He was *so* not a people person.

"If Silas captures Raven, he will create oaths between himself and anyone who needs her blood," River explained. "We are asking that you help us prevent that from happening. Our requirement is far less than what Silas's demands will be if he finds her."

"Wouldn't you rather be in favor of the Dark Half-Witch instead of a demon?" Jeanine asked, softening her tone. "Raven is kind, Larinda. She can help you."

Larinda contemplated, looking at each of us before focusing solely on me. "Go to my cottage. Your Phantom Prince knows where it is."

"Boy, does he ever?" Luca muttered behind us.

I sat beside *my* Phantom Prince around a small table, glancing around the tiny cottage. The five of us took up the majority of the space in the living area. Zeke had my legs draped over his lap, his fingertips grazing my thighs while we waited.

He was becoming impatient for all sorts of things.

His shadows were lingering in a dark corner of the room, blending in so well that I had trouble spotting them. It wasn't until the top of one of them hooked and barely crept out of the darkness that I flinched. Zeke followed my gaze, his cheek pulling up in a slight grin. "Frightened, little demon?"

"No," I lied.

The cottage's front door squeaked, and we all twisted to see Larinda walking in, followed by a witch that looked close to my age, but I knew she was much older. And when she noticed Zeke and me, she gasped, her hand flying up to cover her mouth.

I would never become used to that. I still saw myself as the orphan dropped off on a porch who grew up confused and misplaced. I spent the majority of my life feeling unseen and unwanted, and now, my blood was wanted so much that it gave me severe whiplash.

I hadn't even found time to reconcile that my father wasn't my father and that my actual father was locked in a forest and needed my blood to be freed.

It was a wonder that I hadn't imploded from the pressure placed upon me.

Larinda guided the witch around the table to sit across from us. I moved to put my feet on the floor, but Zeke stopped me with his hands around my legs. He started to introduce himself. "Hello, I am-_"

"I know who you are," the witch answered with her gaze, one of awe and wonder.

I narrowed my eyes, powers pulsating through me as my jealousy flared. "Mine," I finished for him. "He is mine. And I am unaware if it is you who wants him or the spirit living within you."

Jeanine bristled.

"Blair," Larinda said in warning. "The Dark Half-Witch has returned. It is best to remove your gaze from the prince and focus solely on her."

Blair sheepishly moved her eyes to me, though the blossom in her cheeks told me she was still thinking about my husband. I wanted to leave from here as quickly as possible. "I need to speak with Morana and only her. I will not need your input."

Zeke brought my hand to his lips, kissing the backside of it while we waited for Blair to stop gawking at us. It took another warning from Larinda before she shifted in her chair and closed her eyes.

And when she opened them, I recognized the black eyes staring back at me. "Hello, beautiful stranger," she hissed, moving her gaze to the corner of the room where Zeke's shadows hid. "Only you are not a stranger anymore, are you? Have you come to dance with my ribbons once more?"

"No," I snapped, my patience wearing thin.

"She's going to set something on fire soon," Jeanine whispered to Luca.

"I have come to inquire about that," Zeke answered. "When did they... *dance* together?"

He said it so awkwardly that I smiled.

"Many, many moons ago. The Phantom Prince required the help of my ribbons to eliminate a breed of beasts." Her eyes flickered quickly to River. "Do you remember the beasts, Prince of One?"

"I have tried to forget," River replied.

"What kind of beasts, Morana?" I asked.

"Beasts with fangs and fur," she hissed, dragging her nails across the tabletop. "Beasts who fed on mortals and took from the Phantom Prince."

Zeke raised a brow. "Took what?"

"The Phantom Prince only fed from mortals," Morana answered, reaching for him across the table.

I turned her hands to ice with only a look. She screeched as I trapped flames within them, the heat unable to escape and burning her. "You will not touch him," I said calmly. It was the most power I had used since the unbinding.

And I enjoyed it immensely.

"Morana will not touch! Morana will not touch!"

I freed her hands from their icy confines. She dragged them back quickly and blew on them as if that would soothe the burning. Zeke dug his fingers into my thighs, impressed and most likely aching for me. When he shifted my legs across his lap, I felt precisely how desperate he was for me when his cock pulsed against my thigh.

Wanting to skip any further story times, I put my feet on the floor and leaned over the table. "Morana, I require your assistance. In exchange for your allegiance to me, I will offer you a physical body that you will be able to control. No more sharing or splitting minds with someone else. And especially no more altering memories."

Her black eyes narrowed on me. "You want my ribbons to defeat the leader of the Undead."

I nodded. "I want complete control, Morana."

Larinda interrupted with, "Morana lives within Blair now. She can assist you in fighting the Undead with Morana's ribbons."

Zeke shook his head. "No other female is allowed to *dance* with my shadows. If Raven does not possess Morana, we do not have a bargain."

Morana looked between Zeke and me. "Morana does not want another body. Morana wants to live within the Dark Half-Witch only. Morana wants to play with the Phantom Prince."

"No," Zeke said quickly, "absolutely not."

"You tried to kill all of us," Luca spoke up.

"You manipulated her, Morana." Jeanine placed her hands on my shoulders. "You tried to turn her against everyone she loves. This bargain allows you to live forever inside a physical body. Raven is out of the question."

"Morana, your song can solve our issues with the Undead. You can help eliminate them and prevent harm from befalling anyone else. Does it not upset you that the Undead take lives when you are so much better suited for it?"

Morana tapped her fingers together, a malicious smile widening her cheeks at the compliment. And I meant what I said — I loved taking lives, but Morana was terrifying with how easily she coaxed others to give their lives for her. "Morana will help the Dark Half-Witch under one condition."

Zeke sighed but gestured for her to continue.

"Morana will be free to roam. No traps, no dungeons, no threats." Her eyes flickered to Zeke. "Morana will be free to mate."

"He is off-limits, Morana. I will agree to the rest, but you will stay away from the Phantom Prince."

Morana's sigh was more of a screech, but she nodded. Before coming here, River taught us how to swear oaths. It seemed too simple, but oaths could not be broken unless you wanted to welcome death with open arms.

I wondered how that would work with a spirit *of* death.

I placed my wrist on the table. "Swear an oath, Morana. Fight with us, and we will ensure you have a physical body. Deny me, and you will be an enemy of the Phantom Prince and his mate. And," I added, shifting into Blaze to hopefully strike fear with my fire, "You will leave Zeke alone."

For a moment, I thought she *would* deny us. I worried we would have to add learning how to kill a spirit of death to our never-ending list of tasks, but then, slowly and eerily, two black ribbons left Blair's fingertips and twisted tightly around my wrist.

Zeke's shadows crept out of the darkness, prepared to strike if needed, but when the ribbons uncurled, I stared at a black mark on my wrist in the shape of an octagon with a skull in the center.

"Memento Mori," Larinda whispered, "the symbol of inevitable death."

"Cheery," Jeanine said.

River stopped anything further from happening by placing his finger on the mark and closing his eyes. Encasing the coin, a wave of water curved around it. "If she changes the oath, she will be faced with the wrath of the Fae."

Since the only Fae I knew were the two in this room, that didn't hold much weight with me. River was powerful, but he had only shown us drops of what he could do, and maybe turning people into drops of blood and being able to drown them was the extent of it. That didn't bode well in my favor when it came to hazy ribbons.

And, well, Zeke's shadows were a whole other issue.

"Wonderful," I muttered, keeping my right hand on the table in anticipation of her seeping into my skin and unaware that oaths could be changed after they were made. But just as before, Morana sought my left arm. "It's broken," I said, wincing as the ribbons wrapped around my hand.

But that didn't stop her as I felt the familiar draft of Morana's bitterness and chill seep into my skin.

When my eyes rolled back, Zeke pushed into my mind and stood with me in the black room of our dreams and nightmares, holding my hand as Morana cloaked my skin, bringing with her the void feeling of emptiness as a harsh reminder of the pain that accompanied carrying her within me.

"Stay with me," he said, pulling me flush against him while the darkness wrapped around my heart. "Control her, Raven."

"Sing," I whispered. "Tether me."

Leaning down, he kept his lips pressed against my ear as he began humming the soft melody from my dreams—the one that found me when I needed to rest, the song he couldn't explain. I wanted no one else to ever hear the passion this melody held.

It was a melody of euphoria, strength, seduction, sin, and everything he was made from. It overtook the chasm of despair, weaving around my body and calming my fears of losing myself to the melancholy again. And he didn't stop, even after she entered me wholly, making herself at home once more, the ribbons wrapping around the bones of my arm and healing my broken fingers.

He didn't stop until I opened my eyes and kissed him, weaving my arms around his neck and threading my fingers through his hair. After pulling away, I stared into his eyes. "Bargain with me, Zeke. Make me a promise we cannot break."

Taking the wrist devoid of Morana's mark, he placed his fingertip against my skin. "Together, my love," he said, creating a marking of shadows entwined through a flame.

"Beyond the end," I whispered.

"THESE SHADOWS WOULD LOVE A CHANCE TO EXPLORE MORE OF YOU." "IF YOU'D STOP BREAKING, I AM SURE

65

RAVEN

Before departing Reine, Zeke and I sat inside Larinda's cottage with only her, dismissing the rest to wait outside while we pleaded with her to break the curse on our strand. Genuinely apologetic, she informed us that a curse could not be broken until the caster's or receiver's death, which meant that our curse would remain unless Silas or one of us died. Silas had threatened the demise of her entire coven if she didn't assist him in tearing Zeke and me apart and promised blood to her upon my capture.

She agreed in her desperation to protect her coven and, with the enticement of my blood, to restore their waning magic. But Larinda didn't realize I would've provided what they needed without any threats. All we would've needed was information, but we were cursed because of her impatience. And until Silas's death, the curse would continue to weaken our pull to one another.

Still shifted as Blaze, I informed Zeke that I would remain as her until I was positive I could keep Morana controlled. Blaze was the only shift ever stubborn enough to fight against Morana and would be my greatest defense against the untrustworthy spirit.

Upon our return to Thoya, Zeke demanded one last night with me, but when we arrowed back to the kingdom, we were surprised to find Melik speaking with Edmund. Behind him, waiting hundreds of yards away was what looked like the entire kingdom of Nova.

Melik waved when he spotted Zeke, then swallowed from fear at seeing me. When I burned him that day in Reales, it was under the assumption that he could not be trusted. But after giving Zeke a place to rest during his travels, I considered us even. "Ezekiel," Melik greeted Zeke, then dipped into a deep bow. "And his mate."

I smiled, then reached for his arm. He flinched but allowed me to push his sleeve up. Still visible on his arm laid the words I had written in flames across his skin. "I can heal this for you," I offered, "if you'd like."

Melik looked at Zeke for permission, then nodded once. "It would be nice not to overdress in the sweltering heat."

The vast pool of my healing energy had grown substantially since our magic was freed, and though Melik was mortal and my blood would do nothing for him, I could heal the skin around the scar with my fingertips. The words started fading into a pink, puckered welp. "It will fade," I assured him. "And then you will never again be reminded of our meeting in the forest."

"You are not that simple to forget," Melik said, stepping back as Zeke moved forward. "I mean that with the utmost respect, of course."

I rolled my eyes. "He will not harm you, Melik. He does not hurt our friends."

Even with the guarantee, Zeke slid an arm around my shoulders and tucked me against his chest. Melik, discarding his jacket now that his arm was healed, nodded up toward Zeke's ears. "Avalie was correct in assuming the Phantom Prince's bloodline was strong."

"Appears so," Zeke answered, not speaking further about the change in his physicality. "Have you come here to seek refuge?"

"May I ask who else you've invited to my kingdom, Ezekiel?" Edmund asked, exasperated. "You are wearing your 'best friend' card very thin these days."

"I invited him before the shield around Thoya broke, Edmund. The Undead were murdering his people," Zeke replied. "Will you fight with us, Melik?"

Melik nodded pridefully. "Of course. We have brought weapons and wagons. I have three-hundred men at your disposal."

Edmund clapped his hands together. "That brings our total to over a thousand. Surely with that many, we will come out victorious."

Exhausted by the talk of war and intrigued by the idea of having me alone, Zeke took my hand. "We leave tomorrow evening. Now, if you'll excuse us...."

When Edmund called for us to wait, Zeke hung his head and sighed. We hadn't been alone in days, and Zeke was addicted to more than just my blood. The longer he went without touching me, the more unbearable he became.

"Petra offered more soldiers to us, but she said these are not..." Edmund cleared his throat, lowering his voice, "She said only you would understand, Ezekiel."

Zeke stiffened, his hold tightening on my hand. "Where is Petra?"

Tipping his head toward the castle, Edmund said, "Dining with my father and Elric."

Zeke tried to pull me to accompany him to the castle, but I placed a palm against his chest. "I will stay here, my love. I need to speak with John about how our people are adjusting to life here."

"I will not be longer than an hour," he promised, kissing me once. Twice. "Wait for me in our manor. I do not have time to chase you tonight."

I dragged a finger down his chest. "I wouldn't dream of wasting any more time." And then, I smiled sweetly. "Can you please take these with you?" I motioned to the shadows wrapped around my waist. "I have my own ribbons now."

Zeke chuckled, then sighed. And slowly, the shadows unraveled from around me to linger almost invisibly behind him. My lips parted as I stared at the three fierce creatures before me. Since the shadows had been released and had stuck to me, I had yet to see them with Zeke. And he looked every inch the intimidating phantom of death the stories painted him out to be.

"Are you sure you need to speak with Petra?" I murmured, sliding my hands underneath his shirt and grazing the indentions of his abs.

Shaking his head, he leaned down to kiss me, but Edmund interrupted us with, "Ezekiel, we have a war to fight."

Zeke growled against my lips in frustration. I kissed him anyway, my nails scraping across his chest like claws. "One hour," I said. "Do not keep me waiting. I want you to be the first person I unleash upon."

"Raven," he groaned, squeezing my waist. "I could kill them all," he offered, teasingly I hoped, but I couldn't be sure anymore.

Smiling with a shake of my head, I removed my hands from his chest after shoving him a step away. "Go, my love. I'll be here."

He hesitated, glaring at Edmund when he told him again to leave, but then winked at me before he vanished into a black cloud of smoke. Once more, I stared in wonderment. Melik stood beside me, watching as the smoke cleared into nothingness, leaving no hint that Zeke had just been here.

"I spoke more with my scholar about the Phantom Prince," Melik said. "I believe Zeke holds back when you're near. I am eager to see what he can do once we reach Reales. There is a reason he was once feared and why Silas was so desperate to kill him."

"Zeke before becoming... whatever this is"—Edmund waved his hand through the empty air—"was intimidating. I want to be beside him on the battlefield. I might not need to fight at all."

I frowned deeply. Through the chaos of the last few days, I had forgotten that my dear friends and family would be battling the Undead and only had a week to prepare while on the move. And even though Zeke was intimidating, he still hadn't learned how to use his powers, which meant we would likely lose many men.

I said nothing else except, "Edmund, where is John?"

"No, Raven. I refuse to entertain this."

I followed John through the crowd of mixed people from multiple kingdoms coming together. The differences between our realm and the people of Nova were easy to spot. Petra had supplied our domain with such unique clothing that the loose and airy outfits looked out of place against the bright, fitted garments the Novans were wearing. They looked prepared for both labor and battle, whereas our people appeared more relaxed due to living peacefully for so many decades, untouched by the kingdoms outside ours.

I nearly tripped over the piles of trunks, shifting around as I chased him through the crowd. "John, please! You must understand where I'm coming from. I need to ensure a leader for our people if something happens. I need to make sure Zeke has blood—"

"No!" John shouted, turning around to face me. "It is already enough that I am about to send all of my children off to battle creatures that have proven to be untouchable, and now you're asking this of me."

Sighing, I ran a hand through my hair and tried to think of what I could say to make him listen. "John, this is the responsible thing to do. And for once, I need to do the responsible thing. It is only a precaution but a necessary one. There must be a plan in place if something goes wrong. If I die, I can be brought back. Zeke can't. And I refuse to let that happen."

"You need to speak with him first," John argued.

I shook my head. "I can't. If he knows, he will insist I remain in Thoya. He will not allow me to fight or go with him to Reales. I don't intend on losing, John, but the Undead are strong. Silas might've been able to kill all four of us in Scolia if he hadn't been shocked by Zeke's shadows. We are about to battle hundreds of them, John."

His expression was frustrated, and his eyes began to gloss with tears. And logically, he knew I was right. We couldn't risk Zeke, nor any of our people. What I was asking from him was frightening, but it needed to be done.

"This must remain a secret between us." I squeezed his arm gently. "We've always been a team, John, even before I realized it. Even with no kingdom left to rule, I want it to remain so."

Lowering his eyes to the ground between us, he was quiet for a moment while the loud chatter of people around us blurred into memories of when Seolia was once full of laughter and joy.

Finally, he nodded once. "I'll start the preparations."

~

I DID NOT WAIT in the manor for Zeke. Instead, I sat before Isla's grave and ran dirt through my fingers. There hadn't been enough time for me to grieve her death properly, nor had I let the weight of guilt fully settle on me. Isla already gave me so much of her life and then in the end, sacrificed it entirely.

Before learning what kind of man Cade was, he and Isla were my family. Thousands of memories were made with them, separately and together, and she was the last remaining component of my life before Zeke. "I wanted to believe I had more time with you," I shared with her sorrowfully. "I hope wherever you are, you know how grateful I am for your belief in me. You did not have to love me so much, but you did. And I pray you felt it was reciprocated, Isla, because I loved you so very dearly."

"It is almost unfair," I said with a breathy laugh, "how I wield death, yet I cannot speak to the dead." I dusted the dirt from my hands. "You would insist that I not, but I will bring meaning to your death, Isla. I will remember what he did to you."

Shifting into Terra, I raised to my knees and placed my palms against the ground. And closing my eyes, I pulled droplets from the deep well of power within me and pushed them into the ground. Terra was a force of nature, but I wanted to honor Isla with stillness and beauty, an ode to the peace she brought to my life. All around her grave sprung flowers of violets and primrose in colors of ivory and gold.

"Rest well, Aunt Isla."

~

ZEKE WAS WAITING for me on the back porch of our manor, smiling as I neared him with a bouquet of lilies hanging from my hand. And for only a moment, I imagined our life here years from now.

He would watch our children play in the fields while I visited Isla, anxiously awaiting my return so we could read to them in front of the fireplace before he visited their dreams while they slumbered.

It was the last moment of peace I would have.

"You could've come to me," I said, somewhat surprised his shadows hadn't sought me out.

"I knew where you were," he returned, beckoning me to him with a hook of his finger.

I climbed one step before straddling his lap, placing one of the lilies behind his ear. He held his breath as I touched the pointed tip of one, and my lips parted as I explored the smooth, slanted shape.

"How do they feel?" I asked, touching both ears.

"Very sensitive," he breathed, closing his eyes.

"I like them," I assured him, leaning forward and kissing the delicate skin at the point. "I love them."

"You're biased," he replied, as goosebumps rose on his neck. "I am not fond of them."

I snorted. "You're not fond of change, period."

He grinned, opening his eyes to stare into mine. "River says the Fae are immortal. It seems you got your wish, little demon. You are stuck with me."

I sighed, throwing my head back dramatically. "Just when I thought I'd find freedom."

He chuckled, but then slowly, a frown appeared. I mirrored it with a frown of my own, resting my hands on his shoulders. "What is it?"

"I didn't want to be this," he whispered, shifting me closer. "I knew who I was. I could've protected you as I was. Now... I am a Fae. Or a vampire."

I nodded with a small smile. "Welcome to my life. We can both move forward with no truth about who or what we are, but I know something constant if you want my secret."

"Tell me."

"I love you." I brushed my fingertips across his jaw. "Man, Fae, Vampire, Buffoon... I love every version of you. You are *my* Zeke, just as I am *your* Raven. None of the rest matters."

He kissed the oath we swore to one another on my wrist, staring at the shadow-covered flame. "Remind me every day?"

I pushed his hair back with my fingers, curling them around his neck as he leaned forward to rest his forehead on my shoulder. Our last night alone together should not be so heavy, yet the sun that was lowering across the horizon and eliminating the light left on his skin did not bring the peacefulness I wished for.

"Love me," I murmured.

Wordlessly, he stood from where we sat on the steps while I kept my legs locked around his waist. And the silence remained between us while he carried me inside but did not go upstairs. Neither of us could face what we created the last time we were in our bed, nor were we sure it could ever be recreated. Instead of facing the unknown, he parted with me to set me down in front of our fireplace.

Shifting from Terra to Blaze, I lit it aflame. The fire sparked and sizzled against the logs, nearly pouring out before settling down and immediately filling the room with warmth. The colors changed swiftly from orange to purple and back again, and I gave him an apologetic grin. "I haven't learned yet how much to use since the unbinding. If you thought I was chaotic before…"

Grinning, he backed away until he sat on the sofa, spread his knees wide, and discarded his shirt. "I want all of you, Raven. Every shift, even the deadliest."

With a tilted head, I blinked in confusion. I didn't like how his request felt more like a goodbye. "Zeke, what did Petra say to you?"

"We're not going to talk about that," he responded, loosening the waist of his pants. "The only name you're allowed to say tonight is mine. Now, undress. Slowly."

Bare and waiting, his cock hardening in anticipation, he crooked an arm to rest against the back of the sofa as he waited for me.

Fingers trembling from his darkened stare, I slowly untied the laces of my bodice. He watched so intensely that I pulled in the corner of my lip, very much on display, while I shimmied the top down my arms, gasping in surprise as his shadows curled over my shoulders. "I thought you couldn't control them."

"I'm not," he admitted.

"Does it not worry you how they have minds of their own?" I

asked, staring at one as it snaked across my breasts, my eyelids fluttering from the sensation.

"Keep going, Raven."

Sliding my hands into the waist of my pants, I pushed them down over my hips until they pooled at my ankles. He didn't move, cocking his head to the side as the shadows circled my waist and lingered closely to my core.

The shadows felt like silk against my skin, their exploration over every inch of my body bringing goosebumps. When I tried to touch one, I felt nothing but skin. Zeke watched with burning intensity. "For months, Raven, you begged for these shadows. You found them before I did."

I nodded, eyes widening when one curved around my throat. "Zeke," I rasped.

"You have no reason to be frightened, Raven." He leaned forward slightly, curling his fingers into fists to keep from touching me. "I was envious, Raven, of how much you wanted them."

"I wanted all of you," I corrected.

A dark, foreboding grin spread across his mouth. "Do you still?" Waiting for my nod, he dipped his chin toward the floor. "Then crawl."

"I WANT ALL OF YOU, RAVEN. EVERY SHIFT, EVEN THE DEADLIEST."

66

RAVEN

The shadows left me and slithered across the floor to linger at his ankles. I scrunched my nose in confusion. "*Crawl?*"

"On your knees," he demanded.

Gods, if this were anyone else...

Dropping to my knees, I tried to keep from rolling my eyes as I moved to all fours and slowly crawled toward him. He leaned back again, a combination of amusement and lust in his eyes. "I can't wait to inform your fucking Fae father that his daughter only bows to one man."

I scowled and raised to my knees, but he lunged forward and

grabbed my elbows, pulling me between his legs. "Isn't that right, baby? You only kneel for the Phantom Prince."

I fought against him, trying to pry my wrists free. "You are just as fucked up as I knew you'd be."

"Put your mouth on me, Raven."

"You do not deserve...."

He shoved his tongue into my mouth and melded it with mine, melting me with a single, heart-stopping kiss. And I hated him for it; how easily he could switch my allegiance back to him. Threading his fingers through my hair, he tugged my head back and dragged the tip of his tongue across my lips.

"You feel so fucking good, Raven. I want your mouth around me, so I can show you how much I love your spitfire tongue."

Biting my lower lip to keep from smiling at his praise, I lowered my eyes to his throbbing length and nodded the best I could with his grip in my hair. He guided me down, shifting closer to the edge of the sofa to allow me a better angle at attempting to take all of him in my mouth.

He was so thick that the back of my jaw ached as I took him in. But when I shifted into Frost and ran my cold tongue across the tip, he hissed and cursed at me, trying to pull me off.

I stayed right where I was.

Swirling my tongue around the length, I soothed the chill with fire, shifting into Blaze and warming my hands on his thighs. He relaxed his grip on my hair and sighed from satisfaction, assisting in a steady bob of my head. "You're beautiful," he murmured.

"This is all I wanted, Raven." He paused to draw in a breath, his free hand closing over the edge of the sofa. "When I saw you for the first time, I got off to the fantasy of your mouth around me as Blaze."

I wanted him to stop talking. I wanted him to be so satisfied that he couldn't find words. I wanted to see his eyes roll back for once instead of remaining focused on me, but I flinched when I felt a shadow crawl over my legs.

"Relax," he whispered, stroking my hair.

The shadow moved between my legs, gliding across my thighs. "You know I can't come unless you do," he reminded me with a cocky grin, foiling my plan.

I narrowed my eyes at him until the shadow slithered across my clit, causing me to moan around him. He breathed my name, closing his eyes but continued moving my head. Hollowing out my cheeks and loosening my muscles the best I could as a foreign... creature edged me, I took him until my mouth covered his base.

My gag made him groan.

And then, swiftly, the tip of his shadow entered me. I jumped at the contact, in disbelief that something I couldn't touch could bring me pleasure like this. "Breathe, Raven. It's me."

The shadow stopped when Zeke opened his eyes to stare into mine. "I will fuck you with a shadow while you fuck me with your mouth, but you must relax, or it breaks my concentration."

Baring down slightly, I rolled my hips. He grinned, relaxing his head against the back of the sofa. With each bob of my head, the shadow would match it with an airy thrust. And within a solitary moment, we were nothing but moans and whimpers.

I rolled my hips against the shadow, trying to grab it to hold it still, but caught nothing but air. Zeke thrust into my mouth; his jaw slack, his breathing labored. "Come, Raven," he demanded huskily. "Fuck, your mouth..."

My eyes rolled back, my climax tightening my stomach and pulsing through me. The intensity was mind-boggling and over-whelming, the shadow not slowing until Zeke came in my mouth, the warmth shooting down my throat and pooling in my mouth.

I coughed as I swallowed, pulling up to swipe the back of my hand across my mouth but fell backward in shock. Zeke opened his eyes, his head whipping back and forth in alarm until he laughed.

He waved his hands through the flames on the sofa as they engulfed it but kept away from him. And then, he looked at me in amusement and lowered to the ground, thrusting his tongue into my mouth.

I couldn't focus on the kiss, instead keeping my eyes behind him as the fire spread to the floor. I shoved at his shoulders to stare at my hands in bewilderment. "I didn't touch anything," I whispered.

"I was hoping to piss you off enough for a reaction like that," he answered, laying me down.

"You are such a bastard," I snapped.

"You say the sweetest things to me, Raven Audovera." He didn't ask me to stop the fire. Instead, he said, "Dance with me."

Shifting into Morana, the ribbons immediately poured from my left hand and entwined with his shadows. He slid into me, interlocking our fingers and raising our hands above my head.

The ribbons and shadows wrapped around us, and he loved me as death danced, as we felt the immense power between us from their reunion. The wood cracked and popped from the flames, and our bodies were nothing more than sweat, but he kissed me.

Each thrust was filled with passion. Each kiss seared and bruised my lips. He loved me through each shift, crying only my name as the flames morphed into purple, spreading across the floor and engulfing our bodies.

Until we were nothing but fire and death.

The way it always should've been.

We were strangled in our need for one another, our moans mangled, the room falling to pieces, but he didn't come until I shifted into myself. Only then did he whisper my name and bite my shoulder, sucking blood between his teeth while coming inside me.

And I shook and trembled in his hold, tears falling down my cheeks from pleasure and pain, love and longing; every emotion a person could experience was coursing through me like a winding river.

And when the second orgasm hit me, I shifted into Terra from the uncontrollable pleasure. And as I did, my eyes filled with gold, and my skin emitted a gentle glow. He licked across his lips as he raised his head, the black of his eyes harsh against the soft radiance of my skin, but he looked at me with recognition.

Shocked by what happened, blinking as I stared at my body in bewilderment, the shadows uncurled from around us. The air around us felt thick, and when he demanded I shift into Frost, he rose to his knees. The snowflakes in my eyes were reflected in his, and the glow encasing my body was fading. He smiled then, dragging his finger down my chest. And with it, ice followed.

"Our powers are connected, Raven." He drew shapes and curves across my skin, watching the frost that followed his touch. "Every emotion *you* feel, *I* feel, and my magic reacts to yours. That is why the shadows cling to you. Fear, love, hope, despair, they want it all."

"Pleasure," I whispered.

He nodded. "Especially pleasure." Breathless, he returned to me, tracing what felt like snowflakes across my cheeks. "Controlling that one shadow was difficult, but not impossible. I need practice."

The fire died out as I drew in breaths, blinking and clearing the haze of lust. "Practice on me as much as you'd like," I offered enthusiastically.

Chuckling, he looked around at the charred remains of furniture and books that were falling from the bookshelf to the floor beside us. "You broke our manor, witch."

Wincing, I shrugged. "Gisela will be delighted to redecorate it." I smoothed his hair back but then frowned. "We have to leave, don't we? You're taking me to Perosan."

Dropping his head, he kissed my shoulder and remained with his lips pressed against my skin. The realization of this being our last few moments together before being thrust into final preparations for war made me burrow into him as much as I could, crying from the warmth of his arms enveloping me.

"I'm scared," I whispered. "I'm so frightened, Zeke, and I am trying not to be."

"It will be okay, Raven." He tightened his hold on me, resting his chin on top of my head. "Baby, I have loved you through so many lifetimes. The shadows hold memories, and I can see them."

My heart ached.

"And gods, Raven, our love has lasted through many trials. You are stubborn in each life, and I love you every time. You are beautiful and mine, Raven. Nothing about that will ever change."

"I am always yours," I murmured, closing my eyes and inhaling our scent. "I promise my heart will always belong to you."

"Even if I am cruel?"

I smiled, laughing through my tears. "Especially if you are cruel, my love."

Taking my chin between his fingers, he lifted my head and kissed me tenderly. "I will never be cruel to you, Raven, only to those who try to take you. And anyone who looks upon you, those who dare to speak to you...."

"Kiss me," I begged quietly. "Kiss me and stay with me until they drag us away."

Covering our bodies with the remains of a charred blanket, he made one final promise to me, "Together, Raven. Beyond the end."

THE SUN still hadn't broken across the horizon as we stood on the murky shores of Perosan. Edmund would lead our armies here and meet us in a day, but Petra and Zeke knew the secret of the army that lived within this forest.

The army that only answered to me.

River stood at my side, staring into the darkness with me. He hadn't been inside the forest in over a century, only returning here once to help me escape Cade. His home hid behind this forest, through the skeletal army, yet he could not return. Not yet.

"Blaze," I whispered, as I shifted into her and freed her from her physical confinement. She landed on the shores in a pool of fire, quickly taking the shape of my fox.

"You mustn't give blood," River reminded me. "If you do, the realm will unseal, and they cannot fight, Raven. They're too weak."

"How do you even know they're alive?" I asked.

"I have been keeping communications," Petra said behind me. "They are alive, but not for much longer. The bulk of their powers have been put into the army that is guarding the forest. Honestly, I am not sure there is much more of a realm to protect."

"The survival of the Fae rests solely on my shoulders." I looked at River, frowning. "I feel no allegiance toward them, River. I am not warring against Silas for their sake, yet my brother and husband are Fae. You must understand how difficult this is for me."

His eyes lowered. "I do, Raven, but *I* feel allegiance toward them, and you *are* a Fae too. We were raised as Fae until Celestina took us to Seolia. Our father..."

"Do not speak of him," Zeke warned, touching my shoulders. "No father barters his child's life, River. If the army in this forest refuses to fight for Raven, it gives us a good indication of exactly who your father is."

"Zeke must stay behind," Petra said.

"No," Zeke growled.

"You must," River said. "You were viewed as an enemy to the Fae. The forest may have accepted you in mortal form, but they will not take kindly to a vampire entering."

"But his ears...." I started to say.

"Zeke is only partially Fae," Petra interrupted. "And he is already reverting back to his ways of distrust and misunderstanding."

I looked over my shoulder at Zeke and then his shadows. *Shadows hold memories*, he'd said. And when I turned to face him, I crossed my arms over my chest. "What aren't you telling me?"

"What happened lifetimes ago does not matter now," he answered. "I do not trust creatures who could bargain with the Undead for the sake of their own kind. The Fae do not love Raven because she is their princess; they need her for her blood."

"Do not speak of which you do not know," River said, his voice dropping an octave. "Your shadows may hold pieces of memories, but they do not remember everything. You should be cautious when speaking of a species your future children will embody."

Typically, I would do what others asked without question. And I had made the mistake too many times of asking Zeke to stay behind while I walked into the unknown, believing that nothing would happen to me, but I would not keep doing that going forward. Once we defeated Silas, Zeke would bloodmate with me and be given the respect of being my mate.

"Zeke is not an enemy," I said, holding Petra's gaze. "He will bring no harm to those who are loyal to me. If you insist he stays behind, I will not go without him. Where I go, he follows."

Petra exchanged a glance with River before she sighed. "I guess I will follow you, too. The army will not take the Phantom Prince's entrance kindly."

"Gods, what did you do to them?" I muttered, shaking my head at Zeke.

"Tried to murder your father for killing my mother," he answered dryly. "He is the reason Silas found us, Raven. He is at fault for our deaths."

I whipped my head toward River for confirmation. River simply sighed. "A witch in your coven was paid in favors from our father for information on Celestina's whereabouts. She betrayed her, and when our father learned you planned to bloodmate with Zeke, er, the Phantom Prince, he alerted Silas."

"That sounds like more than a misunderstanding! They killed his mother *and* his mate!" I snapped. "Zeke has every right to loathe the Fae!"

"Zeke *is* a Fae!" River shouted, not backing down when Zeke moved to stand between us.

"Do not raise your voice at her," Zeke demanded with a throaty tremor. "I became the monster you wanted me to be, and not you, nor your aunt, get to decide how I respond to the memories these shadows hold. They have given me more insight into previous lives than you ever have."

I called the shadows back when they stood erect behind Zeke, ready to strike at River as the tension between them built. The shadows recoiled slightly, slithering backward to be closer to me.

I placed a gentle hand against Zeke's back. "You are absolutely correct, my love. No one can take away the pain we endured lives ago, nor should they justify it. However, it is up to us to forge ahead and forgive." I looked at Petra. "*All* of us."

Having spent her years protecting the Fae realm and me in her own catastrophic way, Petra knew I was right. Zeke was the Phantom Prince again, but he wasn't the same man. He was still terrifying and intimidating, yes, but his love for me softened him into becoming the man who at least listened to others before offing them.

"She's right, River," Petra said gently. "I have known Ezekiel as a man, and he is worthy of forgiveness for the wrongdoings from another life."

"I was willing to let you bloodmate with my sister against beliefs of the Fae tying themselves to demons," River added, continuing his stare-off with Zeke. "Despite what transpired between you and my father, I did not let it stand between you and Raven. I would hope that would earn me a sliver of your trust."

Exhaling, Zeke turned from River to face me. He stared intently into my eyes, speaking through his. I wished we could push past the curse and my bond with Silas to have the mind bridge other mates were gifted with, but I had become great at reading his expressions. And when he leaned in, kissing me softly, it was his way of telling me he would at least *try* to get along with River.

Taking his hand, I tugged him toward the forest. "Let's go speak to some skeletons, shall we?"

~

THEY WERE MORE INTIMIDATING than I expected, towering over me while standing shoulder-to-shoulder in a group of three, staring at me with hollowed eyes and blocking us from going further. I tried to reason with them once, but they didn't move from their post.

"I don't think this is working," I said, glancing at River, who looked at Petra in confusion. Blaze bounded behind them, chasing what looked like a golden butterfly.

"They know who she is," River said. "Why aren't they answering her?"

"Because of me," Zeke answered with a sigh. "We didn't exactly get along when I was mortal. I am positive my current persona doesn't bode well with them, either."

I stepped forward, flicking a shadow off as it wrapped around my wrist and tethered me to the ground. "Zeke," I said in gentle warning. "Let me speak with them, please."

Rumbling a hoarse snarl in response, he uncurled his shadow from my wrist to allow me to take three steps forward until I stood directly before the center skeleton. It lowered its chin substantially to stare at me. He had a slight crack above his left eye in the shape of an upside-down V, and I wondered if he received it before death or after.

"He is not your enemy," I started, pointing to Zeke. "He is my love. You know him as the Phantom Prince, but he is my twin flame."

The skeleton on the left tilted its head as if balking at the idea, so I moved my gaze to him. "It's true. He died during our blood-mating ceremony because of Silas, and I sacrificed myself to be with him in death." I focused again on the center skeleton, who seemed

665

to be the leader. "The gods blessed us with a strand that Silas has cursed."

Puffing out my cheeks, I bravely stepped forward and grabbed the bony fingers of the center skeleton. It shifted its head to look at our locked hands.

"Raven," Zeke growled.

"You cannot truly be jealous right now," I snapped, glancing over my shoulder.

Zeke crossed his arms with a glare.

"I need your help," I pleaded, refocusing my attention on the guard. "I am your princess. If you follow me into battle..." I paused, closing my eyes and drawing a deep breath through my nose. "I will free the Fae realm from the confine my mother placed them in."

A moment passed, and their stature didn't change. As Zeke stepped forward to drag me back, my hand was caught in a bony grip as the skeleton's fingers wrapped around mine. "Thank you," I murmured as I pried my hand free before Zeke could find a way to saw it off.

I jumped and placed a hand over my heart as the center skeleton banged its fist twice across his chest, followed by the two on either side and so forth until the noise echoed throughout the forest. And as the sound of rattling bones surrounded us, Zeke grabbed me and pulled me to squish against his chest, his arms and shadows locked around me.

I wanted to assure him they wouldn't harm me, but it would've fallen on mute ears. As far as the eye could see, skeletons stood erect behind the initial three, grouped in hundreds. My eyes widened, my lips parted, and I suddenly was not *as* fearful of Silas.

Because I controlled a skeletal army.

WITH WHATEVER MAGIC THEY POSSESSED, the skeletons could Arrow on their own, which left the seven of us with the task of moving the armies to the outskirts of Reales. Only a quarter of them left the forest to assist us, but it was better than none. Seven days had passed, and though we wanted to become familiar with our powers, Zeke and I were instead split apart to prepare everyone else.

Zeke was the most knowledgeable in the layout of Reales, so he spent his days with Edmund, Elric, and Melik, planning their spread. We would draw the Undead into the forest with the scent of my blood after killing Mira, which was what I was planning with Jeanine. Eliminating her first was imperative. If we failed, the realm could not be left in her hands. If she had willingly sacrificed her own people for consumption, we did not doubt she'd do the same for the rest.

We needed more time.

Zeke and I were absolutely unprepared. His shadows still preferred to be beside me instead of listening to him, which didn't give him much time to practice with them. They would behave if he drank enough of my blood to satisfy them, but it wouldn't be long before they were wrapped around me again.

Blaze played with them sometimes, setting them on fire and chasing them across the empty fields as we moved across lands. But now, as we stood hidden behind the cliffs in Reales, I was shifted as Morana so Silas couldn't feel me.

As Morana, our scent was disguised as death, and there was nothing the Undead feared more than death itself. They wouldn't seek us out.

Gathered in a small circle with the leaders of our kingdoms, Jeanine detailed our plan for killing Mira first. It would require us to arrow into Mira's bedchambers, where Jeanine believed she'd be at nightfall.

"The second the oath is broken, Silas will know," River said. "Raven will immediately need to Arrow to the forest so she could draw in the Undead."

"Do not give him time to find you within the castle," Elric added. "If he realizes you're so close, this will end before it begins. Mira is the only thing stopping him from taking you."

"He won't touch her," Zeke said.

I appreciated the confidence but would be lying if I said I wasn't nervous. If killing Mira could end it, I would be more willing to believe we would walk out of this unscathed.

But Silas would fight for my blood.

"Your, uh" — Edmund glanced over his shoulder at the skeletons as they stood as still as statues, far away from the mortals who feared coming too close — "army of remains, what can they do?"

I shrugged. "I'm not really sure. They don't bleed or tire, so I hope they are useful."

As it quieted, we waited for one another to pose further questions, but nothing was left to be asked. This was it. This was the moment we had known was coming for months. Since Zeke found me in Seolia during the Festival of Dreams, this was what he knew would happen.

A war between kingdoms, three against one, and a legion of Undead who wanted my blood.

It all came down to this.

As the night neared, we knew we had to move quickly. Since they were not suspecting we would arrive so soon from Thoya, we had an advantage, but we needed to move smartly.

"A moment," Zeke demanded.

Everyone around us dispersed, reconvening far enough away to give us a respectable distance while he took my face between his palms and kissed me. A last kiss, I realized, before we battled for our freedom. Before we risked... everything.

After he pulled away, he stared into my black eyes while the same blackness flooded his. We would have to maintain our deadliest personas until the end so Silas wouldn't scent me. Morana had behaved and let me control the ribbons — she'd stayed buried within — but that did not fight the chilly bleakness that embodying death always brought.

"We're going to win this, Raven."

"I need you to stay in the forest with the army," I said, placing my fingers against his lips when he tried to argue. "Jeanine will stay with me inside the castle. You have to protect our friends, Zeke. They can't be out there alone with only River."

"No," was precisely what I expected him to say.

So, I played my last card. "If you stay in the forest with them while I kill Mira, I won't fight."

He stilled, with disbelief in his eyes as he searched my face. "You would do that for me?"

"Zeke, I would do anything for you."

His eyes flickered over to Jeanine, who was in deep conversation with Edmund and Melik. Until finally, he nodded once. "Very well, but I want to see you before you go. And you mustn't be long."

Tearfully, I tried to nod. "Zeke…"

"No, baby." He shook his head, pressed his lips against my forehead, and held me there momentarily until he whispered against my skin, "There is no need for goodbyes. I will stand with you in the end."

"Can I just tell you then" — I inhaled a stuttering breath, unable to control the tears falling down my cheeks — "how wildly unhinged you've made me?"

Chuckling, he kissed my tears away one by one. "Likewise, little demon. So very wildly unhinged."

UNTIL WE WERE NOTHING BUT FIRE AND DEATH. THE WAY IT ALWAYS SHOULD'VE BEEN.

67

Raven

J eanine Arrowed me into Mira's bedchambers. The less I moved
alone, the better our chance of not alerting Silas. Thoya's army
lined the cliffs in the forest, waiting for our return to begin the
battle, and my stomach was twisted into so many knots that it
was a wonder how I didn't vomit upon landing.

The skeletal army along with the armies of Seolia, Nova, and
Perosan were instructed to remain behind the cliffs until needed,
after which they were to come into the forest in increments.

Mira was startled upon seeing us but seemed unsurprised by our
intrusion, moving to stand in front of her bed. "I knew you'd come
for me."

"You lied to all of us, Mira." I stepped forward. "All because of your disdain for a decision Zeke had no choice in. He did not want to be king, yet you decided to punish him for the choices made by your father. You lied about being Celestina's daughter."

"It was an elaborate plan, yes?" Mira turned to face us. She looked sicker than our visit weeks ago, almost as if she were nearing death.

"You let them feed from you," Jeanine said. "I should've realized you would try to become one."

Mira pulled up the sleeve of her dress, revealing scarred bite marks along her arm. "Silas wanted to ensure I could be controlled. Each bite was only for a second as to not kill me, but enough to create a link between us." The way her voice softened had me raising an eyebrow. She sounded as if she had fallen for his charms.

"He does not care for you, Mira," I said, wanting to give her no hope for anything prior to death. "He used you the same way he wanted to use me."

Mira's expression turned into the scowl she was known for. "You have hidden well, little bird. His inability to find you is what saved me thus far."

I curled my fingers into loose fists. "I am not your little bird, nor have I kept you alive by choice."

Jeanine stood beside me. "All of this for a throne, Mira. A throne that you will never sit on. Was it worth it?" She gestured to the dark, empty room. "All of this to end up alone and right back where you started."

Mira cackled. "I might not end up on the throne, but I accomplished my tasks of making Zeke miserable and selling Celestina's daughter. All I wanted was a mother and a father who appreciated me." She stepped toward us, and Jeanine pulled me back. "I was the bastard of a woman who favored Celestina due to Rudolf's sick obsession with a blood witch, and she was killed for producing a female heir."

"But it did not have to lead to all of this!" I shot back. "The choices of our parents were not ours!"

"Someone had to pay," Mira hissed. "The Undead will win, Raven. And your mother will lose her daughter to them, just as she always feared. Ezekiel will lose you and this kingdom, and my father will rot in the ground as the failure he is."

"You are a wretched, evil woman," I said, "And I am going to enjoy this very much." Raising my left hand, the ribbons left my fingers to wrap around Mira's throat, silencing her. She would not be promised a peaceful afterlife.

And then, Jeanine moved before I could blink. I turned away, closing my eyes at the sound of teeth piercing into the skin and at the gurgled cries Mira choked out as Jeanine bit her.

It should've only taken seconds for the venom to kick in, but when we neared a minute, I said Jeanine's name in warning. And when I turned, I clutched a fist against my stomach at the sight of Mira's lifeless body, her eyes rolled back—Jeanine drinking from her like a rabid beast.

Because even if Mira was sour in personality, human blood was still a treat for any Undead. And Jeanine couldn't stop, her blue eyes flushed red, her nails digging so deeply into the skin of Mira's throat that blood trickled down. "Jeanine," I said calmly.

Sighing, I wrapped the ribbons around Jeanine's throat and fought against her as she tried to pry them off, her grasp slipping from Mira's body to claw at them around her neck.

"I need more!" she growled.

I ran to Jeanine and wrapped my arms around her, attempting to stop the thrashing. "Jeanine, I can't shift without alerting Silas that I am here!" I whisper-shouted. "But I'll have to if you don't calm down!"

I shook Jeanine as hard as possible, which didn't do much since she was made of rock, but it was enough for her to lock eyes with me. "Enough, Jeanine! You've had enough." The ribbons loosened as she stopped fighting me, blinking as she focused. "You made me a promise, remember?"

She settled, clutching my arms as her chest heaved. But then, her eyes filled with water. I immediately shook my head. "No, Jeanine. This is what has to be done."

"It doesn't!" she shouted, wrapping her arms around me. "Raven, we can fight him; we can win."

Swallowing thickly, I took her face between my hands. "We can't,

Jeanine. Not yet. Petra knows the plan, and John has vials of my blood stashed in Thoya. Give enough to River to unseal the Fae realm and ensure Zeke has the rest."

The only sounds she could make were weak cries and blubbered arguments as her fingers clawed at my arms. "Listen to me," I pleaded, holding her steady. "Jeanine, Zeke is going to fall into darkness and despair. He isn't going to understand why I did this, so you have to ensure he gets my letter."

She nodded the best she could, her eyes squeezed shut as tears rolled down her cheeks. "He is going to kill me, Raven. He will kill River—"

"He won't," I argued, wiping tears from her cheeks. "Jeanine, he won't. He'll watch your memory and see that it was my choice. John believed I was only taking precautions. He didn't realize I wouldn't be returning. Zeke must understand that. Do not let him hold another grudge against John."

I kissed her cheek and wrapped my arms around her neck. "I love you. You will find me, Jeanine, but you must go. Find Felix, restore your bond. It is the only way you'll be able to locate The Great. Allow River to help you, Jeanine."

"What if we don't find you?" she squeaked.

"No one in any universe has ever loved someone as much as Zeke loves me," I whispered. "He will not rest until I am in his arms again. Now, go."

Tearfully, she took a small step back. She drew a deep—albeit unsteady—breath as she wiped the tears off her face. "We will find you," she promised.

I forced a smile. "I know you will."

The second she Arrowed to locate Felix, I fell to my knees beside Mira's lifeless body. I gave myself a moment to doubt my decision, but I knew I was right. We weren't prepared. We would lose every man against the Undead because we weren't familiar enough with our powers and did not have enough magic to use against them in the first place. Our realm would be nothing but blood.

Zeke needed time.

The Fae needed freedom. River would demand they assist in finding me and helping Zeke. I made the skeletal leader trust Zeke's intentions, and he had Petra and Elric on his side. And unbeknownst to Zeke, River had made time to work with me on shielding my emotions.

I hadn't veiled all of them when I promised Zeke I wouldn't fight —just enough for him not to taste the lies and unease. I was fighting, just not in battle.

We just needed more time, and I could provide it.

And never again would I be taken against my will. I would protect the people of this realm from death and bargain with my life to do it. I would be the queen that Seolia always needed.

Because Zeke was right. Queens didn't belong on battlefields. I would stay in the black tower within The Great while he fought to find me.

After all, I was his favorite thing to catch.

So when I Arrowed into the throne room, shifted into Blaze, and bit my own palm, it was only seconds before Silas found me. I stayed beside the throne, perched on the arm, and stared him down.

"Mira is dead," I informed him. "And I would like to bargain with you."

When he stepped toward me, I held up a hand and swallowed my fear. "I would like to do this civilly, Silas, and not against my will. If you make a move to take me, I will leave with Zeke and hide so well that you will never find me."

He flashed a wide smile, his pristine fangs giving me pause and causing me to almost reconsider this entire idea of mine. "You would leave your people behind so easily?"

"For him, I would." For him, I truly considered it, but the idea of never seeing Jeanine, Edmund, Gisela, Luca... it was too much to bear.

His smile faltered at the heavy truth behind my words. "What do you wish to bargain, witch?"

"Me," I stated. "If I agree to go with you, the Undead will not return to this realm. You will leave my people alone and look for blood elsewhere. And you are not to bite me against my will. I will provide the blood you need without your touch."

He rolled his neck, watching blood dripping from my open cut to the throne. I had kept the wound open on purpose, hoping the scent of my blood would work in my favor. "Those are heavy asks, little poppet."

"For *my* blood? I haven't asked enough."

He clenched his jaw, his chest unmoving from the breaths he did not need to take before releasing the tension with a sigh. "I have a request of my own."

When he again moved toward me, I stood from the throne and stepped back. His lips widened into a grin of faux amusement. "I agreed to behave civilly."

Blinking and full of distrust, I allowed him to take three more steps until he remained only a body's length away. And then, he lifted a hand and pointed it at my chest. I cried out in pain as his fingers curled, my insides crushing as he crawled through with unfathomable power, falling against the throne as he extracted a screeching Morana from within my body. I fell to my knees, panting and aching from the intrusion and exorcism of death from my body.

The black haze curled into itself as he balled it in his fist, bringing it to his face. "Do not believe I will forgive you for your oath against me, Morana." And when he launched her away, she teetered and howled before flying out the door.

The mark of her oath remained on my wrist. She hadn't defeated Silas while within me, hadn't even fought him, so she would remain tied to me until she completed her tasks. And with her oath came a promise that whatever body she took residence in next would not touch Zeke.

It was a needed assurance. A painful one, no less. But I grinned despite it, trying to find humor in the amendment I'd made Jeanine promise me in the fields between kingdoms.

She would drain any woman who dared take my place at his side, no matter how long we were apart. Her oath was beside Morana's, marked on my skin in the shape of a sun. And it made me smile to see the marking of her oath, because Jeanine was a sun. Her bright blond hair, her enchanting smile, and her gift of continuing to burn brightly, even after being handed such darkness.

She would find me.

Silas kneeled and grabbed my wrist, yanking me toward him more forcefully than needed. And I would've been lying if I said I wasn't afraid of him. I was terrified of what would happen in the days to come, but I couldn't continue risking the lives of the people who always stayed by our side. At least, not until they were better prepared.

Beside Zeke's oath on my wrist, a new one formed. It was not black or gray but red and shaped like a bladed star with four ends. "I will not bite you, beloved." He held onto my wrist as if fearful I might flee. "But you will someday ask that I do."

Grinding my teeth at the thought, I said, "I can guarantee you that will never happen."

"Dear little poppet, I hope you know what you've gotten yourself into."

Closing my eyes as he pulled me up, his hand left my wrist to wrap his arm around my waist. I flinched but remained still, turning my head from his as a tear rolled down my cheek.

I would have to tear The Great apart from the inside out.

In the corner of my mind, where I always heard Zeke's voice, where we were supposed to have a bridge to speak to one another—the place Silas had blocked with his curse and our bond—I whispered to him, *I love you. Find me. Find me, my love.*

And like the stars when they faded as the sun rose each new day, Silas laughed, and we vanished.

EPILOGUE

Zeke

AND I WAS NOT MADE to let her go.

As darkness fully enveloped me once her scent faded from the realm, from the protected dome where we had spent only months together, I couldn't fathom the distinct hatred I felt toward her — for not trusting me enough to protect her. She wanted me to accept this shadowed man within, to become the one others feared, and for her, I would.

For her, blood would spill.

Souls would fade.

And I would become her nightmare.

THE END

RAVEN AND ZEKE'S STORY CONTINUES IN
A KINGDOM OF SHADOW AND SACRIFICE
RELEASING 2024

About the Author

Whitney has been an avid fantasy reader since she was seven years old. Never in her wildest dreams did she believe she would ever publish a book, or create an entire new fantasy world from the depths of her brain.

When not writing, she's most likely visiting worlds and lands of imagination, or dreaming up more scenarios to share with all of you.

Follow her on:

WHITNEYDEAN.COM
INSTAGRAM (@AUTHORWHITNEYDEAN)

ALSO BY WHITNEY DEAN

THE FOUR KINGDOMS SERIES:

A Kingdom of Flame and Fury

A Kingdom of Frost and Fear

A Kingdom of Death and Despair

A Kingdom of Shadow and Sacrifice—releasing 2024

THE DARK HEARTS FAIRYTALE RETELLINGS:

Rise of the Cinder Fae—releasing 2024

Made in the USA
Middletown, DE
10 September 2024

60123756R00406